GHOSTS OF ZION

BOOK 2

Ryan Duval

MONKEY MONKEY PUBLISHING

No Artificial Intelligence was used in the conception and writing of *Ghosts of Zion*.

Sale of this book without front cover may be unauthorized. If this book is coverless, it may have been reported to the publisher as "unsold or destroyed" and neither the author nor the publisher may have received payment for it.

Ghosts of Zion is a work of science fiction. Names, characters, places, ideas, technology, recipes, and incidents either are the product of the author's imagination or are used fictitiously. Any resemblance to actual persons, living or dead, events, ideas, technology, cuisines, or locales is entirely coincidental.

Copyright © 2025 by Ryan Duval

All rights reserved. No part of this book may be reproduced or used in any manner without written permission of the copyright owner except for the use of quotations in a book review.

First paperback edition October 2025

Timeline Art by Ryan Duval
Cover Art by Ryan Duval

ISBN 979-8-9892400-4-3 (paperback)
ISBN 979-8-9892400-3-6 (ebook)

MONKEY MONKEY PUBLISHING
www.monkeymonkeypub.com
firstcontact@monkeymonkeypub.com

For Quinn, to prove that following
a dream is always worth it.

GHOSTS OF ZION

BOOK 2

CHAPTER ZERO

"Listen up, you little shits! We're hitting a seed bank today!" the old woman barks from the cockpit of their stolen refuse barge slowly nearing a gray speck in the vastness of space. "So, say your prayers! Send those messages to your mommies! For only half of you might return!"

Thirty young men and women, recruited from the streets of Hardsill, nervously glance at one another.

"You've got to be kidding me..." a boy of seventeen years whispers in the deathly silent cargo bay directly behind the cockpit.

"So, that's what all the secrecy was about," says another.

"But a seed bank... That's a death sent—"

"Shut your traps!" cries the old woman. "You signed up for this! You knew a seed bank was possible! My Sol, you're a bunch of wimps! And you call yourselves soldiers!?"

No, we don't, the boy thinks, his stomach twisting until pain and nausea is nearly overwhelming. He imagines they all feel this way. They all were tricked. *More like we had no choice.* The boy's mother comes to mind, the hoarseness of her cough worsening with each passing day, and the medicine draining their life savings. *But everyone from Hardsill has a story like this. So, a seed bank makes sense,* the boy admits, knowing the value of the ancient kernels, pits, grains, and nuts, ones untainted by centuries of genetic modification, locked behind several meters of sicklecell titanium.

"The moment that cargo bay hatch opens, we storm!" the old woman continues, her voice hardening. "Don't give them a second to think! A second to respond! Be fast! Be efficient! Be just as ruthless as they've been to you!"

"But they'll have an entire regiment guar—" a recruit begins.

"How do you know that!?" spits the old woman. "Are you a mole or something!?"

"E-everyone knows this," the recruit dares respond.

The old woman whirls from her cockpit chair, raises her rail-pistol, and clicks. A projectile silently passes into the recruit's head, melting through skin and bone before splintering within their brain. By the time the rest understand what happened, the old woman is back in her seat, staring at the gray speck in space growing larger by the second.

None of them say a word or move a muscle.

"Helmets on!" barks the old woman, sealing her own. "Rail-guns coiled!" she calls through com.

They don helmets and retract coils without question.

A light blinks on the cockpit dash.

"Vessel three-six-foxtrot-whiskey," comes through the com. "This is Eden Bank. Please, state your business."

The old woman clears her throat and dashes an icon. "This is Refuse Barge three-six-foxtrot-whiskey, requesting routine docking with Eden Bank's refuse bay. Sending encryption code now. We apologize for arriving out of sequence, we had to navigate a patch of micro-meteorites."

The com is silent. The recruits glance at one another.

"Clearance granted," finally comes. "Transferring you to dock master."

The gray speck grows larger, appearing like a perfect circle.

The seed bank's cylindrical end, the refuse bay, the boy recognizes.

"Bring it in nice and easy," says the dock master. "Now, match gravitational rotation."

The old woman rotates the barge and weight appears in the boy's gut.

"That's it. Docking in three, two, one..."

A clunk resonates through the refuse barge's cargo bay where the recruits wait facing the hatch in formation, rail-guns raised and ready.

"Docking complete. Equalization commencing," the dock master says. "Any crew transports today?"

"Negative on crew, sir," the old woman casually responds. "We're just here for pickup."

"Roger that. Equalization will complete in approximately five minutes."

"Thank you, sir." The old woman closes the feed and turns to the recruits. "I know that you're scared... I know that a seed bank has never been hit before... But I've been raiding for over two-hundred years and can tell you they have no idea what's coming."

The boy's arms and legs begin to shake, his rail-gun rattles. He believes it is only him until he sees the shoulders of recruits in formation ahead shifting nervously, too. He peers to his right to see the person next to him is crying behind their visor. *Trained to use envisuits, trained to use rail-guns, trained to follow orders and read schematics, but never trained to handle fear...* the boy realizes. He feels strangely comforted in knowing he is not as terrified as those around him. He breathes deeply. His shaking subsides.

The cargo bay hatch whines with the increased pressure of the airlock beyond. An indicator light shifts from red to yellow, then green. The whining stops and the heavy knocking of deadbolts releasing is felt through the boy's feet. His breathing increases. His hands shake again.

"Steady..." whispers the old woman through com.

Seconds feel like an eternity, until, with a sudden jerk, the cargo bay's hatch opens to reveal a young janitor, no older than the recruits, guiding a cart overflowing with trash.

"Welcome to Eden Ba—" the janitor trails off.

The recruits stare confused.

They're supposed to be soldiers! the boy thinks.

"Fucking go!" shouts the old woman. "Shoot him!"

The recruits do not budge.

The old woman pushes through them, her rail-pistol drawn, and clicks at the young janitor. He winces with each projectile silently penetrating his skin and crumbles to the floor. His mouth opens to scream but only blood comes gargling forth. The old woman kneels to the convulsing janitor, pries a holotile from his pocket, rushes to the refuse bay's back door, and swipes it across the lock.

The door goes green and slides open.

She turns back to the recruits. "Come now or we're all dead!" She bolts down the hallway, clicking her rail-pistol at more workers in maintenance uniforms.

Shit! the boy thinks.

The recruits in front of him snap into action, shifting formation, becoming a two-by-two line and funneling into the hallway after the old woman. The boy moves as if on autopilot, what little training received actually coming back to him. They flood from one room to the next, filled with workers ducking below desks, and send projectiles.

But none of them are military! the boy knows, unable to pull his trigger, his finger frozen.

Just then, they round a bend to meet a shower of bullets from a regiment guarding the entry to Eden Bank's control room. Holes appear in the recruits in front of the boy. Light shines through them like swiss cheese. The rail-pistol in the old woman's hand shatters and spurts of blood erupt from her arm. She lurches back, stumbling over fallen recruits, pushing against those still standing.

They retreat around the corner to the screams of those left behind. A second volley silences them.

Blood gushes from the old woman's arm. *She's done for,* the boy is certain until she presses a button at her shoulder. Her face contorts as smoke seeps from her envisuit's shoulder joint. Then, her arm drops to the floor and the seam seals tight. The old woman does not give a second thought to the arm, kneeling to pull a rail-gun from a dead recruit's grasp. She flicks out the old magazine, leans the gun against her chest, pulls a fresh mag from the dead recruit's belt, and shoves it into place. Then, she rests the butt of the rifle on her thigh, its tip to the ceiling, and pulls its coil into ready position. She stands, faces the remaining recruits, makes eye contact with the young boy, and winks.

Her attention snaps to the ceiling hosting several pipes, fixating on one painted red, and follows it to the bend where the regiment waits. "Those of you who can move, get in line!"

They fall in behind her.

"Ready in three… two… one… go!" she cries and bolts around the corner, the rest following in haphazard formation. She raises her rail-gun to the ceiling, as the regiment opens fire, and snipes out the red pipe. A spray of gas washes over the regiment and ignites.

The recruits shoot through the flame-screen hoping to hit something as the old woman continues forth. Her rail-gun runs out of ammo. She discards it to the floor and jumps through the wall of flame.

The recruits come to a screeching halt and stare bewildered at the blaze.

The regiment is no longer shooting back, the boy realizes.

A flailing arm comes through the wall of fire, then a soldier's helmet is pushed into the spray. The gas dissipates and the fire clears. The boy makes out the old woman among the soldiers, parrying their moves with her single arm and striking back with precision. Their bodies pile around her.

A god among mortals, the boy thinks.

The sight of the old woman boosts the recruits' morale. They rush forth, clicking at the soldiers on the floor, putting them out of their misery.

But the boy hangs back, his gun pointed to the floor, staring at soldiers being overwhelmed by their rush. *No... overwhelmed by the old woman,* he corrects himself.

Wild cries come through com as the last soldier falls, a mixture of cheers and screams. The boy cannot tell which is which.

The old woman grabs a soldier's heavy blaster, looking massive in her grasp, but she handles it with ease, and they funnel into Eden Bank's command room.

"Lock down the barracks before the rest of their regiment comes!" she orders, pointing at a central hologram. "The rest of you, follow me! The seed banks are just beyond this door!"

We actually did it... the boy thinks, astounded.

They fall in behind the old woman as she inputs a code. Hissing and a series of mechanical thumps and clicks, like an ancient clock, comes. Then, the door, nearly a meter thick, slides to the side. Dim lighting marks hundreds of smaller vaults down a long corridor.

Each contains a different variety of seed, the boy knows.

"Let's go!" the old woman cries, hustling down the corridor.

They pass wheat, barley, teff, sorghum, corn, soy, and more but do not stop. The recruits look side to side confused.

This is what we came for... the boy thinks. He builds his courage and says, "Shouldn't we open the vaults?"

The old woman whirls about. "Did I give you permission to speak!?"

The boy timidly shakes his head.

"Then, don't!" The old woman continues onward until the end of the long corridor appears with a vault several times larger than the others. It takes them nearly ten minutes to reach. She gently places her hand on its metal surface. "Behind this door is salvation... You should consider yourselves lucky to be in the presence of such greatness."

"Greatness?" a recruit responds. "I thought this was a raid... Aren't we here for the goods?"

The old woman grins. "You might be." She inputs a code. "I, on the other hand, have loftier aspirations." The old woman kneels, raising her heavy blaster as the vault shudders. "Against the walls!"

The remaining recruits press to the sides of the corridor, and kneel, their rail-guns fixed on the massive vault door groaning open. The room beyond is pitch black, appearing endless, save for a pulsing orange light on the back wall. The old woman does not move a muscle until a metallic tumbling breaks the silence and a fruit-sized orb bounces out from the darkness.

"Grenade!" the old woman cries and opens fire.

The grenade tumbles towards the boy. He has no time to think, but the muscle memory from eight years of competitive Ganyball kicks in. He whips the butt of his rail-gun, cracking the metallic orb, sending it hurtling back through the open vault door.

"Hell yeah!" cries the old woman.

The boy curls on the floor just as the grenade erupts. Even through the helmet his ears ring and his retinas burn, but for a moment he sees several soldiers within the darkness dropping. The old woman shouts orders, but the boy cannot hear a thing. She rushes into the vault.

Move your legs! the boy commands himself. With all his willpower, he stumbles into the vault after the others to meet a line of muzzle flashes. The recruits ahead flutter into the air like a gust of wind catching leaves. Then, a mighty punch slams the boy's thigh, sweeping his feet out from beneath him.

Floor, ceiling, floor, ceiling, floor...

The wind knocks out of him upon landing. His leg is completely numb. *What in Sol was that!?* After several agonizing seconds, he regains his breath and grasps his thigh, but his hand falls into a gaping hole, instead. He stares, then removes his hand to see the floor on the other side. Blood gushes. *No, no, no!* The boy desperately pinches the hole, trying to stop the blood. *I'm dead!* But then, he remembers the old woman's arm dropping to the floor and her suit sealing tight. *The leg must do it, too!* He searches around the suit's hip, but his blood obscures all color and fills all creases. His gloved hands shake, his metal fingertips slip about. *Calm down! Think...* He breathes deeply, removes his gloves, and slips his fingers into the pouring blood. He discerns a little circle on the hip.

The moment he presses, a message appears on his visor reading, *"Do you wish to sacrifice?"*

"Y-yes," the boy whispers.

The suit cinches tightly around his hip and needles prick his thigh. The smell of barbecue hits his nose. He desperately tries pinching his nostrils, but his helmet is in the way. He fumbles to unlatch and tears it off. After several seconds, the searing stops and his leg loosens free. There is no pain. *This can't be real.* He looks at the other recruits for confirmation but finds their bodies strewn motionless about the vault. *I'm the last one,* the boy realizes. *Well, almost.*

The old woman still fights in close quarters with the soldiers, a heat blade in her hand, slicing at joints, spines, and necks. She is shot point blank in the chest and drops to a knee. Somehow, she stands back up.

Soldiers continue to fall.

Four left, three left, two left, now one, the boy counts.

The last is out of ammo and cautiously circles the old woman, staring at her heat blade, seemingly at a loss as to how she still breathes let alone fights. As he lunges for the blade, the old woman lets it go and shoves her palm under his helmet's chin, snapping his head up and knocking him back. Just before the blade hits the floor she kicks the handle, sending its heat edge through the soldier's ankle. He steps back to regain balance, but there is no foot to step upon. Instead, he slides on his stump and crashes to the floor. The old woman is quick and jabs her metal fingertips into his neck. He squirms, trying to release his helmet, then convulses. His arms drift to the floor.

The old woman drops to her hand and knees, coughing up blood and splattering her visor. "Not yet!" she gurgles and unlatches her helmet, letting it tumble to the floor. She crawls to the pulsing, orange light on the back wall, reaches up, pushes, then crumbles.

The back wall shudders and cracks. Snow spits as the wall parts. Beyond appears like a blizzard, until the rush of decompression subsides.

The chill air prickles the boy's cheeks and when he peers into the opening, he gasps. The silhouette of a man, well over two meters tall, with bulging, inhuman muscles, becomes visible. Soon, the boy discerns long, red hair. *Locked in ice, in hibernation,* he understands.

An orange glow surrounds the massive man. Water pours across the vault floor. The ice groans and cracks. Chunks fall. The man's gargantuan arm moves ever so slightly.

The boy tries to climb to his feet, momentarily confused when he cannot, and shuffles to the vault's side wall, instead.

"Ah!" comes from the massive man, echoing down the long corridor. A low growling follows.

The boy freezes.

The old woman straightens her back and presses her fist to her missing shoulder. Ice crashes to the floor before her, but she does not move. Tears run down her cheeks, yet she smiles.

A massive leg moves from the wall. A foot thumps to the floor. Once free from the ice, the man slumps down and retches a mouthful of strange liquid. He begins breathing deeply and powerfully, like a horse. Red hair masks his face, but the boy can sense the strength of his jaw.

The old woman looks upon the monster of a man with such love, such admiration. "Fores le Derecoture," she whispers in a strange language. "Condra feen array tole sun."

The massive man slowly looks at the old woman, his hair parting to show pale eyes. He slides a knee beneath himself, matching her position, and gently places a paw-like fist to his opposing shoulder.

"Condra feen array tole sun," he responds.

The old woman cries out and falls forward. The giant man catches and helps her back into position. He stares into her eyes and smiles sweetly. They whisper back and forth, laughing, crying, and touching each other's face as if they cannot believe the other exists.

The boy does not comprehend a word they speak, but understands their closeness. *Is he her great grandson?*

The old woman reaches into a compartment on her utility belt, retrieves what looks like a syringe, and presents it to the massive man. He stares at it in disbelief. He does not take it. She sets the syringe on the floor, instead, and leans forward, almost bowing. Turmoil crosses the man's face. He sighs deeply and slowly cups his paws around the old woman's jaw. With a quick jerk, and a crisp snap, her body goes limp. He gently lays her to the floor, covers his face with his paw, and sobs.

Such ferocity, such fragility, the boy thinks.

After several minutes, the man delicately grasps the syringe and brings its point to the old woman's temple. "Zun dah!" he shouts and pushes the needle deep into her brain.

The syringe beeps and blinks red.

The massive man rips fabric from his faded uniform, pulls his long, red hair back, and ties it into a bun.

The syringe again beeps. Its light becomes solid green.

He pulls the syringe from the old woman's head and brings it to his own temple. He breathes in once, out once, and in again. "Zun dah!" He plunges it into his brain. He moans. He twitches. He shouts. He wails. He goes to pull the syringe out, but fights himself at the last second. "No! No!" he cries and falls to the floor, writhing like he is on fire. And then, he is still.

The syringe beeps a final time.

Is he dead? the boy wonders, not sure of what he should be thinking anymore. *Am I dead?*

As if to answer, the man's paw twitches. He calmly pushes himself to his knees and removes the syringe. He looks upon the old woman.

"Sister," he whispers in Interspeak. "Your sacrifice will not be in vain."

"Sister?" the boy inadvertently says.

The massive man snaps his head towards the boy and closes the gap between them in a flash. A fist, larger than the boy's head, hurtles towards his face, but at the last moment it shifts to crash into the wall behind him, instead. The impact chatters his teeth and blurs his vision.

"Are you scared, boy?" says the massive man, with his face just centimeters away, pale eyes burning.

The boy opens his mouth, but no words come.

"That's a *yes,*" the massive man answers.

The boy finds his voice. "Y-yes."

The man inspects the boy's face, his severed leg, and his utility belt. "You helped my sister, yes?"

The boy nods.

"Did you know my sister?"

The boy shakes his head.

"Did you know about me?"

"No…" the boy timidly says.

"Then, why are you here?"

"The seed…"

The man looks about the vault, then down the corridor. "A seed bank?" he says with discovery in his voice. "Brilliant." He turns back to the boy. "But not brilliant enough. They should have destroyed me when they had the chance."

"Are you going to kill me?" the boy squeaks.

The man ponders this. "Your magazines are full. Why didn't you shoot?"

"The soldiers did not deserve to die," the boy says.

"But they were trying to kill you."

"They were defending."

"So, did your comrades deserve to die, then?"

The boy thinks long about that and says, "Nobody deserves to die, including my mother. She's sick. That's why I came."

The massive man sits back on the floor, giving the boy some space. "What's your name, boy?"

"Samuel."

The man's eyes brighten. A smile spreads across his face. "That's a *magnificent* name."

CHAPTER ONE

"Clara Ocol, thank you for granting us this exclusive interview," TWN anchor Celina Cobalt says. "But why now, nearly twelve years after you published Zion's biography?"

Clara glances at the cameras and lights, masking the audience beyond. "It was time I set the skeptics straight."

Celina brightens. "We all found it fascinating when you published his biography as a work of fiction. I know it's far fetched, but are you certain there's no truth to Zion's stories? A growing number of historians are finding they answer some of Earth's mysteries."

Clara grins. "We must remind ourselves that Zion was a genius researcher and storyteller, unlike any the galaxy has ever known. He spent nearly three centuries digging into the histories and cuisines of thousands of cultures. It's how he was able to establish galactic stability after the Arkathy Empire fell. Regarding human history, there is nothing in Zion's tales that did not exist in what was already recovered after The Fall. He merely told it in a cohesive manner, with heart and soul, and a touch of fantasy."

"I'd say a little more than a touch," Celina quips.

"What's life without imagination?" Clara responds.

"But, Clara, aren't some of the characters based on real people?" Celina continues to prod.

"Loosely. And then, there's Mermer, whom Zion completely ripped off from the cartoon."

"Mermer the Genius, my daughter loves that show," Celina adds.

"So you see, while Zion told incredible stories, he never told anything new."

"I… suppose so," Celina says with a narrowed brow.

Phew, Clara thinks, relieved to dodge yet another bullet.

"It's just…" Celina hesitantly starts again. "How Zion describes the Arkathy Empire's dismantling strangely makes sense."

Shit…

Celina senses Clara's anxiety and grins slightly. "I mean, of course it's fiction… Supreme Minister Hjordiana said so herself."

Clara does not miss Celina's hidden message, but hopes Supreme Minister Hjordiana, watching this interview's taping, does.

"The Sorgan species perished long before that event," Clara carefully responds. "And they had no vocal chords. They could not audibly speak. So, it's physically impossible one could have convinced the galactic empire to rebel."

"Then, why did Zion dream that up?"

Clara nods. "The greatest discovery I made about Zion, was that he suffered from Kaladian Degradation Disease, an extremely rare condition that unravels one's DNA, having a particular effect on a patient's mind. As one brain synapses uncouples, it tries desperately to reconnect, often finding the end of another uncoupled synapses to bond with, resulting in the crossing of memories. And we now know of Zion's many psychotic episodes during his tenure, ones the council covered up. Truth is, he was sick his entire life."

"But Zion was a genius," Celina interjects.

"Yes, he was. Now imagine a genius who specializes in research having KDD, and how scattered and confused their mind would become."

Celina's eyes go blank for a second.

Her earpiece, Clara knows.

"Thank you, Clara, for clearing that up. You've certainly given us all a lot to consider." She turns to the audience. "And that concludes this week's episode of *Behind the Curtain.*"

◆

Clara's LightCab nears her apartment building at the top of Cobble Hill and navigates around paparazzi clustering the drop off. They lean towards the car, trying to catch a glimpse through its privacy windows.

Already? Clara thinks and sighs deeply. "Change of destination…

Tempest University, Archaeology Center."

"Destination accepted," chimes the LightCab, turning back onto the street and to the upper ring road.

Clara's eyes become heavy as she stares across Tempest City's reservoir filling the basin below, reflecting skyscraper lights from across the water. It is mid-afternoon. *But it might as well be midnight,* Clara thinks whenever Titan reaches peak darkness of its eight day long night cycle.

The LightCab takes the university exit and plunges into a bamboo forest. Her view of the basin and skyline scrolling by is replaced by dark trunks furiously passing her window. It wakes her up.

"Coffee black, please," she says.

"Coming right up," chimes the LightCab and a humming comes from a synthesizer embedded in its central console. It dings, and a travel cup's outline appears beyond the synth's translucent door.

Aizen would be disappointed in me, Clara thinks, having spent a decade drinking her son's true artisan blend. She opens the synth door, retrieves the artificial coffee, and sips. *Now, I'm disappointed in me.*

University lights twinkle through the bamboo and Clara's cab passes the front gate unveiling the campus in full. Students traverse a quad between classes, navigating statues of archaeological heroes, many adorning patches of the History Recovery Guild upon their lapels. In the darkness they resemble a coven of vampires coming out to mingle.

The cab comes to a stop in front of the University's Archaeology Center and its door lifts. Several students do double-takes as Clara enters. She makes her way from a large central atrium to the many lecture halls, and stops to check the schedule on hologram. *Where is he today?*

A lecture door swings open and students depart.

"And don't forget..." comes a professor's familiar voice, "...Your essays are due first thing on..."

Clara cups her hands around her mouth and calls, "Kip!"

"...Mon—" the professor silences. Hustling footsteps come and Jonathan appears in the doorway with a huge smile. "I thought you had the interview today!"

"Wrapped up an hour ago. Thought I'd catch a lesson," she responds.

"You just missed Paris's catacombs!" he says, but his smile dwindles.

His next lecture is on Paris itself, Clara knows, and that this is where Jonathan's lessons diverge from the truth. *All to keep the Sorgans' existence a secret.* She remembers how devastated he was when the creatures destroyed the perfect buildings, bringing them back to the state of rubble humanity would expect. "This is how Paris was supposed to be found," she had argued, trying to help Jonathan reconcile its destruction. *Still, he refuses to return.*

"Was home infested again?" Jonathan asks.

Clara nods. "And that was only after the taping."

Jonathan shakes his head. "We'll have to align our trip to Earth with the interview's airing, then."

Clara thinks about that. "Aizen still needs time alone."

"You'd think a year is long enough," Jonathan snips.

She gives him a look. "It took you fifty-four years to reconcile your own past, and you're not even in touch with *them.*"

His brow wrinkles. "I know… It just feels like the moment I take a position that doesn't require the year-on year-off schedule, Aizen leaves, instead."

"Maybe this is our punishment," Clara jokes. *Kinda.*

"I just miss him," Jonathan says.

"Me too, hon. We can send a message."

"And hope he responds," Jonathan grumbles.

♦

Remnants of Addis Ababa appear just as the History Recovery Guild described, its city a pile of rubble beneath a glass dome and the anchor point of its great elevator obliterated.

I wish you could have seen it in its heyday, Sha sadly responds in his mind. *Addis Ababa used to be magnificent. Paris, too.*

And New York City, Justin chimes in.

And Toronto, adds Kwai Lan.

But it's all destroyed, Aizen thinks back. *Earth holds no answers for me.*

Mermer comes into view at Aizen's feet, staring at the barren crater. *What were you expecting to find?*

A clue as to how you exist within me.

We've tried answering that question before, the crustacean says.

And? Aizen asks.

I don't think there's a point to it, other than to keep going.

Aizen sighs deeply. *But it's got to mean something.*

Does it?

Aizen kneels to the little crustacean. *Your home is the next to explore.*

If we can find it, Mermer responds.

How can you not recognize your own home? Justin scoffs.

Mermer points its claw at the crater. *You saw this through Sha's eyes. Do you recognize it now?*

Justin quiets.

Aizen thinks about that. *Actually, Justin, you might know where this all began. Mermer must have lived near your childhood home.*

Justin darkens. *I'll never return to that shithole! I'd rather die!*

You're already dead, Aizen states. *So, where is that shithole?*

Justin glares. *Near Portland... Oregon,* he mumbles and fades away.

Aizen looks to the others for clarification.

It was a city on the west coast of old Usonia, Kwai Lan says.

Well, that's a start, Aizen thinks and takes one last look across the crater. *It really stretched all the way into space?*

It certainly did, Sha says.

Crazy, Aizen thinks and boards his shuttle.

◆

Aizen wakes in a cockpit seat to magnificent snow-capped mountain peaks holding clouds at bay below, reminding him of his Blood Mountain trek over a decade ago. His shuttle dips through the clouds alongside steep slopes, their barren rock quickly replaced by sparse trees, then thick forest as oxygen increases. When the coastline becomes visible in the distance, everything feels specifically *Earth* again. Soon, rugged stone cliffs hold an ocean at bay, sea foam spraying above as waves concuss. Even from the shuttle, Aizen can feel its ferociousness.

Are you sure this is Oregon? he asks.

According to the coordinates... yes, Kwai Lan says.

How are we going to find Justin's home? he thinks to Mermer. *You must remember something from your time with him.*

Mermer fades into view. *It's been over a thousand years... Erosion is far more aggressive on Earth than other planets. Any remnants of his hometown are likely gone.*

But the towns were never hit by the light beams, Aizen responds.

Dione appears. *That's part of the problem. Although the light beams decimated Earth's major cities, their destruction was preserved within the glass domes, while the settlements outside have deteriorated to dust.*

Then, again, there's nothing for me here, Aizen thinks.

Justin slowly fades in, wearing a horrible frown. *It's on Sayden Island, off Braxis Point.* He fades away.

Aizen searches the shuttle's archives to find an old map from just after

The Fall. *There are several islands along the coast, but nothing indicating Braxis Point.*

And everything's different with sea rise, Kwai Lan says. *The island must be underwater now.*

Aizen strafes the coastline in his shuttle, analyzing the water depth to determine where an island might have once existed. He comes across another shadow below the surface.

The shuttle chimes, *"67% match."*

Is it enough to warrant an investigation? Aizen thinks. "Simulate sand erosion back to the year two-thousand."

"Simulation commencing." A hologram projects an ancient island's outline below and applies arrows in the water to indicate current. The outline shifts, the water level lowers, and an island appears. *"Simulation complete, 84% match."*

Better, Aizen thinks. "Let's check it out."

The shuttle lowers to the churning water and Aizen makes out long linear formations below its surface.

Petrified trees! Sha says.

Aizen slips on his envisuit and hits a button, cinching it tightly around his body, then dons his helmet. His excitement surges as the shuttle hatch opens, revealing the chopping waves. *This must be how Dad felt when he discovered the WorldRing entry!* Aizen makes a note to send his father the recording. He freezes, realizing that he misses his parents for the first time since arriving to Earth. He frowns, pushes the thought from his mind, and dashes *Record* on visor. He clips a tether from his suit's coiler to the ship's frame and dips into the water. He leans forward against the current and lowers his head below the surface to see the petrified trees. His feet suddenly lose their grip and the waves pull him from the shuttle. The tether catches, and Aizen flails, trying to find the bottom with his treads. A foot makes contact with an old tree. Aizen quickly activates its grip. Then, his other foot finds a home. Slowly, clumsily, he traverses the ghost of an island, searching for any clue of ancient habitation.

He covers it all in three hours.

This isn't it, he concludes. *Did you know?*

Justin appears. *I must admit, Mermer was right about not recognizing home. I have no idea where it was.*

Aizen boards the shuttle, pulls off his envisuit, and takes the cockpit seat. His stomach growls as the shuttle rises. He studies the coastline, finding a break in the rocky shore to make camp. When he lands and the hatch opens, Aizen is struck by the sound of crashing waves. Memories from a life beneath the water, of traveling from one rock to the next, dodging pelicans, falling in love, then losing that love, race through his mind.

For the first time, Aizen senses that Mermer is afraid. *But he's our pillar...* He cautiously steps upon the sand, feeling it shift beneath his feet. *Off with the boots, away with the socks!* Now, granules slip between his toes and stick to his soles. He breathes deeply, taking in the salty scent mixed with healthy decay. *Low tide.* He spies rocks covered in seaweed with water collecting between them. *Tide pools.*

He grabs his pack from the shuttle and sprints across the sand, marveling at how it feels. By the time he reaches the rocks, his thighs burn. *Earth gravity just cannot be replicated.* Even after a year, his stomach still feels like a rock and his heart exuberantly pounds. "Magsuits do little for internal organs and the weight of blood!" suddenly comes from an ancient memory. *But who had said that?*

He navigates the slick rocks, finding small pools hosting tiny fish. He dips his hand into a pool, closes his eyes, and listens for their voices.

Nothing.

Why is that? Aizen wonders.

He's so scared, Aizen thinks and opens his eyes.

He catches a scurrying in a pool ahead. An armored creature crawls into the crack of a stone. *It can't be!* He climbs closer and kneels, trying to get a better view. His heart races. Movement comes and a spiked leg emerges from the crack, then a claw and an armored head. Aizen holds his breath.

Don't get your hopes up, comes Justin's voice. *It's a Dungeness crab.*

Aizen thinks about that. *But it looks just like a grodote.*

That's because you've never seen them with your own eyes.

Aizen rummages through Justin's memories until a grodote appears. *Yeah, not even close.* He stands and breathes deeply, trying to subdue his adrenaline when a monstrous shadow passes overhead, sending his nerves through the roof, instead.

My god! A Pelican! Justin cries, pointing at a prehistoric looking creature drifting comically slow in the sky, as if suspended by cables. It teeters left and right adjusting to offshore winds, then circles above a tide pool, squawking.

"Ahlongee!" cries a voice from below. "Eh! Eh! Ahlongee!"

The bird squawks again and flaps away.

Aizen's eyes drop from the pelican to the pools to find a young woman with a fish writhing on her spear. She is dressed lightly despite the chill, and each item strapped to her leather belt appears to have a purpose. Her skin is weathered, her muscles are defined, and her hair is braided back tight. Aizen's excitement surges. *Not even Dad has seen a native Terran!*

The Terran whirls in Aizen's direction.

Shit! He ducks and stumbles into a pool. All is silent but the waves. Aizen closes his eyes and slips into meditation, but there is so much life on Earth that he is overwhelmed. *Just like every other time I've tried.* He drops his meditation and slowly peaks his head above the rocks. The woman is gone. He studies the ocean waves framing one side of the tide pools, then the rocky cliff framing the other. *Where'd she go?*

A powerful hand snatches Aizen's hair, pulling his head back, and the unmistakable edge of a blade meets his throat.

CHAPTER TWO

The cafe is dimly lit, as Samuel knew it would be, and the old don, dressed in a Hardsill tunic with a cartel pin on the breast, sits at a table in the back calmly sipping coffee affront a wall of artisanal Ganymedan blends. *Illegal on other worlds,* Samuel knows. Several large enforcers sit at adjacent tables looking like they could snap a person in two.

"Don't be afraid…" says the massive man in Samuel's earpiece. "…I'm just outside. I can hear everything you can hear. If there's trouble, I'll know it long before you do."

I'm not afraid! This is my home! These are my people! Samuel wants to respond. *But he won't listen to me. I'm just a 'Boy' to him.* Strangely, despite knowing little, Samuel feels he can trust this monster of a man. *But what kind of a name is Ulysses? And why is it familiar?* Samuel hobbles closer to the old don, still adjusting to the prosthetic leg he found in their refuse barge's infirmary.

Baristas stare, waiters glance, and the enforcers frown. The only one that smiles is the don, revealing missing front teeth.

Samuel stops across the table from him, reaches into his pocket, and retrieves an embroidered patch depicting a seedling, one he tore from a soldier's uniform before departing Eden Bank. He tosses the patch on the table.

"My, oh my, this is certainly a surprise," the don says. "What happened to the old woman?"

"Caught in the crossfire," Samuel answers, as he and Ulysses prepared. "I'm the sole survivor."

The don peers down for a moment, then his eyes pop back up and search over Samuel, fixating on his pant leg. "Barely a survivor at that," he says and motions to a chair. "Please, have a seat."

Samuel awkwardly sits, his prosthetic leg having not been properly calibrated. A waiter places a cup filled with black liquid in front of him.

Coffee... Samuel does not touch it.

The don leans close. "My boy, how much seed did you get?"

Samuel places a holotile on the table next to the embroidered patch, opens the refuse barge's inventory, and slides it over.

The don's eyes light up as he sifts through each variety. "This is far more than expected." He again fixates on Samuel's leg. "How did you move so much cargo on your own?"

"Ambushed by a second team," Ulysses whispers into Samuel's earpiece.

"There were two regiments, not one," Samuel says. "We were ambushed by the second regiment after we loaded the seed."

"I see." The old don sits back and taps his thumb to each of his fingers, his eyes staring upwards, lost in calculation. He stops and brings his eyes level. "I put this at fifty-seven million credits."

Ulysses gasps. "That's incredible!"

Maybe several centuries ago, Samuel thinks, knowing the true value of the seed. "Unacceptable," he says, staring down the don.

"What the hell are you doing!?" Ulysses hollers through the earpiece. "That's a great price!"

"It's worth at least two-hundred million," Samuel states, unshaken.

The old don's gap-toothed smile dwindles. His eyes darken. "Who do you think you are, demanding such a price!?"

The enforcers flanking the don stand.

"Abort! Abort!" Ulysses cries.

Samuel ignores Ulysses and says, "I'm Samuel Kell."

The old don's eyes go wide. "A Kell?" He motions for the enforcers to sit. "My boy! Why didn't you say so!? Please, your full legacy name! Do tell!" The old don clasps his hands. Even the enforcers smile.

"Uh… What's happening?" Ulysses asks.

Samuel grins and says, "Guilhadenpicardinesinkell."

The don cackles with excitement. "And how many years are you!?"

"Seventeen," Samuel responds.

The don looks up at the ceiling. "Praise Sol! You hath delivered!" He sets his gaze back on Samuel. "Two-hundred million it is, my boy. And, please, see The Augmentor about that abomination of a prosthesis." The don retrieves his holotile and flicks the payment to Samuel's. "It is done, my boy. I hope you understand how happy you just made this old man."

"I do," Samuel says, stands, and hobbles out of the cafe.

The streets are dark and moist from a fresh simulation rain. Samuel walks in silence, replaying the moment in his mind. *It actually worked.*

"You have some explaining to do," Ulysses says into his earpiece, breaking the serenity.

Before Samuel can respond he registers Ulysses's monstrous frame from his peripheral down an alleyway off the main street. He glances over his shoulder to see that he is not being followed by enforcers. *Such trust in tradition,* he thinks and hobbles down the alley. He removes the earpiece from deep within his canal as he nears Ulysses.

"I told you," Samuel says shortly. "Even if you incorporated your sister's memories, you still know nothing about Hardsill."

Ulysses clenches his jaw. "Why does your name hold such power?"

"It's only in this situation," Samuel says. "Only a few families survived on Ganymede after The Fall, forced to interbreed. To ensure the genetic pool remained strong, they kept all of their previous family surnames, shortening them to a single syllable, so that they always know who to match with. Now, it's become more of a tradition."

"So, who do you match with?" Ulysses asks.

He catches on quick, Samuel thinks. "Don Credence's daughter is a *Car,* which is in perfect sequence with a *Kell* if the ages align."

Ulysses cocks his head. "So you'll be married to his daughter?"

"Think of me more like a prized bull whose sole purpose is to provide his cartel with a strong heir."

"That doesn't sound like a good deal."

Samuel shrugs. "I'm protected and my family will be rich."

Ulysses gives a look. "Why did you go through with the raid if you had this at your fingertips?"

Samuel grins. "There are thousands of Kells my age. But the dons only accept genetics from donors who prove themselves worthy."

Ulysses mouth opens with sudden understanding. "So the raid itself was the reward for you, not the seed."

"I didn't even know we were hitting a seed bank until moments before. If I had, I would have certainly backed out."

"Fascinating…"

Samuel retrieves his holotile. "Shall we get this over with?"

Ulysses slowly lifts his holotile. "What happened to that scared boy I met not long ago?"

"Well… you spared me, which means you either value or pity me. Both are forms of trust."

"What if it's only to get my half of the payment?"

Samuel thinks about that. "You seem like a person who values principle over money."

Ulysses lets out a little laugh. "You're an interesting one."

"So, we split fifty-fifty. Which means twenty-eight point five million credits for you," Samuel says.

"That's not fifty-fifty," Ulysses says darkly. "It's a hundred million each."

Samuel grins. "Didn't you say fifty-seven million was a great price?"

Ulysses's pale eyes burn into Samuel's.

Oh shit, too far, he thinks.

But then, the massive man smiles. "I am a man of principle, just as you said. And one could say that I owe you my life. Therefore, I accept your split. But, mark my words, this will be the one and only time you best me, boy."

Still a 'Boy,' Samuel thinks, but he cannot help feeling proud to have tricked this powerful man. He types, *"28.5,"* and flicks it to Ulysses's tile. "What should we do with the refuse barge?"

Ulysses nods when his holotile beeps. "We compromise its fusion drive, so that it must be scrapped."

Samuel makes a face.

"What?" Ulysses asks.

"We stole the barge from impound in Puck's orbit and overwrote its registration with one that frequented Kuiper Belt stations. That was just a few weeks ago." Samuel searches for the original barge's registration tag. He smiles. "Looks like nobody's checked the inventory. It hasn't been reported stolen yet."

"Are you suggesting we simply return the ship?"

"Well, someone's gonna figure out a barge with a duplicate registration docked with Eden Bank. But, if it leads back to impound and we revert the barge's registration, then Hardsill will not be on anyone's radar."

"What about the port? There's a record of us docking here."

Samuel motions to himself. "I'm a Kell... and Don Credence owns the port."

There is a sparkle in Ulysses's eyes. "You're starting to impress me... Sam."

♦

Clara and Jonathan stare at a creature lounging on their sofa with curled, quadrupedal legs, a strangely human torso, and swirling red eyes.

"Clara Ocol," says the creature in a raspy, Arkathy voice. "It's been too long."

"Supreme Minister Hjordiana," Clara mutters. *What is she doing here!?*

The minister looks at Jonathan. "Give us the room."

"No... he stays," Clara says.

The minister tilts her head. "There are things we must discuss that cannot risk additional ears."

"I know everything," Jonathan says, standing his ground. His eyes wander from the minister to the dark corners of their apartment.

Cloaked soldiers are around us, Clara realizes.

Minister Hjordiana smiles wickedly. "You only know the end of a very long and unfortunate history, I'm afraid."

"History repeats itself," Jonathan responds.

"I don't think you realize how dangerous of a saying that is," she snips. "It assumes the worst."

"But also the best," Clara says. "What do you want? I gave nothing away during the interview, which I'm certain you oversaw."

"You did well in navigating Celina's questions," the minister says. Her demeanor changes. "But, I am not here to discuss the interview... I..." the minister pauses, searching for the correct words. "I need your help."

My help? Clara doesn't know what to say.

"Please, Clara, I must talk with you privately," she urges.

This is serious, Clara realizes and glances at Jonathan. "Okay..."

"But—" Jonathan protests.

Clara touches his shoulder and turns back to the minister. "Only if your security detail uncloaks and leaves the premises."

Minister Hjordiana's eyes bore into Clara. "Very well."

Four Arkathy soldiers appear from thin air as their cloaks deactivate. They slowly leave the apartment, giving Clara cold stares along the way.

Clara points at the kitchen where she notices a light distortion by the synthesizer. "That one, too."

The minister bears her teeth. "Fine!"

A fifth soldier appears adorning captain stripes on their armor.

Captain Witteksam… The minister's second in command, Clara realizes.

Instead of a cold stare, the captain gives Clara a respectful nod.

"Now, Jonathan goes," the minister says, seething.

Jonathan steps outside after the soldiers and shuts the door.

Minister Hjordiana leans forward and places an orb on the coffee table. She opens a hologram, selects *Play*, and motions for Clara to sit.

A recording appears following a group of soldiers investigating a cylindrical station littered with bodies where a massacre looks to have taken place. They continue through a command room into a long corridor hosting hundreds of vault doors.

"Someone attacked a seed bank?" Clara says. "That's suicide."

"It was," the minister responds.

The recording comes to a large vault where a last stand had taken place. The back wall hosts a massive hibernation chamber.

The minister pauses the recording. "Whoever attacked this bank was not after the seed. They freed whatever monster was locked away."

Monster… Clara thinks about that. She peers into the hologram at a figure on the floor with gray hair. "Who's the old woman?"

Minister Hjordiana tilts her head. "Old woman? We only found humans."

To you, we're all the same, Clara thinks. "Where were the bodies taken?"

"Is this one special?" The minister points at the old woman.

"Perhaps."

"I will take you to the morgue myself."

Herself… Clara thinks about that. "Who else knows this happened?"

"I've assembled a task force to investigate the rest of the seed banks in the Kuiper belt to see what other secrets are hidden within their vaults. Besides them, it's just you and I, Clara."

Clara gives a look. "Of all the people you could have reached out to, why me, given our history?"

"It's because of our history, actually. There is no record of this monster and why it was locked away. According to the council's records, this thing never existed." The minister's red eyes focus on Clara. "But you, Clara, have a knack for discovering things that don't exist."

◆

I know him, Jonathan thinks, staring at Captain Witteksam, appearing more machine than creature in his auto-armor. *But how?*

"What are you staring at, Sapien!?" the captain rasps.

Why am I not afraid? Jonathan wonders. He continues to stare.

The captain squares up.

What am I doing? Look away. But Jonathan feels compelled to stare.

Just when Captain Witteksam steps closer, the apartment door swings open and Clara and Minister Hjordiana emerge.

"Thank you for your cooperation, Clara," the minister says, then snaps her fingers at the soldiers. They vanish in an instant and follow her down the corridor, but not before Jonathan is shoved at the shoulder.

Jonathan turns to Clara. "So, you're helping her now? Why?"

Clara remains silent until the elevator doors close. "I can't say."

"But… You said that I'd know everything," Jonathan says in frustration. *She promised me there would be no secrets!*

"It's a matter of galactic security."

"All the more reason," he says, standing his ground.

Clara purses her lips.

Oh, she actually wants to tell me, Jonathan realizes. "That serious?"

She timidly nods. "But there is something you can do."

Jonathan feels his heart lift. "Yes, anything. What do you need?"

"Find Aizen. We need *their* help."

She's going into harm's way, Jonathan knows it to his core. "Just when life normalizes," he says and takes a deep breath. "Be careful, hon. I have a funny feeling about all this. And there's something about the captain."

"You be careful, too," she says and gently kisses his lips. "Kip…"

"…Kip," he whispers, lost in her taste.

CHAPTER THREE

Waves crashing against rocky cavern walls greet his ears and their vibration meets his feet, but he cannot see a thing in his pitch-dark prison. And when he slips into meditation he still cannot sense anything with clarity.

Earth, you are a surprising world, Aizen thinks.

The sound of sliding metal comes and footsteps enter.

"Uddan!" cries the young Terran woman, her first word spoken since catching him at knife point.

Is this ancient English? Aizen ponders.

"Ud-dan!" comes again followed by a firm kick to his leg.

Well that certainly means, 'Get up!' He places his feet beneath himself and rises. Cloth slips over his head and rope is tied around his wrists. She leads him blind through passageways. Sounds of life come sparsely until the sun's warmth hits his skin and its light glows through the fabric. The Terran's footsteps stop and her firm palm presses against his chest.

"Sin jaden soned," she says, the words directed towards someone else.

"Con seed, comen down to," responds a withered man's voice.

I think you're right, Zion says. *This sounds rooted in English, but seems to have become its own thing.*

Can language really change so much in so little time? Aizen asks.

A millennium is not a short time, Zion says. *Especially with isolation. Listen through me.*

Aizen melds into Zion's senses.

The grammar is backwards, Zion says and Aizen becomes aware of it. *The consonants have been jumbled and many words are new, likely developed after The Fall.*

Little by little, some of the Terran phrases make sense.

She's asking the old man if he's ever seen a creature like me, Aizen thinks.

Yes, Zion confirms. *They're trying to determine if you are human or a creature they call a Sendu.*

Should I say something? Aizen thinks.

It would be good to establish that you are in fact human.

Aizen licks his dry lips, stretches his jaw, presses his tongue to the top and bottom of his mouth, then side to side into his cheeks.

"I… people… am," he awkwardly mutters.

The Terrans silence, then the old withered voice says, "Creature noise reminiscent of our dialogue, must be mimic like Sendu."

Aizen further stretches his jaw. "Not Sendu… I people… outside… world be… from."

The young woman pulls off Aizen's cloth hood, revealing her face only centimeters from his.

"Cannot be that outworlder understands us!" she snaps.

It's becoming more clear, Aizen realizes, maintaining his partial meld with Zion. "I am outworlder, with ability to learn languages. I learn now your language as we speak."

"That's impossible!" the young Terran cries.

Aizen feels like he has it and releases the melding. "It's not impossible, just difficult," he says in their language.

From beyond the young woman comes wheezing laughter from an old man with gnarled muscles and calloused skin, appearing like a spindly tree. "You are indeed no Sendu," he says. "But what business does an outworlder have here? We are no glass city. We have no answers."

Aizen thinks about that. "You have many answers, perhaps more than the cities, for this is where Earth's people still exist. You are the keepers of knowledge so many seek. But I am not here for this."

"Then, why are you here!?" snaps the young woman.

Aizen focuses on her. "I want to understand where I come from."

"How can we trust that you won't tell others about us!?" she asks.

Aizen pauses. "I wish I had an answer for you… but I don't."

"…You must be thirsty," the old man lightly says.

The young woman whirls to the old man. "No! We cannot trust him!"

Aizen catches a scent and licks his dry lips. His stomach growls.

"And hungry, too, I see," the old man says with a confident smile. "Come." He waves for Aizen to follow.

The moment Aizen steps forth, the back of his knee is struck, buckling his leg, and sharp, powerful fingertips grasp his throat.

"Stay put!" the young woman orders.

"Thalee, let him be," says the old man. "He is not the first outworlder to discover us and will not be the last."

Shock spreads across Thalee's face. "He's not the first!?"

"Please, Thalee. If he is going to tell others about us, let him speak of our hospitality. Not this." He points at her hand.

"To hell with you, old man!" She releases Aizen and storms off, pushing into lush shrubbery towards the heavenly smell.

The old man gives Aizen a funny look. "You've been holding back. I can tell by your stance that you are a warrior. Though you do not look it."

Aizen grins. "Were you a warrior, too?"

"I was a hunter. The best. Once upon a time." The spindly, old man turns down a path. "Come. You're starving."

Aizen follows the old man. The heavenly smell intensifies and the sound of fire popping and people chopping comes. They enter a clearing with stone benches lining its perimeter and a fire going strong beneath a large basin of boiling water. A young man rattles away at a heavy block of wood with a knife, chopping what looks like greens. Then, Aizen spies Thalee gutting fish with lightning efficiency. *But everything on Earth is toxic.*

Zion comes into view, studying the fish. *Let's see how she prepares it.*

Between cuts, Thalee gives Aizen hard looks. Eventually, she points her knife at him and says, "Be useful or leave!" She waves her blade at another spot with a wood block, knife, and a pile of tubers.

Aizen grins and hustles to the station.

"Make it like sand!" she commands.

"Yes, chef!" Aizen responds, snatching the blade and balancing it on his index finger to find its center point. *Impeccable!* He studies the tubers having several bulbs clustered together. *What is this?*

Give it a taste, Justin responds.

Aizen breaks a bulb from the cluster, cracks its shell, cuts a bit, and places it into his mouth.

No! It can't be! Justin cries.

It is! Kwai Lan suddenly jumps in.

Do you know what this means!? Sha adds.

Garlic didn't go extinct on Earth after all... Allessandra finishes.

"It grows wild here," the old man says as if reading Aizen's thoughts.

Incredible, Aizen thinks and channels Allessandra's experience, cracking and deshelling each clove, and crushing them with the flat of his blade. Then, he machine-guns away at a forty-five degree angle. Crushed cloves become diced, then minced. *She said like sand!* Aizen picks up speed. His hands are a blur. He abruptly finishes, sets the blade on the block, and says, "Ready, chef!"

Thalee no longer frowns. The old man no longer smiles. The young man no longer chops. Instead, they stare at him wide-eyed.

They weren't ready for that, Aizen realizes. "I'm a professional chef," he says, hoping that might explain.

"What's a *sheft*," the young man whispers.

"It's a person whose profession it is to prepare food," Aizen says.

The young man stares blankly, then says, "What's a *pro... fa... shun?*"

Aizen thinks about that. "A profession is your purpose in society."

"You only have *one* purpose!?" Thalee snips.

"Well, no," Aizen responds.

"So you have more than one *pro... fa...shun!?*" she asks.

"Well... no."

"Then, you only have one purpose, idiot!" she struts over to study the garlic, then the blade. She grabs the knife and a clump of the minced garlic and heads to the large basin. She throws the clump into the boiling water, then stuffs the knife into her leather sack. "Can only do one thing," she mutters with a short laugh and goes back to cleaning her fish.

The sound of the young man's chopping returns.

The old man approaches Aizen. "You seem confused."

"I am," Aizen responds. "About many things. But mostly, why are you preparing fish despite their toxicity?"

"This word... Are you wondering why we don't get sick?"

"Yes."

The old man smiles wickedly. "That's a secret we never tell."

"I'll just figure it out, then," Aizen says.

"If you think you can," quips the old man.

Aizen snaps his attention to Thalee, studying her cleaning technique. But he cannot find anything special. He looks at the garlic he minced, instead, then at the young man and his piles. "What are those greens?"

The young man gives Aizen a funny look. "Just feldhart, drinksimp, and shengert."

That looks like a type of sea-stalk, Mirko says, pointing at a pile of chopped rings.

Agreed, says Kwai Lan.

And that's cilantro, Sha suddenly says, pointing at another pile.

What do Garlic, cilantro, and sea-stalk have in common? Aizen thinks.

Perhaps we should look at what toxins are present in the fish, instead, says Zion, and the others pause to consider.

Dione appears. *Despite the nuclear fallout, Commander Meeks and his crew found the most prolific toxin on Earth was methylmercury discharged when the Terrans desperately reverted to coal power.*

Are you certain of this? Aizen asks.

Dione pauses. *Almost all the Terrans had perished when Commander Meeks arrived. So, I'm not sure. Nobody is.*

But methylmercury and radiation were issues before The Fall, says Sha.

And what was the solution? Aizen asks.

Limit consumption, Kwai Lan says.

Or... Contain the toxin, Zion adds, pointing at the third unidentified pile.

"May I taste it?" Aizen asks, pointing at the third pile.

The young man nods.

Aizen takes a pinch and gives it a sniff. A vision of a lawn and the roar of a combustion engine comes. *Justin's memory...* He places the green on his tongue.

Ha, Justin reacts. *It actually is a lawn... Well, it's a type of milkweed... it's dandelion.*

So, they're all packed with phytonutrients, antioxidants and amino acids, Sha says.

And sea-stalk is full of alginates, Mirko adds. *Oh my Sol...*

What? Aizen asks.

This would have saved us on Enceladus... he whispers.

I don't understand, Aizen says.

These chemicals naturally combine with radioactive particles and methylmercury, among hundreds of other toxins, including the hydrocarbons that Mirko experienced, Sha says.

And once combined, they harmlessly pass through our digestive systems, Kwai Lan adds.

Aizen looks into the boiling basin, then at the old man. "The chemicals in feldhart, drinksimp, shengert, and wild garlic combine with the toxins in the fish, allowing your bodies to harmlessly pass them."

The old man's smile drops. "What's your name, young man?"

"Aizen Ocol," Aizen responds, realizing he doesn't know any of theirs, save Thalee's. "What are yours?"

"I'm Kune," says the old man. That young man is Tadem. And you already know Thalee." He tilts his head. "Aizen Ocol… are you *The One?*"

Aizen's heart skips a beat. *How could he possibly know that!?*

The old man smiles. "It's a pleasure to finally meet you."

CHAPTER FOUR

"There it is," Samuel says, pointing out their refuse barge's window at a cluster of ships orbiting Puck, tinted blue by Uranus's glow.

"It looks like a ball of trash," Ulysses responds.

"That's the idea." Samuel checks the scanners. "No active ships present."

"Shouldn't this place be swarming with police?"

Samuel points at a dot beyond the ball of trash.

Ulysses squints. "I see, there must be thousands of these impound clusters orbiting this moon."

"Patrol will eventually make their way here, but not for another week or so," Samuel says. "It's not their main form of security anyway."

A flicker of light comes from the impound cluster ahead.

"Containment field detected," chimes the ship.

Samuel opens his holotile and dashes *Negotiate*. His holotile pokes and prods the containment field until finding a signal matching its registry.

"Containment field opening at slip 43," says the ship.

Ulysses watches as an empty section appears. "Slip 43, I presume."

"Yep." Samuel nudges their refuse barge into position, pointing its nose at the anchor point. Barges to either side lie dormant, ghostly, their noses gripped tightly by impound claws.

"Docking in three, two, one…" the ship chimes.

A firm nudge comes as contact is made. Mechanical jaws close around the refuse barge's nose and lock tight.

"That's it," Samuel says. "Registration is set back to its original. As far as anyone knows this ship never left impound."

"Well done," Ulysses says.

"Not done yet." Samuel hobbles to the barge's rear hatch and takes his helmet from the wall.

Ulysses gives Samuel's leg a skeptical look. "Didn't The Augmentor say your new prosthetic would be like the real thing?"

"It's on battery right now. Once synced to my envisuit it'll have access to a stronger power source," Samuel says and dons his helmet.

"Do you wish to pair with Debilitator 5000?" appears on visor.

"Yes," Samuel says and the leg becomes nimble. "See?"

Ulysses crams on a helmet over his large cranium and hair. "Doesn't seem very good in a pinch."

"Good thing I intend to live a quiet life after this," Samuel says, feeling freedom right at his fingertips.

They step into the airlock and purge atmosphere. The outer door opens. Ulysses clamps a paw on the hatch jamb, turns his leg ninety degrees, and places his boot's magnetic rollers against the hull. When they snap onto the steel he pushes with his other foot, shifting his entire body perpendicular to the hull, and glides off.

He makes it look so easy, Samuel thinks. He sets his boots to *Spacewalk,* but struggles to get onto the hull. A sudden yank comes from his collar and Samuel knows Ulysses has picked him up. He proceeds to turn Samuel ninety degrees and plants him on the hull.

"You've never done EVA before," Ulysses states.

"And never doing it again," Samuel responds.

They slide their feet as if skating, maintaining constant contact with the hull. A tiny two-passenger craft appears mag-locked to the barge's backside. They open its hatch, which is nearly the entire back half of the craft, and climb in. Once sealed, Samuel takes the cockpit seat while Ulysses curls next to him where a copilot seat once resided.

"This thing sucks," Ulysses says.

"Standard issue tug, it's the only craft allowed in and out of the containment field," Samuel says, starting up its system. He takes the stick and releases its mag-lock. The tug drifts away from the barge with little puffs of gas. As they near the subtle light of the containment field it opens just wide enough to let them pass.

"How do you know all this?" Ulysses asks.

"My late father was a tug operator. I inherited this craft from him. That's why your sister recruited me." Samuel sets the tug to cruise, kicking its little fusion drive into action.

"And this can make it back to Hardsill?"

"Absolutely," Samuel says. "It can even act as a life raft with enough emergency rations for two months." He catches the look on Ulysses's face. "We'll be back on Hardsill in three days."

"Three days?" he groans. "I can't believe I let you talk me—"

Blinding light pierces through the tug's windows. Ulysses and Samuel duck to shield their eyes.

What the hell was that!? Samuel thinks. When the light dissipates he whirls around to see the cluster of impounded ships behind them shattering into thousands of pieces.

"Is that thermonuclear!?" Ulysses shouts.

In space? What's the point? Samuel thinks, knowing the most destructive part, the shock wave, is nonexistent in a vacuum. He then realizes that it was the reactor cores of the impounded ships that detonated. *But what set them off?* He searches space around their tug until finding a patch above them devoid of stars. He points and whispers, "What's that?"

Ulysses is already staring at it. "Can this tug go any faster?"

"No," Samuel says, watching the stars in front, behind, and to either side vanish like a curtain is dropping.

"We're inside a ship," Ulysses says under his breath.

The tug lurches as its mag-lock is remotely engaged. Its fusion engine cuts. *Commandeered,* Samuel knows. Strange thumps are felt through the tug's floor.

"Switch to hyperthermic view," Ulysses whispers.

Samuel does and a shuttle bay with several silhouette's marching forth becomes visible. *Their legs are quadrupedal.*

"The Arkathy!?" Ulysses growls.

"I think so," Samuel says.

The silhouettes stop short and raise rifles. The tug's rear hatch opens.

"You are in violation of article 244 subsection C of the Council of Colonies!" comes a raspy voice. "Come out with your hands up!"

They'll open fire on Ulysses for sure, Samuel thinks. *I'm on my own.* He opens his tug license and registration on his holotile.

Ulysses spies the registration and nods.

"I'm coming out," Samuel says on a public frequency, trying to mask his anxiety. "But I can't see anything."

One of the Arkathy motions and lights turn on to reveal six Arkathy soldiers in heavy auto-armor.

Samuel inches out and around the tug with his hands up, projecting his information above. His heart pounds, his stomach cramps, and his remaining leg shakes. The soldiers aim their rifles as he nears. They seem just as nervous as he is.

"Stop there! Turn around! No sudden movements!"

One approaches to read Samuel's registration, then stretches their hand shifting side to side from Samuel's head and working down. The soldier pauses at Samuel's prosthesis, then continues to his feet. A beep comes. The soldiers relax and lower rifles.

"What are you doing here!?"

Their commanding officer, Samuel realizes. "Routine maintenance on the impound clamps."

The commander looks at the tug. "We'll escort you to Miranda where you can take a ferry out of the Uranian system."

"What's happening?" Samuel dares ask, fighting his anxiety, finding that his voice sounds strangely innocent. "Why was the impound cluster detonated?"

The commander's helmet shifts slightly, focusing more on Samuel. "This system is on lock-down. That's all you need to know. Come with us."

They quickly surround Samuel, snap about, and march, nudging him along. But just before passing through the bay doors, entering deeper into the ship, one of them stops. They rasp back and forth, seemingly arguing and pointing at the tug.

Shit, Samuel thinks.

The one approaches the tug and scans.

"Sam… Get out of the way," Ulysses whispers on a private frequency.

Samuel studies the Arkathy soldiers and their rifles fixed upon the tug. *They're not watching me.* But when he is about to run for it, the Arkathy commander waves a hand. A pulling comes against his suit, dragging him across the floor and pinning him flat against the back wall. *Magnetism!?*

"That'll do," Ulysses whispers.

The Arkathy form a semicircle around the tug as the one continues forward.

"Come out with your hands up!" they rasp.

Ulysses does not emerge.

"Last warning! Come out with yo—"

As if hit by a train, the one is sent rocketing across the bay, slamming into the wall beside Samuel and knocking out the magnetism holding him. He drops to the floor and sees a massive fist indentation in the soldier's chestplate. The soldier groans, slowly places its quadrupedal feet beneath itself, picks up its rifle, and gallops back into the fray. More soldiers are tossed about by a force Samuel cannot see.

Because Ulysses is cloaked, he realizes.

Two soldiers converge electrical shots.

"Fuck!" Ulysses grunts and suddenly becomes visible.

The soldiers jump back when they see how massive Ulysses is, but keep firing. Others, in dented armor, pick themselves up and add their shots.

"Fuck! Fuck! Fuck!" Ulysses shouts as they press him against the wall. He raises his forearms to take the brunt.

He's losing... A sudden horror fills Samuel, realizing his newfound confidence is because of his invincible partner. But there is another feeling deep in his gut, new to him. *I must protect my friend!* Samuel stands, ready to jump into battle, to do whatever he can. *Maybe get a hold of a rifle!* Instead, his prosthetic leg locks to the floor.

"Debilitator 5000, Asset Protection Protocol initiated," spreads on visor.

What the hell! "Release my leg!" Samuel orders.

"No," D5000 responds.

"What do you mean, no!?"

"No, meaning the opposite of, Yes," it responds.

Ulysses drops to a knee, the Arkathy shots wearing him down.

"Release my leg! I must help Ulysses!" Samuel pleads.

"No, protection of asset is top priority."

"What asset!?"

"Samuel Kell, holder of prime genetic material, property of Calvin Credence," D5000 informs.

Don Credence... Samuel finally understands why the don was so insistent that he see The Augmentor. "So, you're here to protect me!?"

"Affirmative."

"But if Ulysses dies, I die!"

"Situation understood."

"So, release my leg!"

"No."

"You are not protecting me, then!"

"Alternate suggestion, enter Defense Mode. Do you wish to engage?"

"Yes!"

"Defense Mode activated."

Finally! Samuel thinks. His envisuit tightens around his upper thigh, then tears away from the hip down to reveal his prosthesis. The leg splits, forming a tripod, anchoring into the floor as its inner components flip up. The ankle points at the Arkathy soldiers like a gun barrel and the hip faces Samuel's chest, splitting into a double-handle.

"Choose your weapon," Debilitator 5000 says, then lists, *"Sniper, Shotgun, Anti-tank, Gatling..."*

"Gatling!" Samuel shouts and grasps the double-handle.

A spindle drops to the floor, shredding metal and passing the shards up to the gun. The barrel splits into several and spins. Samuel braces himself, breathing deeply, and aims at the Arkathy soldiers.

"Please, identify Ulysses," comes on visor.

"The big one!" Samuel shouts.

The Arkathy highlight in red as Ulysses highlights in green. Then, all hell breaks loose.

Samuel's teeth chatter and his hands go numb as shards of metal spit. Through blurred vision, he sees a soldier fall to the floor, and fixates on them, keeping them pinned. Another whirls around. Samuel shifts the gun's spray onto them, instead. The soldier jerks side to side as each shard makes contact, unable to aim its rifle, but also not going down. The previously pinned soldier is back on their feet. *Their armor is too strong,* Samuel realizes. Dread mixes with adrenaline. He feels nauseous. But then, his eyes drift to the side of his visor, to the options. *"Sniper, Shotgun, Anti-tank..."*

"Anti-tank!" he cries with his voice in vibrato, sounding like an Arkathy.

The barrels cease spinning and combine into one large cannon. The spindle continues collecting floor material, but the chamber now compacts it into one condensed projectile. Several agonizing seconds pass. The two soldiers give their rifles hefty recoil pulls.

Switching from stun to kill! Samuel assumes.

As they aim their rifles, the cannon kicks. Samuel's helmet cracks against the back wall. He fights to maintain consciousness and searches for the soldiers.

Only their quadrupedal legs remain.

The rest are knocked to the floor and quickly scramble to their feet. They stare at their dismembered comrades with horror.

Ulysses peaks from behind his forearms, first at the Arkathy, then at Samuel and his Debilitator 5000 cannon. "No fucking way!"

Beyond them, lies a meter-wide hole in the wall, traveling through several layers of the ship. Sirens wail, lighting flickers, and the artificial gravity cuts.

The Arkathy activate magboots and form up.

The barrel of Samuel's cannon glows red hot. *"2m45s remaining for cool-down,"* appears on visor.

"It needs to cool!" Samuel says.

"I'll take it from here!" Ulysses glides off on his mag-boot rollers, pushing side to side, circling the perimeter of the shuttle bay and picking up speed.

The Arkathy are unable to pinpoint his location, their shots hitting the walls, instead. On the third lap, Ulysses presses hard on the floor, dashing to the center, and lowers his shoulder into the cluster of soldiers. Their commanding officer is sent crashing against the wall so hard purple blood spatters from the auto-armor's joints. Ulysses continues orbiting and dashing to the center. The next soldier is met with a knife-hand strike at their armor's waist and their torso tips over like a broken tree limb. Another's helmet is struck in the chin, twisting their head around with an audible snap.

Only one soldier remains, Samuel thinks as the lighting momentarily cuts. When it returns, the Arkathy's arms dangle. *Pulled from their sockets?*

Ulysses picks the soldier clear off the floor by its head, disengaging its magboots from the floor.

"What are you doing here!?" Ulysses cries, his mighty fingers flexing around the helmet, causing it to creak.

The Arkathy lashes its quadrupedal legs, trying to kick Ulysses, then convulses and goes limp.

"…Suicide pill!?" Ulysses tosses the body across the shuttle bay.

The Arkathy ship suddenly shutters.

"Shit, what the hell was that!?" Ulysses cries.

"We're caught in a gravity well!" Samuel says and scrambles to deactivate the Debilitator 5000. "Asset is protected!"

"Confirmed, do you wish to return to normal function?"

"Yes!" Samuel says.

The cannon flips vertical and the tripod closes to reform the leg. Samuel bends the knee. It seems to function normally again.

"We must learn what they were after!" Ulysses says.

They race through a tight corridor passing an empty barracks, canteen, engine room, and into a vacant bridge with holograms flashing red. Uranus's Nu ring comes into view through its window.

Ulysses finds a hologram highlighting several locations in the Kuiper belt. "They're all seed banks! What are they searching for!?"

Prisoners like you, Samuel realizes and spies another feed of the ship's cargo hold with four cryotubes. He zooms onto one and mutters, "Khasi Sinam..."

Ulysses turns to him, a hard look on his face. "What did you just say?"

"Khasi Sinam," Samuel repeats and points. "That's this man's name."

"...The Butcher of Earth," Ulysses gasps. "He's the one I must find!"

"Is he one of you?" Samuel asks.

"No, but he has invaluable information!" Ulysses says.

The ship begins descending into Uranus's Nu ring.

"We have to go!" Samuel says. "The particle field will pulverize us!"

Ulysses stares at the hologram. "Not without Khasi!" The massive man bolts down the corridor to the cargo hold.

Samuel desperately tries to catch him. *We don't have time!* He enters the cargo bay to find Ulysses staring through a cryotube's window at an old man built like a laborer. A hologram flashes, *"KHASI SINAM—CRITICAL!"*

An alarm wails from the adjacent tube. The person within lashes about, then becomes still. Its hologram melts to, *"DECEASED."*

Another cryotube sounds its alarm.

"No!" Ulysses cries and paws at Khasi's tube. "They're not modified! They can't survive thaw without medical intervention! We must get Khasi's tube connected to stable power!" He turns to Samuel. "Can you negotiate with the cryotube's computer!?"

I can! Samuel quickly connects to the cryotube, finding its firewall is non-existent. He switches from the ship's failing power to the cryotube's emergency battery. "It's old technology! Its internal cells can't hold sufficient charge! We have two minutes to hook him up to the tug's auxiliary power!"

"Get the tug ready! I'm right behind you!" Ulysses says and grasps the cryotube, twisting and pulling until its mag-locked cleat shears off the floor. "Go!"

Samuel shuffles back to the shuttle bay, keeping his magboot's roller locked to the floor and pushing with his prosthetic leg. Ulysses grunts through com and the screeching of metal comes as the cryotube presses through narrow corridors. Samuel enters the shuttle bay, weaves around

Arkathy bodies, and enters the tug's open hatch. He takes the cockpit and starts.

"Access denied!"

It's still commandeered! Samuel realizes.

The cryotube comes pressing through the shuttle bay door, bending the opening into an oval shape, followed by Ulysses.

"What's taking so long!?" he shouts through com.

Samuel opens his negotiation program. *Never thought I'd use this on my own tug!* he thinks as his hand races across his visor. But when he penetrates one fire-wall, the Arkathy ship's computer puts up another.

"Oh no…" comes through com.

Samuel turns to find Ulysses at the hatch and sees the problem. *The cryotube won't fit.*

"Is there a way to expand the hatch!?" Ulysses asks.

"No!" Samuel says. "Strip the tube!"

"It's already stripped!" Ulysses cries.

"Access granted," suddenly spreads across Samuel's visor.

"We're in!" he says and looks at the cryotube. "There's no time! We must leave him!"

"Like hell we do!" Ulysses digs his fingers into the cryotube's hatch, bending its metal and breaking its seal. "This tug has an auto-med, right!?"

Samuel slams his fist onto the wall where a square reading, *"Medical,"* resides. The wall splits and a table with straps unfolds.

The cryotube's hatch bursts open, spilling foul cryogel across the shuttle bay. Ulysses pulls the quivering man from within, rips off diodes, and tears a throat tube with a heaving of liquid from the ancient man's lungs. Khasi's eyes pop open. He screams, gurgles, and sputters, then convulses. Ulysses straps him on the med table and says, "I'll save him! You save us all!"

Samuel spins to the cockpit, seals the tug's rear hatch, and warms the fusion drive. The moment the mag-lock disengages, the shuttle bay rotates around them. The exterior doors are opening and Samuel nudges the tug into alignment.

"Keep it steady!" Ulysses shouts above Khasi's screams.

Samuel hears the whining of a defibrillator and its thud of discharge.

"Fuck!" Ulysses shouts as the defibrillator whines again.

Focus! Samuel thinks. His eyes lock onto the opening doors, then the gleam of particles outside. *We've already descended into the Nu ring!* "Hold onto something!" he says and kicks on the fusion drive, blasting from the bay and into the Nu ring.

The first particles harmlessly bounce off the tug's hull, then one the size of a house collides with the Arkathy ship behind them, shattering it like glass. More come and it is with every ounce of luck that Samuel tracks and dodges. His adrenaline skyrockets. Time appears to slow. *But what about Ulysses!?* He glances back to see him with an arm and legs braced against the circumference of the tug and his other arm holding Khasi to the table.

The particles cease and their ride smooths.

"We made it!" Samuel says with excitement.

Ulysses is quietly staring at Khasi, who neither convulses nor screams.

Samuel sets the tug to cruise and heads back. "Is he okay?"

"He's dead!" Ulysses barks.

"I'm sorry he was lost," Samuel says. "But we made it free of the particle field. It will be smooth sailing back to Hardsill."

Ulysses darkens, his jaw clenches. "You don't understand! Khasi was key to my people's salvation! Without him, we are truly lost!"

Samuel looks at the floor like a scolded child. But then, a thought creeps in. *Ulysses needs the information, not the man.* "Can you do the memory immersion thing that you did before?"

"It doesn't work on just anyone!" Ulysses snaps. "You must share DNA, like my sister and me!"

You must share DNA, Samuel ponders that, then studies Khasi's features. "What's his last name again?"

Ulysses gives a confused yet fuming look. "Khasi Sinam!"

Sinam... Samuel deconstructs the name. *Nam, no... Na, no... Sin...* "He's a *Sin!*"

"What the hell does that—"

Samuel points at himself. "I'm a *Sin!*"

Ulysses furrows his brow. "I thought you were a Kell!"

"Guilhadenpicardine-*SIN*-kell!" Samuel rattles off. "That means I can do the memory immersion thing, right!?"

Ulysses's furious expression melts into fright.

"...Right?" Samuel quietly repeats.

Ulysses hesitantly says, "It has to be now. Are you certain you are related?"

"Absolutely," Samuel says.

The massive man pulls the syringe from his envisuit belt and activates its blinking red light. He places the tip against Khasi's temple.

"Zun dah!" He plunges the syringe deep into the ancient man's brain. Once it becomes green, Ulysses delicately pulls it from Khasi's flesh. "Samuel, you will experience everything this man lived as if it were your own life. But, it will be spotty and confusing. Memory immersion is not a refined technology. It is a last ditch effort. And… This will hurt."

Samuel digests Ulysses's words, but does not feel afraid. Instead, he feels like he has waited his entire life for this moment. "I understand," he says and slowly removes his helmet. He takes the syringe from Ulysses's paw and brings it to his temple.

"You are one of us, now, Samuel Kell." Ulysses kneels and presses his fist against his shoulder in salute.

Samuel breathes deeply, then cries, "Zun dah!"

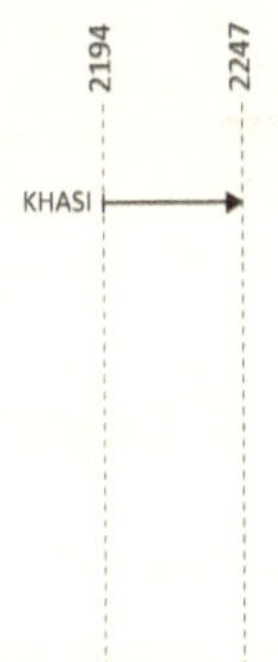

KHASI's TALE
Earth: 2194 - 2247

The mare cried out as it lay on the pavement, lashing her front legs, and when I searched farther down the freeway, to where the wrecked auto-truck had stopped, I found her hindquarters kicking just as wildly in a ditch. A line of entrails stretched across the freeway connecting the halves. The man who led the mare was nowhere to be found, and no one would look for him, for his life meant nothing. The loss of a horse, however, was a tragedy.

I was summoned to clean up the mess.

◆

"Some asshole tried crossing the freeway!" said a guard wearing lightweight armor with a New Horizons logo on its breastplate and holding a stun rifle.

This is an aboriginal crossing zone! The auto-trucks are supposed to yield! I thought, wishing I could say that aloud, but I valued what semblance of a life my family and I still had.

The two guards jolted when they noticed my presence.

"Sneaky bastard!" one snapped, grabbing my collar.

"What do you want?" said the other with lieutenant stripes.

I remained silent, grinding my teeth.

The lieutenant sighed. "You may speak."

I slowly pronounced their syllables, "I am a butcher."

"A butcher?" said the guard clutching my collar.

"For the horse," said the lieutenant.

The guard grunted. "So, why aren't you butchering?"

"Need the knife," I responded.

The guard looked at his lieutenant, whom nodded. He released my collar and rummaged through the back of their Dongfeng truck. "Where did it... Here it is!" He raised a short knife riddled with nicks and rust.

My heart sank, knowing the disrespect it would give the mare.

"Don't try anything smart or you'll need to be cleaned up, too!" the guard said and reluctantly handed me the rusty knife.

"I must sharpen," I said, studying the horrid blade, trying to keep my voice steady.

"You have one hour for the entire cleanup," said the lieutenant. "If you're not done by then, we'll scrap the horse's remains."

No time to sharpen, I knew.

I cut the entrails laying across the road first and carefully coiled them like rope. Then, I raised a privacy curtain around the front half of the mare, so that traffic could partially restart. I gently stroked her mane, as her legs continued to kick, and looked in her eyes, but she was already gone. *Just neurological twitches,* I knew, having seen it before with the sows I butchered. I slowly sawed the rusty blade through her throat for good measure, imagining the pain it would have caused. And the disrespect.

"I'm sorry," I whispered as hot tears rolled down my cheeks.

"Are you crying?" said the guard, approaching the privacy curtain.

Pull back those tears! Don't let him see! I quickly wiped them away. But I did not need to, for the moment he peered over the curtain and saw the mangled mare, his face went pale. He reeled back and vomited on the pavement.

"You better clean that up, too!" the guard spat as he shuffled away.

I went quickly to work, separating out the prized cuts of meat, ears, and tongue into one container to be given to New Horizons's upper management, while the lesser parts went into a second container to be distributed to the company guards. The junk pieces would be given to the families that worked this sector. *Like mine.* I could not help glance at the intestines, knowing what they considered garbage were the best parts. *They'll let me have it for certain!*

I rolled up the mare's skin for processing into luxury bags, then pondered the hooves. *Yes, that would be perfect with the intestines.* I sawed through the tendons and cartilage at the mare's ankles, then tied the hooves together and placed them alongside the intestines.

I lugged the containers to the Dongfeng truck, headed to the mare's hindquarters in the ditch, and raised another privacy curtain. *I've got time!* I thought and quickly went to work.

Thick evening smog was rolling in as I finished the hindquarters and I slipped a respirator over my nose, mouth, and eyes. I loaded the final containers onto the Dongfeng truck, turned to the guard, and extended the bloody knife hilt first.

"I'm not touching that," he muffled through his military re-breather designed to recycle his breath instead of filtering the toxic smog.

"Take the knife," ordered the lieutenant. "And mark it as returned."

The guard snatched the blade so quickly he could have sliced open my palm. "You better get going, curfew is eighteen hundred!"

The smog will be deadly tonight, I knew. "What time is it, now?"

"Seventeen-twenty," said the lieutenant.

No time to clean the blood off my hands. "Thank you," I said and hustled down the freeway shoulder as traffic resumed in full.

More than once, cars veered close to me, one brushing my elbow, and I saw its passengers laughing within. The exit came. I huffed through my respirator's restrictive filters, feeling about to pass out. Then, the silhouettes of my township faded into view through the smog, but it did not last long, for it was growing heavier by the second, blotting out the evening sun. Only a tower's light was visible in the distance, twinkling through the particulates.

I turned down the township's main street towards the elementary school as fine, gray particles began to flurry like snow. The school's front steps became visible, then the outlines of children wearing respirators waiting for their parents appeared. *I'm early,* I realized and slowed, giving my lungs a break. I looked over the children. *Kandara must still be in class.*

"Khasi!" came a muffled, foreign voice in my people's language. "What happened to you!?"

I turned to find Professor Shu wearing her re-breather not far away, but made sure no eye contact was made and not to answer.

"…You may speak," she added.

"There was a horse," I muffled between deep breaths.

She waved me closer and pointed at a trough of soapy water inside the school's entry. "Clean your hands before your daughter sees!"

"Yes, Professor. Thank you," I said and did as ordered, dunking my hands and furiously scrubbing, but the blood had already dried and flaked off in patches. I quickly wiped my hands dry as Kandara appeared.

"Daddy!" she muffled through her little respirator, skipped closer, and clasped my hand.

"Are you ready to go home?" I asked.

"Yep! Let's go!" she said, pointing in the direction of our camp and tugging me along.

I glanced back at the school to find it already lost in the smog.

When we turned off the main street, Kandara stopped in her tracks, pointing at the tower's twinkle of light in the charcoal sky, and her little ears rose as she smiled beneath her respirator.

"Is that!? Is that!?" she said with so much excitement she could not utter the word.

"Why yes, that's a star," I lied.

"I knew it!" she declared.

My stomach twisted, remembering a time when I gazed upon the entire arm of the Milky Way in the night sky before New Horizons turned our lush lavender fields into factories. Now, witnessing a single star was impossible. *But how could I bring myself to tell Kandara the truth of what it was?*

The road collected gray particles, mapping the footsteps of people ahead, reading, *"Converse, Nike, Reebok."*

Tourists, I knew.

I heard them before I saw them and their silhouettes faded in from the haze. They wore full helmets with oxygen tanks feeding purified air as they posed for holopics in front of an old mosque I attended in my childhood. *Now partially demolished for a new Buddhist temple to take its place.* My blood boiled and I glared at them despite the law.

"What are you looking at!?" one snapped. "Know your place, old man!"

What are you doing!? Think of your family! I scolded myself and lowered my gaze. "Sorry," I said in their tongue.

"Did you just speak without permission!?" the one said.

I shook my head and trotted along.

"Better not have!" he called after me.

We made some distance and I timidly looked back. They were obscured again. I felt a tug on my arm. Kandara was looking up at me.

"Why do they hate us?" she asked.

"It's a long story… for another day," I said.

Major Gao, the gatekeeper of our camp, nodded as we approached and his kunming dog sniffed through Kandara's clothing.

"Hi, John," she said, gently patting his fur.

John licked her hand, then turned to me and sat.

"Arms out," Major Gao ordered.

I raised them like airplane wings and felt the major rummaging through my pockets and patting down my legs and groin. He grasped my wrist and upturned my palm.

"Khasi, this is blood, explain."

I remained silent.

"You may speak," he added.

"There was a horse," I said.

Major Gao's demeanor lightened. "That's right… I'm supposed to give you this, actually. You may lower your arms." He handed me a tightly wrapped bundle of cloth. "But, what good are feet?"

"Good for flavor," I said, unwrapping the cloth to see the hooves I cut from the mare. *But no intestines.* "Thank you."

John whined, looking at me with hopeful eyes, prancing his front paws and licking his chops. I gently extended a hoof to the dog, who happily took it, wagging his tail.

"That's kind of you, Khasi. Better get home, smog is coming in thick tonight," the major said.

Kandara and I passed several brick boxes with corrugated steel roofs and small plastic windows until reaching ours. We entered its airlock. When the particulate laden air was purged, I opened its inner door. The air-purifier inside was running strong, adding white noise like old radio static. Kandara ran to her brother Juna at the stove with the night's stew simmering away, as I removed my respirator and hung it on the wall.

"Juna, look what I brought home," I said.

He looked my way and smiled when he saw the hoof. I handed it off to him. He inspected it thoroughly and gave it a good rinse. Then, into the stew it went. "I heard about the horse at the greenhouse today and thought they might have sent you," he said. "Was it bad?"

I made a face. "We should pay our respects."

Juna nodded, then made a circular motion around his eyes with his finger. I got the hint and moved to the washroom, ducking under the door frame to check my reflection in the cracked mirror. *Pollution goggles.*

I was washing my face when I heard Kandara yell, "Mommy!"

Saundi entered wearing a standard issue mathematician's uniform and removed her respirator. She had the same pollution goggles as me. She lifted Kandara off the ground and gave her a hug. Then, she returned our daughter to the floor, approached me in the bathroom, and gently squeezed my arm. I could not wait for her to wash so we could kiss. But I never got that chance, for Juna called, "Dinner!" and everything else fell to the wayside.

He set a towel onto the table, then the heavy steel pot atop.

Imitation lamb stew, I saw when I took my seat. *The hoof should add flavor.* I noticed fresh carrots and greens. *Juna must have smuggled them from the greenhouse.* I frowned, knowing what danger he put himself in. Juna ladled stew into four bowls and passed them around. But, before we dug in, we lowered our heads and thought upon the poor mare.

"...May you find peace," I finally said.

I spooned my stew, soaking in its warmth, relishing the bone and cartilage taste in the broth, and how it made even the imitation lamb taste like heaven. I finished the solid pieces, then tilted back my bowl, sucking in the broth.

Kandara was racing me, and when she finished, she smiled at her mother and said, "We saw a star today!"

"You did?" Saundi responded, looking at me with concern.

"Yep, it was twinkling and everything. I'm gonna become an astronaut and go there!" Kandara declared.

This was news to me. News to Saundi and Juna as well, judging by their worried expressions.

"...Hon," I began, setting down my bowl. "Maybe we should consider mathematics, like your mother."

"They need mathematicians in space. Trajectories," Kandara emphasized and waved her finger in circles, tracing orbits around imaginary planets.

I could not argue with my daughter's logic.

"So, an astronaut," Saundi said. "When did you decide this?"

"Today, with Daddy," Kandara said, bouncing in her chair.

◆

"Khasi, I must speak with you privately," Professor Shu said when I dropped Kandara off at school the following morning.

I nodded, then looked at my daughter. "Make sure to wash."

"I will, I promise. Bye, Daddy!" She dashed through the entry and joined a crowded trough of children washing arms and faces.

Professor Shu led me to her office, closed the door, and offered a seat. But I remained standing.

"We need to talk about Kandara," she said.

Professor Shu was one of the few New Horizons employees who learned to speak our language and she had always treated me with respect. I dared eye contact.

She grew nervous and evaded her eyes. "Your daughter's scores are off the charts. We've never seen anything like this before."

I was silent.

This made her even more nervous. "You can talk to me like a normal person, you know."

"Is that true?" I said, not believing those words passed my lips.

Shock washed across her face, but she thought about my words. "You're right, we're not equals. Nevertheless, I am looking out for your daughter's interests."

"What do you mean by that?" I asked.

"Her mathematics scores are beyond measure," she stated.

"That sounds good. What's the problem?" I replied, playing up to my expected naivety.

Professor Shu hesitated, then whispered, "They will want her."

My ears grew hot, remembering the day New Horizons ran for office, promising my people our homeland of East Turkestan returned to us for our support. *A promise they made to all the minorities.* But many of us could not read the contract's fine print, could not read its characters. And from what I now gather, the translated version was quite different from the original. To this day, I remember reading, *"In return for the restoration of Uighur culture and its homeland of East Turkestan, the Uighur people must aid New Horizons in preparation for interplanetary colonization."*

Nothing about this slavery... My eyes met the professor's again, this time hers held. "What can we do about this?"

"I can lower Kandara's most recent scores," she said. "But she's been testing absurdly high for some time now. The real problem is that she's expressed interest in becoming an astronaut."

"I'm sure thousands of children have said the same," I argued.

"But they're not scoring like Kandara is." Professor Shu shook her head. "If they have not already discovered her, they soon will."

And I will never see my daughter again... My anger flashed. "I would rather die than let them take her!"

Professor Shu raised hands to shush me. "Khasi, don't say such things. They would prefer it that way."

◆

"You're late!" Foreman Feng cried as I entered the pig hotel, coming furiously my way.

I felt my ears grow hot and my hands shake. *Breathe, let the anger flow out of my fingertips,* I thought, trying to control myself.

"What's your excuse!?" he barked.

I remained silent.

"You may speak!"

"Dropped daughter off at school. There was a problem."

"Is that a tone in your voice!?"

Breathe... "Sorry, sir." My hands still trembled.

"Not as sorry as you'll be by week's end! Your tone just cost your family a day's worth of rations!"

My arm almost lashed out, but I caught myself, masking it like a twitch.

"What's this!? Do you want to lose another day!?"

Breathe, dammit! "No, sir. Sorry, sir. Will not happen again."

"It better not!" The foreman smiled wickedly. "You're on piglet duty this morning!"

No! Please, no! I thought, feeling my stomach churn, remembering my training there as a younger man. "It's to toughen you up!" they had told us, but we all knew it was to break us down.

"Th-thank you, sir," I said, my voice cracking.

The foreman nodded, knowing he did his job well.

The smell of urine and feces grew as I descended several levels of staircase. Muffled sniffles and sobs of new trainees echoed in the otherwise silent basement. I took a long blade from the wall, found a place in line, and faced a series of freight elevator doors. The elevators hummed and I heard squeals from the pens on the hotel's upper floors echoing down the shafts. The humming stopped in front of us and the elevator doors parted, spilling hundreds of confused piglets. Electric pulses in the floors sent them scurrying from the cabs and through funnels, squeezing them into single file lines, one in front of each butcher.

Squeals became gurgles as we methodically picked up piglets and slit their throats, and they thrashed like fish on hooks as we tied their hind legs to racks above collection drums. *One hour. Two hours.* After the third, all the piglets were sent up a level for processing.

Tension in my throat and jaw was unbearable. A migraine was coming on. But I still had the afternoon ahead of me. *Not with the piglets,* I hoped, trying to convince myself that Foreman Feng would return me to my usual station processing the large sows upstairs.

The timer chirped, signaling us to report for lunch.

We trudged up the stairs to the ground floor canteen covered head to toe in piglet blood with tear tracks running down our cheeks like river deltas. We met pitiful looks from the other butchers when we joined the line for the day's meal — *pork dumplings*.

♦

Home… I just want to go home…

I waited for Kandara at the school's front steps, trying to keep my migraine at bay. Smog was rolling in again, not as thick as yesterday, but enough to blot out the sun and buildings. I donned my respirator.

Children appeared, greeting their parents and skipping off to one of the camps New Horizons built around the old town center.

I waited.

Professors departed in autocars.

I waited.

Janitorial crew began leaving.

Now, I panicked, checking the time, checking the day, checking the address. I paced back and forth, tempted to bolt into the school to search the classrooms.

"Khasi? Why are you still here?" someone said in my tongue.

I snapped my head up to find my camp neighbor, Ghetar, in his janitor uniform. "I'm… I'm waiting for Kandara," I said, my voice quivering.

"All the children have left," he responded.

No! I paced more furiously and heard myself whining like a dog beneath my respirator.

"It's okay, Khasi," Ghetar said, holding my shuddering arms. "I'm sure Saundi picked Kandara up."

I raised my arms, breaking his hold. "No! Only I pick her up!"

Ghetar looked nervously around us. "Khasi, calm down, if they see you like this, it's over…"

My eyes met his. I breathed in deeply and out at length, and crossed my arms to keep my shuddering less noticeable.

Sharp, echoing steps of dress shoes came from the school's hallway, and I knew Principle Zhang was on his way out. The steps stopped next to me.

"We're closing up the school now. Best be on your way."

Neither Ghetar nor I responded.

"Is something the matter?" the principal asked.

We remained silent.

"You may speak," he added.

"My… my—" I stammered.

"Khasi's daughter Kandara has not come," Ghetar said for me.

Principal Zhang thought about that. "Let's have a look at today's attendance, shall we?"

"Th-thank you," I managed to say.

The principal opened his holotile and scrolled through the names. "Kandara… Kandara…" he muttered under his breath. "Ah, yes, she's been marked absent today."

My adrenaline surged, my hands furiously shook. "No… no… Professor Shu was here when I dropped Kandara off. She knows."

"Careful with that tone, Khasi," the principal warned, but scrolled through another roster on his holotile. "It appears Professor Shu was absent today as well."

"No… We talked today," I again argued.

"Watch that tone!" the principal snapped.

Another figure approached from my peripheral.

"Is everything all right?" said a voice I knew, and I heard a sniffing around my legs.

"This Uighur is questioning my roster!" the principal hollered. "You must detain him!"

My anger skyrocketed. *This is the last straw!* But just before I lashed out, I felt a nose nudging my clenched fist. I looked down to see John staring up with innocent eyes.

"Khasi," said Major Gao. "Come with me." The major turned to Ghetar. "Go home, now!"

Without a word Ghetar hustled off.

"Make sure this one gets what he deserves!" Principal Zhang furiously said, pointing his finger at me, then marched to his autocar.

I maintained eye contact with John, letting my fist loosen, and scratched behind his one floppy ear. My shaking subsided. My rage dwindled. *Thank you, John…*

"Khasi, I must bring you in," Major Gao said. "Do you understand? You may speak."

"I understand."

He grasped my upper arm and pulled me along in silence until the New Horizons disciplinary office appeared in the smog.

"Khasi, before we go in, you must know something," Major Gao whispered. "General Xi arrived yesterday and has been evaluating student performances."

I stopped in my tracks and looked straight into the major's eyes. "Major Gao. Where's my daughter?"

"I don't know." His eyes intensified. "But I can help you find her, so long as you are processed without incident."

The major again grasped my upper arm, trying to pull me along, but I remained motionless, like stone. I watched his sudden comprehension of my strength, one developed from thirty years of grappling two-hundred kilo sows, and that I could easily overpower him should I choose. He let go of my arm and gave me a hard look.

"Khasi, will you please accompany me inside?" he politely asked.

All this time they've required submission. Yet, what they respect is defiance, I thought, but the major's voice conveyed more.

"I'm on your side," he nervously whispered. "Professor Shu and I work together."

They work together? I sensed truth behind his words.

"You trained in the military, right?" he then whispered.

Mandatory training when I was eighteen, before New Horizons took power. "Yes," I whispered back.

Major Gao rhythmically squeezed into my arm. It took me a moment to realize that it was Morse code.

"Play along," he was saying.

I took a step forward and lowered my eyes.

"You better listen when spoken to!" Major Gao shouted and shoved me forth. "Next time, I'll sic the dog on you!"

I stumbled as if weak and squeaked, "S-sorry, sir."

I felt John nipping at my heels. *Playing his part, too.*

Major Gao led me up the front steps and through the Disciplinary Office's main entry.

"Event," he informed through my arm. *"Gen Xi, here. You, listen."*

We passed several detention cells to one at the far end. He unlocked the door and shoved me in. "You better keep your mouth shut!" He locked the door and strutted away.

John gave a confused look, lowered his head, and followed his master.

Did he just trick me? My anxiety again swelled until I heard a faint voice coming from a ventilation grate in the ceiling. I removed my respirator, closed my eyes, and cupped my ears with my hands.

"You're late!" shouted a voice, sounding far away.

"Sorry, sir, there was an incident at the school," I heard the major say.

"Fall in and listen up!"

That must be General Xi, I thought.

"We have a situation! Our best prospect has disappeared!" said the general. "These cockroaches think they can hide her from us, but they do not know the depths we will go to ensure our victory in this war!"

War? I thought, taken aback. *What war?*

"Take a good look at this face!" the general continued. "This is Sonya Shu, the professor who took the child!"

My breathing escalated. *Kandara's with Professor Shu!*

"She's a corporate terrorist now! Shoot her on sight! This child is the future! She will shift the tide against the Hermians! We cannot afford her being smuggled out of New Horizons's territory!"

◆

I woke to a kick in the leg.

"Get up you piece of shit!" cried a guard. "You're released!"

Only took four days, I thought and peeled myself from the concrete floor. "Thank y—"

The guard cracked me in the jaw. "Did I give you permission to speak!?"

I remained silent, my cheek throbbing and tasting of blood.

"That's better!" He shoved me along, from the cell and through the front door to a regiment of New Horizons paramilitary in the street, each with a kunming dog. "Does anyone know which camp this prick is from!?"

"That's enough, private!" came Major Gao's voice. "He's from my camp. I'll escort him there, myself."

I felt a change of hands, one releasing my collar, the other taking my arm.

"No time," Major Gao squeezed. *"Come."*

I hustled beside the major, keeping my eyes down, hearing the whispered conversations of the guards as we passed by. Then, we were on our own, not a soul in sight. *The entire town is on lock down,* I realized.

"They haven't found Professor Shu or Kandara yet," Major Gao whispered. "But much is happening. You must get your family out of New Horizons's territory."

"No. I must find Kandara," I grumbled. "Where is she?"

"There are several places she might be right now, but we must stay away from them should they have any chance of escape. You must leave for the

Kazakh border. If Professor Shu is successful, they will meet you there."

"No," I said and planted my feet, becoming an immovable object again.

"Khasi, you don't understand the situation."

"Then, explain."

"Will you promise to keep moving if I do?"

"Yes."

"We're raiding the camps tonight," he quickly whispered. "This entire region is being liquidated."

I let the major lead me and asked, "What will happen to us?"

"The weak and old will die. The strong and skillful will work. And the young and brilliant—"

"Will fight in your war," I finished.

This time Major Gao stopped. "It's everyone's war, Khasi."

"When did it start?"

"Around the time you were born."

Almost fifty years ago... "Who are you fighting? People like me?"

"Khasi, we don't have time. We must—"

"Tell me!" I growled.

The major's look hardened. "It's bigger than your people. Bigger than my people. The Hermians started a war with all of System Sol."

With the whole solar system? "Did we already settle the planets?"

"Yes, over a century ago."

That cannot be! I thought, but sensed it was true. "What are Hermians?"

"They're the people who settled Mercury and, because of their proximity to the sun, they gained immeasurable power. That's why we need your people's cooperation. Earth must be a united front."

By any means necessary, I realized. "What exactly is New Horizons?"

"They're a metacorporation originating from Japan owning most of Asia, Oceania, and Australia. They're one of seven metacorporations that acquired Earth's countries."

"Who owns Kazakhstan?" I asked.

"Iranian Sun. That's why you must go there."

"Won't we be going from one bad situation to another?"

Major Gao shook his head. "Iranian Sun is Islamic owned. You will be treated like royalty and your story will be heard, for they would love nothing more than to weaken their competitors."

We reached the camp's gate.

"Be quick Khasi, I'll meet you at the northern edge of the fence with the equipment you will need," the major said.

"So, you know of the drop hole?" I asked.

"I've been covering your son's escapades for some time now."

"Thank you, Major Gao." I thought about the paramilitary amassed at the Disciplinary Office. "What about the dogs?"

Major Gao nodded. "Don't worry about them. Every year, Professor Shu has the children make chew toys for the young pups we train, so that they grow up immersed in the scents of your children. If a moment comes when the dogs' loyalties are tested, they choose the children."

◆

"Dad!?" Juna cried when I came through our airlock.

"She's not with you?" Saundi said with pleading eyes.

I shook my head. "Professor Shu hid Kandara when General Xi arrived."

She processed, then asked, "Where?"

"Nobody knows. That's why everything is in lock-down. But Major Gao believes they're going to Kazakhstan."

"Why would he tell you that?" Juna asked.

"Major Gao is working with Professor Shu. We can trust him."

"Can we!?" Saundi challenged.

I thought about that. "He had every opportunity to betray me and didn't."

"Because you're playing right into their hands!" she argued. "They probably think you hid her!"

"We have no time to debate this! There's going to be a raid at any moment!" I strutted to Kandara's cot and snatched her blankets and stuffed bunny. "We must tie Kandara's blankets around our waists. Major Gao trained the dogs to know our children's scents."

"Have you lost your mind!?" Saundi cried.

Frantic banging rattled our front airlock. We froze.

"Khasi!?" came a muffled voice.

Saundi peered through the window. "Ghetar!? What's he doing here!?"

I raced to the airlock, letting him in.

"Khasi, there's an entire platoon with dogs at the gate!" he said.

Saundi snatched one of Kandara's blankets and wrapped it around her waist. Juna did too. Ghetar gave them a confused look.

"Ghetar, New Horizons is liquidating the camps," I said, and saw his blank expression. "They're going to imprison us all."

"How's that any different from now?" he responded.

"We've been lied to. Humanity already settled the planets of the solar system and have been at war with Mercury for fifty years," I said. "They'll put our children on the front line."

"You're not making any sense, Khasi," Ghetar said with the same skeptical look as Saundi and Juna.

I sighed. "What matters is that there's paramilitary at our gates."

The whining of stun rifles firing, the ferocious barking of dogs, and the cries of people, came abruptly in the distance. We snapped our heads to the window.

"What do we do!?" Ghetar asked.

"Wrap Herta, Carste, and yourself in your son's blankets, pack your things, and meet back here in five minutes. I know a way through the fence."

Ghetar dashed through our airlock.

I turned to Saundi and Juna. "Pack only non-perishable food, an extra pair of clothing, and winter gear. I don't know how long it takes to get to the Kazakh border, but we must account for weeks while also packing light."

"How do we get there? No road is safe," Saundi said.

"Major Gao knows." I hoped that was true.

Saundi pursed her lips. "You better be right about him, Khasi."

I took a paring knife from the kitchen counter and ran my finger perpendicularly across its blade, testing its sharpness. "They don't consider kitchen knives a threat because their blades are only six centimeters long. But, like a sow, a person's jugular veins are less than a centimeter deep."

"Dad…" Juna gasped.

"I don't think it will come to that, but we must be ready," I responded.

After we packed and selected blades, we met Ghetar's family on the road. Evening smog was rolling in and we strapped on respirators. Growls and barks sounded just around the corner as paramilitary shouted muffled orders through re-breathers.

"Follow me!" I said and led the opposite direction, deeper into camp where a large bramble patch was.

"On the ground! Now!" a voice shouted.

I turned to see two guards with rifles raised behind us and kunming dogs bounding our way.

"The dogs are our friends! Our blankets are our shields!" I cried. "Around the house!"

Stun shots impacted the ground and brick wall, and I could hear the dogs' panting. *They're right behind us!* We plunged into the brambles, hoping to conceal ourselves. The dogs came sniffing at the edge of the patch, refusing to enter, and gave whining barks.

"What's gotten into you!? Get them!" a guard ordered, but their whining only grew.

The second guard neared. "What's the matter?"

"The dogs won't go in!"

"Then, you go in!"

"But—"

"That's an order!"

"Y-yes, sir!" The guard came crunching through the brambles, stumbling over gnarled limbs and catching his uniform on thorns. His footsteps approached Saundi, Juna, and myself, and I readied my paring knife, waiting for the guard's legs to appear, but he took a sudden turn.

"Let me go!" cried a young boy.

Carste, I realized.

"I got the little one!" the guard announced and started back to the road. "The rest of you better show yourselves or we'll feed him to the dogs!"

Wild barks came as the guard approached them.

"...And boy do they sound hungry!"

"We're right here!" Ghetar shouted from several meters away. Brambles crunched as he and Herta stood.

My heart sank, but I could not blame them.

"Too late," the second guard said.

Loud cracks were followed by heavy thuds.

Pistol shots! I realized.

"Mom! Dad!" Carste shrieked as the guard dragged him into the road.

The dogs barked ferociously and their claws scraped against the dirt as they bolted forth.

"Enjoy your din… No!" the guard sharply screamed.

I leaped to my feet and bolted through the brambles towards the screaming. A guard, thrashing on the ground with two dogs tearing into his arm and leg, faded into view. Carste appeared on the ground a few meters away, looking bewildered. Then, I saw the second guard with a pistol in hand, pointed at the boy.

"Don't!" I shouted.

The second guard snapped his head up and swung his pistol my way as I closed the gap. I ducked low, sinking my shoulder into his stomach, and grabbed his legs behind the knees, as if I were flipping a sow. *But this man is so much lighter.* I lifted him clear off the ground and back several meters, slamming him into a brick wall. His pistol tumbled into the brambles. I pressed my forearm into his neck, shifting up beneath the chin of his re-breather to expose his throat. He lashed his arms, striking my head, and his feet, striking my groin, but it felt like nothing to me. I pulled the paring knife from my pocket and pressed its edge against his neck.

"Wait! I'm sorry! I'm… ghurrllers!" he shouted as my blade ran across his throat.

I let him drop and watched him wiggle and convulse, until he was still. "Just another piglet," I whispered, feeling no remorse. *They conditioned me well.* My eyes drifted to the stripes on his breast. *The lieutenant from the cleanup,* I realized, and became aware of the first guard's screams. I slowly approached him. His arms and legs gushed blood from where the dogs had torn holes. His pack was on the road a few meters away. I knelt and rummaged through its compartments until I felt a familiar handle. I pulled out a rusty, nicked blade.

The guard's frantic eyes met mine. "H-help me!"

The dogs whipped their heads, baring their teeth at me. But then, they wildly sniffed the air and fixated on Kandara's blanket around my waist. I snapped my fingers and pointed at Carste. They quickly positioned next to the boy like sentinels. The guard looked relieved until he saw my eyes beyond my respirator's goggles. I knelt next to him and lifted the rusty blade.

His eyes shot from the blade to the captain lying motionless, then back to me. "W-what are you doing!?"

I studied the rusty blade as the shouting of more guards and the barking of their dogs grew. "No time to sharpen."

The guard's eyes widened in recognition. "What kind of monster are you!?"

"I am a butcher," I said and sawed the rusty blade through his neck. Tranquility washed over me. I was a different person. *Confident. Powerful.* Everything became clear. *I know what I must do,* I thought as the guard's gargles dissipated.

"Khasi?" said Saundi's faint voice. "Are you okay?"

"Stay there," I said and looked at the boy, who blankly stared at the blood-soaked dirt. "Carste is okay, we're coming back to you." I picked up the boy and trudged into the brambles, the two dogs obediently following.

"Where are Ghetar and Herta?" Juna asked.

"The guards used pistols, not stuns… They're gone," I whispered, hoping Carste did not hear me. *But how could he not know?*

"Where are the guards?" Saundi asked, giving me a hard look.

"The dogs got one, choosing to defend Carste, just as Major Gao said they would. I… stopped the second."

"Stopped?" Saundi challenged.

"What do you want me to say?" I responded.

She looked at the blood coating my hands and her eyes averted.

"We must move. There's a trail in the brambles that cuts to the opposing side of the camp to a drop hole under the fence. Our struggle here has caught their attention. The other end should be clear."

"I know it," Juna said. "That's how I get fresh vegetables in. I'll lead."

I clenched my jaw, but nodded. "I'll take the rear."

I handed Carste off to Saundi, who took him in her arms, her head turned away, refusing to acknowledge my existence.

No… My heart ached.

We slowly crunched through the brambles until Saundi and Juna's footsteps quieted ahead, and I knew they were on the path.

"This way, stay low," Juna said, crouched.

Sirens blared. Stun rifles winding up and releasing switched to pistol cracks. Shouts became blood curdling screams. *They must have found the slain guards!*

Saudi and Juna turned their heads and froze.

"Keep going!" I whispered, snapping them back into action.

Pistol cracks shifted from beside us to our rear. Then, barking came from the brambles. *They've picked up our trail!*

"Faster!" I whispered.

We were sprinting when the camp's perimeter fence became visible.

"Almost there!" Juna cried.

Scampering came from ahead and a kunming dog bounded towards Juna. My adrenaline surged. But, instead of tackling my son, the dog playfully circled around his legs, prancing its feet.

John! I realized.

"You've caused quite the commotion. We must move fast," came the major's voice and he faded in from the haze holding a large sack. "Saundi, Juna. You don't require my permission to speak."

"Thank you, Major Gao," Saundi said.

The major nodded, then saw the boy in her arms. "Carste?"

"His parents were killed," I whispered.

"I thought it would just be you three," Major Gao said. "I'll need to pick up another envisuit."

"Envisuit?" I asked.

The major handed me the large sack. "They're like re-breathers, but for your entire body. You can even recycle excrement into nutritional drink for several weeks. There are three envisuits in here. The way across the border is by traveling at the bottom of the Ili River. It will take two weeks for the currents to deliver you to the Kapchagay Reservoir in the Almaty region of Kazakhstan. Make sure you never come up, there are guards patrolling the entire way. Once reaching the reservoir, you must make contact with a Sergio. He manages the marina's slips. Do you understand?"

"Yes," I responded.

Major Gao looked at Saundi and Juna. "Do you understand?"

"Yes," they both responded.

"Good. I must retrieve a fourth envisuit for Carste, but John can show you the way to the river's launch point. I will meet you there. Be quiet. Be mindful. Our fates are tied now." With that, Major Gao took off, disappearing into the haze.

John watched the major leave, then circled about. The two other dogs joined in his circling and followed John through the drop hole, appearing on the other side of the fence.

"Let's go," I said.

Saundi set Carste on the ground. "It's going to be okay, the nice dogs are going to help us. Let's follow them through."

Carste kept his eyes down, but he knelt on all fours and crawled through the hole. Saundi went next. Then, it was Juna and me.

As soon as I emerged the dogs formed a triangle around us. John took the lead running ahead and coming back when the coast was clear. The other two flanked us, keeping watch to either side, sniffing the air wildly, and nipping at our heels when we were too slow. The alarm dwindled. Screams faded. Gunshots became distant. Town structures came into view, but we did not enter. The dogs led us into shrubbery at the southern edge of our township and down a steep hill. Large trees enveloped us. A river's whooshing grew.

Water is high. Current is strong, I gauged.

John stopped a few meters from the shore, laid into the bushes, and rested his head on his front paws. We ducked down, too.

The sun began to set, coloring the smog crimson, and when it dipped below the horizon, all went black. After several hours, John snapped his head up, and I heard crunching.

"John," whispered the major's voice.

He bolted into the darkness.

And then, the major appeared. "Sorry for taking so long, but General Xi called in the reserves." Major Gao lit a dim red light that illuminated our faces. "Take out the envisuits," he instructed and pulled a fourth envisuit for Carste from his pack. He gave a quick, but thorough instruction of how they worked, and helped Carste to don his.

I marveled at the symbols on its visor and how it changed visually to show things otherwise invisible.

"It's time," the major said. "Your journey will be terrifying, it will be lonely, for you cannot use communications without being detected."

I gave Juna a long hug. Then, he sealed his helmet, waded into the rushing water, and dipped beneath the surface.

That's one, I thought.

Saundi held Carste tightly to her chest as Major Gao clipped them together. I went to give her a hug, but she shrugged me off, not once glancing my way. She sealed her helmet and waded into the water.

Two and three…

"Major Gao," I whispered. "I will never forget this kindness. You are a rarity among your people…" I faced him. "…You have my deepest—"

Major Gao's eyes went wide.

"Major Gao? Are you okay?"

He raised a shaky arm to his earpiece.

I grasped his other arm. "Major. What is it?"

His eyes slowly met mine. "Khasi… I'm sorry."

"Sorry for what?" My heart pounded.

Cheers came abruptly from the paramilitary in town.

"They found them… They… hung Sonya… They… have Kandara…"

My body went cold.

Major Gao snatched his pistol and raised it to his temple.

"Don't!" I shouted, realizing what kind of partnership he had with the professor.

A crack rang and the major tipped over.

John barked wildly, running to his master and licking his face. All three began whining. I desperately tried shushing them, stroking their backs. Then, I had a thought. I rummaged through the clothes we intended to sink to the bottom of the river and gathered Kandara's blankets. I tied one around each of the dog's necks, looking like ponchos. They sniffed into them and curled to the ground.

I studied the rushing river, knowing my wife and son were swept away to a better life. I knew I would not follow them. I faced the paramilitary cheering in the darkness. The moment I sealed my helmet, figures patrolling the town's perimeter became bright points of light, and the silhouette of a woman swaying from a construction crane's boom by her neck appeared.

When I faced the dogs, *"John, WaiWai, and Serena,"* materialized on the visor. And when I turned to the major, *"Major Chuanjie Gao—Deceased,"* came.

I knelt and gently picked up his body. "I will always remember you," I whispered, waded into the water, and let the current pull him from my arms. I gathered the major's pistol, stun rifle, and utility pack. Then, I clipped Kandara's bunny to my envisuit.

The dogs were standing at the ready, looking to me for direction, but John's tail was low.

I removed my helmet and scratched behind his floppy ear. "It's going to be all right," I said. "Major Gao has gone to a more peaceful place. We will make time to mourn him..."

John looked deeply into my eyes.

"...But right now, I need your help." I brought the stuffed bunny to John's nose. "We must find a little girl."

◆

They called me *The Butcher of Earth*, but I was no such thing, for I held the natural world dear. *It is people that must be culled.*

Everywhere I went I saw my face, but I could not recognize myself, for the wanted images were taken from New Horizons's records before the rebellion began, before Kandara was taken from me.

That was five years ago...

I wondered where my daughter was, what she was doing, if she was okay, if I would recognize her, if she would recognize me, and if she would hate me for what I had become. *As Saundi certainly did.*

I watched John, standing like a statue and peering into the distance. Perhaps he was the only one besides me who knew how this all began, how my plight became everyone's, how a little girl saved millions from bondage, purely by existing.

Our homeland was ours again. Not returned as promised, but liberated by those who understood that promises are not designed to be kept. Our air was clearing. Our mosques were being rebuilt. And our cuisine was being rediscovered. But life would never be restored to its ancient glory. For our borders were under constant attack by either force or finance. Nevertheless, after two and a half centuries of communist and corporate rule, East Turkestan now stood tall as the only free country on Earth.

My liberation army, nearly ten-thousand strong, was camped outside of the ancient Chinese city of Xi'an. We had the same weapons New Horizons had and the same reserves, but we were still terribly outmatched. Our only advantage was the desire of those within New Horizons's own ranks to win their freedom. And it was working. Half of my army consisted of those who once oppressed us, either seeking redemption or looking to rid their own lands of their CEO masters. And as we pressed north, east, and south into old Chinese lands, we learned more of that even greater threat Major Gao spoke of—*The Hermians.*

The chain of oppression runs long, I thought, wondering if the Hermians had someone lording over them.

Dawn came and we marched towards Xi'an's walls with our chameleon cloaks activated, our artillery reflectors at the ready, and our cannons broken down and carried by teams of twenty, designed for quick assembly and disassembly. But before we could use them, white flags were raised along old fortes built within the city's ancient wall. A gate opened and an auto-dump truck zoomed out.

"No weapons detected," came on visor.

"Don't trust it, assemble cannons four and seven," I ordered.

I watched teams four and seven coalesce on visor, each member adding the next component, perfectly sequenced. *"21 seconds,"* appeared when team seven finished. *"26 seconds,"* for team four. The cannons trained upon the truck as it stopped. Its bed tipped up and people wearing suits rolled limp to the ground.

A projection above the truck read, *"The heads of New Horizons – Xi'an Division, welcome you!"*

"What's happening?" I asked Juna on our private frequency from across the Kazakh border.

"This is incredible," Juna responded. "Reports are coming in from Beijing, Shanghai, Chongqing, Shenzhen, Guangzhou… All of old China is liberating as we speak."

"At once?" I thought about that. "No… This is not liberation. New Horizons would never give up their space elevator. Something's happened."

"What could it be?" Juna asked.

"I don't know."

New Horizons paramilitary, perhaps two-thousand soldiers, emerged from the gate with arms raised and white fabric in their hands.

"Move to intercept, break them into smaller groups, search them thoroughly," I ordered.

Teams released chameleon cloaks and surrounded fifty soldiers at a time.

My eyes wandered back to the dump truck, then to the bodies on the ground. *It would have been better to keep them alive,* I thought, knowing their deaths would be linked to me.

"John, search."

He ran ahead, sniffing the ground around the truck, as I followed with Terkat and Batuhn, my most trusted freedom fighters. John did not sit.

"It's clear," I said, deactivating my chameleon cloak and unclasping my helmet, and studied the bodies. *They were beaten to death,* I knew by the puffiness of their faces.

"They're all New Horizons upper management," said Terkat, once a butcher at a pig hotel like mine.

"You'd think they'd protect their own," said Batuhn, a thickly muscled hay baler from Inner Mongolia.

"That is what's special about New Horizons," I said and knelt to a man in a Gucci suit. "Nobody is safe." I searched him over, finding a holotile in his pocket with, *"Yujin Mitsuki, Managing Director, New Horizons, Tokyo,"* engraved on its back. "He's from their Tokyo Headquarters."

"So, this is what our slavers look like," Terkat said.

"Skinny little thing," Batuhn added.

John barked sharply, causing us to jolt, and stuck his nose into the holotile. Then, he sniffed deeply into the man's blazer.

"What is it, John?" I said, backing away. *He's not searching for explosives or munitions,* I realized. *He's tracking something...*

John whipped about, facing me, and began whining.

It can't be... My hands trembled. My heart raced. I retrieved Kandara's stuffed bunny from my pack. John sunk his nose into the bunny, then reared onto his hind legs and bolted towards the city gate.

"Follow John!" I cried and quickly sealed my helmet, watching his beacon race through the streets.

We activated cloaks and brushed by hundreds of soldiers in queue for surrender. A blue line superimposed onto the streets, leading us into old districts. Super-tall skyscrapers became crumbling stone buildings. Multilane streets became tight alleyways. We zigged and zagged, cutting corners in case of an ambush. *But John would have sniffed that out.* We turned down a dead-end alley to find John scraping the end wall with his claws. My visor put the stone at twelve-thousand years old.

"Analyze mortar," I said.

It confirmed the sidewalls were reconstructed fifty years ago, but the end wall was only two days old.

"Something is hidden behind this wall!"

Terkat and Batuhn retrieved hand-held battering rams and pressed their thumpers against the stone, letting them calibrate to the wall's resonance. Where at first it seemed futile, a stone shifted and mortar crumbled. A few seconds later a gaping hole vibrated open, revealing a man curled within. Terkat pulled him out by his foot as Batuhn peered into the cavity.

"There's more of them!"

◆

Thirteen in total, all high-ranking New Horizons employees, all out of Tokyo. And now, I was staring across the table at Takamoto-san, Head of Space Development.

"This is an old East Turkistani drink called *kumis,*" I said, sliding a small bowl to him. "It's fermented mare's milk."

Takamoto-san glanced at it. "Do you think I'm a fool?"

I calmly lifted the bowl and sipped. "It's not laced."

He inadvertently licked his lips, let out a sigh, and reached for the bowl. He sniffed, then sipped. "I taste alcohol," he said. "I thought Muslims didn't drink."

"You say *Muslim* as if billions of us across the world are the exact same people. East Turkestan once hosted countless vineyards with its own grape species and viticulture practices independent from Europe." I slid a basket containing several large dumplings across the table.

"They look like empanadas," Takamoto-san said and timidly took one. He smelled, then nibbled. His face melted. "This is incredible."

"It's another traditional food of my people called *samsa.*" I took a dumpling, sinking my teeth into its baked bread casing, feeling the spiced tender lamb within roll over my tongue.

"Why are you feeding me?" Takamoto-san asked.

"Our cuisine was nearly lost during your occupation of our lands," I said. "I want you to understand what you tried to destroy."

He finished the dumpling and wiped his hands on a napkin. "I'm sorry for what happened to your people, but we inherited this problem from communist China. It was not us who enslaved you."

"But you chose to continue it, systematize it, perfect it!" I snarled.

Takamoto-san raised his arms slightly. "I'm a scientist. I dream of reaching the stars. I don't have anything to do with this."

My anger spiked. "When you take little girls from their families, you have everything to do with it!"

He gave a confused look. "Who did I take?"

I ground my teeth. "My daughter, Kandara Sinam."

"I'm sorry, but there is no one in our program by that name."

"Of course not," I growled. "She would be twelve now, with my complexion, my eyes."

Takamoto-san thought about that. "There are thousands of young cadets in the program, I don't know them on a person by person basis. Do you have an image?"

"No," I said bluntly.

"How can you not have an image of your own daughter?" he scoffed.

I nearly ended him there. "You did not allow us to have pictures! And the images taken for your records mysteriously vanished when she did! You erased her from the system!"

"Then, I don't know how I can help you," Takamoto-san said, looking me straight in the eye. "If you're going to kill me, please get on with it. But spare the others, they know nothing."

I thought of all the ways to dispose of him. But then, I studied Takamoto-san's jawline and brow. *One of the younger employees had similar features.* "No… You're going to help me find my daughter."

"And why would I do that?" he asked.

"If you don't, Misato dies."

Horror flashed across Takamoto-san's face. "You wouldn't… You're a father, too…"

"So, now you understand," I said.

"…What do you need from me?" Takamoto-san quietly asked.

"Where are the cadets being held?"

"They're stationed in Shenzhen, next to the space elevator's anchor so they can be quickly sent up for zero-g training," he said.

I shook my head. "Shenzhen was abandoned by New Horizons, just like Xi'an was. They pulled out of old China completely."

Takamoto-san thought about that. "Why would they abandon the elevator?"

"You tell me," I said.

He rubbed his forehead. "Shenzhen is where they were. I don't know where they might have taken them since."

"Then, you are useless." I lifted my paring knife.

Takamoto-san stared at it. "Get me to the elevator's zero-g station and I can find where the cadets were transferred to."

◆

Power generation was gone. Mass transit stopped. Water purification ceased. The list went on. *China is dying*, I realized.

Takamoto-san peered out the window of our resurrected gas truck, in the middle of a twelve vehicle caravan, at millions of refugees in pop-up camps in the distance.

"New Horizons did this?" he whispered. "How could they?"

I turned to him. "Everyone is sacrificial when it comes to their quarterly projections. Even their most loyal workforce. But this is nothing compared to what's happened to the minority groups."

He glared at me. "You're no better, slaughtering as you go, abandoning those who cannot keep up with your campaign."

"We're not abandoning these people. Half of our liberation army is made up of former New Horizons employees from China. They intend to rebuild their homeland, just as we have rebuilt ours. We are not conquerors, this is not a campaign, we're simply protecting our homes."

Takamoto-san thought long about that.

A thin strand appeared in the sky ahead, stretching through the clouds.

"Is that it?" I asked, pointing.

"Yes…"

Impossible, I thought, yet there it was before my eyes. "And there are seven of these things?"

"Eight, if you consider the elevator on Luna," he said.

Hundreds of bodies in New Horizons uniforms littered the ditches on either side of the road as we neared Shenzhen.

"You barbarians," Takamoto-san whispered.

"This wasn't us." I pointed at several buses blocking the road ahead.

"We're detecting generators," Terkat called from the lead truck.

"Stop here," I ordered, and stepped from my truck to study the blockade. *Thick trees line either side of the road.* "They're in the woods."

"What do we do?" Terkat asked.

I looked at Takamoto-san in his scuffed suit with his head held high. "Takamoto-san and I are going to say hello. The rest of you stay here."

Takamoto-san snapped his head my way, his mouth dropped. "You cannot expect them to be civil."

"Don't you know who they are?"

His face was blank.

"New Horizons employees did this to other New Horizons employees. Your employees," I said, pointing at the bodies alongside the road. "This is your people's doing… Why can't you grasp this?"

He stared at me. "Will they be with you or against you?"

"We're going to find out." I opened the door, backed away, and motioned my hand in a manner saying, *after you.*

Side by side we walked to the lead truck where Terkat and Batuhn sat.

"Are you sure about this?" Terkat asked.

"If they're revolutionaries, we have me. If they're loyalists, we have him." I pointed at Takamoto-san.

Batuhn handed us lengths of white cloth. "We'll be ready to engage, just in case."

With white flags raised, Takamoto-san and I approached the blockade. The greenery to the right of the road remained still, but the leaves on the left rustled with a nonexistent wind.

I grasped Takamoto-san's arm and whispered, "Cloaked soldiers are coming from the left. Keep moving forward. They've cut off our escape."

When I was certain they had surrounded us, I lowered my flag and raised my chin. "Many of you know me as The Butcher of Earth… But I am also Khasi Sinam, father to a little girl named Kandara Sinam," I announced, letting my voice project. "I do not come today to quarrel. I don't know if you're loyalists or not. Honestly, I do not care." I turned to Takamoto-san. "This is Takamoto-san. Many of you know him as New Horizons's Head of Space Development. But, like me, he is a father. My daughter was taken from me for New Horizons's space program and Takamoto-san has been kind enough to help me find her. But we must access the space elevator to learn where she was transferred to. Please, grant us safe passage."

A soldier released their cloak right in front of us. Takamoto-san reeled back, nearly tripping, but I did not flinch.

"Khasi, we've been waiting for your arrival with much anticipation, welcome to newly liberated Shenzhen…"

♦

"You've restarted the old coal plants," Terkat said. "You think it's safe to revert back? Those things are ancient."

"No, it's not safe… It'll choke the air even more than it already is, but we don't have much of a choice, do we?" said Commander Sen, as we sat in his war room, abandoned by New Horizons.

"It doesn't have to be this way," I said. "You could live a simpler life, rid yourselves of unnecessary comforts."

"I wish it were that easy, Khasi," he responded. "But we're caught between two wars here. Your campaign on the ground and the Hermians above."

A hologram materialized on the war room's central console depicting the space elevator's entire length, from anchor to zero-g station halfway up its tether, and continuing to its counterweight.

The commander highlighted hangers at the elevator's base. "We must continuously charge four hundred thousand mech units to keep up the fight." He zoomed into the elevator's counterweight. "But New Horizons shut down the elevator's fusion reactor at the counterweight during their abandonment, disabling its auto-defense system and our ability to properly recharge, making us extremely vulnerable to Hermian attack. We must get the elevator's power back online."

"How do we do that?" I asked.

"The coal plants can provide just enough power to get a platoon and engineering crew to the zero-g station. From there, we must use the elevator's natural centripetal force to fling us to the counterweight. Once our engineers arrive, they can get the reactor back online."

I thought about that. "Please, allow Takamoto-san and I to join you."

"No, you'll slow us down."

I shook my head. "Takamoto-san is familiar with the elevator and, as the Head of the Space Program, has access to areas and programs you do not. With him, you can reach the reactor more quickly."

The commander grunted. "I assume your condition is to come along."

"It is," I confirmed.

The commander gave me a hard stare. "You and Takamoto-san will report to the hangers. You must have a crash course in mech training. I will not have you becoming a hindrance."

"And Terkat and Batuhn," I added, pointing at them. "That's only an additional four to your platoon of a hundred."

The commander clenched his jaw. "Very well."

The world disappeared beneath my feet. Trees and roads became textures. Towns and cities were tiny blemishes. *East Turkestan is so small,* I realized as I identified its borders. We plunged into low cloud cover, and when we rose above, the sun washed it in tangerine. I turned to Terkat and Batuhn, in their mech units, to see tears rolling down their cheeks. After an hour, the curvature of the Earth was apparent and a blue haze glowed at its horizon.

"It's so beautiful," Batuhn said. "You can't even see the pollution."

"This is what we fight for," Commander Sen said. "This is why metacorporations enslave people like you. It's all to defend Earth."

"Yet, it was you who rebelled against the loyalists," I retorted.

He gave me a stare. "I am neither a loyalist nor a revolutionary. I am a soldier sworn to protect this world. So, that's what I do. The loyalists wanted to abandon the elevator. But that is a death sentence."

He's one of us, but doesn't know it yet, I realized.

Earth became a sphere beneath our feet. I braced my hands against the elevator wall. My head spun and my legs shook. I could see Terkat and Batuhn struggling to keep upright as well, but the commander's platoon remained unfazed. A dusk line crept across Asia. City lights hinted at country borders and landmasses. China was dark, like a footprint.

It took nearly a full day to reach the spaceport, my weight noticeably lessening and my gut progressively fluttering with each passing hour.

"Listen up!" the commander barked. "There may be loyalists still on the station. Be prepared for an ambush!" He turned to us four. "And you stay at our rear until called upon!"

"Yes, commander," I responded, fighting to keep my breakfast down.

"Activate magsuits!"

I dashed my finger across my visor, just as we had trained, and felt weight return to my shoulders and extremities, but my stomach remained fluttery. I glanced at Terkat and Batuhn, who looked pale.

"Drink from your reservoir," Takamoto-san said. "It's filled with electrolytes and ginger extract to help with space sickness."

I did and felt the liquid calm my stomach.

We positioned at the very back of the lift as we docked with the zero-g station. Commander Sen's platoon formed up and raised rifles.

"Ready in five, four, three, two, one!" the commander called.

Doors snapped open, revealing the lower elevator lobby with emergency lights illuminating ten lifts around its circular perimeter.

Completely empty, I saw, breathing a sigh of relief.

"Keep alert, they may be held up elsewhere," said the commander.

We passed through customs and its security tunnel, then entered a multi-tiered arrivals and departure hall with cafés, bars, boutique shops, waiting areas, and food and beverage.

"It's like an airport," Terkat whispered.

The platoon fanned out.

The next level up hosted twenty-four airlock gates positioned equally around the ring-like station. Platoon soldiers rounded the perimeter, checking each gate, determining they were sealed and, more importantly, empty.

An engineer approached a heavy blast door, leading to a space traffic control room at the station's center, and hardwired his holotile. "Omega class encryption," he said. "This will take hours."

Commander Sen faced Takamoto-san. "I hope you have clearance."

Takamoto-san approached the door with four soldiers positioned just behind him. I could hear the old scientist's heavy breathing and see his legs shaking between his mech's hydraulics. He slowly unclasped his helmet, holding his breath like the air was poisoned, and leaned his face to the blast door. A hologram projected, analyzing his features.

"Welcome, Takamoto-san," chimed the door.

"…And guests," he muttered.

"Welcome, Takamoto-san and guests. Please, enter." Deadbolts released and the metal door slowly swung open.

The four soldiers brushed past Takamoto-san and swept the control room.

"Takamoto-san," the commander said. "We'll need your assistance readying the service lifts for the counterweight." He turned to Terkat, Batuhn, and I. "You three, stay here. Once power is restored, you will have your chance to search the logs."

I nodded. "Thank you, Commander."

We pulled off helmets, stepped from our mech units, and found seats among the soldiers.

"Hey, Khasi," said a young corporal. "They say we should fear you. But I don't get why, looking at you."

I grinned and approached her. "I don't get why either."

She made a face. "Aren't you some sort of conqueror?"

I shook my head.

"Then, what are you?"

"A father looking for his daughter."

"Bullshit. Why are you occupying China?"

"Many of your people helped my people liberate East Turkestan," I said. "And now we're returning the favor. We don't intend to stay."

"So you'll abandon us just like New Horizons did?"

"No, we will help rebuild your infrastructure."

"And then, you'll just leave?"

"Yes."

"What happens after that?"

I shrugged. "You become China again."

"Fuck China," she scoffed, and several others nodded.

"You're Cantonese?" I asked.

"Yeah," said another.

"Well, it's a good time to bring an independent Canton to life."

"You can't just make a country from nothing."

I chuckled. "The world considered East Turkestan nonexistent until we dug our heritage from the ashes and declared ourselves a country."

"Yeah, how'd you do that, anyway?"

"Honestly, it started with our food."

The corporal rolled her eyes. "China made sure to destroy Cantonese cuisine long ago."

"But you still have Dimsum," I said.

She shook her head. "That was the first thing they destroyed."

"No," I firmly said and they turned to me. "My son, Juna, escaped to Iranian Sun seven years ago, where he became like a celebrity, telling our story to the world. When he was in Paris, advocating for our people, he found a Dimsum restaurant completely run by ancestors of Cantonese immigrants. Their creed is by protecting their food, they protect their heritage. It was this little restaurant that inspired my people to do the same."

"But…" she stopped and thought about that.

The commander came into the fold. "Corporal Young, the maintenance lift is ready. Prepare your engineering team."

Corporal Young stood, and with twenty others, stepped into their mech units. But, before she sealed her helmet, she turned to me. "Dimsum really exists?"

"It does," I said.

"You better not be fucking with us!" She donned her helmet and followed Commander Sen to the maintenance lift.

◆

"Reactor is ready," Corporal Young reported from the counterweight twenty hours later.

"Well done, corporal," said Commander Sen. "You're cleared for restart."

She pulled switches, lowering rods into the reactor. Power indicators flashed green on the space traffic control room's central hologram.

"Takamoto-san, you're up," said the commander.

He neared the hologram, letting it study his face.

"Welcome, Takamoto-san, please enter your password."

He entered his password and the system's bios appeared.

"Thank you," the commander said. "We'll take it from here."

Lights came on full. Ventilation hissed. Refrigerators hummed to life. And music pumped through speakers.

"I hate this song," said one of the soldiers.

"Get that defense system up," the commander growled and pointed out the window at several blue specks in the distance. "We must make contact with the fleet, they may be in desperate need of resupply. They're our only line of defense right now."

"Working on it, but there are several preliminary systems we must revive first," the engineer responded. "The service lift is back online."

"Corporal Young, lifts are working," the commander called.

"Roger that," the corporal responded. "We'll be roughly twelve hours."

"Twelve hours." Commander Sen turned to the engineer. "Work faster."

"Yes, sir," he responded.

"Can we access the entry-exit logs?" Takamoto-san quietly asked.

The engineer paused. "Yes, but do it from another console."

Takamoto-san and I met at a side console.

He took the seat, signed into the system, and navigated to the logs. "Departures from basecamp are marked with a C-BC, standing for Cadet – Base Camp. When arriving at this station the letters become C-ZS. When leaving for training you have C-DT. Returning it's C-RT. C-RBC indicates a return trip to base camp."

Hundreds of thousands of markers appeared.

"How can this tell us where my daughter might be?" I asked.

"When fleet personnel or cadets transfer, a destination marker is applied." He selected a filter focusing on transfers only.

Thousands of logs still remained.

"There must be an easier way," I said. "Don't you have cadet pictures? I can pick her out of a lineup."

"You don't understand," Takamoto-san said and pulled up the cadet roster.

I peered at the corner, reading, *"1,237."* "See, much better to work with."

"Khasi, these are pages." He opened one of them and thousands of faces appeared. "Sifting through them would take months."

"Can you download this to your holotile, then?" I asked.

The scientist nodded, started the download, and reopened the transfers page. "It's best to understand where they might have gone. We do exchange programs with Earth's other elevators and even Luna's…" The old scientist quieted.

"What is it?" I asked.

"This is strange… The logs indicate New Horizons's entire roster is in Lunar orbit. Personnel and cadets."

Commander Sen stiffened, about faced, and marched over. "That cannot be!" he cried and studied the hologram. "Fuck…"

"What's happening?" I asked.

"It would require the entire fleet to transfer them," Takamoto-san whispered.

I peered out the window at the blue specks looking slightly larger than before. "If that's not your fleet, then who's is it?"

Commander Sen faced the window. Takamoto-san peered out another. The soldiers at the gates slowly stood and pointed out several more.

"Yes, I got it!" the engineer proudly said. "Defense system up in three, two, one!"

Sirens blared and the floor rattled as anti-spacecraft cannons sent shots screaming into space.

"Enemy vessels approaching! Contact imminent!" came through the speakers as twenty-four incoming ships highlighted on the central hologram.

We stared, silently processing what this meant.

They have one for every gate... I realized. "Who are they!?" I said, hoping to get some sort of clarity.

Commander Sen snapped out of his shock. "To your mech units!" he ordered and his soldiers rushed. "I want four soldiers at each airlock!"

"No, Commander! That—" I began.

"Khasi, shut the fuck up! These are Hermians!"

"But you're spreading us too thin!" I argued.

"You and your friends are on gate thirteen! Be good little soldiers!" He marched from the control room and stepped into his mech unit.

I found Takamoto-san head down on the console, sobbing. I grabbed him by his collar and pulled him to his feet. "We will survive! We will see our daughters again!" I dragged the old scientist from the control room and shoved him into his mech unit.

Terkat and Batuhn approached in their mechs, rifles in hand.

"The commander is spreading us too thin," Terkat said.

"I know," I responded. "He won't listen."

"Shit…" Batuhn muttered.

"We must follow his lead if we are to have any chance," I said. "We're covering gate thirteen."

The blue specks became large circles. One flashed brilliantly, breaking into several pieces. Platoon cheers came through com. But then, the cannons ceased.

They're too close to the elevator, I realized.

"Enemy vessel will make contact at gate sixteen in ten… nine… eight…" chimed the defense system.

At five, the enemy ship's blue skin melted to bright red with a white cross on its front airlock.

They announce their arrival, I noted.

The station shuddered as they made contact and the shredding of gate sixteen's outer lock door came.

"They're in!" cried the commander. "Convene on gate sixteen! We'll take them out as they come!"

The Hermians can't be that stupid, I thought.

A chanting came from beyond the gate. The inner hatch did not open.

"Enemy vessels approaching gates three and seven…"

More outer doors were cut and more chanting began. They did not open their hatches either.

"Enemy vessels approaching gates nineteen, twenty-two, and eleven…"

"Commander!" I called.

"Khasi! Shut up!"

"No! They're waiting for all their ships to be docked!" I shouted. "They're going to come at once! This is a stampede tactic! We'll be overwhelmed!"

This time, the commander was silent.

The chanting grew. A word with two syllables, I could feel it in my chest. *Honor…*

"Enemy vessels approaching gates thirteen, two, nine, seven, twenty-

four…"

"Commander, I know how to stop them!" I sternly said.

"What do you suggest?" he responded on a private line.

"How many will come from each ship?"

"Twenty. They're small, designed for ship to ship insurgency. So, nearly five-hundred total."

"We must control their flow," I said. "At the pig hotel we used barricades to funnel hundreds of piglets into single file lines ahead of slaughter, keeping those farther back ignorant of what's to come."

The commander paused. "How does this translate to our situation?"

He's with me, I knew. "We retreat to the lower elevator dock, and use our mech units to funnel them into the lobby. The lifts have doors made of heavy steel. They become our bunkers. From there, we pick off the Hermians as they enter single file."

"We can't do that forever," the commander said.

"Just for twelve hours, until Corporal Young returns with her engineering team from the counterweight and strikes them from above. It will be like shooting fish in a barrel, as the Usonians say."

"This might work. Hermians refuse to retreat. It dishonors them." The commander switched to the public line. "Listen up! We have a change of tactics!"

♦

"…Honorrr! Honorrr! Honorrr!…" shook the station.

Then, silence.

"Get ready…" I said on the platoon line, peering from behind lift five's heavy steel door, cracked just enough for me to survey the lower elevator lobby. Eight of us were inside each of the ten lifts and our mech units were positioned at the customs passageway with their joints locked and their cleats biting into the floor, creating a rigid funnel. "…Do not waste ammo and trust in our shooting sequence."

I could hear their steady breathing, almost in unison. *Yes, one breath,* I thought, and breathed deeply, audibly, for them to hear.

Muffled explosions, shuddering the gate level, were followed by hundreds of footsteps. Shots fired. Glass shattered. *They're taking the control room,* I knew, and that they could not see it was empty. *Now funnel down.*

A howling came from the food court.

"They're close, ready yourselves," I said and heard the platoon's breathing intensify. Footsteps grew, sounding like a waterfall. *Come like rushing water,* I thought. *Crash into us.* Metal detectors rang as they passed security. And then, I saw them sprinting through customs.

"y'Attack!" they cried and heavy fire rained upon our mech units, splintering off pieces of armor, several catching fire and filling the lobby with smoke. Just as I hoped for.

"Let them come!" I said, watching the Hermians drop their rifles, pull glowing knives, and come crashing into the mechs. "Just a little longer!"

Like a faucet turned on full, the bulk of the insurgency came, pressing those already at our mechs and squishing them through the funnel.

"It's working!" I cried. "This is our moment! If they want to take this elevator! If they want to start a ground war on Earth! Then, let's give them a taste of the nightmare to come!"

"Yes, sir!" the platoon responded in unison.

The first Hermian pushed through the funnel and wrapped around the mech units, slicing them from behind. More spit through and attacked the mechs, turning their backs to the lifts.

"Lifts one through five! Open!" I ordered.

The lift doors at one side of the lobby parted, revealing our soldiers aiming rifles.

"Single shots! Now!"

Forty shots let fly, sounding like one cannon blast. Two dozen Hermians fell to the ground, writhing, reaching for their backs. Ones at the opposite side of the lobby spun in confusion.

"Close!" I shouted. Our doors slammed shut. "Lifts six through ten! Go!"

I heard them open across from us and fire single shots. Then, their doors slammed shut.

"Now evens! Go!" Once they opened and shut, I cried, "Odds! Go!"

My door opened again, revealing the panic. Bodies lined the floor. The Hermians no longer attacked the mech units but were trying to report back.

"Get them before they warn the others!"

Another forty shots and another chunk of Hermians fell. The moment the doors closed something slammed into mine and grinding came.

They change tactics quickly, I noted.

"Open cracks! Send grenades!" I ordered.

Remote grenades were sent into the lobby.

"Detonate!"

Deafening pops rang, followed by silence.

I cracked my door to see the lobby filled with thick smoke. My visor displayed, *"127 dead, 54 wounded."*

"That's almost a *third* of them," one of our platoon said.

I found the rest of the Hermians kneeling in the customs hall as smoke slowly ventilated away, their fists pressed against their shoulders. "Don't get excited. They're acting weird."

"They're praying to The Director," Commander Sen said. "The true battle begins now."

◆

One hour remains...

The lobby was littered with Hermian dead. Lifts four, seven, and eight were decimated, and our soldiers within were torn to shreds. Commander Sen was gone and our mechs no longer provided the funnel.

It's us versus them, now. Plain and simple, I knew.

Customs hall was quiet, as if the Hermians had finally given up. *But they never retreat,* I remembered the commander saying, and that had certainly held true so far. *What are they scheming?*

Heavy thumps shuddered the floor, different from before. I opened the door a crack to see two monstrous soldiers sprinting down the hall, clad in thick, red armor. Their helmets skimmed the ceiling and their shoulders scraped the walls, sending sparks.

"Equalizers!" one of our platoon cried and panicked breathing came through the com. "We're done for!"

"No, we're not!" I responded. "They're nothing more than big sows. Sweep out their legs! Get them to their backs! Slit their throats!"

"We can't!" the one said. "Their armor self-destructs if their heartbeats stop! It'll take out the entire space elevator!"

"Good! If this is their point of entry to Earth! Then, we destroy it!"

Gasps came across the line.

"That's suicide!"

"Yes, exactly! We must beat them at their own game!" I said.

The com became silent, all but our synchronized breathing.

The equalizers entered the lobby, shouldering through the remaining mech units like cardboard cutouts.

They're coming for me, I realized. *They know I'm giving the orders!*

"They're heading for lift five!" I shouted. "All other lifts, open fire!"

Their doors whipped open as mine sealed shut. I heard shots bouncing off thick armor. Then, the thumping steps halted and two armored fists punched through the lift's doors. We scrambled to the back as their metal fists opened

GHOSTS OF ZION | 79

into paws, turned back upon the doors, and pulled. The lift groaned and the heavy steel doors creased like tin foil.

I pointed at two platoon soldiers. "Use heat blades to cut their Achilles' tendons!" I pointed at another two. "Shoot their faces! It will knock their balance back and obscure their vision!" I turned to Terkat and Batuhn. "Terkat and I will flip the right one onto its back! Batuhn, you do the same for the left, show us your strength!"

Batuhn gave a devilish grin.

The doors tore away, revealing the equalizers, their helmets at the door header and their legs like tree trunks.

"Ready! Char—"

A massive paw thrust into the lift, clamping around Batuhn's head, and sharply twisted. A pop rang and Batuhn went limp. The equalizer pulled him from the lift and chucked him across the lobby like a piece of trash.

"Legs!" I shouted.

Soldiers dove to the equalizers' ankles, as others opened fire at their helmets. Terkat and I lunged forth, each taking one of the two equalizer's tree trunk legs in our arms and pressing our shoulders into their groins.

They did not budge.

A deep chuckle came from above me. The monster lifted his other leg and stamped upon the soldier cutting at his ankle, smushing his head.

Use it! I turned my weight, locking up the monster's knee. His foot slid on the blood. *Harder!* With every ounce of strength I pulled back at his knee while pressing forth with my shoulder. Pops ran down my back. A twinge shot through my knee. And my shoulder dislocated. *Keep going!* His foot again shifted. I quickly repositioned and yanked with everything I had. The leg slid more. *I have him!* But then, his boot cleat crunched into the floor and all movement ceased.

"You'rrre strrrong, little man," said a bellowing voice.

Dread percolated through me until the equalizer grunted and turned to find a platoon soldier sinking a heat blade into his hip.

From another lift, I realized.

More converged, ditching their rifles for blades and swarming the equalizers like ants devouring a locust. For every devastating strike they gave, a body part was lost, until the two equalizers fell to their knees and their arms dropped limp, their tendons severed.

"y'It's too late!" one laughed. "The rrrats y'arrrre flushed y'out!"

We're exposed! I realized.

A flurry of shots came from customs and I whirled, expecting to find Hermians coming to finish us. Instead, the gunfire dwindled and twenty soldiers in mech units came marching into the lobby.

"Corporal Young!?" I said.

"Khasi…" the corporal gasped, looking at the bodies strewn about the lobby and the two equalizers on their knees. She made eye contact with me, but instead of respect or the excitement of victory, I saw horror.

"This is how you beat the Hermians…" I said.

"You have not won," said the bellowing voice. "This y'is y'only y'one y'of severrral waves to come. We will take this y'elevatorrr."

He's right… I knew and faced him. I signaled for their helmets to be removed. Magnificent jaws and eagle eyes revealed. *Superhuman,* I understood. I pulled out my paring knife.

"y'Acting tough with that little thing, little man. You wouldn't darrre kill y'us," he said with a grin. "You don't have the—"

I slit his throat.

The platoon soldiers flinched.

I stared into the mighty man's confused eyes as his blood poured into zero-g and said, "I hear that when you die, you self-destruct, killing us all, destroying this entire space elevator. How long does that take? Thirty seconds? A minute?"

His eyes became vacant and his body went limp.

I dabbed my finger into his floating blood and drew an, "*E,* " on the chest of my gray, battle jacket. I approached the second equalizer, calmly counting, "Fifty-nine… fifty-eight…"

By the time I reached forty, he was no longer grinning. When I hit twenty, I saw a flicker of uncertainty. At ten, he looked at me like I was crazy.

"…Three… two… one… kaboom," I quietly finished, staring into the monstrous man's eyes. He looked like a scared boy now.

All was silent.

"That's what I thought," I said, knowing the space elevator was too valuable to destroy. "You sacrificed your lives for nothing."

"…We still have y'ourrr honorrr," he said.

That's what we must take from them, I realized.

I pointed at the Hermian dead. "Strip their armor, we're taking their bodies. Our pigs are hungry," I said to everyone's horror.

"W-what?" the equalizer said.

I stared him down. "You will stay and explain to the next wave of

Hermians exactly what happened here, and what we do to you when you die. Tell them, The Butcher of Earth is waiting.”

◆

She's on the moon... I thought, staring at its glow like I did as a child, fixating on Sabine Crater, where Luna's space elevator anchor resided. I held Kandara's bunny in one hand and scratched behind John's ear with the other. “How do we get there, now that the Hermians occupy Shenzhen's elevator?”

Takamoto-san sat beside me, also staring at the moon. “We'll know more when the metacorporations announce their ruling.”

“I wouldn't expect much,” I responded.

“They will take action against New Horizons for recklessly abandoning the elevator,” Takamoto-san argued. “And strategize how to retake it from the Hermians.”

A soldier approached with a confused expression. “They've made their announcement…”

Takamoto-san opened his holotile. “Yes, they just posted.” His mouth dropped open.

I thought about the timing of New Horizons's abandonment of China and their fleet being in Lunar orbit. “New Horizons sold China to the Hermians, didn't they?”

Takamoto-san looked up. “The metacorporations say the sale is legal. That the Hermians now own all of China, including the elevator. They're a metacorporation now…”

“It's not just China,” I said. “This ruling gives the Hermians precedent to purchase more of Earth to conquer.”

“But this can't happen!” Takamoto-san said. “Someone must stop it!”

“Someone will,” I said and slowly stood, taking one last look at the moon. *Kandara, I'm sorry… I need more time…*

◆

“Did your contacts on Luna discover anything?” I asked Takamoto-san before we met with Europe's freedom fighters who were about to engage the Hermians at southern Spain's elevator, having been recently sold off by SudsiCo.

Takamoto-san shook his head. “They've searched everywhere for her.” He paused. “Can you go through the images again?”

“I've gone through them countless times, I thought picking her out would have been easy… but,” *I'm a bad father...* “she would be nineteen now, a changed person, a different person. I don't know if I'd recognize her.”

Terkat approached. "Khasi, they're expecting the Hermians to make contact at any moment."

I sighed deeply. "Please, keep looking."

"I'll do my best," Takamoto-san said.

I followed Terkat through granite tunnels beneath the ancient city of Chongqing as the Hermians shelled us from above. *Still a fortress,* I thought, having learned it was the capital of China during World War II because of its impregnable nature. Lights flickered, tunnels shook, and granite dusted our hair. But, I barely noticed, having listened to it for two years straight.

Terkat opened the door to our war room hosting representatives from across China, Mongolia, Siberia, Southeast Asia, and Australia. Every country that New Horizons had at one time or still occupied. All considered corporate terrorists now. Two holograms hung above a central console—the first, a window into Paris where Europe's freedom fighters had assembled; the second, a diagram of Spain's space elevator.

"Khasi, thank you for joining us," a young freedom fighter named Cane said from her hologram. "Do you have any last insights?"

I watched as Hermian ships simultaneously approached their elevator's zero-g station, its counterweight, and maintenance ports along the tether. *They've changed tactics.* "The Hermians will not make the same mistakes twice, so we must force them to make new ones. Treat your soldiers on the elevator as guaranteed casualties. If the Hermians look to take the elevator, destroy it first."

Horror washed across Cane's face. "Khasi, we can't do that!"

"This was the mistake we made at Shenzhen," I said. "The Hermians have space superiority, but we have atmospheric control. It's why they need the elevators. Destroying them keeps the Hermians off of Earth."

"But the elevators are our lifeline!" she argued.

"Lifelines are weaknesses," I snapped back.

"Contact imminent," chimed the hologram, displaying the elevator's defense system barrage as Hermian ships closed in. They made contact, gate doors were cut, and a firefight ensued. The diagram suddenly flashed at the elevator's counterweight. *"Enemy ships dock—"* The hologram froze. Feeds from within went blank. The counterweight became dark. Then, the anchor became unresponsive.

"Commander, come in!" Cane called to her team.

Only static returned.

They EMP'd several points simultaneously, I realized. *It's over.*

Earth was rotten, soft, corrupt. Like an orange growing patchy mold. The Hermians infiltrated strategic points across the world, purchasing every elevator save Addis Ababa's, making Earth's metacorporate CEOs ungodly rich. But we, the people who actually inhabited the land, still fought.

"Iranian Sun is hosting this year's metacorporate summit," Juna said during a holocall, an older man now, a father himself.

I missed everything... I thought.

John perked up when he heard Juna's voice.

"Yes, that's Juna, old boy," I said.

"Hey, boy," Juna said.

"Will the Hermians be there?" I asked.

"They're a metacorporation. So, they must attend," Juna responded. "Iranian Sun is hoping we might accompany them as a show of good faith."

My blood boiled. "Good faith!?"

John flinched and I gently scratched behind his ear to calm him.

Juna raised his arms. "I know… But I had to ask."

I thought it over. "It might be good to get eyes on who's there," I said. "You think they'd agree to let John come?"

"Why?" Juna asked.

"He's the only one who can track Kandara."

Juna's face hardened, his eyes blazed. "Consider it done."

♦

I could not hug my grandson, afraid I would taint him. And I sensed that Juna and his wife preferred this, for even my own son flinched at my embrace. *I'm a monster, after all.* They treated John like royalty, having a lavish doghouse built in their garden and feeding him choice cuts of meat. *A better life...* I thought, angry at my son for living exactly how I hoped he might. A part of me felt he was erasing the past, erasing me.

Samsa, lamb stew, and more Uighur dishes sat atop a long dining table separating my son and I. This was Juna's contribution to our people, rediscovering and archiving our traditional recipes. *So, how can I be angry with him,* I thought, yet I could not shake my frustration.

"How's your mother?" I asked, trying to distract from it.

"She's teaching at the Kazakh National Conservatory," Juna said, then made a face. "She's getting married to the Dean."

But we're still married... I thought.

"How's Carste?" I grumbled, trying to distract from my distraction.

Juna winced. "He's been in and out of rehab. I haven't seen him in years."

Did I really save him? I thought.

A servant approached Juna. "Sir, Mr. Shirazi will be arriving in twenty minutes."

"Thank you," Juna said and turned to me. "It's time."

We followed the servant to a fitting room where Uighur ceremonial garb lay upon an upholstered table next to a tailor.

I stopped at the doorway. "No."

"We must represent who we are," Juna urged.

I ground my teeth. "Neither of us are good representations of our people. Our people are peaceful..." I said and waved at the lavish clothing. "...And live simple lives."

Juna pursed his lips. "It's expected of us."

I breathed deeply, keeping my anger at bay as Juna dressed, looking like a caricature of our culture. Then, the tailor fitted clothing around me. He lifted a cloth hat from the table.

"I'm not wearing that fucking thing!" I snapped.

The tailor looked at Juna, who reluctantly nodded.

I grabbed my small pack.

"You can't bring that," Juna said.

"Sir," the tailor interjected. "There is a traditional sack that accompanies the garb."

I thought about that. "I'll put my pack into the sack. Is that acceptable?"

Juna breathed deeply. "Fine."

We exited Juna's estate as a caravan of black armored vehicles arrived. Corporate soldiers in white mech units, with Iranian Sun's logo upon their chest-plates, surrounded the vehicles. John was brought from the garden, wearing a traditional jacket and hat of our people fitted to his anatomy. I snapped my head to Juna.

"Okay, that's a bit much," he admitted.

A soldier opened the central vehicle's door to reveal Mr. Shirazi, newly elected CEO of Iranian Sun, mid-call on his holotile. Instead of traditional Persian clothing, he wore a white t-shirt and jeans with a cheap blazer and surfing sandals. *We're the only ones in costume,* I realized and slowly turned to Juna, who refused to make eye contact with me. We sat across from Mr. Shirazi and waited for him to finish his call. The vehicles took off.

"Uh-huh," the CEO kept saying with a serious look. "Three scoops. It's three! Just make sure Peanut doesn't die!" he snapped and ended the call.

I sucked up my pride and said, "Thank you, Mr. Shir—"

"You'd think people could feed a fucking cat," he said, cutting me off. He reached into his blazer jacket and pulled a bag of white powder and a little metal spoon. He scooped and sniffed, then casually handed the bag and spoon to Juna.

Juna was like a deer caught in the headlights.

"What?" Mr. Shirazi said. "It's the usual."

Juna slowly scooped the powder and sniffed.

My heart sank and my hands trembled. *This is the better life!?*

"So you're *The Butcher,*" Mr. Shirazi said with a grin.

I stared at him, breathing my breaths to keep from lunging across the seat and snapping this little boy's arrogant neck.

"Say *I'm The Butcher Of Earth* for me," he teased.

I heard a growling and thought it was John until Juna nudged my leg and I realized it was me.

"Would you rather bark like a dog?" the young CEO asked.

I breathed deeply again. "Thank you for inviting me to this summit," I grumbled. "But I am not your fucking toy. And neither is my son."

"Oh, but you are," he responded lightly. "And tonight, you're going to show everyone that you're not the cold-blooded killer everyone thinks you are. That you are a reasonable man." He paused. "Or am I wrong?"

His playboy persona is a cover, I realized. "What do you stand to gain by parading me around?"

"Respect." He took another hit from his spoon. "I have no intention of selling our space elevator and lands to the Hermians, but the other CEO's held this same conviction before they ultimately did. The Hermians know how to twist arms. Sometimes, literally." He pointed at me. "I need them to see me with you to show them they are not the only bully around."

I thought about that. "So, I nod and smile…"

"And you have a chance to find your daughter," he said.

I snapped my head to Juna.

"I had to tell him," he quietly said.

"Okay…" I grumbled. "I'll play along."

Mr. Shirazi smiled. "You'll have fun."

The vehicles entered barren desert as the sun dipped below the dunes. The sands became pitch dark. *They'd never find us out here,* I knew and began questioning the young CEO's motive, until we took a sudden turn and passed through a gate. Darkness was overcome by flashing lights and tremendous commotion. The vehicles came to a stop and the door opened to cameras and reporters. Men and women, dressed in their finest, strutted down a red carpet, periodically facing the cameras, positioning their legs, and giving dashing smiles.

"Let's give them something to gossip about," Mr. Shirazi said, dashing his own smile and stepping from the vehicle with a hand raised. Cameras swung his direction and cheers came. He took a deep bow to hundreds of flashes.

"Did you come stag!?" a reporter shouted.

Mr. Shirazi turned their direction. "I came prepared!"

"That's our cue," Juna said and stepped from the vehicle.

I timidly followed, gripping John's leash.

"May I present to you, Juna Sinam of East Turkestan!" the young CEO announced. "And the reputable Khasi Sinam, *The Butcher of Earth!*"

I expected tremendous fear to cross their faces, for them to reel and scream. Instead, laughter came.

"You're too funny!" one cried.

"Who's the third dog, then!?" shouted another.

Mr. Shirazi chuckled. "That would be John."

I was too stunned to be furious. I saw my reflection in the vehicle's window, looking ridiculous. *They don't believe it's me...* John was sniffing wildly. *Use it,* I thought.

We passed security and entered a gargantuan fabric tent with hundreds of Persian rugs overlapping one another on the floor. Groups lounged upon large pillows around low tables, taking long drags from hookahs and swirling glasses of wine. Soldiers in differently colored mech units followed their CEOs like remoras on a shark. I found Amazonian One, Inuit Fire, Stoll, AdventureStop, SudsiCo, and New Horizons. I stared at New Horizons's CEO, CFO, and small entourage, trailed by their mechs. They approached tables, smiling pleasantly, clinking glasses, and introducing their members. A chill ran down my spine remembering when they were our greatest foe. *A joke now...* I searched for the color red, for that newest metacorporation, but could not find them. *Are the Hermians not here?*

A hologram opened, spanning the entire tent canopy, displaying the young CEO of Iranian Sun with two awkward people and a dog.

"Welcome Hisha Shirazi, CEO of Iranian Sun, and his friend, Khasi Sinam, The Butcher of Earth!"

Laughter erupted. CEOs threw their heads back and wiped tears.

"They even did the dog!" one cried.

Among the laughter, I found a group in the back, perfectly still, dressed all in black and holding impeccable posture, each built like an Olympian. *The Hermians...* They were not laughing. In fact, they seemed terribly offended. *The only respect I get is from my enemy.*

As each CEO approached the Hermians, a massive equalizer blocked their way, pointing for them to move along. And even with their soldiers in mech units, the CEOs obeyed.

Juna and I followed Mr. Shirazi from one group of fake smiles to another. I nodded at their comments and jokes, all the while allowing John to mingle among them. When we met New Horizons, I was certain one would recognize me. When no one did, I felt disappointed. *But they never considered us human... So, why would they remember?*

John playfully nudged hands and let them pet his fur, but not once did he circle, whine, or sit. Not even among New Horizons.

I sighed deeply, scratched behind John's ear, and whispered, "It's okay, boy. It was a long shot anyway."

When all of Earth's CEOs were met, Mr. Shirazi set his sights on the Hermians. "This is it, behave yourself," he warned with trembling hands.

This won't work, I knew, and that the Hermians would view this charade as disrespectful to their comrades whose lives I had taken. As we neared, I discerned a man at the center with long, gray hair pulled into a bun. *The Director,* I realized, astonished he would come himself. Then, I saw the young General Kase, the scourge of Earth, the Director's own daughter, by his side. But my heart nearly stopped when I saw the woman accompanying them. She appeared about my age, with long, black hair going gray. I did not recognize her face, I never met this woman before, but something deep within me said that I had. I was about to dismiss my gut feeling when John began prancing.

"What is it, boy?" I whispered.

John spun and stopped with one leg up, pointing right at the Hermians.

I must get close. I looked at my garb. *But not like this.* I slowed my pace, letting Juna and Mr. Shirazi move ahead, and noticed the mech units were focused on the equalizer. I fell behind, then casually turned away unnoticed with John. I headed to a long buffet table where fabric quickly parted beyond. *The servers are cloaked.* I slipped through the fabric to a kitchen with cooks and servers racing about. A few glanced my way but did not seem to care. I found a prep table covered with hundreds of cheese boards ready to be served, each with a small, curved cheese knife. *Short, sharp, perfect...* I palmed one, found a janitor closet, and entered. I tore the ceremonial garb off John and myself, then reached into the sack for my pack, and my battle jacket within. Blood stains, from hundreds of encounters, riddled its front, written as small *E's* for each equalizer I had slain since Shenzhen. Its smell was metallic. I slipped it on.

Servants were coming down the hall with the cheese boards in hand when I emerged from the closet. Horror struck their faces.

They finally see me...

I marched back into the tent as Mr. Shirazi was reaching the Hermians. The big equalizer stood to his feet and pointed for Mr. Shirazi to head back. Instead, Mr. Shirazi turned to introduce me, only to realize that I was not there. His frantic eyes shot about. The equalizer grasped Mr. Shirazi's collar, effortlessly lifted him from the ground, turned him a hundred and eighty degrees, and set him back down.

"Go!" came his monstrous voice.

I expected Iranian Sun's soldiers to intervene, to at least surround their CEO, but their eyes went wide and their mech units trembled.

They've never seen action before, I realized.

All was quiet, except for my subtle footsteps. Heads turned as I approached. People's faces became horror. Mr. Shirazi's eyes locked onto me, then shifted to my battle jacket. He went pale. Even Juna looked as if he had seen a demon.

The Hermians abruptly stood and the equalizer snapped my way. I calmly closed the gap, coming within the monster's striking range. Then, I turned to Mr. Shirazi and said, "Leave."

The young CEO quickly backpedaled.

I felt the equalizer's gaze burning upon me and his breath against my face. I made eye contact and gently tapped the *E's* on my jacket, one at a time, watching him increasingly tremble with rage.

Twenty-four was his limit.

He thrust a paw to break my neck, but John snapped into action, sinking his teeth into the man's gigantic finger. I dropped low, gripping my palmed cheese knife, and ripped its short blade through the equalizer's hamstring. He dropped to a knee, putting his neck right in front of me. I quickly flicked up, catching his right side jugular veins, and when he tried to stop the blood, I flicked the left side of his neck, too. The equalizer furiously gargled, holding both sides of his neck, and began army crawling towards me.

They're all watching, I realized. *CEOs and Hermians alike.* I slowly stepped back, staying just out of the equalizer's grasp, and watched the light fade from his eyes. He finally slumped to the Persian rugs. I knelt, dabbed my finger into the blood-soaked fabric, and drew another, *"E,"* on my jacket.

Hermians formed up on my right, their eyes blazing, their bodies trembling. *Ready to end me.* But then, heavy footsteps came from my left, from mechs of many colors, from several metacorporations, standing side by side with stun rifles raised, pointed not at me, but at the Hermians.

The CEOs have finally grown spines, I thought, then saw them hiding behind pillows. *No, but their soldiers have...*

"You have my attention," said a composed voice. The Hermians parted, revealing The Director, his daughter, and the mysterious woman still seated. "Come join us."

Every step I took was matched by a flinch. John grew more excited as we neared, tugging on his leash. When I sat across from The Director, John went into play posture in front of the woman.

The Director tilted his head. "Your companion has taken a liking to Miss Kessler."

I stared at Miss Kessler, looking over her features, feeling as if this might be a big misunderstanding, until we made eye contact.

"I'd say Khasi has taken y'a liking to you, too," General Kase quipped with a smug grin.

"What's the dog's name?" The Director asked.

"John," I responded and watched Miss Kessler's eyes avert, down and to the left, just like she had done long ago, before whatever facial reconstruction she must have undergone.

"There are only two people in this system that give me pause," The Director said. "Mirko Obradovic, *The Harbinger of Death.* And now, Khasi Sinam, *The Butcher of Earth...*"

I continued staring at Miss Kessler, ignoring The Director, as John nudged his nose under her hand.

The Director looked at Miss Kessler then back at me. "You're not here to speak with me, are you?"

I slowly shook my head.

"Told you," General Kase said.

The Director grimaced. "I'll take my leave, then. These CEOs sicken me, anyway."

As The Director and General Kase stood, the Hermians knelt and pressed fists to shoulders. Most of the soldiers departed, leaving just enough to encircle Miss Kessler and I. The more I studied this woman, the more I recognized her younger self.

"Professor Shu…" I said in my native tongue. "…How could you?"

Tears welled in her eyes. Her lip trembled.

I gazed through her, slowly piecing things together. "You got out with Kandara. But not to Kazakhstan like Major Gao thought…" She flinched at the major's name. "…New Horizons would never admit to losing you. So, they fabricated your capture and hung some poor woman in your stead..." She remained silent, a confirmation that I was correct. "…I don't know how, but you reached the Hermians and brokered a deal."

She opened her mouth slightly.

"Am I wrong?" I asked.

"We went to Usonia instead of Kazakhstan," she responded in my people's language, sending shivers down my spine.

The Hermians' focus shifted from me to her, confused expressions crossing their faces.

They don't know who she is, I realized. "Why?"

"It was another point of escape Major Gao and I developed if the Kazakh border was deemed too dangerous, which was the case. There were others at New Horizons who could help, even among upper management. They smuggled us across China, Mongolia, and into Siberia."

"You passed through Xi'an," I stated.

She tilted her head. "How do you know that?"

"John picked up Kandara's scent on one of New Horizons's employees when we searched the city."

"Yujin-san helped us," she said.

The body from the truck. "But something went wrong."

Professor Shu pursed her lips. "Our contact in Anchorage proved to be a Hermian agent. He provided us with a secure passage off Earth via Hawaii's elevator, but the vessel he smuggled us on was heading to Mercury instead of Ceres."

"Why would the Hermians go through such trouble for Kandara?" I asked. "She couldn't have been that unique of a child."

Professor Shu shook her head. "She was, but not for the reasons we thought."

"What the fuck does that mean?"

"There's something about Kandara's DNA that Dr. Kaladian needed for a special project."

My rage surged, my hands shook. "What did they do to my daughter!?"

The professor raised her palms to calm me. "Nothing monstrous. They only took blood samples. It was on someone else that they experimented." Her eyes shifted towards The Director and General Kase at the far end of the tent.

General Kase, I realized. "Who does Kandara go by now? Where is she?"

A single tear rolled down the professor's cheek. "She was brilliant and so eager to travel to the planets and moons of System Sol. She was recruited into the Hermian Navigational Academy at age six, and… underwent their genetic modifications."

I furiously stood. "You said, nothing monstrous!"

The Hermians stepped forth, but so did several mech units. *Calm down…* I told myself, knowing that without The Director present they were likely to strike. I sat back down.

"Continue…" I growled, staring daggers at the professor.

"Kandara was valedictorian of her class. So, when the time came to place her, the Hermian Armada in the Jovian System was the natural choice." She paused. "Kandara quickly rose through the ranks and by age twenty-one she became Admiral."

Abigail Kessler… I knew the name well, for she was a demon to be feared, just like me. My eyes drifted to the floor. *Everything has been taken from me, my childhood, my homeland, my culture, my soul, my wife, my son, and my daughter. Only a butcher remains…*

◆

One by one, the metacorporations collapsed, their paramilitary overthrowing their CEOs and adding their forces to my fight against the Hermians.

At last, an Earth united. No borders or red tape. Prejudices forgotten or forgiven. A single mind…

It took six years to drive General Kase's forces back to the elevators. All but Addis Ababa's, still owned by Iranian Sun, the only metacorporation still in existence, having never sold to The Hermians. And the young CEO now listened to every order I gave for fear of losing his dynasty. *Well, almost…* He still had access to metacorporate information no one else did, to all of Earth's dirty secrets compiled into something called *The Terran Files*, as Juna had discovered during one of their drug parties, no doubt.

His final cling to power.

I stared at the young CEO among my liberation army generals in the war room. *I must get my hands on The Terran Files! But first...* "We must secure Earth's atmosphere."

"But the Hermians control it," Cane said from Paris's hologram.

"No, they control the elevators, not the atmosphere," I corrected.

"Khasi," said Vasili, a general once under Stoll control. "What do you suggest?"

"We destroy the elevators."

They stared at me, stunned.

But I always say this, I thought, annoyed.

"That would be a death sentence!" Cane cried, just as she had years ago.

I shook my head and looked again at Mr. Shirazi. "We would still have Iranian Sun's elevator."

"That's one of seven. We cannot survive with only one," Cane argued.

I frowned. "We did just that for decades with a population similar to what we've reverted to because of this war."

Cane scoffed. "If we compromise an elevator's tether, half will fall back on Earth, destroying everything in its path, including us."

I shook my head again. "If we sever their anchor points below ground, then they will fling into space entirely."

Vasili gave a look. "But that's where The Hermians are strongest. There's no way we can attack on the ground."

I clenched my jaw. "The WorldRing was decommissioned decades ago, but their tunnels still connect to underground stations below the elevators. That's how we get in."

Cane fumed. "The anchors are made of thousands of filaments extending kilometers into Earth's crust. You can't sever them all."

"Yes, we can." I turned to Mr. Shirazi. "If we use *them.*"

Mr. Shirazi grimaced. "No."

"No... what?" Vasili asked.

"Khasi wants to use the nukes," Mr. Shirazi said.

Horror spread across their faces.

I did not let it deter me. "For decades, the metacorporations have stockpiled old nuclear arsenals to keep each other in check. If the Hermians are indeed a metacorporation, then let's get them in check."

Mr. Shirazi turned red. "No, Khasi. Just... no!"

"Then we lose this war!" I exploded, raising my hands in frustration. "I've given you the answer! This is how we beat the Hermians!"

"By destroying ourselves!?" Cane asked.

I faced her hologram. "Earth has survived thousands of subterranean nuclear tests that most people don't know about! There would be no radiation cloud! No atmospheric contamination!"

"What about the water table?" Vasili said.

"Well…" Takamoto-san quietly responded. "An underground detonation would vaporize local water and rock, and form a molten cavity sealing any radiation. It would essentially contain itself."

"It does not matter!" Mr. Shirazi shouted in a rare display of defiance. "I will not give them to you!"

My throat tensed. "You fucking CEOs! Willing to eradicate entire cultures for a tenth of a point on your stocks! But when it comes to saving this world, you suddenly gain a conscience!?" I stared him down. "I did not know such cowardice existed!"

♦

"Juna, I need your help," I said, alone in his estate's lavish kitchen.

He did not acknowledge my words, focusing on painting a spicy marinade onto a leg of lamb rotating above a flame coming through stainless steel vents. *The furnace likely cost more than our family's entire worth under New Horizons's rule.* I felt frustration climb. But then, I caught the lamb's scent and was shot back to my childhood, visiting my grandparent's lavender farm, and when my grandfather would cook this same leg of lamb over a campfire. *The world has changed so much, yet this remains.* I glared at Juna's expensive furnace. *Let it go…*

John pranced his feet, licking his chops and whining.

"Not for you, John," I said, and his ears and tail lowered.

Juna opened the furnace door and added more pear wood logs.

"When did you learn to make this one?" I asked.

Juna pointed at a deteriorated recipe book on the counter. "Mom's husband found that in a junk store when they visited her childhood village."

I winced, having not thought about Saundi in over a decade.

Juna smiled. "Mr. Shirazi is uploading our recipes to The Terran Files for safe keeping. Mom and I hope to archive our entire culture's cuisine!"

To The Terran Files? I tilted my head. "I thought those files contained military secrets."

Juna nodded. "Mr. Shirazi describes them as containing all of Earth's information, including military secrets. When I told him about the recipe book, he asked me to digitize everything Mom and I find."

I thought about that. "Do you have access to the files?"

Juna shook his head. "I send the recipes to Mr. Shirazi's personal assistant. Then, someone from their team uploads them."

"So, you don't really know if they're being uploaded."

Juna shrugged. "I guess not."

But this might be a way in, I realized. "There are a few recipes I remember from childhood I'd like to add," I innocently said.

Juna froze mid-stroke and turned to me. He knew I was scheming something. He thought long, then said, "Send me the files and I'll add them to the next batch."

♦

Two months after I gave Juna my recipes, my holotile beeped, indicating they had been uploaded.

"It actually worked," I said in disbelief.

Takamoto-san sighed. "If we get caught, we're done. The others would consider this an act of treason."

"Treason? Against who?" I scoffed.

"Except for you, Khasi, the liberation army generals agreed to never use nukes," the old scientist said.

I grimaced. "Then, we might as well bend over for the Hermians."

"I agree with Khasi," Corporal Young said and started her program, searching for the backdoor code she wrote into the files I gave Juna.

I opened my holotile, displaying The Terran Files login page. The corporal hardwired to my tile and ran through millions of lines of code.

"Four," she said.

I input the number into the username field.

"T," the corporal followed up. "H… E…"

I input the letters, then muttered, "Four the…."

"D… I… R—" the corporal suddenly stopped.

"For the director?" I said, feeling my breath leave. "This is Mr. Shirazi's personal login. He was always against Hermian control. Why would he have something like this?"

We stared silently for several seconds.

"He became CEO of Iranian Sun after The Hermians became a metacorporation," Takamoto-san finally said. "He must be a plant."

"That actually makes sense," I admitted. "They couldn't find a way to exterminate us. So, they fabricated an ally to control us, instead." My mind raced with all the conversations we had had with the young CEO, how he was deep within our operations, and how The Director did not seem surprised to see me at the summit. "The Hermians must know everything."

"Except, they think we're ignorant," the corporal said. "I… N… T…"

"Into the light," Takamoto-san said.

I input the password and selected *Login*. I held my breath as its icon spun. Then, to my simultaneous disappointment and satisfaction, we were in.

"Look at it all…" Corporal Young said.

"How long will it take to download everything?" I asked.

"It's over three zettabytes… So, a month."

"Do it," I said. "We'll sift through it all later."

Corporal Young started downloading the files to a small yet mighty hard drive powered by its own curium isotope generator, able to fit within the palm of my hand.

♦

I came by Corporal Young's quarters each evening to check on progress, and spent my days in the war room discussing tactics against the Hermians as Mr. Shirazi listened. I tried not to glare, tried not to break his little neck, and tried not to give away my best strategies.

"Khasi, look at this," the corporal said after two weeks.

I peered into her holotile to see a folder entitled, *"Operation Eraser."*

She opened the folder, then the first of several recordings.

The Director appeared mid-conversation. "…Earth is dead. Humanity is sick. If we are to be worthy of a future, these corrupt governments, companies, industries, and militaries, all across System Sol, must be destroyed. We must restart humanity with only the best of us."

"And who are the best of us?" Mr. Shirazi responded.

"Certainly not you," The Director snipped.

"Then, why should I help?"

"The only reason you exist is because you are useful to me," The Director said. "The moment that stops, I take over."

"So, no choice."

"Mr. Shirazi, did you give the people you oppressed a choice?" The Director asked. "Consider your service to me a privilege, for this is only a fraction of the pain you caused millions."

"Will you let me live?" the young CEO pointedly asked.

The Director ground his jaw. "You may live."

He sighed. "What's my part?"

The Director smirked. "When the time comes, you must turn Earth's nuclear arsenals against Mars and Ceres."

Mr. Shirazi paused. "Ceres will detect them long before their arrival and intercept."

The Director narrowed his eyes. "I'm sending you the schematics for a prototype cloaking software that will circumvent their detection systems."

The recording cut.

The corporal and I stared at the now blank projection.

"What the fuck..." Corporal Young whispered. "Khasi, we must do something. We must tell the generals."

I gritted my teeth. "No... Our war room has been compromised. We can't tell anyone. We can't risk the Hermians discovering that we know." I breathed deeply. "But we can do something ourselves."

"Like what?"

"I don't know just yet. But the moment you finish downloading these files, delete the source."

"No, Khasi," she said. "They'll know they've been hacked."

I had a thought. "Can you create an auto-erase trigger for a later date?"

"Yes... yes, I can."

◆

We must destroy ourselves to save ourselves, I reminded myself as Corporal Young, Takamoto-san, Terkat, Juna, John, and I watched seven clusters of missiles launch from AdventureStop's abandoned site in Usonia's Sierra Nevadas, hosting over ten-thousand decommissioned warheads now reactivated and updated with The Director's cloaking software. *The first cluster will hit Hawaii's elevator,* I knew from Takamoto-san's simulation. I stared at its thin tether rising from the pacific ocean to outer space in the horizon. *That's when the source code will auto-erase.* I scratched behind John's ear, then studied the hard drive containing the only copy of The Terran Files strapped securely around his neck.

"They should have made contact with Hawaii," Takamoto-san whispered.

"The source files have begun auto-erasing," Corporal Young confirmed.

A series of flashes came from Hawaii's elevator at the horizon and a mushroom cloud rose like a seedling's germination. But the elevator did not budge.

"Was it enough?" Juna asked.

A slow wave appeared in its tether traveling upwards. It began writhing like a serpent. Then, the engineering marvel, Earth's greatest achievement, shot into the sky, and out of sight. Several minutes later, its sonic boom ravaged the mountains around us, rattling our brains even through our hearing protection. The shock wave dissipated and we stared at the mushroom cloud climbing into the stratosphere.

My holotile lit up with calls from Cane, Vasili, Mr. Shirazi... I silenced it. "They'll know it was us soon enough."

"Cuba's elevator was just hit," Takamoto-san whispered, watching his simulation. "Spain's, too." The old scientist rubbed his temples, processing the moment. "Now Brazil, Addis Ababa, Liberia, and Shenzhen."

"It's done..." I said. "We've cut The Hermians on the ground from their fleets in orbit. We've secured Earth. But life without interplanetary trade will be hard. And the fallout will one day have its affect." I thought about that. "If only the others listened. We could have done this cleaner."

"What's done is done," Takamoto-san whispered, looking pale.

"Dad," Juna said. "What now?"

"We've just committed high treason. So... We run."

◆

From one mountain peak to another, we trekked north through the Sierra Nevada mountains into Oregon's Coastal Range, watching from our new campsites as Iranian Sun paratroopers raided our previous ones. They caught Terkat just outside of Reno, and Takamoto-san near Redding, but Corporal Young, Juna, John, and I kept on. If it weren't for John's nose, we would have been caught months ago.

"We can't keep up this pace," Juna said one night in my cloaking tent. "We're not sleeping, we're not eating. We should turn ourselves in."

I gave my son a hard look. "We must keep The Terran Files out of their hands at all costs." I turned to John curled on the ground with the hard drive around his neck, snoozing away.

"Then, we destroy them," Juna argued. "Isn't that your thing!?"

"No! They contain humanity's greatest achievements, our history, everything! Destroying them would be like destroying humanity's soul!"

"Since when do you care about that!?" he challenged.

I gritted my teeth. "Since Kandara was taken."

He frowned. "You use her as a means to justify your revenge!"

"You can't be serious!" I snapped.

"Look around... All of this is because of you! All of this is in her name! Yet, we don't even know if she's alive!"

I tried not to blurt out the truth and shook my head. "Defeating the Hermians is the only way to save her."

"…Another justification." Juna stood and left my tent for his own.

If only he knew, I thought, having never told a soul about what I learned from Professor Shu. I studied John's fur. Much had become gray. I scratched behind his ear but he was so exhausted he did not stir. I lifted his floppy earlobe and read its tattoo. *"Kunming - 6834026 - Enhanced."*

He's old… And I wondered how much time he had left.

John's nose wiggled, his eyes shot open, and he let out a howling bark so loud my ears rang. Before I could react, torrential wind tore my cloaking tarp from its stakes and blinding light struck. *Paratroopers!?* Mech units dropped to the ground outside our encampment. *How did they find us!?* I thought, knowing I had perfectly masked our presence.

Corporal Young came tearing out of her tent with her rifle raised and peppered the approaching mechs. They returned fire, shearing off her limbs and eroding her torso.

Fuck! I turned to Juna's tent, with its cloaking tarp torn away, but he was nowhere to be found. I frantically searched for him as the mechs thumped forth, until I saw his pack was also gone. *He left us… Just before they struck.* My heart sank as my fury rose. I wanted to slap my son. *But I must survive first!*

I snatched my pack and spun to John. "John, go!"

He bolted into the woods, doubling back to make certain I was following. The paratrooper ship's torrent lessened but I heard branches clinking against metal and stun shots crackling against pine needles, unable to penetrate the thick vegetation. But just when I thought the terrain was protecting me a flurry of projectiles came. Pain plowed down my arm and John yelped, but there was no blood. *Rubber bullets,* I realized. *They want us alive.* I checked John's hip where I saw instant swelling, but he was a tough old boy and stood back up.

"It's going to be okay, John," I said, looking into his eyes, realizing that in all these years, he was my one true friend, my rock.

He hobbled on, zigzagging down steep mountain slopes where the mechs were having difficulty. They cracked open with a distinctive whine and more nimble footsteps pattered. But then, John came to an abrupt halt and I nearly toppled over him.

"What is it, b—" I froze as heavy steps came from lower down the slope. *I've fallen right into their trap!*

I made eye contact with John and brought forth my holotile. "John," I whispered. "It's up to you now." I synced with the hard drive around his neck, where our final gambit lay, should we face this very situation. I stared at *Activate* on hologram. "If the Hermians seek to destroy us, to erratic our entire way of life, do they not deserve the same fate?"

John looked at me with innocent eyes.

I dashed the icon, starting the process, its hologram displaying millions of nukes aligning into silos from every missile site across Usonia, each uploaded with The Director's cloaking software, now tuned to evade Hermian detection as well. But it felt like a game or simulation, for I would never witness their departure. *Nobody will see this coming*, I knew. *Not even The Director.*

Footsteps from above and below closed in. There was no time to watch the arsenal calculate trajectories. I unlinked my holotile, set it on the ground, and aimed my rifle. The shot fried its circuits.

"They'rrre y'overrr herrre!" came a distinctly Hermian voice.

Iranian Sun and The Hermians... I knelt and scratched behind John's ear with one hand while running my other along his collar until I found the hard drive's thumbnail key. I removed it and flipped its switch. John's collar blinked green. I quickly turned it off, placed the key into my mouth, and took a deep swig from my canteen, flushing it down my throat.

John watched me with sad eyes, like he knew this was the end.

"John... You've been the best companion I could have ever asked for." I kissed his forehead. "But we must go our separate ways now." I breathed deeply. "John, go!"

John whined. He did not move.

"Please, you must leave." Tears ran down my cheeks. "John, go!"

He gently nudged my hand with his nose.

"Go! Git!"

Limbs snapped as paratroopers and Hermians closed in.

I pointed my rifle at John's feet, sending stun shots into the dirt. John leaped back, giving me a confused, scared look, before disappearing into darkness.

"y'I have him!" I heard just before my body was racked with electricity, becoming jelly, and I slumped to the ground.

◆

"The Butcher of Earth lives up to his name..." said a composed voice.

Searing pain racked my joints, where they had stretched me, and my jaw throbbed, where they repeatedly struck. The weight on my body and in my gut felt strange. Which meant only one thing. *I'm not on Earth.* But how they got me here without the elevators eluded me. *Mr. Shirazi's personal shuttle?* I thought and slowly peered through swollen eyes to see the old Hermian dictator.

"...How you stole The Terran Files, how you discovered Operation Eraser, then used our cloaking software against us, was masterful." The Director inspected my battered face. "But it is your willingness to destroy your own lands, your own elevators, dooming your own people to achieve victory, that truly impresses me."

"F-Fuck you..." I managed to say, studying The Director's strange show of respect.

"We are more similar than you realize," The Director continued. "For I also believe humanity must make sacrifices to survive. That the worst of us must be purged. That our species should restart without the burden of prejudice, greed, jealousy, inequality, or corruption. You see, Khasi, what I bring, what *Operation Eraser* brings, is not an end, but a new beginning."

I stared at the old dictator, processing his words. "No..."

"No, what, Khasi?" he responded. "Be more specific."

I chuckled. "You cannot break me... For I am already broken... I am dead... I will tell you nothing."

"I see," he said lightly. "Perhaps you'll tell *her,* then." The Director grinned, about-faced, and approached a woman in a crisp uniform hidden within the shadows of the interrogation room. I had not noticed her until that moment. She pressed a fist to her shoulder and The Director responded in kind. Then, he left the room.

I studied the woman, trying to understand how she might be different from the others. She was much shorter, but still held that Hermian posture. She stepped towards me. Something in the way she moved gave me pause and when her eyes came out of the shadows, I gasped.

"Dad? Is this really you?" she whispered in our people's tongue.

My jaw dropped and the air hit the exposed nerves of my broken teeth. "I-It's me, Kandara..."

Her lips pursed. "Prove yourself."

I looked into her eyes, those beautiful eyes. "You were five and we were walking from the school when you saw a star in the sky through the smog. That's when you decided to become an astronaut."

Her brow softened, her lip trembled, and her posture slouched. "No," she muttered. "You can't be him. My father was gentle..."

"Until they took you from me," I said.

She darkened. "I'm the reason you became a monster!?" she snapped, taking me aback. "You're putting this all on me!?"

"It's not like that," I stammered. *But what did I expect?* "I was searching everywhere for you, but roadblocks kept arising that I could not ignore. So, I plowed through them. I never meant to lead a war. I never meant to hurt anyone."

Her eyes blazed. "Yet, you massacred hundreds of thousands! Many were my comrades! You were supposed to be a butcher by title, not in your soul!" She turned away. "You disgust me..."

No... But even I considered myself a monster. "I'm sorry about your comrades." I thought about that. "So, you're truly one of them."

Her jaw clenched. "You wouldn't understand."

"Professor Shu said you were tricked into coming to Mercury," I responded. "It must have been tough hiding who you truly are."

She faced me again. "How did you find her?"

"The summit with Iranian Sun. John sniffed her out."

She paused. "I hope John had a proper burial."

And now she's interrogating me, I knew. "You don't mind that I buried your stuffed bunny with him so he'd have a friend in the afterlife, do you?"

She grinned. "That's okay."

I could tell from her eyes that she knew I was lying.

"He would have been what? Twenty-seven now?" she asked.

"That sounds about right."

"How long do Kunming dogs live for?"

"Fifteen years, I think," I carefully responded.

"But wasn't John enhanced?" she asked.

"Perhaps," I said. "That would explain why he lived to twenty-three." I again saw that she knew I was lying. *But how?* I suddenly remembered Professor Shu saying that Kandara had undergone their modifications, which meant heightened senses. *She's listening to my heartbeat.* "Kandara, can we stop this? I'm not going to tell you where John is."

She frowned. "We know he has The Terran Files."

Juna talked... "How's your brother?"

She cocked her head. "You know it was him?"

I nodded.

"He'll be relocated to Icarus and watched," Kandara said. "What an interesting creature he turned into."

How can she talk about Juna like that? "You don't know him. Yes, he betrayed me. But he's a good father, far better than I was," I responded, watching her face become blank. "Yes, you have a nephew. Maybe if you had children of your own, you'd understand why he did what he did." The corner of her mouth twitched. "So, you're a mother…"

"I don't remember you being this perceptive," she said.

"I've interrogated thousands," I said. "So, what's their name?"

"Her name is Dione," Kandara carefully said. "She's almost six."

"Dione…" I repeated. "What's her real name?"

Kandara gave a sharp look. "That is her real name."

I sighed. "Please, if not for your sake, or our people's sake, then for Dione's sake. The Director is insane. He's planning to destroy all of humanity with Operation Eraser. If you find The Terran Files, you must ensure he never gets his hands on them."

"I'm afraid it's too late for me," she said. "Whatever The Director asks, I must do."

I thought upon the arsenal I unleashed slowly nearing Mercury and that there was no stopping them. I felt horribly sick. My body quivered. I pulled against my restraints with all my strength but they did not budge. *After a lifetime of trying to save my daughter, I've only succeeded in destroying her…* I slumped, letting myself dangle like a doll.

"Kill me," I whispered.

"No!" Kandara sternly responded.

"Please, I beg you. Give me this one mercy."

She grimaced. "You know exactly where The Terran Files are! Therefore, you will never die! You will live in hibernation for however long it takes to crack you!" She snapped her fingers and two equalizers entered the room.

"Kandara, you can't do this!" I shouted.

"When you wake, remember that it was you who forced us to take such drastic measures! It was you who forced us to create Operation Eraser!"

"That's not true! That can't be true!" I cried. "Please, you must stop him! You must—" I saw a pulsing in her irises. *A pattern… Morse.*

"*.. Blink .-- .. .-.. .-..* " they went, shrinking and widening on command.

"*I will…* " she was saying.

She has a plan, I realized and her behavior suddenly made sense. *This is as much of an interrogation of her as it is of me.*

She turned to the equalizers and, with a thick Hermian accent, said, "Put him y'into stasis! y'Add him to The Dirrrectorrr's collection!"

They released my restraints, dropping me to the floor, and with mighty paws dragged my battered body from the interrogation room and down the hall, Kandara leading the way. Doors at the end opened, revealing hundreds of cryotubes, each with someone locked in ice, contorted in agony.

I studied their faces, each of different ethnicities, wearing Terran, Lunan, Ceran, Martian, Jovian, or Saturnian uniforms. *All enemies of The Director.* A familiar face caught my attention. *Takamoto-san,* I realized. I saw Mr. Shirazi a moment later. Terkat's upper torso and head were in another. Corporal Young was just a head. And then, I saw Juna.

I've failed you all.

The equalizers stuffed me into a cryotube, holding me still as they strapped down my limbs. But I did not struggle. A breathing tube slid down my throat and diodes seared into my skin. I barely felt it. The hatch sealed.

Among the grinning equalizers, I saw Kandara, my beautiful little girl, fighting desperately to hold back her tears.

Frigid cryogel pooled around my feet. A chill crept into my toes, climbing up my legs and into my torso. My stomach stopped digesting. My lungs no longer swelled with breath. My tongue locked tight. And my eyes faded to nothing.

Goodbye...

CHAPTER FIVE

Samuel wakes to Ulysses staring at him with a shaken expression. Without a word, Ulysses hands him a bottle of colored water.

"…Thank you," Samuel says and swigs, imagining its electrolytes are percolating through his body. He still feels weak, famished. *But I am more alive than ever before.* "That was terrifying, yet incredible."

Ulysses still stares at him.

"What?" Samuel asks. A glow catches his eye and he turns to see a ringed space-port from his peripheral, then Ganymede's capital city below. *We're back at Hardsill already?*

"You were out for three days straight, reciting pivotal moments in Khasi's life," Ulysses mutters. "How did you do that?"

Samuel shrugs. "I just watched."

Ulysses narrows his brow. "You didn't experience his memories as if they were your own?"

Samuel thinks about that. "I knew it wasn't real."

"But it was…"

"Not for me." He looks at Khasi's body preserved within clear plastic on the auto-med's table. "He was terrible yet somehow great." He then ponders the end. "You want The Terran Files, don't you?"

Ulysses gives a hard look.

Samuel frowns. "You said that I'm one of you now. So, I have a right to know what we're searching for."

Ulysses slowly nods. "The Terran Files are our people's path to salvation. Everything depends on their retrieval."

Samuel thinks upon Khasi's memories. "There was a remote key, but Khasi ate—"

Ulysses raises the small black key.

Samuel snaps his head to Khasi's body to find an incision at his abdomen. "How do you intend to use these files to save our people?"

Ulysses grinds his teeth. "I don't know just yet. We get The Terran Files first, then figure out the rest later."

Samuel ponders this. "We go to Earth, then." He glances down upon Hardsill. "But first, I must help my mother."

♦

It's been far too long, Jonathan thinks. The solidness in his gut, the heaviness in his heart, and weight of his blood, is strangely comforting. *Real gravity...* Paris's dome is visible from the stratosphere, its rippling surface slowly defining as Jonathan's shuttle approaches.

"Welcome back, Jon," comes through com.

"Angela!? Is that you!? I thought you'd never return!"

"I could say the same about you, but here we are," she responds. "I caught wind you took a shuttle from Luna and figured there's only one place you were headed."

"And you up and left New Delhi?" Jonathan asks. "Is the dig paused?"

"Vincent's holding the fort while I'm away."

"Auto-pilot engaged," chimes the shuttle. It navigates around several large oaks, touching down on the grass where Angela waits. The fusion engine winds down and the shuttle's hatch opens.

"Hey you," Angela says, looking tanned, borderline burnt.

"Hey," Jonathan responds, taking a confident first step from his shuttle, but stumbles. He catches the shuttle's hatchway jamb.

"Now that's the Jon I remember," Angela quips.

He grins, feeling embarrassed. *But she's seen me at my worst.* "I'm rusty." He smiles wide and comes in for a hug.

"And, you've gotten soft," she says, patting his back, then she pushes him off to get a better look. "We're going to have to whip you back into shape."

"I'm sure Earth will do that on its own." Jonathan suddenly thinks upon Aizen, wondering how he might have changed.

Angela gives him a look. "It's good to see you, and here of all places, but

GHOSTS OF ZION | 106

why now after avoiding Paris for so long?"

Jonathan's smile dwindles. "I'm not here for Paris, actually."

She cocks her head. "Explain..."

"I'm afraid I can't."

Angela rolls her eyes. "You must at least go inside."

"Oh, I'm going in, but only to talk with *them...*"

It takes Angela a second. "How you can trust those creatures?"

"I trust Zion, and he trusted them," Jonathan says, then smiles. "Dinner?"

Angela checks her holotile. "You have impeccable timing."

Young archaeologists give Jonathan and Angela stunned looks as they pass through basecamp, and when they enter the canteen, they stare.

"They're kids. You think they're up to the task?" Jonathan says, thinking about Hazel, and how she came fresh from school, but proved ready.

"They're trained as much as they can be," Angela responds. "Now, it's up to them to prove their mettle."

"Hazel and Vincent should be here," Jonathan says, getting in line.

"You know Vincent. When he gets his mind on something, he can't let go. I tried to get him to come," Angela says. "It's not personal."

"Oh, I know," he says and smiles, remembering when he would find Vincent asleep on the tables of London's library, practically drooling on priceless texts. "What's Hazel up to?"

Angela gives another look. "She's leading the dig of Prometheus on Luna. I'm surprised you didn't stop by during your transfer."

"I didn't know." Jonathan thinks about that. "We haven't been the best at keeping in touch."

"Speak for yourself, Jon," Angela quips. "Even Aizen checks in."

Jonathan's heart leaps. "Really? Do you know where he is?"

She purses her lips. "He asked me to keep that a secret..."

"Please, it's important that I reach him. He's not returning any of my calls or messages." Jonathan hears the panic in his voice. "I must know if he's okay."

Angela sighs. "Last time Aizen checked in was at Addis Ababa. I'll send a message." She retrieves her holotile and quickly dashes into its projection. "Sent." The moment she stuffs it into her pocket, it dings. She timidly pulls it back out. "It bounced back."

A pit forms in Jonathan's stomach. "So, he's offline."

Angela thinks for a moment. "Are you going to meet them, to find Aizen? Do you think they can detect his location?"

"Their ability to sense vibrations is incredible. They might already know I'm here."

♦

Angela and Jonathan suit up early morning and enter an airlock a hundred meters below grade, separating basecamp from Paris's catacombs.

"Beats crawling through hundreds of kilometers of tunnel barely wide enough for our shoulders," Angela says.

"I don't know," Jonathan responds. "The journey is always fun."

The airlock opens and they step inside. It seals behind them and ultraviolet light brightens to kill any contaminates they might bring in.

Such a waste of resources, Jonathan thinks, knowing Paris is a charade. When the light dwindles, the inner lock door opens, revealing the catacombs just as he remembered.

"See?" Angela says. "Some things are still real."

"I suppose," Jonathan responds, trying to mask his excitement. He sees several skulls shaped like a doorway among a wall of bone. "Look! The skulls are held in place by hip joints! I didn't notice that before!"

"You're like a kid sometimes," Angela says with a grin.

They move through catacomb corridors, closer to the staircase ascending to Paris itself. *Are they still there?* Jonathan's hands quiver as he searches for the strange orange orbs. They round one curve, two curves, three curves. Then, they meet the stairs.

"They're not here…" Jonathan whispers.

"They can't be, you know that," Angela says.

Jonathan sighs. "Let the disappointment begin."

They ascend the staircase to Paris's streets, but instead of the perfectly constructed architecture, breathable air, and impeccable cleanliness, Jonathan finds crumbled ruins with skeletons strewn about in positions of agony and an atmosphere filled with noxious gasses associated with decay. But it all feels like a children's haunted house. Jonathan sits upon a bench in Vincent's Plaza and knocks a pattern in old Morse code.

"There's no need, Jonathan," comes an impossibly deep voice. A black creature appears from the shadows. "I sensed your arrival yesterday. It's good to have your company again. You, as well, Angela."

"XT, I apologize. I should have returned years ago," Jonathan says.

XT tilts its featureless head. "It's only been twelve years, three months, seventeen days, ten hours, thirteen minutes, and thirty-seven seconds. A blink of an eye, as your kind says. There is no need for an apology."

"I sometimes forget that your lifetime spans millennia."

XT tilts its head again. "Yours does, too."

Angela gives XT a curious look. "What do you mean by that?"

Jonathan clears his throat. "Angela doesn't know."

"You humans and your secrecy. I do not understand the point of it."

Angela faces Jonathan. "What in Sol are you two talking about?"

"Later," Jonathan says, feeling a lump in his throat. "XT, I need your help finding Aizen. You must know his location."

"Correct, Jonathan. We know exactly where Aizen is. However, he requires solitude and we intend to grant him just that."

"The situation has changed," Jonathan says and glances at Angela. *She already knows so much, might as well let her in.* "The Arkathy Minister requested Clara's help with an investigation. I don't know the details, but Clara asked me to retrieve Aizen."

"This is concerning." The black creature paces back and forth. After a moment it stops. "I will relay your request to Aizen, but you must respect his choice should he deny it."

Jonathan nods, thinking about his encounter with the Arkathy. "Also… I recognized Minister Hjordiana's captain as someone I know."

"What was recognizable about this captain?" XT asks.

"Its vibration was different." *What the hell did I just say?*

XT zeroes in on Jonathan. "Fascinating." With that, the dark creature turns and melts back into the shadows.

"Um… Jon," Angela says. "You have some serious explaining to do."

♦

Aizen wakes to a child standing next to his cot inside his lean-to.

"Hello," Aizen says.

The child scampers through a fabric entry flap as heavy footsteps approach. The flap whips open and a silhouette of a strong woman appears. His eyes adjust to the sunlight. *It's Thalee.*

"Old man wants to see you!" she snaps.

"Oh, thank y—"

"He's waiting by the caves!" She whips the flap closed.

Aizen rolls from his cot and rubs the sleep from his eyes. *Earth you are a natural sleep aid,* he thinks, having had the best sleep of his life every night there, until just now. He dresses in fabric, borrowed from Tadem, marveling at its craftsmanship, how it feels on his skin, and how it breathes.

It's wool, Allessandra says.

From sheep? Aizen asks, wondering how he missed the entire fold.

Or alpaca, she says. *Either way, it must have been acquired through trade with another tribe.*

That would suggest a larger network of Terrans, Aizen thinks and stands, almost knocking his head against the angled ceiling. *Why am I so uncoordinated here?* He opens his lean-to's flap and steps into cool morning air that seeps through the wool, juxtaposing with the sun's warmth. *I'm wearing wool from now on.*

Fires are being lit and the smell of singed wood invades his nose. Tribespeople watch as he heads to the caves. Some grin, others frown, a few wave, and Aizen waves back. *Do they all know who I am?*

The roar of waves comes before he sees the cave's opening.

"Good morning, Aizen," says Kune in his wheezy voice, emerging from the darkness. "Today is an important day, for what I show you is not known by my kin. Come." He descends into the cave.

Aizen follows, marveling at how the waves reverberate against the stone, until the old man slips into a solid wall. *What?* Aizen stops to inspect. From straight on the wall appears like solid rock but its texture shifts slightly as he turns. He traverses a narrow passage between two overlapping walls, coming to a chamber dimly lit by a glowing source.

An ember! Anda cries, coming into Aizen's view, staring upwards.

The old man points. "A gift from a friend."

"You know the Sorgans?" Aizen asks.

Kune chuckles. "You mean the Sendu? More like they know of us." He turns down another passage.

The waves quiet, replaced by dripping water. Frigid air brushes Aizen's skin. A fishy scent hits his nose.

"These chambers are used for preservation," Kune says, passing one packed with fish beneath another glowing stone, emitting cold this time.

How are they working with the Sorgans? Aizen thinks.

It makes sense, Zion responds. *I tasked the Sorgans with repairing Earth's ecosystem and cities in preparation for our potential return. It seems they deem the native Terrans essential to this effort.*

You don't know for sure? Aizen thinks.

I'm not omniscient, he responds. *But I trust there's a reason.*

"You're talking to them, aren't you?" Kune suddenly says.

Aizen snaps back to the moment. "…Yes."

"All of their questions will be answered in time," he says, leading out from the chill passageway into a chamber the size of a stadium with hundreds of crisscrossing stalagmites and stalactites, some coming together to form natural columns.

The lighting is different, rippling upon a ceiling of chandelier formations. Aizen looks down to find glowing stones strewn across the bottom of a large pool of water. His hair stands on end. "This is a power plant..."

"Very good," Kune responds. "The Sendu introduced us to the transmitters, but we had to create the power source."

"Transmitters? You mean the embers?" Aizen asks.

"*Em–berz,* a strange name," Kune points at the water. "The energy we create is absorbed by the *em–berz* and sent to several locations becoming light, heat, cooling, or power sources. What we choose, they become."

Just like on Sorgan, Anda says.

Images of Anda's life, from when he discovered the ember powering the Coms Tower on Sorgan and used it to manipulate the rock, come.

Transmutation, Aizen realizes. "But the embers are alive."

"They are not alive," Kune corrects. "But the power source they transmit from certainly is."

Aizen peers into the water. A shadow zooms by and he jumps. More follow like a swarm.

"There must be millions. What are they?" Aizen asks and turns to Kune.

The old man is gone.

Aizen feels eyes upon him and peers back into the water. The shadows have stopped zooming and stare at him from the pool's edge. Each has several arms.

My Sol! Mirko suddenly says. *I know these creatures. They're rainbow squid, introduced on Enceladus because of their ability to electrogenerate and receive, allowing them to navigate its ocean in pure darkness.*

Great white sharks also use electroreception to detect prey, Dione adds.

Does that mean... Aizen approaches the pool and slowly dips his hand into the water. Several squid approach, extending tentacles to investigate.

Hello, he thinks.

Hello, hello, hello, echoes back. Their bodies ripple with light and the embers send rays bouncing through the chamber like a laser show.

CHAPTER SIX

"These are the insurgents we found on Eden Bank," Minister Hjordiana says with a disdainful rasp.

Clara looks upon young boys and girls, barely adults, on metal tables with gaping holes through their torsos. A wave of nausea hits her. She feels ice cold, but starts to sweat. Her legs wobble. *Pull yourself together!* She takes deep Ergonos breaths, calming her stomach and quelling her mind. *It's purely scientific,* she tells herself. Her legs steady. She looks at the bodies again, finding the old woman among the young adults. *Her arm was sacrificed, and she took several shots to the chest, arms, and legs, but seemed to fight on,* Clara judges. *Nerve augmentation?* She points. "The old woman was their commanding officer, the rest are practically children."

"I see," says the minister. "These others are indeed hatchlings."

Clara spies a table in the back with a single leg and hustles over to it. Minister Hjordiana cocks her head and follows. Clara inspects the leg. *Medically amputated at the hip.* "Whose leg is this?"

"One of theirs," the minister says, motioning to the bodies.

Clara shakes her head. "This is cauterized. None of these bodies have cauterization, save the old woman at the shoulder."

"What does this mean?"

"One of them might have survived." Clara turns to the supreme minister. "Which means, you're searching for two people. A monster and a one-legged person."

Minister Hjordiana smiles wickedly. "You are good, Clara."

"Do you know where the insurgents are from?" Clara asks.

The minister's smile dwindles. "According to the Council's registry, they do not exist."

Clara thinks about that. "Can I take DNA samples? I know someone who can help."

"Be quick about it," the minister responds.

♦

"Mother," Samuel says to a shriveled woman hooked to a decrepit re-breather that occupies half of their living stall.

"I've never seen this before," says a doctor. "And the equipment needed to properly diagnose her is not available."

Samuel gives the doctor a hard look. "What would it take for the equipment to become available?"

"More than you can imagine."

"Try me," Samuel says and raises his holotile.

The doctor gives a strange look. "At a proper hospital, with the necessary equipment, and a full medical staff... Four to five million credits."

Samuel types, *"7 million,"* into his holotile and flicks it to the doctor.

Her holotile beeps and she timidly raises it. "...How?" Her face melts to realization. "Are you thee Kell?"

"The extra two mill is to never ask that question again," Samuel says.

The doctor quickly opens her com. "Emergency ambulance requested, alpha class." She turns to Samuel. "We'll do everything in our power to save your mother."

Incredible weight lifts from Samuel's shoulders. *I did it...*

Moments later, paramedics rush in, quickly replacing the old, rusty re-breather with a state-of-the-art mech-lung that straps lightly around his mother's torso. Then, they place her on a hover gurney and rush her into an ambulance that resembles a limousine.

"Mr. Kell, the hospital address and your mother's room number are on your receipt." The doctor flicks the information to Samuel. "Not a soul besides you and my medical staff will know she is being treated."

"Thank you, doctor."

She nods and enters the ambulance. It lifts vertically, then cloaks.

"We must go," Ulysses says into Samuel's earpiece. "Earth cannot wait any longer."

"We still have time…" Samuel responds.

"That is literally the one thing we don't have!"

Samuel feels a presence and realizes Ulysses is right next to him, cloaked. He nudges Ulysses's hidden arm. "Let's see The Augmentor, then."

Samuel hobbles through dark, derelict streets to a rusty door framed by two enforcers.

"Arms out," one says and moves to search Samuel.

"Nope," comes Ulysses's voice and the enforcer lifts into the air.

The second one steps forward, but is also lifted.

"Stand here," Ulysses says, placing the two befuddled men on the street.

They stare for a moment, then one stammers, "Y-you may enter…"

As the rusty door opens, a waft of grease, welding gas, jazz, and men and women hollering back and forth for tools, envelops them. A cavernous hanger stretches into the distance, each bay hosting different items from cybernetics to custom ship modifications.

"Samuel Kell!" cries The Augmentor, hustling from a bay hosting a black ship looking made of stone. "It's a pleasure to have you again." She wipes black dust from her hands with a rag and turns to the air next to him. "Who's your friend?"

Ulysses releases his cloak.

"My Sol, you are massive!" The Augmentor says. "Who are you?"

"Ulysses," he shortly says.

She stares in awe. "…May I touch you?"

He nods.

She snatches his paw, feeling up his fingers and into the knuckles, working her way up his forearm to his elbow. Her awe melts to confusion. She stops at his shoulder. "You have no implants…"

"I do not," Ulysses confirms.

"Are you…" Sudden understanding crosses her face. "I never thought I'd meet one of your kind." She turns to Samuel. "You are a fantastic gift giver."

"I'm not a gift," Ulysses grumbles.

Samuel grins. "We need your help."

She gives Ulysses a final glance. "Can you be more specific?"

"My leg's restrictor nearly got us killed. I had to convince it to give me control."

"I see… Come." She abruptly marches to a bay hosting hundreds of cybernetic limbs on racks.

Samuel hobbles to keep up.

She points at a table. "Sit."

When he does, she hard-line connects her holotile. A hologram pops up and she quickly scrolls through. "Gatling, nice," she says. "And Anti-tank… Interesting. What in Sol were you doing?" She opens a recording of Samuel shooting Arkathy soldiers.

It took a fucking recording!? Samuel thinks.

She slowly closes it. "I saw nothing…"

"Can you remove the restrictor?" Ulysses says.

She gives him a look, then dashes several icons. "Restrictor's off. I deactivated its recording function, too. Ignorance is bliss."

"Can you also do something about the battery power?" Samuel says.

She thinks about that. "The prosthesis's auto-defense system is always on standby, using most of the battery power. I can turn off the defense system, giving full power to basic mobility, but you must remember to reactivate it before entering another situation." She dashes more icons. "It's set."

Samuel hops off the table and moves side to side, the leg no longer lagging, feeling truly like his own.

"Is that all for today?" she asks.

"We also need a ship," Ulysses says. "Small, fast, armed, and cloaked."

"I have a Fersandan Racing Corsair being outfitted with rail-guns."

Samuel looks at The Augmentor's blackened hands, then at the black ship peaking over the bay dividers. "What about that one?"

"Not available," she quickly says.

"Why?"

"You can't afford it."

"Try me," Samuel retorts.

"Seventy-eight billion creds."

Samuel's grin dwindles. "Oh…"

The Augmentor's eyes drift to Ulysses. "I might consider a trade for him…"

"Absolutely not!" Ulysses snaps.

"Shame," she says. "It's Don Credence's ship, anyway."

♦

"Jon, where are you going?" Angela asks, looking at his packed gear.

Jonathan looks up from an old map. "I cannot simply sit by and wait for Aizen to respond. This is too important."

Angela gives him a worried look. "What's going on?"

"I can't tell you," he says.

"Well, what were you and XT talking about with your lifespan?"

"I can't talk about that either."

Angela crosses her arms. "I know Aizen is special. I know Zion was special. I've read his biography. I know it's all true despite what Clara says. But what I don't know, is what's happening with you."

She won't quit, Jonathan realizes and sighs deeply. "Have a seat."

As Jonathan explains how Zion lived previous lives, how Aizen is the next lifetime, and how he himself is the link, Angela's face grows more confused, concerned, and questioning.

"So, you can't access the lifetimes like they can?" Angela asks.

"That ability never developed for me," Jonathan responds. "I'm just a genetic carrier."

"But, maybe it comes through your instincts, like when we used the painting to find the WorldRing tunnel," she follows up. "You knew it was the right location before we analyzed the cliff. That can't be a coincidence."

"Maybe…"

"What do your instincts say about Aizen's location?" Angela asks.

"He came to Earth to discover how this all happened. So, he would have searched all the cities of his previous lives."

"He checked in with me at Paris, Addis Ababa, New York City, and Toronto," Angela says. "So what's next?"

"I think he's on the coast, searching for either Mermer or Justin's home."

"Which coast?"

"One of old Usonia's." Jonathan points at the ancient map. "But the shoreline was different then, its level waslower. When he lived as Justin, he went to university in the city, but was close enough to return home on the weekends."

"What city was that?" Angela asks.

Jonathan closes his eyes, racking his brain. "Zion never disclosed that information to Clara, but I can't help thinking it began with the letter *P.*"

Angela looks at the map and points at a city on Usonia's northeastern coast. "Portland."

Jonathan makes a face. "I know, but…" He points at the northwestern coast. "Also Portland."

She makes a face. "Two Portlands? That's so stupid."

"And…" Jonathan points down the Northeast coastline. "Portsmouth, Providence, Province-town… There are thirty-seven cities on Usonia's east and west coasts that begin with *P.*"

"This will take forever," Angela says, then suddenly looks closer at the map. "Wait a minute." she pulls out her holotile, using it to further zoom. "Look at the water next to east coast Portland. These drawings look like crabs."

"I think those are smudges," Jonathan says.

Angela selects *Enhance*. Slowly the smudges become round bodies with many legs, claws, and tails. *"Lobster,"* appears on hologram. "It's in the archives!" Angela pulls up images from when the archaeological team had entered Portland, the creatures appearing throughout the ruins. "It's even on the identification panels of their combustion vehicles!" She squints. "Ma… in…eee," she pronounces. "Do you think *Lobster* is another name for a grodote?"

Jonathan thinks about this, but cannot shake a feeling in his gut. "They might be similar, but I feel like we should investigate the other Portland."

"But it's clear these people worshiped this crustacean like a deity," Angela argues. "This must be the place…"

"Didn't you just say I should listen to my instincts?"

"Yeah, but this is actual proof." She points at the images.

"It feels wrong," he says.

Angela frowns. "We must pass over the east coast Portland on the way to the west coast Portland, anyhow. It's not far out of the way."

Jonathan's archaeological brain knows Angela is right, but still, his gut. "Okay, we'll stop by."

◆

"Clara! I'm so happy you called!" cries Dr. Lee.

Clara grins. "How have you been?"

"Good… Great! I've uncovered incredible things in the DNA samples you sent!"

"What do you mean?" Clara asks.

"Samples one through twenty-nine were nothing special, except that they share genetic markers common on Ganymede," Dr. Lee says. "But then, there's sample thirty."

The old woman, Clara knows.

Dr. Lee shakes his head in disbelief. "I don't know how you obtained ancient Hermian DNA in such perfect condition. Is this something Jonathan found?"

"This sample is from someone who recently passed," Clara says.

Dr. Lee chuckles. "You still have that sense of humor."

"…No, Dr. Lee. This sample is only a few weeks old," Clara says. "I studied the body myself."

His grin dwindles. "No… This person is actually from The Fall."

"Are you certain she was not just a descendant?" Clara asks.

Dr. Lee nods. "Very few Hermian modifications from before The Fall were inherited by their descendants. Sadly, more of the repercussions were, like Zion's degradation disease." He takes a deep breath. "Sample thirty has clear marks where heavy genetic modification took place, meaning it was actively changed. Not inherited." He opens the genetic code and highlights a section. "These muscle proteins are literally taken from chimpanzees. And there's more from frogs, horses, eagles, bats, owls, whales. The clarity is incredible."

The old woman looked strong, but not comically so. Clara thinks about that. "Are there any gorilla genes?"

"No…"

"So she's not an equalizer. She didn't have super strength."

"She's likely Hermian infantry," Dr. Lee says. "But she was super strong. The chimpanzee DNA compounds with that of a horse, making her several times stronger than a normal person, with nearly unlimited endurance. Meanwhile, appearing like a typical soldier." The good doctor pauses. "But, there's also something strange about her chromosomes. She has a double-set of *X…*"

"Meaning?"

"She was born without a father."

"How is that possible?" Clara asks.

Dr. Lee shrugs. "Some reptiles from old Earth can reproduce this way. It's called Parthenogenesis."

Clara ponders this. "If she has chromosomes from only her mother, then is she a clone?"

Dr. Lee's eyes widen. "Yes! My Sol, I didn't even think of that! This changes everything! She's roughly two-hundred and fifty years old, but if she is cloning herself through parthenogenesis, then her modifications might transfer, too!"

But why would she pick now to attack a seed bank? Clara thinks.

Dr. Lee opens another DNA strain. "But, perhaps even more incredible than the Hermian sample, is sample thirty-one."

The severed leg? Clara thinks, confused.

"I have never seen anything like this." Dr. Lee seems at a loss for words.

"This young man's entire body behaves like stem cells during early formation of an embryo."

"I don't understand," Clara says.

"I performed several tests, injecting the cells from the other samples, even from the Hermian woman, into this young man. In every case, the boy's DNA adopted the injected cell's attributes, perfectly matching them, essentially becoming them."

"What does this mean?" Clara asks.

"Using this boy's DNA, coupled with the Hermian sample as a road map, we can regrow organs and limbs, maybe even brains, to be rid of Kaladian Degradation Disease." Dr. Lee saddens. "I wish we had this sooner... We could have saved Zion."

♦

Clara enters Minister Hjordiana's flagship bridge to the minister and her officers huddled around several holograms. Anxiety permeates the air.

Minister Hjordiana snaps her head up. "Clara! We found them!"

Clara squeezes in between Arkathy officers to see a battle taking place between Arkathy black ops, a massive man, and a one-legged boy. *This is live,* she realizes, watching the boy's prosthetic leg become a gatling gun, then a cannon, splattering two Arkathy soldiers.

The officers next to her shout and raise furious arms.

The massive man picks up speed, rounding up the remaining black ops, then dashes into the center, one by one, smashing them.

That's an equalizer for sure! Clara thinks.

When the last op falls, the soldiers beside Clara silently back away from the hologram.

They're terrified, she realizes. *I'm terrified.*

The equalizer and one-legged boy rush to the bridge, then to the cargo hold where the equalizer rips a cryotube from its cleat and presses it through a corridor to the shuttle bay. They pull a convulsing man from the tube, enter a small tug ship, and blast from the Arkathy cruiser. Seconds later, the holograms go blank.

A silence hangs heavy.

"Who did they take?" Clara whispers.

Captain Witteksam accesses the pod's information. "A human criminal from long ago, Khasi Sinam."

Why do I know this name? Clara thinks.

"Clara," comes the minister's quiet rasp. "Please, tell me your contact learned something from the DNA samples.”

"The insurgents were from Ganymede…" Clara says, but keeps the rest of Dr. Lee's discoveries to herself.

CHAPTER SEVEN

Aizen floats on his back staring at light refracting through the cavern's formations and feeling electric currents flowing through his body. He closes his eyes and slips into meditation. Instead of the cacophony of life he had been experiencing, he finally senses Earth with clarity. *They calibrated me...*

Mermer appears resting on Aizen's chest.

Did you know your species was electrogenerative? Aizen asks.

No, Mermer says. *But it makes sense.*

But it does not explain how the transfer happens, Kwai Lan says. *Electrogeneration is not DNA.*

I thought grodotes communicated with chemicals, says Justin.

One mystery down, Aizen thinks. *Many more to go.*

Giggling and splashes come from the pool's edge and Aizen stretches his senses that direction. Several younger tribespeople are swimming. Thalee is among them.

"How was it when you first met him?" one asks.

"Did he try to fight you?" asks another.

"I don't want to talk about it," Thalee groans.

"Come on, you have to tell us."

"Is it true he learned our language after hearing it once?"

"Yeah, that's true," Thalee reluctantly answers.

They pause for a moment.

"He's kinda cute, don't you think?" one says.

Thalee scoffs. "He's not cute!"

Aizen grins devilishly, gently curls into a ball to change his buoyancy, and slips beneath the water's surface. He kicks like a frog, following the natural current within the pool, making his way closer to them. He senses their ankles in waist-deep water and picks out Thalee's. He brushes his hand against her calf.

"What was that!?" her muffled voice says.

"What was what?" says another.

Aizen brushes her other leg.

"There it is again!"

"Maybe it's the squid."

"They never come near us!"

Aizen goes in for the kill, grabbing both of Thalee's ankles, planting his feet on the bottom of the pool and lifting her into the air.

"Squid attack!" he yells as he breaks the surface.

The others scream as Thalee takes a plunge. Before Aizen knows it, knives are drawn. Thalee scrambles to her feet and pulls her knife, too. *Maybe that wasn't the best way to make friends*, Aizen thinks.

"Aizen!?" Thalee shouts. "How did you get here!?"

"Kune showed me," he timidly responds.

"No! This place is sacred! You cannot be here!"

"But—"

"Out! Now!" Thalee points at the exit with her knife.

"Sorry," Aizen quietly mutters and makes for the pool's edge.

Why you leave? say the squid.

I'm not welcome, he responds.

You welcome, you welcome.

I promise to come back.

Okay. We miss you.

"They're glowing," one of the tribespeople says and the rest gasp.

Aizen turns to the pool to see the squid rippling with color. The moment his foot leaves the water, they go dark. The tribespeople now stare at Aizen as he heads back through the cave system.

"Did you enjoy yourself?" comes Kune's voice at the cave's mouth.

Aizen faces the old man, suddenly feeling something off about him. "You disguise yourself well. Do any of them know what you are?"

Kune's confident smile dwindles and his posture straightens. "Thalee has always questioned me. The rest believe what they see. Come." Kune leads to his lean-to and motions for Aizen to enter. When they sit upon the wood floor, he says, "Your father is looking for you."

"He's early." Aizen thinks about that.

"Are you ready to see him?"

"I don't know…"

"How did you not immediately know your father was here?" Kune asks. "R9 should have detected him… Have you not taken the spore?"

The spore… Aizen thinks, feeling tendrils of fear creeping in. "R9 hasn't come to me since Mars. It felt best to let it be."

"You're afraid of it, you mean," Kune says, and Aizen nods. "I hope you're safeguarding it, then."

"It's in the shuttle."

"That's not a very safe place."

"What would you suggest?"

"Take the spore."

"What will happen?" Aizen asks.

"It will replace every cell in your body in a matter of seconds, including that of R9's."

"Won't that reduce my lifespan?"

"By several years, yes," Kune confirms. "But it's a small price to pay to access R9's ability to repair and enhance your body."

"I'm not ready…" Aizen says, trying to find a way to change the subject. "Where's my dad now?"

Kune tilts his head. "He's in Portland."

"Oh, that's not far," Aizen says, impressed by his father's deduction.

"No, the east coast Portland."

Maine… Aizen realizes, pulling from Justin and Kwai Lan's memories. "Why is he looking for me?"

"Your mother needs your help with an investigation," Kune says.

Aizen ponders this. "Investigation into what?"

"Supreme Minister Hjordiana asked for Clara's help and she in turn requested that Jonathan finds you. He does not know the specifics."

Aizen's veins run cold and the consciousnesses within him squirm. Even R9 stirs. "I must leave immediately, then!"

Kune raises a palm. "There is one more thing left to do before you go," he says. "You must dive to a most sacred place. A place called *Beesa.*"

"What? Why?"

"It's essential to discovering what you are."

Aizen thinks about this. "Will it be quick?"

"That depends entirely upon you."

◆

"The Corsair will be ready at any moment," Ulysses says, nervously shifting on a bench pulled up to a bar table as golden oldies play. "We shouldn't be out in the open like this."

"Relax," Samuel says. "I'm under Don Credence's protection. And no one is insane enough to pick a fight with an equalizer."

Ulysses snaps his head to Samuel.

"Yes. I know what you are," Samuel says.

"From Khasi's memories?" he asks.

"And Zion's biography, now that I think about it."

"Zion's biography?" Ulysses tilts his head.

Samuel points at a hologram on the bar wall with the caption, *"Clara Ocol Tells All, An Exclusive Interview! Tonight at 22:00!"*

"I don't follow," Ulysses says.

"She wrote a fake biography about Zion Wright, our previous minister who went crazy, with stories of his supposed past lives. There's one from a Hermian's perspective just after The Fall..." *With a perfect description,* he now realizes. "...A captain named Dione Sharpe."

A look of horror crosses Ulysses's face. He lurches from his bench, knocking it over. "No! Dione sold us out! This is all because of her!"

"Wait, you knew her!?"

Ulysses darkens. His muscles ripple and flex. But then, he takes a deep breath, barely maintaining control. "...Where can I find this biography?"

Samuel retrieves his holotile and flicks a copy to Ulysses's tile. "It's free to read."

Ulysses studies the title, then swipes to the author. "Clara Ocol..." he says and faces the advertisement on the bar's hologram.

It suddenly disappears, the bar lighting cuts, and the music stops.

"What the hell!?" Ulysses snaps.

A power outage? Samuel thinks, but notices that his holotile is also out. He tries to move his prosthetic leg to find it offline, too. *An EMP...* Thumps come in the distance. Samuel envisions dark tunnels and dust falling upon his head. *Khasi's memories.* "Carpet bombing..."

"They've found us!" Ulysses begins growling like a wolf.

The bar shudders, knocking bottles off shelves. Samuel's prosthetic leg snaps back into action, as its system reboots, and projects light, revealing Ulysses with his teeth bared and his shoulders shaking.

"Ulysses! Get a hold of yourself! We must get to the hanger!" Samuel says. "But first, we get my mother!"

Ulysses takes several deep breaths. His shaking subsides. "No, the hanger is on the way!" he says. "Corsair first, then the hospital. Follow me!" He takes off through the bar's darkness.

Samuel can barely see Ulysses ahead, and it is all he can do to not stumble, trip, or collide into another person as he scrambles after him. Flickers from outside the bar, illuminating Ulysses's silhouette, are followed by deafening cracks and a shaking of the ground. People run in every direction in the streets, each saying the siege is coming from different directions. Samuel looks up. Hundreds of light streams descend from several dots in the sky. *An armada...* The bombardment lands in several locations at once, indiscriminately, with no obvious logic. *It's what I would have done,* Samuel thinks, then shakes his head. *What Khasi would have done.*

A concussion almost knocks Samuel to the ground. He whips around to find the bar missing.

"Hanger's this way! Let's hope it still stands!" Ulysses cries.

Between every explosion that chatters Samuel's teeth, vibrates his stomach, and shakes his feet, he can only think of his mother and if the EMP cut off her re-breather.

"We're almost there!" Ulysses shouts as he rounds a bend.

An artillery shell shatters the building at the corner showering Samuel with shrapnel and stone. Searing pain rakes his arm and when he grasps his elbow, nothing exists. *Not again!* He quickly pulls a belt from his trousers and cinches it tight around his arm as blood pours. He screams out, but cannot hear his voice. *Calm down!* he breathes deeply, focusing on his stump, watching the blood slow, then stop.

The shelling ceases.

"Sam, stand up!" Samuel orders himself. "Dammit Khasi, stand up!" His shaking stops and he rises to his feet.

Building rubble scatters the street and the hanger is blown to smithereens. *No Ulysses anywhere...* Samuel searches the debris, his nose clouding with noxious gasses. When he steps upon a segment of collapsed wall he feels it shift. A tremendous groan comes from beneath. Samuel backs away. The wall tips up and over to reveal Ulysses with his arm limp.

"Are you okay?" Samuel asks.

"I think my arm is dislocated," Ulysses says, feeling his shoulder. "Yeah… It's fu—" he silences when he sees Samuel's arm is gone.

"The hanger was hit," Samuel says, not a second thought given to his arm. "We must find another way."

A beeping comes and Samuel looks down to see a blinking red light through his trouser's fabric. *The prosthesis?*

Pitter-pattering rises in the distance like an approaching storm. Thousands of objects are dropping from the sky. Two crash to the ground next to Samuel and Ulysses, but do not explode. Each is shaped like a sunflower seed, three meters tall. The seeds crack open and Arkathy soldiers leap out.

"On the ground!" one rasps.

The other calls out in its Arkathy tongue. Nearly fifty soldiers gallop from streets in every direction, their rifles trained on Samuel and Ulysses.

"They have us!" Ulysses says.

"No..." Samuel responds, staring at the light through his trousers, now solid green. "You're forgetting who I am and how much I'm worth."

Rail-guns unleash from above, shredding through auto-armor. The soldiers try returning fire, but cannot find a target. The last Arkathy is mowed down and Samuel and Ulysses stare, frozen in place. A hatch cracks open in the black sky with a thin, old man standing in an airlock.

"Samuel, my boy! Praise Sol! You're still alive!" says the old man.

Don Credence... Samuel realizes.

A small ship uncloaks and lowers to the ground.

The black ship from the hanger, Samuel realizes.

"Come quickly! You and your friend!" the don says.

Samuel and Ulysses rush through the airlock. The ship lifts and its hatch seals.

"To the cockpit!" the don announces, leading the way.

The ship's small, simple, Samuel notes. *So, why does it cost so much?* He sees two passengers already strapped into seats, their heads locked within immobilizers. He recognizes The Augmentor in the pilot's chair, her hands moving quickly across the controls, still stained black. The other is a young woman Samuel's age.

The don takes his seat, straps in, and makes eye contact with Samuel. "Strap in, my boy!"

"Not without my mother!" he responds.

"There is no time!"

"Then, leave me!" Samuel says.

The don grimaces. "Where's your mother!?"

"Saint Cader Medical Center!"

The Augmentor turns around. "You can't be serious! This ship is a prototype! We're lucky to have made it this far!"

"Appease the boy!" the don snaps.

She rolls her eyes but turns the ship around. Samuel straps himself in as quickly as he can one-armed. A hand reaches over to help. It's the young woman.

"How are you alive?" she says, studying his stump.

"I've had worse," Samuel responds.

Her eyes are full of worry and, strangely, respect.

The ship kicks forth, zooming just above burning rubble until they reach a hospital complex to find its buildings pancaked.

"Where is she!?" barks The Augmentor.

"Penthouse suite, building C!" Samuel shouts but only sees debris.

"Penthouse is now in the basement!" says The Augmentor.

Samuel scrolls through the events leading up to now. Horror grips him. *I killed her…*

"Sam! Immobilize! We gotta go!" says The Augmentor.

Samuel keeps staring, hoping to find building C miraculously standing among the chaos.

"Sam," says the young woman. "Sorry about your mum, but you *must* immobilize if you are to survive launch." She places a gentle hand on his intact arm. "Sam…"

He takes a deep breath, leans back, and a halo drops over his skull, cinching tight.

The ship turns upwards, pointing directly at the armada in orbit and a whining grows so loud Samuel can no longer think.

"Launch in three! Two! One!" shouts The Augmentor.

◆

"You can't do this!" Clara yells.

"This is a matter of galactic security!" Supreme Minister Hjordiana rasps. "I can do whatever I like!"

"But these people are innocent!" Clara argues, pointing at Ganymede's capital city of Hardsill from the minister's flagship window.

"They are not innocent! They're harboring fugitives!"

Clara shakes her head. "They likely don't know the fugitives are there!"

"That's enough, Clara!" the minister snaps. "Your insight is no longer welcome!" She turns to Captain Witteksam. "Kenton Zhart!"

An EMP emits from the flagship and city lights below systematically cut. Then, several heavy cruisers beside the flagship open bay doors and unleash hundreds of artillery shells.

Clara rushes to the hologram, determined to disrupt the bombardment, when one of the minister's secret service intercepts her. She instinctively grasps his incoming wrist, crosses the Arkathy's hand to his opposite shoulder, twisting his torso, and flips him to the floor. Then, Clara turns to meet a flash. Her body goes numb and she crumbles.

"Strap her to a chair!" the minister says. "I want her to watch!"

"Zion would have never stood for this!" Clara groans.

The minister's red eyes furiously swirl. "Zion's dead, Clara! What do you not understand about that!"

Clara peers out the window as the shells make landfall looking like marigolds blooming in time-lapse. She imagines the destruction. The screams. *This is all my fault!* she thinks, wishing she never gave a location.

"Launch the first wave!" the minister says in Interspeak.

For my torture, Clara knows.

Thousands of pods drop from the cruisers and land throughout the city. Their vantage points appear on hologram, depicting chaos in the streets.

"Clankhata sedan!" Captain Witteksam rasps and expands a soldier's feed, displaying the massive man and one-legged boy.

The boy's arm is missing, now, Clara notes.

"That's how it's done, Clara!" the minister cries. "Jhiyy Dant!"

Soldiers amass around the fugitives and raise rifles, but before they open fire, the feed cuts.

"Ghatabf!" the minister cries.

Another soldier's feed opens, showing thousands of rounds coming from a source above. The captain opens his platoon's indicators, showing greens quickly becoming reds. Only two remain in yellow.

The man and boy, Clara knows.

The yellow indicators suddenly vanish. The captain frantically runs through optical modes searching for them, but nothing.

Clara humphs.

The minister snaps her direction. "Is there something you know!?"

Clara shakes her head.

The hologram detects a burn signal from the surface, but cannot determine the ship's make and model, only that it is heading straight at them.

"Rtegorts!" shouts the captain.

The flagship sends another EMP, tracking on hologram. It crosses the mysterious ship, but does not effect its progress.

"Ghotrertenda!"

A cruiser flanking the flagship opens its bay doors and launches a missile, again tracking on hologram. It passes harmlessly by.

They can't track it! Clara realizes.

"Kiddona!" The captain manually detonates the missile creating a brilliant white display out the bridge's window.

A black speck reveals, rapidly growing in size, looking to collide with the flagship.

"Florattuenits!"

The flagship dips hard to the left. The Arkathy soldiers' boots grip the floor and they lean into the g-forces. Clara feels her guts squish to the side and she almost screams out.

A black object flashes past the window.

The flagship settles and all is quiet. The hologram no longer detects the burn signal. Instead, it displays a blurry image of a little black ship.

The explosion's light does not reflect on its surface, Clara notes.

"Clara!" the minister shouts. "What kind of ship is this!"

Clara shrugs.

"Don't pretend you don't know! Never has a ship escaped us! How did it evade detection!?"

No signals can sense it, no reflections can be seen, nothing is emitted, and everything is absorbed. Clara thinks long, rolling back to her interview on Parliament Station. *Jupiter marble...* She locks eyes with the Supreme Minister and says, "I have no idea."

CHAPTER EIGHT

Jonathan stares at Aizen's incoming call in the corner of his visor. *Can he sense that I'm close!?* He quickly answers and Aizen's face materializes.

"Hey, Dad…" Aizen says.

Jonathan does not know what to say except, "Hey, buddy…"

Aizen seems to be at a loss of words as well.

"You've gained muscle," Jonathan awkwardly says.

Aizen shrugs. "I've lost weight, actually."

"Oh…" Jonathan scrambles for something else to say. "I'm sor—"

"Are you in Portland?" Aizen asks, cutting him off.

He's hiding something, Jonathan knows. "How did you know? Are we close to you? Can you sense us?"

"No… And Justin's from Portland, Oregon. Not Maine," Aizen says.

Jonathan sighs deeply and looks at a brick wall hosting a giant mural of a lobster in front of him. "I thought that might be the case."

"Jonathan, you okay?" Angela calls on com and waves from down the street. "You're staring at that wall and it's spooking me."

"I'm fine," Jonathan responds. "I'm talking with Aizen."

"Aizen!?" Angela shouts. "Let me in! Let me in!"

"You're added." Jonathan says.

Angela's square appears beside Aizen's.

"You were supposed to check in a week ago! Remember!?" Angela scolds, but she smiles.

"Sorry," Aizen says. "But I've discovered something incredible and couldn't use my holotile."

Jonathan studies Aizen's background. *Calling from his shuttle.* Then, he notices his son's shirt. "What are you wearing?"

"It's wool," he says.

"Like, the ancient cloth?" Angela says.

"Where did you find that?" Jonathan asks. "It looks pristine."

Aizen gives a serious look. "...I found a tribe of Terrans."

Jonathan's heart skips.

"Oh, come on, Aizen," Angela scoffs.

"I'm serious," Aizen defends.

Angela crosses her arms. "Prove it."

"I can't... I promised I wouldn't tell the outside world." Aizen frowns. "I should not have told you."

"Wait, you made contact with them!?" Jonathan asks.

"I didn't mean to," Aizen says. "I discovered one fishing in the tide pools and the next thing I knew, there was a knife to my neck."

Jonathan gives a look. "Did you escape?"

"They let me go as a sign of good faith," he says.

"Well that's certainly convenient for your story," Angela quips.

"Dad, I've discovered something about us," Aizen timidly says.

Jonathan refocuses. "The grodotes?"

Aizen stays silent. His eyes flick to Angela's square.

"She knows," Jonathan adds.

"Yep, I know all about your past lives," Angela confirms.

Aizen takes a deep breath. "I discovered how we can communicate with certain creatures. Grodotes are electrogenerative and receptive."

Jonathan thinks about that. "Does that explain the transfer?"

"I don't know, but Kune is helping me discover how everything works."

"Kune?"

"He's their village elder. Well... he's actually a Sorgan in a human body," Aizen says. "He said you were searching for me..."

Angela's skeptical grin dwindles.

"Jonathan, we can't let Clara help Minister Hjordiana," Aizen suddenly says with a different voice. "The Arkathy always have a second agenda."

That's Zion! Jonathan realizes. "Clara conveyed it's a matter of galactic security."

Aizen shakes his head. "I hate when you do that!" he says, looking to the side. "Sorry, Dad. Zion is a control freak."

"That's alright…" Jonathan says.

"Stay where you are," Aizen then says. "I have one more thing I must do here, then I'll come to you."

"Okay. Be careful, Aizen," Jonathan says. "I've missed you."

Aizen grins. "…I've missed you, too, Dad."

His son leaves the call and Angela's square shifts to the center. Her face is white, almost green, looking like she's seen a ghost.

◆

Aizen leans back in his cockpit chair replaying his conversation with Dad. *I must help Mom… But there's the dive.* Aizen thinks about how Kune said it would uncover what he is. *Why is everything a right of passage?* He rummages through his shuttle's compartments, searching for anything he might need, when he sees his small lock-box. He inputs its code. A seal hisses. He opens its lid to reveal the black spore bound within a titanium cage attached to a neck chain. *R9… You there?* Aizen thinks, waiting for a response.

Nothing.

Kune is right. You must keep it more safe, Mermer says.

Aizen reluctantly lifts the chain and latches it around his neck, tucking the spore beneath his shirt. Then, he exits the shuttle and sets it to hibernate. His return to the village is accompanied by the rhythm of the waves crashing upon the rocks and the calls of birds in the air.

Kune is waiting at the edge of the woods. "You ready?"

"Are we ever?" Aizen responds.

Kune leads down a path. A waft of breakfast strikes. Aizen detects cod and clams alongside garlic and greens. The clearing opens with all fifteen tribe members around the central fire with the basin going strong. They give Aizen funny smiles, except for Thalee, whom looks away.

He peers into the basin. *A chowder,* he thinks, studying its thickened soup.

"This meal is especially prepared for when one of us makes the journey to Beesa," Kune says. "Each of us has added an ingredient with either an intention or defining who we are, so that you take a piece of us with you."

"That sounds wonderful," Aizen says.

"I added garlic," Kune declares. "For it is the lifeblood of cooking and cleanses the heart."

Well said… Justin responds.

That second part is actually true, Kwai Lan adds.

"I added the greens, so that you may always know balance," Tadem says and turns to Thalee.

She rolls her eyes. "I did the fish, okay…"

They wait.

"…To give you strength… whatever," she grumbles.

Aizen can't help but grin.

After each member describes their ingredient, Kune turns to Aizen.

"And what will you add?"

Aizen ponders the combination of flavors and what might round them out.

Spice, Aizen, spice, Allessandra says.

He removes his pack, retrieves a small container, takes a pinch of ground red seeds, and sprinkles them into the pot. "Mala peppercorns, to remind us life is always better with a little kick."

The tribespeople giggle.

"Very good," Kune says. "Would you do us the honor?" He motions to a wooden ladle and clay bowls.

Aizen takes the ladle, gives the stew several turns to mix in the peppercorns, then serves it into bowls and passes them around.

Kune raises his bowl high, smiles wide, and says, "Let's eat!"

They take quick spoonfuls, not shying away from what disaster it might be, but rather, eager to see what they've invented. Aizen takes a spoonful, nearly searing the roof of his mouth. Each ingredient swirls across his tongue like waves, each slightly different. *Like a kaleidoscope.*

"Aizen," Kune says after several minutes. "You should know that this journey is only reserved for those within our tribe."

Aizen sits up. "Does this mean… I'm one of you?"

"No!" Thalee snaps. "The old man went crazy and is giving you special treatment."

"Thalee," Kune says. "Times are changing. We must adapt."

All is silent.

"Aizen," Tadem meekly says. "Make sure you return with something that proves you found Beesa."

Aizen cocks his head. "Did all of you bring back something?"

"Yep." Tadem pulls an old pistol from his sack. "It doesn't work, but I'm sure it has an incredible story."

"Each item serves to teach us something about ourselves that we did not previously know," Kune says. "Turns out, Tadem is an incredible historian. But he did not know this until he found the pistol."

Like Dad, Aizen thinks. "Will it help me find answers?"

"Yes," Kune definitively says.

"And it was like this for all of you?" Aizen asks the group.

They each eagerly present their items. All but Thalee, who stares blankly into her bowl.

"Thalee… what did you bring back?" Aizen ventures.

She flicks the contents of her bowl into the fire and marches off.

The others go quiet.

"I didn't mean to offend," he says, helplessly.

"It's not you," Kune replies.

"What is it, then?"

The old man sighs. "There was a young man who attempted this journey a year before Thalee did, but he got lost in the caves." Kune makes a face. "Instead of bringing back an item from Beesa, Thalee brought back that young man's skull."

Aizen is silent, processing it all. "Was he her brother?"

Kune shakes his head. "Her intended."

♦

Aizen wades into the cave's pool, illuminated by hundreds of embers and with the entire tribe at his back. The water's chill prickles his skin and tightens his chest where the spore rests. The squid approach, but do not ripple with color or whisper. Nevertheless, the tribespeople gasp at their congregation.

We can help, says Mermer, appearing in the water.

No, this is my journey, Aizen responds.

Okay, you're on your own, then, Mermer says.

The souls go silent in his mind. Aizen stuffs his anxiety down as he slips on diving flippers made of leather and bone, goggles from old glass, and a deerskin diving sack containing food, water, and a knife.

He dives, feeling the water fill his ear canals, pressing harder as he descends to the dark bottom. Temperature layers sweep across his body. His ears feel like they will implode. He searches for the first air pocket but can barely make out the rock beside him. His lungs already protest, his mind sounds the alarm, and he is tempted to ask Mermer for help. *No! Figure it out!* he orders himself and lashes his legs, descending deeper, until he spots a tunnel opening. The rock levels out within, then turns back up. Dull, rippling light catches his eye. *The surface!* He propels upward, feeling like a dolphin about to burst above the waves, but he knows it is only a trapped pocket of air.

He pops into it, gulping its mystery air, then waits. *It's breathable,* he determines after several seconds, and takes more breaths as he treads water. He realizes the dim light is not coming from above or below, but beside him. He ducks below the surface and peers towards the source. *At the end of another tunnel?* he guesses. *Only one way to find out.*

With long, strong lashes of his legs, he propels horizontally along the tunnel. *Ten seconds. Twenty seconds. Thirty seconds.* Another air pocket ripples ahead. After more breaths in this new pocket, he dives to another. *Ten pockets, twenty pockets.* Soon, he understands the light source is from a shaft above a fork in the tunnel.

Left or right? He looks up the light shaft and closes his eyes. Before long, he notices warmth brushing gently against his legs. *The tide is coming in from the right tunnel,* he realizes. Nothing comes from the left. *Because that's a dead end.* His progress is slow, his arms and legs tire, and his stomach growls. He finds another pocket with a light shaft and ledge to rest upon. He opens his deerskin sack, finding it perfectly dry within, and retrieves fish jerky.

"How much more is there?" he whispers, studying the light well's rocky walls. He notices the shaft is not as tall this time. *The hillside is lowering,* he determines, watching a little cumulus cloud scoot by.

Three air pockets and two more forks later, he finds the tunnel's end.

He takes another moment to conserve energy, bites into his fish jerky, and rehydrates. Then, he dives, stopping at the tunnel's end to survey the open ocean outside. Sunlight speckles a coastal floor hosting squares filled with the crumbled concrete of ancient foundations. At the far end is an intact structure looking made of stone or concrete, somehow impervious to erosion. Above a large opening, in English letters, is, *"BESA 12."*

Beesa... Aizen grins. Large fish enter and exit through the opening. *An airlock,* he identifies. He judges its distance and if he can make it there and back in one breath. *No...* He peers at the surface, but determines the distance from the waves to the structure is the same. He returns to the last air pocket and floats on his back. *There must be an air pocket inside. But just in case...* He unstraps his sack. *Can I fill it with air?* Aizen thinks, knowing it will take extra effort to dive. *Unless, I offset it...* He finds several loose stones on the tunnel floor and stuffs them into his sack, then raises it overhead, opens its mouth, gives it a whirl through the air, and rolls its mouth to create the watertight seal. He straps the sack across his chest, for easy access to its mouth, and takes one last breath from the air pocket.

He lashes through the tunnel and grasps large stones, making him slightly negatively buoyant. He enters open water, marveling at how sunlight ripples upon the ancient debris below. As he descends the air within his pack compresses, causing him to become more negatively buoyant. He releases the stones to level out.

Midway across the open water, his lungs begin to scream. He opens the corner of the sack's mouth and exhales hard, adding compression so he can physically breathe it back in. It's slow, agonizing, but he manages a partial breath. *Two more before risking carbon dioxide poisoning,* he knows, and presses on, trying to keep steady, straight, and calm.

He enters the ancient township, flipping along a sandy pathway between foundations, stirring granules in his wake. Large fish hover like submarines in the airlock ahead.

What is this place? Aizen thinks, as eagerness returns to his lungs. The airlock's inner hatch is open and the first thing he makes out are skeletal remains. *Shit!* Aizen is certain no air bubble lies within. He fumbles with his sack. It bursts and his captured air escapes. *No!* Aizen thinks, watching it bubble away. His lungs tremble. *Mermer, I nee—*

The bubbles coalesce above him.

Aizen ditches the sack and rockets upward, reaching hands above his head to take the impact against a concrete ceiling. He twists his head so his nose and mouth face up to reach the tiny pocket and takes a massive breath.

Just enough oxygen remains for one more, he knows. He faces down, submerging his goggles. The skeletal figures are wearing deteriorated uniforms and their feet are in boots. *Not tribespeople.* Debris is strewn about the main corridor. *A battle took place here,* he realizes, finding bullet holes in the concrete and several rusted pistols on the floor.

A blinking light registers out the corner of Aizen's eye. He peers deeper into the facility. *Must be my imagination.* Several seconds later, another blink comes. *Or not...* A third blink comes and Aizen sees ripples on the ceiling just above. *An air pocket!*

He takes one last breath of stuffy air and kicks towards the blinking light. Before long he makes out a skeleton grasping a strange black ring. The light blinks from a bulge along its circumference. The skeleton's uniform is strangely intact, with a name on its breast. Another blink and Aizen reads,

"Eva Jain – Marine Biologist."

He carefully unfurls the woman's fingers, disturbing as little as possible, and takes the ring. Then, he looks up, locating the air pocket, and rises into it. He pops off his goggles for a better look at the ring. *Rubber?* It disintegrates in his hands to reveal an inner structure of untarnished metal. When the blink comes, he reads, *"Warning! Curium isotope housed within!"*

All of Aizen's past lives come rushing forth.

That's nuclear! Mirko cries.

CHAPTER NINE

Samuel studies his new prosthetic arm, wondering what hidden tracking devices, security protocols, and weapons might lie within. He then peers at Earth shining brightly below them.

"My boy! You better be right about these files," the old don says. "My fortune depends on it."

Samuel faces Don Credence. "I've seen them through Khasi's eyes, I know what they contain. They will grant you the riches you seek."

"Ah, but young Kell. Fortune is not riches, but richness, which comes in all forms..."

Samuel catches a glare from Ulysses and cannot blame him. The Terran Files are his people's key to salvation, not Don Credence's path to fortune. But Ulysses and Samuel had no choice, it was either using the files to lure the don into going to Earth, or rebuilding a ship that is hardwired to obey only the old don.

Don Credence slaps a palm on Samuel's shoulder and waves at the young woman. "...Like my daughter, Faith. Isn't she a rare fortune?"

Samuel sets eyes on Faith and can sense her discomfort, rivaling his own. "Yes, Don Credence, she certainly is," he manages to say.

Ulysses clears his throat. "We must descend, there is not a second to waste."

The don turns to The Augmentor. "Where do we stand?"

"It'll take time to prep the ship for Earth's atmosphere and gravity," she responds.

"Some ship," Ulysses grumbles. "Can't even land on a planet."

"Nobody expects to come to Earth except those history geeks," The Augmentor snaps back. "This ship's hull is made entirely of Jupiter Marble, which is how we escaped the Arkathy. But the trade-off is weight. In space, who cares. On Earth, it's insanely heavy."

Ulysses frowns. "How are you fixing this?"

"I'm creating a low-emission setting for the fusion drive to act as landing thrusters. This has never been done before, so give me a break."

Ulysses raises his paws. "We simply don't have the time."

Samuel eyes two hatches beyond Ulysses and The Augmentor. "Can we use an escape pod to land while you calibrate the ship?"

The Augmentor ponders that. "Yeah... That can work, but they're rated for four people." She looks at Ulysses. "Which is essentially just him when considering weight."

"We have two pods," Samuel says.

"One must stay. I won't strand us here," she says.

"How much weight exactly?" Ulysses asks.

"On Earth... About four hundred kilos."

Ulysses faces the pod, opens its door, grabs his pack, and steps in.

The pod's indicator says, *"336 kg."* Samuel squeezes in next to Ulysses. The indicator flashes red. *"414 kg."*

"Damn," Ulysses mutters.

"Wait." Samuel removes his prosthetic leg and tosses it from the pod. The weight drops to, *"398 kg."*

Ulysses grimaces. "Looks like I'm carrying you."

Don Credence gives a hard look. "Don't do anything stupid... You're my investment."

Samuel returns the look. "And you're mine."

The don nods. Ulysses seals the door. They pull on envisuits and strap in.

"Where are you heading?" The Augmentor asks through com.

"The west coast of old Usonia, near a city once called Portland," Samuel responds. "That's about where Khasi parted ways with John."

The Augmentor punches the coordinates into the pod's computer and gives a mischievous grin. "Enjoy..."

She pulls a lever and they drop.

Samuel's stomach flutters and his mouth hangs open. Earth's upper atmosphere skips them like a rock across a pond. Flames lick the pod's windows. His foot warms. They hit a cloud layer in the stratosphere, replacing fire with rain, and again, knocking them about. Retrorockets thrust, controlling their tumble, and when the pod rolls Samuel glimpses vivid green and blue through its windows. Parachutes deploy. Chaos becomes tranquility.

But now, Samuel's stomach is a rock and his heart is like iron. They pass magnificent mountains peaks towards a glistening bubble in the distance. *Portland,* Samuel realizes, marveling as the glass dome grows larger. The pod drifts to the coastline. *Sand... Ocean...* Samuel stares bewildered as waves concuss against rugged cliffs, shooting sea foam skyward. Even having witnessed this world through Khasi's memories, Samuel is overwhelmed.

The pod levels out above a patch of sand and lowers. Its landing gear unfurls. A final nudge comes and the thrusters wind to silence.

"Landing sequence complete," chimes the pod. *"Please exit carefully. Emergency survival kit is located in the rear payload."*

Samuel looks at Ulysses. They remove helmets.

"Are you ready?" Ulysses says.

"I think so," Samuel responds.

Ulysses yanks the hatch lever and the pod door pops off.

Sunlight blinds and the crashing of waves, sharp cries, and a constant buzzing and clicking, deafens. Samuel shields his eyes from the sun, letting them adjust, and realizes the sharp cries are from flying creatures.

"Birds…" Samuel whispers.

A ladder extends from the pod to the sand, but Ulysses jumps, landing as if the crushing gravity does not exist. Samuel grips the ladder's side rails and hops down one rung at a time, instead. When he touches sand, it shifts beneath his foot. He watches Ulysses casually rummage through the survival kit.

"Why are you not affected by the gravity?" Samuel asks.

Ulysses lifts his head. "Oh, I'm designed to handle twenty G's for evasive maneuvers during ship to ship combat." He thinks about that. "I feel it in my stomach a little."

Just how strong are you? Samuel thinks.

More than you can imagine, an invasive thought responds.

Ulysses motions to the survival kit. "This should keep us warm and fed until The Augmentor can adapt the ship." He opens his holotile and Khasi's remote key, and gives Samuel a look. "This is as good of a time as any." He places the ancient key into the holotile, giving it the minuscule juice it needs.

Samuel holds his breath and notices that Ulysses is, too.

"Syncing initiated," says the holotile and an interface opens.

"Uh, what language is this?" Ulysses asks.

The symbols feel familiar to Samuel. "I think it says *Username.*"

Ulysses gives a look. "You know Khasi's native language?"

"I guess I do," he responds, closes his eyes, and runs through Khasi's memories. "John… I think that's the username."

Ulysses opens a strange keyboard and hands it to Samuel.

Samuel slowly types, *"John."*

"Access denied," pops up.

Samuel realizes his mistake and types, *"Kunming–6834026–Enhanced."* The screen melts to a password page where Samuel then inputs, *"John."*

"Access granted," the interface fades to a map of western Usonia with a green dot blinking in the mountains several thousand kilometers southeast of their position. *"Searching… Searching…"*

The missile site, Samuel realizes.

"What mountains are these?" Ulysses asks.

"The Sierra Nevadas. This is where Khasi launched the nukes that took out the elevators."

"I thought they moved north afterwards."

"They did," Samuel says, confused as well.

"Searching… Searching…" suddenly melts to, *"Updating… Updating."*

The green light moves north along the ridge of the Sierra Nevadas while displaying the date. Two months pass. It pauses at a city called Reno, then Redding.

"That's where Takamoto-san and Terkat were captured!" Samuel excitedly says. The dot continues into the Coastal Range mountains. "We're near the end." The green dot veers west. "This is just John now!"

Months pass. John is making a mad dash to the coast, where he diverts north towards Portland.

"It's coming closer to us!" Ulysses says, smiling.

The dot settles on a beach several kilometers south of their position. But just when Samuel thinks it's over, it races east, crossing the Rocky Mountains, the Great Plains, all the way to Usonia's Eastern coast, to another city called Portland.

"Two Portlands?" Samuel says. "That's so stupid."

Ulysses raises his hands in frustration. "We're on the completely wrong side of the continent!"

"Wait…" Samuel says.

The green dot dips south to Georgia, then west to Louisiana and Texas, north to Colorado, and back over the Rockies Mountains to the little beach just south of them.

"I'm so confused," Ulysses says.

The green dot remains still for several months.

"Something happened." Samuel opens the settings, switching from months to years, then decades.

Centuries pass and the dot does not move.

"It's still there!" Ulysses exclaims.

Sea levels rise, covering the dot's resting place.

"But it's underwater," Samuel says.

As the timeline meets present day, the dot suddenly shifts.

"What in Sol?" Samuel says. "Why would it suddenly move now?"

Ulysses clenches his jaw. "We're not the only ones after The Terran Files! Someone's beaten us!"

♦

Cheers erupt when Aizen breaks the cavern pool's surface, holding the metal ring triumphantly above his head. His body trembles, his teeth chatter, and his hands and feet are numb. When he reaches the pool's edge, the tribespeople pull him out and hand him a canteen. He chugs deeply, feeling bitter liquid course through his body, replenishing his cramped muscles. He returns the canteen and reaches to his feet, tearing off the flippers. Abrasions around his ankles drool blood. When they help Aizen to his feet, he wobbles. *How drained am I?* he wonders. Tribespeople race into the cavern with hot fabric to swaddle him.

"Well done!" Kune shouts, smiling wide. "Now, to the sand!"

They rush through the cave system. Blinding afternoon light strikes him at the mouth. They do not stop, racing to the beach where they tear off the swaddled fabric.

"Lay on the sand!" Kune instructs.

Aizen stumbles ungracefully to the ground and rolls to his back. They push sun-baked sand across his body. The heat is like fire, but he welcomes the warmth seeping into his core. His hands and feet prickle as feeling returns. His teeth stop their chatter.

An hour later, after telling them about his journey, the sun begins to set.

"What about your object?" one says.

"Yeah… where is it?" says another.

Aizen realizes the ring is still in his grasp. He lifts it from beneath the sand.

They stare confused.

"What is it?" one asks.

"I don't know," Aizen responds.

"Then, why'd you choose it?"

"It's still functioning," he says.

"Maybe you were hallucinating," Thalee snaps, breaking her silence.

The rest nervously giggle until the ring's LED blinks.

"Ah!" they shout and backpedal, all but Thalee who comes rushing forth to investigate, instead.

It blinks again.

"What's it doing?" she quietly asks.

"I'm not sure," Aizen says. "But many gadgets do this to indicate they're functional."

"What's its purpose?" she follows up.

Curiosity has gotten to the best of her, Aizen realizes. "Beats me."

She gives him a sudden glare, her moment of curiosity passing. "Are you stupid or something?"

Aizen grins. "Kinda."

She scoffs and leaves the beach.

After the sun sets, they dig Aizen out of the sand. And when he stands, he feels strangely rejuvenated.

Sand… We'll have to remember that one… Zion says.

They head to the village where a rising thumping is accompanied by metallic clashes. Several people await Aizen wearing a mix of flora, fauna, feathers, hides, and scales. They throw hands into the air and circle around the clearing's center where the fire once was.

"Come, Aizen! This is for you!" Kune says.

Leather straps, with feathers and flowers, are wrapped around Aizen's knees and upper arms, and a wreath-like band is placed upon his head. He is pulled into the circling to cheers of, "Aizen!" barely audible above the thumping and clashing. They grab his arms, lifting him into the air. But after the fourth lift they stop spinning, go silent, and back away to form a ring. Aizen now faces Tadem in the center whose hands are up and front foot is lightly touching the ground.

Um… Mirko says. *This is Muay Thai.*

What? No way, Aizen thinks. *It's the wrong continent.*

These tribespeople likely descend from soldiers trapped on Earth during The Fall, he says. *They would be trained in many martial styles.*

Tadem lunges with a jab that grazes Aizen's cheek, then comes a cross.

Aizen snaps into action, redirecting the cross with the ulna of his forearm, and steps in close. He places his lead foot behind Tadem's heel and presses the young man's chest, tripping him to the ground.

Well done, Aizen! Mirko cries like a proud father.

Tadem stares back stunned, then smiles wide, climbs to his feet, and jumps up and down with hands raised.

They lift Aizen and beat their drums, until the next opponent comes. Time and again he fights, but none of it feels threatening or like a test of skill. For when he holds back, his opponents do the same. *It's just fun...* They go through every martial style, and each time they cheer when Aizen proves masterful. Soon, neither he nor they hold back. Sticks are tossed into the center. It becomes an escrima match.

Hours pass, Aizen is exhausted, but he does not want it to end. Again, they stop and pull away to form the human ring, but this time only Aizen stands at the center. They look around, trying to see who is next. A flickering comes from above and a blade sinks into the sand.

Instead of cheers, the tribespeople are silent.

"Let's see what you're really made of!" comes Thalee's voice and the ring of people quickly parts, letting her through.

She unsheathes another blade, twirling it effortlessly through her fingers, then snatches the handle.

Kali Salat... Mirko says. *Aizen, this is real now, I must take control.*

Don't you dare! Aizen thinks back. *I owe her a fair match!*

But in every knife fight even victors expect to be cut! Mirko says.

I know! Aizen kneels, taking the knife from the sand, and when he matches her stance, the tribespeople gasp. He fixates on Thalee's hips, where her motion generates, but he cannot help glancing at her cold eyes.

She's killed before, Dione says.

They circle one another. When Thalee turns her heel, Aizen does, too, and she turns it back.

She's a master, Mirko says with both respect and worry.

Thalee lunges mid-step, catching Aizen off balance. *Slash, slash, thrust.* Aizen narrowly dodges, but now Thalee is right in front of him. She ducks low for his hamstring and Aizen barely parries her wrist with his palm. He wastes no time, bringing his own blade to her neck. She is fast, her palm knocking his hand higher. He whiffs above her head but uses the momentum to twist out of range. He glances at his leg to see that she cut the leather strap from around his knee.

The rest watch, baffled as to how Aizen escaped.

Thalee begins circling again.

Aizen can't help grinning as well. For despite all his time training with Mirko he did not know if he could handle a true opponent. He takes Ergonos breaths and stays on his toes.

She shifts her ankle.

Aizen lunges, catching Thalee off guard this time, sending her stumbling back. He ducks low, slicing at her ankle, but hesitates. It gives Thalee a fraction of a second to send a wave of sand into his face. *She has the upper hand again!* But Aizen has an idea. As Thalee's blade comes, he thrusts the butt of his knife upwards, cracking her wrist.

It sends her reeling and she nearly drops her blade. She shakes with rage and goes straight for his heart, coming so fast Aizen barely twists his torso. The back of her blade runs across his chest, then her hand and arm. With her elbow at his ribs, Aizen grasps her wrist, straightening her arm, locking her elbow, and forcing her to turn with him. Then, he drives her shoulder down, bringing her stomach to the dirt. But at the last moment, Thalee plants her feet and yanks back up.

She'll let her arm break! Aizen realizes. He reverses direction, swiveling his grasp on her wrist, curling her arm towards her, instead, and places his foot behind hers so she cannot step back. He topples to the ground atop of her, with his weight driving down, bringing the tip of Thalee's own knife to her neck.

"Yield," Aizen whispers.

Her eyes rage and tears well. "No!"

"You must yield, I've won," he says.

She clenches her jaw. "Finish it!"

What? Aizen removes the knife from her neck and backs away.

Thalee stares blankly at him, then fury crosses her face. She jolts to her feet, about faces, pushes through the ring of people, and disappears into the dark woods.

The tribespeople disband, giving Aizen confused looks.

It wasn't supposed to end like this, he understands.

Kune approaches. "Well fought... But why did you let Thalee live?"

Aizen is taken aback. "Why wouldn't I?"

Kune tilts his head. "She came with the intent to kill."

"That's not a reason to end someone."

The gnarled old man thinks about that. "She was prepared for anything, except mercy. You must talk with her." He waves a hand to the woods.

Aizen sighs, gives the two blades to Kune, picks up the ring he took from BESA, and presses into the darkness after Thalee. He closes his eyes and senses her not far off, sitting on a cliff edge overlooking the beach. He lets his meditation slip away and approaches.

"What do you want!?" she snaps.

"I don't understand what just happened," Aizen says and she turns to him. He can see in the moonlight that she is crying.

"Of course you don't," she retorts.

"Why were you trying to kill me?" he asks.

"I wasn't trying to kill you."

"Then, who were you trying to kill?"

She glares.

"You wanted me to end you," Aizen answers himself and points at the ground next to her. "May I?"

"You can do whatever you want, apparently," she says.

"What happened that makes you want to die?" he asks and sits.

"Didn't the old man tell you?" she says.

"He told me about your intended," Aizen carefully says.

She chuckles. "That bastard…"

"Bastard? Was he not good to you?"

She gives a hard look. "Why are you being nice? What do you want?"

"This is just who I am," Aizen says. "Actually… I'm like my dad," he admits. "But we haven't talked in over a year, until just recently."

"What did he do that was so bad?"

Aizen knows she only asks to get out of talking about herself. "He was always leaving us. Everything would be great, then he would just up and go."

"And he never came back…" Thalee states.

"No… He always came back," Aizen says.

She gives a look. "But what did he do that was bad?"

"That… That was it," Aizen says, feeling silly.

She darkens. "You are such a baby! At least you have a father!"

Aizen does not know what to say. Silence envelopes them. They watch the ocean waves below gently lapping the beach.

"His name was Liontas," Thalee finally mutters. "He was beautiful."

"That's a great name," Aizen responds.

Thalee looks at the ring. "Can I see that thing?"

Aizen grins, knowing what little information he got was victory. He lifts the ring for her to see. It blinks red again.

"How is it still working?" she asks.

"There's a curium isotope within." Aizen points at the warning label. "Which will give off enough heat to generate minuscule power for roughly fifteen million years."

"How do you turn it on?"

"I have no idea," Aizen admits. "Kune just said it will teach me everything I need to know about myself."

Thalee snatches it from Aizen's grasp.

"Hey!" He reaches, but Thalee holds it out of range. He scrambles forth, tumbling on top of her. She masterfully bucks and rolls and is now on top. Aizen wraps his legs around one of hers, lifting her slightly off the ground and paws at her wrist. She stretches it further. *Her balance is off.* He gives a buck of his own. She fights, not letting him get top position, but by doing so brings the ring within Aizen's range. He grips tight. Neither let go. They lay on their sides facing one another, breathing heavily. Her stomach and hips press against him. Tension suddenly dwindles. Their bodies soften. Thalee's muscular thighs melt into his.

What's happening? Aizen thinks. Her lips are right in front of his. He feels her breath. Their noses gently brush. The ring's red light blinks again, highlighting her features. Her eyes are locked onto him.

Aizen leans in, catching her lips with his.

◆

A sharp beep jolts Aizen and Thalee awake.

A green light ferociously blinks from the ring, then a hologram emits.

"What is that!?" Thalee cries, giving Aizen a confused look. She realizes her legs are still entwined with his. She wiggles out and searches for her clothing. "How did you turn it on!?"

"I… I did nothing," Aizen says, pulling his clothes on.

A woman appears in the projection wearing a tattered uniform. *"Eva Jain – Marine Biologist, "* reads on her name tag.

"This woman! Her skeleton was holding onto this ring when I was in Beesa!" Aizen says.

The projection moves, and Aizen realizes it is a recording.

"My name is Eva Jain, and if you are watching this, then that means I am long gone…" the woman says in ancient English.

Aizen and Thalee look at one another bewildered.

"…My research is of the utmost importance, for what I have discovered will change humanity. Bio-immortality, enhanced sensory perception, telepathy, and genetic teleportation. This is what I've unlocked. Or I should say, what they've unlocked. But the path of discovery was difficult, confusing, and unexpected. I ask that you keep an open mind." She takes a deep breath. "All my research has been compiled onto this hard drive. But be forewarned, whoever holds this device will never know peace. Other things live on this drive added long before it came to me, and people have spent years hunting me to obtain it." She looks sadly to the side. "I am at an end now, they have me cornered. But before my time is done, I must tell you everything about my discoveries, exactly how they happened, when they happened, and why they happened…"

EVA's TALE
Earth: 2302 - 2334

After the space elevators were lost and the cities were glassed, life did not change all that much. After toxins settled into our soil, rivers, lakes, and oceans, things went on more or less the same. After the displaced soldiers grouped into ronin bands roaming the countryside in search of the less fortunate, I would call it normal times. Because, for us biologists at BESA 12, life after The Fall was not so different from life beneath the metacorporations.

But that all changed when I met a dog named John.

◆

"It's okay, old boy… or girl?" I cautiously said. *What's with the massive collar?*

The old dog faced me, sniffed the air, and slowly hobbled closer.

How has it survived? I thought, outstretched my hand, letting the dog sniff, and scratched behind its one floppy ear. "My goodness, you're skinny," I said, feeling the boniness of its skull and vertebrae. *Boy,* I saw when checking around his ribs. His fur was thick, his toenails were strong, and his gums looked healthy. *No radiation exposure.* I investigated his collar, looking made of black rubber, locked tight around his neck. A label read, *"Warning! Curium isotope housed within."*

A power source? Why? I thought. *I need Charlie.*

"Come on, old boy," I said. "It's getting dark."

The dog slowly laid on the dirt, exhausted, instead.

I sighed and knelt. "We must go. You know what happens if ronin find us in the open." I again scratched behind the dog's floppy ear, then peered inside to see numbers and letters tattooed within.

"Kunming–6834026–Enhanced," the first line read with, *"John,"* below.

"John…" I whispered.

The dog lifted its head and looked at me.

"Come, John," I said.

John let out a sigh and begrudgingly stood, his back legs trembling.

He's toast, I realized, gently wrapped my arms beneath his chest and hips, and lifted him from the ground. He melted into my body like a newborn infant, resting his head on my shoulder and beginning to snore.

I navigated old town rubble, careful not to trip, and when I reached BESA 12, the sunset colored the offshore radiation cloud a brilliant fuchsia. *One day it'll make landfall,* I knew. *But when?*

I input my code into BESA's pin pad, holding John as still as possible, afraid to disturb his slumber. The heavy metal door clunked, then screeched open. I winced, certain it would wake John, but he continued to snore. *So tired. Poor thing…*

I stepped into the airlock and sealed the outer door.

"Eva, what the hell is that?" said Nick, our station manager, over com. "Is it dead?"

"Nearly," I responded. "It's an enhanced Kunming dog, from before The Fall… I think."

"Can't be. No dog could have survived that long."

"It must have. Its collar has a power source. I've never seen anything like this," I said. "I need Charlie to have a look."

I heard background discussion, then Nick returned. "Fine, but it's your responsibility, its food comes out of your rations."

"Understood," I said.

"Radiation exposure?" he asked.

"Nothing abnormal."

"Geiger count looks good," Nick confirmed from his control room. "You're cleared for entry."

The inner door groaned open, revealing dim emergency lighting and several biologists hustling about, carrying on with their research despite our dwindling resources and the apocalypse outside. A few glanced my way.

Rachel was shaking her head. "I swear, every time you go out, you come back with something new," she said, approaching me.

"That's part of my research," I responded.

Rachel crossed her arms. "How is a dog going to help you unlock the biological secrets of crustaceans?"

I sighed. "I don't know just yet."

Rachel rolled her eyes. "Do you still need my help catching those weird crabs you found?"

"Yeah," I said. "I swear, they work together."

"I have time tomorrow," Rachel said.

"Great. But I'm hoping to get out early, it's quite a hike." John stirred in my arms. "I gotta find John something to eat. Hope the canteen is still open."

"You've named it already?" Rachel snickered.

"It's tattooed in his ear." I flipped up his earlobe.

She made a face. "Weird."

"Yeah." I gently stroked John's head to settle him down. "Have you seen Charlie?"

"Nope."

"So, see you at six tomorrow morning?" I asked.

Rachel made another face. "I guess…"

The canteen was nearly empty and I saw only a few pots out. Our cook, Tate, came from the freezer.

"Hey, Eva. I was just about to pack that up for tomorrow," he said.

I grinned. "If you have extra, you think John can have some?"

Tate looked at the dog. "You can't help yourself, can you?"

I frowned. "All the others were for research."

"Sure they were," Tate said, pulling pieces of Spam from an old tin and wrapping them in cloth. "Tell no one."

"Thanks, Tate."

"What about you?" he asked.

"I made dinner outside."

His eyes went wide. "That's so dangerous. You could be poisoned."

"Only if you don't understand how to counter the toxins," I said.

"You're insane…"

"Yep," I agreed, taking the Spam. "See you tomorrow."

"Later," he said and started packaging up the rest.

I passed several researchers on the way to my quarters and asked where Charlie might be. Someone finally told me he was at the observatory for the month.

I looked at John curled in my arms. "Well, I guess you should meet the family."

I entered my small research lab, now doubling as my living quarters, packed with small aquariums hosting several species of crustacean I collected over the years.

John stirred, opening his eyes into slits, then yawned. I lowered him to the floor, but he stayed curled in my arms, giving me a disappointed look. I spread a blanket on the floor and set him on top. Only when I placed the Spam on the table did John snap up his head and sniff. He stretched his legs and sluggishly stood. I filled a bowl of water from my reservoir, put the Spam on a plate, and set them on the floor.

John went for the water first, his tongue sounding like small waves upon a shore, then he sniffed the Spam and snatched a slice.

"Feel better, John?" I asked.

His eyes wandered my room and he limped to the aquariums.

"That one has hermit crabs," I said, pointing at a dry tank with critters lugging heavy shells. "They're not crabs in the conventional sense, they're more closely related to lobsters." I pointed at another water-filled tank. "These are dungeness crabs."

John followed my finger but did not seem interested in my crustaceans. *Just like everyone else,* I thought. He turned to the empty plate and whined.

"That's all Tate gave us," I said. "There will be more in the morning."

John slumped back onto his blanket.

I unrolled my bed mat beside him, laid down, and stroked his hair. Movement caught my eye. I squinted and leaned closer to see little specks bouncing from his fur. *Shit...*

◆

The more I scratched, the more raw my scalp became. I studied John's fur reflecting the foggy morning light outside of BESA 12's airlock, looking as if years had melted away since I washed and combed out matted patches earlier that morning. He even pranced on his front paws.

The airlock door opened behind me.

"You're bringing the dog?" I heard Rachel say.

"You bet," I said. "He's the best warning system we could ask for."

Rachel studied John. "He looks better."

The itching in my scalp was growing.

"Which path are we taking?" Rachel asked.

I swore something crawled in my hair.

"Hello… Eva… which way are we going?"

I could not take it anymore and furiously scratched.

Rachel stepped back and looked at John. "Do you have fleas, again!?"

I quickly retracted my hand. "No…"

John sat, stuck his hind paw beneath his collar, and scratched.

"That's what!? Three times now!" Rachel said.

"It's not fleas! I swear!" I argued. "And, we take the caves up north, trek the woods to Braxis Point, then cross to the island."

"The caves…" Rachel said. "You sure you can navigate through them?"

I nodded. "It's not that hard once you climb the cliff."

"How do we do that?"

I pulled a length of climbing rope from my pack.

"I can't believe I agreed to this," Rachel scoffed.

"It's well worth the journey. I promise."

"I'm out," Rachel declared, about to turn around.

"I'll make you fresh crab stew," I said.

"So you can poison me?" she jabbed.

"I know how to clean them. I've been doing it for almost a year now."

Rachel's stomach growled. "Fine! But if you give me fleas, I swear to god I'll have you kicked out of BESA!"

"It's not fleas!" I said. *Please, don't be fleas.* "Let's go."

I led through the fog-covered town, turning at familiar landmarks, keeping my steps light and watching for debris. John stayed right by my side despite me never commanding it.

"How can you see?" Rachel said, stumbling to keep up with me.

"Keep quiet," I responded. "They like to ambush in the fog."

"Then, maybe we should wait until it burns off," Rachel whispered.

I ignored her, not chancing any further speech.

John bolted into the fog ahead, showing no hint of his limp, as if he were a younger dog.

"And… he's gone," Rachel whispered.

No, he didn't abandon us, I thought, feeling there was a purpose for his sprint. John came back into view and sat. I stopped in my tracks and Rachel almost ran into me.

"What the hell are—?"

I whipped around and cupped my hand over her mouth.

Heavy steps crunched. Metallic clanking of old battle armor came.

John circled and quietly moved off the path. I waved for Rachel to follow him. Several sets of heavy steps approached. Then, they were beside us. Soon, they were behind us. The steps slowly faded away.

I scratched behind John's ear. "Good boy."

Once back on the path, we continued until the town's rubble became lush vegetation. The sun rose and the fog burned away, revealing a cliff face above the treeline.

"You've got to be joking," Rachel grumbled.

I faced her. "Why did you come if you're just going to complain?"

Rachel gave me a look, but remained quiet until sufficiently far from town. "Work keeps me in the bunker almost everyday," she said. "I'm losing my mind."

"When was the last time you were out?"

"About two years ago," she muttered.

I thought about how all the Quantum Mechanics researchers had sickly complexions. "Just, try to keep an open mind about all this."

"Mind open," Rachel begrudgingly said.

We reached the cliff face mid-morning and took a moment to replenish fluids and take stock of our climbing gear.

"Okay, so it's not a sheer cliff, and there's kinda a path," I said, clipping two tethers onto my harness with a carabiner at their ends. "You see these loops anchored into the rock? Make sure one of your carabiners is always connected. Two is better." I wrapped a makeshift harness with two straps around John and hoisted him on my shoulders like a backpack. He did not struggle. I clipped my carabiners onto the first anchor loop. "When you move, clip one carabiner at a time." I performed a few maneuvers. "Got it?"

Rachel looked even more pale.

I sighed. "It's okay if you want to head back."

She furrowed her brow and clipped her carabiners. It was slow going at first, but Rachel was getting the hang of it. We zigzagged up the rock, taking several water breaks, with John snoozing on my back.

At the midway point Rachel said, "This is kinda fun."

"Now that's more like it!" I responded.

We reached the top by noon and turned around to view the derelict town that once housed BESA 12's researchers.

"What happens if someone comes up as we go down?" Rachel asked.

"We don't take this way down," I responded, approaching a portion of the cliff with a single anchor at its edge. "We rappel down the sheer cliff, here."

Rachel grimaced. "You could have mentioned that before we climbed!"

I shrugged. "We can go down the other way, but it'll take longer."

A chill emanated from the mouth of the cave, sending goosebumps across my skin. I set John on the ground, keeping his harness on, and pulled a sketched map from my pack.

"It'll take two hours and stay tight with me. If you make a wrong turn you could be lost forever," I said and faced John. "That goes for you, too." I linked a tether to John's harness so he could not run off.

He immediately sat, awaiting instruction.

"That's a really well-trained dog," Rachel said. "Who raised it?"

"I'm hoping Charlie knows that, too," I said.

We donned headlamps and plunged into darkness. Birds chirping and leaves rustling were replaced by eerie drips. It cooled as we descended. Our breaths became visible clouds. The tunnel wound back and forth.

I stopped at the first fork, making sure it matched the map.

"Eva, it's freezing," Rachel said.

"We're at the bottom, it'll warm soon."

After an hour, jagged rock abruptly gave way to a large chamber with stalagmites and stalactites coming together like the jaws of a crocodile, some joined into columns. When I shined my headlamp upwards, light scattered across the chamber, refracting through crystals resembling intricate chandeliers.

Rachel stared with her mouth open.

"Told you it was worth it," I whispered.

"Yeah…" she muttered.

After several minutes I said, "Rachel, we gotta go."

"Okay," she said, her eyes locked, her legs not moving.

"Rachel, let's go," I repeated.

Her eyes drifted from the ceiling and she reluctantly followed me into another tunnel. Several forks later and the sun's rays percolated through a light shaft above. *We're close.* The chill lessened and woodland sounds grew.

"That's it," I said.

"That was so cool," Rachel whispered.

I grinned, knowing I made her a convert.

We shielded our eyes from the sun as we exited the cave system and were immediately swallowed by a coniferous tree forest. Sounds of birds, rodents, and insects enveloped us as yellow pollen filled the air. Crashing waves soon came and we exited thick forest onto sandy beach. Pelicans crossed overhead on their way to an island off shore. A charred sign, barely clinging to existence, read, *"Braxis Point."*

"Is that the place?" Rachel asked, studying the island.

"Yeah. There used to be a town accessible by ferry, but we have to wade through the water at low tide to get there, now."

"When is low tide?"

"In about an hour, but time is tight. The beach quickly becomes rock, slick with seaweed and algae. It will be slow going."

Rachel pointed at the pools next to us. "These crabs of yours must be here, too."

"I searched this entire shoreline," I said, shaking my head. "They're *only* on the island."

"Weird."

"Yeah…"

"Can we take a boat?" Rachel asked.

"Yeah…" I said. "You have a boat?"

Rachel's lips tightened.

"Let's go, our window is short."

The sand was still cool from the night and I removed my shoes, letting it slip between my sweaty toes.

"This feels great," Rachel said, prancing her feet, exciting John, causing him to prance, too.

The cool sand soon gave way to heavy rocks covered in razor sharp barnacles and slick seaweed. *The perfect combination.* "Boots back on," I said to Rachel. "And John… stay?"

John gave a disappointed look and laid on the sand.

"You think he'll actually wait for us?" Rachel asked.

"I hope so." I brushed sand off my feet and pulled on my hiking boots.

◆

I dunked my head into a tide pool, when Rachel was distracted, letting the salt water soothe my scalp's horrible itch. *And getting rid of fleas,* I thought, hoping to god Rachel does not catch them.

We trapped several dungeness crabs and stored them in a catch bag for afternoon super. We had yet to find those strange ones. Rachel glanced more frequently at my pouch as we doubled back through the island's crumbled town, using its streets to reach the next length of shore.

"How'd you learn to clean the crabs of toxins?" she eventually asked.

"Um…" I inadvertently said.

"What do you mean, um?"

"You're not going to like the answer," I said.

She gave me a hard look. "And why is that?"

"Promise not to judge me?"

Rachel sighed. "I promise."

"I learned by watching the crabs we're searching for," I said with an awkward smile, like that would gloss over its ridiculousness.

"You what!?" Rachel blurted. "Have you completely lost your mind!?"

"Hey, you promised!" I hollered back. "I know it sounds insane, but they do it every time they eat."

Rachel stopped on the old street. "They do what!?"

"I swear, whenever they find dead fish, they don't eat it right away." I thought about how ludicrous my next sentence was. "They collect algae and seaweed and cut them into little pieces, mixing them with the fish. Then, they eat them like a sandwich."

Rachel's face became furious. "That doesn't mean a thing!"

I raised my arms. "It does…"

She focused on me and quieted.

"I've tested the fish they eat. They all contain high levels of methylmercury and radiation, among several other toxins. I then combined it with the same algae and seaweed and fed it to my dungeness crabs at BESA. The toxicity levels in the fish they ingested matched almost perfectly with the amount in their feces."

Rachel looked up, processing it all. "But not the exact amount."

I smiled and opened my findings on holotile. "There's always slightly more toxin in the feces, meaning the combination of algae and seaweed not only pass the toxins harmlessly through their bodies, but also serve to remove any toxins previously accumulated. After a few days, the crabs are no longer toxic."

"And you ate them?" Rachel asked.

"They were delicious."

"But, that's so dangerous…"

"No, it's not," I said. "You're a scientist. Look at the science."

She read through everything and snapped her head up. "And this works for human anatomy, too?"

"I found that we require a more complex combination of ingredients – a mix of garlic, cilantro, milkweed and the seaweed, and it must be cooked for at least twenty minutes. But yeah, it works for us, too."

"So, how do these mystery crabs know to do this?"

"That's what I want to find out."

Rachel closed my holotile and moved along the road with renewed vigor. She took a sudden turn down a narrow street overgrown with brush and whose pavement was crumbling to dust. I was about to correct her when I saw a small beach at its end. *I haven't checked here before.* Deteriorated homes appeared overlooking the coast, their roofs green with moss and bowing, on the verge of collapse. Waves crashed upon rocks with a distinctive fizzle when passing through seaweed. A parking area opened with shrubbery growing through the rusted holes of old cars.

"This looks promising," I said, climbing onto the first tide pool rock. "Really promising."

Rachel beamed a smile.

"Keep an eye out for movement. Their shapes are between the dungeness crabs we caught and large shrimp," I instructed as I moved farther into the tide pools where the waves were crashing, using the low sun to cast my shadow across the rocks. "I'll guide them with my shadow. You, stay right where you are."

"Okay," Rachel said and knelt.

I waved my arms, scuffed my feet, and moaned.

"Do you actually think this will—" Rachel squinted. "Oh! I see one! Two! More!"

"Where are they heading?" I whispered back.

Rachel got the hint and whispered, "A few are in the pool where your right hand is casting a shadow. Try moving more to the right." She watched. "Yes, they're cornering themselves beneath a rock." She continued to watch. "I think I can grab… What the?"

"What is it?" I asked.

"They… uh… made a circle. One is wiggling its claws at the others," she said with a confused look.

"See? They work together," I said, feeling vindicated.

"Reaching in," Rachel narrated, but quickly retracted her hand. "They're looking at me."

One rushed up from the tide pool to a rock. Rachel backed away. The little creature raised its claws, snapping them strangely.

"I think it's trying to protect its friends!" I excitedly said.

The crustacean spun to me and started squeaking, like an alarm.

There's rhythm to it! I realized. "Quick! Grab it!"

The moment Rachel reached, several more came rushing from the pool, bearing their claws.

"Ah!" Rachel backpedaled, stumbling into the pool behind her. "I thought they were supposed to run away!"

They are... I thought as they squeaked in unison. I saw movement out the corner of my eye. More were rising out of the pools. *Hundreds...* "Rachel! Run!" I cried and leaped from one stone to another.

Crustaceans, as far as I could see, raised their claws and squeaked. Then, they rushed.

"Shit! Shit! Shit!" I yelled, feeling pincers snipping at my boots and the cuffs of my pants.

"What the fuck!?" Rachel hollered as little crustaceans clipped onto her pant legs. She started panicking and slipped into another pool.

I caught her arm. "Careful! Rocks are more dangerous than they are!"

"Are you sure about that!?" she yelled, looking beyond me.

I turned to see an army. "Forget what I said!"

We scrambled over rocks and stumbled through pools. Several crabs clipped higher onto my pants and I saw Rachel getting weighed down. I dragged her along as best as I could, until we were on land.

"Quick! Take off your pants!"

We fumbled with buckles and tore off our pants. The moment we did, the crustaceans let go and scuttled back towards the pools.

This is the perfect opportunity to catch them! I thought. "Don't let them get away!"

Rachel turned to me. "Are you insane!?"

"Yes!" I chased, but they juked left and right, impossible to grasp.

"How are they so good at this!?" Rachel said and I knew she was trying to catch them, too.

When all seemed lost, when I felt failure trickling in, the sound of paws on sand and a blur of fur appeared.

John! I realized.

He cutoff the retreating crustaceans and circled them like a sheepdog. I lifted my pants from the sand and tossed them atop the creatures, then pressed down on the fabric to isolate a few.

"Got one!" Rachel cried, holding it by its shell so that she could not be pinched. "Why do they reek of onions!?"

I caught the smell, becoming stronger by the second, invading my nostrils, and causing me to cry. I continued cordoning off sections of cloth.

There are three under here! I was certain. One slipped out and ran off. *Now two!* Another ran off just as my hands clamped around the last.

"I got it!" I triumphantly said. "Quick, get the catch bag!"

Rachel looked around. "Where is it?"

"It's clipped to my pack!"

"Uh… Where's your pack?"

I became aware that no straps were on my shoulders. I snapped my head up and surveyed the tide pools. In the distance, bobbing up and down with the waves, I saw my pack drifting out to sea.

◆

We camped in the mouth of the cave, for I would not risk being caught in the open and did not have the courage to navigate the caves by memory. John kept a watchful sniff as Rachel and I took turns staring into the moonlit forest. But I could not sleep, replaying all the times I made this journey, convincing myself I knew the way by heart. But, there was also the rappel down the cliff. *And the equipment is gone…* The dull glow of dawn came and I knew sleep was futile. Rachel was passed out. John was snoozing. *At least they got some rest.* I studied the crustaceans tied within the pant legs I tore from my trousers, turning them into cutoff shorts. They no longer reeked of onions. The fabric wiggled and I noticed the knots were nearly undone. I quickly tightened them. *How can they be so smart?*

"They still there?" Rachel groggily said, stretching her arms.

"Yeah."

"I'm starving," she then said. "Should we eat them?"

"Absolutely not!" I snapped. "Water is more important, anyway."

"The caves have pools," Rachel said.

I shook my head. "We lost the testing kit."

"Then, what do we do?" she said.

I sighed. "We navigate the cave system."

"Without the map? That's insane."

"I know the way," I confidently said, but I was freaking out within.

Every turn was full of distrust. Every fork only confirmed to be correct when we reached the next. The chill was welcomed against my sweaty skin, but I stared at pools of water with lust. John approached several. I scolded him until realizing he was only sniffing and backing away. *He can smell the contamination.*

After several slow hours, we entered the large chandelier chamber. Without our headlamps, we relied on sparse sunlight percolating through natural shafts above. I pawed at the walls, searching for the correct path out.

John suddenly whined, circled, and sat.

A shuffling came from one of the tunnels, its echo making it impossible to determine which. Distinct footsteps followed.

John growled, and I desperately tried shushing him. Then, he barked.

We gotta run! I thought, squinting through the darkness, trying to see which tunnel led back to the forest, but I was disoriented. The footsteps grew and my anxiety went through the roof.

"Evaaaa!" echoed like twenty people calling at once.

Wait… I know this voice, I realized.

"Evaaaa!" came reflecting again, closer this time.

That's… "Nick!" I called back, my voice bouncing.

A light appeared from a tunnel on my right.

"Eva! Are you okay!?" Nick called, barreling into the chamber out of breath. "Is Rachel with you!?"

"Yeah, and we're thirsty."

He aimed his headlamp up to refract against the formations and illuminate the chamber. He pulled a canteen from his pack. "We were worried sick about you two!"

Rachel took the canteen first, chugging. She finally pulled it away, but looked about to take more. I snatched it from her, downed some, and gave John the rest.

John slowly approached Nick, giving him a good sniff.

"Be good, John. Nick's a friend," I said.

John wagged his tale and spun around, going into a play stance.

"I need to check you over, just in case," Nick said, and searched Rachel's hair, fingernails, and gums. "You're good." He turned to me.

My stomach filled with dread as he ruffled through my hair. At least his fingers gave relief to the horrid itching.

Nick paused and quickly backed away. "Are these radiation burns!?"

I clenched my jaw. "No… It's raw from scratching… I think, maybe… I might have fleas."

Rachel shot me a glare. "What the hell, Eva!"

Nick sighed deeply. "I hope you enjoy quarantine." He glanced at John. "That goes for you, too."

♦

Rachel slipped a breakfast of oatmeal, re-hydrated eggs, spam, and instant coffee through the quarantine room's double-sided transfer hatch.

I retrieved the tray and set it on the table. "Thanks."

"So…" Rachel began, pointing at the aquarium Nick let me lug into the room. "Have you discovered anything?"

"Not really. They've been staring at me for the last four days. When I try feeding them, they don't budge." I thought about that. "I'm worried they might starve to death."

John whined and nudged his nose at my tray.

"No, John," I said. "This is my breakfast. You already had yours."

He gave pleading eyes.

"Oh, all right." I reached for the Spam, to find it gone. I faced John. "Did you steal it!?" I looked at Rachel. "He's been doing this all week."

John again whined and spun in circles.

"I guess all that training was for nothing," Rachel said.

I pointed at John and with a stern voice said, "No, John, no."

It sent him whining even more, his eyes were begging now.

"What's gotten into you lately?" I asked.

"Um, Eva?" Rachel said and pointed at the aquarium.

I heard a little splash and turned around to see the two little crabs facing me, still as ever. "What?"

"I swear, one of them was out of the tank," she said.

I turned back to her. "There's a lid."

Rachel gave me a pleading look not so different from John's.

Okay, I'll bite. "In order for them to get the lid off, they'd have to first unscrew the water bubbler." I walked to the tank. "And, as you can see, the bubbler is… unscrewed?" I stared at it confused. "Even if it's unscrewed, they'd have to…" I saw a tiny piece of Spam wedged behind the tank against the wall. The two crabs scuttled around like they were hiding something behind their backs. My excitement surged. "You magnificent little bastards!"

◆

"Is this one of yours?" Tate said through the quarantine room glass, holding tupperware containing Frank. "Found it in the kitchen trying to pry open a can of Spam."

"So, that's where you've been," I said, peering through the clear plastic. "Thanks, Tate. How'd you catch him?"

"Took the entire cooking staff two hours to corner this little delinquent. A few were tempted to serve him up for lunch," he said. "What are you doing with them anyway?"

"I think this is a new species, somehow overlooked, probably because they only exist on one specific island.”

“You serious?” He slipped the tupperware container into the transfer hatch. “You’d think someone would have figured that out long ago.”

“They’re really similar to another species called a grodote. They could have easily been misidentified. But I don’t really know just yet,” I responded. “Thanks for not cooking him.”

“Nah, we wouldn’t have done that. Too dangerous.”

“Right…” I said, thinking about how these creatures were devoid of toxins. “I gotta get back to testing. Sydney is waiting.”

“Who’s Sydney?” Tate asked.

“The other crab.”

Tate rolled his eyes. “When do you get out, anyway?”

I frowned. “I don’t know how, but John is clear of fleas and I’m not.”

Tate grinned. “Maybe you gave them to him.”

I shot Tate a glare.

“Later.” He quickly turned and headed back to the canteen.

I peered into the tupperware at Frank. “You are one slippery little dude.”

He lifted his large claw and tapped the tupperware lid.

“You’ve already figured this out, haven’t you?”

“Mer!” Frank called and I jumped a mile.

◆

“How does it feel to be out of quarantine?” Rachel asked, staring at my buzzed hair.

I rubbed my head not sure how I felt about it, but it proved the only solution to kicking the infestation. “Good, I guess.”

“So, why haven’t you moved back to your quarters?”

“This quarantine room’s observation side is perfect to study Frank and Sydney incognito.”

“You’ve named them?”

“Yeah. Check this out,” I said, pointing at their tank.

We watched through the one-way glass as Frank and Sydney eyed a piece of spam I left on a plate, having pretended to go use the bathroom.

Sydney crawled to the bubbler at the tank’s corner, as Frank kept watch, and said, “Mermee.”

Rachel gave me a questioning look.

“I installed microphones to pick up their calls,” I informed.

“EeeMer,” Frank responded, scurried to Sydney, climbed onto her back, and reached for the bubbler.

"Are they talking to one another?" Rachel asked.

I grinned. "I've recorded over two-hundred variations."

"Have you deciphered what any of them mean?"

I shook my head. "Not exactly, but they always say *Mermee* and *EeeMer* just before they start their great escape."

"Maybe it's something like *Clear?* and *All Clear*," Rachel suggested.

I raised my eyebrows. "That makes perfect sense, actually."

Sydney spun, rotating Frank with his claws clamped to the bubbler.

"They're unscrewing it!?" she cried. "How do they know!?"

"When I clean the tank, I unscrew the bubbler before removing the lid. They've been taking notes," I proudly said. "What I've yet to figure out is how they lift the lid."

The bubbler sprung free, but instead of spitting out of the tank, Frank held on, using its jet to launch himself to the lid. *But he'll never fit through the bubbler's hole,* I thought. Frank released one claw as he reached the hole letting his other slip through. With a claw outside, he repositioned the bubbler's spout, wedging its end at an angle. *Like a pry bar.*

Wrenching, twisting, bouncing. The lid popped open in one corner. Frank pressed his way through the gap, stretched his claw to the back wall, and tipped over the edge.

"No!" I cried and covered my mouth.

He pressed his legs against the tank's glass, wedging himself between the tank and wall, and slowly lowered himself to the floor.

"Shit, he's smart," Rachel said.

Frank wasted no time, scurrying to the table and clamping his legs and arms to the inside corner of its leg, and climbing.

"He's keeping the claw marks hidden from us," Rachel said.

He's doing just that, I realized.

Frank did one last maneuver and he was up.

"This is incredible!" Rachel leaned closer, posting her hands on the control table, right on the transparency switch.

The glass became clear.

Frank turned sharply, making eye contact with me, with a piece of Spam in his claw. The moment I twitched, he bolted, scrambling down the table leg and racing back to the tank.

I whipped open the door and cried, "Frank, stop!"

He froze.

Did he understand me!? "Frank, turn around!"

He slowly faced me.

I knelt and tapped the floor. "Come here."

He lowered his stalk eyes, like a scolded dog would its ears, and approached. When he reached me, I upturned my palm. He placed the Spam in my hand, then somberly headed back to the tank.

My gut sank. "Frank, wait…"

He looked back at me.

I broke the Spam into four equal pieces, placing the first on the floor. "Eva," I said, then placed the next. "John." I placed a third. "Frank." Frank perked up. I placed the fourth piece. "Sydney."

"Mer!" Sydney called from the tank.

I pushed the two pieces for Frank and Sydney towards Frank.

"Mer! Mermee Mer mere Mer!" Frank raced to the Spam, taking a piece in each claw and raising them triumphantly over his head.

♦

"May I have your attention, Please! Charlie's back!" Nick called across BESA 12's com. "Meeting in the canteen in ten minutes!"

Finally! I thought and looked at John. "We're going to figure out what this collar is." I set Frank and Sydney on the floor, then stored the samples I took from tiny spots on their bodies.

They scurried back to their lidless tank, up a plank of wood I added for access, and into the water.

"I'll be back soon," I said to them. "John, let's go."

We joined a stream of researchers in the corridor and packed into the canteen against the back wall. John sat between my legs to not take up space. Across the canteen was Charlie with two others from his crew, looking haggard, exceptionally old, as if they aged a decade in a month. *Where are the others?* I thought, knowing he set out with ten.

"Thank you for coming on such short notice," Nick said. "What Charlie's team discovered is crucial to our future." He turned to Charlie.

The old survivalist gave a quiet stare, then slowly stood. "I wish I could say that humanity's chances of survival are looking better, that we are coming to a turning point, an upswing. But when we revived the observatory…" Charlie took a breath. "…We confirmed our worst fears. It was not only Earth's cities that were struck by the light beams. It happened to Luna, Mars, and the Jovian and Saturnian moon colonies as well. All glassed. All lost."

Gasps circled the canteen.

"You can't be serious!?" someone shouted.

"What about Ceres!?" another blurted.

"Ceres was different," Charlie answered. "We observed thousands of continuous explosions in its orbit for two weeks straight. Then, when it settled down, there was too much debris to study the surface."

All was silent until Rachel said, "And Mercury?"

Charlie faced her. "That's where it gets confusing. It appears like thousands of thermonuclear events occurred across the planet's surface. The Hermian's solar fields have vanished and their cities were burnt to a crisp. They somehow suffered the worst of it."

Murmurs went all around.

"Does that mean the war is over!?"

"More than over! It means everyone lost!"

"But how could this happen!? Who struck first!?"

"Are we the only ones left!?"

"Yes!" Charlie cut in and everyone quieted. "We must assume no one else made it. We must assume we stragglers caught outside the cities during The Fall are all that remains of humanity. And... We have descended to barbarism." He breathed deeply again. "I lost seven of my crew to a band of ronin on the way back from the observatory. They were heading to the coast."

"More are coming? What for?" someone asked.

"General Kase has them searching for someone who supposedly has all the answers to our situation. Some guy named John."

"Me?" John, a kelp scientist, responded.

"Maybe it's me," said another John, from water salinity.

Charlie gave them both looks. "I'm sure it's neither of you, but let's talk in private tonight. We must take extra precautions."

The crowd burst into scared complaining.

Nick stood, raising his arms. "I know you have many questions that we will try to answer!" he called above the fear. "You will each have time to discuss your concerns with us in private, but appointments are first come, first serve." He raised a clipboard and pen and set them on a table.

A stampede of researchers made for the sign up sheet. *And I'm in the back.* By the time I reached it, names filled the first six pages. I added mine on page seven and saw a subject line. I studied the previous ones, all saying the same thing, many using quotations to reference above, all for either clarification of System Sol's observation or the ronin situation.

I wrote, *"Dog collar identification."*

"How'd it go?" I asked Rachel when she entered my observation room.

"Not much different than the canteen," she responded. "I cried a little."

My frustration rose. "Did you ask Charlie about Enceladus, Europa, and Ganymede? I saw your subject line was about System Sol."

She gave me a funny look. "No… Why would I?"

"They established aquaculture research stations far below the ice. Not only did they perform similar research to BESA 12's, they might have survived," I said, appalled. "Ganymede even had your sister Quantum Mechanics program."

Rachel's face went blank. "Maybe they'll let me back in."

"Nope, you had your chance," I said.

She sighed and looked into the quarantine room at two separate tanks with a crustacean in each and a soundproof wall separating them. "What are you doing?"

"Remember how they have hundreds of variations for *Mermer?*"

Rachel slowly nodded.

"Do you also remember how I installed microphones to hear their calls from inside the tank?"

"Yeah," Rachel said.

"Well, as I've been more closely studying their anatomy, I discovered their hearing is not great, yet they can communicate with each other through the tank's glass when Frank is off stealing Spam. Which makes me think they're not communicating with sound at all."

Rachel cocked her head.

"I discovered tiny spots across their bodies resembling electroreceptors you might find on the snout of a shark. I then set up electrical sensors. Check this out." I entered the room, towards Sydney's tank, completely out of sight and hearing from Frank, and set Spam on the floor. Then, I returned to the observation room and pulled up a hologram. A cluster of electrical pulses, the makeup of Sydney's body with electrical signals running from her brain to her extremities, formulated. She neared the edge of her tank, looking at the Spam.

"Mer!" came through her mic.

The hologram displayed sound waves stopping at the soundproof wall but an electrical pulse went right through.

Frank abruptly turned and responded, "Mer mee!"

Another electrical pulse shot back to Sydney.

Rachel's face went blank. "So, why do they make noise, then?"

"I think it's a byproduct. Like, when humans speak, you can see us moving our mouths, but the visual is not required for communication," I said. "It gets even more amazing. Watch." I isolated Sydney's call, placing the sound waves alongside the electrical pulse. "To us, Sydney said something simple, a single syllable, taking a fraction of a second to create, emit, and be heard. But in that same amount of time…" I zoomed into the electrical pulse. "…she emitted thousands of electrical pulses."

"What does this mean?" Rachel asked.

I grinned. "In the time it might take humans to utter a single word, these creatures can have complex conversations. To them, *Mer* is probably something like, *Hey Frank, this human put another piece of Spam next to my tank. What's her deal? Why is she so strange?*"

Rachel gave me a look. "I agree with Sydney."

I dropped my grin. "You know what I mean."

Rachel pointed at the hologram. "Have you noticed when Sydney emits electricity, Frank's body also reacts. Is that electroreception, too?"

I paused. "I haven't noticed that." I opened a dual feed from when they spoke. I stopped the recording just as Sydney emitted her electricity.

"Whoa… Look at that," Rachel said, pointing at Frank. "Frank's brain is responding before Sydney's signal reaches him."

I stared at the diagram. "The test must have been compromised."

"How?" Rachel said. "If they're communicating through electricity, then its almost at light speed. But Frank is reacting immediately, faster than the speed of light. The only way to achieve that is with quantum entanglement."

Her area of expertise, I knew. "Can you test something like that?"

"Let me talk with Dr. Fennel!" Rachel excitedly said.

◆

"Please, let us at least try," Rachel said to Dr. Fennel, head of Quantum Mechanics. I stood in the doorway with Frank and Sydney in my arms studying the priceless equipment.

"No, Rachel," Dr. Fennel responded. "We're strapped for resources as it is. This little hobby of yours has gotten out of hand." The doctor turned to me. "And I've been hearing complaints from health and safety about those crustace—" his eyes shot to Frank and Sydney. "You brought them here!? Out! Now!"

"Wait!" Rachel said. "I'm calling in my coin…"

Oh, shit… I thought, knowing she only had one.

Dr. Fennel turned beet red. "You have one hour! Then, never again!" He opened his palm.

Rachel placed her coin, with its distinctive groove down the center, into the doctor's hand. He twisted, snapping the coin in two.

"Rachel, I —" I began.

"Don't," she responded. "This is my choice." She smiled sadly. "Let's get to work."

We set up a similar experiment to the one I performed in the quarantine room, but with equipment designed to create true isolation. I placed Frank into one tank and Sydney into another.

"We can cut all forms of communication with this system," Rachel said. "Whether it be auditory, visual, electrical, everything. The only thing that can work is quantum entanglement."

"Which is why your hobby is a waste of time," Dr. Fennel snapped from his station.

I ignored him. "What is quantum entanglement, anyhow?"

Rachel beamed. "That's the question we all have! What we know is that when you split a quantum particle the pieces are still somehow linked."

"Meaning?"

"When one half rotates, flips, or performs any type of movement, its counterpart reacts instantly, no matter the distance apart or what's between them. But entanglement's hurdle is that if the first half does a flip, then the second half does not necessarily match."

"So, how do you know it worked?" I asked.

"By recording the fact that they moved at the exact same moment."

"Didn't we have this figured out before The Fall? We had quantum relays," I said.

"But we couldn't achieve long distances, hence why we had to relay them. And we were constantly updating our prediction models... It took us half a century to figure out how to stimulate the first half of a particle to either flip or spin, and then assign Zeros and Ones."

"Binary..." I said.

"Yeah. And then, it took another century and a half to come up with a database of trillions of possible reactions the particle's counterpart might perform to start predicting results from the other side. And, there were so many errors. It was why we still used tight beam, keeping quantum relays strictly for entertainment purposes."

"The quantum relays are gone now."

Rachel grimaced. "But the research continues. If we can develop a flawless system of interpretation, we can rid ourselves of the need for relays, and have true, instantaneous communication into the farthest reaches of space. It could change humanity as we know it!"

"Hurray," Dr. Fennel sarcastically said.

Rachel gave cut eye. "Let's perform the same test as before."

I opened the hologram with Frank and Sydney's electrical signatures. I placed Spam inside Sydney's tank, then sealed it tight.

"Mer mee Mer me," she said.

"Eeemer mere," Frank responded.

Dr. Fennel turned from his station. "Are they talking to one another?"

"Yep," I answered.

Dr. Fennel frowned and returned to his work.

"Okay," Rachel said. "Cutting sound and sight in three, two, one..."

Frank and Sydney went silent, but their electrical signals continued shooting back and forth.

"Electroreception as a means of communication, confirmed!" I said.

"Wait, what?" Dr. Fennel said, now watching our hologram.

I grinned, knowing the doctor could not help his curiosity. "Their sound is a byproduct of their electrical pulses."

"Fascinating," said the doctor, then snapped out of his intrigue. "Still a waste of time."

He started to leave when Rachel said, "And now, cutting all possible communication routes."

Dr. Fennel stopped to watch.

Frank and Sydney suddenly looked around themselves, startled when their electrical pulses ceased. But then, they relaxed and moved their claws as if conversing. Their brain activity kept going, still in sync, still flashing.

"That's it!" Rachel cried. "They've maintained communication!"

"What's the time delay!?" Dr. Fennel shouted, rushing forth.

Rachel quickly pulled up the reading. "There's literally zero delay!"

"How!? How!?" Dr. Fennel shouted with his hands on his head as the rest of Quantum Mechanics gathered. "Eva, how!?"

I looked long and hard at the hologram, at the portions of Frank and Sydney's brains flashing in sync. "I've never seen this before in any creature," I responded. "I think we just discovered an organ capable of sending and receiving information directly from one mind to another."

"Biological quantum communication..." Dr. Fennel whispered, looking about to pass out.

♦

The entirety of Quantum Mechanics crammed into the canteen watching Frank in his isolation tank with several cards depicting a bird, boat, sun, rock, fish, and crab. On hologram was Rachel with Sydney in the lab. Rachel faced the hologram and showed a card with a small boat for us to see, then placed it inside Sydney's tank.

As Sydney approached the boat, Frank approached the many cards in his tank. He raised his claw and pointed at the boat.

The canteen erupted in cheers.

"They did it again!" one cried.

"Is this something all crabs can do!?" said another.

"It's only these specific creatures," I said. "We don't know how it developed or what its capabilities are. All we know is that they can convey basic ideas."

"Yeah," Rachel said on hologram. "We really should be testing longer distances. Like, from here to the observatory."

"I'll make sure to bring that up with Charlie and Nick during my appointment today," I said.

"If you haven't been bumped," said Tate from the kitchen.

I snapped my head to him. "What do you mean?"

"It happened to me. Nick said there were more important things."

"Like John's collar," I said.

"Is that what you wrote as your subject line?" Tate asked.

"Yeah… why?"

"You're bumped for sure, then," Tate said.

"Shit…" I whispered as I pulled Frank from his isolation tank.

Frank gave me a funny look.

Shitshit, flashed into my thoughts.

I turned to John. "John, with me."

The three of us traversed BESA's main corridor to the management wing. Voices were arguing ahead. *From Nick's office,* I knew.

"It's just too dangerous," I heard Nick say.

"But, this is a breakthrough unlike anything we could have imagined!" said another voice. "I guarantee this is worth the risk!"

Dr. Fennel! I realized.

"No!" Nick harshly said.

Dr. Fennel came huffing down the corridor, made eye contact with me, and muttered, "I hate this place."

I entered the office.

Nick faced me. "What do you want!?" he snapped, then saw Frank. "No! I just went over this with Dr. Fennel! We can't risk sending another team out right now!"

"It's not about that," I said.

Nick rolled his eyes. "What, then!?"

"It's my appointment…" I realized Charlie was quietly standing in the back, staring at the wall, still as a statue.

Nick snatched his clipboard and flipped pages. "…A dog collar? Eva, no. We have serious matters at hand. This appointment is over."

I felt my anger swell. "I've waited two weeks to speak with Charlie! This collar has some crazy tech I've never seen before!"

"It's a shock collar, Eva!" Nick yelled back. "Mystery solved!"

"Would a shock collar have a curium isotope generator!?"

Charlie turned my way.

"Whatever that means!" Nick said. "You're dismissed!"

"But Ni—"

"I said, dismissed!"

My hands trembled. I turned abruptly. "John, let's go!"

"Wait…" said a quiet voice.

Charlie, I realized and stopped.

"The dog's name is John?" he asked.

Nick scoffed. "She gives all her pets human names." He pointed at my arms. "She named that thing, Fred."

"Frank!" I corrected.

"See?"

"Oh," Charlie said.

"No, no!" I desperately said. "I didn't give John this name! It's previous owner did!"

"Who's the previous owner?" Charlie asked.

"…I don't know. I found him roaming the town."

"Then, how do you know his name is John?" Nick snickered.

I furrowed my brow. "It's tattooed in his ear, you asshole!"

"How dare you—"

"Nick, Shut up!" Charlie scolded. He approached John and knelt. "May I see the tattoo?"

I flipped up John's floppy ear.

"Kunming… 6834026… Enhanced," Charlie muttered and looked into John's eyes. "My god…"

"What is it?" I asked.

Charlie looked at me, then Nick. "John's an old war dog."

"What?" Nick said. "That's impossible. That would make him at least fifty years old."

"It was believed they all died in battle, never reaching their potential lifespans," Charlie said. "Nobody knows how long they can live for."

"Incredible," I said, then pointed at John's collar. "Do you know what this is, then?"

Charlie felt around the collar, working his way to the bulge. "Sicklecell titanium, military grade, within high density silicon." He read the warning label. "It's a generator, all right." Charlie sharply stood and stepped back.

"What?" I whispered.

"John…" Charlie raised a hand, pinching the bridge of his nose. "Fuck. I know this dog…"

Nick gave a look. "Like, personally?"

Charlie grunted. "I know who this dog once belonged to. His master stole something valuable from the metacorporations." Charlie breathed deeply. "The ronin we encountered. I think this is what they're searching for. But, they believe they're after a person, not a dog."

"What could be so important about this collar?" Nick asked.

Charlie shook his head. "I don't know. But, my ex might."

"Where can we find her?" I asked.

"Him," Charlie corrected. "Hector runs BESA 1 outside Portland."

"That's not far—"

"Portland, Maine," Charlie said. "At least, he was there the last time we spoke." He gave the collar a hard look. "We must discover what this is."

"So an expedition?" Nick said. "It's too dangerous right now."

Charlie glared at him. "It's about to get a lot more dangerous should the ronin find out who John actually is."

"I'll go to Maine," I said. "But can I make a request?"

"Ask away," Charlie said.

I pointed at Frank. "I know you don't understand the importance of what's happening with these creatures, but testing their ability to quantum communicate over significant distances could lead to reestablishing communication across System Sol." I breathed deeply. "This is more important than anything we've ever discovered."

Nick turned an unbearable shade of red.

Charlie thought about that. "Okay, if we're going out anyway, then we should make the most of it. Gather a small team and itemize only the equipment you absolutely require. We move fast."

♦

"Eva, look!" Dr. Fennel cried, pointing at the observatory peaking above the rugged mountain trees as dusk approached.

"Keep it down!" Charlie snapped. "These hills are crawling with ronin!"

The others stared daggers at him as they huffed and puffed, carrying the isolation tank, associated gear, and Frank watching through the tank's glass, marveling at the trees and rocky cliffs.

"Sorry, sorry," Dr. Fennel whispered.

John froze with one leg up and we crouched alongside the trail.

"John, search," I whispered.

He took off, swiftly, silently, like an owl. A minute turned into several, until, at last, John's pattering paws were heard. He returned from the shrubs with a mass of fur in his mouth.

"What is that?" someone said.

"Shh!" the rest collectively scolded.

But what is it? I thought. John came to a stop in front of me and dropped the mass of fur, then pranced proudly. I knelt, feeling its softness, then I discerned four limbs and long ears. "It's a hare. A big one."

"Check it," Nick whispered.

I pulled test tabs and a small knife from my pack. I sunk the blade in several spots, then inserted the tabs. They turned green. My heart fluttered. "Good boy," I whispered to John.

The crew came to study the hare, their smiles flashing brightly in the dusky light, and they scratched behind John's ear. His mouth opened wide and his tail wagged.

If there is a dog heaven, this is it, I thought.

"Does that mean it's all clear ahead?" Charlie whispered.

John wagged his tail so vigorously his entire butt swung side to side.

Not sitting. "Yes, it's clear," I said.

"Let's move," Charlie whispered and we continued on.

Shrubs and stunted trees gave way to bare rock where the observatory's rusty dome stood like a monument.

"Secure the perimeter," Charlie said and his crew took off with pistols drawn, pointed at the ground. "Eva, John, with me."

"John, let's go," I whispered.

We followed Charlie, stopping to plant stakes in the ground.

"Vibration sensors," he whispered for my benefit.

John kept a constant sniff and did not whine or fuss as we rounded the observatory. Soon, I saw Nick approaching from the other side.

"They're all set," Nick said.

"Let's get closer," Charlie responded.

We inched towards the observatory's entry door hosting a massive padlock. Charlie knelt and drove a vibration stake so deep its head disappeared, and covered it with dirt. He pulled a key, relinquished the lock from duty, opened the door, and waved for us to enter. Once inside, Charlie closed the door and used the padlock to lock us in.

"Okay," he said at a normal volume. "Shield your eyes."

Heavy clunking and light blasted all around. After a moment, I peaked from beneath my hands. Old construction lights flooded the inside surface of the observatory's cylindrical wall and highlighted a metal staircase winding to a mesh mezzanine above. Through the mesh I saw a massive telescope resting upon rusty gears.

"Will ronin see the light?" I asked.

"No," Charlie said. "The observatory is specifically designed to cut external light pollution. Therefore, it also works to keep interior light from shining out, especially when its viewing slot is closed." He pointed at the closed slot above, then at a series of power cells on the floor. "We set this up last time. It should have enough power for Dr. Fennel's equipment. When is the experiment?"

Dr. Fennel perked up. "Eight tonight."

Charlie checked his old wind-up watch. "That gives you two hours to set things up. I hope that's enough, we won't spend more than one night here."

"That's enough," Dr. Fennel confirmed.

"Good." Charlie turned to Nick. "Let's cook up that hare."

◆

"The first transmission will come soon," Dr. Fennel announced.

Nick stopped skinning the hare and made a face. "If we can't contact Rachel in BESA. How will you know if it worked?"

"We've coordinated a sequence of sixty images with her ahead of time," Dr. Fennel said, opening them on holotile for everyone to see. "At every minute, beginning at eight, Rachel will show Sydney an image. Then, Frank will select a matching image from within his isolation tank here. We will know the instant a transmission occurs by watching this spot in his brain." He pointed at the diagram displaying Frank's brain activity. "The accuracy of what they transmit will be tested with the images."

"So, it's the same thing you were doing in the canteen," Nick stated.

"Exactly."

"What's the point of doing it again?"

Dr. Fennel grinned. "Distance is key to understanding how well they're communicating on the quantum level. At BESA, the distance from the lab to the canteen was too short. We cannot properly measure time delay. Distance also serves to remove any possibility of the test being compromised. But, the real experiment will be when Eva reaches Maine."

"Uh… okay," Nick said, going back to skinning. "Isn't it strange that these crabs use both electricity and quantum to communicate?" he suddenly asked. "Why complicate things? Just pick one."

"It's not complicated," I responded. "It's actually far more simple than how humans communicate."

"How so?" Charlie asked, coming into the conversation.

"Human communication starts as thoughts transmitted electrically from ours brains to our lungs to mechanically push air through vocal cords, vibrating in specific ways to produce sound-waves that travel through the air. These sound-waves then vibrate tiny bristles of hair inside another person's eardrums, sending electrical signals to their brains for interpretation." I pointed at Frank. "Frank and Sydney only need to think about something to one another, using electroreception to add more detail to their conversations, which is why these quantum tests are so basic when the electrical component is removed. Their communication is a two step process, where humans have a six step process."

Charlie humphed.

Dr. Fennel raised a hand. "The first image will be displayed for Sydney in three, two, one…"

The diagram of Frank's brain flashed, and he approached the cards. He raised a claw and pointed at a fish.

Everyone turned to Dr. Fennel.

He smiled wide. "The first image is a… fish!"

"What about time delay!?" I asked.

Dr. Fennel studied the moment the flash occurred, comparing it to the schedule. "There's a microsecond between the two, but that aligns with Sydney's ability to see and understand. If we subtract that, then the transmission of information from Sydney to Frank is literally zero!"

"So the experiment worked?" Charlie said.

"It did!" the doctor cried. "We just confirmed without a doubt that Frank and Sydney are communicating via quantum entanglement!"

The crew was quiet.

"That's so anticlimactic," Nick said.

"Not everything is a celebration," I snapped, then eyed the hare, now rotating above Nick's smokeless furnace. *Or maybe it is!*

Dr. Fennel and I spent the next hour recording every image Frank selected, cheering with each one correct. Charlie's crew dwindled off, finding the hare more interesting. Soon, charred barbecue combined with baked beans hit my nose. I found myself turning several times and saw Dr. Fennel doing the same.

"That's the final image," Dr. Fennel said, closing down his holotile. "Frank got everything right."

"What's next?" I asked.

"I don't know, Eva… Not in my wildest dreams did I imagine biological quantum communication existed… Thank you for this." The doctor closed his eyes and breathed deeply. "Christ, I forgot how good real meat smells."

Nick gave the baked beans one last stir and removed them from the burner, then cut a small piece from the hare to inspect. He smiled. "Come and get it!"

Dr. Fennel and I joined the others with stainless steel mugs. Nick ladled beans into each, then placed chunks of meat on top. He turned to John.

"Hey, boy! Come get yours!" he said, holding a rabbit leg.

John bounded over, coming to a skidding stop, and delicately took the leg from Nick. We sat on old observatory chairs, situated in a circle, and devoured our meals.

Smiles all around, I thought, marveling at the power of meat. *If only they were this excited about the experiment.*

Meat, flashed into my thoughts.

I looked around, searching for who said it, but everyone was shoveling down food.

"Hey, look," one of Charlie's crew said. "Little guy wants some."

"Can they eat rabbit?" another asked, turning my way for an answer.

I looked beyond them at the isolation tank where Frank was tapping the glass, but there was no sound.

Dr. Fennel's eyes met mine.

"Frank is still in isolation," I said. "The glass is opaque from his side."

Dr. Fennel bee-lined to the tank to confirm. "He shouldn't be able to sense anything."

"Is it just a coincidence?" Charlie asked.

"Frigging incredible coincidence," I responded.

Dr. Fennel stuck his fork into his mug, fished out a piece of rabbit, and lowered it to the opaque glass. Frank turned towards it, raising his claw.

Meat, came again, but no one else seemed to hear it. My hands began to shake. *What's happening?*

"Has the isolation tank been compromised?" Charlie asked.

"...It's working exactly how it should," Dr. Fennel said.

"Is this part of the experiment?" Charlie followed up.

"No," I said, trying to remain calm. "This is… just happening."

"So, what does it mean?"

"More questions than answers," Dr. Fennel said.

◆

Growling... My eyes cracked open to find John next to me. His teeth were bared, his hair stood straight up, bristling, and his muscles rippled. *A werewolf,* I thought, then realized this was not a dream.

"y'It's y'a fucking warrr dog, y'all rrright," said a hoarse voice, rolling his *R's,* his accent unlike anything I ever heard before.

"y'I thought they y'all died," said another, just as strange.

"G-guess n-not," stuttered a third.

"Good to see the y'old rrrabbit trrrick still worrrks," said the first.

I peered beyond John to see Nick with his pistol drawn.

"Eva," came a whisper. "Sit up slowly. Make no sudden movements."

Charlie, I recognized. I faced him on the other side of me, his pistol drawn, too. I realized they were all drawn, even Dr. Fennel's.

A thump came through the ground.

"y'And y'a sweet little woman," the hoarse voice said.

Ice ran through my veins. I slowly sat up to see three old soldiers in deteriorating armor, scars and wrinkles riddling their faces, and their massive rifles pointed at me. My hands shook. I began hyperventilating. *Why didn't the vibration stakes sound!? Why didn't John warn us!?*

"Stay calm," Charlie whispered.

"G-get y'over herrre. l-little w-woman," the stuttering one said.

Think! I felt John's breath against the side of my buzzed hair. "I'm not a woman," I said as masculinely as possible.

The first ronin chuckled. "Herrrmian women y'often shave theirrr hairrr. You'rrre not fooling y'anyone." He stepped forth. "You belong to y'us now."

John crept closer, his jaws opening and his growling rising.

"Call y'off yourrr dog," he said, training his rifle on John.

I stroked John's bristling fur, but he did not acknowledge my touch. *He's in battle mode,* I realized. "Lie down, boy."

He did not budge.

"Be good, boy. Lie down," I said more sternly.

John crept forward, looking about to lunge.

"Last chance," the ronin warned.

"John…" I reluctantly said. "Lie down."

John ceased his growling, his fur fell flat, and his muscles relaxed. He laid down next to me.

"No fucking way…" the ronin said. "…That's The Butcherrr's dog."

"John…" the second one muttered.

"W-what's the thing y'arrround y'its n-neck?"

The first one smiled. "Generrral Kase y'is going to be happy y'about this." We made eye contact. "You have no y'idea what you possess, do you?"

I stared back at the ronin, silent, frozen.

Scared… came into my mind.

Beyond the ronin, in the shadows, I saw Frank in his chamber, holding his claws up against the glass.

I… help… came to me.

What's he doing? I thought and realized the chamber was not in isolation.

Frank clacked his claws against the glass, sounding like a machine gun piercing through the silence.

The ronin whirled, turning their backs to us.

It's now or never! "John! Attack!"

He bolted off as Nick and Charlie opened fire, followed by the rest of the crew, their bullets bouncing off the ronin's armor, chipping away at the rusted portions. The ronin flipped on their helmets, but not before John leaped, sinking his jaws into the nearest one's neck and tearing at his jugular. The ronin dropped his rifle, grabbed John around the torso, and tumbled to the ground, pinning him to the floor. Then, a dagger sunk into John's side again and again. But, John refused to let go.

"No!" I cried, and lurched forth, only to be caught by Charlie.

"John's gone!" Charlie shouted, shooting at the other two.

"But, his collar has what they want!" I pleaded.

Charlie grimaced. "Stay here!" He let me go and clasped two hands around his pistol, closing one eye, lining up a shot, and pulling the trigger. The pistol barely made a sound above the cacophony, but the ronin's head snapped back.

John let go of their neck and thrashed on the floor.

"Fuck!" came from my right. Nick dropped to the ground holding his stomach. Then, I saw Dr. Fennel lying motionless.

The two remaining ronin knelt behind their dead comrade's body, using it as cover, and aimed their rifles.

Left! came into my head, and I obeyed, lunging to the side as the ronin unleashed destruction.

Charlie rolled to the left with me, narrowly evading the onslaught, and aimed again, two hands, one eye. A spurt of blood burst from another ronin's neck, at the seam of his helmet and pauldrons.

Forward! came to me. Again, I listened and Charlie followed.

We flanked the last ronin and Charlie pinged shots off his helmet. The ronin swung his rifle our way, letting random shots fly, hitting the observatory's cylindrical wall.

Right! the voice shouted, leading me straight at the ronin.

I closed the gap with my hands raised, grabbing the ronin's rifle barrel and searing my palms. I pushed it to the floor, ignoring the burning.

Charlie leaped over me, tackling the ronin. John was suddenly there, too, sinking his teeth into the ronin's free hand. With the tip of his pistol, Charlie flipped up the ronin's crusty helmet and released several shots.

All became silent and I rolled to find everyone lying motionless.

"Shit…" Charlie said, holding his ribs. "Eva, go… They weren't alone… Go, now!"

I watched blood pour from his chest. "…Where?"

Charlie coughed a mouthful. "…M… Maine… Find Hector… Give him your coin… to prove you're… from BESA 12."

My coin… "I lost it years ago," I whispered.

Charlie grunted and reached into his pocket. "Take… mine." He placed it in my palm and curling my fingers into a fist. He winced hard, rolling to the floor. "Go… go… go…" He relaxed, as if falling asleep.

"Charlie?" I whispered and dropped to my knees.

John whimpered and crawled towards me with his front paws, dragging his hind legs. His nose nudged my hand and I turn to him. I touched the deep gashes at his hips, but he did not flinch. Not until I was midway up his back did he yelp.

No, John, I thought.

Safe... came to my mind.

I faced Frank beyond his chamber's shattered glass. I carefully reached inside to retrieve him, my hands shaking. *He smells like onions again...*

We... Go...

"Yes," I whispered and silently gathered my pack, two pistols, all the ammo I could find, dehydrated meats and vitamins, Charlie's map, and Dr. Fennel's holotile containing our findings. I kept my thoughts on the trek to Maine, or on the smell coming from Frank, not letting myself dwell on what just occurred. Frank latched onto my pack's shoulder strap.

All the while, John whimpered, his claws scraping the floor as he dragged himself, following me. My lip trembled. I found leftover rabbit in a pot and took a bone.

"C-come, John," I managed to say, setting the bone on the floor.

He dragged himself closer and slumped to the bone. I gently scratched behind his ear with the tip of my finger as he licked the gristle. Then, I replaced my finger with my pistol's tip and looked up at the blue sky peaking through the observatory's open slot.

◆

I set fire to the observatory, burning my comrades, the ronin, anything that might give clue as to what happened, but I cremated John outside, giving him what I felt to be a hero's goodbye.

Friend... came to mind.

"The best kind," I whispered, knowing Frank and I must move fast, that the smell and smoke would attract more ronin. John's collar trembled in my burned hand, wrapped tightly to keep dirt from my weeping wounds. I looked at Frank, clamped to my shoulder strap, and said, "Let's go..."

Charlie's map led along old trails, overgrown and barely legible, crossing more defined roads, but never following along. *To avoid ronin,* I knew, but the temptation for a smooth trek was nearly overwhelming.

Silence became my agony, for without distraction, the observatory massacre constantly replayed in my mind. Thankfully, as my dehydrated foodstuffs dwindled, the anxiety of my next meal consumed my thoughts. *I must get over the Rockies,* I knew, for game on the grasslands would be plentiful and clean. *If the rumors are true.* The next checkpoint was BESA 07 outside Denver, taking me right through ronin territory. Without Charlie and John, I was not certain of my chances.

Me... came to mind.

I tried ignoring it, but saw Frank staring at me from my shoulder. Eventually, I turned to him. "Yes, I still have you."

He pointed his claw off the trail and twitched an antenna.

Smell...

I thought long about that, knowing a crustacean's sense of smell was incredible. "Is it food?" I timidly responded.

Yes...

I've officially become a lunatic, I thought and stepped off the trail into a small clearing with a doused campfire, wisps of smoke still rising. I ducked down, listening. I turned to Frank. "Is it clear?"

Yes...

Eva Jain, cause of death... stupidity. I moved to investigate. I smelled barbecue and found several large boot prints. *Ronin.* But then, I saw three familiar ones, sizes seven, eight, and eleven imprinted at their arches. I realized my prints were identical. *They're from the BESA program, but which facility?* The prints led along the trail, heading the same direction as me.

I came upon another camp the following day with embers looking about to reignite. *Only hours old. I'm catching up to them.* The barbecue scent was strong, but I could not discern what they were eating. The large prints were the same, but I saw only two sets of BESA prints now.

Frank pointed into the woods.

I cautiously approached, covering my brow, and peered into the brush. *A pair of boots.* When I neared, I realized there was no body. I flipped over the boots to find, *"SIZE – 8."* I sighed deeply, knowing they died on the trail. *But why only leave the boots?*

I found bones in a smoldering fire at the next camp. A tibia, fibula, and the metatarsals of a foot. I stared at them, feeling like it was some sort of prank, until I realized the tibia was hollowed out for marrow. I retched into the embers sending a sickening wash of steam into my face, causing me to vomit again.

◆

I was not sure how long it had been, but I was almost out of The Rockies. I maintained a slower than desired pace, hoping I would not turn a corner to find the ronin waiting. Frank smelled ahead, confirming all was clear. I found more human remains at each campsite. And then, only one set of BESA boot prints were in the dirt.

My hair grew shaggy. My food supply was gone. But I knew how to trap.

Thankfully, the game was clean. *But would that last?*

Frank abruptly raised his claws.

Stop! came to me.

A scream cut through the night. I crouched, and there I stayed awake until dawn.

◆

The clattering of armor and the sizzling of a fire being doused came as the ronin broke down camp.

"Come, you piece y'of shit!" one said.

A moan followed.

"Quit yourrr complaining! You y'ate, too!" said another.

I crept downhill after them, trying not to make a sound, until I found a break in the trees where forest was overtaken by grassland. I waited for hours until the ronin appeared in the grass. I peered through my binoculars. *Five ronin and a woman in a BESA uniform,* I determined. I zoomed onto the scientist. A chain dangled from a metal collar around her neck, held by one of the ronin, and when she turned, I realized her right arm was missing from the elbow down. *"BESA 07,"* read on the breast of her jacket. When the sun peaked its head above the horizon, the woman snapped her head up, looking right at me. I sprawled to my stomach, knowing she must have caught sunlight reflecting off my lenses. I timidly picked the binoculars back up and focused on the group.

Heading south to Denver, I realized.

I caught more glimpses as they crested grassy hills in the distance. After a few days, the woman's upper arm went missing. Another day and her left arm was gone. Then, her ears and nose disappeared. She could barely walk.

One morning, she simply vanished altogether.

◆

Grassland became bushes and brambles as I closed in on Denver. I glimpsed sunlight reflecting off the city's glass dome. *Almost there…*

Frank stood vigilant on my shoulder, his antenna twitching with every gust of wind, pulling odors from water molecules in the air. With such low humidity, I was not certain what he could discern, or how long he could survive. But the more I studied him, the more I realized his body was changing. And then, he molted during our second night in the bushes. His gills were practically gone, his lungs were more powerful, his shell was harder and sealed up, and his antennae were short and stubby, perfect for capturing molecules in low humidity. *Just like land crabs.*

Smoke rose from several kilometers out from BESA 07. Barbecue came strong in the wind. Everything in me wanted to pass by, but a tight beam system was there that I needed to send a warning back home and to notify BESA 01 of my coming arrival.

Every step I took, I questioned, like I had tempted fate for far too long. But every time I asked Frank if ronin were there I would hear, *Gone…*

♦

A BESA facility, just like ours, but built into a rock face, was now before me. Its hatch was blown open and bodies laid charred on the ground, carved of meat. But it felt no worse than the observatory or the campfires. My stomach did not churn. *I've grown accustomed*, I realized, feeling sadness for the innocence I lost. Smoke no longer poured into the sky. Instead, little puffs came with each breeze that passed through its entrance. I opened my holotile, knowing ronin could theoretically detect it, and accessed its chemical analysis program. As I navigated BESA 07's central corridor, the diagram spiked, but never above yellow. In the canteen were three bodies hanging by their ankles. They were not burned or carved of meat. They were skinned.

Alive… came to me.

One opened his eyes into slits as I neared. His eyes drifted to my waist, then back to me.

My pistol, I realized.

"P-please…" he weakly whispered.

"Why did they do this to you?" I asked, drawing my pistol and aiming.

His eyes pleaded for me to shoot. "J-John," he whispered.

I pulled the trigger, but missed. I stepped closer and took another shot. A hole appear in his skull and his eyes become vacant. I holstered my pistol, and found a table hosting BESA uniforms. I read their name tags.

"John Bailey, Biologist."

"Jonathan Klouse, Radiologist."

"Cadence Johnson, Botanist."

Everyone with a name close to John, I knew, feeling dread wash over me. *I must get to Maine…* I stocked up on canned garlic and cilantro, for when food must be cleansed, and found their tight beam system. A gaping hole was in its console.

Leave… came to me.

"Yes…" I whispered.

♦

A year had passed since I departed BESA 12, and when that rocky east coast beach appeared I raced to kiss its salty stones. I stuck to the coast to hunt in the tide pools as I worked north, Frank guiding me along, helping to locate prey, seaweed, and algae to combine with my garlic and cilantro, until I finally glimpsed the glass dome of Portland, Maine.

I woke on a white sand beach one morning to Portland's dome looming large. *I should be there by noon,* I knew, feeling my first sense of calm since the observatory. I broke down camp, strapped on my pack, and set Frank on his shoulder perch. I was about to head north, when a vigorous flapping and high pitch cries came. I turned to see a flock of seagulls heading straight at me. I dropped to the sand, grabbed Frank from my shoulder, and curled around him. But the gulls went by us, neither after me nor Frank. Strange tremors came through the ground.

I stood and scanned my surroundings until I saw a speck along the beach to the south with dust clouding the air behind it. I retrieved my binoculars. There was a blur, tipping side to side like a seesaw. I focused. "No!" I cried, almost dropping my binoculars. A man, larger than I had ever seen, was barreling my way, his shoulders dipping deeply with each powerful thrust of his legs. His eyes were like an eagle's, locked onto me. My stomach sank, my legs felt weak.

The monstrous man raised a hand and several more ragged people appeared from behind him, fanning out into a line. They were not wearing armor and held no rifles, but they were the most terrifying thing I ever witnessed. The monstrous one pointed its finger at me and moved his mouth.

"Little girrrl!" rumbled seconds later, with such force my chest felt about to explode. My legs seemed paralyzed. I could not think let alone breathe.

From within I heard, *Run! Run! Run!*

The onion smell came from Frank, pulling me out of my daze. I tore the collar from my pack and secured it to my belt, then stuffed Charlie's map and ammo into my cargo pockets. I loaded a pistol, trained it on the monstrous man, and unleashed the entire magazine, my hand knocking wildly with each shot.

Collective laughter shot back.

"Little girrrl! Little girrrl! Join y'us forrr dinnerrr!" the big one cried.

I scrambled, slipping in the loose sand.

Water! came the voice.

I moved closer to the waves, feeling firmer sand beneath my feet, and finding traction. I glanced back to see my assailants had gained significant ground. *Move, Eva!* I imagined every muscle in my body contributing to each stride. *You can hike forever! You can outlast them!* I tried convincing myself, but my muscles were burning.

"Little girrrl! Just give y'up!" came the booming voice, so close I could hear their breathing.

There was a sharp bend on the beach ahead, marked by jutting rocks land-side that would trap me to the sand, but I knew there could be more ronin in the woods waiting. *No choice…*

As I rounded the bend, a swipe knocked my kick-backed leg, tumbling me to the sand. I rolled with my pistol drawn, ready to fight to the bitter end, but the monstrous man was looking beyond me with startled eyes, instead.

Deafening cracks rang.

I dropped my pistol, covered my ears, and watched holes appear in the monstrous man's chest. He leaped over me, as the rest backpedaled, sliding on the sand. Limbs tore off, and heads popped. A few managed to limp back around the bend. I rolled to my stomach to see the monstrous one charging two dozen soldiers, organized in two tiers, the front kneeling, the back standing. They did not waver as he closed in. Instead, they aimed their rifles up, taking his head.

"After them!" one cried, and the kneeling row sprinted by me.

They formed up at the sharp bend and sent another volley at the fleeing ronin.

"You! Hands where we can see them!" the one commanded.

I starfished on the sand as barrels aimed upon me. The commander's name tag read, *"Sergeant McKenna – Head of Security, BESA 01."*

"Name and rank! Now!" the sergeant ordered.

"E…Eva Jain," I stammered. "BESA 12, Marine Biologist!"

"Twelve!? What the fuck are you doing here!?"

"Ch…Charlie sent me!" I blurted. "I'm looking for Hector!"

♦

"Charlie would never send a courier, he's a face to face kind of person," said an older man in a quarantine room, identical to BESA 12's. "So, I ask again, how did you acquire his coin?"

"I told you, we were ambushed by ronin at the observatory. Charlie gave me his coin just before he died."

"Charlie would never risk going to the observatory twice."

"Well, he did in this case," I snapped.

The older man calmly nodded. "It's just that, without your coin, we cannot confirm who you are and if you are indeed from BESA 12. You managed to cross the entire country, through ronin infested lands, and did not check in at BESA 07. You could very well be a ronin, yourself."

"BESA 07 is gone, their tight beam was destroyed," I grumbled.

"How convenient."

I raised my palms. "Send a message to BESA 12. Ask for Rachel Mendez. She can confirm who I am, and that we left for Portland to ask Hector about this collar," I pointed at it.

The older man glanced at a table where it lay alongside everything else either on my person or in my pack when Sergeant McKenna arrested me. "Our tight beam went down in a fire last year," he said.

"How convenient," I bitterly retorted. "Are you a ronin?"

The older man pointed at the collar. "What's so important about this?"

"That's what John was wearing when I found him. That's what the ronin are searching for."

"Wearing?"

"John was a dog…" I said, and remembered what the ronin said at the observatory. "…The Butcher's dog from the war. There's a hard drive with a curium isotope generator, but the encryption is beyond us. Charlie said that Hector is the only person who might help."

"The Terran Files…" the older man whispered in terror.

"You're Hector, aren't you?" I stated.

He made eye contact with me. "I am."

"What are The Terran Files?" I then asked.

Hector shook his head.

I raised my hands. "Everyone I was with died trying to learn what this is and why the ronin are searching for it. I have a right to know."

Hector took a deep breath. "They contain Earth's greatest achievements and greatest horrors. Whoever possesses them, has the power to either raise humanity from the ashes, or destroy it once and for all."

◆

There was a knock on the quarantine room's door in the middle of the night, and when I opened my eyes, I saw Hector peering through the glass with a horrid expression.

He opened the door and whispered, "Come with me."

I donned my uniform, picked Frank up from my pillow and followed Hector to his office.

He shut the door, locked it, and motioned to his desk where John's collar lay. "Please, have a seat."

I sat in an old chair as he took another.

"Eva… There are things about my past that nobody knows. Things not even Charlie knew," he paused. "You see, Eva, I have a key that opens The Terran Files."

What!? I thought, feeling my heart race. "Are you a ronin, after all?"

He gave a look. "No, Eva. The opposite." He breathed deeply. "My mother was a corporal once working for New Horizons as a military engineer at the height of The Hermian War. But after New Horizons sold China to the Hermians, she began working with The Butcher to liberate countries held in corporate bondage."

I stared at Hector. "But, you're a scientist…"

"I am. Which was quite the issue for my mother. For when the time to accept a position within New Horizons's paramilitary came, I chose to immigrate to AdventureStop and work as a climatologist for their new BESA program, instead. That's where I met Charlie." He looked through me, lost in memories. "I hadn't seen my mother in ten years until AdventureStop's paramilitary joined Khasi's fight against the Hermians. I was at BESA 14 in Nevada, when she appeared at my room one night. I almost didn't recognize her. It was just after the elevators were blown and she was on the run. She simply gave me a key, saying I must protect it with my life, that it was a copy made without The Butcher's knowledge, for she did not fully trust him. That it could locate and unlock The Terran Files, and that someone named John was safeguarding them. Then, she disappeared into the shadows. I never saw her again." Hector looked at the ceiling and chuckled. "The dog… How did I not make the connection?"

He lifted a box from beneath his desk and leaned his face over it. *"Access granted,"* projected and its lid lifted with a hiss. A tiny black rectangle, no larger than a thumbnail lay within. When he placed it atop his holotile, a green light furiously blinked from the bulge of John's collar.

"Fucking Christ…" Hector gasped. "…It's real."

◆

The next evening, a young woman strolled into Hector's office with a pleasant smile and gentle demeanor, but she appeared oddly athletic.

"Carter, lock the door," Hector said, and the woman's smile vanished.

"What is it?" she said and flipped the door's latch.

"We're hoping you can help us figure that out." Hector swiveled his holotile around, displaying a login page. "It requires a username and password. Can you hack this?"

Carter's eyes went wide. "I'm just I.T... not a hacker..." she looked at the collar. "What's that?"

"It's a hard drive that contains incredible information. Something called The Terran Files."

"Fuck me…" Carter said and went pale.

"You've heard of them?" Hector asked.

"In my circle, they're rumored to contain all of Earth's information, uploaded to the most sophisticated of hard drives." She studied the collar, reading the warning, and looked up with wonder.

"Can you get into it?" Hector asked.

She pursed her lips. "I hope so."

The first day came and went, with Carter vigorously working with her holotile daisy chained to the hard drive.

The second day appeared like progress had been made, Carter clapping her hands several times and hooting. Coffee mugs and empty plates littered the desk.

The third day, she fell asleep.

The fourth day seemed hopeless until Carter suddenly raised hands with a surprised look on her face. "We're in! I think..."

Hector and I raced over, expecting to find The Terran Files up and ready to read. But, there was only code.

"I don't understand," Hector said.

Carter pointed at a line. "The username is twenty-one digits long."

"That's pretty long," Hector said.

She made a *not really* face. "The weird thing is that the password is only four digits."

"So… What are they?" I asked.

She shrugged. "No idea."

"I thought you got in," Hector said.

"I did, but we still have to figure out the username and password."

Hector sighed. "What information can you get?"

Her eyes lit up. "You wouldn't believe the capacity of this drive. Just over three zettabytes are being used, leaving another zettabyte free."

"Is that a lot?" I asked.

"Is that a lot!?" she said in shock. "All of BESA's research from every facility across North America, adds up to a few petabytes. One zettabyte equals a million petas." She thinks about that. "If we can get in, then we can upload all of our research from the last seventy years."

"What's wrong with our current storage system?" Hector asked.

"Hard drives don't last. They get brittle, they crumble." She pointed at the collar. "But this thing can last for centuries. It must be made of high density carbon."

"Diamond," Hector muttered.

"Yeah," Carter said. "But we'll need incredible energy to write new data."

"Like from a curium isotope generator?" I said, pointing at the label.

◆

We spent every waking hour racking our brains for what the username and password might be. But, after three days, we were spent.

I stared at the collar, feeling hopelessness sinking in.

Dog... came from within.

I turned to Frank.

Miss...

"I miss him, too," I whispered. "John was a good... *John!*"

Hector lurched from his slumber and Carter nearly spilled coffee onto her lap. They gave me confused looks.

"John is four digits long! That must be the password!" I shouted.

"Eva, that's way too obvious," Carter said.

"Is it? We knew John was carrying it and, still, it took us this long."

"Then, it's gotta be one hell of a weird username," Carter said.

"Might the username also be related to the dog?" Hector suggested. "Do you know what kind of dog he was?"

I nodded. "An enhanced kunming dog."

"How do you know that?"

"It was tattooed in his ear..." I froze and closed my eyes, trying to visualize the serial number. "Kunming 6834026 Enhanced."

"What?" Carter said.

"That was John's serial number! It's twenty-one digits long!" I said.

Carter stared silent for a moment, then typed the serial into the username field and, *"John,"* in for the password, then selected *Login.*

The Terran Files' main page opened.

Hector clasped a firm hand on my shoulder. "Good work, Eva! No... great work!" He turned to Carter. "You, too!"

"Look at it all," Carter said. "Where do we begin?"

I had a thought. "Maybe we search for things we need. Something like, *repair tight beam after fire.*"

She typed that exact phrase and manuals for hundreds of models, complete with step by step tutorials, appeared.

"Oh!" Carter cried. "This is exactly what we need!"

◆

The tight beam was running and Carter messaged every BESA location, including BESA 12, but no one responded.

"The satellites aren't working," she said.

"How do you know?" I asked.

"I sent a ping this morning that should immediately return, but nothing."

"Is it a temporary problem?" Hector asked.

Carter grimaced. "We haven't been able to perform routine satellite maintenance for decades, and there may be significant debris in orbit from when the elevators were destroyed. There's no way to know for sure."

"Then, we can't get the network back up," Hector responded.

"Well," Carter said. "If we revert to old radio, we might."

"Radio?" Hector gave her a look. "How so?"

"Unlike tight beam, which relies on direct line of sight, radio waves are dependent upon an atmosphere and will follow Earth's curvature."

"But the range," I said.

"We'll have to refurbish old radio towers in the Midwest to relay radio waves to our west coast locations." She looked at John's collar. "And I'm willing to bet everything we need is in there."

"Not ideal," Hector said. "But it's a beginning."

Hector and I asked every department what they needed to repair equipment, maintain the facility's small reactor, and cleanse the soil outside to farm. Meanwhile, Carter went to work building a radio transmitter and receiver from spare parts. Then, she compartmentalized The Terran Files' hard drive, giving a petabyte over for uploading BESA 01's research, with no login or password required, making it accessible to everyone.

◆

"Radio is ready," she said one morning. "But we won't know if it's working unless someone is listening."

"How do we know if they're listening?"

"They either respond, or we go to another location and build a radio there."

"Nobody's responding, right?" I asked.

Carter nodded.

"I'll talk with Sergeant McKenna about an expedition," Hector said. "How's the uploading of BESA 01's research going?"

"It's nearly done," Carter responded, looking extremely tired.

"We bring The Terran Files to the other BESA facilities," Hector said. "We establish radios there, help their crews with repairs and maintenance, and upload their research."

I pulled Charlie's drawn map and laid it across Hector's desk. "Which location should we go to first?"

Hector looked over Charlie's notes with a sad expression. "BESA 02 in Portsmouth, New Hampshire is within the region secured by Earth's soldiers after The Fall, just like here."

"What about the ronin that were chasing me?" I asked.

Hector paused to consider. "That was strange, an outlier, an act of desperation. That big equalizer was already dying."

"From what?" I asked.

Hector shrugged. "Nothing contagious."

◆

BESA 02 was abandoned, neither attacked nor starved out. *Just empty.* But its foodstuffs were still good, its storage rooms were still equipped, its archives were still intact, and its reactor was still operational. I stocked up on pickled garlic and cilantro again, and replaced my tattered undergarments.

"Well, something must have happened," Sergeant McKenna said after he swept the facility. "Their tight beam was shot."

"Just like at BESA 07's," I said.

Hector turned to the sergeant. "Are you certain this area is clear of ronin?"

"Absolutely," he responded.

Again, I thought upon the monstrous ronin on the beach.

"Then, there's no time to waste." Hector faced Carter. "Let's get that radio built and send a message home. We're desperately overcrowded there. This facility would be a welcomed relief."

As Carter again worked to restart the reactor and build the radio, I was archiving research into The Terran Files. And when Carter called BESA 01, and they responded, we breathed a sigh of relief. Three weeks later, fifty scientists arrived, claiming departments and repairing abandoned equipment.

"We must reach BESA 03," Hector said, pointing at Savannah, Georgia on Charlie's map.

"I've never gone farther south than New York City," the sergeant said, giving a stern look. "I suggest using the Appalachian trail to avoid detection." He eyed each of us. "It will be an intense two month hike." He focused on me. "Do you think you can handle it?"

I cocked my head. "I just crossed the entire country while navigating ronin, including through these little Appalachian hills you call intense," I pointed at the sergeant. "Do you think you can handle it?"

He grinned.

♦

The sergeant came rushing out of BESA 03. "Eva, there are four bodies hanging in the canteen, stripped of their flesh, just like you described at BESA 07."

My stomach dropped. "Are any of them alive?"

The sergeant shook his head. "There's heavy decomposition."

"They were likely tortured for having *John* in their names," I said.

The sergeant made a face. "Eva, you better take a look yourself."

The hair on my neck stood on end as I faced the entry.

Safe, came to mind, and I saw Frank twitching his antennae.

I slowly approached the door, catching a waft of death. The walls of the central corridor were black with mold. Bodies were strewn about in positions of agony. *A massacre...* I saw a flickering light beyond the canteen's door. I entered to find the bodies hanging, just as the sergeant said, and their limbs shriveled and covered in mold. Movement caught my eye. Their skin seemed to crawl. *Maggots,* I knew. I looked away to find a table with uniforms laid out. I studied their name tags.

"Eva Campbell."

"Sara Evagel."

"Jace Eva-Smith."

"Evan Djardins."

We burned the bodies, archived BESA 03's research, and left as quickly as possible.

♦

BESA 04, outside of New Orleans, was completely underwater, the levees that once held the ocean at bay now crumbled away.

BESA 05 was raised to the ground.

We followed the Colorado river north to Austin, Texas, domed like every other city, then into Edward's Plateau. There, BESA 06 lay completely abandoned, leaving foodstuffs and equipment behind. Once we uploaded their research and stocked up on food, we were off to BESA 07.

♦

Low bushes and shrubs overtook the blackened ground, obscuring the corpses I found eight months ago. A flurry of snow granted the landscape a strange tranquility. *But how can there be snow in August?* It wasn't until we entered the canteen that the horror returned. The three bodies still hung by their feet, but their dangling arms, faces, and midway up their torsos, were picked clean. I imagined wolves and coyotes leaping to grab flesh.

"Okay," Carter said. "We must do things differently here. First, I'll get the reactor online while you download their research, then we head to the Forte Radio Tower northeast of here to refurbish its transmitter."

The sergeant nodded. "In the meantime, I'll familiarize myself with BESA 07's surroundings." He turned to me. "Eva, you're the only one who's been here, your insight would be greatly appreciated."

"Sure," I said, and turned to Frank. "You gotta stay. It's freezing outside."

"Mer!" Frank protested, but climbed down my arm to a canteen table.

"It's like he really understands you," Hector said.

If only he knew, I thought.

The sergeant and I exited the facility to strange darkness looming above despite it being noon. I looked towards the mountain peaks, finding them completely obscured.

"What is it?" the sergeant said, giving me a concerned look.

"The Rockies should be clearly visible," I responded.

A gust of wind struck my cheeks, prickling my skin, and particles clinked against BESA 07's metal door.

"Sleet!? Now!? What's happening!?" Sergeant McKenna cried.

I racked my brain trying to understand. *The radiation cloud!?* I thought. The sleet became hail the size of marbles. Soon, golf balls thumped into the ground. "Get inside!" We quickly hid to either side of the open entry, pressing against the walls as hail shot down BESA 07's main corridor. "We gotta close the door!"

"How!?" the sergeant shouted over the cacophony. "No power!"

I pointed at a large wheel against the corridor, its gears looking orange and crunchy. I tried cranking, but it would not budge.

Sergeant McKenna leapt across the corridor, taking a baseball-sized chunk of ice to the thigh. He grimaced and grasped the wheel.

Still, it would not budge.

We're going to die!

A rapping came from deeper down the corridor. I looked its way to see an overturned steel table coming towards us, the hail denting its surface. When it passed us, I realized Carter and Hector were on the back side, pushing.

They nestled to the side of the corridor, using the wall to partially brace the table and deflect the hail. Carter joined us at the wheel.

I felt grinding and giving, until the wheel lurched. A quarter turn became a half turn. A full turn became another. The door slowly crept across the entryway.

A deafening bang came, and I saw Hector reel back, barely holding the table upright, and a basketball sized piece of hail rolled down the corridor. More bangs racked the exterior door as it closed and its metal vibrated like a speaker.

Hector ditched the table and we raced deeper into the facility, navigating treacherous ice balls. Only when we entered the reactor room and Hector sealed its door did the racket finally dampen. "Is everyone okay!?"

Sergeant McKenna pointed at a swollen knot midway up his thigh. "I think it's fractured!"

◆

The percussion stopped early morning. Hector lit a heat cube as we woke in the old reactor room.

"Hector, Carter," I said. "Thanks for coming to our rescue."

Hector was quiet for a moment. "Believe it or not, it was Frank."

"What?" I asked, looking at my little companion.

"We couldn't hear the hail back here and would not have come in time. But Frank was tugging at our pant legs, desperately pulling us to the door, and stunk of onions. It wasn't until I entered the corridor for fresh air did I realize what was happening."

I looked at Frank stretching his claws to the heat cube for warmth. *He knew I was in danger even when isolated.*

Frank turned to me. *Safe.*

"Thank you, Frank," I said, then turned to Hector. "What caused this?"

Hector frowned. "We hypothesized something like this might happen after nuclear fallout. But after a hundred years. I thought we were in the clear for several more decades." He gave me a concerned look. "The hail was getting tremendous by the end. I fear we might be blocked in."

"Only one way to find out," I said. "Supply room has winter gear."

We emerged from the reactor room, huddled around Hector's heat cube casting soft light and illuminating massive chunks of hail frozen solid in the corridor. We entered the supply room and eagerly donned heavy undergarments and coats. I placed Frank inside my coat's pocket.

"The hail near the door is melting. It's warm outside," I said when we reached the dented front door.

"So, the hail should melt away," Carter responded.

"Or refreeze to become one giant block," the sergeant said. "Let's open the door."

Together, we cranked. Dull sunlight peeked through the door's crack, but the hail had warped it so much it wedged tight at a half meter open. Monstrous chunks of hail piled above the door's header.

As Carter and Hector raced to restart the reactor, Sergeant McKenna and I chopped the ice, breaking off chunks and sliding them down the corridor. But as nightly refreezes came, the ice was becoming glacier-like.

After a week, the reactor roared to life and the heating system furiously went to work. We cranked it to full and cracked the door at night to keep the ice outside from refreezing.

By the second week, we cleared enough to see bright blue sky.

After week three, we dug a tunnel wide enough to squeeze through.

◆

"When should we make for the radio tower?" I halfheartedly asked, convinced it no longer existed after the storm.

Hector sighed. "Carter's still building the new components. Until then, we sit tight."

I turned to Frank on my shoulder. "We'll be in Quantum Mechanics, uploading research, then."

Hector nodded.

I entered Quantum Mechanics, linked the hard drive to their mainframe, and watched its download begin. "And now, we wait," I whispered to Frank.

He perked up and pointed at an isolation tank in the back of the room.

I felt a sudden yearning to know if he was still speaking with Sydney. I dusted off the tank and connected it to power. Then, I placed Frank inside and opened a hologram displaying his brain activity.

Nothing appeared.

Are they no longer linked? I thought.

A flicker appeared in Frank's brain.

There we go, I thought. *Is everyone okay back home?*

Frank's brain flickered again.

Be okay, came to me.

My gaze shifted from the hologram to the isolation tank. Frank was staring at me through the glass despite it being completely opaque from his side. I raised my hand and waved. Frank lifted his claw and waved back. I breathed deeply and eyed several electrical sensors in the second isolation tank. I retrieved one and another hologram projected. When I placed the sensor at my temple, thousands of electrical signals formed a distinctly human brain.

Frank? I thought and saw several portions of my brain flicker. At the exact same moment, that spot in Frank's brain also flashed.

Eva... returned to me alongside another flash.

My lip trembled, my eyes welled.

What... wrong? Frank said.

I'm scared, I thought back.

Me... too...

I quickly approached Frank's tank and opened its hatch. He was at its edge with claws raised like a baby welcoming a parent. He smelled of onions and I felt oiliness on his shell. *Every time he's scared,* I realized.

I cut the download and unlinked the hard drive. Then, I bee-lined to BESA 07's biology department to its electron microscope and DNA sequencer. As they booted, I found a swab, wiped Frank's shell, then placed it into a sterilized glass tube.

What do? Frank asked.

I'm trying to understand how we're linked, I thought back.

Oh... Frank gently tapped the glass tube containing the swab.

I placed Frank on my shoulder and captained the microscope. *Like riding a bike,* I thought as my hands found the controls. Its hologram was up and ready. I opened the sterilized tube and inserted the swab into the scope's analysis port. It went to work, breaking down chemicals and proteins.

"97.2% Plasma," appeared on hologram, listing the usual suspects. But after several minutes it flashed, *"Unknown Object Detected!"*

"Isolate," I commanded.

It switched from chemical breakdowns to magnification. Strange cells appeared. *Or is this a separate organism altogether?* I pondered, watching these strange cells use cilia to swim. *If only the net still existed. I could run—The Terran Files!* I connected the hard drive and breathed deeply. "Compare unidentified object to all information within The Terran Files."

It sifted through thousands of files in the blink of an eye. Minutes passed. An hour came and went. The hologram updated from, *"Unknown Object,"* to, *"Unidentified Virus... Waterborne—Confirmed... Airborne—Pending Further Analysis."*

A virus? I studied the files currently being compared in The Terran Files.

It was research from a multi-billion dollar company called Spare Parts. I opened a third hologram and sifted through the company's research and development.

"Kwai Lan," I whispered. I dug further into her Regenerative Cloning thesis, noting how she pioneered DNA transfer from flatworms to humans using RNA, mimicking a virus's ability to horizontally transfer DNA from one creature to another. I looked at the isolated virus from Frank.

"Analyze the DNA within the unidentified virus," I commanded.

"Secondary DNA detected," appeared. *"Unidentified Crustacean."*

My heart raced. "What part of Crustacean DNA is this?"

"Brain cell — 94.87% Probability."

I clenched my jaw and eyed a pack of auto-syringes. I slowly pulled one out. *I must know...* I thought as I peeled its seal, removed the syringe, and activated its extraction function. A red light flashed. I brought the syringe to my temple.

"Fuck!" I pushed it in, feeling a sudden migraine hit. I listened to its mechanism gently extracting brain tissue accompanied by a flashing light. Its light went green. "Fuck, fuck, fuck!" I pulled the syringe from my temple, and the migraine ceased.

Frank looked at me with concern. *Why?*

I'm getting to the bottom of this, I thought back, and placed the syringe into the microscope's port. "Analyze brain tissue for anomalies."

"Anomaly Detected," immediately displayed, then, *"Unidentified Virus."*

"Compare unidentified viruses from Sample A with Sample B. Are they the same virus?" I asked.

"99.9% match."

"Is crustacean DNA within Virus B as well?" I followed up.

"Negative."

What? I thought. *Maybe it's already delivered.* "Analyze my brain tissue for crustacean DNA."

"DNA match found." It highlighted a portion of my brain with Frank's DNA spliced in.

"Holy shit," I whispered, watching the small portion of my brain flickering in sync with Frank's. "You built a quantum connection in my head, you little bastard."

♦

Carter completed the radio components, and Sergeant McKenna found the best route north to the tower. Each step upon the hail felt more treacherous than the tide pools I negotiated with Rachel. Wyoming's Badlands appeared like an endless ice sheet.

After two days, the radio tower stood ominously in the distance, seemingly unharmed, but as we neared I saw that the tower's members were bent and dented. The station itself was pulverized.

"We don't need the station, just the tower," Carter said before we could ask. She gazed upward. "But we must climb to its top to install the new components."

"That's if it's salvageable," Hector said.

"Yeah," she responded.

"How tall is this thing?" Sergeant McKenna asked.

"Over three hundred and fifty meters," Carter squeaked. "I don't know if I can do this…"

"Are you kidding me!?" Hector snapped, giving her a death stare. "You were the one who dragged us out here!"

Carter's hands trembled.

"I'll go with you," I said, and they turned to me. "I have the tethers and carabiners we need, and experience climbing." I gave the tower's endless lattice of horizontal and diagonal members a hard look. "I estimate five hours up and four hours down. Which means, we must start before dawn. It will be physically grueling and deadly cold. If there is any reason to turn back, we turn back." I stared right at Carter. "Understood?"

Sergeant McKenna, Hector, and Carter looked at me blankly.

"Understood?" I repeated.

"Understood," Carter muttered.

♦

We bundled in extra layers and donned goggles, face muffs, and thick mittens. It was an hour before dawn. Frigid wind sent pins and needles across my cheeks despite the face muff, and our breaths appeared like snuffed campfires. Carter's posture gave away her terror.

"Listen to my instructions and we'll be okay," I said and pulled tethers from my pack, strapping two to each of our harnesses. "Each tether has a carabiner at its end which must be attached to a structural member at all times. Two is better," I demonstrated a few maneuvers. "Use your arms as little as possible, especially your grip. If you must rest, loop your arm, using the crux of your elbow to hold your weight. Your legs are your climbing force, no matter how tired they might get. I will set the pace. We must go slow to prevent sweating. Sweating kills us."

"Okay," Carter whispered. "But… Can you take the equipment?"

I remembered carrying John strapped to my back up the cliff side. *Once upon a time...* "How heavy is it altogether?"

"About twenty kilos," she said.

"Done," I responded and saw relief in her eyes.

The first fifty meters was not so bad. But then, the steel's frigidness seeped through my mittens, and the wind picked up, causing a sway in the tower that grew more present as we climbed.

At a hundred meters, the sun rose, its rays piercing through my goggles, but it did not provide the warmth I hoped for. *At least the wind died down.* I dared a look down to see a world of ice shimmering in the sunlight like an ocean.

Massive pops rang at two hundred meters, shuddering the tower.

"What the fuck was that!?" Carter cried.

"Metal expanding in the sunlight's warmth," I said.

"But it's freezing!"

"It's less freezing than before," I replied.

"Should we turn back!" Carter asked.

"The tower undergoes contraction and expansion everyday. So, no."

Carter quietly muttered, "Okay."

We climbed for the next hour in silence, glancing down at the landscape.

"What's that?" Carter asked, pointing to the northeast.

I shielded my eyes from the sun. Among the endless sea of white was a minuscule patch of rusty land.

"No idea," I responded. "We'll have a better view from the top."

"How much further is it? My fingers are numb and my soles feel like I'm stepping on daggers," she grumbled.

"About a hundred meters more," I answered.

Wind picked up again and the temperature plummeted. The tower swayed deeply and, with no reference to judge movement, my stomach gurgled.

"I'm gonna be sick," Carter whined. "Can we turn back now?"

I peered at the rust colored patch of land and noticed the coloration had bands to it, like the rings of a tree. "If you keep your eyes focused up, the nausea will dissipate," I said, not sure if that was true.

The wind eventually died down in the afternoon. I finally saw the transmitter at the top. "Carter, we're almost there!"

No response.

I looked down. She was gone. I began hyperventilating, imagining her falling to her death. But then, I caught movement along the structure. I looped my arm through a member and fumbled into my jacket for my binoculars. When they auto-enhanced, I saw Carter uncoupling and coupling the tethers, working her way down. *She must have turned back an hour ago,* I realized and whispered, "So close." I locked my two carabiners, leaned back to rest my hands, removed the pack with the radio components, and strapped it tightly to the tower.

I was about to start back down, when the rusty patch of land again caught my eye. A portion was black now. *Shadow?* I raised my binoculars, focusing on the patch. *It's a canyon...* I further zoomed, making out vehicles at the canyon's floor parked along a road. *How is this place free of ice?* I recorded the road winding in and out of canyon walls, ending at a gray square built into the rock. My binoculars measured the square to be thirty meters tall by thirty meters wide.

My holotile buzzed, signaling our point of no return. *We didn't even make it to the top let alone install the equipment.* I took coordinates of the canyon, then stowed my binoculars into my heavy coat.

My fingers were numb and my feet were throbbing as I worked my way down. The sun dipped low by the time I caught Carter. Not a word was exchanged. The sun set and our headlamps came back on. My teeth chattered. More pops shuddered as the tower's steel contracted. Finally, thirteen hours after we began, we touched down.

Sergeant McKenna and Hector rushed us into our basecamp tent, stripped off our heavy coats, and wrapped heat blankets around our shuddering bodies.

Hector gave a concerned look. "I didn't realize it was going to be this dangerous." He paused. "Didn't people once do this for a living?"

"It w-was the m-most dangerous j-job in the w-world," I responded through shivers.

"Well, I'm glad its over," Hector said, handing us mugs of steaming tea. "I'm guessing the new components were installed without a hitch?"

"Uh…" Carter said.

"We d-didn't reach the t-top," I said.

Hector cocked his head. "Where's the equipment, then?"

Carter looked at me.

"I l-left it on the t-tower for w-when we return."

They gave me horrified looks.

"No point in carrying it up t-twice," I argued.

"I'm n-never doing that again," Carter muttered.

"What!?" Sergeant McKenna blurted. "We spent months getting out here, specifically for this! We can't just chalk it up as a loss!" He composed himself. "Is there another way to establish a relay?"

As Carter said, "No," I said, "Maybe."

They turned to me.

"We f-found a red p-patch in the ice-field. I took a r-recording." I retrieved my binoculars and tried pairing to my holotile with shuddering hands.

"I'll set it up," Sergeant McKenna said.

My recording opened, following the canyon walls and vehicles, all the way to the massive square.

"What is it?" Hector said. "How's it free of ice?"

I shrugged. "Maybe there's a significant heat s-source."

"This looks military," the sergeant said. "Do you have coordinates?"

I nodded.

"Let's see what The Terran Files say," he said.

I unlatched the collar from my belt and handed it to the sergeant. He linked it to my holotile, then input the coordinates.

"Access Denied."

"And that would mean military," he said. "Carter, can you get through?"

With shaky hands, she opened her negotiation program, but nothing happened. She made a face. "It's n-not even allowing me to start."

"What do you mean?" Hector asked.

"It's blocked through its h-hardware."

"Can you fix that?" Hector followed up.

"No…" Carter flipped the collar around, to the key and looked at Hector. "You said y-your mother made a c-copy of the original. There might have b-been hardware inscription designed to limit duplication."

"So there's no way of finding out what it is," Sergeant McKenna said.

"We c-could go there," I said. "It didn't l-look more than a f-few day's t-travel." I looked at Carter. "It's t-too windy and cold to climb the t-tower again right now. We can use this t-time to check the canyon out. If there's n-nothing there, then w-we come b-back and install the t-tower components as originally p-planned."

♦

For three days we negotiated melting and refreezing ice. Every slight incline or decline was treated like we were crossing a glacier's crevasse.

On the fourth day, patches of mud appeared. And then, we crested a hill and the canyon revealed like the page of a pop-up book. I pulled my binoculars and focused on the vehicles.

"Definitely military," I said.

Is anyone there? I thought to Frank.

No tell, he responded.

"At least the mud didn't completely consume them. I guess that means it's not deep," Carter said.

I focused on the trucks' wheels. "Actually, it looks dry."

"What?" Sergeant McKenna said, and I handed him my binoculars. "How is that possible? Ice melt should be draining into the canyon. It should be a swamp."

Hector cleared his throat. "I think you're assuming that this canyon resides at a lower elevation than the surrounding landscape."

"That's a good thing to assume," the sergeant responded.

Hector shook his head. "These are the Black Hills. What you are calling a canyon is actually a ravine whose floor resides at a higher elevation. Ice melt would flow out, not in."

"But we're looking down upon it," the sergeant said.

"Are we?" Hector challenged.

As we approached, the ground began to incline, and the sound of rushing water came. It was not until a portion of the ice opened that we understood we were atop a river. A warm draft seeped between the seams of my goggles and face muff, and the ice thinned until, at last, we stepped upon dry earth at the mouth of the ravine. We removed our jackets and I placed Frank on my shoulder.

Weird, he said to me.

Very weird, I responded.

No... Frank said. *Warm weird.*

I thought about that and turned to Carter. "Do you have a geiger counter?"

She gave me a strange look. "I have an old refurbished one." She pulled it from her pack and flipped it on.

"Radiation Detected!" opened on hologram.

She froze. "There must be a reactor inside. It might be leaking."

"How bad?" the sergeant asked.

"Two hundred forty-seven rads," Carter said. "It could cause cancer if exposed over time."

"Is it safe to investigate, then?" the sergeant followed up.

"Yes, if we are quick about it."

"That explains the warmth," Hector added.

We continued onward with Carter's geiger counter monitoring, rounding twists and turns along the ravine's central road with military trucks rusted through. Finally, a massive steel door revealed at the end.

"Its gears are fused," Sergeant McKenna said as he inspected its jamb. "There's no way to open it."

"There might be another way in," Carter said, pointing at a ladder next to the door, running up the side of the ravine.

"I thought you hated climbing," I said.

"This is only fifty meters, not three hundred and fifty," she said. "I think we should try."

The sergeant turned to me. "Do you still have the climbing gear?"

"I do," I responded, "Carter and I can go first and set a belay for you and Hector."

"Sounds good to me," the sergeant said. "But if there's nothing at the top, come down immediately."

"Understood," Carter said.

She took the lead this time, quickly climbing the ladder. *Expertly climbing the ladder,* I noted.

"We're almost there!" she excitedly said, and when she reached the top, she pointed. "There's a way in!"

What's happening? When I joined her I saw hundreds of rusty domes, each of them four meters in width, stretching into the distance. Carter was peering inside one that was cracked open.

She turned to me. "It drops straight down! Let's set the belay!"

When Hector and Sergeant McKenna reached the top they paused.

"What?" I asked.

"These are missile silos," the sergeant said.

"But, look here!" Carter beamed. "This one is open. We can rappel down with Eva's ropes!"

Hector gave Carter a strange look.

He senses it, too, I realized.

"This seems extremely dangerous," Hector said.

"The rewards might be worth it," the sergeant reluctantly responded.

"I'll go first!" Carter turned to me. "Can you belay!?"

With her helmet lamp on, Carter dropped into pitch darkness.

"Whoa," she said after a few minutes.

"What is it?" Hector called through the open panel.

"There's a missile," Carter said. "It's huge."

When she reached the bottom, I recoiled the rope and belayed Hector. Then, I went down and set a bottom belay to lower Sergeant McKenna.

He touched down with horror on his face. "That missile is a nuke."

Carter checked her geiger counter. "Still the same rads."

We placed our gear on the concrete floor, then passed from one silo after another, with missiles so tall our headlamps could not illuminate their noses.

A sudden cry came from the darkness ahead.

"Sounds like a bird." Carter cupped hands around her mouth, and cried, "Coo-rah!"

There was a pause, then several more bird calls came.

"This way!" Carter pointed in the direction of the calls. "They likely nested in the warmest spot, which might be a control center with a radio."

We timidly followed her, glancing at one another.

Not bird! Frank shouted in my head.

"Stop! Something's wrong!" I said.

Hector and Sergeant McKenna froze.

Carter calmly turned around with a nervous smile. "It's okay… This is my home."

"Carter!" a woman's voice pierced the darkness. "You cerrrtainly took yourrr time!"

The sergeant, Hector, and I jolted.

A tall, old, but incredibly strong woman, emerged from the darkness. More people followed. *Tens. Hundreds.* Each was built like a former Olympian. Several were impossibly large.

"Mom!" Carter excitedly said. "I brought Eva! She has The Terran Files!"

The old woman spun my way and her eyes dilated like an owl's. "y'Is this trrrue? Do you possess the files?"

I backed away until metallic footsteps thumped behind me.

"Well!?" the woman urged.

"It's true…" I squeaked.

Thunderous cheers echoed from the darkness, followed by an incredible chanting of, "Honorrr!"

The old woman raised her fist, silencing them. "Then y'Eva, you must help y'us."

"W-Who are you?" I dared to ask.

The woman grinned. "y'I was y'once y'a grrreat generrral, leading y'a campaign y'against y'Earrrth, beforrre The Fall."

"General Kase…" I whispered.

"Mommy!" came, and from the sea of ronin bounded a little girl, perhaps four years old.

Carter's face lit up. "Beverly!" She knelt to receive her daughter's reckless embrace.

♦

"I'm sorry that I lied," Carter said as she escorted us to a room converted to a cell, flanked by a massive man, reminding me of the one who chased me on the beach. I could not help notice that his hands constantly shook.

"Was everything a lie?" I pointedly asked Carter. "Are the satellites really gone? Is radio our only means of communication? Was the tower just a ploy to get me to see this ravine?"

She gave a shameful nod. "The satellites are gone. Radio is our only communication. But the tower could have never become a relay. The distance is too great."

"But you spent all that time building the components," Hector said.

Carter shrugged. "They were just junk parts I found lying around."

"Fucking hell!" Sergeant McKenna snapped. "How did you get past our security in the first place!?"

She sighed. "My mother is Hermian, but I was born here. I'm Terran, just like you."

The sergeant shook his head. "You're a ronin!"

Carter raised her arms. "We're just trying to survive."

"By murdering everyone else!?" the sergeant spat.

"y'A necessarrry y'evil," General Kase abruptly said and entered. "y'Eva, come with me."

I did not budge.

She paused in the doorway and pointed at the monstrous man. "Don't make Loyd drrrag you."

I followed the old woman down tight hallways, with Loyd thumping behind me, to mechanical rooms below the missile silos, and growing warm. Kase opened a hatch with a heavy clunk and a waft of heat brushed my cheeks. Amber light washed across concrete walls and ceiling. A sphere at the center of the massive chamber glowed white hot. Around the sphere were hundreds of people laying on cots looking horrifically sick.

"Is it a plague?" I asked.

"y'In y'a mannerrr," the general said. "y'It y'is y'a plague y'of y'our y'own making, y'a plague y'of genetics. y'Our grrreat Dirrrectorrr believed human potential had y'only just been scrrratched, that with the correct y'adjustments, we could become gods. And doctorrr Kaladian was the conduit for which The Dirrrectorrr's vision became rrreality." She sighed. "But y'our gifts come y'at y'a grrreat cost, y'especially forrr y'ourrr y'equalizers." She motioned to Loyd. "You see, y'Eva, therrre comes y'a time y'in y'all y'of y'ourrr Herrrmian lives y'in which we y'abrrruptly crrrumble frrrom the y'inside y'out."

"Kaladian Degradation," I whispered.

"So, you know."

"I've heard the rumors."

"But what you don't know, y'is that The Dirrrectorrr was searrrching forrr y'a currre, y'even going so farrr y'as to collaborrrate with doctorrr Sharrrai y'on Earrrth."

"Did he find one?" I asked.

"They found y'an y'avenue that might become y'a currre, but this rrresearrrch was lost durrring The Fall. y'Or so we thought." Kase lifted John's collar. "y'If The Terran Files trrruly hold y'all y'of y'Earth's knowledge, then y'it must contain this rrresearrrch y'as well." She took a deep breath. "y'Eva, will you help y'us?"

◆

"Dammit!" Carter cussed.

"What's the prrroblem?" Kase asked.

"It won't let me access Dr. Sharai's research."

Kase gave me a burning look. "Why can't we y'access them?"

"There's something wrong with the copied key," I said. "It can only access non-military information."

"But this isn't military," Carter said.

"It's for the Hermian Infantry, right?" I retorted.

The old general thought about that. "Might you know wherrre the y'orrriginal key y'is, then?"

I thought about when I first found John. I shook my head.

"Let me rrrephrrrase." Kase leaned closer. "Wherrre did you find The Terran Files?"

I remained silent.

"y'Eva, must y'I rrresorrrt to morrre perrrsuasive tactics?"

"I…I found them outside BESA 12, where I was stationed," I confessed.

"We've scourrred that y'arrrea y'and found nothing. How y'is y'it that you found them?"

I tried to choose my words carefully. "They were not hiding in a specific location. They were mobile."

"How can that be?" Kase followed up, tilting her ear.

She's listening to my heart beat, I realized. "I got them from John."

"So, John does y'exist," Kase said. "How did you convince him to give them to you? y'Or did you take them by forrrce?"

"Uh…" Carter said.

Kase gave her daughter an annoyed look. "Well, y'out with y'it."

"John was a dog," Carter said.

Kase narrowed her brow. "What?"

"The Butcher's dog," she clarified.

Kase looked up at the ceiling, her eyes darting side to side, racking her brain. "The Butcherrr's dog… y'Of courrrse," she whispered. Her eyes lowered, focusing on me. "y'It must still be with the dog. Wherrre y'is it?"

My lower lip trembled. "He… died a year and a half ago."

"Wherrre!?" she snapped.

"In the Coastal Range… At an observatory," I quietly said.

Kase's eyes widened, her jaw clenched, and her hands trembled. "The Glendale y'Obserrrvatorrry!?"

How did she guess!? My breathing escalated. "Yes."

The old woman furiously paced back and forth, waving her hands wildly and moaning. The others stepped back, even Carter. She suddenly whirled my direction and closed the gap between us. Her eyes dilated rapidly, her face contorted. "y'It was you!" she shouted, her spittle sprinkling my face. "You killed my husband!" Kase looked to the ceiling again and breathed deeply. Her trembling subsided. She slowly grabbed my uniform collar and effortlessly lifted me from the ground. "y'Eva!" she said with terrible coldness. "Show me y'exactly wherrre John died!"

◆

Everything within me wanted to bolt off the trail, but I knew the ronin would either hunt me down or harm Hector and the sergeant in retaliation. Kase led the way to the observatory with several of her best soldiers in heavy armor and monstrous Loyd at our backs.

The trees shrunk as oxygen reduced. Barren rock replaced dirt trails. And then, the observatory's blackened dome appeared.

Here? Again? Frank asked. *Why?*

We're looking for John, I thought back.

John... Gone.

I know, I thought.

Kase silently approached the observatory's metal door, warped by the heat of the blaze, and tore it from its hinges. The rest quietly knelt outside with fists upon shoulders.

"Fuck!" Kase finally cried and exited, her hands black with soot and grasping something gray in her hands.

A skull, I realized.

She locked eyes with me, lifted the skull, and turned its features my way. Its jaw was magnificent and its brow was proud, but its most striking feature was a pea-sized hole between the eyes. "y'A twenty-two?" she said. "y'A fucking twenty-two!? He deserrrved betterrr!" She gently touched the small entry hole. "But, you have y'one hell y'of y'a shot!"

"It wasn't me," I squeaked.

"Then, who was y'it!?" she snapped.

"It doesn't matter. He was killed, too," I said. "I'm the sole survivor."

"Give me y'a name! y'I must know who killed my husband!?"

"Charlie..." I said.

"What!?" Hector blurted.

Kase faced him. "How do you know him!? y'I thought you werrre frrrom differrrent facilities!?"

Hector silenced.

Kase pulled her pistol from its holster and aimed it at my head.

Hector sighed. "We were lovers, a long time ago."

"y'Is that so?" Kase raised her husband's skull and lunged.

Hector did not try to run. He simply closed his eyes as the skull crunched into the side of his head, toppling him to the ground.

Kase mounted him, pounding the skull deeper into his face, crushing his nose, shattering his teeth, and breaking his orbital bones. With a final crunch, she stopped and rose to her feet, holding the bloodstained skull high above her head. "y'In death! Patyrrr finds his honorrr!"

"Honorrr! Honorrr! Honorrr!" the ronin chanted, their voices rumbling in my chest. "May he be shepherrrded y'into the light!"

I stared at Hector's mutilated face and the blood running down the rock. I did not wince or cry. I felt nothing.

Kase tossed her husband's skull like it no longer held value and pointed at Hector's body. "Clean y'and quarrrterrr him! His meat y'is toxin frrree!"

My stomach finally turned. I fell to my knees and heaved.

"y'And you, y'Eva!" Kase shouted. "Show me wherrre John is!"

I pointed and muttered, "The rocks."

The old general ordered two ronin to pull the rocks away.

John's charred bones slowly appeared. Ronin furiously searched the ground and rocks around his grave. When they found nothing, they pulled mallets and began cracking his bones.

"y'Eva!" Kase said. "y'If we cannot find this key, then this y'is what happens to you!" She pointed at Hector's body, arms already cleaved off, and his muscle being carved from bone.

I met Sergeant McKenna's gaze and we held for what seemed like hours.

"Therrre's nothing herrre," the ronin finally reported.

She turned to me. "y'It's time you take y'us to BESA 12!"

♦

Waves crashing against rocks and sifting through barnacles and seaweed was the most beautiful sound in the world. A lone, tranquil moment, until I glanced at Kase.

She gave an excited look, as did all her ronin.

"We make camp herrre tonight!" She set her pack on the sand and plopped onto her butt.

I spied Kase's pack where John's collar now lived.

Her ronin set up tents and gathered firewood. And my disgust reached new heights when they started dining on the jerky made from Hector's flesh.

Loyd caught me glaring. "What y'are you looking y'at!?" he snapped, then studied his jerky. "You must be starrrving. You surrre you don't want to trrry? Yourrr frrriend y'is delicious."

The sergeant and I were running purely on water, having refused to consume Hector's flesh, of which I knew the ronin were running low on. *It'll be the sergeant next,* I thought, knowing Kase wanted me alive to find the key. *If it even exists.*

Make food, Frank said in my mind. *Food for all...*

I studied the tide pools. *Yes, I can do that,* I thought and placed Frank on my shoulder.

"Eva, you can't swim away," the sergeant whispered, watching me study the shoreline. "You'll freeze to death in the water."

"That's not what I'm thinking," I responded, pulled a towel and twine from my pack, and approached Loyd.

"What do you want!?" he said.

I pointed at the jerky. "You're almost out of this, right?"

He gave me a skeptical look. "Yeah, why?"

"Can I have this piece before it's gone?" I asked.

"Well, y'I'll be damned." He handed me the piece, waiting for me to try.

They're all watching, I realized. I pointed at a large cook pot.

"Surrre, cook y'it y'if you must," Loyd said with a grin.

I took the pot and jerky and turned to Sergeant McKenna. "Come."

He timidly stood and followed me to the tide pools. I handed him the pot and lined the bottom of it with the towel.

"Fill it half way with seawater," I said.

The sergeant lowered it into a tide pool.

"You betterrr not waste that!" Loyd shouted after us.

"y'It's y'a burrrial y'at sea!" Kase snapped. "Let them have theirrr custom!"

"Weirrrd fucking custom," Loyd grumbled.

"Eva, what the hell are we doing?" the sergeant whispered, awkwardly holding the pot.

Frank pointed his claw at the nearest tide pool. *There.*

"Watch," I said and maneuvered over the first rock. Frigid ocean spray speckled my cheeks and wind chapped my lips. I knotted the twine around the jerky, knelt, and lowered the baited line into the water. For several minutes, nothing, then legs slowly emerged from beneath a rock followed by an armored head. *Dungeness crab...*

"Oh…" the sergeant muttered.

It extended its claw to the jerky and the moment it clamped, I slowly reeled the line, pulling the crab to the surface, hoping it would hold tight.

"Bring the pot closer," I whispered.

The sergeant lowered the pot to the water's surface.

"We don't have a net, so get ready to catch," I instructed.

"Okay," he responded.

The crab broke the surface and I flicked it towards the pot. Its legs scrambled about, but the sergeant maneuvered the pot to catch.

"Nice one!" I said.

"Now, what?" he asked.

"We go again," I said and moved to the next pool, lowered my line, and snagged another.

Two quickly became several. The ronin were on their feet, staring perplexed. When the pot was full, we returned to camp and set it next to a fire being lit.

"How y'in Sol did you do that!?" Loyd hollered.

"y'It doesn't matterrr, they'rrre toxic," said another.

I ignored them and returned to the tide pools.

Sergeant McKenna followed. "Eva, they're right. The crabs are toxic. What's the point of all this?"

"See this seaweed?" I said, pointing at a tubular plant on the rocks.

"Yeah…"

"Collect as much as you can."

"Have you lost it?"

I did not answer him and began collecting. We returned, with arms full, to a fire going strong and I waved for the ronin to step aside. They snapped their heads to Kase.

She raised a hand, signaling for them to move, then said, "You know you'll die, rrright?"

I rolled two large pieces of driftwood to each side of the fire, creating a stable base. Then, I bundled the towel ends hanging out of the pot and pulled the crabs from the seawater, letting the water drain back into the pot. "Don't let the towel touch the sand and don't let them escape," I said to Loyd, handing him the bundled crabs.

He looked at Kase, whom nodded, and he took the bundle.

I set the pot above the fire and faced Loyd. "Knife."

"y'I don't think so," he grumbled.

"Are you afraid a little girl will best you?" I asked and heard snickers.

Loyd clenched his jaw and handed me his skinning knife.

"Sergeant," I said, waving him closer. I took a tubular seaweed stalk from his arms, placed it into my mouth, and bit.

"What the fuck?" ronin whispered.

I chopped the stalks into little rings, letting them drop into the pot. The water began to steam, then boil. I broke down several more and added my own seasoning and the pickled garlic and cilantro I had foraged from BESA storerooms. I then collected milkweed from the edge of the beach and added that, too. The ronin were entranced by the boiling water and heavenly smell. After ten minutes, I turned to Loyd and extended my hand.

"This y'is the strrrangest way to commit suicide," he said, handing me the bundled towel.

I positioned the crabs above the pot, then dipped them into the boiling water. I let go of the bunched knot and removed just the towel. The crabs thrashed for several seconds, then they became still and turned bright red.

"Fucking chrrrist!" a ronin said, sniffing the air.

"This y'is not suicide, this y'is murrrderrr!" Loyd quipped.

"y'Only y'if you'rrre dumb y'enough to trrry," said another.

"y'I think y'I might be dumb y'enough," Loyd said, inhaling the scent.

Kase silently stared at the stew. I could see the wheels turning in her head, trying to comprehend my insanity.

Is it ready? I thought to Frank.

His antenna twitched. *Close.*

The sun was low and we huddled around the fire for warmth.

Frank's antennae twitched. *It's ready.*

I calmly stood with my stainless mug and tongs in hand. Ronin eyes locked onto me as I retrieved a crab, several chunks of seaweed, and a garlic clove. I sat on the sand and popped a piece of stalk into my mouth, breathing heavily as it seared the roof of my mouth. Then, I flipped over the crab, collected its legs in one hand, and held its armored head down. When I pulled, the shell split, revealing freshly cooked meat. I pinched with my fingers and inserted it into my mouth.

Gasps came from around the fire.

"Eva…" the sergeant whispered in disbelief.

I ignored them and gave a piece to Frank to munch on.

"y'I did not think you'd go thrrrough with y'it," Loyd said, astonished. "You, young lady, have y'earrrned my rrrespect."

"I'm not committing suicide, you idiot," I said and sucked meat from one of the legs.

Silence all around.

"Test the stew," Kase ordered.

The ronin looked at her confused.

Her eyes narrowed. "y'I said test y'it!"

Loyd pulled a tab and slowly dipped it into the stew. It turned red. "Toxic." He faced me. "You'll be dead y'in y'an hourrr."

"You sure about that?" I took another bite.

He narrowed his brutish brow and placed another tab into my mug. Again, it turned red. "Yep."

"y'Eva, y'explain yourrrself," Kase said.

I sighed deeply. "The molecules within seaweed, milkweed, cilantro, and garlic bond with methylmercury and radiation, among thousands of other toxins, helping them to pass harmlessly through our systems."

"y'I don't believe you," Kase said.

"In an hour, you will," I fished out another crab. "Whose hungry?"

The sergeant lifted his mug and I served him crab with seaweed and a garlic clove. He gave it a long stare, then flipped over the crab, gathered its legs, and cracked its shell. When he inserted the meat into his mouth, his eyes closed and his posture slouched. Then, he moaned.

An hour came and went. A second hour passed. The sergeant and I ate seconds. Then, thirds. The ronin restlessly stirred. And then, the growling of one's stomach came.

"Don't y'even think y'of y'it!" Kase snapped. "y'Everrryone, to yourrr tents, now!"

♦

Sergeant McKenna and I crawled from our tent at dawn to find Loyd staring into the pot. I approached and noticed a few crabs were missing. The sergeant restarted the fire, bringing the pot to a boil, and we had breakfast.

"Fuck me…" ronin moaned from their tents.

They emerged, giving us perplexed looks.

Again, Loyd tested the meat. "Still toxic y'as hell."

"Your loss, then," I said and fished out the final crab and seaweed as the ronin nibbled the last of their jerky with disappointment.

That evening the sergeant and I ventured into the tide pools again, using bits of dungeness crab from the previous stew to capture more. Again, the ronin watched us eat as their stomachs growled. I knew they were out of jerky and would be looking to butcher the sergeant, but they did not look his way. *Because they're entranced by the crab.*

The next day, the ronin were sluggish and distracted as the sergeant and I marched strong. At one point, we were in front of the ronin.

I spun and shouted, "Aren't you supposed to be superhuman!?"

Not one of them had the energy to argue. *Maybe we can escape?* I thought. The moment I turned around I came face to face with Kase.

She grabbed my collar tight, lifting me off the ground. "Don't y'even think y'about y'it!"

We stopped at noon and I unwrapped another crab meal.

"Fuck y'it! y'I'm having some!"

I lifted my head to see Loyd barreling my way.

"Don't you darrre!" Kase shouted.

Loyd did not acknowledge her, as if rank no longer mattered. He stopped before me, his eyes locked onto the crab. "May y'I have some? Please?"

"I made it for you," I said, handing a crab to his jittery hand.

Loyd cracked its shell and furiously sucked its meat. He moaned, then let out a sharp laugh. Beyond him, the rest were watching with wide eyes. Kase turned red with fury.

Her hold on them is weakening, I knew.

That evening, the general ordered us to camp far from the beach.

We huddled around the fire, staring at the dancing light, but it brought no comfort, for I felt the tendrils of hunger creeping in and could only imagine how hungry the ronin were. Each looked exhausted, famished, defeated.

I stood, ignoring my anxiety, knowing Kase was already on the edge of madness trying to maintain her dominance. *Pack animal behavior,* I realized and that they must be modified with wolf genes or similar to prevent insubordination. *But what if they find a better leader?* "I'm going to the beach to collect more crab. Anyone care to join?"

The ronin snapped their heads up with hopeful looks.

"y'I forrrbid y'it!" Kase snarled, her eyes blazing.

"You need to eat," I said as calmly as possible.

She gritted her teeth. "You'll die frrrom pois—"

"Within the hour, right!?" I cut her off and saw the ronin's eyes widen. I pointed at myself, then at the sergeant. "It's been two days. We're fine." I pointed at Loyd. "He ate some for lunch. He's fine." I waved my hand around the campfire. "And I know some of you snuck crab. You're all fine."

"y'Anotherr worrrd y'and you'll rrregrrret it!" Kase shouted.

"I'm going crabbing whether you like it or not," I said. *Keep your hands at your side! Lift your head high!* I ordered myself.

The ronin held their breaths and glanced back and forth between Kase and I.

Don't look away! Don't blink! I kept my eyes locked with Kase's.

"Well, y'I'm fucking starrrving," Loyd said, breaking the tension. He stood and collected the cook pot. "Let's go, y'Eva…" He looked at Sergeant McKenna. "…And whateverrr the hell yourrr name y'is."

Another two ronin stood.

Kase did not say a word.

The five of us bushwacked through the woods, Loyd leading the way with his owl eyes, until ocean waves met our ears.

"So, what do we do?" Loyd asked when we reached the beach.

"Crabbing is simple," I started. "Lower baited line into the tide pools, wait until one of the crabs comes to investigate and grasps the bait, then slowly pull them up."

"Uh, won't they let go?" Loyd said.

"If you pull too fast, they will. But if you're careful, they hold on tight. You must understand that most crabs are too simple to understand they're being hunted."

"y'It can't be that y'easy," Loyd said.

"You watched me do it twice already," I responded. "Loyd, with me. Sergeant McKenna, can you teach…" I realized I did not know the others' names."

"Jameson," said the first.

"Kelsey," said the second.

Sergeant McKenna stepped forth, holding command in his posture. "Jameson, Kelsey, on my six," he said and dashed into the tide pools.

The two ronin snapped into action.

They're following us already, I knew and turned to Loyd. "I usually crab during the day so I can see, but you should be fine, right?"

Loyd nodded. "y'Ourrr modifications trrransition y'our rrrods to cones y'almost y'entirely. Which means, y'ourrr night vision y'is based y'upon movement." He peered into the pool. "So, y'if they move, y'I'll see them."

Fascinating, I thought.

Loyd lowered baited line into the water and waited like a stork, terrifyingly still, his shaky hands becoming like stone. After several minutes, he delicately reeled the line with a good size dungeness crab clamped onto the bait. He was so gentle the crab did not realize it was out of water. He grasped it with his bare hands. "y'Eva…" he whispered and I saw a tear run down his cheek in the moonlight. "y'I didn't know y'it was this… simple."

"You okay?" I asked, taken aback by his vulnerability.

"y'I spent my y'entirrre childhood learrrning to be y'a masterrr hunterrr, but y'of people, not y'animals. y'And, y'I was cerrrtain y'everrrything y'on y'Earth was toxic. That the y'only sourrrce y'of food was y'otherrr people. Kase told y'us this was the y'only way to surrrvive." Loyd sobbed. "This y'is why we do horrible things… y'I'm sorry forrr what we did to yourrr frrriend… y'If y'only y'I knew this was y'an y'option."

"Loyd," I said, feeling tension in my throat. "Now you know."

"Fuck me," Loyd whispered and wiped his tears. He moved to the next pool and dropped his line.

We returned with two full pots of crab and armfuls of seaweed and milkweed. Loyd went quickly to work starting the fire, while I demonstrated how to cut the seaweed and milkweed, and taught them the importance of finding garlic and cilantro whenever they could.

"y'It doesn't grrrow wild?" Jameson asked.

"We've domesticated the wild species so much they cannot survive without constant upkeep."

Jameson thought about that. "But that means y'it could be domesticated back to y'its y'orrriginal wild state."

"That's correct!" I excitedly said and saw Jameson restrain a grin, like a proud student. "Though it might take decades."

Loyd looked at Jameson. "We have decades…"

Yes! I thought. But then, I saw Kase pacing in the back, her face barely illuminated by the campfire, her eyes glaring at me.

A waft of stew washed over the ronin and their eyes lit up.

I pointed at our two bundles of crab. "It's time."

Jameson went first, untying the end and shaking the crab into the pot. "How long do we let them cook forrr?"

"I give twenty minutes so the compounds within the seaweed, milkweed, cilantro, and garlic seep into their bodies completely and bond with the toxins in their systems."

Jameson's eyes suddenly widened. Kelsey dropped his towels of crabs to the sand and they scrambled off. The ronin opposite me stood from their seats and stepped back.

What's happening!? I thought, studying the fright upon their faces, then the woods behind them. *Where's Kase!?* A solid thud hit the ground beside me and I peered down to see Sergeant McKenna staring wildly about with his body quivering and his neck kinked.

Eva! Run! Frank shouted.

Before I could react, I was lifted into the air and slammed to the ground, the wind knocking out of me and my vision flashing.

"Hold herrr down!" Kase cried, and felt a change of hands.

I looked around bewildered, finding the sergeant's face next to mine, his eyes lifeless. I craned my neck, looking up to see Kase with a hideous grin. In her hand was Frank frantically wiggling his legs.

"You want to y'eat crrrab!?" she shouted. "Then y'eat this crrrab!"

The ronin yanked me to my feet as Kase marched to the pot.

"Nnnno…" I groaned, trying to pull free, but my limbs felt like jelly.

"y'I told you that you'd rrregrrret this!" the general shouted.

She's winning her ronin's loyalty back, I knew. Even Loyd looked at her with devotion again.

Onions hit my nose and my head began to clear. Frank no longer wiggled in Kase's grasp. He was unbelievably calm.

I'm sorry, Frank, I thought to him.

It okay, he responded. *Life be happy.*

You're lucky, then.

You be lucky, too, he responded.

I wish that were true, I thought. *Goodbye...*

No goodbye, Frank said. *I come with you.*

What?

"Rrrememberrr, y'Eva! You brrrought this y'on yourrrself!" Kase dropped Frank into the pot.

I made eye contact as he fell. Time appeared to slow. Happiness coursed through my veins like dopamine. Thousands of visions flooded my mind. *Swimming, eating, mating, meeting new creatures.* A century passed by all at once. Then, visions of myself came, looking down like I was a giant, and John came into view, sniffing my shell with vigor.

"Frank?" I whispered.

"We're together now," he responded more clearly than ever before.

I breathed deeply, feeling strange new sensations. My eyes were closed, but I could see in every direction with unbelievable clarity. *Through the pores of my skin.* Everything was in slow motion. *But how can this be?* I thought. *Electroreception...*

Frank plunged into the boiling water and thrashed about. I felt it all, as if I were in the pot with him, and I screamed like I never knew I could.

"It's okay, Eva," Frank calmly said. "That's not me anymore."

I focused on the horrific burning. *It's not real...* I thought and it subsided. All was silent around me. I sensed the ronin staring. When I opened my eyes, the world sped back up. Kase was no longer smiling. Instead, she looked like she had seen a ghost. I stared her down, peeling back the layers of her mind, looking right into her very soul.

She averted her gaze and pointed at the sergeant's body. "You know what to do!" she ordered. "y'Eat y'up! Rrrest y'up! Tomorrow, we navigate the caves! y'And then, we strrrike BESA!"

◆

I breathed deeply, discerning the pine of the woods, the muck beneath my boots, the salt and decay of the beach behind us, and the dampness of the caves ahead. It was so potent, so obvious. I knew exactly where each ronin was along our caravan and what conditions they were in, as if they were hooked to sensors and I was a computer. *All creatures emit minuscule electrical signals,* I knew. *This is how Frank saw others.*

"Partially," he responded.

I thought about how that might be, then remembered Rachel explaining how quantum relays used binary to transmit data. *Consciousness is information,* I realized. *We're just Ones and Zeros.* My head pounded, but I was not sure if it was from Frank's memories forming millions of new synapses in my brain, or the concussion Kase likely gave me.

I focused on the old general, feeling her heartbeat, her anxiety, her bad knee, and her cesarean scar, among a thousand other tidbits of information. I knew she and her ronin could hear a pin drop and remembered what Loyd said about their night vision being based upon movement. *What are the chances they're modified with shark, cephalopod, or crustacean DNA?*

"None," Frank said. "We would sense the emissions from their bodies."

I felt the cave's chill.

The ronin stopped and turned to me.

"You betterrr rrrememberrr the way," Kase growled.

"I do," I flatly said.

The old general made a face. "Don't trrry y'anything, y'or y'else!"

I made eye contact with her. "Or clse what?"

Her mouth twitched. "We'll kill y'everrryone y'in yourrr beloved BESA."

"You can't get inside without me."

"We'll wait y'until they come y'out!" she snapped.

"We have several years of supplies. You'll starve first."

"Then, we'll y'eat you!"

"And never find the key," I responded. "You're not very good at this."

One of the ronin gave a chuckle.

Kase snapped her head their way, but could not determine who it was. Her eyes returned to me. "y'I'll slowly peel y'off yourrr skin and consume you while you watch! y'I'll forrrce you to y'eat yourrrself! You will beg forrr death, but y'I will keep you y'alive, y'until you give y'us the location y'of the key y'and the code y'into BESA!"

I thought upon the bodies in BESA 03 and 07. I donned my headlamp and pointed. "Let's go."

The chill enveloped us and, after rounding a few bends, sunlight no longer existed. I kept my headlamp pointed ahead, illuminating the pathway, knowing the ronin had their night vision. *But how long does it take for them to adjust?* The first fork came. I quickly faced the ronin behind me, flashing my headlamp upon them.

They winced and covered their eyes.

"We'll be passing hundreds of forks, just like this one," I said. "Make sure that you stay tight to me. If you veer down the wrong path, you could be lost forever. Understood?"

They were silent.

"Understood!?" I repeated, my voice echoing down the tunnel.

I sensed Kase's seething. "y'Underrrstood."

"Good." I faced forward, taking the right path.

The ronin stumbled into one another as their eyes were switching back to night vision. Eventually, they moved along with ease again.

Nine seconds, I noted.

After an hour, we reached the massive chamber with its chandelier formations, exactly as I remembered it. I stopped at its center. "This is a special place, for only a handful of people have seen these formations. Consider yourselves lucky." I looked up, sending my headlamp light into the crystals.

"My Sol..." one of them whispered as light shimmered and spread.

"y'Incrrredible," said another.

I gradually maxed out my headlamp, refracting light around the chamber like a disco ball. At first the ronin covered their eyes, but when they adjusted they stared, entranced.

"And check this out." I cupped my hands around my mouth, and let my best wolf howl fly, sounding like an entire pack.

The ronin were silent for several seconds, then...

"Aooooooo!" one howled.

"Hooow! Hooow!" shouted a second.

"Oooo! Oooo! Oooo!" bellowed Loyd, sounding like a tribe of gorillas.

Laughter erupted, becoming more insane than the animal calls.

I closed my eyes and opened my new electroreceptive sense. I recognized each of their electrical currents and discerned where they were by minuscule disruptions in the rock formations, creating a clear picture of the terrain. I breathed deeply and let another wolf howl fly, holding it as long as I could. Loyd joined in. Several more came. Kase was howling, too. I focused on her, standing across the chamber, and the bright ball of current in her pack. *John's collar...*

This is it, Frank, I thought. *Are you ready?*

"More than ever," he responded.

My howl dwindled, but the ronin continued on. I reached to my head lamp, switched it off, and bolted. Echoes masked my footsteps and their adjusting eyes became my veil. I crept closer to Kase, counting, *One, two, three!* I sensed them spinning around disoriented. *Four, five, six!* The howling was dissipating, replaced by Kase's frantic shouting.

"What!?" the ronin responded, adding to the cacophony.

Seven, eight! A few were moving, reaching out with their hands, and grasping air. I was only a few paces behind Kase.

Nine! I ducked low and froze.

The ronin silenced. I sensed them waving their hands back and forth. *They can see again,* I knew, and that they were communicating non-verbally. They dispersed in several directions. Kase spun around, facing me. My heart leaped into my throat. Everything in me wanted to run, but I willed myself into stillness. Kase's eyes averted, but she cocked her head, turning her ear my way. *She can hear my heartbeat!* She peered at me again, squinting hard this time. And then, she grinned. *What do I do!?*

"Blind her," Frank said.

I switched my headlamp on full, blasting rays into her face.

"Fuck!" Kase shouted, covering her eyes.

I aimed my light at the crystals. "Aoooo!" I shouted, filling the chamber with echoes and switched off my light again.

"God fucking dammit!" Kase cried.

One, Two, Three! I bolted to her as she wildly lashed her arms, and slipped to her backside. The Terran Files were right there, within arms reach, but when I tried to grasp them, I got handfuls of canvas. *Four, Five, Six!* Kase whipped about. *Seven, Eight!* I found a stone on the ground and chucked it between her legs. *Nine!* I froze.

Kase listened to the stone's echo, sounding like a landslide. I concentrated hard, trying to discern the details of her pack, feeling how the electrical signals being shed by the curium isotope generator were seeping through the fabric and zippers. I snatched a zipper pull, yanked it open, and grasped the collar.

"Duck!" Frank shouted.

My body dropped, as if it were being controlled, and a blade sheared off locks of my already short hair.

"You sneaky little shit!" Kase shouted, creating more noise pollution, and lunged.

I flashed my headlamp, but it didn't stop her.

"Left!" Frank shouted, and I obeyed, barely evading another slash of her knife. I switched off my light and raced between rock formations. *One, Two, Three!* I searched the many tunnels around the chamber's perimeter, trying to discern which was correct. *Four, Five, Six!* I finally locked onto one with a subtle shimmer.

"That's the way!" Frank said.

Seven, Eight! I sprinted towards its mouth. *Nine!* I was in.

"She's y'overrr herrre!" one bellowed.

I traversed the tunnel, sensing tight walls and ceiling, and navigated twists and turns by feeling my own electrical currents reflecting off minerals in the rock. I passed a fork and knew the ronin's chances of becoming lost grew exponentially. I met the second fork and felt my chances increase even more. But then, my hamstring seized. I gritted my teeth and limped along. My heart felt about to explode. I gasped for air as quietly as possible, knowing every sound I made was reverberating back to the chamber.

"y'Evaaaaa!" came Kase's voice, ricocheting from behind.

I sensed something massive coming through the tunnel, somehow navigating the two forks behind me. *No...* I picked up my pace, but it was gaining fast, impossibly fast. I heard heavy breathing on my tail. I spun and flipped on my headlamp to blind whoever was there. I opened my eyes to find Loyd charging with arms covering his face.

So close... I thought.

Gigantic paws grasped my legs. A bulging shoulder planted into my midsection. I was certain he was about to slam me into the rock, but he kept sprinting, instead.

"Turrrn y'off the light," he whispered.

I looked down the path behind us. *It's only Loyd...*

"Please, y'Eva, y'I need to see," Loyd urgently whispered.

"He's helping us!" Frank said.

I flipped off my headlamp and closed my eyes, slipping back into electroreception.

"Betterrr," he whispered.

We came to a third fork. I tapped Loyd's left shoulder, hoping he would understand, afraid to let my voice fly. Loyd went left. He moved with such speed, such consistency, I began pondering what animal genes were in him. When we negotiated another fork, the electrical signals ceased. I was utterly confused until I realized it meant there was no rock to reflect. I yanked both of Loyd's shoulders and opened my eyes to see sunlight at the end of the tunnel. Loyd planted his feet but slid on the rock's slickness. We burst from the opening, sliding up to a cliff edge.

"Shit!" Loyd yelled, waving his arms as we teetered.

I twisted my body and stretched my legs back towards the cave. It was just enough weight to tip us onto safe ground.

"That was close," Loyd said, peering over the edge. "How do we get down?"

"We rappel," I said, pointing at the anchor. "But we don't have ropes."

"y'Evaaaa!" came from the cave, sounding right behind us.

Loyd peered over the edge again and whispered, "We can make y'it."

"Make what?" I asked.

He spun me from his back to a cradle in his arms. Then, before I could process, he leaped off the edge.

Wind rippled through my hair and clothes. I furiously gripped Loyd's arms. As the cliff side crept close, he kicked against it, slowing our descent, but in doing so, tumbling us. He kept his arms wrapped tightly around me, taking the hits with his massive frame. The cliff became a steep incline. Loyd found his footing and braced his legs, sliding down its face. I dared peek through his arms to see the incoming treeline. We plunged, snapping limbs, and Loyd grunted with the larger ones. Then, we hit a trunk, knocking him off his feet and tumbling us again. Somehow, he held me tight, protecting me.

We finally came to a stop.

Loyd's breath was ragged and when my eyes focused, I saw blood drooling from his mouth.

"Loyd!" I cried.

He released me and rolled to his back, revealing a tree limb protruding from his chest. "That sucked…" he grumbled and coughed up blood. He grasped the branch, gritted his teeth, and snapped it short, keeping the lodged portion in place. To my amazement, he sat up, then stood. "You y'okay, y'Eva?"

I became aware of pain radiating from my shoulder. "I think my shoulder is dislocated."

"Lucky…" he snatched my wrist and yanked.

I cried out as my shoulder popped back into place. *But this is nothing compared to what Loyd must be feeling.* I whimpered, took a deep breath in, and let it out slowly.

"Which way, y'Eva," Loyd said.

I pointed through the woods, where I knew we would meet up with the trail. We hurried off, both limping, but after an hour Loyd began to slow.

He suddenly stopped and looked back the way we came, then at his bleeding chest. "y'I'm bleeding y'all y'overrr the place, they'll trrrack y'us."

I saw drops in the dirt and more pooling at his feet.

He gave me a sad look. "y'Eva, thank you forrr showing me therrre's still good y'in this worrrld, that therrre y'is y'anotherrr way. You have done morrre forrr me y'in this shorrrt time than you will y'everrr know." He winced hard and gave John's collar a look. "You must not y'allow Kase to y'access The Terran Files. She says she wants to currre y'ourrr sickness. But herrr trrrue y'objective y'is to gain y'access to the nuclearrr warrrheads y'and finish what The Dirrrectorrr starrrted."

"Why would she do that?"

"Because… Kase y'is the Dirrrectorrr's daughterrr, his special prrroject, modified y'in strrrange ways the rrrest y'of y'us don't y'underrrstand. y'All y'I know y'is that Carrrterrr was borrrn with no fatherrr, y'and Beverrrly was borrrn like that, too."

Parthenogenesis!? I thought, knowing the phenomenon from studying crayfish. "Okay," I said. "I'll try my best."

Loyd gave a sharp look. "Therrre's no rrroom forrr trrrying. Prrromise me that Kase will neverrr get them…"

I stared silently.

"Prrromise me!" he shouted, his voice rumbling.

I unclipped John's collar from my belt and pulled Hector's key from its slot. "Your pistol," I said, outstretching my hand.

Loyd pulled it from its holster, quickly checked the chamber, and secured a silencer. Then, he spun it around and handed it to me hilt first.

I took the heavy pistol, twice the size of my BESA twenty-two, and I tossed the key to the dirt. I held with both hands and sent a shot. Its kick sent searing pain through my shoulder, but I refused to wince. I looked at the ground to find the key unfazed.

"Switch hands," Loyd said.

"What? Why?"

"You'rrre rrright handed, but left y'eyed. That's why you can't hit y'anything."

"Oh…" I switched my grip and aimed again. Despite feeling awkward I could clearly see down its sight. I pulled the trigger and absorbed its kick. The key shattered. "It worked!" I snapped my head up.

Loyd was gone.

I turned about, trying to determine which way he went, wondering how such a large man could have moved so silently. I found his holster and ammo belt, with several clips, at the base of a tree. A line of blood veered away from BESA 12. A terrible sadness for Loyd came over me, sad that he only found hope at the end.

"But he killed thousands of your people," Frank said.

I know, I thought back, remembering him eating the jerky made from Hector's flesh. *Yet, he sacrificed himself to save me.*

I strapped his holster and ammo belt around my waist, cinching them all the way, and I holstered Loyd's massive pistol and silencer, its combined length equal to my thigh. I faced the cliff peeking between gaps in the tree canopy, where a figure stood at its top, peering over the edge. *Kase...* I limped through the woods, glancing back every few minutes, certain she would be right there. An hour turned into two. The afternoon sun dipped, highlighting the clouds in pink.

A deep howl pierced through the air sending birds fleeing.

Loyd... I knew, and that he was trying to lead them away.

Another round of adrenaline coursed through my veins. I was almost at the old town when I heard heavy footsteps and branches snapping behind me. *What am I going to do once I get to BESA!? Can we really outlast them!?*

"We won't need to," Frank responded.

What do you mean!?

"I warned them."

I burst from the trees into the old town, to face a line of BESA uniforms with pistols drawn.

"Eva! Duck!" shouted a voice I never thought I would hear again.

Rachel! I realized and dropped.

Hundreds of twenty-two pops came, their little bullets whizzing into the trees. I rolled closer to them, catching glimpses of the woods behind me with each revolution. When the first ronin emerged, my old comrades converged shots, but it took nearly twenty to drop him. I reached their shooting line and they ushered me through.

"Eva! Are you okay!?" Rachel asked, looking so different now, with her hair short and her coat tattered.

"I'm okay!" I shouted above the gunfire.

"Then, get inside!" She yanked me to my feet and practically dragged me to BESA 12.

Another round of pistol shots rang from the front line. I realized there was a second and third line. "Who are all these people? What happened here?"

"They're from BESA 13 and 14 out of LA and Vegas. When we got word you were heading our way with General Kase herself, we sent couriers to gather reinforcements." She pointed at the lines. "Reinforcements found."

BESA's heavy steel door groaned open.

"But how'd you know we were coming?" I asked.

Rachel breathed deeply. "…Sydney told me."

"Fall back!" came just before heavy machine gun fire unleashed. I spun to see puffs of red erupting from scientists on the front line. The rest backpedaled to BESA as Kase and her ronin emerged from the treeline with automatic rifles, one in each hand, spraying the town.

"Everyone, inside!" Rachel yelled, then turned to me. "Eva, get as far back as possible! Get inside the reactor core if you must!"

I hobbled down BESA's main corridor as the rest came pouring in.

"Close the door!" I heard Rachel shout.

I disappeared into the reactor room and hunkered down, listening to slugs peppering the heavy metal door and the cries of those being hit. I closed my eyes and covered my ears, tapping into Frank's electroreception.

Forty-eight of us left, I determined, then I sensed several ronin outside BESA, approaching the door. The pelting ceased. One grasped the door's edge and tried wrenching it open, only to take several shots to the face. *We're not getting out of this.*

Frank's apparition appeared before me. "I know…"

But this can't be the end! I thought. *We've come so far and learned so much! We have a way to reestablish communication with the other colonies!*

"But we can't survive…" Frank said.

I sighed deeply and touched The Terran Files clipped to my belt, knowing the chances of someone accessing its contents was little to none without the key. *But it's compartmentalized now!* I suddenly remembered and I knew that my research of Frank's species held the secrets to humanity's future. That even if I perish, my discoveries should not die with me. With my hands covering my ears I raced from the reactor chamber to my old quarantine room.

"y'Evaaaa! y'I see you!" Kase cried from the entry door.

I leaped into the quarantine room as machine gun fire came.

"Mer!" came from an aquarium.

I spun to find Sydney. I knew what she said, I sensed it clearly. "Yes, I'm back! But there's no time!" I removed the aquarium's lid.

"Mere me emer?" she asked as I picked her up.

"I'm sorry… Frank didn't make it, but he's a part of me now."

"Merrrer mere me?"

"I know it's scary. There's ronin at our doors, and it looks like they'll get through."

She looked at me with pleading eyes.

"Sydney… You must find a way past the ronin. Return to the island where I found you and get your kind as far away from humans as possible. Your species must survive."

Sydney gently rested her claw on my wrist, accepting her mission, then hopped off my hand, scurried to the darkest corner of the room, and hunkered down. I found my terminal, turned it on, and linked The Terran Files.

A monstrous crash rang and heavy shots fired.

"They're inside!" Rachel yelled from the corridor.

I opened the hard drive, quickly selected my folders, and dropped them into the hard drive. *"Transfer initiated, 1h27m until completion."*

So, now we wait, I thought, feeling Frank in the back of my mind squirm. *What is it?*

"How will anyone understand your research if nobody can explain what happened?" he said.

Right… I thought. I navigated to *Record* and dashed. A hologram opened, displaying my face looking distraught, older, broken. *I'm a different person now.* I took a deep breath. "My name is Eva Jain, and if you are watching this, then that means I am long gone…" I paused not knowing how to continue.

"With us," Frank said.

I looked into the hologram. "…My research is of the utmost importance, for what I discovered will change humanity. Bio-immortality, enhanced sensory perception, telepathy, and genetic teleportation. This is what I've unlocked. Or I should say what they've unlocked…"

CHAPTER TEN

Aizen breathes heavily as the hologram fades away, thinking upon Eva's story and everything he has just learned about himself, The Terran Files, and how they can be tracked by a remote key. He stares at the green light furiously blinking from the collar. "We must get this hard drive as far away from your people as possible!" he says to Thalee, "Someone's tracking it as we speak!" The light abruptly stops. *What does that mean?*

Thalee gives a determined look. "I'm coming with you."

"No, Thalee, you cannot come," Aizen says. "It's against protocol."

"What is *pro... to... col?*" she asks, frustrated.

"It's a set of rules the Council established if someone makes contact with native Terrans."

"Why do they get to decide what I can and cannot do!?"

Aizen thinks about that. "It's just... There's a delicate balance to ensure everyone has equal protections."

"Everyone!?" She looks ready to explode. "Or do you mean your people!? Because your Council is keeping us in the dark, forcing us to stay on Earth! I don't know what's happening out there, but I do know that this is not protection, this is control!"

Aizen silences.

She's right, Zion says. *We have no right to shelter them.*

Weren't you the one who established this protocol? Aizen thinks back.

That was under different circumstances. Zion pauses. *It might be time to bring the Terrans into the Council.*

Aizen makes eye contact with Thalee. "Get your things and say your goodbyes. We leave immediately."

♦

"It appears we took care of their cartel problem, as well as exposed our fugitives," Minister Hjordiana says amid a hanger's rubble, where the Arkathy soldiers had discovered the massive man and one-legged boy. "Look at all these weaponized prostheses? All illegal. And I'm willing to bet we can track that one-legged boy through his prosthetic leg."

"You assume too much," Clara says.

"And that's why I always win!" the minister snaps back. "Now, search the rubble! Look for clues about that ship!"

I shouldn't be here, Clara knows but feels compelled by what she saw on hologram. *A ship made of Jupiter Marble and the boy who has now lost an arm...* She walks among the destruction, passing both Arkathy and human remains, keeping her calm, channeling her Ergonos training. Two Arkathy officers flank her, making certain she does not run. Clara does as she is ordered. *For now.*

From one pile of rubble to another, they search. Clara asks the officers to lift debris that she cannot, knowing their auto-armor adds tremendous strength to their otherwise fragile bodies. A speck of red among the sea of charcoal catches her eye. She casually strolls closer, not looking directly at it to keep her escorts ignorant of its existence. At first, she thinks it might be another piece of debris, no larger than a marble. But then, she recognizes the shape of a fingernail. *It's just the tip,* she realizes, and that none of the bodies in the area have lost an arm, hand, or finger.

She points at a slab of wall laying on the ground and looks at her escort. "Can you lift this? I need to take a look beneath."

The Arkathy officers study the slab. "Too heavy."

"Please? Just a few centimeters so I can have a peek?"

They holster their rifles within their complex armor and grasp the corners of the slab, using their armor's hydraulics to lift.

Clara plants hands on the ground, one strategically atop the severed fingertip, lays on her stomach, and peers underneath. "It's clear."

The Arkathy drop the slab, sending a gust of debris into Clara's face. She spits charcoal and feels grit in her eyes. *But now is not the time to complain!* She stands and wipes soot from her tear ducts with her shirt cuff as she slips the fingertip into her pocket.

"Move!" the soldiers order, pushing her along.

By day's end, they convene with the minister, speaking back and forth in their native tongue.

Minister Hjordiana grimaces and turns to Clara. "For discovering the fugitives' origin, I will forgive your little insurrection on the ship and send you home. But there you will stay. Should you even think about what you saw here today, if you attempt to leave the confines of your little moon, consider your life forfeit."

Clara processes the warning. "Understood."

Captain Witteksam steps forth. "Clara, we leave now."

No time to gather my things…

◆

Tempest City's inverted dome glows brightly below them as they drop from Captain Witteksam's Arkathy Corsair in Titan orbit.

Clara's eyes drift from the city glowing brightly out the shuttle's window to the captain sitting across from her. "It's an honor having you personally escort me home," she says, looking at his featureless helmet. "But you must know that Minister Hjordiana's actions on Ganymede are criminal."

Captain Witteksam tilts his armored head. "Not when Martial Law has been declared."

"When did that happen?" Clara probes.

"A moment before the invasion."

Clara shakes her head. "That's impossible. The Council must vote on the matter, which would take weeks at best."

The captain remains silent as the shuttle plunges into Titan's soupy atmosphere. The ground eventually appears and splits apart, welcoming them into an underground platform.

Captain Witteksam stands. "Clara, you must stay on this moon as Chancellor Hjordiana has instructed. But, you will have freedom here."

Clara slowly stands. "*Minister* Hjordiana, you mean."

The captain nods in a respectful manner, just as he had when they first met in her apartment. "I know there are differences we can never overcome, but you must understand that we Arkathy admire you, in our way. As we admired Zion. We would hate for you to do anything stupid."

Admired as an adversary, Clara understands. "And I have admiration for you, captain."

"…You learn fast," Captain Witteksam states and waves his hand.

A sleeve extends from the underground terminal, sealing around the shuttle's hatch before opening. When Clara departs, it quickly closes and the sleeve retracts. The platform splits open above her and the shuttle rises into the thick atmosphere, disappearing from view.

Forward, move forward... she mantras as she struts through baggage claim into the station's shopping center, keeping her eyes straight, letting her peripheral vision do its job. A billboard, advertising Cindar's thermal baths, shedding bright orange light, appears. She stops before it. *Nothing.* She wanders by holographic food court signs. *Not a blur or a shimmer.* She then spies a duty free appliance store and remembers when she met the minister at her apartment and how the synthesizer's light obscured the captain's cloak.

"Welcome, Clara," a holographic host says. *"What interests you today?"*

"I'm looking to replace my synthesizer," she responds.

"Right this way." A light on the floor leads Clara to a wall of synthesizers.

"Thank you," Clara says.

"You're welcome," says the host. *"I am here if you have any questions."* The floor light fades.

Clara starts at the far left, noting that each synth has a, *"Try me!"* button. *Here goes nothing...* She presses the button, watching its dull light emit through its translucent door. She wastes no time, pressing the next model, going down the entire display wall, and activating several at different heights. She then turns around and gazes unfocused with the synthesizers humming behind her. *Where is it?* she thinks, focusing on her peripheral vision, ignoring the customers looking at her strangely.

Nothing... nothing... no—

A blur from the edge of her right eye comes, just enough to think one's mind is playing tricks. *A cloak.*

◆

"It's on the move again," Samuel says, strapped on Ulysses's back with his holotile out and navigating as they bound through the forest in the night. More than once, Samuel thought he would strike a low branch, but Ulysses's awareness is incredible.

"They still heading in the same direction?" Ulysses asks.

Samuel zooms into the green dot. "They've localized around a porous cliff-side."

"Porous?" Ulysses ducks, and a tree limb brushes Samuel's hair.

But I did not flinch... Samuel pushes it from his mind, analyzing the geological breakdown displayed on his holotile. "Porous as in... limestone. It's suggesting a cave system."

"The perfect cover," Ulysses grunts.

The forest opens to a sandy beach washed in moonlight. Ulysses halts, nearly throwing Samuel from his shoulders, and points at a shuttle.

"Set me down," Samuel says, squinting, barely able to make out the shuttle's outline. "It looks Lunan, designed for travel between the moon and Earth." He notes the large landing thrusters. "And hop around in Earth's gravity."

"I thought Earth was not to be touched," Ulysses says and sets Samuel down.

Though the gravity is oppressive, Samuel finds his traction is incredible, trusting that when his foot plants, it stays. He hops closer to the shuttle, keeping a hand on Ulysses for balance, and makes out more details. Three letters stand out.

"HRG..." Ulysses mutters. "What is that?"

"History Recovery Guild," Samuel says.

"Those nerds?" Ulysses says and grins. "If they have The Terran Files, then this will be easy."

"Let's hope that's the case." Samuel analyzes the shuttle's engines and hatch. "It's not so different from my tug."

"You think you can hack into this?" Ulysses asks.

Samuel whips out his holotile and connects to a port below the hatch. "It's in hibernation... Smart."

"Why is that smart?"

"If we activate it, the owner will be alerted."

"Meaning?"

"We can't get inside the shuttle," Samuel answers. "But we can access its basic information." He navigates to a registration. "History Recovery Guild shuttle 26671. Model S12, year 3417. Registered to an Aizen Ocol," Samuel says and studies the name.

"What is it?" Ulysses asks.

"He's kinda famous, I think." Samuel searches, *"Aizen Ocol,"* on holotile. "Yeah, he was a child chef. The only human to beat the machines in competition."

Ulysses peers into the hologram. "Wait... Is he the son of Clara Ocol? The one who wrote that biography?"

"I never made that connection before." Samuel accesses information on

Aizen's family. "Yeah, that's what it says. And his father, Jonathan Zaid, is the famous archaeologist who discovered Paris."

Ulysses darkens. "Clara's description of Hermian life was perfect, as if she lived it herself... And her descriptions of Paris must have helped Jonathan find a way in." Ulysses gives a concerned look. "Sam... I don't think that biography was fake. It can't be a coincidence that her son is here the moment The Terran Files moved."

"But Aizen's just a chef," Samuel dismisses as a waft of vegetables, fish, and a familiar spice comes. "Mala peppercorns," Samuel mutters, pulling from Khasi's memories. "He's not far."

CHAPTER ELEVEN

"I'm going to miss this," Aizen says, looking at the tribespeople grinning with empty bowls in their hands and the smell of spiced fish hanging in the air.

Their eyes shift from him to Thalee.

"It's not like that!" Thalee snaps.

Not like what? Aizen thinks, studying their grins.

Kune flashes a smile. "Both of you are embarking upon a new life together. It will be joyous and perilous, but no matter what, you will endure side by side." He pauses. "Aizen, who would have thought an outworlder could learn our ways so quickly." He turns to Thalee. "And Thalee, who knew you would find love again."

Oh... Aizen glances at Thalee, realizing what their upcoming journey looks like to the tribe. Aizen has a mischievous thought and says, "I will protect Thalee with my life."

Their grins become bright smiles.

Thalee snaps her head to him, her face turning red.

Aizen tightens his lips to contain his laughter, knowing what wrath he will receive later.

"Aizen," Tadem hesitantly says. "Do you think I can see the galaxy, too?"

"Yeah," says another.

Aizen's heart sinks, realizing what dreams they are formulating, and what laws that will break. "Life outside of Earth is not perfect. In fact, we are trying to live in harmony with our worlds as you have achieved here."

Tadem's nervous smile dwindles. "Does that mean, no?"

Aizen sighs. "I cannot stop you, but there are others who will try."

"Why?" he asks.

"They think that by keeping you ignorant they are protecting you and your way of life. To them, Earth is a preserve," Aizen says.

"A zoo, you mean," Tadem responds.

Aizen's heart sinks further. He does not know what to say.

"Yes, like a zoo!" Thalee spits, staring daggers at Aizen. "That's why I must go first! I will show them we are not weak, we are not ignorant! That we deserve just as much the right to explore the galaxy as they do!"

Aizen sees nods all around and realizes they are changed forever. He checks the stars. "Thalee, it's time…"

Kune presents two wooden boxes. "We have a gift for each of you, to aid in your journey. Having been inspired by your match, we felt that two master knife wielders deserve the best we can craft." He opens the boxes, revealing two sets of knives, each of their blades short, wide, razor sharp, and black as night.

That's hyper compressed carbon! Mirko blurts. *Pick it up!*

Aizen does, feeling its balance and seeing fibers running along its blade.

It's like diamond! Mirko says. *Compressed flat and folded over hundreds of times!*

It must be quite strong, Aizen thinks back.

Stronger than you can imagine! Mirko says, *I've never seen anything like this before!*

Have any of you? Aizen asks.

They all respond, *No.*

Then, a stir comes from deep within.

R9, that's the second time I've felt you this week, Aizen thinks.

"These are incredible," Thalee says, staring at the blades. "How did you craft them?" Her eyes land on Kune.

He smiles. "When you return, I will teach you myself."

"Okay…" she whispers, lost in the blades' craftsmanship.

"We must go," Aizen sadly says and stands.

They converge around him and Thalee, placing hands upon their shoulders, like a gigantic hug. Then, they release and trickle away from the campfire, leaving only the two of them.

Aizen dons his pack and places the collar around his neck so the isotope hangs just above the spore upon his chest. He stows the knives in a leather sheath and secures it around his thigh. He turns to Thalee, who is staring into the fire. "You ready?"

"No," she quietly says. "This has been my entire life."

"Take all the time you need," Aizen responds.

She scowls, stands sharply, grabs her pack, and marches into the forest.

Aizen sighs and follows, listening to the symphony of insects and birds as they near the beach. But then, the symphony abruptly stops. Only the waves and wind exist. An uneasiness grows within Aizen. He races to catch Thalee before she steps onto the beach, grabs her arm, and pulls her back.

"What the—"

He cups a hand around her mouth and stares fiercely into her eyes. She calms. He releases his hand and points at the beach where a figure leans against his shuttle, barely visible in the moonlight. *One leg. No crutch...*

He's not alone, Dione says.

"Become invisible," Aizen whispers to Thalee, and before he blinks, she silently melts into the woods. He focuses on the figure and steps upon the beach. "Can I help you?"

The figure stirs. "Aizen Ocol… Who would have thought someone like you would be here."

"I'm on vacation. My dad is part of the Guild. I wanted to come see what all the fuss was about," Aizen casually responds and closes his eyes, slipping into meditation, finding the one-legged man's point of light and Thalee's working its way through the tide pools to flank him. But then, a massive light appears at the edge of the forest.

Aizen! Mirko cries. *That's an equalizer!*

What's it doing here!? Dione says.

I imagine we'll find out soon, Aizen thinks back, remaining calm and taking Ergonos breaths. He locks onto the equalizer's massive light and opens his eyes, holding partial meditation.

"A vacation?" the one-legged figure says, then darkens. "You have something I need."

"You can have the shuttle, I don't want any trouble," Aizen responds.

"Not the shuttle." The figure raises a hand and green light emits.

The hard drive around Aizen's neck suddenly activates. *He has the key!* Aizen realizes. "Who are you?"

"Well, that's just it, Aizen," the figure says. "I'm nobody, representing an entire population of nobodies. A people without rights, without consideration, without acknowledgment. According to the galaxy, we do not exist. But our voices will be heard, by any means necessary. Give me The Terran Files."

Aizen steps forward and says, "No."

♦

Three... definitely three, Clara thinks, approaching her building's front door after a full day of browsing appliance stores and testing synthesizers. She finally purchased one to not give herself away. She opens her building's door and watches it close before starting up the stairs. She opens her apartment door and enters, leaving the door agape.

"It's incredible how far we've come, technologically," she says aloud as she enters the kitchenette. "But you see, the more advanced we become, the more weaknesses we develop. Humanity made this mistake a millennium ago, resulting in The Fall." She opens a utensil drawer and searches its underside. *My pistol is gone.* "You might consider humanity simple because we have not significantly progressed these past few centuries. But, you see, that is intentional." Clara finds Aizen's knife set and pulls one from the block. "The best example of this is when you Arkathy tried to conquer humanity with hypothesis and the galaxy's most advanced technology, only to be thwarted by a cookie." She moves to a switch on the wall, raises her finger, and faces the living room to see the door has been closed. "And now, a light switch."

A flurry of steps comes as Clara flips the switch, sending an EMP ripping through her apartment, down the building, and out into the neighborhood. Lighting cuts, ventilation stops, and three quadrupedal figures in auto-armor appear frozen like statues in her living room. One of them is just arm's reach away from her with their rifle raised. Clara knows their armor is completely shut down, trapping the Arkathy soldiers within. *But their systems will soon reboot!*

She dashes to the hallway closet, pulls down the ladder, and climbs into the attic, but she cannot find her sniper gear. *They thoroughly searched the place... But maybe.*

She leaps from the attic into the closet, bounds to the bathroom, and flicks on the light. Nothing happens. *Right...* She fumbles through towels, her fingers feeling folded ends of tufted fabric until touching a thinner material. *Yes!* She pulls it from the pile, spilling towels across the floor, and wraps the thin fabric around her shoulders. She searches for a seal and slips it from her feet to her chin, then flips a hood up and over her face. *Please be operational!* she hopes, knowing the EMP might have fried its circuitry. She turns it on and holds her breath. An interface opens displaying body coverage, charge, and enhances her vision, revealing clutter on the floor. She selects *Activate* and peers into the mirror. *No reflection.*

She passes silently down the hallway to the living room and slinks by the frozen Arkathy. She is tempted to swipe a rifle, but knows they are DNA locked. *Better to be undiscovered.* She quietly opens and closes her apartment door, then sprints through the corridor, down the egress stairs, and out its emergency exit.

♦

Dr. Lee prepares for another late night in the lab, watching the break room's synthesizer as if lab results were about to come in. The synthesizer dings and Dr. Lee retrieves a bowl of granola and milk.

"Cereal for dinner? Really?" Clara says.

Dr. Lee flinches, nearly sending his bowl across the room. He frantically searches for the voice's origin. Clara releases her cloak and Dr. Lee flinches again. She pulls back her hood.

"For the love of Sol, Clara!" Dr. Lee says. "Could you at least announce when you're coming?"

"Sorry, Dr. Lee, but this is an emergency. I need your help." Clara raises her hand from beneath her cloak holding the burnt fingertip.

Dr. Lee adjusts his glasses and comes closer. "Is this from sample thirty-one?"

"That's what I need help determining," Clara says. "The one-legged boy is now a one-armed boy as well."

Dr. Lee rises up and down on his toes like an excited child. "Come!" He hustles off, forgetting the bowl of cereal in his hand, spilling milk on the floor.

Clara carefully follows down the corridor to his lab. *But it's just Dr. Lee at this hour,* she realizes. Once in, she closes the door and removes her cloak.

Dr. Lee sets down the bowl and quickly opens the holograms of the previous samples Clara sent him. "I'm so glad you're here! The sample from that boy has been doing some interesting things since we last spoke! Check this out!" He starts a recording of several cells clumped together, looking like nothing special until a flush of different cells appears. "Because of how easily this boy's cells were accepting other's DNA, I tried going outside our species to see what happens," he says. "These are from chimpanzees!"

The boy's cells reach out, bonding with the introduced cells and transferring their information.

"This boy is now a chimpanzee," Dr. Lee says.

Clara stares at the recording. "Can this be used for genetic modification?"

Dr. Lee smiles wide. "Among so many other things! This boy might be the key to our future as a species! To all species! We could even resurrect extinct animals on Earth! We must find him!"

Clara raises the fingertip. "Next clue is right here, hopefully."

Dr. Lee points at a box and Clara places the fingertip inside. He closes its lid and dashes *Sterilize.* A laser races across the fingertip. Then, Dr. Lee remotely cuts a microscopic bit of flesh and places it into a drop zone. He claps his hands and opens a fresh hologram above his terminal. "Okay… What…? Okay," he mumbles to himself as the cells appear. He pans over. "What…? Okay?"

"Are you able to determine anything?" Clara asks.

"Kinda," he says. "This sample is definitely from the boy, but it's different now."

"Different how?"

He points at an area of cells. "These are his cells, same as before." He pans to the right. "But here, they're changing…"

"Into what?"

"I don't know." Dr. Lee keeps panning. "Wait!" He points. "That's a brain cell!"

"In his fingertip?" Clara asks, beyond confused.

"It likely migrated through the boy's blood stream. But, instead of matching the introduced brain cells, the boy's cells are becoming muscle tissue, instead. He's literally turning into someone else as we speak!"

Clara has a sinking feeling. "Who?"

Dr. Lee uses micro-scissors to delicately isolate the brain cell, then runs it against DNA archives. "Male," he mutters. "Genetic markers from Earth, but from some time ago. Around The Fall, actually."

The hologram slowly matches proteins, creating a genetic image of an ancient man.

"Central Asian," Dr. Lee says. "One of the old Stan countries, maybe."

The hologram halts and a face appears, wrinkled and scarred by decades of brutality.

"We have a match?" Dr. Lee whispers, beside himself.

"Khasi Sinam, The Butcher of Earth," appears.

The man they took from the Arkathy ship… Clara realizes.

"It says he was executed for his war crimes," Dr. Lee says.

A cover up, Clara knows. "Why would this boy have Khasi's DNA? What purpose could it serve?"

Dr. Lee ponders that. "If brain cells are in his system, then perhaps he was trying to recover information."

Memory immersion... Clara realizes. "Information of what?"

"I don't know."

"If Khasi is from Earth, then this boy is likely heading there, too," Clara says. *Aizen... Jonathan...* She turns sharply to Dr. Lee. "We're heading to Earth, immediately!"

Dr. Lee gives a confused look. "What do you mean, we!?"

CHAPTER TWELVE

Thunderous footsteps come from the forest. Tree limbs snap as a low growling comes, rumbling Samuel's chest. But Aizen slowly approaches, unfazed. Ulysses lets out a howl when he steps upon the beach and charges the lean, young man like a rhino. Still, Aizen does not waver. Samuel's stomach tightens. *This is not right.*

Aizen shuts his eyes.

Is he insane!? Samuel thinks.

Ulysses closes the gap about to end this young man's life, but at the last moment Aizen ducks, spreading his feet and slipping through Ulysses's powerful legs. Ulysses's feet cross. He slips and slides. And to Samuel's shock, his massive friend tumbles to the sand.

Aizen continues his calm approach.

Samuel's adrenaline skyrockets, his mind fills with questions, but above all, he wishes he had his prosthetic leg. *But I have the arm!* He slaps his holotile into its reception port, projecting, *"Heat blade, Stun, Projectile, Flamethrower…"*

Flamethrower! Samuel selects and his arm transforms, the fingers pinching together, becoming a nozzle and shifting forward. A vacuum winds up, sucking the surrounding air, separating out oxygen and compressing it. A blue pilot light flame pops up at the nozzle. Samuel leans against the shuttle's hull, grasps the arm's trigger, and points the flamethrower at Aizen. *But I'll hit Ulysses, too!* Samuel knows, watching his friend regain his footing and lunge at Aizen. But, time after time, he whiffs.

"You slippery son of a bitch!" Ulysses cries in frustration. "You can't keep this up forev—" He tumbles to the ground again, his leg looking out of commission. He makes eye contact with Samuel, the flamethrower's pilot light reflecting in his eyes, and says, "Do it, Sam! Do it, now!"

Samuel grits his teeth and pulls the trigger, hoping he won't melt the hard drive around Aizen's neck and fry his friend. But just before fury unleashes, a second figure comes out of nowhere and knocks his arm skyward, sending hellfire above them, instead. *There are two!?*

Samuel uses the flamethrower's nozzle to deflect her next slash, but her black blade slices clean through sicklecell titanium, lopping it off. The prosthesis jettisons the compressed oxygen cell over the water, where it ignites, momentarily turning night into day and revealing this second figure.

A native Terran!? Samuel realizes.

She slashes again.

"System Override!" emits from the remaining half of his prosthetic arm and it lights up blue along its ulna. Samuel desperately raises it, halting her blade as if the light were solid.

The woman backpedals and grins.

Pain shoots up Samuel's calf. His foot wobbles. All stability is lost. He tumbles to the sand and looks at his ankle to find a gaping cut. *She severed my Achilles' tendon! How!? When!? What is she!?*

She is a butcher, comes the intrusive thought deep within Samuel.

"Sam! No!" Ulysses cries as the woman comes in for the kill, the sheer volume of his voice causing Samuel's ears to throb.

The woman winces, turns, and dashes towards Ulysses to help Aizen, instead. *But he doesn't need it,* Samuel realizes, watching Aizen jab a quick knuckle into Ulysses's shoulder causing his entire arm to go limp. Then, a toe sinks into Ulysses's groin, knocking his other leg out. Before Samuel knows it, his invincible friend is flopping on the sand like a fish out of water.

"Khalun ga dee!" Aizen shouts at the Terran in a strange language and points at his shuttle. They bound through its hatch, the woman giving Samuel a grimace as she passes. Its thrusters come online.

They're going to cook me! Samuel desperately crawls away.

The shuttle suddenly shifts to a safe distance and Aizen comes back through the hatch, dashing to Samuel with a small box in his hand.

"I'm sorry!" Aizen shouts above the shuttle's thrusters. "This is the least I can do!" He places the box on the sand. "Standard med-pack! You must take the foot!"

"What the fuck do you mean!?" Samuel responds.

"Listen carefully!" Aizen says. "I hit your friend's coronary artery bifurcation point! It must be reset! But first, take the foot!"

Samuel is beyond confused. "Why are you helping us!?"

"I'm not your enemy!" Aizen turns and boards the shuttle. Its hatch closes and they zip off. The sound of their fusion engine quickly dissipates.

Samuel studies the med-pack, then his mangled calf. Blood pours from the gash. *Take the foot,* he thinks, knowing he is bleeding out.

"Sam! You okay!?" Ulysses calls out and begins rolling from his back to his front, towards him.

"No!" Samuel cries. "I lost my foot!"

"Again!?" Ulysses says.

Samuel fumbles to open the med-pack with one hand, using his teeth to open its lid. Within are several injection cartridges. *Painkillers.* He pulls one, and looks over his ankle, trying to determine the best spot.

Midway up the calf, comes the intrusive thought.

Samuel jabs the cartridge. Pain from the calf down disappears. *Now for the foot, but how do I stop the blood?*

The heat blade will cauterize the wound, says the thought.

Right, Samuel nervously stares at the blade's blue edge still emitting from his prosthetic arm.

Do it! the thought yells.

"Fuck! Fuck! Fuck!" Samuel slices through his lower leg. Again, the smell of barbecue hits his nose. But this time, he vomits. When the nausea passes, he searches himself for other injuries, finding none. He deactivates the heat blade, detaches the damaged prosthesis, and tosses it to the sand.

"Ulysses…" he quietly says.

No answer.

Samuel turns to find his friend convulsing on the sand. "Ulysses!?" *What did Aizen do!?* he thinks, trying to remember what he said.

We must reset his coronary artery bifurcation point! says the thought.

I don't know where that is! Samuel thinks back.

Then, it's a good thing I do!

◆

Angela gives Jonathan a nervous look from the shuttle's copilot seat. "Aizen's three days late."

Jonathan calls again, but it goes straight to mail. *Clara's have been, too,* he reflects. "They're in danger."

Angela peers into the hologram. "You have several unread texts."

"What? Really? What do they say?"

"Oh, an error," she says. "It's just three letters."

Jonathan thinks about that. "What letters?"

Angela squints. "K. I. P."

Jonathan breathes a massive sigh of relief and whispers, "Kip…"

"Oh my god! Is this that stupid word you say to Clara all the time?" Angela says, rolling her eyes.

"That brilliant word, you mean?" Jonathan responds. "Where are they coming from?"

"First one's out of Titan. Next one is from Europa's orbit. Then, Ceres."

"There's no destination heading." Jonathan has a thought. "Are the messages coming by quantum relay?"

Angela pulls up message information. "There's no marker."

"It's tight beam, then," Jonathan says. "Which means, Clara's in the dark. Can we estimate the rest of their trajectory from these three points?"

Angela is already doing just that. "She'll arrive at Luna in three days."

Jonathan grins. "She's coming to us."

"Um…" Angela adds.

Jonathan faces her. "What?"

"There are several other texts arriving at the same time, also using *Kip.*" Angela brightens. "They're coming from The Rockies! Clara must already be here!"

"That can't be. The timing doesn't work." Jonathan studies the second text chain and lets out a sharp laugh. "It's Aizen…"

Angela frowns. "You three are a weird little cult."

Jonathan grins. "You mean… a family?"

Angela rolls her eyes.

◆

"Clara, we're entering lunar orbit. Should I send another message?" Dr. Lee whispers through the metal casing of his research equipment.

Clara knocks once against the inside wall of the equipment's empty reactor cavity, where she has spent the entire trip within an envisuit, recirculating fluids for almost two weeks. *Once inside a shuttle bound for Earth, I will be free…* she tells herself to keep sane.

"It's sent," Dr. Lee says. "You think Jonathan will figure this out?"

Again, Clara knocks once.

"I hope you're right," Dr. Lee skeptically responds.

"Shuttle seven, four, alpha, tango. This is Sabine Crater Station. We have you on lidar, but not on our schedule," comes through com. "Please, state your business."

"Where is it?" Dr. Lee mutters and Clara knows he is searching for the *Response* icon. "Ah, yes, good sir…" he awkwardly says.

"It's Mam," the dock master corrects.

Clara cringes.

"Uh… Equipment, delivering, science, study—" Dr. Lee stammers.

"Are you here for delivery or scientific study?" she impatiently asks.

"Uh… Science?" Dr. Lee says.

"We're bringing you into platform fourteen. Prepare to be boarded."

Shit! Clara thinks.

"Sorry," Dr. Lee whispers as the shuttle is commandeered.

Clara hears landing gear unfurl, a solid thudding of touch down, and engines dwindling.

"They're coming," Dr. Lee whispers.

A knocking raps on the hatch followed by decompression.

"Dr. Kevin Lee," says the dock master. "Come with us for questioning."

"Please, do not touch the equipment," Dr. Lee says. "It's highly sensitive to even the slightest change in air pressure."

Nice one… Clara thinks, feeling like the doctor is redeeming himself.

"I'm afraid we must search the shuttle thoroughly," the dock master says. "New protocol—"

"That won't be necessary," another voice cuts in.

I know this voice, Clara thinks.

"Dr. Cordon?" the dock master says. "What are you doing here?"

"Dr. Lee was kind enough to lend me his equipment for my work," says the voice.

Who is this!? Clara racks her brain.

"You should have logged its delivery with us," the dock master scolds.

"It's on your schedule under my name," the doctor says. "Equipment delivery, August 24th."

They go silent for a moment.

"There's a delivery on September 24th," says the dock master.

"Oh, I'm so sorry," Dr. Cordon apologetically says. "I swear, I meant it for August, I must have accidentally selected nine instead of eight."

"We still have to search the equipment."

"Again?" Dr. Cordon says. "It went through customs on Titan and Ceres. That certainly meets the new protocol. And as Dr. Lee said, pressure changes have disastrous effects on sensitive equipment like this."

The dock master sighs. "Just make sure it doesn't happen again."

"Thank you, mam," Dr. Cordon says.

Footsteps leave the ship.

"Dr. Lee, shall we get going?" Dr. Cordon asks.

"Uh…" Dr. Lee says.

Clara knocks once against the metal.

"Yes… Yes, let's go, without haste," Dr. Lee exuberantly says.

Before Clara knows it, the equipment wheels from the cargo hold and down a ramp. Then, it hoists up and secure latching comes.

"Clara, you can come out now," Dr. Cordon says.

Clara freezes. A moment passes.

"It's okay, Clara," Dr. Lee says. "It's Hazel."

Hazel!? Clara quickly unlatches the reactor's door, dumping herself onto the floor of a cargo hold. There, before her, is the young archaeologist with hands on her hips and wearing a cocky smile. Clara pulls off her helmet. "Hazel!? How in Sol did you know we were coming!?"

She grins. "Your hubby called a few days ago and I did some magic to get a delivery in the books."

Jonathan, you never let me down, Clara thinks with a grin. "How'd you know we had equipment like this?"

Hazel shrugs. "I didn't."

"That's quite the gamble," Clara says, feeling sudden guilt for placing her in such peril.

"Jonathan once took quite the gamble on me. I suppose this makes us even." Hazel opens the hatch to a moon hauler's cockpit. "There's a guild transfer in a few days that you can join, but until then, you're with me."

"Did Jonathan mention why I'm being smuggled?"

Hazel makes a face. "No, and let's keep it that way."

CHAPTER THIRTEEN

"How did a skinny, little, seventy-kilo boy beat the holy snot out of you?" The Augmentor asks Ulysses as she tinkers with a new prosthetic foot to match Samuel's new prosthetic arm and leg. "Aren't you supposed to be super strong, super fast, see in the dark, taste color, wild shit like that?"

Ulysses turns a deep shade of red. "You don't understand. Aizen's nerve strikes were incredible and he moved with impeccable timing. I couldn't touch him." He presses his lips tight. "Only one other person in history fought like this."

"Mirko…" Samuel mutters.

"…Yeah," Ulysses responds, giving Samuel a look. "You know this from Zion's biography?"

Samuel nods.

The Augmentor laughs. "Wasn't that biography fake?"

"We're not sure about that," Samuel says. "Those characters existed and those stories perfectly captured the events."

"But how can a chef fight like that?" Ulysses says. "It would take decades of intense training. And Aizen seems to be in his early twenties."

"Wasn't Mirko a chef? Maybe that's the secret," The Augmentor quips and makes a final adjustment to Samuel's limbs. "Don't lose anything more. Don Credence is already considering sticking you in auto-armor."

Samuel and Ulysses face The Augmentor. "You have auto-armor?"

"Older models, rebuilt for human anatomy." She eyes Ulysses. "Feeling the itch to get inside?"

Ulysses tilts his head. "Aizen rendered me useless with his nerve strikes." He turns to Samuel. "If you hadn't found the counter points, I would have died. How'd you do that, anyway?"

Our little secret... the voice in Samuel's head says.

"I noticed lumps in your neck and pushed from the opposing sides," Samuel responds.

"Good guess," Ulysses says.

"You think the armor will stop his nerve strikes?" The Augmentor asks.

"I do," Ulysses answers, returning his attention to her. "But can it be modified for my frame?"

She brightens. "I thought you'd never ask."

"Samuel, my boy!" the old don announces, entering the ship's medical bay. "You've become more machine than man!" He turns to The Augmentor. "Can you fashion him armored underwear? I must protect my investment." The don flashes his gap-toothed smile. "I'm off to the bar!" He heads back out. "Join me when you can!"

Samuel grins. "He's funny."

The Augmentor shakes her head. "He just made the call. From now on, you're to wear auto-armor whenever you leave this ship."

Samuel frowns. "I can handle myself."

The Augmentor raises her head. "Remind me again, who took your foot?"

"A native Terran…" Samuel grumbles.

"And with what?"

"A knife," Samuel reluctantly says, knowing he is wearing auto-armor whether he likes it or not.

Ulysses clears his throat. "When might the adjustments be ready for me?"

The Augmentor points at the ship's cockpit. "We were able to land with the initial calibrations made to the fusion drive, but it was at significant cost to fuel. I need to make further adjustments if we are to hop around Earth. I estimate a few days."

"No! Not again!" Ulysses snaps. "We can't keep getting delayed!"

"Be happy you're alive!" The Augmentor responds. "And do you even know where they're heading!?"

"Kinda," Samuel says. "They can't mask the tracker's signature. Last time I checked, they were crossing The Rocky Mountains. I've set an alert should they stop."

"So, they didn't go off planet? Interesting," The Augmentor says.

"Very interesting," Ulysses agrees.

"He's searching for something." Samuel looks at Ulysses. "We must never underestimate our enemy again."

"Enemy?" The Augmentor says. "Didn't he give you the med-pack?"

Samuel frowns. "The worst kind of enemy is a friend, for they will hit you where it counts."

Ulysses gives Samuel a concerned glance.

"Fair enough." The Augmentor motions at the door. "We should join Don Credence. His suggestions are orders."

Ulysses darkens. "We don't take his orders. We have a deal, that is all."

"Still. In his world, not joining is an incredible offense," she says.

Samuel slowly nods. "We should go." He stands from the table, wobbling as his new prostheses calibrate to his weight and gate.

They follow The Augmentor through the ship's corridor to a room resembling an old saloon. The don is behind the bar wearing an apron and wiping down the counter. Faith sits upon a stool watching them enter, locking eyes on Samuel's new foot. Where before he saw respect, he now sees concern.

Don Credence snaps his head up and waves at the stools. "Please, have a seat. I have a wonderful tasting prepared for you."

"A tasting?" Samuel says. "Is now the time to be do—"

"Of course it is! We're on Earth!" Don Credence snaps and places several small glasses on the bar filled with beans of varying shades of brown. "Now, sit."

When they do, Ulysses says, "Coffee beans?"

"Why yes, my gigantic friend. Good eye."

"How does this relates to our situation?" Samuel says.

The don smiles. "I certainly dabble in many ventures, but with the sanctions on coffee exports, it's become like gold on the black market. Thus, my family has spearheaded its cultivation for over five hundred years, with the dream of one day farming like the ancient masters of Earth." He pulls a simple glass canister and plunger from beneath the bar. "If those Terran Files truly contain all of Earth's information, then they no doubt hold the secrets to how our ancestors cultivated their crops. I am especially interested in soil composition, as that is of the utmost importance to flavor."

"Ganymede has soil," Ulysses says.

The don shakes his head. "I would barely call it dirt. But earth… real earth… One can only imagine the possibilities."

"You make it sound like we do not have coffee," Samuel says.

"Outside of Ganymede, we don't," the don responds. "What the rest of System Sol drinks is a sad imitation. The synthesizers infuse artificial stimulants to simulate the effects of caffeine, but the taste is absolutely horrid." The don makes a face, then points at the first glass containing beans as black as night. "This blend is Ganymedan Coal, the darkest roast I make." He pours the beans into a small cylinder which grinds away. When he opens it, the beans are like black sand. "Do not be deterred by its name, coloration, or roast, for the darker it is the more caffeine has been burned off. It is your light roasts you must be weary of."

"Where did you learn all this?" Ulysses asks.

"What kind of businessman would I be if I did not understand my product?"

Ulysses pauses. "I mean, you seem to know exactly how it's done. Your movements are second nature."

The don takes a breath. "I was not simply given the title of don. I had to earn it through blood, sweat, and tears. I spent years working in the fields and with the roasters. Then, I served the scum of the system in cafes across Hardsill, rising from busboy to head barista. All incognito, so I would experience the hard truth of it. Finally, I learned the business firsthand while shadowing my mother," the don says. "So, Ulysses, I know exactly how it's done."

Ulysses nods deeply. "I didn't mean to offend. My people worked the fields, too."

The don looks past Samuel and Ulysses with a lost look in his eyes, then comes back. "Right…" He pours the coffee grounds into the glass canister as an old kettle whistles. The don delicately fills the canister with boiling water, fogging the glass, then inserts the plunger, but he does not press. "We let it steep."

Samuel watches the grounds swirl, staining the water black. "For how long?" he asks, strangely fascinated.

"Until it feels ready," the don answers.

They watch the water become darker.

"Is it ready, now?" Ulysses asks.

"No," says the don.

A few minutes pass.

"How about, now?" Ulysses follows up.

"No."

Another minute passes.

Now it's ready, says the voice within Samuel.

"It's ready," Samuel relays.

Ulysses turns to him. "He just said it's not."

"My boy," the don quietly says. "You're right."

Confusion crosses Ulysses face as the don presses the plunger, squashing the grounds to the bottom, clearing the black water of particulates. He lifts the canister and pours steaming coffee into five small cups.

"There," the don mutters, grasping the loop of his cup and raising it to his nose, letting steam wash his face. He breathes deeply and sips. "Perfection."

Faith, The Augmentor, and Ulysses do the same.

"My Sol!" Ulysses says. "How is this so good?"

"Family secret," says the don.

Samuel looks into his cup, raises it to his nose, and sips. Hundreds of memories flash before him, of a little boy on a lavender farm, sipping coffee with his grandfather. Samuel is consumed by these new memories, until his holotile beeps and he shakes his head, returning to the present. He pulls the tile from his pocket. *The green dot has stopped.*

"Aizen's in the badlands," Samuel says.

"What are bad lands?" Faith asks.

"It's a region of old Usonia where not much grows," Samuel answers.

"Why would Aizen stop there?" Ulysses asks.

Aizen must have accessed The Terran Files to know this place, the voice says from within. *But how if he doesn't have the key?*

"There's an ancient nuclear arsenal below ground," Samuel says and turns to The Augmentor. "How quickly can you calibrate the engines?"

Her eyes narrow. "Keep the coffee coming and I'll turn three days into one."

◆

Aizen's finally here, Jonathan thinks, shifting nervously as a shuttle becomes visible in the sky. *But why is he so late?* The sun's warmth washes his face and he shields his eyes. The shuttle's lettering becomes legible, reading, *"HRG 26671."*

"That's definitely him," Angela says.

"I hope he's okay…"

"He did say he had one more thing to do before leaving. Perhaps it took longer than expected," Angela rationalizes.

"Maybe," Jonathan says, but his gut twists.

The shuttle hovers, then smoothly drops.

Too smoothly, Jonathan knows. *It's on autopilot.* He grips the handle of a med-pack.

Landing gear unfurls and the shuttle nestles into the grass. Then, its engines wind down.

"The privacy tint is up," Jonathan states, waiting for the hatch to open, terrified of what he might find.

The hatch remains closed.

"Um… Is it empty?" Angela asks.

A thumping comes.

"No…" Jonathan responds, feeling even more confused.

The shadow of a palm presses against the window, barely visible through the tint.

Angela gives Jonathan a look. "That's not Aizen."

A black object suddenly pierces the shuttle's hatch from the inside. Jonathan and Angela jolt.

"Is the hatch stuck!? Are they suffocating!?" Angela races to pull the jettison lever.

"No, Angela!" Jonathan says and tries to catch her.

Compressed gas canisters erupt around the hatch, blasting it over their heads, landing nearly twenty meters away. Angela drops to the ground.

Fucking hell… Jonathan thinks, staring at a proud figure in the hatchway with a blade as black as night in each hand. Her eyes pierce through him like a hawk to a mouse, her jaw clenches, and her corded muscles ripple.

She points a blade at him. "Gretan hadeez padre! Aizen!"

A fury swells within Jonathan. "Where is my son!?" he roars, marching towards this terrifying woman, towards this… *Terran?* He stops. *She's a native Terran… She's never opened a hatch before.*

"Gretan hadeez padre! Aizen!" she again cries. She sheaths one of her blades and pulls a card from a leather sack.

Jonathan squints, reading, *"Dad,"* on its front in Interspeak.

The Terran sheathes her second blade, points at the card, and then at him. "Gretan hadeez padre! Aizen!"

Jonathan listens to what sounds like gibberish at first, until it clicks. "Yes! Padre! Aizen!" He vigorously points at himself.

The Terran tilts her head and shakes the card.

Jonathan approaches, briefly stopping at Angela. "You okay?"

"Yeah," she says, her eyes locked on the Terran.

Jonathan continues, stepping within the Terran's range. When he takes the card, she flinches, sending his nerves through the roof, and he quickly backpedals.

She smiles wickedly.

She's messing with me... he realizes and looks at the card. He lifts its fold, revealing both sides and the back written upon.

"Her name is Thalee and, yes, she's a native Terran. They speak a version of ancient English that takes a moment to learn, but I have faith you will. During my last day with them, I discovered something incredible yet dangerous, a hard drive containing a compilation of Earth's entire history, called The Terran Files. We were then attacked by a one-legged boy and an equalizer, somehow tracking the hard drive, which is why I cannot meet you as promised. Please, stay as far away from me as possible. When all is settled, I will send word. I love you, Dad. -Aizen-"

♦

Aizen walks upon scorched earth, approaching black hills while deep in meditation. He lets his bare soles absorb subtle vibrations, trying to sense anything cavernous. But without R9, it seems futile.

Maybe it's time we take the spore, Mermer says, becoming visible.

Aizen grasps the spore dangling around his neck. "I can't."

Why the hell not? Justin scoffs.

"We can do this without R9," Aizen halfheartedly says.

You don't believe that, Allessandra responds.

Kwai Lan comes forth. *No, Aizen's right to be hesitant.*

Why is that? Zion says.

One by one all of Aizen's past lives appear.

Kwai Lan points at the spore. *We don't know what this will do to his DNA. The Sorgans only have a theory.*

Zion thinks about that. *If it weren't for R9 helping you keep my degradation at bay, I would have died young. I imagine this is similar.*

No, Kwai Lan says. *With you, we were constantly repairing the unraveling of cells. The task was clear. But this spore will completely reset DNA. Aizen's, R9's, yours, mine, all of ours... We don't know if we will maintain separate consciousnesses or become one single, different person. And considering Mermer and R9's DNA, we might become a strange hybrid creature. We just cannot predict what will happen.*

Why would the Sorgans design something like this? Dione asks.

Well... Anda responds. *Sorgans perceive the destruction of a body as a mild inconvenience, for they can always regrow a new one.*

Then, we don't take the spore, Zion says. *How can we find this facility without R9's senses?*

Aizen looks at the collar and its isotope warning. "Maybe we're overthinking this."

How so? Zion says.

"Mirko, you have knowledge of nuclear physics growing up on Ceres, right?" Aizen asks.

They drilled it into us at the academy, Mirko says.

"How long might an old reactor maintain its radioactivity?"

He thinks about that. *Earth's reactors were made before The Hermian War, in the twentieth century. Their technology was outdated compared to what we developed on Ceres. They would have likely used Uranium 228 or Plutonium 248, each having half-lives in the millions of years.*

"So, they would still be radioactive today?" Aizen follows up.

Yes. Mirko says. *But without continued upkeep, the housing around their nuclear cores would be in extreme disrepair.*

"Would they be leaking radiation?"

Possibly, he responds.

"Envisuits have a geiger counter," Aizen says, looking back at the supplies he gathered from his shuttle before sending Thalee to Maine. He dons his envisuit and helmet, clips The Terran Files to his utility belt, and walks the barren surface, following minuscule radiation bumps, hoping they lead him in the right direction.

What do you intend to achieve by coming here? Zion asks.

"I need to know if Eva's story is true," Aizen responds. "And if the boy and equalizer are after The Terran Files, then they might be looking for places like this to finish what The Director started. Just like General Kase was. We must know if the arsenals are salvageable."

And if they are? Zion challenges.

"Then, we destroy them," Aizen says.

Easier said than done, Mirko interjects. *You would need to access The Terran Files. They might contain the process in which to decommission them.*

"They're tracking me with the key…" Aizen mutters, knowing there is no avoiding another conflict. *But how much time do I have to prepare?*

Not much, Zion says.

Sha comes forth. *Why did you help them in the first place?*

Aizen pauses. "There's something about the boy that feels familiar."

Familiar how? Sha asks.

"I don't know…" Aizen says.

What will you do when they arrive? Zion asks.

"Take the key from them, like I should've done before." Aizen approaches the hills. His geiger counter ticks up. Several ravines are before him. *It's the one straight ahead,* he determines and enters its mouth. Granite walls rise tall. When Aizen extends his glove to the ravine's path the geiger counter shoots into the yellow. "It's high."

But not too high, Anda responds. *Your envisuit will protect us.*

"Okay…" Aizen continues onward.

The ravine leads the way. A mound of red dirt registers out his peripheral. He discerns tires in the pile. *Old military trucks, rusted to dust, leaving only their rubber components behind.*

The configuration suggests a semi-truck and trailer, Justin says.

To transport a nuclear missile… Aizen knows.

More rust piles litter the nooks and crannies of the ravine until Aizen wraps a final bend to find a gaping square hole. *Where are the doors?* Aizen thinks. He approaches the opening nearly thirty meters in width and height. Within, the facility widens and its ceiling leaps to fifty meters high. Thousands of ancient missile bays line either side of the facility's main hall, each scalloping the rock walls, designed to hug armament. Sunlight washes down each bay through launch doors above, their metal hatches deteriorated to dust.

They're all gone, Aizen realizes. *Missiles and their cores.*

The blinking green light suddenly emits from the collar, followed by a thunderous crack from outside. Aizen whirls to the entryway to see a tiny, black ship tumbling from the sky. *They're here! But what happened!?* Aizen thinks, watching the ship level out at the last moment and make an emergency landing in the distance.

Aizen! Zion says, coming into view and pointing up at a subtle bending of light descending into the atmosphere. *That's an Arkathy warship!*

Aizen's stomach drops, and he reaches for Mirko's rifle strapped to his back. *We'll need a lot more than this!* He knows and clutches the spore beneath his envisuit's fabric. He breathes deeply, trying to remain calm. Again, R9 stirs. Aizen removes his helmet. He lifts the chain from his neck and out of his envisuit, and opens the cage housing the spore. It resonates in his hands. *I have no choice!* Aizen closes his eyes, opens his mouth, and pops the spore in. *Swallow, dammit!* Aizen reseals his helmet and swigs from his reservoir, feeling the spore painfully slide down his esophagus. He braces for whatever might happen, for his body to change, for cell division to accelerate, and for his entire genetic code to be torn apart and rebuilt.

But nothing happens.

CHAPTER FOURTEEN

"I cannot thank you enough," Clara says to Hazel as she enters a shuttle just outside of Prometheus.

Hazel grins. "Just tell Jonathan he better come visit next time."

"That, I will," Clara says, and she and Dr. Lee strap into their seats next to three guild archaeologists, destined for Paris.

Hazel seals the hatch and heads to a launch bunker.

"Good luck," Hazel says through com as shuttle engines wind up.

They lift from the surface.

Clara turns to the window, watching the extent of Prometheus's old elevator coiled beneath them in ruins as they rise. *It's the only one left to investigate,* Clara thinks, knowing Earth's elevators were sent whipping off into space. She turns to Dr. Lee to find him staring at his holotile, instead.

"Is everything all right?" Clara asks.

"My equipment has been in and out of pressure zones and through filthy loading docks," he snips. "When we get to Earth and find that boy, I'm afraid our tests will be compromised."

Clara thinks about that. "So, your concern before was not a ruse?"

Dr. Lee gives a funny look. "Why would I lie about that?"

To save our butts, Clara thinks.

"Paris's basecamp has a clean room," says one of the archaeologists. "Are you biologists or something?"

"Yes," Clara quickly says, and turns her attention to Earth far in the distance.

Hour by hour it grows until after half the day they slow into orbit.

"Please, prepare for atmospheric entry," chimes the shuttle as Europe rotates into view below.

"I'm here," Clara whispers, thinking upon Jonathan and Aizen, hoping she is wrong about the fugitives coming to Earth. Hoping that her anxiety is just that. She takes a deep Ergonos breath as flames lick the shuttle's windows.

◆

"I see the ravine!" Ulysses cries, pointing through the ship's cockpit window at a thrust of rock in the otherwise barren landscape. "That must be where he is!"

"How in Sol did you see that!?" the don says. When he notices Ulysses's pupils twisting like a camera's iris his mouth drops open, revealing his missing front teeth. "Oh…"

The ship's sensors analyze the rock.

"It looks like solid granite," The Augmentor says from her pilot seat and turns to Samuel. "Can you confirm this location?"

Samuel pulls his holotile with the key attached and opens its hologram. "Aizen will know we're here the minute we activate its homing beacon."

"Do it quickly. Allow only a few seconds to confirm the location and maybe Aizen won't notice," Ulysses says.

Samuel nods and activates the remote key.

Its green dot flashes right at the end of the ravine.

"Confirmed!" Samuel terminates the program and returns the holotile to his pocket. "Let's hope Aizen didn't notice."

Ulysses points at his pants. "Sam! You didn't turn it off!"

Samuel sees a blinking red light through his trousers. He frantically retrieves the holotile, but no light emits from it. Dread fills him as the light beneath his pants becomes a solid green.

An alarm cries.

The Augmentor's face goes blank, then she whips around. "Missile closing in fast!"

"Isn't this ship supposed to be untraceable!" Ulysses says.

"It's not locked onto the ship!" The Augmentor responds.

"Then, what is it following!?"

"The boy's leg! Obviously!" the don says and makes eye contact with

Samuel. "Off with your pants! Follow me!"

Samuel slaps his holotile into his prosthetic arm's interface, fumbles to undo his belt, and frantically kicks off his pants, revealing his prosthetic leg and foot. He chases Don Credence down the corridor to the cargo bay.

"Evasive maneuvers!" The Augmentor shouts. "Brace yourselves!"

The ship rotates ninety degrees. Samuel's weight feels quadrupled and he squats down, bracing his hands against the corridor walls, and sees Don Credence doing the same. *He understands evasive maneuver protocols*?

When they level out, the don turns and shouts, "Move, now!"

They enter a cargo bay filled with heavy farm equipment, like the don had known they were heading to Earth all along and prepared accordingly. Samuel spies large forest mulchers and tilling blades on the walls.

The don loops an arm around a metal handle on the back wall and hits two switches. The inner and outer bay doors simultaneously open, revealing blue sky and the sun shining. Wind tugs at Samuel's shirt and freezes his bare legs and cheeks. Tilling blades clank against the walls. A tiny black *X* appears in the distance with a bright white halo. It takes Samuel a moment to realize it is the missile coming straight at them. He sees Don Credence shouting, but cannot hear his words. The don points at Samuel's leg and then out the open bay.

Move your ass! shouts the voice from within.

He snaps into action, looping his arm around a metal handle and grasping his prosthetic leg. He twists, disengaging it from his hip. The *X* quickly grows. Samuel takes the heavy metal leg by the ankle and chucks it through the cargo bay door, watching it tumble into the sky. The missile swerves towards the leg as the bay doors shut. Blinding light comes through the door's crack as it seals followed by its concussion.

The ship somersaults.

Samuel's prosthetic foot and hand automatically bite into the floor and wall, anchoring him down. Farm equipment tears from their cleats, flying across the cargo bay and crashing into opposing walls. Tilling blades whirl, one hurtling towards Samuel's face. By sheer reaction, he shifts his head. Searing pain comes from his ear. *It's gone,* he knows and imagines Don Credence forcing him into permanent auto-armor. But then, Samuel sees the old man come flailing across the cargo bay.

A tilling blade whips by. The don's leg spins separately from his body. Another blade comes. The don's arm is off. Then, his torso splits at the belly. Finally, his head is separated.

A low altitude warning sounds.

This is it! Samuel braces for impact.

At the last moment the ship snaps level and Samuel knows The Augmentor managed a final correction. The ship's belly touches down, sounding like a grinder against a metal drum. Pain ripples through Samuel's shoulders and hips as he desperately hangs on. His teeth chatter. With every clunk, Samuel is certain the ship will tear apart. Instead, they begin to slow. Then, they stop. Alarms sound and shouting comes from the cockpit.

"Samuel! Credence!" Ulysses booms. "Are you okay!?"

Samuel checks himself over, his joints aching, but nothing is torn from his body. *Well...* He reaches for his ear to find it missing. Then, he sees pieces of the don everywhere and his head on the floor.

"I'm okay!" Samuel calls back. "But Don Credence is dead!"

A sudden silence comes, then Faith limps into the cargo bay, blood gushing from her nose. She lets out a blood curdling scream. Ulysses follows looking relatively unscathed, then The Augmentor appears, cradling her arm.

"Where is he!?" The Augmentor shouts.

"Everywhere!" Faith cries, running from one piece to the next.

Searching for his head, Samuel knows. When Faith makes eye contact with him, he points to where it lies.

She races over, drops to her knees, and gently picks it up. She calms, cradles the head like a baby, and kisses its forehead. Then, she breathes deeply and stands up straight. "I will not let the family down," she whispers, then snaps her head to Samuel. "My father took a liking to you, but I do not care if you are my perfect genetic match!" She steps closer. "You have singlehandedly destroyed my family! You and Ulysses must leave, immediately!"

"But—" Samuel begins.

With lightning speed, Faith pulls a pistol, points it at Samuel, and shoots.

Heat comes from Samuel's other ear and wetness pours down his head.

"That's your final warning!" Faith hits the bay door switch with the butt of her pistol, but nothing happens. She hits it again to no avail. She snaps her head to The Augmentor.

"Don Carlyle," The Augmentor carefully says and bows. "The family network is still loyal to Don Credence. Which means the transfer of power never happened between you two." The Augmentor pauses. "This ship, along with everything else, went into lock-down the moment your father's heartbeat stopped."

"Meaning!?" Don Carlyle snaps.

"We're trapped."

"And whoever shot us down is on their way!" Ulysses says.

The Augmentor nods. "It was a trans-orbital missile, launched from space, designed to disable its target. We don't have long before they arrive."

"I can smash through the hull!" Ulysses says.

The Augmentor shakes her head. "Beneath this ship's stone exterior is an inner hull made entirely of sicklecell titanium. It's how we survived the detonation and crash landing. Even you cannot break through." She turns to the new don. "The only way to get out of this ship is to transfer power from Don Credence to Don Carlyle."

Don Carlyle makes a face. "How is that done!?"

"That's a family matter," The Augmentor says. "He must have told you something."

She looks at her father's head in her arms. "No…"

Samuel soaks it all in. "Don Carlyle…" he says and she trains her pistol on him again. "…If it's a family matter, then at some point Don Credence underwent the same transfer of power from his mother."

"How does that help us!?" the new don says.

"Don Credence was a *Cre…*" Samuel says and studies the don's head with his mouth hanging open. Then, he looks at Ulysses. "…And I'm a *Cre…*"

CALVIN's TALE
Ganymede: 3287 - 3418

When people think of organized crime, they imagine drugs, alcohol, and promiscuity. Bank robberies and extortion. But that is not what we do. We are not thugs. We are not criminals. *Well*... Technically we are, but not by choice. We simply provide what others endeavor to destroy. In the past, it has indeed been drugs, alcohol, and sex, hence why my predecessors dealt in such practices. But today is different. Today, we are on the brink of a new existence, meanwhile clinging onto age old habits. Addictions, I dare say. For when sugar was banned, humanity nearly self-destructed. And when poppy seeds were driven to near extinction, we almost lost our civilization. Now, they are trying to take the most essential of chemicals from us. Remove a product that keeps the entirety of humanity running. It is an addiction we hold most dear.

Welcome to the Caffeine Cartel.

◆

"Don't you ever ask me why again!" the don snapped.

"But, Mother, I—"

She narrowed her eyes, bending down to my ten-year-old height, her nose nearly touching mine. "What did I just say!?"

"I'm not asking why," I said, standing my ground, staring right back into her menacing eyes.

"Then, what are you trying to say!?"

I carefully formulated my words. "I want to know for what reasons I am being sent to the fields."

Mother slapped me across the face. *Once, twice, thrice.* "You just asked why in a different way, you arrogant prick!" she hissed. But then, she sighed. "All the dons do this at your age. If you are to take over the cartel, then you must learn it from the ground up, literally."

"It's dangerous," I complained.

"So, what!? Our entire operation is dangerous!"

I tried to find another way out. "But I'm your son. It's beneath me."

Mother furrowed her brow. "Bean picking is not beneath you. These laborers are not beneath you. A cartel is a family. And these people are part of it just as much as you and I. Be thankful that you were born at the forefront, relish in the luxuries at your fingertips, but understand that you will one day protect these people, like a sheepdog guarding its fold. And that we are nothing without them." She stood up straight. "You will be known as *Franco*, just another abandoned peasant boy. You will feel their pain and experience their strife, firsthand. And then, you will learn to make them love you."

I studied my tattered canvas clothing. "Franco…" I muttered.

"Say it without that fabricated accent!" Mother snapped.

"Franco…" I repeated, all the while thinking that I speak this way because Mother does.

"Again!"

"Franco," I said, just like I heard the laborers say when we had previously visited the plantation to oversee production.

Mother smirked. "Better." She handed me a dirty pack. "See you in a year." She boarded her shuttle without a glance over her shoulder, lifted from the grass, and activated its cloak.

A gentle rattling of coffee plants ripe with beans accompanied a quiet showering of artificial rain in the distance. The sun was rising, but granted no warmth. A chill shuddered through me. *But now is not the time to complain,* I thought. *Franco would not complain.*

I walked in darkness for an hour before I saw the skiff I was to rendezvous with silhouetted against dull sunlight. The movement of several people came, one of them tall. *The foreman,* I assumed. Children's voices grew as I neared. One pointed my way.

The foreman cupped hands around his mouth. "Hurry up!"

I felt my body obey. I started to run.

Children were scrambling onto the skiff's bed when I arrived, and a girl, about my age, extended her hand. Her palm was like sandpaper against my delicate skin and she yanked so hard my shoulder felt about to dislocate. I tumbled onto the skiff's bamboo planks to their snickering.

"Shut up!" cried the foreman. "You're new! Who are you!?"

I propped into a sitting position and thought about his accent.

The foreman cocked his head. "Are you mute or something!?"

"Franco," I said, trying my best to sound like them.

The foreman gave a hard look. "Franco here has made you all late! Which means, no breakfast!"

What!? I thought, watching scowls form on the children's faces.

The foreman entered the skiff's cab and we lifted from the ground, hovering just above the coffee plants. Then, it took off, almost tumbling me off the bed.

"You've never worked the fields before," stated the girl who pulled me onto the skiff.

I watched the crops racing by, feeling like we were about to crash. I looked at the others still scowling. "I'm sorry, I didn't mean to be late."

They gave me weird looks.

"So… He is slow, after all," said one, looking older and heavily muscled.

I tried not to give a smart response, for he would certainly do more than slap me. I stared at Ganymede's indigo sky, instead, studying its almost nonexistent atmosphere, having been terraformed just enough to make life possible without domes, allowing us to utilize Ganymede's entire landmass. "Making us the agricultural dynasty of the outer system," Mother had said numerous times. *But how did our ancestors do it?* I thought, knowing they barely had the resources to survive let alone accomplish such a feat. *Nobody cares how it happened, so long as it provides enough produce for System Sol.*

The skiff stopped at a section of coffee plants looking weighed down by fruit. The foreman stepped from the cab.

"Line up!" he barked.

The children spilled from the skiff and formed up alongside the road. I grabbed my pack and raced into line.

"Leave the pack, Airhead!" the foreman scolded, pointing at the skiff where the other packs lay.

I tossed my pack onto the flatbed, or so I thought. My anxiety skyrocketed as my toss came up short, my pack landing on the dirt, instead.

"More like, Airball…" the muscular kid snickered.

"Shut it, Brent!" snapped the foreman.

I scrambled to place my pack on the skiff and got in line.

The foreman eyed me. "I will only go over this once! The fruit on these plants are extremely delicate! Treat each like they are eggs!" He tossed a wooden crate to the ground. "Once you fill a crate, place it on the bed and make sure you write your name on its face! No name! No credits!" He paused. "Any questions?"

"How much do we get paid?" I asked.

"Ten creds," he said.

"Per bean? So low," I said, forgetting to keep my smart mouth shut.

The foreman grew furious. "That's per crate!"

♦

It was almost noon and I winced with every bean I picked, my delicate hands raw. Rawness turned into blisters. Blisters broke, becoming sores. Sores became open wounds. The others were on their fifth crates, while I was a quarter through my first. *Not even ten creds*.

"Are you bleeding?" said the girl, coming out of nowhere.

I flinched and tried hiding my hands. "No…"

She tightened her lips. "Don't try to be tough. If you bleed on the beans, they're ruined."

Oh… I thought. "How do I make it stop?"

She reached into my crate, retrieved a few beans, and inspected them. She sighed. "None of this is salvageable. You're in a lot of trouble."

My stomach sank. "What will happen to me?"

She gave me a hard look, then knocked my crate to the ground, spilling the beans across the dirt, and stomped on them. "Airball! You idiot!" she yelled. "Can't even tell these are infested with mites!"

Chuckles came from the other kids.

Tears welled in my eyes. I wanted to run, give up my rights to the cartel if I must. *Nothing is worth this humiliation!*

"Shut your traps!" cried the foreman, heading straight for us.

The girl quickly grabbed my wrists and yanked me to the ground, rubbing my palms into the dirt. I wanted to cry as granules ground into my wounds, but I noticed the blood disappear. My hands just looked dirty.

The foreman stopped before me. "What happened!"

"The bushes in this row have mites," the girl said.

"Are you certain!?" he barked.

"Yes, sir," she responded, deadpan.

"Fuck… Which row?" he said, looking at me.

I was in shock, but pointed at my row.

"Okay… okay," he muttered, deep in thought. "Tamarind… Teach Franco how to detect the mites."

"Yes, sir," Tamarind said and turned to me. "This way."

I robotically followed her, still processing what just happened.

"Hey, the crate," she said.

Right… I raced back to pick up my crate, making sure all the supposedly mite infested beans were out, and caught up to Tamarind. *She just saved me… I think.*

"Work here." She pointed at the row she was picking.

"What about the mites?" I asked.

She picked a bean and pointed to where the flesh met its stem. "If you see little holes here, it means mites have burrowed in. You must stomp them into the ground, they cannot survive in the soil. They spread by jumping from one bush to the next. Which means, we must burn the whole row."

A wash of heat came against my back. I spun to see our foreman in a reflective suit, with a fuel tank backpack, spitting fire from a handheld nozzle onto my row. My jaw dropped, knowing how much it was worth.

Tamarind frowned. "You owe me." She pointed at my hands.

I upturned my palms.

She sighed deeply. "Just pretend to pick today."

I nodded and followed closely behind her. As she picked, she would periodically turn to me, pretending to teach something, but really deposit beans into my crate.

The sun soon set, and I finally set my one and only crate onto the skiff's bed as the rest loaded their eleventh or twelfth. I started writing, *"CALV…"* when I felt a nudge.

"I thought your name was Franco," Tamarind whispered.

I froze, searching for an excuse. "I can't write my name."

Tamarind gave a funny look. "You really are slow." She crossed out, *"CALV,"* and wrote, *"FRAKO,"* instead. "That's how you spell your name."

I suppressed every urge to correct her. "Thank you."

We piled upon the skiff bed among the full crates and zipped back the way we came. Then, we veered down a lane opening to a clearing hosting two shacks I assumed were to house the skiff and crates. But once our crates were placed upon a wooden platform in the grass and covered in plastic, and the skiff was parked beside it, I looked upon the shacks with newfound dread.

"Tamarind! Find Franco a bunk and teach him the routine!" the foreman called, then marched to the less dilapidated of the two shacks and entered, slamming its door shut.

Tamarind pointed at the other shack. "We're here."

I studied the shack's rotted siding and bowing roof. "Home, sweet home," I whispered.

"We don't have sugar," Tamarind said.

"What?"

She gave an exacerbated sigh. "We don't have sugar, so we can't cook anything sweet."

I zeroed in on her. "You cook?"

She cocked her head. "How else do you make food?"

"With a synthesizer?" I said.

Her eyes darted side to side. "What's a *syndi-cider?*"

My smart mouth had nothing to say.

Tamarind found an empty top bunk with a soiled bedroll and tattered blanket, among twenty-nine others packed together. "We have running water, but only for drinking. We bathe in town once a month." She motioned to a small closet. "And we're lucky to have a built-in outhouse."

"For better or worse," said Brent, pinching his nose.

"For better when the night rains come," Tamarind said.

There was a door to another room emitting clanks and rattles, like a terrible percussion band.

"What's in there?" I asked.

"...The kitchen," she said, then pointed at a wooden slab with mismatching chairs. "Do you know what a dining table is?"

I turned red with embarrassment and grumbled, "Yes."

"Then, set it," she said and disappeared into the kitchen.

I opened the cupboard to find chipped plates, bowls, and cheap silverware with crooked necks or tines, and placed three stacks of plates on the table.

"What are you doing?" said one of the others.

"Setting the table," I responded.

He shook his head. "We need bowls not plates, idiot."

"What are we eating?" I asked, beyond frustrated.

He turned and entered the kitchen without answering.

Tamarind came out with a scowl. "Bowls, spoons, and... Just watch!" She set thirty bowls unceremoniously on the table.

No place mats?

She placed spoons at their fronts.

"Right," I muttered.

"What?"

"...Spoons go on the right," I said.

"Some of us are left handed... So, spoons at the front..."

I opened my mouth in protest, but I knew it was futile.

The crew started gathering around the table as more ruckus came from the kitchen.

"Make way!" Brent cried, coming through the kitchen door with a massive steel pot and hoisting it onto the dining table. "Soups on!"

Soup? I thought, certain they were joking until a spicy scent hit my nose. My stomach growled and my mouth watered. *What is happening to me?*

The crew scrambled to their seats as the smallest of them, wearing an apron, strutted to the pot with a smile on her face. I found a seat at the far end. She raised her hand, smiled wide, and cried, "Minestrone!"

"Minestrone!" the crew echoed back and pounded the table with their fists, then chanted, "Nel-ly! Nel-ly!"

They conveyed bowls to Nelly and she ladled minestrone into each.

"Hey, Airball! Pass it down!" someone shouted and I saw several bowls had piled next to me.

"Sorry." I hustled them along.

Full bowls were rounding the table. My hands quivered with excitement. But, when that first steaming bowl met my palms, I nearly dropped it in pain.

"Come on, Airball!"

I gritted my teeth and handed it off, anticipating the next shot of pain with the next bowl. Soon, there were no more to pass, just the one before me. The others placed fists against their shoulders, closed their eyes, and gave a moment of silence.

But for who? I matched their strange salute.

"Honor..." they muttered in unison and raised their heads.

"Honor," I quickly said.

Some blew across their bowls as others slurped it in.

So eager. Why? I looked into my bowl of red liquid filled with green, orange, and white pieces, none of which I could identify. Again, as I inhaled its scent, my body seemed to understand what I could not. I spooned a bit and blew, then timidly inserted it into my mouth. I shuddered. I moaned. I closed my eyes and was lost in another world. Flavors danced through my mouth.

Why!? I kept thinking. I swallowed and felt heat trickle down to my stomach. When I opened my eyes, they were staring at me.

"You okay, Airball?" Brent said.

♦

The next day was much like the first, my palms screaming, and I rubbed them in the sand to make sure blood would not make it onto the beans.

Tamarind took one look at my hands and whispered, "There better not be any blood on them."

By the end of the day, I had one crate with, *"FRAKO,"* on its side.

The foreman turned my way. "I thought your name was Franco!"

"It is…" I responded.

He pointed at my crate. "That is not how you spell Franco!"

"I don't know how to spell my name," I said, again.

The other kids snickered, but I did not care, for I was lost to the world, imagining what magic was going to be prepared for dinner.

♦

I became more proficient by the week. My palms were stiff and leathery, no longer bleeding. I set my fifth crate of the day on the bed with, *"FRANCO,"* on its side.

"Better!" the foreman shouted and faced us. "Tomorrow is Kontanda! Which means, you all get a day off!"

The kids smiled.

But I'm here for a year, I thought and could not recall any holiday by this name. I timidly raised my hand.

"Yes, Franco!" the foreman answered.

"I have nowhere to go," I quietly said. "I… have no family."

The foreman sighed deeply. "Can anyone take Franco in?"

Tamarind raised her hand.

♦

"I know you don't like strangers, but can my friend, Franco, stay for Kontanda?" Tamarind said while I waited outside a small stable stall.

Where am I? I kept thinking, flinching at every rat scurrying by or drunk worker shuffling in from the fields. *Where are the cows and horses?* I thought, studying the stalls. Then, it hit me. *It's these people's homes.* A pit formed in my stomach.

"No!" came from the stall, followed by shattering glass. "No strangers!"

"But… He has nowhere to go," Tamarind argued. "He's an orphan… He can't even spell his name."

Footsteps came and a woman stepped from the shadowy stall, standing nearly two meters tall, built like a professional athlete past their prime. A half-finished bottle dangled loosely in her hand.

"You're Franco!?" she barked.

"Y-yes…" I responded.

She cocked her head. "Where are you from!?"

My mind raced, trying to remember my backstory. "I'm from Hardsill. I was abandoned by my mother." *The truth hurts…*

The woman cocked her head. "That's real, but your voice is not! Who are you!?"

"Franco," I said.

The woman closed her eyes and turned an ear closer. "Again!"

"Franco," I repeated.

"One more time!"

"Franco…"

"Nice try," the frightening woman said and seemed to calm. "You better come inside."

I slowly entered the stall. Dull light revealed Tamarind sitting at a stained table on a chair whose leg was strapped together with wire. The frightening woman sat across from her and kicked out a third chair. "Sit, Franco," she said, emphasizing my name. "Tell me more about who you are."

I felt like Tamarind had led me to the wolves.

"Well!?" said the woman.

I thought about all the times I was gaslit by Mother. My frustration swelled, overriding my fear. "The best defense is the appearance of complete control," I remembered her saying, and I sat. "I'm sorry that you don't believe me. But that's who I am."

The woman leaned forward. "I know who you really are."

I imagined Mother negotiating with the lesser cartel bosses. *It's all just a game… No matter how scary,* I knew. "That's because I told you who I am," I calmly said, surprising myself. "Who are you?"

The woman took a swig from her bottle. She suddenly seemed less terrifying. "I'm not supposed to be here. If you must know."

"Neither am I," I said, granting her a small concession.

Her eyes narrowed. "Your mother taught you well."

I studied this less frightening woman. "How do you know my mother?"

"From when she worked here, long ago," she grinned.

"She never told me where she was from."

The frightening woman laughed. "You are good. I'll give you that. But, just like your mother, you're here to learn the business from the inside out. That's how this all works, isn't it?"

Tamarind turned back and forth between her mother, or maybe grandmother, I was not sure, and myself. "What are you talking about?"

The terrifying woman glanced at her granddaughter, as I decided she must be, then at me. "Why don't you tell her, Calvin."

♦

Tamarind gave me weary glances the next morning as we headed to the town square for Kontanda, no doubt trying to figure how she should treat me now that she knew who I was. Strange thumps and clashes came ahead, breaking festive music, followed by hoots and hollers.

"Those fuckers started early!" Tamarind's grandmother said, picking up her pace. She turned to us. "Move your asses!"

We hustled, trying to keep pace with her long, powerful strides and plunged into grass well over head height, joining several families along a path cut through the middle. They lit up when they saw Tamarind's grandmother.

"Are you fighting this year!?" a father, trailed by seven children, excitedly asked. I recognized two children from the picking fields, smiling at Tamarind's grandmother like she was a celebrity. They did not even acknowledge Tamarind and me.

"Of course!" she snapped at the father, then strutted faster, forcing Tamarind and I to run.

"Then, my credits are on you, Joan!" the father called after her.

Joan? I had heard this name before, muffled by Mother behind closed doors with a tone suggesting she was a problem.

Music intensified, followed by loud clanks and shouts. Small shacks appeared above the tall grasses. Then, the pathway opened, revealing dozens of food vendors surrounding a large crowd, cheering on whatever was happening at the center.

"Move!" Joan shouted, planting hands on people's shoulders and shoving them aside, making a path for us to cut through the crowd.

They broke to a dozen large people in the middle, clad in heavy armor and wielding melee weapons, appearing made of salvaged farm equipment. All were painted bright red with white crosses on their chests. A few were crawling on the dirt, retreating into the crowd.

"Stay here!" Joan ordered.

We stopped at the edge of the circle as Joan strutted into the center.

A hush came over the crowd and the heavily clad fighters squared up to her. Credits quickly changed on holotiles as bets were being made.

She's not wearing armor and has no weapon, I thought and turned to Tamarind. "She'll be killed!"

"Just watch," Tamarind said with a grin.

I eyed the crowd, certain someone would provide Joan with armor and weaponry. But no person came forth. Meanwhile, Joan calmly stood at the center, with her arms crossed, waiting.

A man, with a helmet shaped like a bull and wielding a gigantic sledgehammer, charged, swinging his hammer down upon Joan's head. *She's dead...* I was certain. But at the last moment, she raised a hand, catching the hammer by its shaft, just below its head, stopping it dead in its arc. Reverberations shuddered through the hammer's shaft to its wielder and he cried out as he lost his grip.

"Is that it?" Joan said and inspected the hammer now in her possession, swinging it effortlessly with one arm. She tossed it to the ground and eyed the rest. "Don't bother coming one at a time. Just attack."

They swarmed upon her, but she was so fast, so direct, and so strong. It felt like I was in the presence of a god. *Or a demon.* The crowd hooted and hollered as armor dented or was torn off by Joan's strikes. Soon, only one opponent remained.

Joan made a hand gesture saying, *come on.*

His legs shook and his armor rattled, sending laughter through the crowd. He raised two mace-like weapons and rushed. I had seen his earlier strikes and knew he liked beating his competitors like a drum. *Will this be Joan's Achilles heel?*

She subtly sidestepped the man, barely evading the first right-handed strike. Then, she pivoted, shoving her palm against the side of his wrist, forcing his mace across his body into the path of his second strike. The man screamed out as he struck his own hand, disarming both his weapons and tumbling them across the dirt. Joan planted a foot on the ground and thrust her palm upwards beneath her opponent's chinstrap, popping off his helmet and whirling his head around. Then, he tipped to the ground with a thud.

A moment of silence was followed by a mighty roar. Spectators raised holotiles, displaying their projected winnings. But their excitement dwindled as a man, flanked by two enforcers holding taser rods, pushed through the crowd to the center.

A lesser cartel boss, I recognized.

The boss raised a hand adorned with gaudy rings. "Joan is disqualified! She did not arrive on time!" he cried. "Therefore, all bets are off!"

The crowd erupted in complaints and stepped forth, until the enforcers ignited taser rods sending visible arcs of electricity to the ground. They cowered back.

"Must I do everything myself!?" Joan marched up to the cartel boss, gripped his collar tight, and lifted him off the ground.

The enforcers thrust taser rods into Joan's gut, but she did not flinch.

"I was on time!" she cried. "You started early!"

The enforcers continued thrusting taser rods, until Joan stomped on one's instep with an audible snap. The enforcer fell to the ground, grasping their foot and screaming. The other backed away and deactivated his taser rod.

The cartel boss's eyes darted around, then settled on Joan. "You know what?" he said, perfectly composed, as only a boss could do. "I think you're right."

Joan set the boss to his feet. "The odds were ten to one against me, correct?"

The boss furrowed his brow. "Ten to one for you."

She slowly lifted him off the ground again.

"My mistake," the boss calmly responded. "You had an elbow injury this year, right?"

Joan grinned. "Sure…"

"Then, yes. The odds would be ten to one against you."

The crowd cheered as their winnings skyrocketed.

I saw seething in the boss's eyes and understood why Mother spoke of Joan with such disgust. *Her acting against a lesser cartel boss is the same as acting against them all.*

We sat at a food vendor as happy gamblers came to thank Joan, each buying her a shot.

"Lunch is on the house!" the vendor said.

Round upon round of food was set before us: fish cooked with citric acid, meats and grilled vegetables on small plates, and then something I could not comprehend – *Ice cream.*

"Are you crying?" Tamarind asked.

"No," I quickly said, wiping my eyes.

As one hour turned into two, the vendor's smile dwindled.

"I'm full," Tamarind said.

"Keep eating!" Joan snapped and knocked back another shot.

"Joan, I'm sorry, but this is the last round," the vendor finally said.

"Fuck you!" Joan cussed. "Give us more!"

The vendor timidly turned to the curtain obscuring the kitchen and said, "Another round of fried calamari!"

"You serious!? We're already into tomorrow's supply!" the cook cried.

"You better believe I'm serious!" Joan shouted.

She's drunk. I checked the time. *Noon. But maybe I can use this.* "Joan is an interesting name," I said. "Where does it originate from?"

Joan did not acknowledge me, but Tamarind turned my way.

"She's named after a woman who lived under a bridge."

"What?" I responded.

"Because of the arches," she added.

Arches? I thought, then remembered history class. "You mean, Joan of Arc! She was a hero! That's a great name!" I beamed a smile, but saw Joan staring daggers at me.

"I am no hero," she said, stood from her stool, and staggered from the vendor's booth.

"Cancel order. She left," the vendor said with relief.

"Who named her? Where were they from?" I asked Tamarind as we followed Joan to the edge of town where the grass grew tall.

Joan spun, grasped my shirt, and lifted me from the ground. "Keep your mouth shut!" she snarled, her spittle spraying my face, reeking of alcohol.

People turned a blind eye and hustled off.

I silently stared back, feeling something within me boiling up. Not rage or frustration, but an understanding. I thought upon the body language of the opponents Joan had fought and the look on the cartel boss and vendor's faces. I remembered their fear. *That's Joan's power.* I did not know what compelled me, but I took a deep breath and said, "No."

Joan blinked. Then, she chuckled and set me down. "Nice to see that someone has balls."

Tamarind was silent, her eyes wide, not believing I just talked to her grandmother like that.

"What is Kontanda celebrating?" I followed up, feeling my heart pounding in my chest.

Joan knelt to my height. "The last rebellion of our people."

"The Bloody Dozen?" I whispered, having studied the event in school.

"How does a child know about The Bloody Dozen?"

"I must know everything if I'm to take my mother's place," I responded.

"Yet you did not know about Kontanda."

"I know now…" I said, letting my smart mouth fly.

"How much do you know about The Bloody Dozen?" Joan asked, her eyes focused on me like an eagle.

"…They were a band of clones named after heroes of antiquity, ones who stood up against the cartels, five hundred years ago. But they failed, despite having been genetically modified to be superhuman. They were all either killed or captured," I said, staring into Joan's eyes, realizing how strange they were, especially when she was drunk.

A prideful grin spread on her face.

I studied her breathing, deep and powerful, and the solidness of her muscles, recalling how she made hulking men seem weak. *She's superhuman, too…* I realized. "You're one of them, aren't you?"

Joan's look hardened. "Now, you know too much…"

◆

Tamarind and I returned to the fields in morning darkness, before Joan woke from her drunken slumber. I felt lucky to be alive. Felt that Joan could have killed me at any moment. But I understood that she had principles hidden beneath her agony. I was almost giddy to meet the other children, but when I climbed onto the skiff I sensed anxiety.

"What's wrong?" I asked. "Did you not enjoy Kontanda?"

Brent glared at me. "Keith is late."

"Who's Keith?"

"The foreman," Tamarind said.

"So, we wait," I said.

"He's never late, Airball," Brent said.

"Someone's coming." Little Nelly pointed at the rising sun.

A silhouette, strange, muscular, and lumbering, appeared. *Not our foreman,* I realized.

"Shit, that's Schunt," Brent said.

"No…" said another.

I noticed the man's lumbering was actually staggering. "He's drunk."

"They all are," Brent said.

I gave him a look. "Then, why are you so afraid of—"

"You!" came Schunt's coarse, slurred voice. "Shut your fucking mouth before I break your teeth!"

The kids silenced, even Brent.

When Schunt reached the skiff, he stumbled, grasping the edge of its bed to remain upright. His immense weight dipped the skiff. "You motherfuckers are mine, now! Do as I say or lose your teeth!"

Keep your mouth shut! I begged myself, but this giant buffoon was going to get us killed. *I must say something!* "Where's Kei—"

Something cracked my jaw and sent me flipping off the skiff, landing hard in the dirt. I did not see what struck me. I was not sure if it was actually Schunt. I felt dirt between my molars. I searched my mouth with my tongue until pain zapped where my two front teeth once were.

"Teeth!" Schunt cried and flashed his own gap-toothed smile. "Get up or you'll really have something to worry about!"

I fought through blinding pain and crawled back onto the bed.

Schunt took the cab, fumbling with Keith's setup. The skiff bucked, then took off. He swerved side to side, almost dumping us. When we finally arrived at the next ripe field, I caught the scent of urine from the other children.

"Get me some fucking beans!" Schunt cried as he emerged from the cab with a fresh bottle in his hand. "I want twenty crates from each of you! If you don't have twenty by the time I return… Teeth!" He placed a massive hand behind the crates and sent them crashing to the dirt. Then, he reentered the cab and took off, leaving us stranded.

"He broke a lot of them," Brent said when the skiff dipped beyond a hill and turned to me. "Good time for you to learn how to fix them." He quickly gathered twenty crates and wrote his name.

The others were doing the same and all the broken crates were tossed in my direction.

I'm screwed no matter what. "No!" I said, air hitting my exposed nerves and I winced. *Fight through!* I ordered myself. "I won't fix them!"

Brent turned to me. "What do you mean, no!? Did you hear what Schunt just said!? Do you want to—"

I smiled wide, revealing my two missing front teeth and fighting back tears. Then, I stuck my tongue through the gap and wagged it at him.

Brent grimaced. "If they're still broken by the time Schunt returns, then we're all fucked!"

I retracted my tongue. "You barely get twelve crates a day, anyway. So, what makes you think you can do twenty now? You might be able to pull off fifteen, but you will still lose your teeth." *Fuck, that hurt!* They were staring at me, letting my words sink in. "The only way we get through today is if we work together."

Brent fumed, looking to end me right then and there, until Nelly said, "How do we work together?"

Brent deflated. "Everyone fixes a crate, then we get to work."

It took an hour to repair them and we dispersed into the fields, each taking a row. I studied Brent furiously picking, but his technique was brutish. He was not filling crates any faster than the younger kids, but he carried them with such ease to the loading zone that he had the most, second only to Tamarind. She was filling crates faster than the others. Her technique was flawless, but she was slow in delivering them.

I lugged my first crate to the loading zone and when I turned back I realized how much of a disorganized mess we were. *We'll never reach twenty...* I climbed atop an overturned crate, cupped my hands around my mouth, braced for excruciating pain, and called, "You are too slow!"

They turned my way.

"We will never meet the quota if we don't help each other!" I added.

"Shut up, Airball!" Brent called back.

"Tamarind has more crates than you and she is half your size! Why do you think that is!?"

They were quiet.

"It's because she has the best picking technique!" I answered for them. "Brent! You have the worst picking technique, but still have the next most crates. Why do you think that is!?"

Again they were quiet.

"Because Brent is the strongest and can quickly haul his crates to the loading zone!"

"What of it!?" Brent hollered.

"Brent is now responsible for collecting and stacking all the crates!"

"Fuck you!" he shouted. "I ain't doing that!"

"Are you not strong enough!?" I asked, letting my smart mouth fly.

"Ooooo," said another.

Brent picked up his full crate with one arm, then marched to another row, picking up one of the smaller kid's crates. He jogged to the loading zone with both and set them at my feet. "See!? Easy!"

I grinned. "I bet you can't do that for an hour."

"I can do this all day!" he declared.

"...Prove it," I said.

His eyes locked onto mine, realizing I had forced him into a position to either do as I say or face humiliation. A smug look grew on his face, as if he found a way out of my game. "I can collect crates faster than the entire crew can fill them."

Is that so? I thought. "Brent says he can collect all of your crates faster than you can fill them!" *Ow!*

"Bullshit!" one of them shouted.

Brent's smug look dropped.

"Everyone, line up in the same row!" I instructed and winced. "When your crate is filled, raise your hand and Brent will collect it. I will provide you with an empty crate to fill next!" They timidly formed up at a single row.

Brent cocked his head. "You're making this easier for me?"

I wagged my tongue through my teeth and then called, "Tamarind, can you teach everyone your picking technique!?"

She nodded, and they gathered around, watching how she rotated the fruit to naturally break their stems.

Crates were filling. Brent was getting nervous. The first hand was raised and he took off, but by the time he reached the first crate another picker had their hand raised. He returned with two as I placed empty crates at their feet. After an hour, the first round of full crates were in the loading zone, and the picking team moved on to the next row.

Brent studied the crates. "How do we know whose is whose?"

"If the total is enough, Schunt won't care," I responded, huffing hard, wincing harder.

"Hey!" came from the field.

Brent and I turned to see more hands were raised. Brent took a deep breath, then raced off again.

Round after round was collected, and by early afternoon, I knew we were turning the tide. The sun started setting as Jupiter grew brighter in the sky. Anxiety skyrocketed as Schunt's impending arrival neared.

I returned to the loading zone to collect more empty crates to find none remaining. *We did it...* I realized and faced our rows of full crates. Some had twenty, most had nineteen, and a few had twenty-one. I quickly redistributed them so each was exactly twenty, except for the last, with thirteen. I plopped onto the dirt as Brent came running with two more crates. He gave me a confused look and set them in the last row. *Fifteen,* I noted. The others were staring at me, waiting for new crates.

"Airball!? What are you doing!?" Brent hollered. "Deliver more crates!"

"Brent..." I calmly said and pointed at the rows. "We're done."

Brent snapped his head to the rows and counted, then threw his hands up. "We did it! We did it!"

The others lit up, until a skiff popped up over the hill.

"Schunt is here!" I called. "Fill those last crates!"

Pickers furiously worked. Brent took off collecting two more crates as the others worked to hustle the rest to the loading zone. I pointed at the last row, seeing the final crates were not quite filled as they were stacked.

Good enough... I thought. "Everyone, stand in front of a row!"

They responded like little soldiers and I took the row with the crates coming up short.

The skiff almost swerved off the lane before stopping past us. It bucked in reverse to align with the crates. Schunt's silhouette sat slouched in the cab, his head nearly touching the steering stick.

He's even more drunk than before, I realized.

He popped open the door and stumbled out, spilling bottles to the dirt. Then, he rounded the skiff. "You little shits!" he cried with unfocused eyes. "None of you got twenty! Which means! Teeth!"

"We all have twenty!" I sharply said, feeling adrenaline course through me, trembling my hands and dulling my pain.

"Who said that!?" Schunt spat, his eyes finally lifting.

"I did," I raised my hand.

He came barreling towards me with his fist cocked back. But, just before he struck, I smiled wide, flashing my missing teeth.

He stopped in his tracks, almost tumbling backwards, and grasped the crates in my row to keep his balance. He began studying them, slowly and deliberately, wiping his face, shaking his head, and squinting his eyes. "One... two..." he mumbled, and I hoped he wouldn't notice the few not quite full. "...Nineteen... twenty." He stopped and stared, then looked at the next row and counted. "Twenty again..." he muttered, with a twinkle in his eye. He studied muscular Brent, then little Nelly. He pointed at her. "You! How did you pick just as much as him!?" He pointed at Brent. "You must have cheated! Which means... Teeth!"

He charged her with his fist raised, but Brent moved fast, passing in front of Nelly and taking Schunt's punch on his shoulder.

"It was me! I cheated! I gave her some of my crates!" Brent said, holding his arm. "But look, we all have twenty, just like you asked. This many crates has never been done in one day before. You'll get the bonus!"

Schunt's eyes lit up at the word *bonus*. "Make sure it never happens again! She must pick her own twenty! No help!" He snatched Brent by the neck. "For speaking out of turn and cheating… Teeth!" His fist sunk into Brent's face. *Once, twice.* Then, Schunt threw him to the dirt. "Load the crates!" he shouted, entered the cab, and opened a fresh bottle.

I raced to Brent laying motionless on the dirt, grasped his shoulder, and rolled him to his back. I was about to shake him awake when he smiled, revealing missing front teeth. He stuck his tongue through the gap and wagged it at me.

♦

We picked exactly twenty crates each for two months straight. And where Schunt was initially furious, taking a few more of our crew's teeth, when that first bonus came in, he was all smiles. He now showed up in his brand new skiff, wearing a new hat or coat, to say a few slurred words. Then, he would return to the bunkhouse to drink himself to death. Meanwhile, we became a well-oiled machine. On top of crate collection, Brent drove the old skiff. And when we found mites, he donned the reflective suit and torched the rows. I was in charge of efficiency. Tamarind was quality control.

But as Schunt's success became known, the other foreman came to watch and learn.

Schunt arrived in his new skiff a few days later, furious. "Who taught them how to pick like you!?" he accused. "I'll lose my bonus!" He knocked more crates from his skiff. "I want twenty-five crates from each of you or I'll take *her* teeth!" He pointed at Nelly, then entered the cab and sped off to the bunkhouse.

We stared at the skiff as it dipped over the hill.

"Twenty-five is impossible," Brent said, giving Nelly a nervous glance.

I thought about that. "Tamarind…"

"Yeah?"

"Can you get Joan?" I asked.

The look on everyone's faces told a story or two.

"She's likely drunk," Tamarind responded.

"Isn't everyone?" I said.

"What should I tell her?"

"The truth of our situation."

"What makes you think she'll come?" Brent said. "She's just as bad as Schunt."

No, she's a principled person, a person of justice, I knew in my gut. "She will help us," I said to skeptical looks. "It's just that nobody has asked her before." I sighed. "Tell her that I will owe her a favor. And where I'm from, a favor is sacred."

"Okay?" Tamarind said.

I turned to Brent. "You think you can give Tamarind a ride?"

"What about the quota? You'll never reach twenty-five without us."

"We won't make twenty-five anyway, just like you said," I responded. "We don't have a choice."

For the next two hours we made due without our best picker and star crate collector. But in their absence others stepped up. *We're making good progress...*

"I see our skiff!" Nelly said.

We gathered by our stacked crates as it slowed to a stop. Only Brent and Tamarind were in the cab, their faces looking defeated.

Did Joan refuse? I thought until a groan came from the skiff's bed. I rounded the cab and caught the smell of alcohol and vomit. Joan was curled around a bottle, asleep.

Brent and Tamarind stepped from the cab.

"I don't think she can help us," Brent said.

"Did she at least agree?" I asked.

"Yeah," Tamarind said. "But I don't think she understood."

"She kept saying, *anything for the king!*" Brent added.

She understood, I knew. "Let her sleep, we have several hours before Schunt returns."

Brent spied the crates and raised eyebrows. "You got a lot done."

I grinned. "I think we'll still achieve twenty a person."

"So, Schunt can't be too mad at us," Tamarind said.

I shrugged. "I don't think it matters."

"Maybe we can almost get twenty-five," Brent carefully said. "Progress is at least better."

Yes it is, I thought, proud of Brent for coming to this conclusion. I suddenly remembered Mother stressing how these laborers are not beneath us. *Maybe I don't give them enough credit.*

We returned to the field, working faster than ever before. Meanwhile, Joan slept through the afternoon.

The sun soon descended and Schunt was coming.

I quickly counted our rows. *Twenty-two or twenty-three each.* "Line up! Schunt is here!" I called and everyone scrambled to a row.

Schunt came to a clean stop and stepped briskly from the cab.

He's sober… I realized.

"You little fuckers had better got twenty-five!" he shouted and faced me. "Well!? You're the fucking leader, right!? Did you get twenty-five or not!?"

At that moment, I understood his behavior was not a result of his drinking. *That's just him…* "We did better than ever before. Twenty-three each," I said. *Wake up Joan!* I thought.

His eyes widened, then narrowed again. "That's not twenty-five! Where is she!? Where's Nelly!?"

I saw her hiding behind Brent. "She's not here."

"What do you mean she's not here!?" He locked eyes with Brent and marched towards him. "Out of the fucking way! Nelly's mine!"

Brent widened his stance and spread his arms like he was a wall. He closed his eyes and braced for the beating to come.

"The Mighty Ox…" came a hoarse voice.

Schunt froze.

"…You picking on little girls, now?"

I whipped my head to the skiff to find Joan leaning against its bed.

"Are you gonna look at me?" she said and stepped closer.

Schunt slowly turned. His face was pale.

"That's better," Joan said, approaching him. "Now, give me a little smile, won't you?"

He did not smile.

"No?" Joan said, feigning surprise. "Oh, that's right. Last time we met was during Kontanda seven years ago… Didn't I take your teeth then?"

Schunt did not move a muscle.

"You've gotten so fat," Joan said and poked his belly.

Schunt slid his foot back, his body language becoming submissive.

"I've heard you've won a lot of bonuses lately," Joan continued.

"Y-yes," Schunt muttered.

"So what's the problem?"

"They were supposed to get twenty-five crates today."

Joan turned to me. "Is that true?"

I saw the opening. "Yes," I said and Schunt relaxed until I followed up with, "but we were told midway through the day." I pointed at the crates. "We have twenty-three each having only half the day to adjust. If we had the whole day, we could have done twenty-five."

Schunt squirmed something awful.

Joan turned to him. "Looks like they are on track for twenty-five from now on." She stared right into Schunt's eyes. "Don't you agree?"

"Yes, you're right," he quietly said, but I could sense his seething. He turned around and marched to his skiff.

"Wait," Joan said, motioning at us. "Don't you owe them an apology?"

No... too far, I knew.

Schunt's gaze rested on me. "I'm sorry." He entered his cab and took off.

We loaded the skiff and dropped Joan off at the stables, then returned to the bunkhouse where Schunt was waiting. My stomach grew more nauseous by the second, not knowing if he would be passed out drunk or ready to collect teeth.

He was standing in his doorway, with a bottle in hand, as we parked the skiff and transferred the crates to the platform, simply watching us with a little smirk.

We entered the bunkhouse in silence, made dinner, and got ready for bed, all the while keeping an eye on the door, expecting Schunt to burst through at any moment.

I desperately fought off sleep, as the others were no doubt doing, too. But, one by one, I heard our breathing become heavy and rhythmic. Then, artificial rain came pattering on the metal roof, drowning out all other sound.

♦

Sharp screams pierced through the sheeting rain, jolting me from my bunk. Everyone was shuffling about, trying to see in the pitch dark.

"Roll Call!" I shouted, then, "Franco!"

"Tamarind!" I heard.

"Brent!" came next.

They each called names, all but one.

"Nelly, are you here!?" I cried. "Nelly!?"

"Her bunk's empty!" Brent hollered back.

Another scream came. It was unmistakable.

"I'm going to kill him!" Brent shouted and I heard his footsteps running to the door. "It won't budge!"

We stumbled through darkness, bumping into each other, until we reached Brent and added our strength, yanking at the door. A splintering slowly came until the door whipped open, revealing the night's torrential downpour.

I squinted, trying to make out what had locked us in. I ran my hands along the floor until I felt wet metal and the shape of a spade. *A shovel through the handle,* I realized.

The piercing scream came again. We plunged into pouring rain, slipping on mud and grass, making for the foreman's cabin. Orange light with flickering shadows shone through Schunt's window. We pounded against the cabin's bamboo siding and locked door.

"Get back to the bunkhouse!" Schunt cried from within.

"Open the door!" Brent shouted, pounding with all his might, cracking its planks.

The door whipped open, revealing Schunt in his underwear, but wearing his new coat and hat. A part of me breathed a sigh of relief to see him somewhat clothed, until I saw his hands. In one was a pair of pliers, dripping with blood. The other was holding a little ankle.

"You want her!?" Schunt lifted Nelly by her leg.

Blood ran down her face and when she opened her mouth, only her gums remained.

"Teeth!" Schunt cried triumphantly and threw her to the sopping wet grass. "From now on, if you ever talk back to me! If you try anything sneaky! I will remove another piece of her!" He looked right at me. "And if you even think about running to Joan, I'll kill her!" He pointed at Nelly. "Clean her the fuck up! I want thirty crates tomorrow!"

Brent rushed Schunt, swinging his fists.

Schunt grinned and sent a fast cross, like a boxer, planting on Brent's jaw and dropping him to the grass next to Nelly. Then, Schunt slammed his door and the clinking of another bottle came.

My jaw clenched. My hands trembled.

"What do we do!?" Tamarind cried.

"Get back to the bunkhouse!" I called above the rain. "Tend to Nelly and Brent!" I turned to our skiff and saw a little orange light. *A reflection of Schunt's cabin.* I marched over to it.

"Where are you going!?" Tamarind shouted, but I ignored her, focusing on the strange orange light.

The reflection suit... I realized as I reached the skiff's cab, finding it laid upon the passenger seat. On the floor was the incinerator's nozzle and tank reading, *"1/8 full."* My mind raced, weighing Schunt's threats and increasing expectations. Then, I thought upon Mother just before she left me here, saying, "You will one day protect these people, like a sheepdog guarding its fold..."

◆

I snuck into the bunkhouse just before dawn, quietly crawled into my bunk, and pretended to wake with the rest of the crew. Despite the night's events I could tell that they had fallen back to sleep. *Good...*

We helped Nelly and Brent from their bunks, dressed them in clean canvas, and spoon-fed Nelly porridge.

"Thirty..." several of our crew whispered.

Tamarind gave me a long stare from across the dining table, but did not utter a word. *Good...*

We exited the bunkhouse to see the artificial rain had stopped right on schedule. Moist soil was the only discernible scent. Another pallet of empty crates was delivered by the collector ships, and I realized that under the cover of night and the torrential rain, they did not notice the mayhem. *Good...*

We loaded the crates onto our skiff as morning light crept upon us. No one dared to look at Schunt's cabin, terrified that he might be standing in his doorway, watching us. *Good...*

Brent drove to the next section of coffee plants ripe with fruit. We set up in our usual way and furiously picked as Nelly and Brent nursed their wounds.

"Mites!" I cried late morning as we started a new row. Everyone emptied their crates and stomped the beans into the dirt without question. *Good...*

Brent sat up, looking about to don the reflection suit.

I raced to him. "Let me do it today, you should rest."

He paused, then said, "Do you know how?"

"I've watched you a hundred times," I replied and slipped on the reflective suit. I primed the tank and strapped it on.

Brent watched, nodding when I did things correctly. He did not check the tank's fuel gauge. *Good...*

"Make sure to use both hands, it has a kick," he instructed.

"I'll be careful." I ran to the infested row, aimed the incinerator's nozzle, and released hellfire. I was sloppy, using too much fuel, and by the time the row was turned to ash, the tank was empty. *Good...*

"Dammit, Airball!" Brent shouted. "That's expensive! Schunt's gonna be pissed!"

"Sorry!" I hollered and hustled back to the skiff. I tore off the reflection suit and empty tank, and rejoined the pickers.

By early afternoon, we were at ten crates each. *On pace for twenty,* I knew, feeling like this would be a terrible haul when only a few months ago, twenty was unheard of. I cupped my hands around my mouth. "We're on pace for twenty despite being shorthanded! Keep up the good work!"

"That's not enough," Tamarind said, giving me a penetrating look.

"If Schunt has a problem, then I'll take the blame," I responded.

"No… He'll take it out on Nelly," Tamarind followed up.

"He won't," I said.

"But… he will," she argued.

I faced her squarely. "He won't."

She cocked her head. "How do you know?"

"I just do." I went back to picking, focusing on the plant in front of me.

Tamarind did not question me further. *Good…*

Dusk came and we stacked our crates in the loading zone. *Twenty each.* But I saw anxiety in everyone's postures.

"We're going to be okay. Nelly will be okay," I said.

They looked at me like I was insane, then faced the horizon, searching for Schunt's skiff. A half hour became a full hour. No skiff appeared. *Good…*

"Where is he?" Brent asked.

"Maybe he's drunk," Tamarind said.

"We should head back before it becomes too dark," I suggested.

They were silent the entire way, anticipating Schunt's fury. But when we arrived, he was nowhere in sight.

"Where's his skiff?" Tamarind asked.

"Yeah, was it gone this morning?" Brent added.

No one could give an answer. *Good…*

We set the crates in the collection zone and covered them, then we bee-lined to the bunkhouse to make dinner. Artificial rain was not scheduled for that night, so we heard every subtle sound. Nobody slept, each listening for Schunt's skiff to return and for him to stumble into the bunkhouse furious. But he never came. *Good…*

◆

We rose the next morning and silently readied ourselves. Our full crates were replaced with another pallet of empty ones. This time there was a note. *"Congratulations on your bonus! Keep up the great work, Schunt!"* it read. Behind the note was a stem-code for deposit.

Our push to twenty-three crates was enough, I realized.

"His skiff is still missing," Tamarind said. She built her courage, approached the cabin, and peeked through its window. "It's empty…"

"Where did he go?" Nelly quietly asked, wincing.

Everyone shrugged.

"What do we do, then?" she followed up.

A few looked at Brent, but Brent was looking at me.

"Let's aim for twenty-five crates today," I said, but saw their looks. I lifted the note. "Schunt still got his bonus because of our push to twenty-three. If we keep the bonuses coming in, then maybe he won't hurt us."

Everyone glanced at where Schunt's skiff was usually parked, then began loading the crates.

♦

We each collected twenty-five crates every day of that week and every night we returned to find Schunt still gone. Another bonus was delivered with the replacement crates.

"What do you think happened?" Brent asked, looking at the foreman's cabin. "Should we check it out?"

"Maybe," Tamarind said.

Nelly made a determined face and strutted across the grass, her little hands in fists. Our jaws dropped as she bounded up the steps and pounded the door. It drifted open. She turned with a confused look.

Brent ran forth, then cautiously stepped inside. "He left his holotile!" He emerged with Schunt's holotile in hand, a note hovering in its hologram.

"What does it say?" I asked.

"Dear, Nelly…" Brent read aloud and turned her way. "I was wrong to hurt you. You did not deserve my rage. I hope that you can one day forgive me. I am so ashamed of myself. Please, as an apology, I give you my life savings. My account information is below. Brent, I leave you in charge. Please, fix Nelly's teeth with the money in my account. Sorry, there is not enough to fix everyone's. Goodbye, Schunt."

Everyone was silent, stunned.

Brent looked at me. "I don't know how to do account stuff. Do you?"

"My mother taught me before I was abandoned," I responded. *Again, the truth hurts...*

"Can you help me get Nelly new teeth?" he asked, handing me Schunt's holotile.

"Absolutely," I said, scanned the stem codes from the two bonus receipts, and watched them deposit into the account.

♦

Nelly returned a week later from the field hospital and smiled brightly, showing off her new teeth.

"Who needs a flashlight when we have you!" Brent laughed.

We began smiling as we worked, the pride of being our own masters fueling us. We reached twenty-five crates regularly. Then, twenty-seven.

With the bonuses rolling in, Nelly and I purchased new equipment and ordered better produce and proteins. Our bodies were changing. I no longer recognized our ragtag crew. I no longer recognized myself. I was rugged. My skin was bronzed. My hands were like leather. I was four centimeters taller. My hair grew shaggy and bleached out. And I had missing teeth.

Three months after Schunt left, we reached thirty crates apiece.

♦

"Who's that!?" Tamarind said, pointing at a ship hanging in the sky above our bunkhouse, as we returned from another record day in the fields.

A cartel gunship, I realized and discerned several figures at our crate platform, all in black, with semi-automatic rifles in hand. *Cartel enforcers…* I saw one dressed more elegantly. *Mother!?*

We slowed to a stop in front of them, but none of us disembarked.

Mother raised a hand and smiled brightly. "Hello, children. I wish to speak with your foreman."

We did not budge.

She laughed lightly. "Of course, I must introduce myself. My name is Don Hayes. I am the owner of this here plantation."

We still did not budge.

Her smile dwindled. "You are not in trouble. In fact, we are here to congratulate you. You've been a great asset these past nine months. We wish to speak with Schunt to learn how he turned our worst crew into our best. Do you know where he might be?"

Brent slowly opened the cab door and stepped onto the grass. He motioned for us to come. Only then did we move, aligning opposite the enforcers. Mother gave each of us an inquisitive look. Then, her eyes lit up seeing our latest haul.

"Schunt left," Brent said.

"I see," the don responded. "Do you know when he'll return?"

"He's not coming back," Brent followed up.

"What do you mean?" Mother asked.

"He left six months ago."

"What?" Mother snapped up straight. "That's not possible. Who's been operating your crew? Certainly not Keith."

"We operate ourselves," Brent said.

"That cannot be!" she spat in the manner I was accustomed to.

"It's true," said a little voice. Nelly reached into her pocket and retrieved Schunt's holotile. "He gave us everything to keep going without him." She opened the message.

"Let me see that!" Mother snatched it from Nelly and read through, laughing to herself until the end. "This message is encrypted with his retinal signature…" She slowly handed it back to Nelly, her eyes darting back and forth, searching for why Schunt might do such a thing. Her eyes fixated on Brent. "Schunt left you in charge. And I see that your efficiency has increased since his departure. Are you the foreman now?"

"We have no foreman," Brent responded.

"But, somebody trained you, right? If not Schunt, then who?"

The entire crew faced me.

Mother turned my way, not a flicker of recognition in her eyes.

"Then, that makes you the foreman," she said shortly and opened her holotile. "What's your name?"

"…Franco," I said.

"Okay, Franco, from now on, you are—" Mother's head snapped up and she locked wild eyes with me. But then, her cartel training kicked in and she composed herself. "Franco, from now on, you are our point of contact, which comes with all its responsibilities and benefits. Is that understood?"

"Yes," I said.

"And…" Mother hesitantly continued. "…Keep up the good work."

She had never complimented me before. My heart fluttered and I smiled.

Mother's eyes went wide with horror.

But why? I thought until I tongued my missing front teeth.

◆

My crew loaded another day's haul to the collection zone and retired to the bunkhouse to make dinner. As much as I wanted to join them, I had paperwork to finish. The moment I entered my cabin, I felt a presence.

"Little Calvin, big foreman," came a hoarse voice.

My eyes snapped to the shadows where an athletic woman stood. "Joan… You scared the shit out of me."

"We can drop the accent now," she responded, dropping hers, sounding strangely proper, like a diplomat.

"I sometimes forget you're from a different time and place," I gave her a weary look. "Are you here for payment?"

She shook her head. "Kontanda grants me more than enough credits." She stepped closer. "It's almost been a year, so, I've come to see you off."

"How did you know?"

She grinned. "Your mother was only here for a year."

"Does she know that you figured her out?" I pointedly asked.

"No, and let's keep it that way," Joan responded.

"Agreed," I said.

"So, what happens to you next?" she asked.

"I'll finish school, then start at the roasters," I responded.

"And after that?"

"I work in the cafes and intern with distribution. Eventually, I'll shadow my mother," I said.

"When will you become the don?"

"I don't know," I said.

Joan thought about that. "Make sure it happens quickly. There's a timeline I'm bound to."

"What do you mean?" I ventured.

She grimaced. "There will be a moment in which I will require your help. When I call in my favor to close out yours."

"So, you are here for payment, after all," I said.

She ignored my quip. "One day, a young man or woman, approximately seventeen years of age, will come to you. This person will embody my people's hopes and dreams. They will be the key to our survival, but they will not realize it." She breathed deeply. "You must help them become the person they were meant to be."

"How do I do that?"

"I will inform you of the specifics when the time comes," she said.

I frowned. "You haven't figured it out, then."

"Nothing is certain until the moment it is. When I know, I will make sure that you know."

I processed the information knowing it was all she would divulge. "A favor for a favor, I will repay, in this moment or the next, on my life, I lay," I recited, having heard Mother say the words countless times.

◆

A year... I woke before my crew, but instead of inspecting the new crates and prepping the skiff and incinerator, I packed my things and headed down the lane on foot. I contemplated leaving a note. *But I must remain anonymous,* I knew. Instead, I left everything they would need to keep going on my desk and hoped they could carry on without me.

The lane was dark and I kept a watchful eye should another crew be traveling at this hour. My holotile indicated Mother's shuttle was hidden where I was dropped off. As the sun rose, I cut through the field. A mound appeared just above coffee plants.

"Calvin," I heard as I arrived.

"Mother," I responded, barely making out her silhouette.

"You can stop with the accent," she said.

The sun further rose and I made out her features. "It feels natural now," I said, reverting to my Hardsill accent.

"That happened to me, too," Mother responded. She waved at the shuttle's hatch. "Let's go."

I sat on the shuttle's cushioned seat, which now felt like a marshmallow, and buckled in. Mother started the shuttle and raised us into the sky.

Dawn cracked and for several minutes we zoomed low above the plantation watching its plants ripple in the wind like ocean waves.

"You're getting new teeth," Mother eventually snipped. "A result of your smart mouth, I'm assuming."

I turned from the window. "I just asked about Keith."

Mother made a face. "So it was Schunt who took them."

"It was…" I thought about that moment, then our original foreman who, in retrospect, was a saint. "What happened to Keith?"

"He died," Mother snapped.

"How did he—"

"You didn't happen to save your teeth, did you?" Mother cut me off. "Our dentists can make perfect replicas if you did."

"I don't want new teeth," I said.

"What!?" Mother turned sharply towards me. "Of course you do!"

"No, I don't," I stated.

Mother thought about that. "Why?"

"I don't want to forget." I returned my gaze to the fields below and found a break where one of Jackman Syndicate's many fishing wells, accessing the liquid ocean below Ganymede's ice, lay. I recognized this particular well and my stomach twisted.

Mother slowed the shuttle, banking around the well's circumference, tilting my window downward to grant me a better view. A massive crane along the well's edge dangled a blackened skiff from its boom.

"They found that skiff at the bottom of the ocean, burnt to a crisp," Mother calmly said. "The serial number was scratched off and no body was found..."

My heart raced and my palms began to sweat.

"...We've searched every bar and brothel in Ganymede since Schunt left your crew. It seems both he and his skiff disappeared into thin air…" Mother remained silent for several seconds, which felt like an eternity. Then, she said, "…Well done."

The shuttle leveled out and we headed home.

◆

My daughter was born early morning and did not come quietly. I watched her mother labor through a window for several hours while doctors tried convincing her to have a cesarean. But she knew what stigma that would create for my daughter and refused, choosing to risk her own life in traditional cartel fashion. I did not know anything about this woman besides her name and the few nights we spent together. In fact, her name was the only reason she was chosen. That and her raid upon a Council yacht in Venusian space. She came to us with a councilwoman's priceless portrait to prove her mettle. She was a *Din,* which matched perfectly to my *Cre.* And so, this stranger, pushing out my baby, was given riches beyond her wildest dreams. And I would be given an heir to the cartel.

The purple beast finally popped out, perpendicular to the vaginal canal, facing me. *No wonder it took so long…* She opened her eyes and roared, and all at once, her skin flushed pink and her skull's platelets began shifting back into place. As the mother reached for my daughter, the doctors quickly cut the cord, took the newborn, and made for the exit. My daughter would never know her mother, just as I never knew my father. The mother cried out, but she was too exhausted to put up a fight and uncontrollably sobbed, instead.

I could not bear it and knocked on the window to get the doctor's attention. I raised five fingers, indicating five minutes.

The doctor nodded.

The mother wiped her tears as he placed the newborn into her arms. She rocked my daughter slowly, wincing as her contractions continued on, and whispered, "You saved my entire family, little one…" After five minutes were up, the mother reluctantly nodded at the doctor, who took the newborn. Then, she breathed deeply, groaned, and pushed out the afterbirth.

The doctor raced through the door and presented my daughter to me. I took her awkwardly in my hands, nervously supporting her head, feeling like she might slip out of my grasp at any moment.

"This way, sir," the doctor said, waving down the hall. "You must bond with your daughter. Time is of the essence."

I stared at the crying newborn, still covered in vernix and with hair matted down. I knew then and there that she would simultaneously be my joy and my downfall. That I would not let this life taint her.

"Sir, we must go," the doctor urged.

"Okay," I whispered.

The doctor led to a dimly lit room, warm and soft, and pointed at a reclining chair. I sat, opened my shirt, and leaned my daughter onto my bare chest. Her wailing waned, and when I nudged the nipple of a bottle to her lips her mouth reached forth. She struggled to understand what it was at first. But then, like a compass needle finding north, she latched. Again, I studied her fragility, her perfection. I was not ready. I was eighteen and still a child myself. But the one thing I already learned of life is that we are never ready for any of it.

I had prepared a name for her. A strong name. One that would strike fear in the hearts of our enemies and make Mother proud. But I realized then that it was all wrong.

"Nelly," I whispered, instead, thinking upon the person who had sent me down the path of protectorate. *Is she okay?* I wondered and I tongued my missing front teeth. *Are they all okay?*

"Nelly? That's a stupid name..." Mother said from the shadows.

I flinched, popping the bottle's nipple out of my daughter's mouth.

"...Are you purposely setting her up to fail?" Mother followed up.

I hushed my daughter as best as I could, until she took the bottle again. "You named me, Calvin," I whispered. "That isn't a ferocious name."

"I named you after Don Calvin Seraden!" Mother snapped, "Your great, great grandfather! The man who extinguished The Bloody Dozen and usurped the governors!"

Nelly began wailing.

I clenched my jaw. "But before him, the name meant nothing. He brought meaning to the name himself, just as Nelly will bring meaning to hers."

Mother grimaced, then left the room in a huff.

◆

"First, you froth the milk," I said, sliding a metal pitcher up the spout and sending steam through the milk, hissing and burbling.

Nelly's eyes widened with each new sound.

I pulled it from the spout when enough had foamed. "Like so."

"What now?" she asked with skeptical eyebrows.

"Watch," I said, giving the metal pitcher several gentle swirls above a cup of freshly brewed espresso.

Nelly knelt upon her stool and planted her hands on the bar, leaning over to get a better view as I slowly poured the milk into the coffee.

"You're just filling it up," she said.

"Wait…"

A white dot appeared in the brown liquid, growing in size, becoming nearly four centimeters in diameter. I undulated my wrist, dashing across the white circle, pulling brown through white like brush strokes. I glanced at Nelly to see her lips pursed tightly. I gave one last dip, creating a dark spot midway up the circle and set the pitcher on the counter.

"Ummm…" Nelly said.

I gently spun the cup around.

Nelly gasped. "It's Jupiter!"

"Yes! Good eye!" I said.

A crash came from the street followed by shouting. Nelly snapped her head toward the entry. I heard my enforcers cussing.

"Never mind that," I said, trusting they would deal with it. "What planet should we do next?"

"You can do more?" Nelly said, turning back to me.

I nodded.

"Can you do Earth?" she whispered like it was taboo.

I smiled. "Let's see if I ca—"

"Let me go, you motherfuckers!" bellowed a man from just outside.

I froze, my ears picking up the accent.

"Daddy, what's happening?" Nelly nervously asked.

"I don't know. Stay here."

I rounded the bar as one of my enforcers came through the door, blood oozing from his nose.

"Sir, we have a situation."

"Nelly, go in the back," I said, my voice deadpan.

She hopped off the stool and took a waiter's hand who guided her through the kitchen doors.

I turned to the enforcer. "What is it?"

"It's one of your bean pickers, a big fucker. He's trying to get in."

"Is he drunk?"

The enforcer thought about that. "He must be."

"They drink homemade everclear. Did you smell it on his breath?"

"No, sir."

"Then, he's sober."

"I need to see Calvin!" came the picker's voice.

Again, it gave me pause. I approached the door.

"Sir, it's dang—"

I lifted my hand, silencing the enforcer, and passed through. The sun was low in the morning sky, casting long shadows from three enforcers trying to restrain a very sturdy man in soiled canvas.

"Let me go!" the sturdy man shouted and leaned forward, planting his legs, and dragging the enforcers along.

"Release him!" I called.

The enforcers snapped their heads my way and quickly let the man go. The sturdy man looked at them confused, then turned to me.

"What do you want?" I asked.

"I need to see Calvin!"

"Why?"

The man seemed thrown off by my willingness to listen. "I was told to find him! There's a problem!"

I thought about that. "Who sent you?"

"You wouldn't know them," the man said, seemingly defeated.

"Was it Tamarind or Joan?" I asked.

His jaw dropped, flashing his two missing front teeth.

My Sol, it's really him... "I'm Calvin," I said. "Please, come inside."

The enforcers gave looks of disbelief and stepped forth to intervene.

I raised my hand, halting them. "It's okay, I know this man."

They backed off.

"Come with me, Brent," I said to his confusion.

Brent took a timid step forth, following me through the door, and looked around the cafe with wonder. I waved at the bar. He cautiously took a seat.

"I don't drink," he said.

Interesting, I thought. "Don't all the foremen drink?"

"Not on my crew," Brent said, studying the bar-top and the cups on the bar back. "What is this place?"

"This is a cafe." I snapped into action, making a cup.

Brent watched me work. "I don't understand."

"We make coffee here."

"What's a *kawfee?*" he quietly asked.

"Coffee is a drink made from the beans that you pick. They go through a process of roasting and grinding, then they're either percolated by steam or steeped in water." I said, packing the grounds into the portafilter and wrenching it tightly into the espresso machine. I placed two cups beneath the portafilter's forked spout as hissing came. Coffee drizzled into the cups.

"It becomes a drink?" Brent asked.

"It does." I placed the cups on saucers and pushed one Brent's direction. I lifted the other and smelled its aroma. "It's quite hot, so be careful, and it might taste bitter to you. Think of it like alcohol, but instead of making you forget and fall asleep, it keeps your mind sharp and awake." I took a sip. "Perfection... You should give it a try."

Brent carefully took his cup and studied its contents. He sipped and made a face.

I could not help but grin. "Well, it's not for everyone."

He gave a look. "Why are you serving me? Aren't you the next don?"

I nodded. "As future don, it is my duty to understand the entirety of this business. To work from the ground up, through every stage, from picking the fields and processing with the roasters, to serving guests. So, serving you is one of my responsibilities."

Brent clenched his jaw. "You never picked the fields. Everyone would remember that."

"Brent..." I calmly said, adopting a picker's accent, and smiled wide, revealing my missing front teeth. I stuck my tongue through the gap and wagged it at him.

Brent's face lit up. "Airball!?" He placed hands atop his head. "I... What... How!?" His eyes darted back and forth. "How did you convince them to make you the next don!?"

I laughed. "Brent, I've always been the next don."

He processed. "That means Schunt took the don's teeth!?"

"It does," I responded.

"He should have been punished, then!"

"He was."

"No, he just disappeared!"

"That was his punishment," I said.

Brent thought it over. I could see the wheels turning. His eyes met mine. "Does anyone else know who you are?"

"Tamarind knew from the beginning," I said.

"Oh... That makes sense."

"And Joan," I added.

Brent's eyes widened. "You're insane."

"Daddy's not insane!" came a little voice.

I turned to find Nelly peeking through a crack in the kitchen door. "Come on out. This is my good friend, Brent," I said, dropping the accent.

Nelly gave me a strange look. "Why were you talking funny?"

"This is the accent used by most Ganymedans outside of Hardsill," I answered, putting it back on.

"Outside of Hardsill," Nelly repeated with eerie accuracy.

"My Sol…" Brent said with a smile. "…What's your name, little one?"

My daughter opened the door and timidly stepped closer. "Nelly."

Brent's smile vanished, his face washed in horror.

"Brent, what's wrong?" I asked, hoping I did not offend him by naming my daughter after his little sister.

"This is why I came…" Brent's lip trembled. "…Nelly's sick."

◆

Brent and I landed in the fields under the cover of night, and I set my shuttle to cloak. I wrapped myself in picker's canvas and trekked alongside Brent through crop lanes to the stables. Commotion of home-cooked dinners being either prepared or devoured came, resurfacing hundreds of bunkhouse memories.

"This way," Brent whispered.

We rounded a divider to find several people dimly illuminated. I started picking out their features, seeing many of them had missing front teeth.

It's the crew! I realized.

"Brent's back!" one said and the others turned.

"Hey dorks. You won't believe who I brought," he said.

"Who? The don?" one quipped, and the others chuckled.

"That's correct," I said, coming into the light. I removed the canvas, revealing my pristine Hardsill tunic with its cartel pin.

The crew reeled back, with their eyes wide and their mouths agape. All except for an athletic young woman in the back, standing with impeccable posture. She stared right through me, into my soul, causing my heart to skip and my hands to shake.

She grinned. "Welcome back, Franco."

I could not help but smile, flashing my missing front teeth. The crew gasped, but I could not take my eyes off the young woman. "Tamarind, I've missed you…" I said, then shook my head and looked at the others. "I've missed you all!" I said, putting the accent on like an old hat.

They bombarded me with questions about who I actually was, why I had come long ago, why I left, and why I was returning now.

"I'm here to help Nelly," I answered. "But I must see her to understand her ailment."

They went quiet.

"What?"

"She's with Joan," Tamarind said. "She's seen this before."

"Then, we go to her," I responded.

Tamarind approached, her eyes locked with mine. "This way…"

I wrapped myself in canvas again and followed. The crew's chatter dissipated. Dull light illuminated Tamarind's lean, muscular shoulders with each stall we passed. When she turned her head, I caught her profile. I was staring. She stopped and faced me.

"What is it?" I asked.

She stepped into a dark stall.

The moment I entered, lighting struck and the sounds from outside disappeared. *An audiosphere and cloak,* I realized. Joan was sitting in a chair, looking me up and down. She pointed at a bed where an emaciated, old woman lay.

I cocked my head in confusion, until the old woman gasped for air and I saw the implants for false teeth. "Nelly?" I whispered, fighting back tears.

Tamarind sat on the opposite side of the bed, dipped a washcloth into water, wrung it out, and patted it along Nelly's skeletal arms.

"How did she age like this?" I said, finding my voice. "Is it cancer?"

"No," Joan said.

I studied Nelly's skin. "Why did you wait so long to contact me!?"

"It's been three days," Tamarind answered.

"That can't be." I responded, looking at Nelly's withered body.

Joan stood. "Calvin, most of these people descend from the original clones sent to this moon after The Fall."

"Meaning?"

"In the past seven hundred years, they've only had each other to procreate with, further stagnating their already stale DNA."

I shook my head. "No, we take great care in ensuring our gene pool remains strong. It's why our surnames are so complex."

"Your people do. But that tradition stops outside the cities."

"Okay…" I said, knowing it was true.

"What you are witnessing is called Kaladian Degradation Disease. Named after a genius scientist who spearheaded gene splicing for the Hermian military. But those modifications caused horrific defects."

The Hermians, I thought, having read about their barbaric practices in school. "Those modifications cannot be inherited."

"But the defects can," Joan said. "And they are becoming more prominent with each generation of interbreeding."

"This is a big deal. How have we not known of this?"

"Calvin…" Tamarind said. "Nobody cares."

"But we would have noticed people dropping left and right," I responded.

Joan shook her head. "Remember Keith?"

I nodded.

"It took only one day for him to succumb."

I thought about when Mother picked me up from the fields and how she refused to tell me how Keith died. *She knows and is doing nothing,* I realized. I spied Nelly. "How much longer does she have?"

"She should be gone already…" Joan said. "…I don't know."

I made eye contact with her. "I'll get the best doctors in Hardsill."

◆

"Sir, I don't know what this is," the doctor said, looking helplessly at Nelly. "Her DNA is just… coming apart."

I sighed deeply. "Is there anything we can do?"

The doctor opened his mouth, but was speechless.

"I see," I said, gritting my teeth, forcing back my tears, not letting him see how broken up I was.

"It must be the plague," he muttered.

I zeroed in on him. "What did you say?"

"There have been reports of sudden deaths across Ganymede. The fishing guilds have seen the worst of it."

My rage swelled. "Why have you never said anything!?"

"Orders from Don Hayes," the doctor said. "And the fishing guilds are in Jackman Syndicate territory. It's their problem."

A memory from when I trespassed into Jackman territory as a kid came to me, marked by the sudden halting of artificial rain at the border when Joan and I drove Schunt's new skiff to a fishing well with Schunt strapped upon its flatbed. So much blood oozed from his mouth as we pulled his teeth, dropping them one by one into the icy water, and I would never forget how he cried like a baby when I donned the reflection suit and lit the incinerator's nozzle.

"Sir, are you all right?" the doctor said, giving me a look.

"I need a moment to think."

The doctor nodded and entered my shuttle.

Tamarind and Brent didn't even look at me when I entered the stall.

"Can he help her?" Brent whispered.

I took a deep breath. "He doesn't know what this is…"

Tamarind scoffed. "Some hero you are."

A knife through my heart. "I'm doing everything I can."

"Everything but helping," she snapped back.

"What do you want me to say?" I asked.

She shot furious eyes at me. "It's not what you say, it's what you do. And what you've done is abandon us to live a spoiled life!"

I could not speak, I could not breathe.

"That was mean," Brent said.

"Am I wrong?" she responded, turning to him.

Brent didn't say a word.

"I will find a way to fix this."

"Stop speaking like us. You're not from here," she added.

"I'll take my leave, then," I said, dropping the accent, my voice quivering. I turned and left the stall.

◆

"Daddy, what's wrong?" my daughter asked during dinner.

I realized I was staring at my synthesized food. *If you can call it food.* "I have a lot on my mind."

"But, you need to eat. Your brain needs food to think."

"You're right," I said, stabbing my fork into synthesized calamari and chomping comically loud for my daughter, but all I could think about was the calamari at Kontanda. Even the bunkhouse food was far better than this. *And they think I'm spoiled?* I thought, irritated, but I knew their food was the only pro to a long list of cons.

Mother's personal attendant, Chandler, entered the dining room. "Sir, may I present to you, Don Hayes."

Mother strutted in with a hard look on her face.

"Nelly," I said. "Dinner's over."

She timidly looked at her grandmother, then pushed back her chair and scurried out of the room with Chandler.

"What the fuck is wrong with you!?" Mother hissed.

I leaned back in my chair. "Can you be more specific?"

Mother huffed. "Never show your face at the stables! It gives them the wrong idea!"

"And what wrong idea is that?" I prodded.

Mother's face was furious. "That they hold value!"

"But, they do hold value."

"Who taught you such bullshit!?"

"You did… You said that we are nothing without them," I retorted. "In fact, you said that it will one day be my job to protect them, like a sheepdog guarding its fold."

"I never said that!"

I gave her a look. "Don't gaslight me."

She huffed. "It was never my intention for you to fall in love with them!"

"But, it is my duty to take care of them, correct?" I asked.

"No!" Mother snapped, pointing at herself. "It's my duty!"

"But you've known about their disease for a long time and done nothing… Since you cannot perform your duties, I took it upon myself."

Mother slapped me across the cheek, like I was a child, but the pain felt like nothing. "I am performing my duties! Whenever this plague shows its face, I dispose of those infected, ensuring the rest remain healthy! That's how you protect the fold! By cutting the weak!"

My stomach sank. My hands began to shake. I slowly stood, eclipsing her, and I saw a split second of uncertainty cross her face.

Mother grimaced. "You are such a child! You will learn!"

My thoughts raced, wondering how she even knew I was at the stables. *The doctor,* I realized. *Nelly…* I clenched my fists and stepped forth. "What did you do!?"

Mother's eyes went wide and I heard the cocking of rail-gun coils.

Cloaked enforcers, I knew and stepped back.

"I cut the weak!" Mother said, spun around, and marched off.

◆

Thick smoke rose from a kilometer out, as I pushed my shuttle to its breaking point. *It's coming from the stables!* I knew, and when I closed in, I saw hundreds of pickers scattering into the fields. Two were on their knees surrounded by three enforcers with rifles aimed at their backs. A fourth enforcer, in a reflective suit and wielding an incinerator, marched around the stables adding fuel to the fire. I circled the enforcers, trying to get a good look at the two pickers on their knees.

An enforcer waved me down, and I landed next to their gunship. When my hatch opened, my ears were struck by the fire's roar and my nose was engulfed by burnt grass.

Keep calm! Keep poised! I told myself, as I disembarked.

"Welcome, sir!" called the enforcer, racing to meet me.

"What's the situation!?" I shouted above the fire's roar.

"These fuckers decided to fight when we came to collect!"

"So you burned down the whole thing!?" I scolded. "Do you know how much you set us back!?"

"It was ordered by the don!"

My mind raced. "Is Don Hayes here!?"

"No, sir! She never comes!" He paused. "I'm surprised that you did!"

"Our best picking crew lives here! Of course I came!" I strutted towards the kneeling figures. I could tell from their backs who they were and realized the man was missing an arm. "Did you collect the infected!?"

"No, sir. They hid her! We're trying to burn them out now!"

I stepped in front of the prisoners. Brent and Tamarind looked up with hard expressions, until they saw it was me, and their eyes widened.

"What did these two do!?" I asked the enforcer.

"They were throwing rocks! Even after we took this fucker's arm!" The enforcer pointed at Brent. "Tough bastards! We were about to execute them!"

I snapped my head to him.

"Is something wrong, sir!?"

I recognized a pistol on the enforcer's thigh harness. "I should be the one to put them down! They are my dogs!" I pointed at his pistol. "Is that a Phantom 20!?"

The enforcer smiled wide. "Yeah! Wow! You know your guns, sir!"

"I brokered the deal to acquire those a few years back!" I responded and extended a hand. "May I!?"

"It would be an honor, sir!" The enforcer lowered his rifle, unholstered his Phantom, and handed it to me hilt first.

I studied it, remembering how it felt when I tested them during the deal. "Do you know why this pistol is so great!?" I asked.

"I just thought it looked cool!" he said.

"It's a magnetic rail-gun! Which means, it can function without oxygen, has no recoil, and produces no sound!"

"Makes sense why it's called a phantom, then!"

"Actually, that's not how it got its name!" I aimed the pistol at Brent, and stretched its coil into ready position. "These rail-guns are classified as mining equipment, but are modified for our purposes. Therefore, they neither have a DNA lock nor take a genetic imprint!"

"Oh! I get it! The user becomes the phantom!" said the enforcer.

I looked at Brent and Tamarind. "Any last words!?"

They stared at me, too shocked to speak.

I smiled wide, revealing my missing front teeth, and cried, "For Nelly!" I whipped the pistol to its owner, clicking thrice, then swiveled to the remaining two enforcers and emptied the clip.

All three slumped to the ground.

I knelt to the pistol's owner, wrenching another clip from his belt and reloading with trembling hands. The clip slid into place, I pulled back its coil, and spun to the burning stables trying to pick out the fourth enforcer in the reflection suit. It took me several seconds to find a figure flickering with as much light as the fire.

The enforcer bolted off towards the grass.

I trained the pistol just ahead of him. *Click, click, click, click... Boom!* A fireball engulfed the enforcer as the incinerator tank ruptured.

My heart pounded, but my mind was disturbingly clear. I turned to Brent and Tamarind. "Where's Nelly!?"

Brent was speechless.

"Joan took her!" Tamarind responded.

"So, she's not in there!?" I pointed at the fire.

"No!"

I shoved the Phantom 20 back into the enforcer's thigh holster. "Then, help me!" I hollered above the roar and grabbed the enforcer's armpits, dragging his limp body to the stable. Brent and Tamarind each took a leg, and together swung him into the flames. We repeated with the other two.

"What now!?" Tamarind hollered.

"Follow me!" I made for my shuttle knowing Brent and Tamarind were on my tail. Once we piled in, I pointed at the back seats. "Strap in! We must leave now!"

Blinking lights of fire brigade ships in the distance were closing in fast. *And I cannot be here!* We barely lifted off and activated the shuttle's cloak when they arrived. I banked hard as water spouts shot from above. The tall grasses scraped the shuttle's underbelly and I hoped pickers were not hiding in our path. The moment we passed beneath the brigade ships, I pulled up, and was clear. I took several breaths, then turned to see Brent and Tamarind watching the waterspouts douse their home. Brent's arm gushed blood and his complexion was pale. I reached over and hit a medical switch on the wall.

"Brent, stop the blood," I said, breaking the silence.

He peered at the equipment with a lost look.

"Tamarind, do you know where Joan took Nelly?" I asked.

"The bunkhouse," she whispered.

Of course, I thought, set the coordinates, and hit the autopilot. I joined Brent at the medical station. "Brent, bite down on this." I handed him a piece of thick fabric, then retrieved a tourniquet, blades, bone saw, and cauterizer.

♦

It was almost dawn when we reached the bunkhouse, nearly rotted to dust. The foreman's cabin was gone altogether.

"We thought it best to destroy it after you left," Tamarind said, stroking Brent's hair as he slept. "You were our third foreman to disappear."

A figure stood outside with arms crossed, staring straight at our cloaked shuttle. *Joan,* I knew, and that she picked up the shuttle's subtle hiss with her modified ears.

We landed, uncloaked, and opened the hatch. Gentle sirens came in the distance, almost drowned out by the rattle of coffee plants ripe with beans. I roused Brent from his induced slumber.

He looked around bewildered, squinting, then slowly stood and stumbled out of the shuttle. He approached Joan. "Is she inside?"

Joan raised a hand. "Brent… she's gone."

His face contorted. He let out a low moan, pushed Joan's arm away, and barreled into the bunkhouse. Tamarind rushed after him. As much as I wanted to go, I knew it was not my place.

"Calvin," Joan said.

"I know..." I responded. "...It's time I teach Mother that actions have consequences." I turned to Joan. "I need another favor."

"You already owe me a lot," she responded.

"Please."

She thought for a moment, then nodded.

♦

"This is not the way," Joan said as we lowered into the back alley of a warehouse.

"We need firepower," I said and opened the shuttle hatch. "And I need you cloaked."

Joan nodded and wrapped fabric around herself, disappearing from view.

Sparse sounds of Hardsill's late night happenings accompanied the gentle hum and hiss of mechanical systems.

I approached two enforcers flanking the warehouse's side entry.

"Sir, is that you?" one said and opened the door.

"Good evening, gentlemen," I said, passing through the door, feeling Joan right behind me. The moment it closed, I opened my holotile and searched for any night workers.

"No personnel present," it determined.

I sent the warehouse into lock-down.

Joan pulled back her cloak. "Smells like a garage."

I grinned and flipped on the lights. Row upon row of weaponry revealed, the closest containing small arms and blades, then long range sniper rifles, grenade launchers, and cannons. Farther down, a cybernetics bay lit, then heavy equipment and corsairs mid-modification appeared. Lastly, at the far end of the warehouse, a wall of armor highlighted.

"Holy shit…" Joan whispered.

I entered *Small Arms*, picked out two Phantom 20's and several clips, and tied a holster around each thigh. Joan entered *Cybernetics*. When I followed around the divider, I found her staring at a small red box.

"As payment for your help tonight, I give you access to this armory," I quietly said. "But should you be caught with these weapons, I'll have no choice but to end you. Do you accept these terms?"

Joan was silent, staring at the little box. She extended a shaking hand.

"We acquired that from a scavenger returning from Mercury. They still work," I said.

She grasped the red box and opened its lid, peeking inside. "Do you know what these are?"

"I do."

"This technology is supposed to be extinct."

"It is."

She sighed deeply. "This… just this… is payment enough."

I thought about that. "I will need one, but the rest are yours."

Joan reached into the box, retrieved a metal cylinder, and handed it to me. "What must I do?"

I studied the cylinder, extended its needle and switched it on. A blinking red light appeared at its base, ready for extraction. I switched it off and slipped it into my tunic pocket. "You must become my shadow tonight, and go where I cannot." I said. "Follow me."

We passed heavy equipment and corsairs, and stopped at the wall of armor.

"Auto-armor," Joan gasped with a disapproving look. "You've been dealing with the Arkathy?"

I shrugged. "They're one of our best customers."

"What are they buying?" Joan asked.

"Politicians," I said and pointed at the armor. "This is one of four units we've acquired. They only cost us Representatives Vesta of Iapetus and Fordham of Puck."

Joan looked to the side, at a black speck within a containment field. "What is that?"

"Oh… that," I said. "It's called a Disruptor. It creates a miniature black hole when released, lasting ten seconds before dissipating into nothing… I think. Nobody really knows. It was a gift from the Cindarians. They called it their insurance policy against the Arkathy."

Joan looked at me squarely. "You're playing both sides?"

"You're one to talk," I casually responded and motioned at the auto-armor. "Mother's enforcers are cloaked, but auto-armor has temporal detectors allowing its wearers to visualize minuscule gravity wells. You should be able to easily deal with them while I deal with Mother. But first, you must extract my daughter."

◆

I uploaded my estate's schematics to Joan's auto-armor and highlighted my daughter's room. "Nelly should be asleep at this hour."

"Nelly?" Joan cocked her head.

"My daughter…" I responded, imagining Joan's expression beneath the auto-armor's faceplate. "Enforcers are situated along the way. You must get Nelly to my shuttle and send her to Tamarind and Brent at the bunkhouse while I confront Mother."

"Okay," Joan said.

I highlighted the dining room. "Then, I'll need you to meet me here and dispose of Mother's enforcers without her noticing. Can it be done?"

"If you knew what I've done, you'd never ask that," Joan said. "What do you hope to achieve by confronting her?"

"I will force the transfer of power and become Don Credence tonight."

"I see…"

I inserted a small com-link into my ear canal. "I can hear your progress, but I won't be able to respond directly without arousing suspicion."

"Understood," she said, her voice in my ear.

I checked my Phantom 20s one last time before donning a long cartel coat over my tunic and thighs to conceal them. "Are you ready?"

Joan nodded and vanished from view.

I strutted from the estate's garage to the main entry, holding my head high, and nodded at the enforcers. When the massive door opened, I felt a pat on my shoulder and knew Joan was off.

Chandler was waiting for me in the grand hall. "Welcome home, sir."

"Mother is expecting me for a nightcap, I presume," I responded.

"That is correct, sir," Chandler responded and extended a hand. "Please, follow me." He led down the grand hall.

I spied the dining room's double doors at the end, expecting the doormen to grasp their handles at any moment. Instead, Chandler stopped, reached for a statue of my great, great grandfather, and pressed its nose.

A section of wall disappeared.

What the fuck is this? I thought. "Chandler, I am not familiar with this passageway, may I ask where we are going?"

Chandler gestured a hand, but did not speak.

"Well, Don Seraden certainly loved his secrets," I said. "And his statue… brilliant."

"Copy that," Joan whispered into my earpiece.

The moment I entered the passageway, the earpiece screeched. Every muscle in my body tensed and I wanted to tear it out. I gritted my teeth and continued through the meandering path. When I rounded the final bend my earpiece went silent. *I'm disconnected from Joan,* I knew, but realized that was the least of my problems.

Seven dons stood around a large holotable projecting Ganymede at its center with several sections highlighted. I knew each don's enforcers were close by, cloaked. Mother stood at the center, watching me with a strange grin. I rounded the large table, taking a place at her side.

"I apologize for my tardiness, Mother," I said, using my calm, cartel voice.

"It is of no consequence," she responded. "We were just wrapping up our plan to eradicate this plague once and for all."

I pushed down my rage. "And what plan is that?"

"It's Calvin, right?" came a rough voice.

I turned to see an old, scraggly man.

"That is correct, Don Jackman," I responded.

"It appears my fishing wells are ground zero for this plague. So, we're burning them to ash tonight."

Keep calm! I could feel their eyes on me. "Don Jackman, with all due respect, won't you be sacrificing a workforce of over two hundred thousand strong. That would ruin you."

Mother laughed lightly. "For Don Jackman's sacrifice in containing this plague, we've all agreed to gift him a portion of our inventory to keep his business afloat."

"But they will not be properly trained to deep sea fish," I said. "There is tremendous knowledge held by these people that cannot be ignored."

"People?" I heard a don snicker.

Don Jackman nodded. "Very perceptive of you, Calvin. I was just arguing this point."

Mother's smile dwindled. "It has been decided!"

Don Jackman bowed deeply. "It has."

I spied Chandler, suddenly touching his ear and disappearing down the entry corridor. A moment later, my earpiece crackled.

"I'm in," Joan said. "But we have a problem. I searched everywhere for your daughter, but could not find her."

My anxiety went through the roof and I made eye contact with Mother.

"There are fourteen enforcers. Two for each don. The dons themself are not armed," Joan said. "I'm taking out the enforcers now."

The com went silent.

I breathed deeply, then faced Don Jackman. "It appears more has been decided than you are letting on," I carefully said. "Are you to ward my daughter?"

"Two down..." Joan whispered into my earpiece.

Everyone's eyes widened. Don Jackman did not respond.

"Your silence is your confession," I continued.

"Five down..." came Joan's voice again.

"You are very sharp," Don Jackman finally responded. "Your daughter will indeed be warded, but not by me. In fact, neither Don Hayes nor myself know who will be raising her. This is the deal we brokered, to ensure my business survives."

"Eight down..."

I pulled back my long coat, revealing one of my Phantom 20s, and heard coil clicks from the cloaked enforcers. *But only from my left.*

"Twelve down..."

Don Jackman made a face. "Just when I thought you were sharp."

"Calvin, this is childish," Mother scolded. "You'll be shot dead before you can touch that thing."

I bored my eyes into Don Jackman's. "Where is my daughter?"

The old salty don laughed. "I truly have no idea, boy."

"All clear," Joan called in, out of breath.

"Then, you are useless." I casually pulled my Phantom from its holster, pointed it at Don Jackman, and clicked.

A small hole appeared in his forehead and his eyes rolled back into his head. He slumped to his knees and tipped to the floor. A silence, louder than any scream, washed over the dons.

I swiveled my Phantom to Don Kaniastan. "Where is my daughter?"

She turned to where she believed her enforcers stood and pressed into her palm. When nothing happened she faced me and opened her mouth, but no words came.

I clicked. She fell.

"Don Greatier," I calmly said and turned to him. "Where is she?"

He raised his hands. "W-wait. I don't kn—"

Click.

I aimed at his son, only a few months older than me.

"I can help you find her!" he quickly said.

I kept my Phantom trained on him.

"Please, spare my life... as a favor," he added.

"Say the words..." I ordered.

"...A favor for a favor, I will repay, in this moment or the next, on my life, I lay," the son recited.

I lowered my pistol. "Have you performed the transfer of power?"

"Not officially, but it can be done without my father."

I nodded. "Congratulations, Don Feldthart, may your reign be glorious."

"May your reign be glorious," the remaining dons recited, even Mother.

"I do not wish to kill the rest of you," I said. "But if you do not swear to help find my daughter, then I will."

One by one, they swore to it. All except for Mother.

I turned to her. "Swear it!"

"No."

I trained my pistol on her.

She grinned. "Go ahead, kill me."

I considered this, knowing if there was any hope of changing this world, if I were to find my daughter, then I needed the transfer of power. I lowered the Phantom. "Leave with your lives, and be grateful," I said to the others.

They made for the corridor, stumbling over cloaked bodies.

"Mother, you stay."

She looked to the floor, where the dons had stumbled, and pressed a jewel upon her ring. The lighting turned red and the enforcers appeared on the floor, their necks kinking awkwardly.

Behind Mother stood Joan in auto-armor.

"How did you do this?" she asked, with strange respect.

"I learned a lot working the fields. I learned to work hard, to adapt, to fight, and to lead. All of which I'm certain you learned, too. But I learned something else that you never did."

"And what is that?" Mother said, strangely curious.

"I learned that those people are the heart and soul of this moon."

She scoffed. "So, you made some fucking friends!?"

"Exactly," I responded. "And I would like you to meet one of them now."

Joan placed a metallic hand upon Mother's shoulder. "It's been a long time, Ashland."

Blood drained from Mother's face. She slowly turned to Joan's suit of auto-armor. "J…Joan…?"

The armor split down the middle unveiling the muscular woman in tight under-armor, and she stepped out.

"Have a seat, Mother," I said as Joan pulled out a chair for her.

Mother stared at Joan, then timidly sat and looked at me unblinking. "You've destroyed us…"

"No, I'm remaking us," I said, looking into her eyes as I took the seat beside her. "You will be retiring tonight."

Mother's eyes narrowed, then she laughed. "You cannot transfer power without my cooperation."

"I don't need your cooperation," I said.

Mother clenched her jaw. "I was trained to withstand interrogation and torture, just as you were. I will tell you nothing."

"I know…" I reached into my pocket, pulled the small cylinder, and extended its tip. I trained my Phantom on Mother's chest.

She became quiet, studying the syringe, then smiled slightly. "Calvin, despite our differences, I am so pro—"

Click...

Her breath let out long, like air from a tire. Red soaked through her blouse and tunic. She gripped the edge of the table and struggled to her feet, staring at a portrait of Don Seraden on the opposing wall. Her arms rested at her sides and she bowed deeply. Then, her knees weakened and she fell to the floor.

"Glorious…" I whispered, beside myself.

"Calvin," Joan said, pointing at the syringe. "It must be done, now."

♦

Mother… You monster…

I woke from her nightmarish life, lying on the floor with Joan and a second figure kneeling beside me. I rolled and vomited as a bottle of liquid was being pushed towards me. I recognized pristine cuffs.

"Ch-Chandler?" I whispered.

"Don Credence, please, drink," Mother's loyal attendant said.

What is he doing here!? I thought. *Wait… He called me Don.*

He read my confusion. "Sir, I serve a house, not a person, not your mother, and not even you. But rest assured, now that you are to become don, I will work diligently to ensure your success."

"I-I…" I tried to speak, but my body convulsed. *The side effects of memory immersion,* I knew. I fumbled for the bottle and took its contents. Heaven poured through my veins, relieving pain and confusion, to an extent. I still shook as if hyperthermic.

"Sir," Chandler said, opening a hologram with the family crest and placing it on the floor beside me. "Did you find what you require?"

I lifted my shaky head, trying to keep still for the retinal scanner.

"Calvin Credence, confirmed. Transfer of power initiated," said the hologram, and a small entry field opened.

I tried dashing the symbols, but kept missing.

"Please, dictate to me," Chandler said.

I gave him a distrusting look.

"Joan may dispose of me should I prove deceitful," he assured.

"F-five… S-seven…" I began reciting, and closed my eyes, holding onto the memory of my mother transferring power from her father long ago. But for my grandfather it was by torture. "…F… L… Three… Eight…" I could hear his weak voice slurring through smashed teeth alongside Mother's laughter. "…Six… K… Nine…" Mother was peeling skin from his face. "…G… J." He begged for death and Mother obliged.

I opened my eyes.

Chandler nodded and dashed *Enter.*

"Transfer Successful," appeared.

"That's it?" Joan said.

Chandler stood and bowed deeply. "Congratulations, Don Credence, may your reign be glorious."

I slowly sat up. "Chandler…"

"Yes, sir."

"Call the dons for an emergency meeting. Tell them we must abort the extermination of Don Jackman's territory. This plague is not contagious. It's inherited."

Both Joan and Chandler looked about to cry.

"What?"

"You've been out for three days," Chandler said. "The extermination is done."

I turned to Joan, noticing she was not in auto-armor and that her arms and hands were burned. *She's been out there,* I realized. "I'm s-so sorry…"

Joan sighed. "Calvin—"

"Don Credence," Chandler corrected.

Joan bared her teeth. "Don Credence… Jackman territory is unclaimed. There will be war to control it."

I placed a leg beneath myself, feeling my trousers sticking to my thighs, and knew I had soiled myself during the immersion. I wobbled to my feet. "That is where you're wrong."

Joan furrowed her brow. "I don't understand."

Chandler cleared his throat. "Don Credence won the rights to Don Jackman's territory by killing him in plain sight, in the old way. Don Credence has also won Don Kaniastan's territory." Chandler grinned. "Sir, your great grandfather would be proud."

"But I cannot govern all three territories myself," I muttered and turned to Chandler. "Please, call upon the late attendant of Don Kaniastan. I will be granting her heir the return of their territory… with a condition."

"What kind of condition?" Joan said.

"That another extermination never happens again."

"Very good, sir," Chandler said and bowed deeply.

♦

We estimated the reconstruction of Jackman territory would take two decades, for much of its underlying infrastructure was also lost in the extermination. And, when it came time to elect a new don to oversee the territory's reconstruction I knew who it should be.

"No!" Tamarind said, standing alongside Brent.

"How can you ask her something like that?" he asked.

I stared at them flabbergasted. "This is an incredible opportunity. Never has this been offered to one of your people."

"That!" Tamarind said and pointed. "That, right there, is the reason why I would never take it!"

"But, someone needs to oversee the reconstruction of the fishing wells."

"They were destroyed by your people…" she said.

"Do you want it to also be rebuilt by my people?" I challenged.

She looked at me hard.

"I'm trying to give you an opportunity to do things right." I pondered that. "Would you at least be willing to oversee the construction as General Contractor?"

She breathed deeply. "Maybe…"

Good enough… I thought, knowing that for her, it was a yes. "We must move quickly, then," I added.

"We?" Brent said.

"I'll be with you every step of the way," I responded.

He gave a gap-toothed smile. "Like the good ole' days?"

I flashed mine. "You know it."

◆

Tamarind assembled our old crew, assigning each of them their own crews to oversee.

"Are you certain of this?" Chandler said, watching Brent's crew assess one of the decimated fishing wells. "They know nothing of fishing."

"Nobody does," I shortly said. "Not anymore."

"And they can learn it?"

I turned to my attendant. "Do you have another workforce in mind?"

He thought about that. "No, sir. It's just… Perhaps you should select Ganymedan foreman to ensure they stay on task."

"Trust me… The last thing they want is some outsider selected by the don."

"But you're considering joining them, is that not the same?"

"I'm joining as Franco," I said. "Very different."

"With all due respect, sir. Franco does not exist."

No… I thought. *Franco is who I truly am.*

◆

Salt sprayed my face as I competed against my old crew, but they had become formidable in my time away. I was not winning the weekly bonuses. In fact, I was dead last and trailing off like a runner who lost the pack.

"You won again, Brent?" I said as we foreman assembled for our first meeting.

Brent smiled wide. "Two arms. One arm. I guess I'm just better than the rest of you."

"More like, I taught you everything you know," I retorted.

"Hey, Franco!" one shouted, and I saw the others. "Are you truly back!?"

"Only until we rebuild the infrastructure," I said.

"Then, do better!" Tamarind snapped, looking at me. "We are running against the clock! So, pay attention!"

Each month we met again, and each month Tamarind had us working on more projects, ones that did not make sense until completed. I watched my crew's results further trail the rest with each meeting. I felt embarrassment taking hold.

The other dons were taking notice of my commitment, and some gave me smug looks during the monthly conclaves.

"They think you've taken one of them in the old tradition," said Chandler.

I gave him a glare.

"It's for the best. It explains your frequency without divulging that you are working alongside them."

"These people are not concubines," I said shortly.

"To the other dons, they are not people," Chandler responded.

♦

In the twelfth year of reconstruction, and after yet another foreman meeting, in which I saw my progress had fallen to fifteen percent of the next worst crew, I adjourned to my cabin feeling like an idiot. A knock came on my door. I climbed from my straw bed and opened it.

"Tamarind?" I said, taken aback.

She placed a finger upon her lip, shushing me as she entered.

"Is there something you need?" I asked.

She gave me a strange look. I smelled alcohol on her breath. She closed the door and locked its deadbolt. I stood frozen, trying to process what might be happening. She stepped towards me, coming into my personal space, and stroked my stomach. "You're fired," she whispered, her hands making their way to my belt line. "Leave first thing in the morning."

"Who will take over for me?" I weakly asked.

"This is my crew, now," she said as her cheek brushed mine, sending lighting bolts through me. "Go back to your world and be a don..."

"Y-yes..." I responded, finding it impossible to argue.

"But, tonight..." she whispered. "...be Franco."

♦

I gently stroked Tamarind's bare, muscular legs beneath my canvas covers, gently kissed the nape of her neck, and whispered, "I love you…"

"No… No, you don't!" she snapped and rolled from my embrace. "I'm just an itch you needed to scratch."

I deflated. "But, that's not true…"

She looked at me square, her naked body barely visible in the morning light. "You're the don! It has to be this way!"

I thought carefully about that. "I have the power to change—"

She shook her head.

"…I want to offer you—"

"No!" she snapped.

"But it makes sense!"

Tamarind shook her head. "I will never become one of you!"

"Then, your people will never be free!" I rolled from bed and frantically pulled on my canvas clothing.

She watched me dress, not moving a muscle.

"At least consider it," I said, capping my frustration.

"This is the last time you ever ask me," she said. "Your dog is waiting outside."

I clenched my jaw and marched from the cabin into tall grasses, where my shuttle was cloaked. I entered to find Chandler ready for takeoff. Without a word, we lifted from the grasses and zoomed over the fishing wells.

"Sir, it pains me to see such disrespect given to you," Chandler said. "Casting aside a don is a terrible offense. Should we make an example?"

I gave him a cold look. "No," I responded. "She can refuse me. In fact, it's okay for any of them to refuse me. I'm Franco to them."

"With all due respect, sir, only you see yourself as Franco. The rest of the world views you as Don Credence. Especially those once close to you."

I searched for examples of how that was untrue. But in the end, everything had worked out to my benefit. My empire was flourishing and they were still property. *Chandler is right.*

"A change of clothing is in the back, sir," he said.

I sighed deeply and headed to my rear quarters. I donned a blouse and tunic, pressed slacks, a long cartel coat, and knee-high boots. I inserted cuff links, then my cartel pin. *My disguise…*

"Sir, you're being hailed," Chandler said.

Never a moment to rest. I left my quarters, retook my seat, and opened the hologram.

Don Feldthart materialized. "Don Credence, I apologize for the intrusion, but I have a pressing matter."

My stomach twisted. "Go on."

"I was attending the auction of Don Seagle's cybernetics lab when I met a young technician," Don Feldthart paused. "There was something about her that reminded me of you."

Another sighting... I frowned, knowing it was futile at this point. "Thank you, Don Feldthart. I appreciate the sentiment. Please, send me the auction's information." I ended the call before his gracious goodbye. A wave of nausea suddenly struck and I gave it to the floor.

Chandler quickly set the autopilot, snatched a vacuum, and began cleaning the mess. "Sir. I'll check it out this evening. If there is any resemblance to Nelly, I will know," he said, retaking the pilot's seat.

"Thank you, Chandler."

Hardsill's granite perimeter wall appeared. City blocks, streets, and landing alleys became visible. The weapons hanger came and went. Then, my estate came into view at the city center, at its highest elevation, like a castle of old Earth.

◆

I woke to garden cardinals calling to their mates and gentle rays of sun percolating through my windows. But, above it all, I felt Chandler's presence. I breathed deeply and rolled to face him. "What happened?"

"Nothing regarding business, sir."

"Is it Tamarind?"

"No..." Chandler paused. "...I met the technician Don Feldthart spoke of." His face twitched. "I think it's her..."

I sat up. "Is Don Seagle's cybernetics lab still up for auction."

"It is, sir," Chandler said. "Don Feldthart currently holds the high bid."

I pondered this. "We must confirm if this technician is indeed her. Please, take me there."

◆

"Don Credence, to what do I owe the honor?" Don Seagle said as we met outside his Cybernetics Research and Development Center.

Don Seagle's attendant scrambled about, juggling several holotiles, handing one off while picking up another from his master.

"You're in a bidding war," I said. "I apologize for the intrusion."

"Not at all," the young don said. "And, yes! I have four new parties interested. Who knew it would become so prized!?"

They know who's here, I realized. "Does Don Feldthart still hold the high bid?"

"Ah, not anymore." The young don gave me a look. "Are you interested as well, Don Credence?"

"I am not sure of that yet," I said. "May I venture?"

"By all means," Don Seagle responded.

I turned to Chandler, who took the lead. We entered the facility, passing corridors filled with technicians racing from one room to another, attending to clients coming in from across the solar system in search of unsanctioned alterations and prostheses.

"These technicians are composed primarily of the same workforce as our pickers," Chandler said.

"But… This is delicate work," I said, astounded.

"Don Seagle's predecessor established a unique program in which city doctors work diligently to train their workforce in medicine, particularly surgery. The results have been incredible. This research facility would be a prize regardless of your daughter's potential presence."

"I see." I peered down the corridor at a series of double doors.

We passed one layer, two layers, and when the third set parted we abruptly transitioned from hospital to hard manufacturing.

"This way, sir," Chandler said, leading to a research booth.

"No, not like that!" came a voice that stopped me in my tracks. "You have to match the patient's specific nerve patterns."

"You can't feasibly do that," said another voice.

"Maybe you can't," said the first voice. "But I can."

"You're going to ruin the prosthesis! You must cease this research!"

"Make me!"

"You're impossible!" shouted the second voice and a man came storming out of a booth. He was cursing to himself until noticing us and his face melted to absolute shock. He stumbled.

I willed my tongue to loosen. "Careful there."

"Y-yes, sir," the man said, staring as I entered the booth.

"Back for more!?" cried a young woman donning magnifying goggles, hard at work weaving artificial nerves with a fake arm. The arm suddenly lurched. "Bam! See!?" She pulled off her goggles and turned my way with a smug grin. "That's how—" she froze, and her eyes darted to my cartel pin. "I'm so sorry, sir."

She doesn't recognize me, I realized, my heart sinking. "It's quite all right," I said, using every ounce of willpower to maintain poise. "I could not help but overhear your conversation. Is it true you can integrate any prosthesis to a patient."

"Yes, and maintain ninety-nine percent functionality. Its wearer would forget their original limb were ever lost."

I studied the fake arm. "You seem to really love your work."

"I do," she said. "But I could achieve so much if I were allowed to."

"What do you mean?" I asked.

She motioned out of the booth. "That was Dr. Bradford. He oversees all of our work. But he doesn't believe we can perfect neural integration. So, he won't allow me to study it further."

"I see."

"Don't get me wrong," the young tech said. "He's been good to me here. He's simply stuck in a medical way of thinking."

It hit me like a freight train. *She's happy...* I wanted to praise whatever god might exist, but I could not help feeling like a failure of a father. *But she's out of the business... She's free.* I thought upon the other dons bidding on the facility. *No... She's not free.* I made eye contact with her. "My primary product is coffee, but my second most profitable venture is the dealing of rare armament, with a fledgling cybernetics department. Unfortunately, we currently have no talent." I took a deep breath. "Work for me and you can practice your craft in the manner you see fit. In fact, you would oversee the entire department."

She stared at me blankly. "But I would still report to you."

"Yes, that is unavoidable."

"Don Credence, here you are!" Don Seagle announced, entering the booth. "I see you've met The Augmentor. I hope you're not trying to poach her! She's our rising star!"

"Actually... I am."

His smile vanished. "But, with all due respect, she's the reason why so many are looking to purchase. I cannot afford to lose her."

I considered Don Seagle's dilemma. "What's the current bid?"

"Sixty-seven billion creds..."

I glanced at Chandler standing quietly outside the booth. He extended five fingers indicating fifty billion as its true value.

"I will bid a hundred billion if you call this auction off immediately."

Don Seagle's eyes widened, but he composed himself. "That's quite the bid. Please, allow me to discuss with my attendant."

I nodded. "Take all the time you need."

The young don raced off, but I knew his answer.

I turned to my daughter. "Can you equip a prosthetic arm or leg with an assortment of weaponry? Meanwhile, maintain equal athleticism to an actual limb?"

She grinned. "I thought you'd never ask."

◆

It had been three years since I last saw Brent and Tamarind, and I held my breath as they entered my hanger. A young girl teetered alongside them, just learning to walk. My stomach fluttered, for a moment thinking she might be my child. But then, I did the math. My hope flashed to anger and I suddenly wanted to strike Brent. *But he knows nothing of our one night romance. If you could call it that...* I studied the little girl, having Tamarind's same red hair and giving me skeptical eyebrows.

"She likes you," Tamarind said, after an awkward silence.

"Doesn't seem like it to me," I responded.

"She's not crying, or trying to hide away. So… She likes you."

"She's shy, like Nelly," Brent said and ruffled his daughter's hair with his one calloused hand.

The young girl lit up, smiling wide.

"What's her name?" I asked.

"Francine," Tamarind said.

I paused. "I see."

"It's not after you, you dork!" Brent said, with a hearty laugh.

"It's after what you once represented," Tamarind said. "Before you abandoned us."

She's never going to let it go, I knew and didn't bother arguing. "Is Joan not coming?"

Brent grimaced. "We haven't seen her in years."

I cocked my head and turned to Tamarind.

"She's taking a leave of absence," she said.

"For how long? Isn't she the backbone of your people?"

"It's how she stays our backbone," she muttered.

Time skipping? I thought, and it all made sense how she could have been one of The Bloody Dozen. "Well, it will be quite the reunion, then."

"Why are we here?" Tamarind said.

"I want to introduce you to someone." I waved to the cybernetics department with a lone technician calibrating equipment, her arms stained black with grease.

"Is that?" Brent muttered.

"She doesn't remember," I responded.

"Nelly…" Tamarind whispered.

"Please, we must address her as The Augmentor," I said. "Nobody can know who she truly is. Not even she."

"Weird name," Brent responded.

I grinned and led the way to my daughter.

She lifted her head as we neared. "You don't waste time, do you?"

"I do not," I said. "Are you ready?"

She looked at Brent's missing arm. "I'm assuming you're my patient."

Brent glanced at the arm. "I guess I am?"

She pointed at a cushioned table. "Please, have a seat…"

"Brent," he said.

She gave a look. "Have we met before?"

Brent sat on the table and shot me a glance. "I don't think so, not unless you worked in the coffee plantation."

"My mistake, then. You just remind me of someone." She scrubbed the grease off her hands. "Can you remove your shirt, please?"

Brent pulled it off, revealing the stump just above his elbow.

She snapped on gloves and examined Brent's arm. "Whoever patched you up did a shit job."

Brent glanced at me again. "It was done quickly. Life or death, you know…"

"Well, I'm glad you're okay," she said. "So, you work in the plantation?"

"I was a foreman there for many years. But I've been rebuilding the fishing wells after the accident."

"The extermination, you mean?" Nelly said.

Brent squirmed.

"Please, hold still," she said.

"What do you think?" I interjected. "Can it be done?"

"Whoever did this really screwed up the nerve endings, but I can manage." She patted Brent's shoulder. "Ready for a new arm?"

Brent's eyes lit up. "What? Really?"

"She's the best," I said. "Would you like to add anything?"

He gave me a funny look.

"…Like a flamethrower," I suggested.

Brent thought about that. "Maybe when I was at the plantation. But I'm working with metals now… Can you add a welding torch?"

My daughter smiled. "Absolutely."

"No!" Tamarind sternly said.

We turned to her.

I felt my frustration rising. "This is necessary for Brent to work at full capacity. The same goes for thousands of others who have suffered debilitating injuries."

"We don't need your charity," she seethed.

"It's not charity!" I snapped. "It's…" I stopped.

My daughter gave me a strange look.

"It's what?" Tamarind said.

"It's necessary to maximize worker efficiency."

"Why?" she followed up.

I have no choice… "Because you are my vassals and I order it."

"That's what I thought," she said and turned around. "Let's go Brent. Calvin must learn he is nothing but a hypocrite."

Brent slowly stood and put his shirt back on. "Sorry, Airball. But she's right," he said and hustled to catch up to her and his daughter.

I sighed deeply and turned to Nelly, who still gave me that strange look. "I was hoping they'd be more open to this."

◆

I kept Nelly busy with challenging projects that only she could accomplish, and found ways to justify her employment in the eyes of the dons. And where I was initially hemorrhaging credits, things finally turned a corner in the seventh year, when Nelly's prostheses showed a direct correlation to productivity. The other dons began putting in orders to aid their own workforces.

But my attention strayed, for the fishing guild was booming once again, and with Tamarind's unwillingness to step into the roll of don, I took on the burden of management myself. I was barely home, barely in contact with my daughter, and barely saw Brent and Tamarind. I was distancing, assimilating into cartel culture, becoming the exact thing I swore to eradicate.

Decades passed by in the blink of an eye. I watched my hair recede, then disappear, altogether. I became a centennial. And this was marked ever more clearly when I entered my bedroom and felt an old presence.

"I don't recognize you," came a hoarse voice and a strong figure stepped into the dim light.

"Joan…" I gasped. "You haven't aged a day."

She looked right into my eyes. "It's time…"

"For what?" I asked.

"Don't play dumb. It doesn't suit you."

I grinned. "You're finally calling in that favor?"

She nodded. "A boy has been born to a frigate family in the poor district of Hardsill."

"Who is he?" I whispered.

"He's a Kell," Joan said. "I need you to ensure that he embarks upon a path to free my people. I need you to guarantee his protection."

I soaked it all in, pondering the options. "I can create another heir. A *Car* to match with a *Kell*. That way, I can protect this boy without raising suspicion. But I must ask, why him? I've been giving Tamarind every opportunity to stand up for your people. But she refuses."

"You've only offered her a cartel-ship," Joan said.

"Which is a far better position to be in," I argued.

She tilted her head. "A don is just as much in bondage as their vassals. You know this most of all. So, why is it so difficult for you to understand that you are merely offering Tamarind different shackles."

I didn't know what to say, except, "How will this boy change things? What can he do that no one else can?"

Joan clenched her jaw. "He possesses unique cells. One's designed to regrow organs and limbs from their most basic stem cells. If applied correctly, they can circumvent the side effects of heavy genetic modification, they might stop Kaladian Degradation Disease."

"Do you know the procedure?" I prodded.

"No," she admitted. "But my brother knows where to find that information."

"Brother?"

Joan glared at me. "Is Representative Fordham of Puck still under Arkathy influence?"

"He is," I answered, knowing that was all the information she would give me.

"Is he providing them with intel on the Council of Colonies?"

"That is correct."

"But, is he loyal to you first?"

"Yes."

Joan breathed deeply. "My brother was the leader of The Bloody Dozen. When we failed, he was imprisoned in ice. But in the chaos of the Arkathy

Blockade, he was forgotten. He's being held somewhere in System Sol, but I don't know where. Representative Fordham is in charge of Puck's extensive prison system. He might know. Can you help me?"

Sam! Wake up! came a distant voice from within.

I shook my head, trying to focus on the moment, and looked at Joan. She was fading away like a ghost. "I will try my best."

"Can you say the words?" she asked.

I breathed deeply. "A favor for a favor, I will—"

Something grasped my shoulders, shaking hard, but I found no hands.

Goddammit, Sam! Wake up! The Arkathy are here!

CHAPTER FIFTEEN

"Goddammit, Sam! Wake up!" Ulysses cries, "The Arkathy are here!"

I am more awake than you know, Samuel thinks as the old don's memories slip away. His eyes open to meet bright rays of sun instead of the cargo bay's emergency lighting. Wind whips across his face and through his hair, but not across his body. *I'm wearing auto-armor,* he realizes and looks up to see Ulysses also in auto-armor. *He doesn't know who or what I am. He knows nothing.*

Barren land races by. Dust flies in their wake. Samuel plants his hands on strangely familiar bamboo planks, pressing himself into a seated position and finds they are sitting on the bed of the don's skiff.

It worked... Samuel realizes. *They got the information. Don Carlyle has transferred power. And we got free of the ship.* He studies the young don through the cab's rear window, sitting next to The Augmentor, staring ahead as they race to the mouth of the ravine. *But Faith is not the heir,* Samuel knows and focuses on The Augmentor. *And she has no idea who she is...*

"It's a fucking warship!" Ulysses cries, pointing up.

The Arkathy... echoes the old don's voice in Samuel's head.

Samuel discerns a shape descending from above, bending the light. *We shouldn't have left the yacht,* Samuel realizes, knowing now that there are things hidden within the farming equipment that aren't what they seem.

Disruptor... comes the old don's voice.

Samuel locks eyes with his massive friend. "Ulysses…" Samuel calmly says. "Get to the missile site. Get The Terran Files… I'll handle the Arkathy."

"What!?" Ulysses responds.

Samuel hits a switch at his armor's collar, materializing a helmet around his head, tucks his arms, and rolls off the back of the skiff.

"Sam! No!" Ulysses shouts.

The auto-armor creates a protective shell before Samuel hits the ground. His world spins. *Don't you dare puke!* he commands himself. When his tumbling slows and the protective shell releases, he spreads his arms and legs to control his momentum, skidding to a stop. Dust is all he can see until his vision switches to temporal. Earth appears in deep blue at the surface, with smaller shrubs and scurrying creatures in light pink. The skiff becomes a point of red continuing to the ravine. The stone hull of the don's grounded yacht is dark crimson. Then, an ominous purple object looms overhead, no longer hidden from view.

But how do we stop a warship!? Samuel thinks.

The Disruptor! the old don voice says, more clearly now.

The Cindarian's insurance policy… Samuel wonders just how much dealing the old don did with those creatures.

There's no time!

Right… Samuel sifts through memories from when the don acquired the auto-armor. He finds the don's mobility training, plants his hands upon the ground, and digs his toes into the dirt like a sprinter. *Auto-armor, show me what you got!* He lunges forth, feeling the armor add tremendous strength, propelling him with ungodly speed.

"*167km,*" reads the armor's visor. "*189km… 215km.*"

I'm moving faster than the skiff! He quickly nears the don's yacht with its cargo bay open. The auto-armor keeps his legs revolving, absorbing impact, and bringing him to a controlled stop.

"Where's the Disruptor!?" Samuel cries, staring at the farming equipment strewn about the cargo hold.

I… don't know, the don says.

Each piece of debris appears in slightly different shades of color depending on their density. Then, among the red, on the floor against the back wall, Samuel sees a black sphere. *That must be it!* As he scrambles over the debris, the sphere scales down, appearing like a grain of sand, but when he grasps it, it feels like an orange. Samuel expects it to be unfathomably heavy, bracing his legs, but it is so light that he nearly throws it to the ceiling.

Be careful! the old don cries. *If the containment field is compromised, you'll be instantly crushed!*

"How do I work this thing!?" Samuel says.

Its launcher should be here! the don cries. *The Disruptor will do the rest!*

Samuel searches the floor. Among the debris he finds the launch tube cracked right down its length.

Shit... says the don.

"There must be another way," Samuel says.

This armor possesses incredible strength, right!? Khasi's voice cuts in.

So what!? the don responds.

Throw the damn thing! Khasi shouts.

Samuel studies the cracked launch tube in one hand and the Disruptor in the other. *No choice.* He ditches the launcher and bounds over the debris. When he emerges from the cargo bay, the Arkathy warship is several kilometers directly above him. *No... It's passing over me.*

"Where's it heading?" Samuel asks.

The armor estimates the ship's trajectory to the hills, meeting the skiff's dust cloud. *"Interception in approximately 47 seconds."*

"Estimate output required to throw the Disruptor at the Arkathy vessel," Samuel commands.

A dashed line appears on visor from the Disruptor in his hand leading to the warship. *"Warning, dangerous proximity to anomaly!"* Flashes in red. *"Output required will place auto-armor into automatic shutdown! Loss of li —"*

"Do it!" Samuel orders, raising his right hand.

Power channels from the armor's cells, vibrating his body and a high-pitched whining invades his ears. He widens his stance, bracing for the send of a lifetime. Anchors drive into the ground from the armor's soles. Output rises into orange, then red. Samuel stretches back his pitching arm.

"Commencing launch in 3... 2... 1... Ignition!"

Samuel throws with all his might, feeling the armor add tremendous force. His prosthetic leg bends out of shape. *Ruined...* His prosthetic foot snaps at the ankle. *They can be replaced!* Horror strikes him when he realizes what is about to happen next. Searing pain rips through his back and hundreds of pops run down his arm.

The Disruptor rockets toward the warship.

Fuck! is all Samuel can think as his back screams, his arm becomes jelly, and his remaining leg goes numb. His head swims. His vision fades.

Stay with us, Sam! Khasi shouts.

"Emergency shutdown initiated," flashes on visor. The auto-armor winds down to silence and its joints lock up tight as Samuel passes out.

♦

"They arrive in Paris today," Jonathan says, closing Hazel's message.

"What do you mean, they?" Angela responds.

"Dr. Lee is coming with his equipment."

"Why?" Angela tilts her head. "I suppose having a doctor might be a good thing." She glances at Thalee, who stares befuddled at the hologram.

Jonathan raises his palms. "My guess is he's helping with her case." He closes the hologram, watching Thalee's brow wrinkle.

"The case you're not allowed to know anything about?" Angela snipes.

"Yeah, that one," Jonathan snipes back.

Thalee turns to him. "Whost ista Clara?"

It takes Jonathan a moment to decipher her words. "Clara is my wife."

"Aizen's madre…" she whispers.

A sudden dread penetrates Jonathan. He begins to sweat profusely. He stands up and looks into the sky, but nothing is there but the clouds. He cannot help thinking, *The Arkathy?*

Both Thalee and Angela give him strange looks.

"What's up?" Angela says.

"Aizen's in trouble!" Jonathan blurts. "I can feel it!"

Angela furrows her brow. "Jon, maybe you should get checked out when we pick up Clara and Dr. Lee."

"No!" Jonathan says. His stomach twists. *They don't understand!* He furiously gathers his gear.

"We just packed that," Angela scoffs. "What the hell's gotten into you?"

"I can't explain it!" Jonathan says. "Aizen needs my help, now!" He straps on his pack, takes a duffle in each hand, and struts to Aizen's shuttle.

"We have no idea where he is," Angela says, marching after him. "Thalee's description could be a million locations."

Jonathan grunts. "I can find it!"

Thalee leaps in front of him like a panther. "Aizen kay sa, No!"

"Thalee, get out of my way!" Jonathan responds.

"No!" she repeats.

As Jonathan goes to sidestep her, she lunges. Jonathan shifts his legs and spins, knocking Thalee off balance, all the while holding a duffle in each hand. His feet move with a mind of their own, one hooking around hers as he uses a duffle's weight to trip her to the ground.

How in Sol did I do that!? Jonathan thinks.

Thalee scrambles to her feet. "Dee *you* tyrain Aizen!?"

Jonathan steps back. *Did I train Aizen?* he deciphers.

Thalee postures for another lunge.

She must know of Aizen's abilities! "I taught him everything he knows!" he lies. "You cannot stop me!"

She studies his stance. Her eyes meet his. Then, she grins. "I cane tont stoppe you… But, I cane helppe you."

"Aizen explicitly said neither of you should go!" Angela interjects.

"Angela," Jonathan says. "We're going to save my son." He breathes deeply. "Can you meet Clara and Dr. Lee in Paris?"

"You should meet them yourself!" Angela furiously says. "They're expecting you!"

"They'll understand," Jonathan says. "Please, tell Clara that I must help Aizen… And that something is happening to me."

"Can you be more specific about that!?" Angela prods.

"Just tell her." Jonathan turns to Aizen's shuttle with its hastily patched hatch, then spies the blades strapped to Thalee's thigh. One of them appears tinted red. "Thalee, is that blood?"

Thalee listens, then nods.

"Whose blood is it?" he follows up.

She pulls the blade from its sheath. "From zede boy wiste un leg." She grins, devilishly. "No leg boy, now."

Jonathan sets down his duffles and extends a hand. "May I?"

Thalee reluctantly places the blade's hilt into Jonathan's palm.

Jonathan turns to Angela.

Angela huffs. "What is it, now!?"

"Dr. Lee came with his equipment, which means he can analyze this blood to determine who we're dealing with." Jonathan extends the blade her way. "Can you bring this to Paris?"

Angela places hands on her hips. "Fine!" She cautiously takes the blade.

"Thank you, Angela." Jonathan turns to Thalee. "Let's go."

Thalee looks longingly at her blade in Angela's hand, turns abruptly, and follows Jonathan into the shuttle.

♦

Hills jut from the barren, flat landscape, just as Thalee described. *This could be anywhere in the Midwest*, Jonathan knows, but his gut says otherwise.

Thalee points out the window. "What isth that!?"

Jonathan only sees blue sky. "I don't see anything."

Thalee grips Jonathan's jaw, forcing his head up. A strange distortion becomes visible above them, like water bending light. *A cloaked ship,* Jonathan realizes. *And it's big...*

A black speck catches his eye, rocketing from the ground. There is no smoke trail. The shuttle detects nothing.

A bird? Jonathan thinks, but it moves perfectly straight and too quickly.

Just before making contact with the cloaked ship, it halts dead in place and swells into a massive black sphere. Panels peel off of the ship like old paint, revealing its frame underneath.

An Arkathy warship! Jonathan realizes.

Structural members rip apart and explosions are instantly extinguished. Everything sucks into the sphere.

Even light, Jonathan knows. "A miniature black hole..."

His body lurches forth. His harness cinches tight, holding him to his seat, but his arms and legs pull straight, feeling like they'll be ripped from his body. The shuttle's hull groans and Jonathan sees its nose stretching. *We're caught in its gravity well!* They gather tremendous speed, racing towards the anomaly. Jonathan sees Thalee with her limbs pulling out straight, too.

"Hang on!" he shouts and slowly maneuvers his outstretched hands to the stick like an infant learning to hold a bottle. His wrists clumsily grip the handle. He pulls back with all his might. His shoulders pop, and the right one is out of socket again. The stick does not budge, but he manages to slide his palms around the handle. *I need more leverage!* He curls his outstretched legs. His hip flexors burn. His right foot slides in front of the shuttle's dash where he presses firmly, lifting his left foot into position. *Here we go!* Jonathan tenses his core, postures his back, and presses his legs like a power-lifter. The stick slowly pulls back, the shuttle's nose drifts up, and all that pulling weight shifts into Jonathan's lap, like a ton of bricks.

"Warning, dangerous g-forces! 8.4! 8.5! 8.6!" chimes as the shuttle slowly faces the glaring midday sun.

Screaming metal comes from the underside of the shuttle. *Landing gear is gone!* With a hand made of lead, Jonathan reaches the throttle and presses forth, maxing out the shuttle's thrusters. The g-forces upon his chest now match that upon his lap. *And we're still being sucked in!*

Then, without warning or reason, the intense pull disappears, sending them tumbling through the sky like a stone from a slingshot.

◆

A dust-cloud disturbs the still, barren landscape, stretching from the small, downed craft in the distance to a skiff racing towards the ravine. And a cloaked Arkathy warship ripples through atmospheric strata above.

How do I fight both of them!? Aizen thinks.

A black speck rockets towards the Arkathy ship, but there is no chemtrail. Aizen slips into partial meditation, but cannot sense anything.

My Sol! Zion cries. *That's a Disruptor!*

The speck halts and becomes a large, black sphere. Panels rip from the Arkathy ship like a child plucking petals from a flower and structural members peel away. Then, wiggling debris sucks from the ship's internal compartments and coalesce around the black sphere like water down a drain.

A gravity well!? Aizen realizes. *How can that exist!?*

I don't know! Zion responds. *But R9 told me there are two unaccounted for in the galaxy!*

R9! Aizen calls within. *Now is a good time to show yourself!*

Silence.

I took the spore! Aizen cries. *Where are you!? We need you!*

Still nothing.

We'll have to make due on our own, Dione says.

How!? Aizen responds, feeling impossibility consume him.

Aizen, Anda says. *We've beaten The Arkathy before, we've beaten equalizers before. All without R9...*

"So, we don't need its help," Aizen says aloud for his own ears, and breathes deeply, regaining his composure.

Brace yourself! Zion say as the dirt below the sphere lifts into the sky.

A tremendous force pulls upon Aizen's body. He spreads his feet to create a strong base, letting his boots bite into the missile site's concrete floor. Nevertheless, he is dragged, passing through the massive doorway, back into the ravine. He flips on his helmet, pulls an anchor bolt from his belt, and secures his tether. He twists the anchor's shaft and squats, shoving its tip into the rock. Spindly legs split from the anchor's shaft, positioning it perpendicular to the ground, then it spins, boring its way into rock.

"One centimeter... Two centimeters..." displays on visor.

The pulling intensifies, lifting Aizen from the ground. His feet become useless, but he does not panic, focusing on the diagram on his visor, and letting out more tether. *Just like fishing...*

GHOSTS OF ZION | 329

"Ten centimeters... Eleven centimeters... Twelve—"

Aizen locks the reel, snapping his tether taut.

"Anchor secured," comes on visor.

Aizen's arms are pulled above his head. Mirko's massive rifle barely dangles by its strap. Then, his legs rise, folding him like a jackknife. His utility belt bites into his hips, the tether creaks, and the exposed portion of the anchor bolt bends like a wilting flower. *But it's holding!* Aizen looks up to see almost half the Arkathy warship has been consumed. Emergency pods jettison from its opposite side, but they arc back into the anomaly. There are no explosions. *Because there is no air,* Aizen understands.

A small craft lifts from the ground, plunging into the sphere.

The skiff! Aizen searches the ground, finding three figures with arms raised, but their feet are anchored. One of them is massive.

It's the equalizer, Dione says. *I don't remember the other two.*

Where's the one-legged boy? Sha says.

Back at the downed ship, Mermer responds.

They're wearing Arkathy auto-armor, Zion states.

So, are they working with the Arkathy or against them? Allessandra asks.

Aizen studies the Arkathy ship being torn to shreds. The black sphere abruptly vanishes. Tension in Aizen's tether snaps him back to the ground, and he twists like a cat to land feet first. He slides along the rock passing the anchor bolt and heading back through the missile site's entry for the third time. The Arkathy ship dips below the ravine's cliff. A moment later, tremors come through the ground. Then, black smoke rises into the sky.

"Aizennnnnn!" rumbles moments later.

Aizen snaps his head down to see the massive man coming full sprint up the ravine, pointing a monstrous finger at him. Aizen slips into partial meditation. The equalizer is vibrant, the two others less so. *One is injured.* He detects a fourth light at their downed ship. Hundreds of lights move within the Arkathy warship. *The auto-armor protected those not sucked into the anomaly.* Aizen then senses two more souls tumbling high up in the sky.

"Thalee?" he whispers. *What is she doing back here?* He focuses on the second soul. "Dad... No..."

CHAPTER SIXTEEN

Clara peers out her shuttle's window, searching for Jonathan among a small gathering at Paris's landing field. *Maybe he's on the other side.* When she looks out the opposing window she makes eye contact with a woman with arms crossed. *Angela...*

Thrusters wind down and seat belt lights turn green.

"Welcome to Paris. You are now free to depart," chimes the shuttle.

Clara releases her harness and gives Dr. Lee a concerned look. "It's just Angela."

Dr. Lee stares back blankly. "Does Jonathan not understand the urgency of our visit?"

Clara thinks about that. "Something happened."

The hatch opens with a whine. Fresh air, and overwhelming scents and noises waft over her. She tries to stand, but stumbles back into her seat. Archaeologists slowly rise and shift their hips side to side.

"Never been to Earth before?" one of them says.

"I had hip surgery not long ago," Clara lies. *A little too easily...*

The archaeologist nods, acknowledging his misunderstanding, then grabs his HRG duffle and departs. Clara carefully stands and shifts her hips like the archaeologists had, feeling Earth's gravity in her joints, in her guts, and in her blood.

Dr. Lee follows her lead, but holds a serious look.

"Hey… Are you coming or not?" says an agitated voice.

Clara finds Angela at the hatchway.

"Nice to see you, too," Clara snips.

"Aizen's in serious trouble," Angela gruffly responds. "And Jonathan decided to go after him instead of meeting you here."

Clara's heart pounds. "Did Aizen encounter an equalizer and one-legged boy?"

Angela's eyes widen. "That's one hell of a guess." She raises a glass tube containing a black knife. "Thalee used this to sever the boy's foot. Blood is still fresh. Jonathan wanted me to give it to Dr. Lee to identify him, but it seems you already know."

Another limb lost? Clara thinks, feeling sorry for the boy. *But he must have attacked Aizen and... Thalee?*

Dr. Lee extends a hand. "May I?"

Angela hands him the tube.

"This is perfect, Clara," he says, "we can track how much progress the boy's cells have made."

Yes... Clara thinks, but something else nags. "Who's Thalee?"

Angela's face flashes with regret, her lips seal tight.

"Angela… You just said my family is in trouble. So, I'm trying not to lose my shit right now," Clara says. "Who's Thalee?"

Angela takes a deep breath. "She's a native Terran that Aizen befriended."

Dr. Lee gasps. "You can't be serious! This is unprecedented! We have zero understanding of their genetics! Where is she!?"

"She returned with Jonathan to help Aizen," Angela informs.

"Then, that's where we must go," Clara says.

Dr. Lee's excitement disappears.

"Kevin," Clara says and turns to him. "How quickly can you move your gear into Angela's shuttle?"

"It can't handle another transfer," he says.

Clara thinks about that. "Then, set up in the clean room here, find out everything you can about this latest blood sample."

Relief washes across Dr. Lee's face. "Yes, I'll do that!"

Clara turns to Angela. "Let's go."

Angela shakes her head. "I'm sorry, Clara. I thought I could handle the Sorgans being on Earth. I thought I could handle Aizen being an incarnation of Zion. And I thought I could handle Jonathan's change. But, this is too much for me."

Clara cocks her head. "What do you mean by Jonathan's change?"

"Something's happening to him, but he won't tell me what." Angela says. "He said you would understand."

"…I do," Clara says, feeling her heart race even more. She snatches her pack and marches off the shuttle, brushing by Angela, and stepping upon real earth. After a few paces she stops. "Angela?"

"Yeah?" Angela responds.

"I hope you don't mind me taking your shuttle."

"It's Jonathan's shuttle. So, go ahead."

Clara eyes the call signs on each hull until finding his. She beelines to its landing zone, climbs its steps, and presses the hatch's release. A retinal scan emits and a deadbolt thunks.

"Welcome, Clara," the shuttle says as the hatch opens.

A light is blinking at the dash.

A message! Clara races to opens it.

"43.7974130, -104.0032770," appears, followed by, *"Kip…"*

Clara plugs the coordinates into the shuttle, then whispers, "Kip."

◆

They were sent several miles back the way they came. His shoulders feel on fire and his lunch splatters every surface of the shuttle. Thalee furiously grips her straps with her legs still curled.

"Thalee, it's okay now," Jonathan says, but he knows he must land without landing gear.

They zip along in silence.

After several minutes, she turns to him. "…What wast that?"

Jonathan searches for the English words. "It appeared like a black hole… like a gravity well… like…"

"Your people controlla gravita?"

Jonathan shakes his head. "No, but other species in the galaxy can."

Thalee faces him. "Wast the bending of elight a different aspecies?"

"Yes…" Jonathan carefully answers, nervous of her reaction.

She uncurls her legs and relaxes her grip. "Ara they after Aizen?"

Good question, Jonathan thinks. "They might be after the equalizer and one-legged boy."

"Then, they ara friends?"

"No," Jonathan says. "They're called the Arkathy, and were once humanity's greatest foe. They were subdued by a great man named Zion. But, after his death the Arkathy chancellor was elected as his successor. It has been a precarious twelve years since."

"I do not comprende this," Thalee states. "But I knowsa Zion."

Jonathan fixates on her. "How?"

"Sendu worship Zion," Thalee says.

"What are Sendu?" Jonathan asks.

"Creatures froma the terra. Dangerous, but helpful."

My Sol! "We call them Sorgans. They're an ancient species almost wiped out by the Arkathy. Zion hid them on Earth for protection."

"Ara the Arkat-hy thata formidable?"

"They are, but in a different way."

"How?" she asks.

"Their bodies are just as fragile as ours, but they have an ability to control the minds of their enemies. Long ago, they used this to create a galactic empire and collect technology from every species to make their own."

"So, theira bodies ara like ours…" She holds up her lone black knife. "Cana theya be killed witha this?"

"If they're not in armor, that would work."

She snaps her head to the window. "Smoke."

"Huh?"

She points out the window. "The gravita isa gone."

Yes it is, Jonathan realizes as a plume of smoke rises from the other side of the jutting hills. When they round the face they find a smaller downed craft. Debris scatters around its cargo bay and a figure in Arkathy armor stands frozen like a statue. Then, the Arkathy warship reveals like a disturbed log with ants streaming from its cracks.

"That's the Arkathy," Jonathan mutters.

"Ara theya insects?" Thalee says.

"They have four legs coming from double-socketed hips. So, they might appear insect-like from a distance."

"But, they're shiny, like beetle."

"That's their auto-armor, which gives them numerous advantages, including super strength."

As they close in on the hills, Jonathan searches its many ravines. He hovers the shuttle then rolls to the side to get a bird's eye view from its window. Petrified trees give the hills a painted look. Ravines cut into the granite, but water no longer runs. *This land died long ago.* He spies hundreds of black dots side by side at the hill's plateau top, each perfectly circular. They suddenly flicker, becoming momentarily white. *But how is that possible?*

"Thera ara holes," Thalee says.

"You're right." More flickers come. *Muzzle flashes!* Dread fills Jonathan. "They've already engaged Aizen!" He pushes the stick, dipping the shuttle's nose, and plummets to the hills. Thalee grips her harness and tucks her legs again. Jonathan levels out a few meters above the holes. More flashes come, but he cannot determine their source. *The holes are deep.* He start the landing sequence.

"Landing gear compromised, auto-landing offline," the shuttle responds.

Jonathan grasps the stick with both hands, keeping the shuttle steady while using foot pedals to control vertical thrust. They teeter like a rowboat caught in a ship's wake.

"Three meters," says the shuttle. *"Two meters... One meter."*

Just before contact, Jonathan presses the right foot pedal, tipping the shuttle to ensure the hatch faces up. A solid crunch comes as the shuttle's underbelly crumples like foil. The right thruster chokes on dirt. Jonathan hits the kill switch, winding them to silence, and pulls the hatch jettison lever, sending its door flying off again. Shuttle components dwindle to silence. A *Ratatat* comes from outside.

Rounds firing! He tears off his harness and races across the shuttle's tilted floor to a compartment in back. He pulls out Mirko's heavy case. *Unlocked,* he realizes. He lifts its lid to see empty divots in its foam beside two stun pistols. *Aizen's armed up.* Jonathan picks up a stun pistol. *Full charge at least.* He grabs the other.

"Thalee, take this," he says, but there is no response. He snaps his head up to find her gone.

CHAPTER SEVENTEEN

Built like a sledgehammer, but he's the tip of the spear, Aizen thinks as the equalizer covers incredible ground up the ravine, leaving his comrades in the dust. The equalizer's cloak activates, disappearing from view. *It's better this way,* Aizen knows, closing his eyes, fully committing to his electroreceptive senses, and focusing upon the equalizer. But his thoughts drift to his father's light in the sky.

Aizen, not now! Zion says.

Aizen shakes his head and activates his cloak. *Mirko, You're up!*

Mirko swivels his rifle from its back harness, telescopes its long barrel, unfolds its butt, and flips down a tripod. He lays Aizen on his stomach.

We're not trying to kill him, Aizen thinks.

You're making this unnecessarily difficult, Mirko responds.

Just promise me.

Kneecaps and spinal cords only, Mirko says.

Aizen feels a rock in his stomach.

I'm kidding, Mirko adds.

How can you joke like that at a time like this!? Aizen responds.

It's how you manage, Mirko says, then quiets.

The equalizer charges up the center of the ravine, fully trusting in his cloak and armor.

Let's break that trust, Aizen thinks.

The rifle butt kicks into his shoulder, sliding both him and the rifle back several centimeters, and the ground beneath the equalizer's foot obliterates, leaving nothing for his stampeding foot to plant upon. His leg dips into the earth, tripping him, and he splays on his stomach. The equalizer scrambles to his feet and dashes to the ravine's side wall.

Nope. Mirko sends another jarring shot.

The rock wall explodes, sending the equalizer flying back to the center of the ravine. He lies still, as if knocked unconscious. But then, he rolls to his stomach and studies the divot in the ground and in the wall. He quickly pulls a rifle from his auto-armor and lines up a shot.

Shit! Mirko rolls off as his sniper rifle shatters.

He determined our position from only two shots!? Aizen realizes. He focuses on the equalizer to find him casually waving. Then, he vanishes from Aizen's senses.

That's not possible! Mirko says.

My Sol... Zion says.

Do you know what this is!? Aizen asks.

The Arkathy once aided the Trogdans' crusade against the Fersandans. But being aquatic plants, the Fersandans were electroreceptive and could easily sense them. The Arkathy must have developed a method to block electroreception with their armor.

Then, we're blind! Mirko says. *Where's R9 when we need it!?*

There's another way, Aizen responds. *Eva discovered that she and Frank were quantum entangled. We must have all been entangled in the same way at one point.* He thinks about that. *There were times when we made the transfer only moments after meeting the next individual... Sha, how long did you interact with Mirko?*

Sha comes forth. *Maybe thirty seconds, and from nearly ten meters away.*

But it was enough, Aizen thinks.

We're not trying to transfer into the equalizer, Mirko says.

But there should be some sort of connection already, Aizen retorts.

Mermer comes forth. *Okay Aizen, I'll try to find something.*

In the meantime, Aizen, you must be cautious, Zion says.

So this is what it feels like to fight me, Aizen thinks and opens his eyes, searching the ravine for little puffs of dust kicked up by the equalizer's charge, but there is nothing. *Because he's not charging,* Aizen determines. He peers down the ravine to where the equalizer's companions were left behind. *They're blocking my senses, too.*

Dione comes. *Aizen, we must get inside and seek out cover.*

I have an idea. Aizen bolts into the missile site, to the very back, where he remembers the old reactor room existed. A heavy metal door barely clings to existence and Aizen slips through its crack, knowing the equalizer must break through. *And there's no hiding that!*

"*Warning! Dangerous radiation levels detected,*" comes on visor.

I have two hours, Aizen knows.

Arkathy armor can withstand this radiation indefinitely, Zion says.

But their ability to detect me will be compromised, Aizen responds.

This might actually work, Dione says.

Aizen races down a staircase to a short corridor. The moment he enters the reactor room, he meets a catwalk's edge once hosting a guardrail. Below is the old deteriorated reactor shell and a sphere of concrete, but he cannot sense the core itself. *Whoever took the missiles also took this…*

All this radiation is residual, then, Mirko adds.

Appears so, Aizen says, studying the concrete floor below, imagining hundreds of sick equalizers from Eva's story. Only bones remain.

A screeching comes and Aizen knows the equalizer has entered. *Are you sensing anything, Mermer?*

It's difficult to pinpoint where he is, the crustacean responds.

A shudder resonates through the metal catwalk. Aizen faces its direction.

"Smart…" comes the equalizer's bellowing voice.

Aizen does not say a word, focusing on the catwalk beneath his feet. Another shudder comes.

"…You fight like a demon of old…" the bellowing voice continues. "…I was taught to fear your style. But I do not fear you, Aizen. Or I should say… Mirko."

How does he know!? Aizen thinks.

He must be from my time, Mirko responds.

The equalizer chuckles. "To think all this time it was electroreception. You Cerans are surprising. Not even our great doctor Kaladian thought of incorporating such an ability." Another shudder comes. "But, with Arkathy armor, I have the advantage now. You are defeated."

I found him! Mermer suddenly says.

Cutting it close there, Zion responds.

Aizen, we can do this, but you must give us full control, Mermer says.

We must meld, Aizen knows, closes his eyes, and goes into full meditation. He navigates to a white void where all of them are waiting. *All but R9.* Mermer melts into Aizen's body. The equalizer's subtle outline becomes discernible.

That's him, Mermer says.

This is not much, Aizen responds.

It will become more…

As each joins, his senses grow, and little by little the equalizer appears like a ghost.

Still… not much, Aizen thinks.

The monstrous ghost steps, sending another shudder through the catwalk. "Give me The Terran Files and I will let you live!"

"You don't know the power within them," Aizen responds. "You don't know what they can do."

"I of all people know!" the ghost shouts. "They will become my people's path to salvation!"

"And how will they do that?" Aizen says.

"…What do you mean, how!? My people are dying! And the answer lies in the files!"

"What answer!?" Aizen snaps.

The ghost stops his forward march. Aizen can sense him thinking, sense confusion and fear. *Coming through our quantum connection,* he realizes.

"I'll figure it out!"

"Figure what out!?" Aizen challenges.

"Fuck you! Give me The Terran Files, now!"

"Not y'a chance y'in hell!" Aizen shouts back, but with Dione's voice in the old Hermian dialect.

The massive man begins to shudder. "How darrre you speak y'in the rrrighteous tongue! You werrre supposed to save y'us y'all!"

Do you know him? Aizen asks Dione.

No… but he certainly knows me, she says.

"y'I did save y'us y'all," she responds through Aizen.

The equalizer releases his cloak and disengages his helmet, revealing a face of anguish.

He's crying, Aizen realizes.

He points at himself. "y'I y'am y'Ulysses! Leader y'of The Bloody Dozen! Loyal serrrvant y'of the Grrreat Dirrrectorrr!" He marches forth. "You, Dione Sharrrpe… You, betrrrayed y'ourrr people! You, betrrrayed y'ourrr grrreat fatherrr! You, sold y'us y'into slavery!"

What does he mean? Aizen thinks.

I don't know, Dione says. *I lived for more than a hundred years after I transferred into Anda. But I only know of a life before then.*

Ulysses thrusts his massive fist, covering incredible distance in a flash, but Mermer is quicker, sidestepping Aizen. Mirko grasps Ulysses's wrist and diverts his power, turning the massive man's balance. But just before stumbling, Ulysses's feet lock to the catwalk.

The armor's magnetic anchors! Aizen realizes.

Ulysses swings his arm like a baseball bat. Aizen tries to shift back, but there is a concrete wall, then he tries moving to the side, but there is another. He drops to the catwalk's grating, feeling a sledgehammer fist graze his helmet. When it makes contact with the wall, rotten cement explodes. Shards fall around him as he rolls away. He regains his footing and spins to face Ulysses, but the monster of a man is cloaked again. A ghostly shimmer registers from his periphery, too late to dodge. Aizen lifts his arm to take the brunt and feels a snap. But there is no pain.

No pain for you! Justin cries.

Aizen tumbles end over end down the catwalk, hitting the opposing wall.

We cannot take another strike like that! Kwai Lan says. *R9 never enhanced your body like we did Zion's!*

Get out of here now! Zion follows up.

Before Aizen can react, his body does. *It's Mermer.* He scrambles across the catwalk, making for the exit, sensing Ulysses right behind him. He slips through the doorway and furiously sprints up the stairs. Ulysses's thunderous steps gain on him. Aizen leaps into the missile site's massive main hall. *Go! Get out!* he orders himself and locates the gargantuan sunlit opening at the far end.

Remember, there's two more of them! Mirko cries.

The whine of heavy stun rifles comes.

Mermer, do your thing!

Aizen jerks left, right, forward, and back as shots rain.

Can you determine where they're are coming from!? Aizen asks.

Working on it! Mirko responds.

A second later, Aizen's hand goes rogue, pulling his holstered pistol, and setting to stun. *Because it will momentarily knock out their cloaks,* he knows. He trains his pistol into the darkness, but before pulling the trigger someone else does.

A cloak deactivates, revealing one of the shooters frozen in auto-armor. Then, a woman's silhouette flashes like a panther in the night and the frozen shooter's rifle is sliced in two.

"He's got backup!" comes a woman's voice.

I do? Aizen thinks, watching as the auto-armor is sliced clean through, again and again.

How is that possible!? Zion says. *Only Sorgan claws are hard enough to penetrate Arkathy armor!*

Aizen studies the panther-like silhouette dancing across the armored foe. *Thalee...* he realizes and thinks upon the knives gifted by Kune... *A Sorgan.*

The mystery shots come again, searching for the second cloaked shooter, but only hit concrete. Aizen senses a soul above him peering through one of the silo hatches.

"Dad..."

◆

I actually got one!? Jonathan thinks, staring at the frozen armor below. He zooms his visor to better study them. *Not the massive man, not the one-legged boy, and not an Arkathy.*

A second later, a figure dashes across the frozen armor, slicing clean through their rifle with what Jonathan swears is a knife. *That's Thalee! How did she get down there so fast!?*

"He's got backup!" echoes a voice from below.

More stuns fire at what Jonathan assumes is Aizen, and he prays that his son is dodging them. *The fact that he's still cloaked is proof he's okay,* Jonathan knows. He aims at what he knows to be another shooter and lets shots fly. *Nothing...* Jonathan shoves an anchor spike into the rock next to the silo's hatch and locks his carabiner. Then, he positions above the edge. *It's just another dig!* Jonathan thinks, building his courage, and jumps through the hole, plunging into darkness. His coiler lets out line. Jonathan switches to night vision and focuses on the battle as he descends. Thalee slices and dices the frozen armor. Blood oozes from the person within.

A boom comes and concrete cracks spider across the floor. *That must be from the equalizer!* Jonathan takes a shot.

A monstrous foot appears, followed by tree trunk legs, and finally a boulder of a human. The equalizer stands frozen, with their arm mid-swing. A slash comes across the back of their knee, shearing off bits of auto-armor, but Jonathan cannot see who struck.

It can only be Aiz—

Jonathan's tether snaps. A gunshot's pop comes a millisecond later. Weightlessness grips his stomach. His pistol flies from his hand as he flails.

But then, he twists like a cat. His feet touch concrete first, taking the brunt of the impact, then his hands plant. He rolls forward, somersaulting until he stops in a crouched position. He remains kneeling, breathing hard, not sure how he survived the fall. "It's finally awakening for me," he whispers. *But why so late?* He looks to where the battle continues.

The first armored shooter lies in a pool of blood, shaking violently. He then peers at the equalizer. Another gash appears in his armor, followed by a deep howl. The armor shudders. Groaning of metal comes. The armor bursts at its joints, and the equalizer is mobile again, swinging his fists like clubs.

"But if his auto-armor is compromised," Jonathan whispers. "Then, he cannot detect Aizen or me."

"But I can," comes a quiet voice, right behind him, and horrific pain rips through his back.

CHAPTER EIGHTEEN

Searing pain rips through Aizen's back and he drops to his knees. He looks down, expecting to find the tip of a knife erupting from his chest, but nothing is there. *What's happening!? Justin! I need you!*

I'm trying, Justin responds. *But this pain is not yours!*

What!? Aizen desperately rolls as Ulysses wildly swings.

It's coming through your quantum connection! Mermer says.

But, I slashed Ulysses's leg, not his chest! Aizen thinks.

It's from a different connection! Zion says.

"Aizen!" cries a woman. "It's over!"

Aizen whips about, clutching his chest where the phantom pain sits, and peers into the darkness.

Two silhouettes approach. Both uncloaked. One stumbles.

Dad! Aizen realizes. A figure stands behind his father in auto-armor, pointing a rifle at his head. Aizen's eyes wander to the tip of a blade protruding from his father's chest.

"Dad! No!" Aizen cries and stumbles forth.

"Don't you dare!" shouts the woman. "You come any closer! He dies!"

Aizen halts. He sees movement in the shadows. *Thalee...*

The woman snaps her head Thalee's way. "That goes for you, too!"

"Stop!" Aizen yells in her language.

Thalee freezes.

Aizen releases his cloak. A second later, the pain in his chest stops and his connection with Ulysses ceases. *Mermer turned off the quantum connection.* He removes his helmet. "Dad?" Aizen says, barely keeping a quiver out of his voice.

His father raises a hand to his helmet and unlatches. When it rolls back, Aizen sees blood trickling from his father's mouth and incredible resolve in his eyes.

"Don Carlyle! Are you okay!?" the armored woman says.

"Oh, no…" comes Ulysses's bellowing voice. He removes his armored helmet to reveal his owl-like eyes. He points into the darkness.

The armored woman becomes furious. "That was the don!" She presses the rifle against the base of Jonathan's skull. "Give us The Terran Files, now!"

Aizen's father raises his hands in surrender.

"Dad, it's going to be okay," Aizen says, slowly removing the collar from from his utility belt and setting it on the concrete. He kicks it towards the equalizer.

"I know," his father responds and smiles. His eyes are calm, focused. He grins, then whispers, "Kip…"

Before Aizen blinks, his father spins, using a raised elbow to deflect the woman's rifle and sending the palm of his other hand into her faceplate, snapping her head back. He then reaches behind himself, yanks the knife from his own back, and jams its tip into the rifle's barrel. He collapses to the floor as the woman pulls the trigger, but instead of a kill shot, the rifle explodes against her faceplate.

Aizen snaps into action, racing to his father, but a paw grasps the back of his envisuit, lifting him clear off the ground, and hurtling him into the air. Aizen pulls his tether, wraps its end-loop over a blade, and whips it at the equalizer. The blade sinks into the massive man's calf, and when the tether pulls taut, Aizen's weight pulls Ulysses's leg out from under him. Aizen lands on his feet several meters back.

Thalee charges the figure in the armor, dazed by the rifle's backfire, but the auto-armor's back splits open. The woman within leaps out and throws something to the ground.

Ulysses covers his ears.

Aizen braces for impact.

A thunderclap comes.

Thalee drops to the floor, covering her ears and rolling in agony. The unveiled woman lifts into the air, rockets thrusting from her hands and feet. In one motion, Aizen pulls his second knife from its sheath, slices clean through the tether connecting him to Ulysses, and whips it at the woman. He does not wait for it to reach its mark. Instead, he dashes at Ulysses, expecting the equalizer to face him head on.

Instead, Ulysses turns to his father.

Make me go faster! Aizen shouts at those within him. He digs deep, pressing his feet into the concrete floor with all his might. But the equalizer is faster, closing the gap to his father. *They were always faster,* he remembers from Mirko and Dione's lifetime. He watches helplessly as Ulysses crunches a sledgehammer fist into his father's chest.

Aizen's legs become jelly. He drops to the floor.

"Not so invincible anymore, are you!?" the massive equalizers bellows.

Aizen bores his eyes into Ulysses's. His rage builds. His stomach boils. His face feels hot. *But... Too hot...* His entire body is burning. Steam pours from his envisuit's collar. He rips off his gloves, to see his hands are black.

"What the fuck!?" Ulysses shouts, snatches the collar from the floor, and backs away.

Aizen grits his teeth. *What's happening!?* He pulls his envisuit off entirely to find steam leaking from every pore of his body. His wool clothing sizzles. He screams at the top of his lungs and realizes every soul within him is screaming, too.

The equalizer's eyes go wide.

The stitches of Aizen's boots break at the seams and he steps out from them. When his bare soles touch concrete, he senses the entire missile site, the equalizer and his companions, one bleeding out on the floor and the other outside limping with a knife protruding from her leg. He senses his father dying and Thalee staring at him. He senses the one-legged boy at the grounded ship, unconscious. He senses the wrecked warship and Arkathy soldiers amassing outside. He senses that one of them is different. Lastly, he senses hundreds of Sorgans all around them, watching.

"Sendu..." Thalee whispers and dashes to his father, grabbing him by the shoulders, and pulling him away.

Thank you, Aizen thinks, barely holding madness at bay. His fingertips sharpen. He increases in height. His eyes meet Ulysses's, whose jaw now hangs open. And then, Aizen is looking down upon the once massive man.

"What the hell are you!?" Ulysses cries and throws a fist.

A hissing comes from deep within, ancient and furious. "Pathetic!"

Aizen's hand thrusts forth with a knife-hand strike. His fingertips meet Ulysses's armored fist, finding the space between the index and middle knuckles. Auto-armor melts like butter, skin splits like pie crust, bone cleaves like firewood. He passes through Ulysses's wrist, elbow, and into his shoulder joint where Aizen twists, severing the equalizer's arm from his body.

Ulysses screams out as blood gushes from his shoulder. He attempts to pinch the wound, but must drop The Terran Files to do so.

"Make a decision, little man," Aizen hisses.

Ulysses plants The Terran Files firmly against his bleeding shoulder in Hermian salute. His face becomes resolute. "I made it long ago!"

"So be it." Aizen opens his claws and slashes.

Ai... zen, comes faintly from within.

Mermer? Aizen recognizes. He feels the crustacean struggling keep fragments of their souls together.

Aizen... Mermer repeats. *We must... purge R9... It's consuming... us all...*

Aizen tries to clear his madness as R9 continues slashing Ulysses. The equalizer's right leg is missing, yet he still holds onto The Terran Files with all his might. *What must I do!*

This is a Sorgan suit! Anda says. *We must redirect R9's next strike.*

Onto itself, Aizen knows.

Aizen now stands atop of Ulysses, his massive Sorgan foot pinning the brute to the floor. Through his sole, he senses Ulysses's heart pounding, his breath wheezing, and his stomach growling. *But it stops too early...* Aizen realizes the equalizer's entire bottom half is gone, yet he still holds The Terran Files tight.

R9 aims its chisel at Ulysses's neck and thrusts.

Now! Aizen cries and feels every soul within him pull the arm back, sending the chiseled hand into his own foot, instead.

R9 reels back. "You fucking humans! Betraying me again!"

Aizen fights R9's movements, his body jerking back and forth.

"I will rid myself of you!" It cries.

"Then, do it already!" Aizen shouts back. "We're separated!"

Aizen feels R9 assessing the Sorgan body covering his.

"...It's true!" the Sorgan gasps in utter disbelief. "...I'm free!"

"So, let us go!" Aizen cries.

Aizen's arms and legs feel like they are ripping apart and his mind is being diced. A moment later, he no longer senses the missile site in the

Sorgan way. The intense pressure and heat subsides. Chill air strikes his bare skin. He spits out the back of the Sorgan suit and falls to the floor naked like a newborn mammal. He discerns R9's massive silhouette standing over Ulysses. The equalizer makes confused eye contact with Aizen, then returns his attention to the black demon.

R9 slowly turns around, kneels to Aizen, and raises its claws. "And now, I will have my revenge!"

"You will do no such thing!" comes a magnificent voice through Aizen.

R9 stands and backs away. "Zion!? You're one of them, now!?"

Aizen stands, feeling Zion assume full control.

"I am, just like you were, just like we all become!" Zion says. "But you have your freedom! You have a second life!"

"But you must pay for your crimes! You betrayed me! You sold my species to the Arkathy!"

"Did I!?" Zion shouts, his magnificent voice causing even R9 to flinch. "Sense around you… Who's here!?"

R9 pauses and turns to the darkness. "They're here?" It raises its hands in disbelief. "They're all here!?"

"And safe. Just as I promised," Zion says.

"But… How did you get their spores from the Arkathy?" R9 says. He suddenly twitches. "Wait! The Arkathy are also here! The Chancellor herself is among them! You led them right to us!"

"Who else is among them?" Zion says.

R9 calms. "One of them is different… Wait… That's…" It faces Aizen square. "You have a lot of explaining to do…"

Zion shakes Aizen's head. "We don't have time."

"Then, we go our separate ways," R9 hisses.

"We will meet again, my friend," Zion says.

"…Perhaps." R9 abruptly turns and melts into the darkness.

Zion relinquishes control to Aizen.

Ragged breathing is all that remains in the silence.

"W-what are y-you?" Ulysses whispers.

Aizen's body shakes, he desperately needs water. He looks upon the broken man, then at The Terran Files clutched in his paw. Aizen's rage becomes pity. *This is all he has left...* He gives the equalizer one last look. "I hope you're happy…"

Aizen faces the missile site's entry and finds a speck in the ravine, dragging something heavy. *Dad...* He dons the remnants of his singed clothing and envisuit, and realizes that his broken arm was somehow mended during R9's extraction. He then staggers through the missile site, passing the frozen armor with the young woman bleeding out.

Thalee snaps her head up when Aizen hits sunlight. A look of horror crosses her face when he nears until she realizes Aizen is himself again. He loops one of his father's arms around his neck, and Thalee does the same with his other, and they move faster.

But to where?

Far away, Zion responds.

It takes an hour to reach the end of the ravine and Aizen monitors his father the entire way. *There's not much time...* They move east, away from the grounded ships and the amassing Arkathy regiment. They find a shady nook.

"Water," Thalee says and points at a shrub.

They gently set Aizen's father against a cool stone and Thalee races to the shrub, digging at its base. She pulls a wood straw from her clothing and sticks it into the ground, then starts sucking through its shaft. Before long water squirts to the dirt. She retrieves a small pouch and fills it one mouthful at a time. Once full, she places the pouch's spout to his father's mouth. Water dribbles out the corners of his lips and down his chin. But then, he coughs, his mouth moves, and a gentle gulp follows.

Thalee thrusts the pouch at Aizen. "Drink!"

Aizen does as ordered, until Thalee pulls it away, taking the last gulp for herself.

"What now?" Thalee says.

"I don't know..." Aizen responds, at a complete loss. He goes into meditation, sensing his father's light, barely a flicker. "He's fading..." Aizen whispers as hot tears roll down his cheeks. His mind races with possible ways to save him, but the closest solution is either infiltrating the Arkathy warship or the small downed ship, to access medical equipment that is likely destroyed. "Dad... I'm sorry..."

His father lies still. His breathing is weak. Aizen is certain each breath will be his last.

"A ship is coming," Thalee quietly says.

Aizen's entire body shakes as hissing engines come and heat grows upon his back.

Thalee stands, unsheathes her black knife, and slides into her fight posture. When the engines wind down and a hatch opens, Thalee dashes off.

Aizen sucks up his tears and breathes hard, building his adrenaline.

Thalee cries out, a few gentle thumps follow, and then, silence.

Aizen reaches for his blades to find them gone. *I don't need them!*

"Aizen, are you okay?" says a gentle voice.

What? Aizen's anger washes away. He spins to see Thalee on the ground, unable to move her limbs, her eyes wandering confused. *Ergonos nerve strikes...* He then finds a figure in an envisuit, breathing slow and deep. *Ergonos breaths...*

The figure reaches to the helmet's latch and lets it roll back, revealing a resilient face, a face Aizen knows, a face he loves.

"M-mom?" Aizen stammers like a child and slowly points at his father.

His mother's eyes follow his finger and all her resilience melts away.

CHAPTER NINETEEN

"System reboot initiated," says a passive voice, followed by whines, dings, and beeps as functions activate.

Samuel sluggishly opens his eyes. Pain radiates through his torso and arm. *The arm...* he thinks, remembering the pops just before passing out. Darkness becomes light as his visor turns on. On the lower right opens a diagram of his body displaying his right leg, left foot, and left forearm missing, as expected. But now his entire right arm is red.

"S-status of right arm," he whispers.

The diagram centers and zooms. Tissue fades, revealing bones appearing like an icicle shattered upon stone. Each fragment highlights. *"Right arm broken in 472 places."*

Samuel sighs deeply. "Just take the fucking thing."

Needles prick his shoulder, but feel like nothing. The smell of burning meat comes, but is commonplace now.

"Amputation complete," the armor says. *"Jettisoning waste material."*

Waste material... Samuel thinks.

The armor splits apart and spits Samuel's shattered arm to the ground.

"Attention required at L4," appears.

Samuel tries moving his legs, but they do not respond. "Status."

"Paralysis of legs – 99%, Paralysis of bladder – 64%, Paralysis of genitalia – 57%, Paralysis of rec—"

"Can I procreate?" Samuel asks, a part of him still believing he might provide the don with an heir.

"Yes, with the aid of stimuli."

Good enough, Samuel thinks. "What's the protocol for paralysis?"

"Amputation of remaining leg required. Nerve integration with Auto-armor suggested."

"Describe the process?"

"Filaments will be inserted into your nervous system to allow Auto-armor limbs to function in place of original." The diagram highlights insertion points, one at Samuel's right shoulder, left elbow, and above the damaged spinal cord.

"Is it permanent?" he asks.

"Field nerve integration is a temporary solution for survival situations. Prolonged integration will result in significant damage to your nervous system. Seek medical help as soon as possible," the armor responds. *"Do you wish to proceed?"*

"Do I have a choice?"

"Survival probability without integration is approximately 13.2%. With integration is 97.5%." It pauses. *"Do you wish to proceed?"*

"If I choose not to, can I still use the armor's limbs?"

"No, your only option is to be placed into suspended animation and await rescue."

I've become more machine than man, Samuel thinks, finding it ironic the old don forced him into auto-armor to prevent this exact scenario.

"We integrate..." he whispers and looks to the sky for the Arkathy warship, trying to distract himself from the surgery. He finds a plume of black smoke where the vessel was when he threw the Disruptor and follows it to the wreckage of a massive ship on the ground. His visor highlighting several jettisoned escape pods, but he does not see survivors. A burnt smell comes and he imagines it is from the warship. A partial leg jettisons from the armor. Samuel grits his jaw, feeling a lump in his throat. A tear rolls down his cheek.

"Waste purged," says the armor. *"Commencing integration."*

Pain zaps down Samuel's arms. *But there are no arms.* Moments later, it rages through his legs like millions of stinging wasps. *But there are no legs.* The pain suddenly dissipates.

"Integration complete," says the armor.

Samuel moves the auto-armor's arms and legs, having the sensation of touch in their palms and soles. He lifts the armor's legs one at a time, balancing on the other.

Samuel, comes a quiet voice.

"Yes, Khasi," Samuel responds.

I'm sorry for your loss, but we must act. We must get The Terran Files from Aizen.

For the love of Sol! Give the boy a moment! the old don snaps.

"No, Khasi's right," Samuel says and opens his com. "Ulysses, do you read?"

No response.

"Status of Ulysses, Nelly, and Don Carlyle," Samuel orders.

"Don Carlyle – Deceased... Nelly Veld – Unknown... Ulysses Williams – Critical Condition... " the armor responds.

"Calvin... I'm so sorry..." Samuel whispers.

Faith did her job! Where's Nelly!? the don snaps.

"Isn't Faith your daughter, too?" Samuel says with disgust.

She's Nelly's bodyguard! the old don says.

"Still, she deserves something..." Samuel grumbles.

Her family is taken care of for several generations to come. She knew what she signed up for, the old don responds. *Find my daughter!*

"Identify locations," Samuel says and three points appear on visor. *They're in the missile site.* "Is anyone else with them?"

"No other lifeforms detected."

The fight is over, Samuel realizes.

Did we lose? the don asks.

We cannot assess the situation just yet, Khasi says.

"I'll check the location of The Terran Files," Samuel says, reaching for his holotile still attached to his prosthetic arm, but realizes it is beneath the auto-armor. "Armor, can you patch into my prosthetic arm."

"One moment, please," the armor says and quickly negotiates. *"What function would you like to access?"*

"The remote key within my holotile."

The interface opens on visor and Samuel enters the username and password. He activates the key's tracker. A blinking comes from inside the missile site, right on top of Ulysses.

We got it! Khasi cries.

But at what cost? Samuel thinks and takes a few awkward steps. After several seconds, the armor's strides feel relatively normal. Soon, he forgets that his legs are gone. He reaches the mouth of the ravine and searches for the skiff, but it is nowhere to be found. Samuel begins the long trek up the winding ravine, catching glimpses of trucks deteriorated to dust.

Halfway up, his visor highlights an impact crater in the ground and another in the rock wall, labeling them as, *"Recently Disturbed."*

These shots came from inside the missile site, Khasi says.

So, from Aizen, Samuel thinks and looks at a massive entry wide enough for a ship to pass through. Smoke trickles from the door's header into the sky like an inverted waterfall, and debris scatters at its threshold. Samuel reaches the splintered remains of a long sniper rifle. "Is this one of yours, Calvin?"

I wish! the don responds. *These rounds are thermonuclear on a microscopic level! It's an ancient Ceran special forces rifle!*

From Mirko, Samuel realizes.

Be careful, Sam, Khasi says. *Aizen might still be lingering despite the armor's reading. They called Mirko 'The Ghost' for a reason.*

"Understood," Samuel responds and steps across the door's threshold into darkness. His visor focuses on Don Carlyle on the floor, blood oozing from several gashes in her armor, as if it offered no protection at all.

What the hell did this? the old don says. *The armor is cut clean through, But not by a heat blade.*

What if a blade were denser than diamond? Khasi says.

Perhaps, the old don responds. *We must find Nelly.*

Samuel scans every nook and cranny of the missile site, until he finds another suit of armor standing frozen. "It's intact…" Samuel reaches around the helmet to its release mechanism. The armor's faceplate splits down the middle and peels away, compacting into the armor's collar to reveal it empty.

Thank Sol, the old don says. *She got out.*

Samuel's armor highlights Ulysses at the rear of the main hall. He approaches the back to see old windows up high where a control room once existed. His visor highlights gashes in the concrete only hours old. "What the hell made these?" Samuel says. "The same wild animal that killed Faith?"

No, Khasi responds. *Look at the claw marks, four fingers.*

An object comes into view. *Ulysses's leg…* Samuel's heart pounds as he studies how his friend's armor, massive musculature, and bone were cut like butter. Another object is ahead. *His arm, split lengthwise.*

"Sam…?" comes a faint voice. "I-is th-that… Ack! y-you?"

A chill runs down Samuel's spine, stopping at L4. "Yes…"

A deep wheezing comes. "Sam… I… I'm d-done f-for…"

Ulysses comes into view – only half a torso, an arm, and a head. His armor looks like shredded cloth. Samuel barely makes out a face.

"W-what happened?" Samuel stammers.

"Ai... Aizen... Ack!" Ulysses coughs blood. "N-not human." He takes a deep wheezing breath. "H-he is l-literal d-demon..."

A white crescent shape appears on Ulysses's mangled face and it takes Samuel a second to realize he is smiling.

"B-but... Sam..." Ulysses raises his remaining arm, his massive paw grasping a ring. "I g-got ...Ack! The T-Terran Files!"

I don't care... Samuel thinks, but knows not to say that. "Then, you fulfilled your duty... Your people will be saved..."

"Not y-yet." Ulysses extends The Terran Files to Samuel. "You a-are the l-last of us... You ...Ack! must f-finish it. B-bring s-salvation to our p-people!" Ulysses drops the ring and presses his palm into his chest. He heaves blood.

Samuel takes The Terran Files in one hand and places his other on Ulysses's shoulder. The massive man's coughing fit passes.

"Sam..." he whispers, sounding far away. "When I was freed on Eden, my s-sister said I w-would meet s-someone special. Someone w-who would sh-show me the path f-forward..." His eyes focus on Samuel. "Y-you're the one... Aren't you?"

The old woman... Joan... Samuel finally makes the connection. "Joan orchestrated my birth, sequenced my DNA to save our people." Ulysses's eyes widen at his sister's name. "And... a bit of you is in me, too..." Samuel breathes deeply. "You're the clone of The Director, a man named Samuel Williams. The Ganymedans use the French pronunciation for William, which is *Guillaume*. So, that means you're a *Guil...* and I'm a *Guil... Guil-*hadepicardocresinkell..."

The monstrous, broken man chuckles and coughs. "I-it has been an h-honor knowing you..." He reaches into a split in his ragged armor, retrieves a syringe, and weakly hands it to Samuel. "...And it w-will be an honor for you to f-finally know me."

"It has already been an honor," Samuel says.

Ulysses slumps to the ground and rolls to his back. His breathing slows, but his wheezing continues. A tear trickles down his temple. "Sam... I'm s-scared..."

"You no longer have anything to f—"

Ulysses's wheezing has stopped.

Samuel's nonexistent hands shake and his heart pounds. He gently closes Ulysses's eyes and sobs. After several minutes, he calms and looks at the syringe. *You have a mission to complete!* He activates its extraction function and places the tip to Ulysses's temple. "Zun dah!"

Filaments spread into Ulysses's hippocampus, gathering his memories before packing them into the syringe. It beeps. Its light becomes green.

Samuel pulls the syringe from his friend's temple and raises it to his own. "This is my purpose," he whispers, then cries, "Zun dah!"

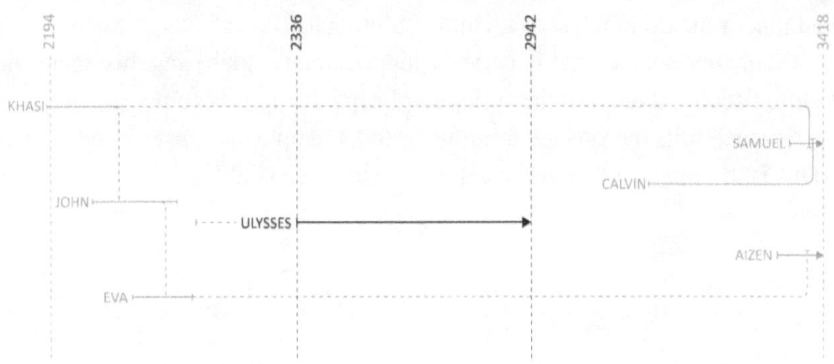

ULYSSES's TALE
System Sol: 2336 - 2942

We Twelve were the chosen ones, named after heroes of antiquity, because, just like them, we would save humanity in its darkest hour. That was what father told us as we slept in our cryotubes, waiting for our moment to shine. And father was always right. But the rest of System Sol could not understand his brilliance, could not comprehend that he was trying to save them. So, they fought against his dream, pushing our people to their breaking points, strangling our supply lines, and stealing our water colonies. They forced us to defend ourselves, then had the audacity to blame us for the subsequent collapse of society. But father had anticipated this very scenario, saying that we Twelve must pick up the pieces of his great dream should he and our big sister fail. That we Twelve were his contingency plan.

But, somehow, the plan changed.

♦

The Awakeners pulled us from our cryotubes mid-cycle. Dreams of our father teaching us horribly interrupted. We were confused, scared. We were teenagers who had never seen the outside world beyond the images fed to us. But, instead of nurturing our integration into a new way of life, The Awakeners only said that our father was dead and there was a celebration to be had.

The most crushing part was that our big sister, the great Captain Dione

Sharpe, the one who was supposed to save us all, killed our father and his dream, instead. Then, for reasons that escaped me, she decided that we clones must pay for father's supposed crimes. That because we held his DNA in our veins we were responsible. That we would work to our last dying breaths rebuilding what was destroyed.

♦

I touched down upon Ganymede's icy surface alongside nine thousand identical faces, sent to rebuild this moon once hosting the great battles between Mercury and Ceres. I searched for The Twelve among the sea of equalizers, and found my sister, Joan, sticking out with her smaller frame. I shuffled through the crowd, my broad shoulders bumping into hundreds of others, to meet her.

"Have you found any of the others?" I quietly asked.

She sharply shook her head, not acknowledging me otherwise.

Right, we must remain anonymous. Joan was so smart, so crafty. And father designed her to be this way. To be the brain to our brawn, having no equalizer genes at all. Instead, she was engineered to be a genius navigator, a leader with infantry athleticism, all within a not too intimidating body. *Able to blend in with our oppressors,* I knew.

I retreated several paces back, but made sure she was still within sight, and waited for our mining freighter's cargo bay door to open and our life of labor to begin.

A heavy clunk came and the door cracked. Its gears groaned. The sun was dim, looking about to rise or set. I was not sure which. As the door lowered I saw an inflatable dome had been built. The door met the ground to reveal a Ceran platoon with rifles aimed our way. *We can easily overpower them,* I thought. But then, I found my sister staring right at me, shaking her head. *What am I missing?* I studied the soldiers in envisuits with helmets sealed. My gaze shifted to the delicate dome again. *They'll rupture it...* I realized, knowing the lack of atmosphere and frigid cold would take even equalizers in an hour or two. I nodded ever so slightly, letting my sister know that I understood.

A little Ceran soldier stepped forth and unsealed their helmet, letting it roll back. He was old, thin, and haggard. He raised a hand and the platoon lowered their rifles.

"I know you've been taught Interspeak on your journey from Mercury," the little soldier said. "I am Commander Meeks of Ceres, tasked with your integration on Ganymede. We will give you food, shelter, purpose, and an opportunity to show us that you are not the same creature as The Director…"

How dare he mention our father! I thought, feeling my anger rise, ready to fight, until a hand grasped my arm. It was Joan, next to me now.

"…All that we ask in return," Commander Meeks continued. "Is that you help us transform this moon into a prospering garden, help it become a sister society to Mars, and provide necessary food and materials to rebuild all of System Sol…"

Slavery disguised as opportunity! I knew. *It will never work! We will never submit!*

"…What say you?" the little commander asked.

"Yes!" came from my left.

"Yes!" came from my right.

I snapped my head to the others. *How can they so quickly agree to this!* I felt my ears grow hot and I clenched my fists. I breathed deeply, preparing to shout a thunderous, "No!" when something struck my throat and a small squeak came out, instead. My eyes darted around to find my sister shaking her head. *I'm missing something, again...* I thought, looking at the others, trying to understand why they were so willing to comply. A memory from my childhood in cryosleep came, one of father explaining how The Twelve were different. "You have the gift of free will," he said, "Different from your brothers and sisters, for they are engineered to blindly follow." I studied the little commander, barking orders like a king, not a fear in the world. *He knows they're engineered this way,* I realized. *But how?* My eyes locked onto a pair of silhouettes behind the Ceran soldiers, one short, but strong, and the other, an equalizer. Ice ran through my veins. *It's them... Our big sister and big brother... Selling us like livestock.*

"Uly, we will have our time," Joan quietly said. "But it's not now. Can you save your rage for another day?"

I breathed deeply again. "Yes… But what about the rest of The Twelve?"

"They will follow our lead."

Commander Meeks raised his hand again. "Your words are a binding contract, and we will hold you to them. But rest assured, once we have built this world into the garden System Sol needs, you will have fulfilled your contracts and earned your citizenship." The commander turned to his platoon and gave a few quick hand gestures.

They parted, framing the two figures in the back.

The two betrayers!

The equalizer slowly walked forth and raised a massive paw to release his helmet, revealing scars across his face and golden irises that pierced like a wolf from the woods. *Taam Kapoor. A brute like the rest of us, but also a master geologist.*

"Comrades!" came his booming voice, holding such force, such certainty. "I see strength in you! I see promise! Are you ready to help rebuild Ganymede!? Are you ready to save System Sol!? Are you ready to become the heroes you were always destined to be!?"

"Yes! Yes! Yes!" thousands of equalizers cried back, shuddering the dome's thin membrane.

Taam stepped aside and motioned to several dozen transport skiffs by a rear airlock, with old envisuits piled atop their beds.

Those around me moved forth, stepping through the mining freight's mouth and down its door like a ramp. I glanced at Joan who began moving with them. I did the same. When my foot met the ground, I realized how strange it was. *Ice, all ice. How can we grow anything here?* I found myself thinking. *No! Stop it! You are not going to help them!* But as nine thousand others blindly obeyed, I realized that I was going to help them whether I wanted to or not.

◆

They split us into hundreds of crews and spread us across the barren tundra to makeshift domes.

"Look starboard," said the driver through com.

I stiffly turned, the ill-fitting envisuit barely containing my frame, and saw a massive, glass dome in the distance, rippling as dull sunlight shined upon its surface and reflecting colors I did not know existed.

"That was once the capital city of Ganymede..." said the driver.

"Sundow," I whispered, having studied the epic battles in hibernation.

"...This was the first city in System Sol to be destroyed by your people during The Hermian War..." the driver continued.

The Ceran War, I thought, realizing they had renamed it.

"...This is just one of twenty-five cities destroyed on Ganymede and one of over twenty thousand across System Sol." The driver's tone said more than his words.

He's shaming us like bad dogs! I restrained from smashing through the back of the skiff's cab and splitting this little driver like wood. *If only Joan were with me!* I looked at the clones making up our crew, each having already accepted their fates.

A white, inflatable dome appeared and, as we neared, I realized it was flimsy like the one we arrived in. The skiff stopped in front of the dome and its seam peeled apart, letting us through. When it healed behind us, another inner seam parted, and we were inside.

"There's a bunk for each of you, with a small kitchen, washroom, and toilet," said the driver, but he did not emerge from the cab. "Please, depart the skiff and remove your envisuits."

Shit... I thought, looking at the flimsy dome.

The others hopped off the skiff, the vehicle lifting more with each, and removed their helmets. Then, they began removing envisuits, not once questioning their new masters.

I cautiously removed my helmet, made eye contact with the clone next to me, and whispered, "We must keep the suits."

He stared blankly at me. "They said to remove them."

"I know," I whispered back. "But removing them makes us vulnerable should the dome fail."

"Why would the dome fail?"

"Any number of things can happen. We must not hand them over."

"They'll let us keep them, then," the equalizer said with certainty, perfectly folding the envisuit fabric, and setting it on the ground with his helmet on top, as they all did.

"Now, place your envisuits on the skiff," the driver instructed.

The one I spoke with hesitated, thinking over what I had just said. Nevertheless, he gathered his envisuit and placed it on the skiff.

"You, too!" cried the driver.

They were all looking at me now.

"You must load it," the one whispered to me.

"So they can take them away and leave us defenseless?" I responded.

They started moving towards me.

"Fine, fine..." I reluctantly removed my envisuit and placed it alongside the others.

"Good! Now, step away!" cried the driver.

We stepped several paces back. The dome's plastic airlock unsealed and the skiff backed out. It healed shut and there was silence. The clone I spoke with shifted nervously.

"He... He took them," he said, stunned. Then, he looked at me. "How did you know he would?"

It was obvious! I wanted to say, but I saw their scared faces. "The signs were there," I said, instead.

Another clone approached. *"Who are you?"*

"Ulysses," I responded. "But you can call me, Uly."

Their eyes went wide like they had seen a ghost.

"You have a name?" said another.

♦

We were left to our own devices for several days. *To adjust to our new domicile,* I assumed. We established daily routines and invented games to keep ourselves entertained. And despite initially judging the clones as imbeciles, they were incredible adversaries. *We share identical DNA except for that one deviation*, I reminded myself. When it came to food, we helplessly stared at the kitchen for not once were we taught how to cook. So, we ate raw ingredients from cold storage, much of it frozen.

On the eighth day, someone finally came.

She entered our delicate dome, appearing just a skinny thing. She was much older than us with hair streaked gray. Her movements were relaxed and she did not hold fear in her posture.

"Hello, young ones," she said with a warm grin.

We stared blankly. She was so unique, so... *Human.*

"All right... I guess I'll start," she said. "I'm Beverly, and even though I am now Ganymedan, I was born a Terran." She calmly turned to the clone I first spoke with, called C1475. "And who are you?"

"I'm... Spaghetti," C1475 said, glancing my way for a split second.

Beverly cocked her head. "Pardon?"

What in Sol? I thought, just as confused.

"I've always wanted to try spaghetti..." C1475 explained. "So that's what I named myself."

"Well, Spaghetti, lucky for you I know how to make that dish," Beverly said and Spaghetti's face lit up. She gave the rest of us looks. "Have you all named yourselves?"

"Only some," Spaghetti responded.

"What possessed you to do this?" she followed up.

Please, don't tell her... I thought, holding my breath.

"Ulysses was given a real name," Spaghetti said, and I felt my stomach turn. "So, I thought I should have one, too."

Beverly looked us over. "Which one of you is Ulysses?"

Don't do it! I thought.

The clones turned to me and I felt such betrayal.

"Fascinating," Beverly said, studying me. "You know, you're not the first

I've met with a hero's name."

I froze, trying not to give a tell, but I was screaming on the inside.

She grinned. "And you all just clam up when I pry." She approached the kitchen. "But I am not here to interrogate. I'm here to teach!" she announced. "Everyday for the next standard month, I will train one of you to make a special dish you can then make for your comrades. Spaghetti, let's start with you."

Spaghetti quickly hustled into the kitchen after Beverly. His excitement was contagious. I even felt my own stomach flutter. An hour later, he strutted from the kitchen with a magnificent smile upon his face, an apron around his torso, and carrying a massive pot. Beverly followed with a grin. He set the pot upon a tabletop and we scrambled closer, peering inside.

"What is it?" one asked.

Spaghetti glanced at Beverly, whom nodded. He turned back to his brothers and sisters and proudly said, "Spaghetti scampi!"

It was so strange, so alien. "It's like hair," I inadvertently said.

"Very good observation," Beverly said like a teacher, and I felt my ears grow hot with embarrassment.

"What are the little, curly things?" another asked.

"That's scampi," Spaghetti said.

"What's scampi?" they followed up.

He smiled wide. "It's shrimp!"

You can't be serious! I thought, staring into the spaghetti and shrimp covered in a red paste. I realized the curls were little tails. *He's serious…* "How can you possibly have shrimp?" I asked Beverly. "Have the printers made exceptional leaps in technology?"

"No, Ulysses," she responded, pronouncing my name with interest. "They live deep in Ganymede's subterranean ocean, introduced by the original settlers of this moon before the war."

She called it The War with no Ceran or Hermian beforehand. I pondered what that could mean. *Perhaps she's neutral.* "Did you learn how to prepare them on Earth?"

She nodded. "When I was the age you are now."

But Earth is a toxic nightmare, I knew from the acclimation videos the Ganymedans had us watch on our way from Mercury. "How did you circumvent the toxins?"

"You ask a lot of questions," Beverly said.

"Oh, sorry…" *Shut your mouth!* I told myself, but I felt more questions building inside me. "It's just…" *Shut the hell up, you idiot!* "…I would like to learn about Earth." *You are so stupid…*

I heard stirring and saw pleading looks upon the clones' faces. *I'm just like them…* I realized to my dismay.

"Can you tell them what you told me?" Spaghetti asked Beverly.

"I sure can," she strutted to the table. "But first… We eat!"

◆

For the next month Beverly arrived each day just before dinner, calling out one of our numbers, and sneaking off to teach them a special dish. When they emerged, they would announce their creation, and that became their new name. During each meal, Beverly told a little more about life on Earth and how she had lived among a group of scientists traveling to South America, trying to rebuild what was lost, with the terrifying ronin at their heels.

One evening, she told us how she lost her mother during a ronin raid.

We stared back stunned, not knowing what to say.

My mouth opened. *Don't say anything!* "I'm so sorry…"

Beverly smiled sadly. "It's alright, Ulysses. No apology is needed."

"But… the ronin were our people," I followed up.

The rest gasped.

"No! Our people would never do that!" Spaghetti said, then looked to Beverly. "Right?"

Beverly glanced down for a moment. "I'm afraid Ulysses is correct. The majority of ronin were Hermian Infantry trapped on Earth after The Fall."

Silence all around. Eyes dropped to the table.

"But it's not your fault," Beverly said. "In fact, it was one of your kind that taught us how to nullify the toxins in Earth's food."

"Really?" said a clone renamed Patatas Bravas.

Beverly nodded. "He was a very old equalizer, one horrifically injured while rebelling against their leader, Kase."

"Rebelling…" I whispered and everyone turned my way.

"How did he figure this out?" Patatas asked.

"Good question," Beverly complimented and Patatas beamed. "It was not he who discovered it, but a person he met in passing who had *'shown him a better way'* as I remember him saying."

"How did you get off of Earth?" asked Spaghetti.

"Not long after my mother passed, Commander Meeks arrived and whisked us away, saying our expertise was needed for System Sol's surviving colonies."

GHOSTS OF ZION | 363

"And you just left?" I asked.

"Anything was better than Earth…"

"Do you still believe that now?" Spaghetti muttered.

"Commander Meeks has given my daughter and I an incredible opportunity to lead meaningful lives." She pursed her lips. "But, there are days when I feel that leaving Earth was a mistake. When I feel this way, I take a look at Earth's ecosystem and see how it's healing." She contemplated that. "Earth is better off without us."

♦

The month was at an end and everyone but I had a dish to call their own. Beverly entered with her usual grin, greeting each of us. She took her usual spot at the kitchen door, raised her thin arm, and called, "Ulysses!"

They cheered and I again felt my ears grow hot with embarrassment, but I could not deny how excited I was. I eagerly followed Beverly through the kitchen door.

"Please, wash your hands and don an apron," she said with a serious look on her face once I entered.

I got the feeling something happened, that perhaps she discovered how I was different. I nervously washed my hands and tied an apron around my torso.

"Ulysses, you're not as naive as the others," Beverly started.

So, she knows, I thought.

"This will serve you well in the coming years upon this moon."

I tilted my head. *Maybe, she doesn't know.*

"There's a reason why I chose you last."

My heart pounded. "What reason?"

"You must take care of the others after tonight," she said.

I thought about that. "Do you have to go?"

She smiled sadly. "You will be okay, because they have you to look up to, you to guide them when lost. For you have been selected as their foreman."

Their foreman? "Does this mean our work will commence?"

"The initial step in a very long journey will officially begin tomorrow," Beverly confirmed and opened a cookbook on holotile. "But it is not my place to speak on the matter."

"Is there anything else you can say?" I asked.

Beverly looked me in the eye and pointed at her holotile. "Everything you need to know is here."

"But it's just recipes…"

Beverly breathed deeply. "It's also a sneak peek into what you will be creating."

I knew she wanted to say more, to tell me something crucial, and that she was not allowed to. I looked at the recipes again, noting there were only thirty dishes and thirty-one of us. "Do I not have one?"

"Here's the thing, Ulysses. I need you to be able to make all of them," Beverly said.

"But… I want something special, too…" I trailed off.

"Go on," Beverly said, staring at me intensely.

"I woke a few times from hibernation before Captain Sharpe reached Mercury."

Her eyes went wide.

"It was just a few days at a time," I carefully said. "To maintain our hibernation chambers. During these times we found food prepared for us."

"What dishes?" she asked.

"My favorite was a fish called Halibut, but it was cooked without heat."

"Citric acid," Beverly said.

"Yeah… How'd you know?"

"It's called ceviche. I learned it in South America."

"Would it be okay if I learned this one?" I cautiously asked.

"I would love to teach it to you," she said. "But we are missing a key ingredient, limes." She looked at the recipes. "Tell you what. If you can get citrus trees to grow on Ganymede, I will personally come teach you."

"Sounds like you'd be breaking protocol," I responded.

She gave me a hard look. "For tonight, we should pick a dish already made. What was your favorite?"

I thought about how all of them were fantastic in their unique ways. "Maybe we do several. Everyone loved the crab cakes, croquettes, cuttlefish ink risotto, and grilled octopus."

Beverly's face lit up. "Very good, Ulysses. This is exactly what I have been preparing you for. These dishes are designed to work together. In old Spanish they're called, *tapas.*"

We feverishly went to work, Beverly commanding as I prepared, using my modifications intended for war to become a sou chef, instead. An hour came and went. Gentle knocks rapped on the door, yet Beverly and I continued, ingredients covering our aprons, arms, faces, and hair.

"Ulysses, it's time!" Beverly finally cried, pointing at several platters with small plates. "The croquettes!"

I gathered the platters and hustled through the door to my brothers and sisters waiting with confused looks.

"We've already had this," Spaghetti said as I spread the platters on the table. "And there's not enough."

"More is coming. Dig in," I said and raced back to the kitchen.

"Grilled octopus!" Beverly shouted and pointed at more platters.

They had barely begun the croquettes when I returned and they snapped their heads up with the same confused looks. I set the grilled octopus alongside the croquettes.

"There's really more!?" Patatas asked.

"We're doing them all!" I responded as I ran back to the kitchen.

All the plates were finally out and smiles were on everyone's faces.

"It's a feast!" one cried.

"It's a bit of everyone!" said another.

"That's the idea," Beverly said and took her seat. "With all of you working together, with all of your individual talents, you will achieve incredible things."

She called us individuals, I noted, taking the table's head as we each did on our nights to cook.

"But does Ulysses not get a special dish, or a new name?" one asked.

Beverly made eye contact with me. "It's your crew, now."

"What does she mean," Spaghetti said.

"I…" I paused. "…Starting tomorrow, we are beginning our work to rebuild this moon, and I have been selected as your foreman. You will each have important tasks to perform. You will each be an essential piece of the puzzle. But it will be my responsibility to ensure we are properly put together. Just like this meal here."

They were silent.

"But, you have no dish. You don't have a new name," Patatas said.

I grinned. "I do have a new name. Not after a single dish, but what they become as a whole." I let that sink in. "I'm Tapas."

When dinner was finished, we cleaned our dishes and the dining table. And then, we turned to Beverly.

"Will you visit?" one asked.

Beverly held a hand to her heart. "I wish that I could, but I have important work to perform as well." She gave each of us warm embraces and had us lean down so she could whisper into our ears. Each lit up and walked off giddy with their secret. She came to me last, giving me a long embrace. I leaned down to hear what she might say, expecting words of wisdom, or perhaps how much she would miss me.

Instead, she whispered, "Joan says, *Hi.* "

◆

"We have asked each of you here today because you were chosen as suitable foreman to lead your crews!" said Commander Meeks to three hundred of us. "This is a great responsibility bestowed upon you. One that comes with great reward or great consequence. Make no mistake, your crew's performance rests solely upon your shoulders. So, listen carefully…"

Temptation and fear. Typical motivators, I thought as I searched the sea of identical faces for The Twelve. I caught someone staring at me. *Liu Bei,* I realized. I nodded imperceptibly and so did he.

"…We have a nearly impossible task," Commander Meeks continued. "To turn this moon into the breadbasket of System Sol, we must first lay a foundation. For we must transform Ganymede's salty ice into fertile land."

I tried to understand where the minerals would come from, how we would raise the moon's temperature, and keep the ice from melting. *They're setting us up for failure.*

Taam walked up beside the little commander, placing a friendly paw upon his shoulder, then set his golden irises upon us. He raised his hand, opening a hologram that occupied the entirety of the dome displaying a cross-section of Ganymede, from crust to core.

"At first glance," Taam said, "Ganymede might seem like Europa or Enceladus, having a solid ice surface separated from a rocky core by a vast subterranean ocean. But where Europa and Enceladus host no accessible aggregate, Ganymede does. We just have to find it." The hologram zoomed onto pockets within the thick ice. "Initial scans show dense material locked within Ganymede's dark ice, keeping it from drifting to the bottom of the ocean. However, what exactly is there remains to be discovered."

I found the concept of drilling water to find dirt amusing, and laughed.

Taam looked my direction. "Every time your crew discovers a viable source of aggregate, you receive a bonus. Every time your crew comes up short, you will be penalized. Take a moment to scope out your competition," Taam finished and a timer appeared in the hologram.

I shuffled among the other foreman searching for The Twelve.

"Who are you?" A clone sister said to me.

Not one of The Twelve, I immediately knew. "Tapas, who are you?"

She cocked her head. "I'm F1395. Why do you have a weird name?"

I scrambled. "We…uh… My crew named ourselves after the dishes Beverly taught us."

She looked even more confused. "Who's Beverly?"

"Didn't someone come to teach you how to cook?"

She shook her head.

"Who told you that you were foreman, then?" I followed up.

"I woke this morning to find soldiers waiting at my bunk." A look of fear crossed her face. "I didn't know about the foreman thing until just now."

Shit… I thought. *Why did my crew get special treatment? Do they know? Am I falling into their trap?* I then remembered Beverly's parting words. *Or is Joan working her magic already?* I searched for her smaller frame, but found someone else grinning at me.

"Ulysses?" she whispered.

It took me a moment. "Oh, Trieu!" I whispered back. "Have you found any of the others?"

She nodded. "Gilgamesh and Boudicca."

"I found Liu Bei, so that makes five of us."

"I'm guessing all of The Twelve of us were selected," she said.

"My thoughts, too," I responded.

"We need to find the others," she said. "But we shouldn't all be seen together, let's meet back here in twenty minutes."

"Agreed," I said and turned sharply away, keeping an eye out for Joan. I found Alexander shortly after.

"Glad to see you're still with us," he said.

"What do you mean by that?" I responded.

"You looked ready to charge The Awakeners when we first arrived."

"I almost did," I admitted. "Joan held me back."

"For what it's worth, I would have been right with you," Alexander said.

"That's why she stopped me," I said. "Have you seen her?"

"No, nothing. I thought she would be the easiest to find."

"Me too," I said. "I found Liu Bei and Trieu. And Trieu found Gilgamesh and Boudicca."

"I have Wallace, Achilles, and Curie."

"That brings us to nine," I said.

"Ten," I heard behind me and turned to find Mulan.

I smiled. "Have you seen Joan or Maximus? They're the only two unaccounted for."

A dark chuckle came from several meters away followed by a menacing voice, "We can hear everything you say."

We turned to find a clone staring back, somehow bigger than the rest of us, with a fresh scar running down his face. Liu Bei, Trieu, Gilgamesh, Boudicca, Wallace, Achilles, and Curie suddenly bee-lined our direction.

"So, there's more of you fuckers," the big clone said, walking towards us.

We remained silent.

"Don't play ignorant," he said. "I heard baby Maximus's name as clear as day. You're lucky the Ganymedans are dull as fuck."

Who in Sol is this!? "You know Maximus?" I pointedly asked.

"He was supposed to be my foreman..."

I stared this clone down, noting his scar ran behind his jaw to a necklace that appeared like a string of pearls. I studied the pearls themself, their shapes. *Maximus's teeth...*

"...But little Maxi did not expect to meet me." The massive clone grinned hideously. "...I'm Z."

Where the hell did he come from!? I frantically thought. *Joan... Where are you!?*

◆

I returned to my crew's dome in a dilapidated skiff, loaded up with drilling equipment from before the war, worn out envisuits, and a holotile containing all the maps and mineral detection programs we required. But all I could think about was Z, his hideous scar, and the necklace of teeth.

Day after day we ventured to spots upon the ice, probing for density, and saw other crews in the distance doing the same. One had their drill mast raised high.

"They're drilling already?" Spaghetti said with an alarmed look. "How did they find aggregate so quickly?"

"They didn't," I said. "They're letting fear get the better of them and digging anything that blips. They're chasing ghosts."

"How can you be so sure?" Patatas asked.

"Has anything we've measured looked convincing enough to drill?"

"No," she responded. "What do you suggest?"

"We devise a better detection method, first."

"You make it sound like we can invent something from nothing."

I pondered that. "Isn't that what our father literally did? He invented LightLine and built the Hermian civilization with nothing but his imagination and math. We have his DNA running in our veins, we were given all the training during hibernation, and we have genetically enhanced memory and physical abilities. Together, we are thirty-one superhuman geniuses, when our father was a single person. We should be able to at least match his greatness."

They gave me strange looks. "You were trained during hibernation?"

Are you fucking kidding me!? I thought and breathed deeply. "I was under the impression we all were."

"No," Spaghetti whispered.

"So, we can't do what our father did," Patatas said.

"You can," I stressed. "You're still geniuses, but you were never given the chance to exercise it. Starting today, I'm teaching you everything I know."

♦

At the end of the month, the foreman gathered again. Taam stood alongside a hologram displaying our crews in order of performance. Only one score was in the hundreds, with most in the mid-twenties. My crew was near the bottom with, *"Crew 136 - 00.00."* But I realized we were not alone, seeing more zeroes. *Ten, to be exact.* I grinned, knowing it was the others from The Twelve likely educating their crews, like I was. I suddenly thought upon Z's necklace of teeth. *From our Eleven...* I corrected myself. *Where's Joan?*

"I know this kind of work is new for you, but I expected more," Taam said. "Only one crew found a viable source of aggregate, a deposit of four hundred thousand tons of ordinary chondrite. Feldspar and iron-nickel." The hologram displayed mineral amounts. "But as you can see, this great find does not account for a fraction of a percent that we require. Therefore, you must work more diligently." Taam took a moment. "But your efforts, as little as they are, will not go unrewarded. Z, step forward."

Ice ran through my veins.

A head, taller than the rest of us, waded towards Taam.

How is he so big? I thought, knowing there were limitations to our modifications that even Dr. Kaladian could not overcome.

Taam extended his hand to shake Z's. "Congratulations Z. I hope this is the first of many deposits you find." He faced the rest of us. "Z's crew is afforded new envisuits designed for your massive frames, and Z will receive five thousand Ganymedan credits to purchase items of his choosing." Taam turned back to Z. "That is all."

Z waded back through the sea of foreman, barely looking at us, like we were beneath him.

But he is supposed to be beneath me! I found myself thinking.

"For those of you who discovered smaller deposits or unusable materials, keep it up. With hard work and diligence, you will strike minerals worth harvesting. You are dismissed!"

♦

Patatas calculated the increased probability of detection should we bore a minuscule hole into the ice and insert a two-hundred meter long rod, to amplify our holotile's signal. And we quickly went to work fabricating the pieces.

"That's it," she said, as we inserted the final section of rod sticking partially above the surface.

I attached our holotile. "Get ready."

A ping emitted, but instead of quickly dissipating, it kept on ringing, and data streamed in.

"Clay… It's definitely clay," I said as the breakdown appeared.

My crew stirred with excitement.

"Should we dig?"

I thought about that, knowing point values were heavily influenced by what was most urgently needed. "No…"

"What? Why not?"

"We will eventually need this clay, but not today. The base is feldspar, so that's our focus." I studied the rod sticking out of the ice. "We mark this location and move on to the next."

Another foreman meeting came and I watched in dismay as my crew was the only one with a score of, *"00.00."* *My brothers and sisters are caving to pressure,* I knew.

Z was at, *"415.00,"* having discovered two more deposits.

Is he getting lucky? Does he know something we don't? I wondered.

He was awarded another bonus and a new skiff for his crew.

But now, with my crew being clearly last, Taam rolled out his consequences. I returned to our dome with several soldiers who waited outside.

"What's happening?" Spaghetti asked.

I gave them a hard look. "We're last. We must give up ten percent of our rations as punishment."

Horror washed across their faces.

"Tapas…. Please, let's start digging."

I shook my head. "The time is not right."

They looked on helplessly as I ordered them to gather rations and send them outside.

♦

We have thirteen clay deposits, four iron sulfate deposits, and one feldspar deposit, I repeated in my mind, as the foremen met again.

"Crew 136!" Taam shouted, snapping me out of my thoughts. "X0471! What the hell are you doing out there!? You have nothing! Explain yourself!"

Shit… I thought as all eyes turned to me. Above their heads, I saw Z looking my way. "I apologize, sir," I started. "We've had an incredible string of bad luck."

Taam looked at me, expressionless. "There is no such thing as good luck or bad luck! If you don't find something by our next meeting, your crew will be disbanded to those who've suffered casualties!"

Like Z's crew, I knew, seeing that they were down ten members already. *The price of reckless success.* I thought about that. *And this is the price I pay for inaction… No choice.* "It will be done."

"It better!" Taam said and waved to the minerals screen. "We're still behind schedule, but we have enough feldspar to create our base. What we need now is silty clay. Finding this is our top priority!"

I grinned until I saw Z staring right at me.

♦

"This is incredible!" Spaghetti said as we drilled the clay deposit we found months earlier, its sludge-like consistency plopping into the first of many collection ships we called to our location.

"And just in time," I said. "We have thirteen confirmed locations."

"Does this mean we'll start winning?" Spaghetti asked.

"It will take time to work up the ranks," I said to their worried looks. "But we're catching up."

They smiled.

"Spaghetti and Patatas," I said and they perked up. "We only need twenty of us here, can you make two teams of five and probe more locations? We must keep our detection system going."

"If we are two teams, we'll need to make more rods," Spaghetti said.

"I leave their production to you, then," I responded and saw a glimmer in their eyes.

"Yes, sir!" They raced off on the skiff.

♦

"We're in fifty-seventh place," I said during dinner, having just returned from another foreman's meeting, one marking the end of our first standard year on Ganymede.

"You were right! We're catching up!"

"We are." I thought carefully about what I was going to say next. "But we must stop drilling the clay."

Their smiles melted.

"But, it's in demand, right?"

"It is," I said.

"I don't get it."

"Only a handful of crews are finding it," I said. "There's a lot of resentment growing among the foreman that are falling behind, and I don't want us to become a target."

"Then, we should drill the low-priority resources," Patatas suggested. "We have a few feldspar deposits."

I was surprised by her instincts and confidence. *She's starting to believe in herself... They all are.* "That's a great suggestion. It earns little points, but prevents us from falling behind. Would you like to lead this dig?"

Her mouth dropped open. "But you're the foreman..."

I nodded. "Several crews have lost their foreman. Should something happen to me, I need one of you to take the reins."

◆

Five years passed quickly. Resource collection was nearly complete and the foundation would soon begin construction. But exactly how we would circumvent the thermal differential, still eluded me.

I was returning with Spaghetti and Patatas from our final probing session, when smoke, above a patch of debris, appeared in the distance.

"That doesn't look right," Spaghetti said.

"We can't get involved," I responded, but my stomach knotted.

"Tapas..." Spaghetti gasped.

I sighed and turned our small probing skiff towards the smoke. Slowly it grew until we made out a boom laying across the ice instead of standing proud. A skiff was aflame with its cockpit glass shattered. Thirty dark lumps splayed across the ice. We stopped and inspected the bodies. I sensed Spaghetti and Patatas's tension as we looked upon the bloodied faces of our brothers and sisters. *Our faces.* Their envisuits were slashed and their visors were smashed. I studied footprints in the ice scattered about, their sizes identical. *But, too many.*

"They were ambushed by another crew," I muttered.

"Why now, when we are nearly finished?" Spaghetti asked.

Among the footprints, I spied a set sunk into the ice slightly more than the rest. "I don't know… Check if they're all from the same crew."

We spread out, scanning bar-codes on envisuit breasts.

"They're from Crew 081," Spaghetti said.

"Patatas, are you getting the same?" I ask.

"Yes," she answered.

Why do I know this crew number? I thought, racking my brain. *They were in second place, nipping at Z's heels,* I realized.

"Tapas," Spaghetti said. "Look at this."

We hustled to where he stood above a small hole in the ice.

"It's just like our probes," he said.

It must be one of The Twelve! I scrambled to each body again, but their faces were so mutated by the cold or brutalized by the attack that I could not identify them. *Only thirty bodies,* I realized, knowing with a foreman a crew is thirty-one. I stood tall and looked into the distance, letting my eagle eyes focus, searching not for color or shape, but movement. *Nothing…* I did the opposite, trying to see where we might not have searched right under our noses. I focused on the burning skiff's shattered glass, but could not see anyone inside. *Still…* I pulled open its door.

On the floor was a body with a hand gripped tightly to their chest. Their helmet shifted.

"One's still alive!" I cried and Spaghetti and Patatas dashed over.

I carefully crawled into the skiff along its seat. They recoiled and I realized their visor was covered in blood. *They can't see.* I reached my paw to their shoulder and gripped firmly. They flinched, but I held on tight, pressing my helmet against theirs.

"Channel three," I said, hoping our helmets made an audio bridge.

They paused.

"Channel three," I repeated, giving three squeezes to their shoulder.

They slowly brought an index finger to their visor. A moment later I heard a woman say, "Who are you?"

"It's Tapas, foreman of Crew 163," I responded.

Her breathing escalated. "U-ly?"

I realized how small her shoulder was. Tears welled in my eyes. "Joan?"

"Yes," she whispered.

"We're getting you out of here! You're going to be all right!" I said, hoping it was true. I navigated my hands around her torso and gently pulled her from the skiff.

Spaghetti and Patatas were watching.

"We must get home immediately and call in the accident," Spaghetti said.

I hesitated, knowing he was right, and that there was no way around it. "Yes, call it in. But wait until we are almost back."

Spaghetti cocked his head. "Why?"

"It's a public line, so whoever did this will know it was us who discovered the scene. I want to be far away by then."

Spaghetti thought about that. "Okay."

Crew 081's skiff and boom, and the bodies strewn across the ice, grew tiny behind us. An hour later, I saw a Ganymedan ship heading that way.

"Looks like someone called it in already," I said.

"I did…" Joan whispered into my earpiece on our private channel.

I gave her a gentle squeeze on her arm to indicate I heard.

"So we don't have to risk discovery," Spaghetti said.

"We'll still have to call it in," Patatas said. "They'll know we have one of 081's crew in our habitat."

Joan grasped my arm. "Uly… don't take me to your dome," she said. "I'm hurt too badly… I'm bleeding out."

"No, Joan…" I said and saw Spaghetti and Patatas's looks.

"Yes, Uly," she responded. "If you call it in, then you become his next target."

His… "It was Z, wasn't it?"

"What are you talking about," Spaghetti said, getting only half of our conversation.

I turned to him. "She's saying it was Z who attacked her crew, and that she doesn't want us to become his next target."

Their eyes widened at Z's name.

"But why does she care?"

"Because she's my sister."

"She's our sister, too,"

"Not like this," I said to their confused looks. "She was named by our father just like I was. I can explain later. Right now, we must hide her."

"We can drill…" Patatas muttered.

"What?" I said.

"We have feldspar only a hundred meters deep, and it's small, so it's worthless. We can carve out a small chamber below and fabricate an airlock."

I thought about that, knowing they were watching by satellite. *But they did not see the attack.* It hit me. *They lied about the satellites…*

I turned to Patatas. "How long will it take?"

"I can finish in a week."

"Do it," I said.

"But, where do we hide her until then?" Spaghetti asked.

I breathed deeply. "We are designed to repeatedly go in and out of hibernation. We turn off her envisuit's heat and keep her out here on the ice. It will prevent her from bleeding out, too."

"That's dangerous," Spaghetti said.

I looked at Joan. "We have no choice."

Joan gently squeezed my arm, then whispered, "Okay…"

◆

Spaghetti, Patatas, and I huddled in a small, carved chamber in the feldspar deposit, with a heat cube slowly thawing Joan out. The feldspar was cool to the touch, but far warmer than the day before when it was dangerous. I studied the makeshift ladder and airlock hatch Patatas rushed together, hoping it would hold.

"Her fingers are moving," Spaghetti whispered.

I returned my attention to Joan. "Be ready with the equipment, we must operate as she thaws, so she does not bleed out," I looked at her blue, vacant face, knowing she might hear me already. "I'm sorry, Joan. This will hurt."

There was a hole through her chest just above her heart, where a length of probing rod was thrust through. Thin trickles of blood came as we cut the exterior tissue wider.

"We must warm the center of her chest, patch her lung and arteries first, then work our way out to muscle and skin."

I slid a piece of warmed rod into the hole and watched on visor as the local tissue thawed. More blood trickled. We did not have a cauterizer, so we dug into our med kit for a needle and thread. For the first time in my life I wished for small, dainty hands. I methodically patched her lung, and luckily her arteries were only grazed. Ribs were broken, but not enough to require reconstruction. I sewed up the last layer of muscle as Joan groaned, and quickly patched her skin.

"Fuuuck," she finally said and brought her hand wavering to the wound, touching it. She looked down, squinting ice water from her eyes. "You suck at this," she added.

"But you're alive," Spaghetti responded.

Joan looked startled, only now realizing there were others present. She fixated on the heat cube, then the feldspar walls. "I forgot this was the plan," she said, looking at Spaghetti and Patatas. "I'm Joan."

"I'm Spaghetti."

"I'm Patatas."

Joan chuckled, then winced. "I forgot about those names, too."

They gave confused looks. "How do you know our names? Did Tapas tell you? Are you 081's foreman?"

"I need water," Joan said, instead.

"No, your digestive system has not completely thawed," I said.

She placed a palm on her heart. "I'm barely awake…"

"We don't have the means to properly thaw you. Give it time."

She turned to Spaghetti and Patatas. "Beverly told me about you. She and I became friends awhile back."

"How?" I said.

She pointed at her leg, where a large scar ran. "I purposely sliced myself to get medical help. Beverly was the one who came. I then started talking as if we were old friends, showing her that we are not mindless clones. Turns out, food is her thing."

She works her magic so fast, I thought. I looked at the wound we just patched. "You did this to yourself, too."

"I did," she confirmed and faced me. "To escape from Z."

All three of us shuddered.

"How does he exist? Who is he?" I asked.

Joan pursed her lips.

"What?"

"We need to speak alone, Ulysses," she said.

I shook my head. "Everyone on my crew deserves to know."

She looked into my eyes, not with frustration or disbelief, but with respect. "Okay…" She tried breathing deeply, but winced. "That hurt…" She took shorter breaths. "Z is my brother."

I cocked my head. "He's our brother, too."

"No," She took a moment. "Z stands for *Zodiac.*"

What? I thought, confused.

"Because he's modified with every creature…" Patatas muttered. "That's why he's so big, right?"

Joan nodded. "That's the rhino genes. Only he has them."

"I don't understand. Why would father create him when he had The Twelve?" I said.

Joan trained her eyes upon me. "Zodiac and I were not created. We are not clones of the director. We are his naturally born children, modified as embryos. Zodiac was to become father's hammer, to smash our enemies, while I was to go into obscurity with The Twelve at my disposal."

I felt my breath leave. I couldn't speak. I found myself kneeling and placing a fist to my shoulder in salute.

"No, Ulysses, don't you dare!" Joan winced. "I am not royalty."

"But you are," Spaghetti said, kneeling in salute as well.

Joan did not have a retort.

"If…" Patatas muttered, then stopped.

"Go on," Joan said.

"If Zodiac is your brother, why did he attack you?" she asked.

Joan pondered that. "My only guess is that because we're not retaking System Sol, as father intended, Zodiac's destructive nature is focusing elsewhere."

"And Taam and Commander Meeks gave him a direction," I said.

"Still, you're his biological sister," Spaghetti piped in.

"That's actually a reason to attack me," Joan said. "If he is truly on a path to dominate us instead of them, then I am in his way."

"That's why you didn't become foreman of your crew. For protection," I guessed.

Joan nodded. "And I achieved much more in obscurity, until he found me." She moved a leg, then her other, slowly placing her feet beneath herself. She pressed a hand against the feldspar wall and stood. "Ulysses, I need you to send a message on the public line. And, for the love of Sol, give me some water."

I handed her the tube from my envisuit's reservoir.

◆

Beverly came in the dead of night, the day after I sent Joan's message, and I could not figure out how she got into our dome and to my bunk unnoticed.

"Where's Joan?" she whispered. "Is she okay?"

I wiped the sleep from my eyes. "Follow me," I responded and crept from my foreman's quarters to the airlock. I turned to Beverly. "How did you get inside without anyone knowing?"

She pulled an orb from her pack and switched it on. Sound disappeared.

"An audiosphere?" I mumbled, confused as ever, knowing it was extinct Hermian tech. *How in Sol did she get her hands on one?*

"It contains the sound of the airlock if we stand close enough," she said.

"I see." I donned my envisuit. "What about the cameras?"

"I called in a favor. The feed is playing from another night, but will only do so until morning."

I nodded. "Let's get going, then."

We took our small probing skiff onto the ice, with its computer and beacon turned off, and headed to the feldspar deposit whose location I memorized by the positioning of stars relative to Jupiter. I kept the internal clock in my head going, thanking Sol for those elephant genes. *Now,* I thought and looked up. The celestial alignments were correct. I turned the skiff slightly left and knew we would hit our target in exactly one hour.

Beverly was looking at me in the pitch black. "I sometimes forget how incredible your gifts are."

"Curse…" I corrected.

"Gifts," she emphasized.

"Have fun convincing all nine thousand clones of that."

She grinned. "Challenge accepted."

I felt the hour end and slowed the skiff. A small divot in the ice caught my eye. "We're here." I made sure the skiff's systems were completely off and took Beverly's hand, leading her through the darkness. I knelt at the divot and placed my hand on the ice, gripping my mighty fingers and crunching through to metal. I cleared the hatch and cranked it open.

"What's that hissing sound?" Beverly said.

I paused, surprised she could hear it. "We built a vertical airlock to a feldspar deposit, hollowed into a chamber. But we must descend one at a time. You go first. I'll close the outer door behind us."

"Okay…" she muttered.

I guided her feet to the first ladder wrung and she dropped down on her own. I followed, pulling the hatch closed and cranking it tight. After a half hour of descent, we reached the lower hatch.

"What now?" Beverly asked.

"Knock, three long, two short. It can only be opened from within."

She laughed, and I realized that she knows Morse Code. She knocked the pattern. I felt pressure build through my envisuit and knew the airlock was equalizing. Pump whines grew as the atmosphere densified. A few thumps and a screech later, and the lower hatch door opened, washing us with dull light. Joan was looking up at us, dressed in light clothing despite the cold, revealing heavy bandages around her torso.

"Joan…" Beverly gasped, staring upon the bandages.

"Hey," she casually responded.

Beverly and I entered, closed the hatch, and removed our helmets.

"Don't *'Hey'* me," Beverly said. "I thought you were done for." She studied the bandages and motioned for Joan to turn around. When she saw her backside she exhaled. "Are you done for?"

Joan grinned. "Four broken ribs, scapula cleaved in two, lung punctured twice, and a mutilated breast. But I'm good."

"My sister's tough," I added.

Beverly turned to me. "You're all scary as hell."

"Yeah, isn't that the whole reason for our bondage?" I said.

Beverly winced. "This is not bondage."

"So we are free to go, then?" I asked.

"It was either this or execution…" She turned to Joan. "I heard there was an accident. The drill shattered."

"Shattered my ass!" Joan snapped.

"What impaled you, then?"

Joan was silent, gritting her teeth. "A drill shard…"

"It was made to look like an accident," I said. "They were attacked by Z's crew, slashed with makeshift weapons to simulate shrapnel."

"Z's crew?" Beverly said and made a confused face. "Why would he do that? He's in the lead."

"And now you know why," I snipped.

"There's no way he would do that," she defended.

"Check the satellites if you don't believe me."

Beverly remained silent.

No satellites, just like I theorized.

"Even if it was an attack, we're barely on schedule. Any derailment for an investigation would mean failure to terraform. We only have fifteen years of supplies left."

I scoffed. "We need a hundred years to get this moon ready."

"No, that's not correct," Beverly said.

"Sorry, ninety-seven years, four months, twelve days, eleven hours, thirty-three minutes, and forty-five seconds," I said deadpan. "Is that correct enough for you?"

She shook her head. "You don't understand the plan."

"What plan!?" My frustration climaxed. "I can do the math far better than your engineers! My entire crew each ran the numbers in isolation with almost no variation in the result! This endeavor is impossible!"

Beverly's lips pursed tightly. "All that matters is tomorrow."

"And why is that!?" I asked.

"Because tomorrow, we begin constructing the foundation."

◆

"We did it! We found the raw materials! And it's all thanks to your efforts!" Taam said to all of us congregated within the same inflatable dome we first arrived in. "I know you have a lot of questions, for these are the very ones we asked ourselves long before you set foot upon this moon!" Taam collected himself. "But we are not gathered here today to discuss how this will be done! We are here to say farewell!"

Gasps echoed across the dome.

Taam raised a paw. "I know… In these five years, we have become a well-oiled machine! A crew! However, Captain Sharpe, Commander Meeks, and I are needed elsewhere in System Sol! But do not fret! We are not leaving you leaderless! Governor Terrence, a scientist born on Ganymede, will continue our work with the help of one of your own…"

One of our own? I thought and felt a pit in my stomach.

A slight, old man stepped forth looking like a child next to Taam.

"Thank you, Governor, for accepting this arduous role," Taam said.

"The honor iz all mine," the governor responded in a strange accent.

A true Ganymedan… I realized.

The slight old man stepped back.

Taam focused on us again. "And now for the one of you who has proven themselves ready to take on my responsibilities, the one who has exceeded our expectations. May I introduce to you, a clone just like yourselves, Administrator Zodiac!"

Fuck… I stood alongside thousands of stunned clones, watching as our worst nightmare waded through us. Zodiac stepped up to Taam and extended his hand to shake, and when Taam presented him with a small box, Zodiac straightened to attention.

Taam proceeded to pin stripes upon Zodiac's uniform breast.

◆

We foremen were stripped of our titles and responsibilities, and replaced by one of Zodiac's most trusted. Then, our crews were shuffled like a deck of cards and organized into work camps of four hundred, each with an enforcer guard of twenty, outfitted with taser rods.

"How could Taam and Commander Meeks be okay with this?" I whispered to Spaghetti.

"Maybe they don't know," he responded.

And then, work began. Work like I had never known. No pride. No regard for health and safety. *True slavery*, I understood, thinking about how right Beverly was in saying it was not bondage before. My muscles ached, my bones felt cracked, and my joints stabbed with pain. And then, we worked more. We spent sixteen hours a day melting down feldspar, pulling molten stone into fine strands, and weaving it into a pillow-soft fabric. Layers were laid directly upon the ice, twenty meters thick, with an R-value of nearly seven hundred and twenty. *Enough to negotiate the temperature differential we'd be creating with a warmed atmosphere*. I thought about that. *How the hell are we going to make an atmosphere?*

Spaghetti gave me a look. "Don't get distracted. If you fall behind, you get left behind. Remember what happened to H4037?"

I looked at him hard, feeling my blood boil, but I spied one of Zodiac's enforcers peering from their gunship, like a lord overseeing their vassals. I hoisted another bundle of rock blanket to Spaghetti situated above me, who then moved it along.

Another day was done.

I sat at our camp's canteen, deep in thought, eating horrendous sludge designed to give us the nutrients we needed, when two people sat across from me. I snapped my head up to see Spaghetti and Patatas.

"Are you okay?" Patatas asked.

I looked to either side of me to see no enforcers close by. "No, I'm not… and neither are you." I thought upon Beverly again and if she knew this would happen. "I need to see Beverly."

"How?" Patatas said. "We're under unbelievable surveillance now."

I thought about how Joan first met Beverly. "Patatas, Spaghetti... Can you cause an accident?"

◆

My leg was broken in three places, and Spaghetti did his best to ensure the accident looked honest and the break was clean. Patatas called it in on the public line, using the same phrase from when we found Joan.

A gunship landed on the ice and two enforcers emerged with taser rods.

"What the fuck happened!?" one snapped.

"He was caught in the drop zone," Spaghetti said, pointing to the location.

"Why the fuck would he do something dumb like that!?"

"T-The way the barges come to drop off insulation is over the areas already installed, which means their approach is blind," Patatas said. "Here comes another now."

The enforcers looked at the twenty meter high wall of insulation, and the clones working to install more. A drop ship suddenly appeared at its edge as clones scrambled to get out of the way. The ship released its payload and turned back as it hit the ice and slid several meters.

The enforcers turned to me. "Just be careful next time!"

"I-I will," I stammered, trying to sound shaken up.

They loaded me onto an immobilizer and placed me into the gunship's cargo hold. *The fucking cargo hold...* I thought, feeling my blood boil again, frustrated to be treated like this by our own siblings. *Save your anger for another day,* I mantra'd the entire way to the hospital. I was delivered like goods to the airlock of a field hospital. The enforcers took off before any doctors or techs appeared.

I sat up, winced, and waited… and waited… and waited.

Finally a young woman exited the airlock and gave me a strange look. She held up two fingers, and I switched to channel two.

"What are you doing here?" she said through com.

"My leg is broken," I muttered. "They dropped me off an hour ago."

"Fucking hell," she said, coming closer. "They do thiz every time." She went silent, but I saw her mouth moving.

Talking on another line.

Several more came through the airlock, each having a strange thinness.

They're Ganymedans, I realized, and my mood simultaneously lightened and darkened. I was rushed through the airlock, stripped of my envisuit, and it took several of them to help me limp to the MRI. When I laid back, a hologram opened, passing through skin, muscle, and into bone, showing my leg broken in three places, just as I knew it would be.

The techs gasped.

I looked at them, not understanding what was so surprising. Then, my eyes darted around, finding a small hologram in the distance with the patient logs. *All are clones, so what's the big deal?* "What's wrong?"

The young tech who found me approached. "There'z nothing wrong. It'z juzt… your bonez have cleaved differently."

"What does that mean?" I followed up.

"You're going to be juzt fine," she said. "More than fine, actually."

Another woman entered in a long white coat, holding command in her posture, and strutted to the hologram.

The doctor, I knew.

"What'z all the excitement about?" she asked.

"Look at how it'z fractured, it'z not like the otherz," responded the tech.

The doctor donned glasses and peered into the hologram, then turned to me. "Iz that him?"

"Yez."

She approached me. "You, my friend, are coming with me."

My stomach sank, I did not know what to say, and I was in no position to flee. My eyes met the doctor's. *Why is she grinning?* I then imagined her coat and glasses were gone, her height was shorter, her eyes and hair color were different, and that she was younger. *How did she do this?* I opened my mouth, about to utter her name, when she placed a finger to her lips.

I felt a slight pinch at my arm and my vision swirled.

♦

I woke to the doctor sitting next to my cot, while hearing high-pitched whines and cries in the background.

"You're an idiot," she said.

My eyes wandered, my head was soupy, and my leg was numb. I reached my paw to feel an immobilizer at my hip. *The surgery is over,* I realized. I studied the doctor. "Why am I an idiot?"

She frowned. "You're different from the others, you've known this since hibernation."

I thought about that. "Sure, I had training, was given a name, and did not receive the submission genes. But there's nothing about my bones being different."

She shook her head. "The submission genes are what cause the difference."

More cries came as a slot opened in my hospital room door and a food tray slid through.

I'm in a cell, I realized. When the slot closed, the crying dissipated. "I'm not following." I slowly pushed myself into a seated position.

"Gene splicing is not an exact science. Each modification has its side effects." She took a breath. "That one extra wolf modification given to the other clones affects their bone structure. One would never notice the difference until the bones are broken."

I studied a diagram showing before and after the surgery. "Just a few pins."

"They'll be removed in a few weeks, once your bones have mended."

I faced her squarely. "How are you a doctor?"

"A long story, for another time," she responded.

My frustration rose but it was immediately quelled by another wave of faint, high-pitched cries. "What in Sol is that? It can't be coming from the other clones." I pondered that. "That's not what I sounded like, is it?"

A devilish grin spread on the doctor's face. "I mean, sometimes you do." She stood and approached a small coffee machine. "They're newborns."

I cocked my head. "Pardon?"

"Every patient in this hospital, besides you, is here to give birth."

"But... they're clones."

"They can still reproduce. Sterilization never interested father."

"So... who are their fathers, then?"

"Other clones," she said, took a sip of her coffee, and grimaced. "These Ganymedans love coffee. Tastes like shit."

She's diverging, uncomfortable, I knew. "Joan, you can't seriously be saying that we've been fornicating with ourselves."

Her expression hardened. "Never use that name here. I'm Genie."

I rolled my eyes. "Answer the damn question."

She sighed. "It's been happening for some time."

"The Ganymedans must be shitting their pants, then," I quipped, imagining hundreds of little equalizer children.

"Not really," Genie said. "Your workforce is doing an exceptional job. Zodiac is doing well as Administrator. If there is a way to perpetuate this situation, the Ganymedans are keen to it."

I gritted my teeth. "We're being worked to death! They can't possibly—"

"I agree with you," Genie calmly cut me off. "But the Ganymedans don't have the surveillance, they don't see it. From their perspective, we've gone from behind schedule to slightly ahead under Zodiac's watch, and that is incredible."

"So... We slip through the cracks?"

"We slip... for now," Genie said, taking her seat again. "As for these children, they become a replacement factor for those who've fallen. And they cannot inherit your modifications. So, they pose little threat. It's a promising outlook."

"It's still slavery."

"Not if you sign a contract, which you did," she responded. "And that's the catch. You agreed to this."

"But the children have not."

Genie sighed. "If this life is all they know, they will likely agree to whatever contract is given to them."

I huffed. "When do I get to use my anger?"

"Not yet, Uly."

"We can't just sit by and be exploited like this!" I grumbled.

"Yes, you can, and you will." Genie sipped her coffee. "If you act now, the terraforming will be left incomplete and everyone, clones, Ganymedans, us, and even Zodiac, will die."

"And after we terraform?" I inquired, barely holding my anger at bay.

"We remind them that although they own this moon, we built it."

"So, we pull the rug from beneath their feet if we must," I said.

"Does that make you happy?"

"No, but I get the logic," I sighed deeply. "But at this rate, we'll be working for a hundred years, just like I calculated, despite what Beverly says. Unless there's something you know."

Genie shook her head. "I haven't figured that out yet. The moment I do, I'll make sure that you know, too."

"Okay…" I looked at my leg in its immobilizer. "Three weeks?"

"Take this moment to rest. You'll need it."

"What's your next move?" I asked.

She grimaced. "Governor Terrence separated from his wife."

I gasped. "No, Jo… Genie, you can't be serious—."

"It's the only way to know the Ganymedans' plan for certain."

"But Zodiac will recognize you," I pleaded.

"Zodiac thinks I'm dead, and you barely recognized me knowing I was alive and well."

"That's because I thought you were hiding in the chamber."

Genie smirked.

"What?"

"I need a favor," she said. "Can you find a way to keep the chamber accessible when you lay the insulation?"

I thought about that. "I'll see what I can do."

◆

I returned to camp and relayed my conversation with Joan to Spaghetti and Patatas.

And then, we worked, heads down, uncomplaining, like mules. Month by month, year by year, I watched as members of our workforce disappeared for several months at a time, returning with a little red-haired infant in their arms. And each time I cringed more.

Infants became children. Miniature envisuits soon joined the sea of clones installing insulation. And they were perfectly sized to run inflatable tubing through tunnels drilled into the ice, ones designed to convey melting saltwater ice to desalination plants and replace with fresh water. *To significantly raise the ice's overall freezing point, ensuring that we don't drop into the subterranean ocean.* I imagined they might propose something like this to circumvent the heat transfer, but I never imagined they would use children. *Cause the Ganymedans don't know,* I reminded myself. As I watched them descend into the tunnels, I realized Joan could fit, too. *Her access point to the chamber.*

"This sickens me," I said to Spaghetti and Patatas at dinner. "Zodiac's using children. He's allowing us to have children. Which might be worse."

They gave each other a nervous glance.

"It can't be that bad, Tapas, right?" Spaghetti said.

"Child labor!?" I snapped, appalled he would say such a thing. I looked around to see the enforcers were not nearby. *Thankfully.*

"No… Having children," Patatas said, placing a hand on her stomach.

I eyed Patatas, her hand, and then Spaghetti. "Tell me you're joking?"

Spaghetti's face turned red and Patatas looked about to cry.

Why did I say that! "I mean… Congratulations?"

They named their son, Ulysses, after their best friend, the only person they said they could depend upon. *Those assholes…* I thought, holding a tiny red-headed infant in my monstrous arms. My heart melted. I started grinning, making little noises, and funny faces. *Why am I being so stupid?*

The little boy simply stared back with eyes full of trust.

"He's beautiful," I inadvertently whispered.

"We want you to be his guardian should anything happen to us," Spaghetti said.

"Yes, of course," I said without hesitation. *But could I truly do that?*

◆

"The insulation is complete! The conveyor tubes are installed! And only five cave-ins!" Zodiac announced, peering across the sea of clones and children, just like Taam did years ago.

I clenched my jaw knowing those five cave-ins resulted in the deaths of two-dozen children. *If we don't get this done, we all die!* I reminded myself.

"And for your hard work! For your sacrifices, I have given you a rare opportunity for your children!"

We perked up and the children stirred.

"Families across Ganymede have agreed to foster your children and give them a proper education!" Zodiac smiled wide. "But the children must come now! There is no time to waste! Come, children! Let's go!"

None moved.

The children know not to trust Zodiac, I realized.

Zodiac's strange smile dwindled. He turned to his enforcers. Taser rods came on and they entered the sea of clones seeking out the children.

"Now's the time," I whispered, searching for any sign from Joan. Instead, I saw little Uly, looking my way, and knew any sort of action would certainly destroy these unmodified children. *So, we hold...*

One by one, the enforcers pulled children from their confused parents.

An enforcer approached us and saw little Uly hiding behind me. She waved for me to step aside.

I did not budge.

The enforcer looked me in the eye. I suddenly recognized her.

"Trieu?" I whispered.

Her mouth dropped open and her eyes welled with tears. "They're going to be okay," she whispered back. "I'll make certain of it... Please, Uly." She again waved her hand for me to move aside.

How can one of The Twelve be an enforcer!? I thought about that. *This must be part of Joan's plan! This must be a way to reach her!* I reluctantly stepped aside, and caught the worried looks of Spaghetti and Patatas.

"It's going to be all right," I said to them, hoping it was true.

Nearly two thousand children formed up behind Zodiac, appearing like an army. A chill ran down my spine.

I turned to Trieu. "Tell Joan, desalination tunnels."

♦

Barge-loads of clay were dumped atop the insulation layer, and we spread it consistently three meters deep across a two kilometer wide strip wrapping the moon's equator. Compared to the mining and thermal blanket installation, it felt like a vacation. When two more years came to an end, we returned to the canteen to find the children waiting.

"And then, and then!" Little Uly said out of breath in his parent's room. "They started teaching us martial arts!"

"Martial arts?" I said and made a fake karate chop.

"Not like that, Uncle Tapas!" Little Uly adopted a Muay Thai stance and began stalking towards me.

I stood frozen.

"Come on, uncle! I want to show you some moves!"

I felt my hands raise and my body slide into the same stance.

"Whoa! You know it, too!?" little Uly shouted.

I knew Spaghetti and Patatas were wondering the same thing.

"Do you know what the best tool in Muay Thai is?" I asked my nephew.

"Leg kicks!" he said and sent his leg whipping towards my thigh.

I relaxed the muscle, so his foot would not break against my leg, and doubled over, groaning.

"I'm sorry!" Uly came over to me rolling on the ground.

"You re-broke my bad leg!" I said.

"I did!?" Uly gasped, looking at my leg with wide eyes.

I stopped writhing and grinned. "Nope." I grasped his hips, tossed him into the air, stood to my feet, and cradle caught him on the way down. "But that was a good kick."

Little Uly giggled as I set him down. "I think you might be as strong as Zodiac!"

My gut twisted as I envisioned him sparring with that monster.

"Mom, Dad! Don't you think so, too?"

"Uncle Tapas certainly is," Spaghetti said, approaching his son. "And, so am I!" It was his turn to toss little Uly.

◆

The children joined us in the fields, but this time spreading seed across a landscape stretching beyond the moon's horizon in every direction, feeling like Ganymede's tundra no longer existed despite being just beneath our feet. We marched side by side, in one long line covering a hundred kilometers of length a day. In a few months we would march clear around the moon's equator following the band of insulated land we created. But by my calculations, it would take several decades to cover a thousandth of the moon's surface. *And they say we will be doing two thirds of it.*

"It's mostly teff, like what they used to terraform Mars, designed for extreme cold," little Uly said, scattering a handful of seed to the ground.

"Is that what they're teaching you?" Patatas asked.

"Mostly grass, soil, and atmosphere stuff," little Uly responded.

"A weird thing to be teaching a nine-year-old," Spaghetti said.

"Not that weird," little Uly responded. "It's going to take almost a century to create enough soil and atmosphere to support crop growth, so it will be a long time."

Spaghetti, Patatas, and I stopped in our tracks.

"Keep moving!" cried an enforcer through com.

We caught up to the line.

"But, we only have a few year's worth of supplies left," Spaghetti said.

Little Uly made a face. "Looked like there was plenty of food in the stores to me."

"You've seen the stores?" I responded.

"Yeah… Haven't you?"

"No, they keep telling us there's a finite amount, that we are racing against time."

Little Uly thought about this. "We should sequential terraform, then."

I was stunned, realizing it had never crossed my mind. "How did you come up with that?"

"A native Martian taught a class on how they terraformed Mars."

"Wish we knew that before we started all this," Patatas said.

No, I thought. *This is purposeful.*

◆

I caught strange movement ahead. A gentle waving back and forth, almost like water. "You see that?"

"Yeah," Spaghetti responded.

Others along the line perked up and pointed.

"Keep steady!" cried the enforcers. "Maintain even distribution!"

We tried to restrain our excitement, but as we neared we realized what it was. For the last hundred meters we ran, the whole line, eight thousand equalizers and two thousand children. And despite all the threats being shouted into our ears pieces, the enforcers were powerless.

"Grass! It's grass!" Patatas reached it first and tumbled to the ground, rolling across little green and red leaves.

The rest of us followed suit, tumbling upon the vegetation like dogs.

"Stop that! You're ruining the grass!" the enforcers shouted. "Ah, fuck it!" They landed their gunships, leaped from their cockpits, and charged. My adrenaline surged, ready for the fight, until I realized they did not have taser rods. They dove to the grass and rolled with the rest of us.

They're still our brothers and sisters, after all, I realized, feeling weight lift from my shoulders.

That evening, we entered the congregation dome, cheering, hugging, all of us together, workers and enforcers, with our children now, to find hundreds of tables set with centerpieces, flatware, and silverware.

A feast!? I thought.

Taam, Commander Meeks, Governor Terrence, and Administrator Zodiac appeared through the airlock at the opposite end. And then, the slaver finally showed her face. "The Great Uniter," as the Ganymedans called her. But she hung back like a skulking troll. Taam spread his arms wide and us clones roared so monstrously that even Zodiac grew wide-eyed.

And then, a chanting began, the only chant we knew, from a lifetime ago. "Honor! Honor! Honor!"

Blood drained from Commander Meeks and Governor Terrence's faces.

Taam raised his hand high, taking the center of a platform, hushing us. He then did something I never thought I'd witness. He knelt and placed a fist upon his opposing shoulder in Hermian salute. "Great saviors of Ganymede!" his voice carried across the dome. "I salute you!"

The clones knelt and thousands of paws pressed into shoulders.

I had no choice, but to do the same.

"Taam Kapoor! May you shepherd us into the light!" we shouted, our voices so powerful the dome quivered like jello.

"You have exceeded my expectations!" he said. "You have done the impossible! And you made it look easy!"

I thought about all who were lost, over a thousand clones. But the others were smiling, enthralled to have their great Taam back.

He stood and waved his hands to the tables. "Tonight we gather to honor this achievement! To honor you! And what better way than to grant you a glimpse of what you will create in the decades to come!"

Decades? I thought and watched dozens of people pour from the dome's rear airlock holding platters overflowing with food, more food than I had ever seen in one place, more food than I imagined possible. *Uly was right, the stores are full.*

"From the elegant floating orchards of Venus!" Taam announced as the platters were set on tables. "We give you oranges! Apples! Pears! Grapes! And bananas!"

A strange chef approached Taam, bowed deeply, and spoke with an exquisite accent, "Take your seats! Indulge! This is our gift to you!"

We raced to seats and reached for the fruit. Sweetness, richness, such as I had never known, invaded my body. I could feel its energy percolating my stomach and bloodstream. I cried out in ecstasy alongside the others.

"This is just the appetizer!" Taam exclaimed. "For the next course, from the deserts of Mars, we serve you, Lamb Stew!"

Spice, heat, and heartiness contrasted with the fruit and we again cried out in joy. More rounds came, each from a surviving colony of System Sol, as if the entire human race had come to congratulate us. And then, a woman I recognized stepped on stage.

"And now, representing our ancient past, coming from Earth itself!" Taam announced, motioning to the woman. "We give you, Ceviche!"

I stared at this woman, remembering her promise to teach me this dish. She did not smile or bow like the other chefs. Instead, she held incredible helplessness in her eyes. *She's been crying,* I realized. She was searching our faces, looking for someone specific. *But who?* Her eyes locked with mine. Her lip quivered and her mouth opened slightly, mouthing a word.

She-Don-Ee, I discerned, but I had never heard this in either Ganymedan or Interspeak. *She-Don-Ee... what could it—* I dropped my fork. *It's Hermian...*

"I'm sorry?" I mouthed back the translation in Interspeak.

Beverly closed her mouth and nodded.

Sorry for what? I thought.

"Mom? Dad!?" I heard little Uly say.

Furious spooning and shouts of joy became heavy breathing and snores. I turned to find Spaghetti and Patatas head down upon the table. More wavered as if drunk. I shook Spaghetti's shoulder, desperately trying to wake him. He was out cold. But the children remained awake. I was awake. And a few other clones were awake. I made eye contact with one. *Alexander...* My eyes met another. *Mulan...* And then, a third. *Liu Bei...*

The submission genes, I realized and saw The Twelve coming to the same realization. I lowered my head to the table, pretending to be a late victim, and saw the others follow my lead.

"Uncle Tapas!? No! Not you, too!" little Uly shouted.

I felt a stab of pain in my heart as I ignored his pleas and felt his tiny hands shaking my shoulders. I matched Spaghetti's breathing and sleep twitches. But my heart was pounding and my mind was racing. *What's the point of this!? Why put us to sleep!?*

"Zodiac, great work," I heard Taam say. "But we must get this moon productive. Can you train the children to do this?"

"I can and I will, sir," Zodiac responded. "What about the clones?"

"Freeze them for another day," Taam said. His heavy footsteps left the platform, followed by a dozen others, and the rear airlock opened and closed.

"Children! Shut up!" came Zodiac's savage, booming voice.

The cries ceased. Little Uly stopped shaking my shoulders. The pattering of thousands of feet congregated around Zodiac.

"I know you do not understand what's happening," Zodiac said. "But this is part of our great plan."

What the fuck!? I thought upon the feast, certainly laced, and Beverly's mouthed word, our argument in Joan's chamber, and how she said I didn't understand the plan. *Did she know about this!?*

"Children, it's time to go," Zodiac ordered. "But rest assured, you will see your parents again."

But when!? A year!? A decade!? A century!? I desperately kept calm.

The children's steps neared the back, and again the airlock opened. A heavy, metallic marching, sounding like a platoon, entered.

"Check them," Zodiac commanded.

Heavy steps thunked down the aisles and dozens of zaps came. I dug into memories of my training. *Mech units,* I realized.

"Ah!" one of the clones cried.

"Found one, zir," came a Ganymedan's voice.

"You know what to do," Zodiac calmly said.

"No, please!" said the clone.

He's one of The Twelve! I recognized.

"You don't understand! I didn't eat, that's why I'm aw—"

A heavy shot echoed through the dome and a thud hit the floor.

Every part of my body wanted to lurch into action, but every part of my brain knew it was futile. I breathed heavily and focused on Joan's words, imagining she was crawling to the feldspar chamber through the desalination tubes, to go into hiding.

A metal fist pressed upon my back and volts rippled through me. *Don't you dare flinch!* I commanded myself. The fist raised and the pain ceased. Soon afterward, the metal steps receded to Zodiac.

"Freeze them," came his menacing voice.

The dome's ventilation went into overdrive. Frigid air numbed my skin. I desperately wanted to bolt. *But they're still here, still watching,* I knew, having not heard another open and close of the airlock.

My limbs became unresponsive. My digestion stopped. My lungs and heart grew sluggish. And my thoughts faded away.

♦

I did not dream, for I was not in proper hibernation. Instead, I was stored away like vegetables or meat, a commodity for another day. *And, apparently, that day had come.*

Distant whispers came first, quickly sounding right next to me as my eardrums thawed. My heart thunked once, heavy and lonely, and after several minutes, it thunked again. I flexed my lungs, feeling ice crystals fracturing within the cilia. *The first breath.*

"Tapas," I heard next to me. "Tapas, you awake?"

Spaghetti. "Y-yes," I responded through chattering teeth.

"What happened?" he asked.

"They d-drugged and placed us into h-hibernation," I said.

"What makes you think that?"

"I heard them s-say it," I responded and made out Spaghetti's silhouette beside me as my eyes thawed.

"But how?"

"On your feet you giant fuckerz!" barked a strange voice.

I saw the shape of a mech unit. "What y-year is it?" I asked.

"No talking!"

I slowly stood alongside what appeared like five hundred of us inside a cylindrical room. The gravity felt weird. "We're on a ship…"

"I zaid, no talking!"

Volts hit my stomach, stiffening my body, and I dropped to the floor.

"Anyone elze!?… Good! Get him to hiz feet!"

Spaghetti grasped my armpits, hoisting me up.

"Line up!" cried the little man. "Now, move!"

Spaghetti helped my half-frozen, half-stunned self along. We passed through the back wall of the cylindrical room to see hundreds of envisuits and equipment.

"Zuit up and get ready! There iz no time to loze!"

"We just thawed, we must eat," one said.

Zaps followed.

"You eat when you accomplish!" came a horrid voice. "You accomplish when you work!"

I lifted my head, fighting my body's sluggishness, to see a hulking man wearing governor attire. His hair was going gray and his wrinkles were deep, but I recognized a faded scar running up the left side of his face. "Zodiac…" I whispered. *How the hell did he become a governor!?*

The monstrous governor smirked. "Well, well, our first dissenter." He peered at me with his eagle eyes. "X0471, do you wish to become this crew's example?"

This crew's? I studied the decades upon Zodiac's face. "No, sir." I quietly muttered.

"Good, boy," Governor Zodiac said, and returned to the group. "Suit up! We must construct and deploy four solar shades in under a year! Do this and we are one step closer to achieving a terraformed moon!"

The wall behind Governor Zodiac opened, revealing Ganymede below with a thick band of green wrapping its equator and several more patches in the northern hemisphere. *Fifty years,* I estimated by the increased grassland. Several smaller patches dotted the surface with texture and color. *Agriculture?* I thought, trying to understand how it might be achieved in such a short time. I searched the moon's horizon for a subtle blue glow, but found nothing. *No atmosphere... They must be in greenhouses.*

"You! Get going!" shouted the little man in his mech unit.

I recognized something in his voice and studied his thin frame beneath the hydraulics and reddish hair. He was maybe eighteen, but I saw the little boy in him. I saw little Uly. *It's not him! It can't be him!* But I remembered how the children were taught Muay Thai and how Zodiac said they would meet us again. *This is how they keep us from mutiny...* I realized and saw the look on Spaghetti's face.

We learned how to EVA on the fly and I thanked The Director for my training in hibernation, but I also cursed his arrogance for not anticipating this scenario.

The first completed shade unfolded its delicate membrane and descended into low Ganymedan orbit. Despite its beauty, all I could think of were the twenty-seven of us lost to malfunctioning magnetic boots, each time listening to their desperate cries as they slowly drifted away. And there were no safety tethers, for that would tangle us up. So, we learned to turn off our coms and keep focused on the membrane within our hands. *Like scared sheep...*

After the fourth and final shade unfurled in orbit, casting equally spaced shadows upon the surface, simulating night and day for the circadian rhythms of crops, vegetation, and people, and creating temperature differentials for artificial rain, we were not met by another grand feast. We were not celebrated as heroes. We were not even thanked.

"They locked us out," I muttered as we pressed upon our construction barge's airlock door and were met by silence on com.

My envisuit's heating system cut and a chill crept into my fingers and toes, but my air was still on. I tried signing to the others as they frantically banged against the hull. *But they were never taught,* I realized, watching us, one by one, succumb to hibernation.

Sewer systems, irrigation systems, golf courses… *What the fuck?*

Cities grew like weeds, hosting tall skyscrapers and castle-like structures. And every time I woke, there were more.

But still within domes, I saw and wondered how much time had elapsed, how much effort was diverting from terraforming to unnecessary luxuries. *Have they forgotten about the atmosphere?*

Most importantly, I studied the wealth.

I woke from cryosleep once again, heaving the usual slurry mix from my stomach and dropping to my knees. *What now?* I thought, feeling blades of grass tickling my bare arms and legs. *Grass... Am I outside?* I instinctively held my breath. *But I should have already suffocated.* I breathed, listening to what I could only determine was wind. Dull light came to my blurred vision.

"Good morning," said a calm voice. "What you are witnezzing iz the dream we all work towardz. Breathe deeply. Lizten to the zoundz around you." She paused. "Yez, that iz wind in your hair. Yez, that iz grazz beneath your bodiez. And yez, that light iz your firzt truly experienced zunrize. Thiz iz what a terraformed moon feelz like..."

Despite knowing it was all for show, I was beside myself.

"...But, do not be fooled," she continued. "For you merely ztand in front of a prototype..."

My eyes were sharpening and I found a small figure in front of the rising sun. *Not in a mech unit,* I realized.

"...Ztand when you can," she said. "Take your time. I'm zure you are very confuzed. Zo, let'z ztart with who I am… I am Governor Verna, one of four governorz who run Ganymede..."

There are four, now!

"… I purchased you hundred from my dear colleague, Governor Zodiac. And at a high price I might add…"

Only a hundred of us this time, I thought. *Where are the others?*

"…Becauze I have been tazked with creating a breathable atmozphere…"

My eyes were clearing. Rippling light appeared on the ground as the sun peaked its distant face above the grass. *Water...*

"...Thiz iz an old rezearch well, twenty meterz wide and dezcending to Ganymede'z ocean zeveral kilometerz below the ice," she said. "Thiz well once granted Ganymedan zcientiztz accezz to the aquaculture below. But, thiz well can alzo zerve to convey oxygen produced by algae introduced centuriez ago, adapted for zero light, feeding upon the ocean'z radioactive decay. More oxygen iz produced in thiz moon'z ocean than even the great algae patchez of old Earth. Thiz iz what you breathe now. But, thiz alone iz not enough to create an atmozphere. Ztray more than a few meterz from where you ztand and you will zuffocate..."

The silhouettes of my brothers and sisters appeared around the well, like a perimeter fence.

"…We are to change that," the governor finished.

The work was mindless, and where a part of me enjoyed the simplicity, it allowed my thoughts to run, to imagine what was happening in those cities.

"What's that thing?" Spaghetti asked, and I was thankful he and Patatas were somehow by my side.

The others… Who knows where they are?

I saw a metal structure far in the distance. I estimated it to be nearly a hundred meters tall by a hundred meters wide. The sun reflected strangely on its surface. *It's a gigantic cylinder,* I realized. "I have no idea," I answered him. "But I'm sure our brothers and sisters built it."

"Yeah," Patatas quietly muttered.

For four years we drilled. And when we could no longer take it, we drilled. A rushing of seawater came each time we cracked through the ice. And each time, a few more of us went missing. *Do I care anymore?* I looked into the depths of our most recently constructed well, imagining what it would feel like to drop several kilometers in complete isolation and darkness. *The same as drifting into space,* I assumed.

"Form up!" cried a little captain in a mech unit. "We have a zhift change! Keep your headz down and your handz to yourzelf!"

We did as told.

I felt footsteps beside me with a gate I recognized. *More clones.* I tried ignoring it, tried keeping my head down. *But who are they?* I turned my eyes, bringing them to their limits. I caught a face behind a beat up visor. *My face…* But it was so different. An eye was missing and scars pocked their nose. Stubble grew on their jaw and upper lip, white as snow. I realized their gate was more of a lumber and limp. *They're ancient, broken, worked to death…* The old man's lone eye shifted my way and I saw his iris focus on me. His mouth opened slightly to reveal broken teeth. His lips moved, mouthing, *"Ulysses."* A rock dropped in my stomach. I searched the old man's face, trying to understand who he might be. Then, I found a little mark under his lost eye, one he acquired during feldspar mining.

"Liu Bei?" I mouthed back.

He closed his eye and a tear trickled down his cheek. Then, he was gone, passed by, just another clone marching to his death.

My entire body shook. I felt a nudge. It was Patatas. *I must regain control!* I knew, but the fire within me that I thought had been extinguished, was resurfacing with a vengeance. *Joan!? I need you! Where are you!? Is now the time!?* Dread percolated through me. I knew the truth to my core. *Joan's dead!*

"Move forward!" ordered the little man, after the broken crew passed.

We trudged into a circular clearing with a hundred cryotubes around its perimeter. *What the f—* The ground beneath us vanished and we fell into frigid water. *A well!?* I realized and that our envisuit heaters were again turned off.

◆

"Oh, zhit! He'z actually waking up!" said a Ganymedan.

My eyelids cracked open and shards of ice slipped from my tear ducts. Nothingness faded to blackness, which became whiteness, and soon, colored shapes.

"Incredible," said another. "I thought they were bullshitting uz."

"Yeah, me too."

"M-me… th-three…" I said through chattering teeth and saw their shapes backpadel.

"He can underztand uz?"

"There waz nothing in the tranzcript about that," said the other.

Transcript? "W-Where am I?" I said.

"We're orbiting Io…" one timidly answered.

Fuck, I thought.

"…It's the innermozt moon of Jupiter," said the other.

"I know w-what Io is," I growled as their shapes sharpened. They were on a raised catwalk allowing them to look me in the eye. "H-How long have I b-been in hibernation this t-time?"

"Almozt a century, we think."

"You don't know for sure?"

The other one shrugged. "They juzt told uz to wake you. That you know how to drill."

"We're s-supposed to be f-finished terraforming by n-now," I shivered.

"We are finizhed."

I gave them a look. "S-So, Ganymede is habitable?"

"It iz."

"Then, we s-start g-growing crops," I said.

They looked at one another. "Cropz are growing."

They fucked something up, I knew, but I needed more information. "Something went wrong, d-didn't it?"

"Yez," they said in unison.

"Ganymede's soil is turning," I stated.

"...Yez," they again said with questioning looks.

They miscalculated the PH levels. "Is the soil too acidic or too b-base?"

One cocked their head. "It'z... too baze."

"And you want to infuse Ganymede's s-soil with Io's sulfur to balance it out," I concluded.

"Were you already briefed?"

I did not answer him. Instead, I clenched my massive paws into fists, feeling ice crack within my muscle fiber. The two Ganymedans stepped back farther. I slowly rolled my wrists, bent my elbows, and flexed my shoulders sending slushy ice to the floor. I stepped from my cryochamber up to the catwalk, rising far above the Ganymedans. Terror spread across their faces. A dark patch grew on one's uniform crotch.

"It's a shame you s-screwed up the soil. That's what happens when you rush these things." I took a deep breath. "I know you think w-we clones are at your disposal, that we will happily c-clean up your mess, but drilling Io is n-not in our contracts."

"What contractz?" one whispered.

I fucking knew it! I stepped forth, but my legs buckled. I barely caught my fall with my paws on the catwalk. Icy bile crawled up my throat and I heaved. Then, my face met the catwalk grating.

◆

"You're okay..." I whispered to myself. I turned my head to see the Ganymedans were gone. *I passed out,* I realized and moved my arms. They felt fully thawed. *I've been lying here for some time.*

Heavy steps resonated through the grating. I looked up to see another frozen clone across from my chamber. When I peered left I saw a long, tight, gradually lifting corridor, lined with hundreds of my kin.

But only I'm awake. Why?

Several soldiers in mech units rounded the corridor's bend and trained rifles upon me.

"Get up!" one shouted.

Easier said than done, I thought.

"I zaid, get the fuck up!"

"I'm trying," I groaned and pressed my paws to the grating, pushing into a kneeling position.

"Don't rezizt!" the soldier shouted.

"For the love of Sol, I'm complying!" I snapped back.

A stun shot hit my shoulder, but did not hurt like it once did. I placed a foot beneath myself as another nailed my leg. *Still, not that bad.* I braced my second foot and stood tall, eclipsing the soldiers in their mech units. Their faces looked much like the Ganymedans earlier, wide-eyed and frantic. *They've never seen an equalizer out of hibernation before,* I realized. I recognized heavy cuffs on one's belt. "If you toss me those cuffs, I'll put them on myself, so you don't have to approach me."

The soldier barking orders moments ago was silent, his mouth agape. Nevertheless, he unclasped the cuffs and tossed them to the grating.

I knelt, pressed my fists into the cuffs, and they cinched tight. I twisted and turned, feeling the metal flex but not shear. *Sicklecell titanium...*

Soldiers scooted around me, turning sideways to clear my massive shoulders, and took my back.

"Clone X0471! You have been called up for zervice!" the barking one said. "We will ezcort you to a holding cell where you will meet Zodiac!"

Fuck me... I did not budge.

"Move! Now!"

Zaps came upon my back, and it wasn't until the fourth that I moved. We walked in tense silence. I felt a slight turning sensation. *Centripetal force gravity...* I realized. *This is a space station, not a ship.* A break in the corridor appeared in the ceiling and the catwalk below became a lift platform. When we stepped within its limits, it raised into the ceiling. Rings of structural titanium gave way to clear poly-carbonate, flooding the lift with light and revealing a swirling orange vortex. I flinched. *Jupiter,* I realized, and that we were so close its hurricane eye filled my entire field of vision. I looked down to see a large ring-like structure. *Holding hundreds of us.* A central hub sat at the ring's center with several more tunnels meeting like the spokes of a wheel. The gravity reduced as we climbed until I felt as light as a feather. When we docked, I became weightless, but the mechs did not, having magnets integrated into their frames. They tilted me forward and gently pushed me along, keeping the walls and floor out of my reach.

Brilliant, I thought, knowing I was completely helpless.

Technicians hustled down the halls, each giving me a wide berth and whispering. A vault door appeared and we stopped. The soldier flashed a holotile and I heard heavy deadbolts release. A meter thick door opened. They pushed me inside. More cuffs were applied to my feet and a large rod was added connecting the two. Then, they placed me at the very center of the room, and let go, leaving me hanging in zero-g.

"When did I become a prisoner?" I asked the soldiers.

"When you were born," came a sudden voice from ahead.

I snapped my head up, finding a window beyond the soldiers with a woman on the other side staring at information on hologram, though I could not make out what. The soldiers filed out of the room and the vault door sealed. I studied the woman's features beyond the window, trying to find any familiarity. *Nothing.*

"X0471?" she asked.

"I am not a number," I responded.

"Yez, you are," she said. "You come highly recommended for thiz tazk."

"I thought Zodiac wanted to see me," I said.

She looked up from her hologram. "That'z why we're talking."

"When do I see Zodiac?"

"Right now."

My confusion was palpable.

She gave me a look. "I'm Commander Zodiac of LKAB Ztation, in charge of all operationz for thiz venture." She paused. "Who were you expecting?"

"A monster of a man who makes me look small."

"Do you mean, Governor Zodiac?" she responded.

"Yes. Why do you have his name? Are you related?"

She let out a sharp laugh. "Many people have been named after that great man. How do you know him?"

"He's one of us… He's a clone."

She squinted and pursed her lips. "It zayz you have a hiztory of paranoid delusionz, and tend to talk back to your zuperiorz."

"Do you consider yourself my superior?" I snipped.

"You live up to your reputation, then," she stated.

I grunted. "Who recommended me?"

"You azk a lot of queztionz."

"I just woke after a hundred years, which was like a blink of an eye for me. I have no idea what's been happening. Of course I have a lot of questions."

She pondered that. "Governor Terrence perzonally requezted you."

Governor Terrence? "That would make him four-hundred years old."

"It'z hiz great, great grandzon."

I thought about that. "Why would he request me?"

"No idea. I zimply have orderz to brief you on your tazk."

"I already know that you fucked up soil alkaline and need us to harvest sulfur from Io to fix it," I said.

She sat back in her chair and crossed her arms.

"We're not going to do it. It's not in our contracts," I stated.

She just stared at me.

"Can you hear me?" I said.

"You're contract ztatez that you gain citizenzhip once terraforming iz complete," she finally said. "It zayz nothing about meanz and methodz."

"But if you hadn't fucked up, terraforming would be done," I retorted.

"Zo, by your own admizzion, terraforming iz not complete."

Shit...

"Once you collect enough Zulfur to infuze Ganymede'z zoil your contract will be fulfilled."

I stared her down. "Can I get that in writing?"

"It'z in your contract," she responded.

"What if that's not good enough. What if I refuse to help?"

She sighed. "We're zending you to Io whether you like it or not. You can either lead thiz effort, or follow... Chooze."

◆

Twenty-five drop-ships fell from the LKAB Station, each containing twenty of my brothers and sisters strapped against their walls, facing a yellow moon spotted by hundreds of active super-volcanoes with vast smoothness between them, appearing like a rotten lemon. *Not a single impact crater...* A surface pushing upwards with the steepest of mountains and volcanoes but not once sinking inward felt like this moon was inside out. At Io's horizon were lava flows glowing brightly and plumes of super-heated sulfur clouds spewing into space. Our drop-ships twisted and turned like a flock of birds, following my commands and navigating the plumes. Temperature bars spiked from, *"minus 100C,"* to, *"positive 1,600C."* Radiation was off the charts. But it was Jupiter's magnetosphere, fed by Io's plumes, that was the real challenge, for our instruments were going haywire. We were dropping in blind and it was never more obvious why they sent us clones for the task.

This is suicide…

I banked hard as a plume became suddenly visible. G-forces ticked up on visor, *"15g, 16g,"* but I simply gritted my teeth knowing our bodies were designed for this. We slipped past the plume, but just barely.

I accessed the rear camera watching the rest of the drop-ships bank, but four were missing. *Eighty souls lost,* I realized. My eyes blurred with tears. *No! Stop it! Focus!* I squinted out the water and kept onward.

We were finally under the plumes and I searched for the features marking basecamp. A dark ring registered out the corner of my left eye. *We're way off course…* I banked that way and what remained of my flock followed. A rusty ring of deposited sulfur appeared among a sea of yellow, surrounding a volcanic caldera that had gone dormant twelve years prior. I searched for a flat yellow plain with enough space to host all twenty-five drop-ships.

Twenty-one ships, I corrected myself.

"Listen up!" I called on the public line. "I've located our site! Remember the briefing! Be ready to perform your tasks the instant we land! We must link the drop-ships together! We must get the geothermal drills in place! And we must get the recyclers primed! Be careful! Be mindful! This moon is unlike anything humanity has experienced before! We are the first people to set foot upon its surface, for everyone else is too chickenshit!" I heard cheers on com, but I knew they were terrified. *Because I'm terrified.* "Here we go!"

◆

"Volcanus Zamama…" I whispered, staring at the steep slopes of its caldera, coated in fine sulfur dioxide snow and twinkling in pre-dawn's indirect light. Then, like the surface of a simmering pot, as the sun crept over the horizon, the snow steamed upwards to form Io's temporary atmosphere. I opened the public line. "We have twenty hours to survey this sector before the sun sets! Drill cores every hundred meters! You know your locations!"

In teams of five, with the same dilapidated skiffs and drilling equipment used to find feldspar and clay, we raced across the smooth surface. But, unlike Ganymede, we were atop a time bomb, ready to erupt at a moment's notice.

Skiffs found their marks and teams quickly unloaded drilling equipment. Tall needle-like erections began spewing yellow clouds. Several teams continued on, including mine, closer to the edge of the caldera's steep slope. Temperature rose sharply, I could feel it through my insulated envisuit.

I glanced at Patatas and Spaghetti sitting on the front of my skiff, then at Trieu and Alexander behind me. *My true brother and sister alongside my new brother and sister.* They were on the edge of their seats ready to bolt onto the surface.

We reached the, *"X,"* on visor and I hit reverse thrusters.

Patatas and Spaghetti leaped from the front, Patatas with her holotile and spike and Spaghetti with the first component of our drill, its cleat. Trieu and Alexander leaped from the sides with massive impact hammers. I dropped the skiff's anchor spike to the sulfur crust and leaped from the cockpit last, carrying the drill's bearing hub. The packed sulfur crunched beneath my feet. A part of me wished we could simply harvest it from the surface, but I knew we must tap deposits from Zamama's previous eruptions and find sulfur not baked by Jupiter's radiation.

Patatas's holotile searched for the best location and, when it flashed green, she dropped to the sulfur, driving her spike. She peeled away, returning to the skiff, not a glance over her shoulder, brushing right by us. Spaghetti arrived next, placing the cleat over the spike, and inserting four heavy stakes in its flanges. He rolled away just as Trieu and Alexander came swinging their impact hammers, driving two stakes deep into the crust. They pivoted and swung again, driving the other two. I came last, planting the bearing hub atop the cleat and twisting, locking it in place. When I turned, I saw Patatas right on my tail with the motor and Spaghetti with the drive-train. Component after component was installed, until, ten minutes later, we had the drill spinning. We continually added ten meter lengths of bit, four of us hoisting them vertically, the fifth locking new ones to the ends of the previous, trying not to damage the connection in the torrent of yellow particles.

After several hours, the first team reached two kilometers, their indicator signaling on my visor.

"J0873, what's your status?" I called to their team lead.

"Just reached 2K, sir," she responded.

"Is the sulfur any good?" I followed up.

"No, it's all irradiated," she answered.

"Stop now, recover the bits and disassemble the drill, head back to basecamp immediately," I ordered.

"Sir, I'm not sure we have time."

"Disassemble as much as you can and leave the rest in the field."

"Copy that."

More teams were reaching their marks, their cores all irradiated. *But they're the farthest from the Zamama's caldera, and we're the closest.*

We hit ten hours, the day's halfway mark, signaling our point of no return. Most were already retracting their components. I glanced into the tenuous Ionian sky, a thin yellow haze, to see LKAB Station above, only a speck of light.

"Team 87 to Tapas!" team 87's lead called in.

"Tapas here, what is it?"

"Our core! It looks good!"

"Send the analysis!" I said, my heart pounding.

I saw that in only the last few meters had they hit clean sulfur.

"Team 88 to Tapas!" called another voice, from Mulan's team.

"Go ahead," I responded.

"We have clean sulfur!"

I quickly checked their position. *Right next to us.* I turned to see all five of their team members waving in the distance.

More called in with clean cores, all next to the caldera ridge.

My team was still drilling as the others were returning to basecamp. *We'll be leaving our equipment,* I knew.

Evening was upon us and the sulfur dioxide atmosphere was dropping like golden snow.

"We gotta go," Spaghetti said.

"We're so close," I said. "We must confirm our core to get a complete map of Zamama's deposits."

"But the snow—"

"Is harmless," I responded, but I knew what was coming next. *We have a little more time!* I saw that Mulan's team had not yet left. "Catch a ride with Team 88."

"We're not leaving you," Patatas said.

Of course they won't.

I felt tremors in my feet and looked to Io's leading horizon. A little white orb, like a golf ball, peaked above. *Europa...* It was growing in size, and, after another half-hour, looked like a baseball hanging low in the sky.

"Uly…" Trieu said on a private line. "We have to go."

I breathed deeply. "Okay, we'll finish up tomorrow."

My feet were numbed by the relentless vibration of the drill, but when it wound down, the vibration continued. Cracks spread on the hard packed surface and soft sulfur began sifting up from the layer below. I peered at Europa. *We shouldn't feel any tidal forces!*

"Shit!" Alexander said, knee deep in sulfur. "It's like quicksand!"

"On the skiff!" I ordered.

Patatas and Trieu were already there and pulled the rest of us from the soupy ground. I started the skiff's systems and retracted its anchor spike when a sudden lurch came. The skiff began lowering. *The crust is biting the spike!* I cut the spike, popping our skiff above the surface, nearly bucking my team. I spun the skiff around and floored it back to basecamp, following yellow rooster tails from other teams doing the same.

Europa was still growing in the sky.

"Look at that!" Spaghetti said, pointing at the caldera.

I glanced to see our booms dropping into the sulfur. *No!* I thought, knowing they were essential for guiding the heavy augers. "Do you have eyes on the six clean locations!?"

My team was silent.

"Answer me!"

"It's difficult to tell," Alexander responded.

I was tempted to turn around and search myself, but the kicked up dust cloud made visibility almost zero.

The cloud ceased, and I faced a sea of skiffs clustered at basecamp's airlock with dozens of clones stumbling about. I came to a hard reverse-thrust stop and shut down the skiff. When our feet met the ground, it felt like a rug was pulled from beneath us. My teeth chattered and my vision blurred, and when I looked up I saw that Europa was now shrinking towards Io's opposing horizon. The tremors reduced. I was able to stand again. Several minutes later, the tremors subsided altogether.

Heavy breathing came through the public line.

"Anyone injured?" I eventually asked.

They were facing the horizon, watching Europa descend.

"I'm taking your silence as *no,*" I said.

"I thought you weren't supposed to feel the tidal forces," one said.

"You're not," said another.

"Well, that theory is shot to shit," said a third.

"Will this happen every time?"

I sighed deeply, knowing Io was in a one to two orbital resonance with Europa, and a one to four resonance with Ganymede. "Let's assume so."

"How does this effect the mission?"

"We must time our work with a two Ionian day and make sure we secure all equipment before we pass Europa again."

"What about Ganymede's resonance?"

"We'll have to wait and see how debilitating it is," I answered.

We entered basecamp to find equipment and foodstuffs scattered about. Without words, we began cleaning and repairing.

♦

"It's buried fifteen meters down," Mulan responded. "We'll have to dig out the area around it to begin excavation. That'll take half a day."

"We have all day tomorrow before we synchronize with Europa again," I responded. "Just excavate as much as you can in that time."

"Got it," she responded. "What's your progress?"

"We still need to finish the initial bore to see if our sulfur is clean," I said. "But it appears like it becomes cleaner in proximity to the caldera."

"Greater the risk, greater the reward," Alexander quipped. He leaned over the edge of the skiff and lowered his impact hammer's head to the soft, yellow ground.

"What are you doing?" Patatas asked.

"I was almost sucked under last time. Not taking any chances."

The hammer's head pressed the granules. Alexander released more weight until the entire hammer was resting. "Hammer is twice our body weight, I think we're good."

I timidly stepped upon the resurfaced land, half expecting violent tremors. I moved my feet side to side, kicking up little puffs of sulfur.

"It's like dust," Spaghetti said.

"It should be easy to clear, then," Trieu responded.

We each took a plow blade from the back of the skiff, and began clearing off the dust, but it was falling back into the holes. After an hour, I knew it was futile.

"Mulan, we're having trouble digging. How are things going on your end?" I called to her.

"Same, Uly," she responded.

"Uh… guys," Captain of team 83, a clone named C8434, said. "You might want to analyze the dust."

I knelt and scooped a bit in my hand, letting my glove analyze.

"Sulfur 4," appeared on visor.

"It's only been mildly irradiated," I said.

"This layer was fifty meters down yesterday," Patatas added.

"It seems like Europa's gravity pulled it through the cracks in the upper crust," C8 responded.

"Meaning?"

"Maybe we don't excavate down to 2K," he said. "We can do a hundred excavations at only fifty meters deep, and Swiss cheese the whole area south of the caldera."

"Why?"

"When Europa passes again, it might encourage the deeper layers to sift up to the surface, like a tidal conveyor."

I grinned. "Check the math! All of you! If we can turn Europa into an ally, we must take advantage of it!"

"Yes, sir!" they responded.

My teammates raised fingers to their visors, running the numbers, and I saw Mulan's team a few hundred meters off doing the same.

Then, I ran the numbers, too.

It should work... I knew as my math came to fruition. "I'm estimating we'll need a few dozen Europa and Ganymede synchronizations to convey the lowest levels of sulfur."

"Same," they each confirmed.

"What will the Ganymedans think?" Spaghetti asked.

"It's their thinking that got us in this mess," Alexander snipped.

"So, what, then?" Mulan responded.

I grinned. "We ask for forgiveness later."

♦

A hundred teams aligned at the caldera's southern face with heavy augers ready, spaced ten meters apart. Commander Zodiac screamed into my helmet, the noise maddening. So, I left C8 in charge of this operation, much to his surprise. Augers wound up, and when they hit the loose sulfur, we were engulfed.

Commander Zodiac's face comically contorted on visor as she screamed. I grinned back, knowing there was not a thing she could do to stop us. *Or so I thought.* A screeching struck my ears. *Coming across the public line!* Commander Zodiac was no longer shouting, but standing motionless on visor with her arms crossed, watching me squirm.

"Use attached! -K6297-" appeared as text in the corner of my visor.

When I dashed *Load,* all sound cut.

Texts scrolled down my visor's edge.

"Woooo!"

"Hell yeah!"

"Well done, K6297!"

A back channel, I realized and that the Ganymedans could not see it.

Commander Zodiac was still staring at me with her arms crossed. *She doesn't know...* I winced, pretending the screeching was still unbearable, letting my teams work as long as possible uninhibited.

After an hour, the commander's mouth moved. I made out her words, saying, *"Turned it off ten minutez ago."*

"Commander," I responded, assuming my mic was still on. "We're doing things differently whether you like it or not. Can you trust me?"

"No," I read from her lips.

"Too bad." I minimized her screen and joined my team.

We hit ten meters by midday, and when it was time to disassemble the drills and head back to basecamp, most of us passed twenty.

A good start, I thought.

♦

A stir woke us in the middle of the night as Ganymede made its pass. I laid in my bunk, holding my breath and gripping the side rails so hard I felt the metal crimp. When it subsided, I heard a collective sigh of relief.

Not that bad...

We raced to our locations the following morning to find the surface only mildly disturbed. The augers were erected and we went back to work, drilling deeper as ejected sulfur was cleared away by a train of clones pushing dozer blades like construction equipment.

Because we are construction equipment.

That afternoon, Commander Zodiac appeared on my visor. I was about to reactivate the silencer program, but she did not look angry.

"You intend to keep at thiz?" she said.

"I do," I responded.

"It doezn't matter how many of theze zhallow holez you make, they will be erazed with Europa'z pazz tonight."

"That's the idea."

She placed her hands on her hips. "If you focuz on the few corez you found with clean zulfur you can ztart pulling it to the zurface."

"It won't establish a continuous supply."

"And how will drilling a few hundred little onez achieve thiz?"

"You'll see," I responded.

Commander Zodiac's face grew red. "Ganymeda'z livelihood, your livelihood reztz upon thiz mizzion!"

"Which is exactly why I'm doing it my way," I said.

She cut the feed.

I hope to Sol our calculations are correct, I thought.

◆

Io synchronized with Europa again, but we made certain no equipment was in the field and basecamp was secured. We closed our eyes, covered our ears, and curled to the floor hoping to find relief from its ruthlessness. Several minutes later, the tremors dissipated and I knew we were in the clear.

"Remember your locations! Remember the calculations! There's no going back now!" I typed on visor as we raced to our excavation holes.

As we neared the caldera I saw our holes had been erased. *But the landscape is a lighter shade of yellow.* We arrived at our location. Patatas hopped down first, running the soft sulfur sand through her gloves.

"Sulfur 16! That's supposed to be eighty meters deep!" she typed.

Each team confirmed the same. I looked across the landscape, completely covered in newly dredged sulfur.

"Today, we plow!" I typed. *"Tomorrow we re-drill the same holes!"*

"Yes, sir," came scrolling across my visor.

We returned to basecamp with our legs and arms shaking, and were out again in the morning with aching muscles.

A third Europa sync came. Then a fourth, a fifth, and a sixth.

Commander Zodiac's calls grew more threatening and frantic as she realized I truly intended to stay the course. And every time I thought she might remotely cut our heating systems, plunging us into hibernation, like they had done so many times, she never did.

Because they have no choice...

◆

Two months passed. We were on sync thirty-one with Europa and we were exhausted. But as we came to the caldera, I saw the sulfur was greenish-yellow. We hovered above our excavation locations, scared to touch this new color. Patatas eventually scooped a handful. Her shoulders started shaking.

"Is everything okay?" I typed.

When she turned I saw tears in her eyes. She raised a hand to her visor and typed, *"We did it!"*

Similar readings streamed in from the other teams.

I looked across the caldera, the greenish-yellow sulfur spanning nearly two thousand square kilometers. *"Check depths!"* I typed.

Readings again scrolled across my visor, putting my elephant brain to the test as I calculated average depth in real time. *Eleven meters...*

I opened a feed to LKAB Station. "X0471 to Commander Zodiac."

No response.

"X0471 to Comm—"

"What the fuck do you want!?" came the commander's voice and a dark video feed opened.

Middle of the night for her, I realized.

"Well!?" she said, wiping the sleep from her eyes. "You better be giving me your rezignation!"

I grinned. "Send the goddamn collection freighters."

She pursed her lips and squinted. "You found Zulfur?"

I nodded and watched the wheels turning in her head.

"How many zhould I zend?" she grumbled.

"All of them," I responded.

She scoffed. "There'z no pozzible way you can fill all twelve."

"We only have twelve!?"

She studied me hard. "Exactly how many do you think we need?"

I ran the calculation. "Four-thousand, three-hundred, and ninety-two!"

♦

"Tapas, wake-up," came a whisper next to my bunk.

I opened my eyes to Spaghetti's blurry silhouette. "What happened?"

"Commander Zodiac is requesting you."

Why didn't she just call me? "Can it wait?"

"She doesn't want to stay long."

I lurched up almost knocking my head on the bunk above. "She's here!?"

"Her squad landed ten minutes ago."

We had found more sulfur than they could dream of and a steady stream of collectors was already delivering it to Ganymede. *What could we have done wrong?* "Okay… Tell her I'll be there in five minutes?"

Spaghetti nodded and was off.

I looked at my two uniforms, one yet to be washed, the other clean but still hosting magnificent sweat stains around its collar, armpits, and groin. *Who am I trying to impress?* I donned the clean uniform, socks, and a pair of basecamp moccasins. I passed from one drop-ship compartment to another, making my way to one designated as Command Center. Five Ganymedan mech units faced Spaghetti. *But he's smiling,* I noted.

He saw my approach and pointed my way.

The mech units turned to reveal the little soldiers within. It took me a moment to recognize the central one as Commander Zodiac. She was smiling, too, and it felt strange.

"X0471, I'll cut to the chaze," she said. "You've been invited to dine with Governor Terrence."

"Uh…" responded.

The commander grinned. "I had the zame rezponze when I woke to find him at my airlock thiz morning."

"The governor wants to meet me?" I asked.

"He certainly doez. Zuit up. We leave immediately."

I stood frozen, stunned.

"We don't have all day!" she snapped.

I sifted through envisuits, finding mine still covered in yellow sulfur. I slipped it on, feeling like a honeybee covered in pollen. *I should be proud of this,* I told myself, but I felt ashamed to be caught unprepared. *That's the point of the governor coming unannounced...*

The ride up in Commander Zodiac's shuttle was far smoother than the ride down in the drop-ships, the shuttle easily detecting and navigating Io's plumes. *They gave us their old, dilapidated equipment for this operation,* I realized. *Expendable equipment for expendable people.* I glanced at the soldiers in mech units. *Clunky, slow. Are they strong enough to hold me?*

"Commander Zodiac, welcome back," chimed LKAB Station's dock master. "Governor Terrence and hiz wife are waiting for you in bay two."

"Roger that," she responded, and turned to me. "Do you underztand the importance of thiz meeting?"

I gave her a look. "Future of Ganymede, future of your career. I understand what this is."

"And the future of your people," she added, giving me a glare.

The shuttle slid into its bay alongside an elegant yacht. The airlock whined and deadbolts knocked. Then, the door slipped open revealing the governor and his wife dressed in elegant layers, like royalty from a bygone era. Frills and buckles. Buttons and ties. Tunics, tights, and clumsy dresses. My eyes locked onto a holster at the governor's hip. I remembered Governor Terrence's great, great grandfather from the feldspar days. He was a simple man, a smart man, efficiently dressed, and armed only with his mind. I respected that man despite his contribution to our suffrage. *So, what changed?*

"Welcome back, my good commander," the governor said with a strange, fabricated accent, not quite the Ganymedan accent I knew. "I azzume your mizzion waz a great zuccezz."

"Yez, zir. We brought the man you zeek," Commander Zodiac responded and stepped through the airlock followed by her soldiers.

"Oh dear, iz zuch an entourage necezzary for one man?" The governor said with a smile. When he saw me come last in my black envisuit powdered yellow, ducking and turning my shoulders to fit through the hatch, his smile melted. His eyes followed me as I stood tall, my helmet almost scraping the ceiling. He snapped out of his awe. "You muzt be X0471, the one I've heard zo much about."

I stood silent, trying to gauge this governor.

"Pleaze, releaze your helmet, I wizh to zee the great man beneath."

I slowly raised my paw and unclasped my helmet, letting it roll back.

"My goodnezz… You appear zo young."

I studied the governor's slight wrinkles and wisps of gray hair, and placed him around fifty years of age.

"Pleaze… Zpeak," he urged.

"Woof…" I responded.

The blood drained from Commander Zodiac's face. "I'm zorry govern—"

The governor sharply raised a hand. "No apology needed, commander. If he wizhez to be treated like a dog, then I zhall oblige." The governor pointed at the floor. "Come, boy."

My ears flushed with heat, I felt the urge to strike. *But this only reinforces their assumptions…* Instead, I recalled my language training. "I apologize…" I said in old English. "…When you have lived in the dirt…" I continued in old Spanish. "…You tend to lose oneself…" I followed up in guttural Hermian. "…I am a man…" I said in Ceran. "…Not a dog…" in InterSpeak. "…And I wizh to be treated az zuch," I finished, matching the governor's accent.

The governor nodded. "Zhall we, then?" he responded, his pointed finger becoming a gracious wave towards his yacht.

I nodded and ducked through another airlock hatch into the elegant yacht, glancing back to see only the governor and his wife following. The governor sealed the hatch and turned to me.

"Whizkey, gin, tequila? Pick your poizon," he said, motioning to several bottles of liquid next to plush chairs.

I studied the bottles. "Do you have dihydrogen monoxide?"

The governor's wife gave a short laugh and held her stomach, which I realized was swollen beneath thick layers of fabric. *Must be eight months along.*

The governor shot her a confused look.

"Dear huzband, our guezt iz azking for water," she said, elegantly walking to a plush chair and sitting.

The governor's face brightened when he made the connection. "But of courze! Pleaze, have a zeat!"

I looked at my filthy envisuit.

"Do not fret, we'll burn the chair," he said.

I sat, feeling my butt smush deep into the chair's cushion and watching its white fabric stain yellow.

The governor glanced down the hallway. He sighed and gave a sharp clap. A few more seconds passed. He grimaced. "Good help iz impozzible to find. Excuze me." The governor disappeared down the hall.

It was silent. I studied the elegant room with its furnishings and paintings. *Where did all this money come from?* My eyes found the governor's wife looking at me, but she did not make an effort to converse.

"I apologize for my behavior before. I've been through a lot," I said.

She tilted her head.

I studied her perfectly manicured hands resting upon her swollen belly. "Congratulations… Do you know the gender?"

"Yez," she said shortly.

"…Boy or—"

"Uly… It's me," she suddenly said, her accent dropping.

What? I studied her features, searching for familiarity, but could not find anything definitive. *But who else could it be!?* I took a deep breath. "J-Joa… Gen—"

"Astrid," she responded.

"Astrid," I repeated. "Does the governor know?"

She shook her head.

I studied her stomach. "How are you faking the pregnancy?"

"Make way for Queen Chase!" announced from down the hallway and the governor appeared with a toddler upon his shoulders.

When the toddler saw me, she pointed and smiled.

"You cry at your grandparentz, but for him you zmile?" Astrid said, putting the accent back on.

"Mumumum," the toddler said and stretched arms to my sister.

She's not faking… I realized.

"Dinner will be zerved in a moment'z notice," the governor said, flying his daughter to her mother like a ship. "And then, we zhall have that round of dihydrogen monoxide."

"Thank you, Governor," I responded.

"Have you taken a moment to converze with my dear wife?" he asked.

"Just a few pleasantries," I responded.

"Well, I'm certain there will be many queztionz during dinner, for my dear wife wrote her theziz on your kind. Quite fazcinating, really. Although, I muzt admit I waz equally fazcinated in making her my governezz."

I thought about that. "Is that how you know of me?"

"Certainly iz," he said. "In fact, my dear wife'z analyziz of Ganymede'z mining phaze revealed an interezting phenomenon."

A thin man in sharp, black attire appeared from the hall with hands clasped. "Ladiez and gentlemen, dinner iz zerved."

I stood and glanced back at the chair to find a monstrous yellow impression.

"Perhapz we leave the envizuit here, after all," the governor said.

I stripped it off, revealing my permanently stained uniform beneath. The governor's expression did not improve.

The hall was short, adjoining a few modest rooms. The dining room, in contrast, opened with such grandeur that I felt like I was inside a building rather than a spacecraft. A wooden table, old and gnarled, blackened with age, rested at its center with enough chairs to host fifty people, but only a few places at the end were set.

Three servants appeared in the same black garb. They pulled chairs and waited for Governor Terrence, my sister, and I to take our places, then pushed them in as we sat. A highchair was brought out for Chasc.

The governor sharply raised his hand. "A toazt!"

A servant poured water into our glasses.

The governor grinned and raised his glass high. "To the next chapter."

Astrid raised her glass, then I did mine.

"To the next chapter," we echoed.

I took a savage gulp, ready to be quenched, but fire hit my throat, instead. I sputtered and searched for a place to spit it out, finding no other container or napkin. *No choice...* I spit it into my uniform's fabric.

"Oh dear, what iz the matter?" said the governor.

I stared at him, trying to understand if he was trying to poison me.

"Dear huzband..." my sister said. "He iz from a different time. He haz not zet foot on Ganymede in a century. He doez not know about the drink."

The governor shot me a mortified look. "I deeply apologize, I did not realize you actually wanted water." He snapped his fingers and a servant approached. "Water!"

"But… zir," the servant said pointing at the glasses.

"Water water," the governor said and waved him off. "It'z impossible to find good help theze dayz!"

"What is this?" I asked, pointing at the glass.

"It'z a drink developed by your dezcendantz," Astrid responded. "A form of moonzhine they call water."

"I thought for certain thiz waz your reference," added the governor.

"Do the other clone workforces drink this?" I prodded.

The governor gave a hard look. "The other clone forcez were called into final action decades ago, to combat the great famine at the end of my father'z governance. But, unlike the other governorz, my father had the forezight to ztore you and your crew for another day." He turned to my sister. "And when I met my dearezt wife zhe told me zomething quite interezting about you."

I soaked it in, feeling terrible dread as the memory of Liu Bei, ancient and broken, resurfaced. "Which is what?" I begrudgingly asked.

"That you actually won that early mining phaze."

I shook my head. "Zodiac won," I grumbled.

The governor chuckled. "Zure, he collected the mozt rezourcez, but my dear wife dizcovered a ztrange dizcrepancy. There waz not nearly enough time to collect the amount he did. The math zimply doez not add up."

"That's because he attacked other crews and stole their resources," I said.

The governor clasped his hands together. "Did you hear that, dear wife!? Your hypotheziz waz correct!"

Of course it was… I thought.

"Which meanz you are the true winner," he said.

"I don't understand," I said. "My crew was in forty-third place when the phase concluded."

He smirked. "Regarding totalz, you are correct. But there are a multitude of other factorz one muzt conzider."

"Such as?"

"Injury, death, rezource intake verzuz output, time, and mozt importantly, accuracy." The governor had a twinkle in his eye. "When placing all theze factorz into the equation, developed by my dear wife, your crew waz the clear winner. Which iz no doubt why my father fought zo hard to purchaze your original crew from the other governorz…"

I stared back not knowing what to say.

"…Now, with Ganymede'z zoil zhowing zignz of degradation, my workforce iz the only one left to correct the problem," the governor said, waving his hand at me. "And my Zol did you deliver…"

Servants entered with platters, hosting several small plates. When they removed their tops, I saw croquettes, grilled octopus, patatas bravas, and many more.

"Tapas," I muttered and looked at my sister, who shook her head slightly.

"A phenomenal guezz! How do you know!?" asked the governor.

"I had it once long ago," I said. "How do you have these?"

The governor grinned. "They're my dear wife'z recipez, pazzed down from her mother. I hope you enjoy them."

Beverly's recipes…

The governor stood. "I muzt be going. Work beckonz." He kissed his daughter on the forehead, then turned to my sister. "Make zure you don't talk hiz earz off, dear wife."

"I'll be careful, huzband," she said, smiling sweetly, performing her part.

The moment he left, the servant's demeanor changed, they gave several quick hand signals and disappeared into doors hidden in the walls. Astrid reached beneath her extravagant dress, pulled a sphere from its folds, and set it upon the table. All sound disappeared.

"Finally," she said.

I looked at the toddler. "What about Chase?"

"She's fourteen months, she won't snitch," Astrid said, parting her daughter's hair with her fingers as she fumbled with her little spoon.

"Bring me up to speed," I said.

Astrid sighed. "That would take too long."

I raised my hands in protest.

She reached into her complicated dress again. "Everything you need to know is here." She placed a holotile next to the audio sphere.

"Okay," I responded, taking the tile. "But how did all this happen? Where did this money come from?"

"From Venus, mostly."

"Venus?"

"Their greenhouses have become like small island kingdoms with little obligation to the rest of System Sol."

"How can they be allowed to exist, then?"

"Because of their investments," Astrid responded. "You don't bite the hand that feeds you."

"But Ganymede is supposed to be feeding *them*."

"Plans change."

"Not that much," I retorted.

Astrid sat back and frowned. "Time and progress are strange phenomenon, for they happen in abrupt steps and cannot be predicted. There can be a thousand years with little occurrence followed by ten years of profound change. And in that change we might turn left when the universe believed we'd turn right. And within great progress can be tremendous regression."

"Is that why you're acting like a renaissance wife?"

"That's the least of it. Ganymede has become feudal, just like Venus." She looks down. "But unlike Venus, it is not a paradise… Rather, it's not a paradise for some."

I clenched my jaw. "And you chose the side of luxury."

She glared at me. "I watched helplessly as you were worked to death. And then, I watched helplessly as your children and grandchildren were worked to death. Then, came the disease. One that only effects you."

"Kaladian?" I whispered.

Astrid nodded. "Even during the height of The War, equalizers were a rarity, a last resort when things went wrong in the battlefield. For the life of an equalizer, although great, does not last long. I witnessed the degradation in the fields. Watched as suddenly, like a switch was turned on, your bodies gave out and your minds scattered."

"How long does my crew have?"

She shrugged. "It is not an exact affliction. It could be tomorrow or a hundred years."

"So what now?" I prodded. "Is father's great revolution extinguished before it even started?"

"It's changed."

"How?"

She took a deep breath. "Your descendants have it, too…"

"That's impossible. Our modifications cannot be passed on."

"It appears the ramifications can…"

I processed. "…Do the Ganymedans know?"

"They know, but don't understand. And now with the workforce becoming mixed with brothel bastards fathered by the governors, the disease is less obvious, appearing like a cold at first."

"So, a wasting death is our great legacy?" I said.

"There is still a chance," she said. "Beverly and I have been developing a cure, but…"

"But what?"

"Ganymedans have a unique naming structure, one devised to manage genetic strength after The Fall. Unlike the rest of System Sol, they actually know their ancestry. Which provides us with a rare opportunity."

I looked at her daughter. "What have you done?"

My sister's look hardened. "Only what I must, Uly. And it's working. Although, slowly. I've seen how my DNA interacts with the Ganymedan's."

I glared at her. "How many children do you have? Who are they?"

She breathed deeply. "It's better you don't know that."

I grimaced. "So, what's the cure?"

She pursed her lips. "I can't tell you that, either."

"Why the fuck not!?" I snapped.

Chase started crying and Joan leaned over to brush her hair again.

"Because I don't know myself," she shot back. "All I can say, is that one day there will be someone with the genetics to save our people. That is when your part begins."

"What? How?"

"It's in the holotile." She quickly pulled the audiosphere off the table.

Servants entered moments later to tend to Chase's crying.

"X0471, thank you for joining uz for dinner," she said, sliding back into her role. "My great huzband wishez to meet with you again in the morning. And pleaze, drezz appropriately thiz time."

◆

Governor Terrence gifted me a room in their yacht for the night, but the ceiling was cramped, the toilet was tiny, and the bed was short. *Designed for Ganymedan physiology.* And although it exuded extravagance, it felt like another cage. Clothing laid across the bed, so large and textured, I initially thought it was the covers, until I made out flared cuffs and collars, and shiny metal buttons.

I removed my mining uniform and magsuit, and my feet drifted from the steel floor. I glided to the steam stall and set it to max, letting it peel years of filth from my body, watching the steam turn black and suck into drainage diffusers. Literal weight melted off. *And the heat.* I waited until my fingers wrinkled before turning off the steam and floated, curled in fetal, imagining I was a child again in hibernation upon Mercury, and that none of this had happened. The steam became chill and I knew it was time to live my nightmare again.

I placed the extravagant clothing into the closet, where I found undergarments for my stature. I felt like a different person, a privileged person, as if the years of indentured servitude did not exist. I sighed deeply, looking at all the comforts of the room, until my eyes set upon the holotile my sister had given me.

"Time to catch up…" I whispered.

The holotile analyzed my face, then projected a shriveled, old woman in its hologram.

Ummm, I thought until the old woman smiled.

"Tapas, my brightest student," she said. "I am sorry for everything that has happened. I did not know you'd be locked away, for I was not privy to that information. And when I finally learned the true nature of the plan, I was powerless to stop it."

Beverly… I realized.

She looked up for a moment. "Where to start? At this moment of recording, it's 2782, which means you've been in and out of hibernation for over four centuries already. Ganymede has not become what we imagined. The terraforming effort was twisted by outside investors. But what I tell you now, is of the utmost importance, for not even Joan knows."

I leaned closer.

She breathed deeply. "I was born on Earth, not by Terrans, but to ronin hellbent on finding information to save our people from the same ailment that afflicts yours. My grandmother was the worst of them, an old general named Kase. She was set on finishing what The Director started long ago at the expense of both our people and the Terrans. When she died, there was a fracturing of power among the ronin and my mother and I had no choice but to integrate with Terran scientists heading to South America in search of salvation. Mother died shortly after, but not after telling me about a man named Khasi Sinam, known as The Butcher of Earth, who stole Earth's most valuable possession, a hard drive called The Terran Files, containing every dirty secret, every achievement. A complete compilation of humanity's history until The Fall. And with it, the research to cure Kaladian Degradation Disease…"

"Khasi Sinam. The Terran Files," I whispered, locking it into my memory forever.

"…Joan is doing great work with Ganymedan genes, creating a person whose DNA could become the cure to your people's plight. But without this research to guide us, that DNA is useless…" She shook her head. "…I don't know how, Ulysses, but you must find The Terran Files. Khasi is the key, but he was locked in hibernation, much like you were, then forgotten..."

I stared at Beverly's ancient face, feeling the first tinges of hope in my life seeping in.

"...I believe in you," she said. "And I believe in Joan. You are opposing sides of the same coin. Heroes in a universe of corruption." She lets out a long breath. "Good luck, Ulysses."

◆

I studied Io from Governor Terrence's dining room window, searching for the cluster of drop-ships we called basecamp, but only yellow and orange sulfur, with pocks of black, were visible. A steady stream of collection barges, ascending and descending from orbit to the edge of Zamama's caldera, was the only evidence of my crew's existence.

"X0471," said the governor, entering the dining room. He gave a quick study of my attire and smiled. "You're a great lord today."

"Thank you, sir," I responded, but wanted nothing more than to tear off this floofiness. *But I must find Khasi...*

"I hope you underztand how great of an importance today iz."

I gave him a look. "I know nothing."

"Ah. Well, the mozt influential men and women of Ganymede have arrived in the dead of night becauze of you."

What the hell? "I don't understand."

The governor grinned. "I think you're brighter than you let on."

"You give me too much credit," I carefully said, knowing there was a purpose to keeping me guessing.

He frowned. "Ganymede'z complete governance, reprezentativez from the Council of Coloniez, and a few unmentionablez are here to review my zulfur operation." He hesitated. "These unmentionablez are the reazon Ganymede exiztz. Bezt be on your guard."

"Understood," I said.

"X0..." he paused. "Zhould I give you a real name?"

"I have a real name," I responded.

His eyes widened. "Really? Do tell."

I clenched my jaw. "...Ulysses."

The governor brightened. "From antiquity? That iz perfection!" He set a hand on my shoulder. "Zhall we, then, Ulyzzez?"

He led from his yacht to the station's docking bay where several more extravagant vessels now resided. We passed a Command Center where I saw

Commander Zodiac deep in discussion. *But with who?* I tried focusing my hearing, but could only hear a mixture of laughter and hoots, ahead.

"It zeemz we're late," Governor Terrence said.

At the end of the corridor were open doors to a large conference room hosting lavishly dressed people. Governor Terrence entered to a turning of heads and a raising of glasses.

"It'z about time, governor," one said with a slimy smile. "Now, why have you called uz here?" His eyes shifted to me as I entered, ducking my head below the doorway's frame.

"Governorz," Governor Terrence said, "reprezentativez…"

I noted the three representatives were dressed in simple white cloth, looking almost like clergy.

"…And family headz," Governor Terrence added.

Family heads?

"…May I introduce to you, my great colleague, Ulyzzez..." the governor paused and turned to me.

"…Williams," I muttered, using my father's last name.

He snapped back to his guests. "Ulyzzez Williamz, foreman of my great venture here on Io."

"You mean your ill-fated venture," said the slimy character.

Governor Terrence smiled. "Ah, Don Zeraden, zkeptical az ever. I azzure you there iz nothing ill about thiz. In fact, I believe I have found the cure to all of our problemz… And it'z all thankz to Ulyzzez and hiz crew, who dredged clean zulfur from itz depthz."

The guests grew excited, all except for Don Seraden. His eyes were on me now, but he didn't hold surprise or fear. "You're juzt a clone," he said with a complete disregard for manners. "We've dealt with your kind before. You have neither the intelligence nor the zkill to achieve zuch a feat."

I felt my anger rise. I opened my mouth to respond, but the governor simply laughed.

"Zee for yourzelf, Don Zeraden," he said and moved to the far wall. He flipped a switch and the wall parted, revealing Io's yellow surface below. A hologram superimposed upon the window, highlighting a train of collection barges rising and falling from Zamama's caldera. It continued highlighting different aspects of our operation, like an advertisement.

But this is live, I knew, judging from the sulfur deposits.

My crew appeared on hologram working diligently to move sulfur into collector ships.

"My goodnezz," said a governor. "How did you get zo much?"

Governor Terrence looked at me.

"Instead of drilling to the sulfur," I said, watching eyes turn my way. "We weakened the southern face of the caldera so that when Io synchronizes with Europa and Ganymede, at peak orbital eccentricity, their tidal forces dredge softer under-layers of sulfur to the surface. It took only thirty-one minor quakes for Sulfur 2 to finally appear."

They were silent, their faces blank.

They have no clue what I'm talking about, I realized.

"How much iz there?" one finally asked.

"When I left, over thirty million cubic meters were on the surface." I heard several gasps. "But with each new quake, more is still being dredged."

"My Zol!" said another.

"Do you have proof it'z in the correct ztate?" Don Seraden asked, vigilant in his skepticism.

"Why certainly," Governor Terrence said and produced a vial filled with greenish-yellow dust from the folds of his sleeve.

The don peered through the vial's glass as if he could determine by sight alone. Then, he opened his holotile and dusted a small amount onto its sensor. All held their breaths as the holotile ran its analysis.

"Sulfur 2, 98.3% purity," appeared on hologram.

His face melted. "It'z real…"

Governor Terrence smiled. "Zo, you zee the importance of today'z meeting, Don Zeradan."

He reluctantly nodded.

"…And my dear governorz, you muzt recognize the great achievement of Ulyzzez. Recognize that he iz one of the few who firzt zet foot on Ganymede and built the great foundation beneath itz vazt fieldz. It waz he who zeeded the firzt zoil. He who created our air. And now, it iz he who comez to zave our cropz from certain dizazter." He paused. "Governor Veranda, what zay you?"

She eyed me. "Aye."

Governor Terrence moved to each governor, asking the same question.

They're voting? I realized. *But for what?*

They slowly turned to the shadows, parting to reveal an old, decrepit man slumped in a hover-chair with skin like melted cheese over his massive skeletal frame. His eyes were barely open, gazing at nothing. Drool oozed from his mouth. A servant quickly wiped it away. Only a few wisps of hair remained on his spotted skull. And an old, peeling scar ran across his face.

My adrenaline surged.

"Governor Zodiac," said Governor Terrence. "What zay you?"

Nothing registered in the old monster's eyes.

"Well, what did we expect?" Terrence quipped to a round of laughter.

I abruptly strutted towards Zodiac, causing the governors, representatives, and family heads to jolt. His servants quickly backed away. I stopped at his chair and knelt to his level.

"Time took care of you," I whispered, using every ounce of self control to not snap his now spindly neck.

The old monster's eyes shifted, looking right at me, and he grinned. Guttural sounds spewed from his mouth. His gnarled hands gripped the arms of his hover-chair, enough to creak the metal despite his frailty. His legs shifted. He planted feet on the floor. His servants looked nervous as his head tilted forward and his balance set upon his legs. I saw tubes protruding from his back to mechanisms built into the chair. He began to rise, his legs quivering. I stood up, giving him something to aim for. He reached the limits of his tubing, and almost fell back into his chair. But then, he gritted his yellow teeth and tubes popped out of his back.

The governors backpedaled as he eclipsed them in height.

They've forgotten who he is, I knew, watching the monster rise.

Zodiac reached my height, and with all his strength, he tried to go beyond. But his degraded spine would not allow it. A servant came to his aid, but the monster pushed their chest, tumbling them to the floor. Zodiac opened his mouth. He grunted, coughed, and wheezed. Then, he flexed his jaw. "Ul…y…sses," he mumbled. "You… cunt…"

I stared into his geriatric eyes, seeing a fire still raging inside his failing body. *His prison…*

"…Now… you… will… see…" he whispered.

Sirens wailed. Zodiac's eyes went blank and he crumbled back into his chair. His servants quickly ushered him from the room.

A silence hung in the air, and when I turned, I found all eyes on me.

"It'z zettled," Governor Terrence said, breaking the silence. "We, the governorz of Ganymede, herby deem thiz contract, fulfilled." He opened a hologram with the words we first spoke to Commander Meeks.

Our contract? I stared in disbelief as Governor Terrence signed his name.

"You are now a citizen of Ganymede, Ulyzzez," he quietly said.

I stood frozen, for never had I thought the Ganymedans would actually keep their promise.

"Ulyzzez," the governor said. "Would you like to zee what you created?"

I slowly turned to him, not knowing what to say.

The governor grinned. "I'll take that az a *yez.*"

◆

Fields stretched to the horizon in every direction, growing thousands of different crops. And within the crops I saw openings that shimmered. *The wells,* I knew, recalling our excavations to reach the ocean below and their monstrous up-rushing of seawater. Their tranquility now was such a stark contrast that I wondered if this was all a dream.

"Ulyzzez," Governor Terrence said as we stood together in his yacht's observation deck. "Bazk in your accomplizhment." He patted my shoulder and left me in solitude.

Workers hustled about the well below, looking like ants operating toy cranes, pulling net balls from the water and dropping them into sorting trays. *Our descendants,* I knew and that they were becoming their own people, for among the sea of gingers, I saw a mixture of ethnicity. *The governors' bastards...*

"Brothels," I whispered.

"Would you like to vizit them," said a gentle voice.

I jumped, and turned to find a middle-aged woman in black servant clothing, standing diligently in the shadows. "I thought I was alone."

"You are alone, my lord," she responded. "Pleaze, conzider me nothing more than furniture."

"I am no lord," I said.

The servant looked at my attire. "Yez, my lord."

I studied this woman, picking out familiar features – reddish hair like myself, but a darker complexion, like Governor Terrence. "You're one of them, aren't you?"

"A zervant, yez."

"I mean, one of the governor's bastards."

She cocked her head. "No, zir. My father died before I waz born."

I retrieved an image of the governor from my photographic memory, overlaying his features upon this servant. There was no argument to be had. *She does not know.* "I apologize. It was not right of me to judge."

"No apology needed. It iz my duty to be judged, if that iz your dezire," she bowed deeply. "Would you like to zee the brothelz?"

"No, thank you," I said and looked at the fishing wells. "Would it be possible to see them work up close?"

"My lord, it iz you who decidez zuch thingz."

"How is it my decision?" I asked. "Wouldn't it be whoever owns this land."

"That is correct," the servant said.

"But…" It hit me with such horror, such terror. "…I'm a governor?"

"Not quite, my lord. But that iz the intention. You have been temporarily gifted a portion of Governor Zodiac's territory to prove your mettle."

What the fuck!? I thought, but I knew if there was any chance of finding Khasi and The Terran Files, if there was any chance of saving my people, that I must play along. "In that case, I must inspect the wells. I must learn the industry I am to govern."

The servant eagerly bowed. "Abzolutely, my lord. Pleaze, follow me to your zhuttle."

We dropped to the surface, landing along the edge of a well. And, when the hatch opened its familiar chill flooded me with memories.

Their foreman scurried over, gave my attire a glance, and soaked in my immensity. "Welcome… Can I azk what the vizit iz for?"

"Mannerz!" snapped my servant. "Addrezz your new mazter az Lord Williamz!"

The foreman gave the servant a look that could kill.

They're the same, but different, I understood.

"It's all right," I said, and my servant bowed. I faced the young foreman. "I'm here for observation only. Please, go about your business as usual. I wish to learn."

The foreman seemed taken aback but nodded. "Az you want… My lord." He hustled back to his crew as another netball dropped into the sorter.

I inspected twelve fishing wells that afternoon and learned what I could about their processes, but I could not shake the feeling that they were staged. I eyed my servant piloting the shuttle as we zoomed into the setting sun.

"Where are we heading?" I asked.

"To your accommodationz, my lord," she responded.

"I'm not staying with Governor Terrence?"

"You have your own manor, my lord."

"You've got to be joking."

"My lord, humor iz not a part of my zervice. Unlezz you wizh it to be." She turned to me. "Do you wizh me to be funny?"

I furrowed my brow. "I wish you to be honest."

She nodded. "We zhall arrive within the hour."

I studied her. "How can I trust you?"

"You cannot," she stated. "No more than you can truzt any ztranger. No more than I can truzt you. But you might truzt the zituation."

"Which is?"

"I zerve a houze, not a perzon."

"Zodiac's house."

"And Zodiac iz no more than zkin and bone."

I faced her. "You were there. You saw him stand."

"I zaw him fall," the servant said. "If hiz great houze iz to continue, there muzt be new, reliable leaderzhip."

"What about his children?"

"He cannot bare children, or baztardz for that matter. A problem that haz vexed uz for quite zome time. But now that we have you, I zee light at the end of the tunnel."

"So, I should trust the house..." I said.

"It iz the only thing to truzt," she finished.

We stayed silent as we neared a patch of land rising from the fields dotted with buildings.

"What if you no longer deem me good for the house," I finally said.

"Then, you will be replaced."

"What if I refuse to leave?"

"Then, my lord, I would kill you," she said, matter-of-factly.

Fuck... I thought, understanding that it was the perfect system to ensure compliance. I scanned the horizon, searching for landmarks that might help me orient to this unrecognizable moon. Several ships were rising into orbit in the distance.

"Is that a mining operation?" I asked.

"In a manner of zpeaking," she said. "They're tranzporting zeed to a zeries of banks in the Kuiper Belt to enzure the protection of food zhould another cataclyzmic fall occur."

I caught a glint in the distance reflecting the setting sun and focused. *The strange cylindrical structure...* "And, what's that?" I asked, pointing.

She looked. "I zee nothing, my lord."

"Large metal object, perfectly cylindrical."

"Oh my, you can zee that?"

"I can. What is it?"

"I do not know," she responded, with a crinkling of her chin. "It waz built before I waz born."

"You never thought to ask?"

"I never dared to azk."

"So who might know, then?" I prodded.

"I zuzpect your fellow governorz." She pointed at a walled estate with stables, vineyards, several buildings around a main square leading to a manor at its center. "I apologize, it iz a lezzer eztate but zhould zerve your needz until your zuccezzion."

"Lesser? It's like a small city," I gasped.

She pondered that. "I zuppoze it might appear that way after your confinez."

♦

I toured several other estates and met with governors and family heads alike. Truth be told, I could not tell the difference between them.

"Face and body," my servant simply said when I asked.

"Can you elaborate?"

"Governorz are the face of Ganymede, who work directly with the Council of Coloniez. The Familiez are the body, who enzure production ztayz on track and lawz are enforced."

"So, they're the military," I stated.

"There iz no military on Ganymede. A requirement of the Council of Coloniez."

"Police, then?"

She shook her head. "They are privately owned and operated."

A mercenary force, I realized. "Are they known by this Council?"

"Only by a few reprezentativez, but officially, they do not exizt."

"Isn't that a risk?" I pointedly asked.

"It iz, but mind you, thiz greatnezz before you waz not funded by Council inveztmentz, but by zhadow benefactorz who require prezence while maintaining anonymity."

"So, you don't know who this shadow benefactor is?"

"We know only the Familiez, nothing more."

I must get in close. "How do the dons and governors coordinate?"

"There iz a zoiree happening tomorrow evening. All the donz and governorz will be prezent. Az a governor now, you are required to attend. I imagine many of your queztionz will be anzwered then."

♦

I traversed a dark, winding corridor, feeling the presence of enforcers around me. *Hearing them...* I realized when I focused. It was Don Seraden's party, thus Don Seraden's estate, and when the other guests continued to the grand dining room, I was directed elsewhere, to this corridor. I moved onward, hearing voices ahead. The corridor finally opened to a large table with a hologram displaying Ganymede at its center, borders and color coding across its surface.

"Ah, Ulyzzez, good of you to join," said Don Seraden from across the table. He waved to an open position next to Governor Terrence.

"Thank you," I cautiously said and squeezed in among the governors and dons, again unable to distinguish them.

"We were juzt dizcuzzing Governor Zodiac'z territory," the don said, pointing at a purple zone spanning from Ganymede's equator to North Pole.

Upon the lighter ice, I knew, and that it was where we had drilled the wells over a century ago. Now, it looked simply like a lakes region of old Earth. Within the purple was a tiny area in orange. I squinted to see a small town and several wells within its confines. *My territory.* I searched for Zodiac in his chair among the dons and governors. *He's not here...*

"I azzume you were briefed on the zituation," Don Seraden said.

"I was," I responded.

"Which iz what?" he followed up.

"I am on trial to determine if I am a suitable replacement for Governor Zodiac."

He nodded. "Correct... partially." He waved a hand and the territories changed, looking completely different. "You zee, my territory crozzez into Zodiac'z, zpecifically upon your zmall allocation. Zo, it goez without zaying that you report to me..."

I gave Governor Terrence a sideways look, to find him staring into the hologram as if nothing were strange. I realized that my servant only knew the half of it. *The dons are in charge.* I pondered when and how this transition happened, and if Joan and Beverly knew.

"...I underztand thiz iz all new to you. Are there any burning queztionz?" Don Seraden asked.

There are so many... but... "This territory granted to us, how will it be governed? My crew can integrate with the current workforce, but they will not answer to someone unknown."

Governors and dons chuckled, all except Governor Terrence.

"Am I missing something?" I asked.

"Ulyzzez, you have no crew," Don Seraden said.

"My brothers and sisters on Io, I mean," I responded.

He flashed a wicked smile. "They proved zo uzeful that I decided to purchaze them from Governor Terrence. They have been tranzferred to my holding facility."

What!? I turned to Governor Terrence, but he kept looking into the hologram, pretending he was deep in thought. "But they're Ganymedan citizens now! They fulfilled their contracts!"

The don laughed. "Only you have won your citizenzhip."

Governor Terrence's eyes shot my direction for a fraction of a second.

I ground my jaw, thinking upon the exact wording he had used, how he insinuated plurality, but never said outright that we had all won our citizenship.

The don raised a hand. "You muzt underztand that Ganymedan citizenzhip iz bazed upon DNA, with one opening allotted for each individual. Zince you clonez zhare identical genetics, you are effectively one perzon, and thuz, fill one citizenzhip opening. Congratulationz on being the bezt of your kind."

I felt the presence of cloaked enforcers with rifles trained upon me.

Don Seraden closed the hologram and turned to the others. "That zettlez thiz evening'z conclave. Now, friendz and colleaguez, indulge yourzelvez. We have much to look forward to."

I stared daggers at Don Seraden as the others left the room. I felt a sudden nudge at my ribs.

"Move," came a whisper, and I realized it was Governor Terrence.

I huffed and slowly turned, following the governor from the room through the dark corridor and back into the mansion's main hall. More guests had arrived, each in elegant or shocking attire with holotiles hovering above them recording their every movement.

"Keep forward, don't look back," Governor Terrence whispered.

Just loud enough for my modified ears to hear, I realized. It took every ounce of strength for me not to break his neck. The dining room appeared beyond two massive doors, filled with piano music and couples waltzing at the center. Governor Terrence moved through the crowd to a standing table with two women chatting away in evening dresses. The governor leaned in and kissed one gently. It was my sister. *She had the baby?* I thought. He proceeded to whisper into her ear. She made sharp eye contact with me. The second woman backed off as I approached, her eyes wide and her jaw dropping.

"What the fuck is happening!?" I whispered viciously to them.

"Ulyzzez, you muzt calm," Governor Terrence said.

I made eye contact and watched his posture melt. "You little insect… How dare you deceive me…"

"Uly, stop," my sister said without the accent and Governor Terrence gave her a look. "There are things you do not understand about this world."

"Like what!?" I stepped closer to her.

Governor Terrence finally found his balls and slid between us. "Ulyzzez, I am deeply zorry to have deceived you. But, pleaze, underztand that I muzt protect my family."

I snatched the governor's collar and I lifted him clear off the floor. "As I must protect mine!" I barked, my voice thundering above the chatter and music. I looked at my sister, while the governor thrashed in my hand, and whispered, "Now's the time!"

Her lips were tight and she shook her head. "Not yet," she whispered. Her posture immediately changed, becoming weak, looking about to faint, and she screamed, "Let go of my dearezt huzband! You brute!"

Fuck you! Fuck this! My entire body tensed, all I wanted to do was crush this governor. Instead, I set him down and let go of his collar. It was deathly silent around me, until I heard a solitary clapping.

"Bravo!" said a voice. "Bravo, my good Ulyzzez!"

I turned to see Don Seraden approaching me with a slimy smile. The guests relaxed.

"Thank you for zhowing uz your ztrength and reztraint," he said, staring at me. He touched my shoulder, leaned closer, and whispered, "I know it'z a lot to take in. Go home, relax, think about the future we are giving you. Come morning, I'm certain you will zee the light."

I glanced at the guests, Governor Terrence and his crumpled collar, then at my sister's pleading eyes. *Pleading for me to comply.* I sighed and faced the don. "I apologize for my behavior. I had too much to drink."

The don nodded. "We have all overindulged before, haven't we!"

The guests nervously laughed.

"Muzic! Drinkz! Dancing!" the don announced and the festivities resumed. He turned to me with a menacing look. "Leave, immediately."

◆

I woke in the dead of night to the subtle yet familiar whining of hydraulics. *Mech units?* I sat up and peered into the darkness. *But it is not my eyes I need.* I closed them and listened to what could only be Don Seraden's enforcers. *How could I not have seen this coming!?* I thought, cursing myself for my stupid outburst the night before, and for my naivety now. *No… focus!* I cleared my mind, letting my ears become everything.

"Twenty," I whispered, hearing the enforcers' cadences upon cobblestone.

I slipped from beneath my bed's plush comforter to the floor, so they could not see me through the bedroom windows, and rolled to the walk-in closet. *But they must know I'm awake,* I thought, assuming they were running thermal alongside night vision. *If it can penetrate this stone…*

Among flamboyant clothing, I saw a box unceremoniously stuffed in the back. I pulled it closer and lifted its lid to find my faded, mining uniform with its eternal stains.

"This is who I am," I whispered, running my thumb across, *"X0471,"* upon its breast. "I am a clone… Nothing more… Nothing less… And my family needs me…" I emerged from the closet in my faded uniform and searched for anything I could use as a weapon. *I am the weapon,* I knew. *But it matters not if they can simply stun me.* I studied the stone wall again, and gave it a firm knock. *Expanded feldspar insulation within off-world granite,* I recognized and grinned, knowing it would shield me. *But I must be delicate, subtle.* I crouched low, staying below the window sills and crossed my chamber to its large, wooden door. When I turned its handle, it squeaked, and when I opened the door, it groaned. I cringed, knowing I gave myself away. I gently closed it, wincing as the latch clicked.

"Thiz way, my lord," came a voice and I jolted.

A face appeared in the hallway just a few meters from me. *My servant, cloaked.* "Do you know what's happening?"

She nodded. "You are being zent into early retirement."

"That's one way to put it," I whispered.

"Pleaze, wear thiz," she said and her hand appeared with a bundle of cloth. "A cloak, like mine."

I slipped it over my mining uniform, watching as each limb disappeared, until pulling the hood over my face. My servant's silhouette appeared on the cloak's visor. *We're synchronized,* I realized.

"The floor iz old, but I know where the creakz are," she whispered on a private line. "Follow my lead."

"Am I still good for the house?" I asked.

"Yez, my lord. Pleaze, we muzt hurry," she responded.

I did not budge. "I need some sort of assurance."

My servant went silent and I felt like my distrust was validated until she muttered, "Joan… iz my great, great grandmother."

Are you fucking kidding me!? I thought, trying to understand how that could be, for my servant was notably older than my sister. *But it must be true if she knows her name.* I followed her, trying to clear my mind of what I had just learned, feeling horrible for not even asking her name. *I'm already acting like a Governor. Already treating those of a lower class like property,* I thought. My servant pointed at a section of floor and it highlighted red. I navigated around.

A sudden creaking sounded and we both froze. I listened intently. Another creak came. *From the other side of the wall,* I realized and placed palms upon its granite, judging its strength. "What's your name?" I whispered on the private line.

"I have no name," my servant whispered back.

I sighed. "Move to the end of the hall, there's something I must take care of here."

Her silhouette faced me and nodded. She delicately maneuvered to the end. I focused my hearing again, imagining the mech unit moving down a hallway on the other side. Another creak came, this time accompanied by the subtle whine of hydraulics. I accessed memories from earlier wakings, determining at what height their pilots resided at. *Head is level with my sternum.* Another step came and I knew they were between my palms. I slowly raised my fist and found a stone at the right height. *Here goes nothing…*

I quickly struck the wall, knocking out a stone like a paper punch. A clunk came a millisecond after, then a thud hit the floor. I held my breath and turned my ear to the hole, listening for hydraulics to whine or an alarm to sound. Nothing.

"Anything ahead?" I asked, but my servant stood stunned. "Hey."

She shook her head. "Zorry, my lord. It will not happen again." She peered around the bend. "It iz clear."

Several more sets of hydraulics entered the estate, but it was difficult to judge exact numbers and locations. When I passed an open window, I heard whispers from outside. I stopped and peered through its opening to find three mechs with their cloaks deactivated, their pilots just standing there with helmets off, their rifles leaned against the wall, passing a flask around. *Waiting for orders? But from who?* I thought upon the one I incapacitated in the hall. An orange gleam in the distance suddenly caught my eye. I focused upon it. *Jupiter? On this horizon?* I thought, confused, knowing it resided on the opposite side of the moon. *No... A reflection... The cylindrical structure,* I realized, and that it lay smack in the middle of Don Seraden's territory. *He said my crew was in a 'holding' facility...* I stared at the structure. *A prison...*

"My lord, we muzt go," my servant urged.

"What's the plan?" I asked.

"To get you out of the eztate," she responded.

"And after that?"

"Off of Ganymede. Zomewhere zafe."

"Safe for me? Or safe for Joan?" I bitterly said, knowing I had become a thorn in my sister's side, a hiccup in her obscure plan.

"For both…"

"No… I will not leave my family to rot." I turned to my servant. "Tell Joan that I'm joining my crew, and that if she truly wants to rescue me, then she'll have to rescue us all."

"My lord! You can't!"

I tore off my cloak and stood tall, no longer skulking like a coward. *If this is the end, then it's on my terms...* My servant's footsteps bolted off. *Good, get out, get to Joan.* I faced the open window and casually stepped through.

The three guards did not notice me.

"What'z going on?" one whispered, taking a swig from the flask. "Haden zhould have reported back by now."

"Don't know if I care," said another and they chuckled.

Thirty meters off, I gauged, and I recalled all that combat training. *I can't reach top speed, but I can get close.* I started at a quiet trot, building to a run, then into a gallop. One of the guards peered at the ground. *He feels it...* I went to full sprint, planting my feet hard, and watching all three of them brace as if an earthquake was on the rise.

The one holding the flask made eye contact with me and his jaw dropped as my fist crunched into his mech's chest plate, launching him across the estate, through a rock wall, and into the town beyond. Clanks rang in the distance as he struck buildings.

The remaining two stood frozen. And so did I, staring at my fist, not believing such power actually existed in me. *Because I've never truly done it before,* I realized. The guards reached for their rifles. I kicked one's hydraulic leg, feeling the metal bend and the man's femur snap beneath, then I snatched the second unit at the waist, pulling both man and mech back. I lifted him off the ground, flipped him over, and spiked him head first into the ground.

Several more mech units rounded the corner, rifles up and shouting orders for my surrender. A gunship panned over the estate with gatling barrels aimed and spinning.

I grinned and raised my hands as electricity racked my body.

♦

Sicklecell Titanium, I knew as I ran my hand along the walls, floor, ceiling, and door of my cell. *This prison is designed to hold equalizers.* The surfaces flexed like fabric, feeling flimsy, but once reaching their plasticity threshold, they were like concrete. When I ceased my pressing, they snapped back to their original positions. *But is the entire structure made of this material?* For every thump and stomp I gave, I immediately froze and listened for their reverberations, only to be met by silence. *Silence means either complete isolation or completely Sicklecell. Or both...*

My door's slot quickly opened and a bowl of slop slid across the floor. I glimpsed a shadow on the other side.

The next day, I laid on my stomach, mentally ticking the time. "Now," I whispered. The slot opened and I saw a pair of boots on the other side upon a metal catwalk, before a bowl slid in.

I positioned differently each day, finding new angles and piecing together more of what lay beyond. I soon understood it was open on the other side of the catwalk. *Maybe an atrium.*

They never collected the bowls and spoons. *Because they're scared.* And so, on the seventh morning, I placed six spoons face down affront the slot, staring at their concave reflections as time ticked. The slot opened right on schedule and the next bowl slid in, knocking the spoons and causing a racket.

"What the hell waz that?" one muffled.

"No idea," came another.

I closed my eyes, focusing on what I saw a split second before the spoons scattered. *Two tall, thin men... red hair... workers uniforms.* My heart sank. *Our descendants...*

The following day, I flicked a spoon out through the slot before a bowl slid in. I heard a crack and saw the bowl split in two, spilling my porridge through the grating.

"Another did the zpoon thing!" the one muffled.

So, it's not just me! I grinned, imagining my entire crew was in cells alongside mine.

"Well, zlide in another," said the other guard and in came a bowl.

They want us fed... I realized. Which meant only one thing. *They're preparing us for another job...*

GHOSTS OF ZION | 435

I studied my spoons, knowing they were made of sicklecell titanium, just like everything else besides the bowls and my uniform, and that no matter how much I wished to sharpen or shear them, it was not going to happen. *Unless I increase their internal heat.* An idea came to me. *Metal fatigue…*

I grasped the spoon's head, bent it over, and released. It snapped straight up. *One…* I did it again. *Two…* And again, not allowing a second to pass. *Three…* Warmth became apparent after five hundred bends, and notably hot after a thousand. By midnight, I hit five thousand. The spoon was glowing orange at the neck. I held its head ninety-degrees and blew across its neck to cool. *Moment of truth,* I thought after the orange dissipated. I let go. The head sluggishly unfurled, closing in on its original upright position. But then, it stopped, slightly kinked. My heart raced. I set the spoon down and paced for nearly an hour. Then, I picked it back up. *Still kinked…* It was cool to the touch now. I bent the head one last time and let go, watching like a hawk as it unfurled, stopping again in the kinked position.

But how can this be applied to the cell? I touched its flexible surfaces. I knew nothing of this prison's construction. *But is that true?* I studied its craftsmanship. *This is indeed our work… And if my siblings built this… Then, I built this.* I analyzed the door, imagining monstrous piano hinges and deadbolts around its perimeter on the exterior side. *Not there.* I racked my brain trying to think of any possible weak point.

"Fuck…" I muttered, knowing where it was. The only place where sicklecell titanium meets another material. *The foundation…*

I spied the kinked spoon, then the slot where I knew hundreds of equalizers were pondering the same thing. *There's no breaking out of this prison… But maybe… Just maybe… We can 'bend' out of it.*

◆

I waited for the perfect moment to act, but could not imagine what it should be. I could almost hear Joan telling me to save my rage for another day. But every time I thought that day had come, she had said otherwise. *So, how can I know when the time is right?*

Fifteen bowls lined the back wall of my cell, neatly organized as I would only have it. Another slid through the slot, cracked and oozing porridge. I sighed and retrieved it, using the spoon to catch the spill.

Why not make this out of titanium, too? I thought, shoveling porridge down before it dripped to the floor. The bowl's porcelain felt inferior in my hands, like a factory defect. *Others had broken, too,* I remembered. I neared the previous bowls lined against the wall, and set the latest at the end, then approached the two other cracked ones. They effortlessly split when I applied force. *Weird.* The bowls to either side appeared different, one glazed and the other more rough. *Why three different porcelain grades?*

I slid a glazed one out to inspect it, then a rough one, but it gripped the floor. I remembered when each had slid through the slot, noting that some stopped shortly afterward, with others sliding nearly halfway into the cell.

I pointed at day one and whispered, "short…" Then, I pointed at the next few, saying, "…short, long… *break,* I guess." I chuckled. *How funny would it be if...* I leaped to my feet and went down the line of bowls assigning short, long, and breaks to them all.

".. - / .. ... / - .. -- . /."

"It is time," it read.

"Are you fucking kidding me!?" I laughed, imagining Joan entering porcelain factories with two little children and blackmailing their foremen.

♦

Up, down, up, down, up, down, I mantra'd, standing at the very center of my cell as I did squat after squat, meanwhile cradling the stacked porcelain bowls in my arms. *Faster, slower...* "There it is," I whispered and huffed.

The floor warped and warped again, as it had for over five hours since I started. But now, I felt resonance bouncing back into my feet, helping my influence build like waves in a pool. Another three hours went by. I felt a slight thudding. *It's the frame...* I closed my eyes trying to feel its resonance, too. *Again... again...* I knew I must maintain my pace, no faster or slower. Sweat beaded on my forehead, but my thighs felt strong.

The frame thudded back, giving a double bump to my feet. *Yes! Build, baby!* But I could not understand how the resonance had grown so quickly. I expected days not hours. *Unless...* "One mind," I muttered, imagining my crew in their cells doing the exact same thing.

"Do you feel that?" I heard from the catwalk.

"Feel what?" said another voice.

Another hour passed.

"Zeriouzly, you don't feel that?"

"Uh, maybe I feel zomething," the other responded.

Two more hours.

"Woah, I feel it now."

"You think there'z conztruction going on?"

Three hours later.

"They zaid it'z not conztruction. They don't know what it iz."

"Maybe it'z zome zort of quake?"

Four hours.

The thudding in the floor became audible, like clashing pots and pans. Footsteps raced down the catwalk. My cell's ceiling shuddered as it made contact with the frame above.

"They zay the quake iz coming from inzide thiz prizon!" said the voice again, panicking now.

Cat's out of the bag... I thought, finally feeling a burn in my thighs. A rattle came from directly in front of as my cell door bound against its frame. The slot flipped open and I saw a shadow.

"What the hell!?" the voice said. "His entire cell iz moving up and down! What are you doing!?"

"Exercising!" I shouted back, with a mighty laugh.

An alarm sounded.

"Attention all perzonnel, evacuate immediately," echoed through a cavernous space, followed by frantic footsteps.

The double tapping at my feet disappeared. *We've matched resonance with the prison's frame,* I knew.

"All prizonerz, ztop bouncing!" came into my cell.

All... I smiled wide and whispered, "Let the games begin."

"Ztop now, or we will uze force!"

The bowls! I placed two stacks upside down on the floor, then I split them into six stacks of three. *You better hold!* On the next bounce I placed my left foot on three stacks. Another bounce and I placed my right foot on the others. *Okay, stand up!* I slowly diverted weight from my hands to my feet. *Trust the porcelain!* I felt the bowls grind and crack. *Now push!* I gave another squat, feeling more crunching, but they held.

"Thiz iz your final warning! Ztop now or face the conzequencez!"

"Bring your consequences!" I shouted.

Twinges shot into my feet as electricity bridged the gap between the metal floor and insulative porcelain. But I knew it was nothing compared to direct contact. "Is that all you got!?"

The voltage increased.

Thank Sol for porcelain! I thought as I grimaced.

Finally, after what felt like an eternity, it stopped.

Are we in the clear? I thought, feeling our resonance regaining strength. The floor was hot. The lighting above cut but the door was warping so much that light from outside was peeking through its gaps. Frigid wind hit my skin, and I knew they triggered a sort of emergency hibernation function. *Keep moving! Don't let yourself freeze!* My hair was frosting, and I wiped it off my arms. *You can fight through this!* The heat at my feet was growing. Soon, the chill was not as harsh. I dared touch the wall to find it wet. *Melted, by constant warping.* The door took on a new sound, cracking instead of screeching. I quickly touched its surface. *Horribly frozen?* I thought, then realized the warmth was not transmitting through the door hinge. *A temperature differential!*

I grinned and shifted my footing, stepping off the bowls, knowing the electricity was no more. I stretched back my fist. On the next rebound, I pressed hard on the floor, generating incredible energy from my legs, through my core and into my brick of a hand. The door's piano hinge shattered, its deadbolts popped out, and the door hurtled across the catwalk, through its guardrail, and down a cavernous atrium.

Row after row of doors across the way were popping off, too, and I saw my beautiful brothers and sisters smiling viciously from within their bouncing cells, squatting in perfect unison. Catwalks tore from their anchors and dropped to the bottom of the cylindrical structure. The atrium floor was shaking. *We're almost there!*

A sudden draft came. I peered up to see the cylinder's top was open to the elements. Several gunships appeared like dragonflies and dropped into the cylinder with gatling barrels protruding from their sides. They stopped halfway down and their barrels wound up.

No! We're so close! I racked my brain for a way to stop them. *But all we have is resonance...* I looked across the way at one of my sisters. She placed a fist against her shoulder. More were doing the same. I remembered the last time we saluted after seeding the soil, and how our collective voices shook the dome. *Resonance is all we need...* I pressed my fist into my shoulder and sucked in all the air I could, until I was about to burst, watching all my siblings doing the same. *Only one word matters.*

"HONORRRRRRRR!" we bellowed, our necks bulging, our lungs quivering, and our heads rattling.

Our voices reflected around the cylinder, building so much power I had to brace forward to keep upright.

Gatling guns went wild, spraying into cells.

Hold it! I ordered myself, my throat and lungs burning. Windshields shattered. Gatling spray went rogue, weaving about. Figures leaped from the ships, with hands cupped around their helmets, and smashed upon the floor.

The ships teetered. Black smoke came from one's engine.

We pushed our vocal cords harder. Our faces turned purple and spittle dripped from our lips.

Gunships tumbled from the sky. Several rogue rounds found my cell, but did not pierce its sicklecell titanium. *Good to know!* Gunships struck the base of the cylinder, one right atop a foundation anchor point.

The entire prison shifted and subsequent anchors sheared off. Our resonance became wobbly. Our bouncing became sloppy. But it no longer mattered. We fell, still trapped inside our cells.

The safest place to be.

◆

"Tapas!? Are you in there!?"

"Spaghetti! I'm here! I'm okay!" I responded from my cell, completely bent out of shape, buried beneath hundreds more.

"The moment we lift the debris, your cell is gonna pop back into shape," Spaghetti said.

I curled into a ball at the very center and covered my ears.

A deafening screech came as the cell popped into a perfect cube once again. I took a moment to appreciate the irony that our cells were the very things that saved us. My body ached, but I never felt more powerful in my life. Light shone through my open door, then movement. Spaghetti's upside down face appeared.

"Hey," he said.

"Hey," I responded.

"Did you hear?"

"Hear what?"

"We took down a prison," he said.

I smiled. "You don't say."

More debris was removed, enough so I could fit through. Then, I helped dig out the others. We separated cells from structural members, laying each piece of this prison out like a kit of parts.

"The bolts sheared when it came down," Patatas said.

"I think that was by design," I responded.

"But not their design," Spaghetti quipped. "The ones who built this prison must have known this day would come and integrated weaknesses."

"The parts are in working order," Patatas said. "We can use this."

"To do what?" Spaghetti asked.

"Whatever it is, we don't have a lot of time," I said. "We need tools to work this material."

"We don't have them," Patatas said.

"But our descendants do." Mulan approached, her arm was lopped off at the elbow with a piece of her uniform working as a tourniquet.

I grimaced. "Glad to see you're alive."

She glanced at her arm. "Many at the bottom weren't as fortunate. We lost Alexander. And we haven't found Trieu yet."

I sighed deeply. "Does anyone know how many we are?"

C8 approached. "Two hundred and seventy-eight have made it out unscathed, a hundred thirty-two are critically injured, and ninety-eight are dead… So far."

"Shit," I muttered and lowered my head. *What have I done?*

"Tapas…" Spaghetti said. "…We all did this on our own accord. Don't let this weigh on your conscience, too."

Still, I thought, then turned to C8. "I need you to take charge of the recovery effort. Gather fifty of us."

"What will the rest of you do?" he asked.

I studied the building elements, then Mulan. "We need to find tools and people who can work sicklecell titanium. We break into teams of thirty and contact the nearest labor villages. They must have the equipment."

"But will they help us?" Mulan said.

I thought about that. "We'll find out."

"The nearest village is fifty klicks west. How do we get there?" Patatas asked.

"We run," Spaghetti answered.

She turned to him. "Are you serious?"

"We don't have a choice," he responded. "And wartime equalizers were known for their ability to run."

"To sprint… This is a marathon."

"But we're much different now," I said, studying my siblings and how their bulky musculature had become leaner over the years. "We have been conditioned for hard labor and grueling hours. To go forever and then some. Spaghetti is right, we run, not just because we must, but because the Ganymedans will never expect it."

♦

We arrived at the first village to meet hundreds of workers outside its perimeter, wielding hammers, blow torches, and more, like a steampunk army.

I raised my hand signaling us to stop. "Patatas, Spaghetti, with me. The rest of you, keep on to the next village."

Mulan nodded and started off around the perimeter.

The three of us slowly approached. I let my eyes zoom and focus.

"That's close enough!" one said, and we stopped. "We heard about the prison break," he continued. "We heard you took the entire structure down with nothing but resonance."

How do they know? "Did some of your people work at the prison?"

The one nodded and came forward, a pickax in hand. He did not seem afraid. "There's going to be hell to pay for that."

"Not the first time," I returned.

The young man grinned. "My great, great, great grandparents were your kind. And I met a few of you from an earlier thaw."

"Then, I hope you will help us. If we are to survive this, we must build our defenses, but we have neither the tools nor the expertise to do so."

The one thought about this. "We must discuss it with the elder. What are your numbers?"

"We have names, not numbers…" Patatas said. "… I'm Patatas Bravas.

"I'm Spaghetti Scampi."

"And I'm Tapas, but some know me as Ulysses," I said.

The young man's eyes widened. "You're the ones! Come now, quickly!" He turned to the others and made a quick gesture. They stood aside.

He's their foreman, I realized.

We followed him, passing hundreds of workers. Tall grasses enveloped us, then gave way to a clearing surrounded by small shacks. *A village center,* I understood. We moved through, getting stares from children peeking from behind shacks and complacent gazes from the elderly. Spaghetti and Patatas looked wildly about, searching for something. *Searching for little Uly.*

"He's not here…" I whispered.

They turned to me with deflating hope.

We passed tall grass at the opposing side of town, opening to a series of stables. *They keep livestock?* I thought, until I realized people were in the stalls. *They are the livestock…*

The foreman stopped and peered into a stable, then turned our way. "She's been waiting for you for some time," he said and stepped aside.

I cautiously rounded the stall divider, terrified of what I might find. But all I saw was a bed unmade, a table stained by years of food, and a chair covered in old laundry. But then, the laundry moved.

"My… my, you still look so young," wheezed the laundry.

I squinted, racking my brain trying to discern the features of a person. A laundry fold wiggled. *A mouth…* Then, I slowly made out an eye and nose.

"Tapas…" she said and her one discernible eye shifted. "…Spaghetti… and Patatas…" the laundry fold twisted up into a smile. "…My most gifted students."

"Beverly!?" Spaghetti gasped.

My Sol!? I thought, then muttered, "How are you still alive?"

"Oh, Ulysses… Take a look around…" Beverly wheezed. "…Don't you know where you are?"

I whipped my head to the stall's open wall. Jupiter shone strongly in the distance and I recognized several stars. I then stuck my head out and looked straight up finding several more key objects. *All in perfect alignment.* I looked at Beverly and said, "The feldspar chamber…"

"Is just beneath this here stable," she said. "We added cryochambers some time ago."

"So, you and Joan have been going in and out of hibernation? You've been time skipping?" Patatas asked.

"Indeed, we have," Beverly confirmed, then grinned mischievously. "But your dear sister and I have another method."

"What kind of method?" I asked, feeling my gut twist.

"That, I cannot say. Not without compromising the efforts we've put forth these past centuries."

"Then, why tell us?" I asked.

"So that when the moment comes, you are looking." She leaned forward and the foreman came bounding into the stall to aid her to her feet. She spread her ragged arms wide. "Now, give me my hugs, you big goofs."

◆

The workers helped us build suits of armor from the prison's scrap sicklecell titanium. They were not what I would consider fine craftsmanship, were nothing like the armor of The Hermian War, but they would get the job done.

Spaghetti paced back and forth, kneeling, twisting, working through his armor's range of motion, and swinging a heavy impact hammer. With each movement came a screeching of metal. He gave a look. "They'll hear us from kilometers away."

"Let them hear," I responded. "Let them squirm in their beds knowing we're coming for them."

Mulan grinned. "I got an idea."

She found industrial painters and set to work spraying Spaghetti's armor bright red, with a white cross running down its front.

"Camouflage might be better," Patatas said.

Mulan shook her head. "They still fear the old Hermians."

I looked at Mulan, Trieu, Gilgamesh, Boudicca, Wallace, Achilles, and Curie, the remainder of our father's Twelve. And I was surprised that the eight of us ended up together. *Joan's maneuvering,* I knew. I spied Patatas and Spaghetti. And then, there was C8, who I was just now beginning to know, working diligently to allot sets of armor for each of us, becoming our de facto human calculator.

Just one more... "We've bled so much," I muttered. "But we are almost whole again."

Mulan glanced at her arm and turned my way. "I guess that makes us the bloody Twelve now."

"Or... The Bloody Dozen," Trieu repeated with a glimmer in her eyes.

"Sounds good to me," Wallace added.

"What do you mean?" Spaghetti muffled, then lifted his faceplate.

"There were once twelve of us," I said. "Chosen by our father to undergo intense training during cryosleep, designed to shepherd all of System Sol to greatness."

He processed this. "So, what happened?"

I motioned to the fields. "This happened."

"But it's not over," said a withered voice and Beverly came into the light, alongside another figure, dressed in Ganymedan elegance, a beacon among our palette of faded uniforms and stained canvas.

My kin gasped, not understanding how an elite could have ventured into our stronghold, passed our eyes and ears, then have the courage to reveal themselves. But I understood.

"Joan..." I said and raced to hug her.

She grinned devilishly. "Sorry I'm late."

"You can't be late when you're pulling the strings," I retorted.

"Joan!?" Wallace shouted. "I thought you were dead!"

"Me, too!" said Boudicca.

I realized not all of us had contact with her over the years.

"Is there room for one more in your little gang?" she said, tearing off her elegant dress to reveal muscular arms and a stomach that was flat again.

It's been two months since the birth of her second child... or whatever number she was on. "You've been preparing…"

"I'm always prepared," she said.

I looked at what remained of my old brothers and sisters, alongside my new brothers and sisters. "Then, welcome to The Bloody Dozen…"

♦

We split off in several directions, each of The Bloody Dozen leading a platoon of forty, running marathons in armor by night and raiding cartel and governor strongholds at the crack of dawn.

We had them on the run. We had them scared.

"Keep up the pressure!" I told runners coming to and from my platoon, relaying orders and outcomes without using coms, keeping our enemies in complete darkness. "Don't stay in one place longer than needed! Keep our enemy running! We cannot give them a second to rest, a second to sleep! Let's see how long they can endure!"

One by one, governors and lesser dons folded, their mech units choosing to flee rather than be smashed by our blitz. And it made sense why. *They are our kin and know we fight for them, too.* Soon, it was clear where the governors and dons were heading.

"Hardsill…" I muttered and recalled that holographic display of cartel territory I had glimpsed during my short stint as governor. *The heart of Don Seraden's territory.*

"What are your orders?" said Mulan's runner outside my habitat as we rested.

"We converge on Hardsill," I responded.

The runner nodded and disappeared. A few seconds later another cloak unveiled.

"Uly," came a wheezing voice and I turned to find Beverly, barely standing.

"How the…" I gasped, not understanding how she could have found me let alone reached me in the dead of night, until a few more uncloaked. *From the village,* I realized and studied their envisuits, from a bygone era, ancient, deteriorating, *Hermian.*

Beverly pressed a finger to her lips, hushing me. "Guess what I found?" she whispered.

"…What?" I quietly responded.

She lifted her glove, holding a little green orb with pores across its surface, and having a stem protruding from its top.

"Is that… a lime?" I guessed and noticed several items in her escort's hands. *Cooking equipment?*

She grinned. "A promise is a promise…" She pointed at my habitat and entered with her escort and equipment.

I scrambled after them, watching as they assembled a simple propane cook-top and opened a box filled with ice and fish.

My heart leaped. "Ceviche…"

Beverly eyed my heavy armor. "Take that off, will you."

I unlatched its heavy titanium buckles and carefully removed my chest and back plates, then my boots and gloves.

"That's better," she lifted a ragged bolt of cloth. "Remember this?"

"You can't be serious!" I said as she handed it to me. I carefully unfolded its fabric, feeling old fibers strain and crack. I found a loop and carefully pulled it over my head. And then, I secured waist ties around my back. My eyes watered as I remembered our first days upon Ganymede, when she had come to us, already an old woman, then.

Beverly's escort left the habitat.

The ancient woman slowly took a knife at a cutting board in one hand and placed a lime on its wooden surface with her other. "Well…" she said, looking at me. "…Get the juicer!"

"Yes, chef!" I answered.

When the prep work was complete, I placed the halibut and marinade into the ice box to cook in citric acid. There was silence. I sat on my habitat's floor, for I had no furniture.

The old woman seemed to melt as she sat beside me. "Have you forgotten?"

I pointed to my head. "I can't forget…" *But what is she referring to?*

"You must have, if this little revolution is your solution."

"Little?" I responded. "We have them running scared. We're winning."

She sighed. "For now."

"What do you know?" I pointedly asked.

"Well…" the ancient woman said. "That's the issue. I don't know. Not anymore. And neither does Joan. These family heads, these dons, have muddied the water. And now, making contact, it's difficult to know what the future holds."

"Contact?" I said. "You mean with other colonies."

"With other species…" she answered. "We've encountered strange beings, one called Cindarians and another the Arkathy."

"That's… incredible…" I did not know what else to say.

"Yes… Yes, it is," she said, but held a worried expression. "But Joan says they met with the dons in secret."

Not with the governors. "What the fuck?"

"My thoughts exactly," she said.

"Still, all of this contact should be good for us," I said. "The Council will rid humanity of its corruption to show these new species how great we are."

"You are so naive, Ulysses," she said. "Don't you see that in all this excitement, as humanity faces other incredible civilizations, that we will be forgotten?"

"…I do, now," I said. "What can we do, then?"

She looked at me squarely. "We take care of our own. We stick to the mission."

Khasi… I knew. "Are we not taking matters into our own hands now?"

"You are, and I hope for the best. But even if you win your freedom your degradation continues. You and your descendants are still doomed." She hardened. "Promise me you will keep to your mission no matter what."

"Okay, I promise," I said, sensing her fear. *Her lack of control,* I realized. I looked at the ground and ran my fingers through grasses pressed flat. "Some dream this turned out to be."

◆

We encouraged the dons in their retreat to Hardsill. *So our hammer only needs to strike once!*

I felt tremors in my feet and I stopped our marathon run. I placed a hand upon the ground and closed my eyes. *A hundred, due east. No mech units.* I stood and curled my paws around my eyes, cutting out peripheral light pollution. Movement registered, tiny specks, like gnats. A glimmer of red came, then a lead figure formed. *One arm.* I grinned. *Mulan must have linked up with Gilgamesh on the way in.*

More tremors started coming from the west. And then, from the north as we closed in on Hardsill rising high in the Ganymedan landscape with floodlights pointing out in every direction. *To blind us.* The sound of hydraulics came as thousands of mech units rushed to meet us in the field.

They know it's now or never, too, I realized.

Several runners appeared beside me.

"It's a fortress," said one. "And there's an army."

"Keep to the rendezvous point," I said, huffing in my heavy armor as we ran. "They're spreading themselves thin, anticipating we will try to overwhelm from all sides."

The runner paused. "I thought that was the plan."

"Not anymore," I responded. "The rendezvous."

The runners nodded and disappeared.

An hour later, I climbed a slight hill in the field, masking our forces' true size from the city's vantage point, to discover C8's platoon already there. Soon, the others started pouring in.

I faced our makeshift army, almost four hundred individuals strong. "Listen up!" I called and they looked up. "I know our tactics so far have been to hit from all sides, to confuse and terrify. But look at them out there." I pointed at the mech units in the dark, highlighted by the many flood lights. "They're spread thin, they're ready for an attrition battle, and they're relying upon that thick granite wall to keep us out."

"So how do we engage?" Patatas asked.

"They're thinking we march through the night because our armor weighs us down, that we only lay siege at dawn after we rest," I looked upon my brothers and sisters, breathing heavily from their marathons just finished. "But you see, despite how much we've changed, we are still those equalizers of old. We are still unstoppable. We can still smash through them in the old way!"

"Pike," I heard murmuring through our congregation.

"Yes! We come at them in Pike formation with The Bloody Dozen as the tip of the spear! Follow us across this field! Be impossibly fast! But be mindful! If we jump, you jump! If we zig, you zig! If we zag, you zag! But most importantly, be ready to push us through enemy lines, no matter what condition of war we encounter, no matter what insurmountable odds we will face!" I paused, letting my breath settle with theirs. "We are not coming back from this… It is either total victory or total defeat… We do not retreat… We *cannot* retreat…" I unclasped the titanium buckles securing my armor's heavy back plate, swung it to my left arm, and strapped it down like a shield.

A symphony of unbuckling and metal sliding to shield arms came as they followed suit. And then, they knelt and placed fists upon their opposing shoulders. I matched them, and there we stayed breathing steadily, calming, preparing. I closed my eyes and listened as we became one matching inhale and exhale, like ocean waves. And between each rise and fall, the whines of thousands of mech units could be heard in the distance.

I stood and stretched my calves and quads, then my hips. *Just like riding a bike,* I thought, recalling old battles of Sundow.

Mulan and Trieu, Gilgamesh, Achilles, Boudicca, Wallace, and Curie were by my side. And then, Patatas and Spaghetti were there, and C8, too. A small figure then came to us. Their face mask lifted to reveal our shadow sister.

Joan made it, I thought, relieved, having been unsure if she could keep up with equalizer speed.

She patted me on the shoulder. "You ready?"

"No… But I suspect they are less so."

"So, you finally have your revolution," Joan said and stepped back, awaiting my mark.

I faced the city of floodlights and the amassed mech units below. *Piloted by our descendants.* My stomach twisted, knowing that some might even be directly related to Patatas and Spaghetti. *…And that's how they've held such power over us in the past.*

I began at a light trot, and felt the footsteps of our army matching stride. "Four minutes, thirty-seven seconds… That's all it will take to reach them," I said to their resolute silence.

We gathered speed, from a trot to a gallop. Then, we leaned forward, driving our feet into the ground, tearing up grass and soil, and coming into a sprint, one that once struck terror in the hearts of old enemies. One that will certainly strike terror again.

I raised a fist and extended one finger.

The Twelve splayed, like geese in *V* formation, with our army lined up behind us single file. *Like a literal pike,* I thought and saw city floodlights whip our direction, but not all of them. *From their viewpoint we appear like a small regiment... They're still searching for the rest of us.*

"Four minutes!" I called out as time ticked away in my elephant brain. "Three minutes!" I called again.

Mech units scrambled into formation, shifting from the east and west sides of the city. Gunships rose from the city walls and bee-lined our way.

So, they know, I realized. "Two minutes!"

The mechs organized into rows, the front kneeling and the back standing. They aimed rifles.

"Shields!" I called out and The Bloody Dozen raised them just before the mechs opened fire. My shield comically dented and shuddered with each round it deflected, creating such a racket I could not hear my own voice. Nevertheless, I cried, "One minute!"

The fire ceased and I took a split second to peek from behind my shield.

They're fleeing! I realized, then saw the gunships above with gatling guns pointed down. *But not from us...*

"Turtle formation!" I cried, raised my shield over my head, and crouched. I felt those behind me converging, becoming one circular mass of people.

Gatling guns unleashed, pressing us with such force our feet and knees embedded into the soil. *How long!?* I kept thinking, as I gritted my teeth, trying to hold my wildly bouncing shield in place. There was a sudden pause and I knew their guns were reloading.

"Return fire!" I shouted and with every ounce of strength I chucked my shield into the sky, watching as it shot towards a gunship, crash through its window, and the pilot's upper torso tumble out.

Hundreds of shields rained upwards, cutting down the gunships.

"Charge!" I hollered, pointing at the mech units who had stopped to watch us get mowed, their faces adopting horrified looks when they realized the turn of events.

Our sicklecell fists, heavy impact hammers, and pick axes met their sicklecell exoskeletons like a freight train plowing through a car. Mech units scattered, either fleeing into the fields or racing to the city gates for salvation.

But they will not open for them, I knew, as we quickly gained ground. "Make for the gate! Pike formation!"

Again, we became a spear and aimed for that gate, hoping our combined mass would crumple it like foil. Floodlights converged upon us, right into our eyes, and I winced, barely making out the terrain in front of me.

Then, as suddenly as they blinded us, they cut.

Shit, I thought as my world went black.

A strange crackling met my ears. The sky lit in furious magenta, and streaming tails of the same hue arced upon us from the city walls. Our armor, holding back everything they threw at us, was now like paper. Gilgamesh took one to the leg and it was gone, the titanium glowing white hot and the nub of his leg instantly burnt to a crisp. Patatas took one to the chest, and it blasted out of her back.

"No!" I cried as more arcs found their marks, homing in on us like they were sentient. *What the fuck is this!?*

Another volley came, landing upon our forces and the retreating mech units, cutting us both down. *Because they don't give a shit about anyone!*

I spun around, trying to take stock of our remaining forces, and caught the dreadful look on C8's face, a second before it was gone.

I bolted to the granite walls, with a few dozen of us, trying to find cover, when I saw a smiling face at the top, looking down upon us. *Don Seraden...*

Then and there, I knew we had fallen right into his trap, had been led to believe we had the upper hand.

Beside him was a strange figure in shining armor, thin and elegant. Their featureless faceplate suddenly retracted to reveal vicious, red eyes. *Red eyes!?* Several more figures, in the same shining armor, appeared, training strange rifles upon us.

Flashes came. And then, nothing.

♦

I woke alongside The Bloody Dozen shackled to the wall with shock collars around our necks. Mulan dangled unconscious. *Likely dead.* C8 was headless. Many were limbless. And I heard Patatas's ragged breathing from the gaping hole in her chest.

"Your kind zhould have known your place!" Don Seraden snapped.

My eyes cleared to find the lesser dons wearing hideous snarls, and the governors with terrified looks, standing behind him. Governor Terrence looked upon my sister with horror, tears washing down his face.

Joan was staring back at him, her jaw tight, her head up proud. She did not cry, but I could sense pain felt for her husband.

She actually loves him, I realized.

Don Seraden turned to the governors. "Zee what happenz when you truzt animalz!" he snapped. "Look at the mezz you've allowed them to make!"

I realized the dons had drawn their pistols.

Don Seraden pointed at the governors. "Line up! On your kneez!"

They obeyed.

He brought forth his ringed hand. "Zwear fealty to me and all zhall be forgiven!" He went down the line, each governor muttering words of loyalty and kissing his ring. All except for Governor Terrence, whom the don had stand off to the side. "The rezt of you are forgiven."

Shots rang and the governors tipped to the ground. Governor Terrence's legs trembled.

Don Seraden faced him. "I have zomething zpecial for you," he said, spun his pistol around and handed it to the bewildered governor. "Zhoot your wife."

"W-what?" he whispered.

"Zhoot… your… wife," Don Seraden repeated. "Do thiz and we will know your loyalty iz true."

Governor Terrence looked at the pistol in his hand, then at my sister.

"Do it," Joan mouthed, and the blood drained from her husband's face.

What is she saying!? I wanted to shout. But then, her eyes darted my way and she winked. *What!? No! This cannot possibly be part of her plan!*

The governor raised the trembling pistol, training it upon my sister's forehead. His breathing escalated and he moaned.

"Clozer," said the don.

The governor obeyed, taking a step forward.

"Clozer," he repeated.

Governor Terrence took another step.

"Clozer," he said again with a wicked smile.

The governor was within arms reach of his wife now.

"I'm zorry," he whispered.

My sister smiled sweetly and closed her eyes.

The governor let out a shriek that curdled my stomach and I had to close my eyes, too. A shot rang. Ten more shots followed. Chains rattled. Then, all was silent, save the sound of splattering on the floor.

I timidly opened my eyes to see Governor Terrence on his knees heaving. My sister hung limply from her chains and the wall behind her was spattered red. The rest of my brothers and sisters were gone. *All executed but me...*

"Congratulationz, Governor Terrence," Don Seraden said. "Or zhould I zay, Don Terrence. May your reign be gloriouz."

"May your reign be gloriouz," the others repeated.

"Come now, ztand up," he urged.

Don Terrence rose upon shaking legs and staggered to the lesser dons. Each patted his back and gave their condolences.

"Now, what about you?" Don Seraden said, turning to me. "Are you zalvageable?"

I pulled against my chains, feeling them stretch and creak.

"Oh dear, I think not."

"Finish it!" I shouted, accepting the electricity ripping through my neck, fighting through it, not letting it faze me.

My voice knocked him back several meters, yet he remained smiling. "Oh, I have zomething in mind for you, the *lazt* equalizer. What a prize you are… And our ezteemed benefactorz indeed love their trophiez." He raised his fist and heavy steps came from the shadows.

Mech units appeared with hatred in their pilot's eyes. *Neither our descendants nor Ganymedans.* It took two units at each of my limbs to hold me still as they unlatched my shackles.

All the while, Don Seraden relished their struggle. "Now, Ulyzzez, you muzt know it iz futile to fight our will.”

Like hell it is! I curled tight, pulling the mech units closer together, and drove my feet into the ground dragging all eight of them along, inching my way closer to the don. But then, I felt a pinch in my neck. My limbs became rubbery and my head began to swim.

They removed my shock collar and dragged me to another room. I was placed within a frigid compartment. *A hibernation chamber,* I knew, but it was different. I opened my eyes to slits into see it was my old chamber from hibernation on Mercury, one built like a tank, designed to survive even a nuclear blast. The hatch sealed.

I failed! It was all for nothing! seeped into my thoughts. I tried to think otherwise, tried convincing myself that we had made a lasting impression. That they would see the immorality of their ways and change. *But they will never see...* I knew, deep down.

A young cryo-tech entered.

“Are you zure you know how to operate thiz type of chamber?” said the don. “It’z been centuriez.”

“I’ve been ztudying them for yearz,” she assured and slowly approached.

I recognized something in the way she moved, the way she turned her head. Then, I remembered what Beverly had said. *I’m looking, Beverly, and I’m seeing, but I’m not believing.* “Joan?” I whispered, knowing the soldiers and don could not hear me through the glass, but that Joan would. She gave me a hard look and that same subtle shake of her head, one telling me to keep my mouth shut.

It’s her! It’s really her! But I watched her die just moments ago! I thought. Then, I studied her uniform, her short-cropped hair, and her smooth skin, looking no older than eighteen.

“How are you young again?” I whispered.

She did not acknowledge me as she tinkered with the old cryochamber.

“Joan, how are you doing this?” I said.

Again, she ignored me.

I lurched my head, cracking my skull against the glass. The soldiers and Don Seraden backpedaled, but my young sister did not flinch.

“Glazz iz dezigned to withztand any ztrike an equalizer might make. You are zafe,” she casually said, then made eye contact with me and mouthed, *“This is not the end.”*

My lip trembled. Tears trickled down my cheeks.

She read my terror. *“Uly, you have a mission to complete. You must save our people, no matter the century.”*

“*But... how?*” I mouthed back.

“*Only you and Beverly know,*” she responded.

Find Khasi... Find The Terran Files... I knew.

“Okay,” I muttered.

“*When the time is right I will come for you,*” she added, then turned to Don Seraden. “Everything checkz out. The zyztem zhould remain operational for zeveral centuriez.”

“Why are we holding him captive again?” a soldier asked.

The don barked, “Not your place to queztion me!”

“Yez, zir! Zorry, zir!”

The don approached my young sister. “Can we freeze him, now?”

“He’z ready,” she confirmed.

“Do it, then,” he ordered, peering at me through the glass. “You will remain a reminder to never truzt your kind again.”

I flinched and watched Don Seraden stumble back and trip to the floor. A grin flashed across my young sister’s face as the cold hit my chest.

My breathing ceased. My heart stopped. And once again, I fell into purgatory.

CHAPTER TWENTY

"Where is he!?" Clara growls through gritted teeth, gripping Jonathan's arm, as he barely clings to life. Her extremities feel cold, like her circulation has stopped.

"W-who?" Aizen stammers, tears running down his cheeks, looking at her scared.

"The one-legged boy!" she says, her eyes furious, her throat raw.

"I-I don't know," her son says.

Come back, Clara! You're still a mom! She breathes deeply and gently strokes Aizen's hair, parting it to the side. "Aizen… I must find this boy. Dr. Lee discovered that his cells have the ability to replicate those of other people. He believes we can use them to grow new organs."

Aizen's eyes twitch. "Like Kwai Lan's research?"

"Yes."

Her son thinks about that and takes a deep Ergonos breath. "You think his cells can save Dad?"

Clara nods and stands. "I need you to get your father to Paris immediately. Dr. Lee is setting up his equipment as we speak. Have Angela come back for me. But before you go, can you locate this boy?"

"Yes…" Aizen meekly says and closes his eyes. "What?… The boy's in the missile site with Ulysses now… And, something strange is happening to him." He opens his eyes. "Mom, you can't go."

Clara listens to Jonathan's shallow breathing. "I have no choice."

"You don't understand what's in there," her son says.

"I know that Ulysses is an equalizer," Clara responds.

"It's not him I'm worried about."

Clara takes a deep breath. "What else is there?"

"R9…" Aizen says with a lost look. "I took the spore, but instead of repairing R9's DNA, it extracted the creature from me completely."

Clara faces Aizen squarely. "How is that possible?"

Aizen's face goes blank. Another voice says, "The spore hyper-regenerated Aizen's cells, using their energy to fabricate a Sorgan suit, meanwhile purging R9's DNA from every corner of his body."

Zion… Clara realizes. "Is R9 dangerous?"

"I don't know, Clara. It's confused. It's furious," Zion says.

"I'm still going in. Don't try to stop me," Clara responds.

"I would never do so," Zion says, "I have all the faith in the universe in you. And you must go… There's something else you must retrieve."

"What?" Clara asks and glances at Thalee, who is watching Aizen with wide eyes, but she does not seem that surprised. *This is not the first time she's witnessed this.*

"They're called The Terran Files," Zion continues. "Existing on a hard drive attached to an old dog collar. They belong to Thalee's people and must be returned before The Arkathy discover them."

So, The Arkathy are here, too, Clara thinks. "What do these files contain that's so valuable?"

"Everything," Zion says.

Clara turns to Thalee, studying her musculature. *A native Terran…* "Zion, please get Aizen and Jonathan to Paris." She makes eye contact with Thalee. "I don't know if you can understand my words, but you're coming with me."

Her son speaks in a tongue similar to ancient English.

Thalee's face hardens. She stands strong, instinctively grasps the handle of a black knife, and nods.

◆

"You cannot be serious!" comes a voice echoing through the missile site's darkness.

"Of course I'm serious," responds the same voice.

Another person? Clara thinks. *No, this person is talking to themself.*

A moment later, her visor detects a body laying in the ground wearing Arkathy auto-armor retrofitted to human anatomy, riddled with gashes.

"Deceased," projects over her. A second set of auto-armor stands frozen like a statue. *"Empty."* She turns to Thalee, not certain how she is seeing in the dark without an envisuit and points at the sets of armor. "Are they the ones?"

Thalee pauses and shakes her head. "Tere ist enoder," she responds, pointing farther into the darkness, towards the droning voice.

They walk cautiously to the missile site's back wall. Clara shifts her head side to side and up and down, giving her envisuit's sensors maximum coverage. Two more bodies are ahead. *"Deceased,"* appears above a massive torso in shredded auto-armor and highlights several body parts strewn about.

The equalizer... Ulysses, Clara realizes.

Next to Ulysses is a small set of armor lying on the ground as if sleeping, with their helmet removed.

"Please, don't leave me…" says a young boy within, looking just like the recruits Clara investigated at the morgue. "…I will always be with you…" he answers himself.

Is he the one? Clara thinks, searching his body for missing limbs. She notes his ears are gone. *It must be...* She kneels, studying his young face, and finds a small syringe laying on the floor. She gently picks it up, then notices three punctures at the boy's temple. *Two fresh, one healed.* Her stomach drops, remembering what Dr. Lee said about foreign brain tissue being in the boy's blood. *Memory immersion...* Clara abruptly stands and looks at the monstrous equalizer to find a fresh puncture at his temple. *The boy is walking through Ulysses's memories...*

"Ah-kat-hee, Ah-kat-hee," Thalee suddenly says.

"Clara Ocol…" comes a raspy voice.

Clara snaps her head up as two quadrupedal creatures appear from thin air, both in auto-armor, one brightly colored, the other with captain stripes and a neuralizer rifle. Their helmets release, revealing red, swirling eyes and smooth skin.

"…Why am I not surprised to find you here?" Minister Hjordiana rasps and turns to Captain Witteksam. "Kthat ghirlly shactch!"

The captain lowers his head like a scolded dog.

Clara studies both of them and the vast blackness beyond, knowing an entire Arkathy platoon stands cloaked behind them.

"You left me no choice," Clara says.

The minister looks at the bodies. "These two are the perpetrators we've been seeking, yes?"

"Yes…" Clara responds.

"Looks like someone took care of the monster human," she says and points at the boy. "But what's happening to the little one?"

Clara studies the minister, knowing she could turn her hypnosis on at any moment. "I don't know."

The minister bears her teeth. "Do you know what this is, then?" She lifts an old, metal ring with a bulge at its center. "The boy was clutching it."

"Ze Tahan Fila," Thalee quietly says.

Clara's eyes lock onto the ring. "I don't know that either."

"How convenient," the minister snarls. "We're taking these two for interrogation and dissection, and this ring for analysis. And you, Clara, are under arrest for treason."

"No," Clara calmly says. "I need the boy and the ring."

The minister cocks her head. "What for, Clara? Are you ready to confess what you know? I might consider a reduced sentence."

I'm at the minister's mercy, Clara knows. *I must find a way...*

"Clara..." Thalee whispers. "Sendu..."

Clara turns to the Terran and notices her hand flexing like a claw. *Sendu...* Clara thinks. *And claws...* She snaps her head to the darkness beyond the minister and captain. Subtle movement becomes visible. Hundreds of heads appear atop massive bodies. Black on black. They move in complete silence, coming to a gentle stop behind the unsuspecting Arkathy. Clara's visor does not detect them. She forces herself to maintain what little composure she has left. *What happened to the Arkathy platoon?* she thinks, until catching wet glimmers from the creatures' claws.

"Well, Clara, are you going to confess or not!?" says the minister.

Clara makes eye contact with her. "I have an alternate proposal," she says, takes a deep Ergonos breath, and steps forth.

The minister flinches. "There is no alternative!"

Clara looks at the captain, right into his swirling red eyes.

He nods slightly. "Your excellency, perhaps we should hear what Clara has to say."

He knows what's happening, Clara realizes. *But why is he so calm?*

"You're useless!" the minister snaps and quickly raises her hand to the captain. A small pistol extends from her elegant armor's wrist, but before she can pull the trigger, her arm tumbles to the floor. Her swirling red eyes widen in disbelief. She stares at her stump, then at her arm still grasping the pistol on the ground. "Gkit dak! Gkit dak!" she cries. When nothing happens she spins around to face her platoon, finding the wall of creatures, instead. She drops to the floor, fumbling for her pistol, then looks at her captain. "Do something!"

"I already have," the captain says and points his rifle at her. "Chancellor Hjordiana, you are under arrest for the murder and enslavement of billions of individuals from countless species across the galaxy."

"What!?" she cries. "You report to me!"

"No, I do not." The captain turns to the dark creatures. "R9, I am glad to see the spore worked, and that you are whole again. Have you been brought up to speed?"

"Not entirely, but enough," says an impossibly deep voice. A Sorgan steps through the rest. "G7… Thank you," It says to the captain, then turns to the minister. "You belong to us, now." It quickly backhands her, rendering her unconscious. Then, the creature faces Clara and Thalee.

Clara's heart jumps, and she can only imagine what Thalee is feeling, but when she glances at the Terran, she looks made of stone. *She's a strong one.*

"Clara Ocol," It says, deeply. "I am told you are the most formidable of your species."

Clara takes a deep breath. "I was told the same about you, R97426."

R9 points at the boy. "You need this one? Why?"

"His cells are special. They can save my husband, Jonathan," Clara says.

"Why is Jonathan worth saving?" R9 asks. The sea of Sorgans stir. R9 raises a hand to calm them. "I am asking purely for my understanding, not to belittle this human's integrity."

"He's the one who found your kin on Earth…" Clara says, grasping at straws. "He's… Zion's grandson."

R9 cocks his head. "How much do you know, Clara?"

He's been out of it for decades, Clara realizes. "Zion told me everything about his past lives. And, R9, you yourself told me your life story."

R9 paces. "Aizen is *The One* now. Is he your son?"

"Yes," Clara says.

It looks at the boy. "Take what you need. But the chancellor is ours."

"She's the Supreme Minister of the council now, she cannot simply disappear," Clara responds.

R9 faces Captain Witteksam. "G7, can you become her?"

The Arkathy captain studies the unconscious minister. "I cannot. Politics play a significant role in Arkathy culture and her hypothesis runs deep. We need her alive and present to maintain the status quo."

"What's the alternative?" R9 asks.

"We stage an Arkathy coup, which is well within my rights as second-in-command. I will become interim minister of the Council until elections are held."

R9 tilts its head. "Then, Clara, we will need yours and Aizen's help." The creature turns to Thalee. "And most importantly, we will need yours."

Thalee's eyes narrow, she stares at R9 with her jaw clenched. Clara doesn't know if she understood any of their conversation. "I will… helppe. But only… jif my people are zet free."

R9 nods and faces Clara. "Go, now. Save Jonathan. Ready Aizen. Ready yourselves. Everything is about to change."

♦

Through glass, Aizen watches his father undergo emergency surgery. *But it's only a temporary solution,* he knows.

"His chances are slim," Dr. Lee says, watching next to him. "But if anyone can survive this, it's them."

Aizen shakes his head. "He could never access their lifetimes, and would need R9 and Kwai Lan's combined efforts. Even I could not access R9."

Dr. Lee studies Aizen's face. "Is this Zion I'm talking to?"

"No… It's me," Aizen snaps.

"...Sorry."

Aizen sighs. "Can they boy's cells really do what you claim they can?"

"I know they can save your father," Dr. Lee says, but gives a troubled look. "But we'll have to develop an entirely new branch of medicine. It'll take time."

"How much time?"

"I don't know. Perhaps a decade."

"A decade!?" Aizen says.

Dr. Lee's mouth drops open. "That's the reality."

Aizen takes several Ergonos breaths. "What can we do until then?"

"After the surgeries, we must place Jonathan into hibernation," Dr. Lee says, waiting for Aizen to explode.

Waiting for Zion to explode, Aizen knows and returns his attention to the perplexed surgeons. *They're not even fixing him.*

Your father was hurt in ways they could not anticipate, Kwai Lan says.

But there are cave-ins, explosions, a multitude of devastating injuries that take place in archaeology, Aizen responds.

Kwai Lan comes into view. *The best they can do is stop the bleeding. That's all anyone can do right now.*

Aizen thinks about that. *Can you help Dr. Lee to develop this new medicine?*

I can, but it will still take time. My Regenerative Cloning was very different, she responds.

"Dr. Lee," Aizen quietly says, facing the doctor. "Kwai Lan can help you, which might streamline your research and reduce time."

The doctor's mouth drops open. "It would be an honor…"

"And we must search The Terran Files thoroughly," Aizen adds. "Eva encountered ronin who were searching for a cure to Kaladian Degradation Disease they believed were in these files. They might help us."

Dr. Lee's eyes widen. "They would."

"Attention all personnel, emergency patient transfer, clear the landing zone," echoes through the hospital.

Dr. Lee snaps his head. "Patient Zero is here!" He dashes down the hall.

Aizen follows, finding the doctor's pace formidable, meeting several techs at the hospital entry. A shuttle descends from the sky. Aizen's mind races, imagining every horrible thing R9 might have done to Mom, Thalee, and the boy. He does not know if Angela is returning with three living people, or three body bags. Techs run to the shuttle once it touches down and, when the engines silence, its hatch opens. Angela appears, hustling to the shuttle's small cargo bay.

"We have two specimens," she announces. "One living, one deceased."

Dread fills Aizen until he sees Thalee come through the hatch next, clutching The Terran Files, and finally Mom. Aizen dashes towards them. "Mom, Thalee, are you okay!?"

"Aizen, we're just fine," his mother says, giving him a warm embrace.

"But, how did you deal with R9?" he asks.

"R9 was not aggressive towards us. In fact, he saved us from the Arkathy when they arrived."

Aizen releases his mother's embrace and immediately hugs Thalee. She stiffens, caught off guard. But then, she relaxes.

"No! No!" shouts from the cargo bay and Aizen turns to find the medical team removing a young man in auto-armor. He lets his embrace with Thalee go.

"The boy is deep in memory immersion," his mother says and motions at a massive torso. "He's walking through Ulysses's life as we speak."

"Take the boy to room two!" Dr. Lee orders, chasing the techs into the hospital. "I must study him in this state!"

"When will he wake?" Aizen asks.

When he's reached present day, Dione says from within.

"I don't know," his mother says. "Is Jonathan holding on?"

Aizen nods. "The surgeons are doing their best to stabilize him. But, Dr. Lee says we'll have to put him in hibernation until the medicine is developed to save him." He spies The Terran Files in Thalee's grasp. "We must scour this hard drive for answers."

♦

Thalee stands in Aizen's doorway at midnight's peak. She neither enters nor leaves.

"Are you coming in?" Aizen says. "I can't sleep anyway."

She timidly enters and sits on the side of his cot. "Your mother is strong... When surrounded by the Arkathy, she did not waver. And when confronted by the Sendu, she stood her ground." Thalee lays next to him.

Aizen opens his covers, letting her slip into his body.

"Does she have the abilities?" Thalee asks, nuzzling her head into the nook of his shoulder.

"No. I was given them through my father," Aizen says, trying to keep his voice from cracking.

"Then, how does she fight like you? How does she know so much?"

Aizen looks at the ceiling. "She's just a one in a billion person."

"Like you," Thalee says.

"No..." Aizen whispers and gently strokes her chin with his finger. "Like *you.*"

♦

Aizen wakes to trickles of sunlight edging Thalee's bare limbs, but all he can think about is if Dad made it through the night. He slips from the cot, careful not to wake Thalee, and dresses in his soiled clothing. *Does it matter?* He gently opens and closes the door and navigates the dark hallway.

A skeleton crew looks his way, but none say a word. When he approaches his father's room, he finds Dr. Lee at the window alongside his mother. Aizen takes deep Ergonos breaths, trying to quell his anxiety. He approaches and peers through the glass to see his father hooked up to a room of machinery. *Much of it is outdated...*

But he's alive, Kwai Lan says.

"Is he stabilizing?" Aizen quietly asks.

"Slowly," Dr. Lee responds. "It will take several weeks before we can move him."

"Move him where?" Aizen asks.

Dr. Lee looks at Clara. "I'll let you two talk."

When the doctor is sufficiently away, Aizen asks, "Are we not taking Dad to Venus? They have the best hospitals in System Sol, and Cillian would help."

His mother shakes her head.

Aizen thinks for a moment. "Mercury would be quicker considering its window with Earth. Its hospitals are also some of the best."

Again, his mother shakes her head, her eyes looking tired, defeated.

"Mom… We're going to figure this out," Aizen says and hugs her. "We're going to save Dad." *Right?* he thinks to himself.

His mother is a ball of tension. She rolls into him and starts sobbing. He holds her tight as her wave of sorrow comes and goes. Her legs are soon beneath her again and he feels her taking deep Ergonos breaths.

"Mom, you need to rest, and not like this, you can't breathe your way through trauma," he says.

His mother gives a sad grin. "And you need a shower."

She's evading... "Where are we taking Dad?" he repeats.

She sighs. "Ganymede."

"What?" Aizen steps back. "Why?"

His mother purses her lips. Her hard exterior returns. "The Sorgans have Minister Hjordiana in custody. They're planning to stage an Arkathy coup."

Aizen cocks his head. "Only high-ranking officials in the Arkathy cabinet can do such a thing."

"Captain Witteksam..." his mother hesitates. "...Is G7. The one who went into hiding to rescue the Sorgan spores centuries ago. The one who created that special spore to free R9."

Aizen feels the souls within him gasp, except for Zion.

Did you know? Aizen asks.

Not for certain, Zion responds.

The Sorgans must have planned this! Aizen thinks, his anger rising.

But I don't think they intended for your father to be hurt, Anda says.

Are you sure!? Aizen responds. *Cause that seemed to be the catalyst!*

Aizen, Kwai Lan cuts in. *Trauma might be the key. But it could have come in a multitude of forms.*

"R9..." Aizen quietly growls.

"...Needs our help," his mother calmly says.

Aizen comes back to the present and faces his mother.

She looks him in the eye. "When Captain Witteksam announces Minister Hjordiana's removal, he is going to explain what she did on Ganymede, and why she went all the way to Earth with a full regiment."

"Okay," Aizen says, processing. "But we cannot give up the Sorgans."

"We won't. But the events on Ganymede and Earth are undoubtedly linked," she says. "There's no avoiding Earth."

Aizen thinks about that. "Zion believes it's time Earth is brought into the Council of Colonies…" He looks down the hallway to his room, where Thalee sleeps. "…And I know who should represent them."

"You're quite taken with her," his mother says.

"I am," Aizen responds, recalling the moment he saw her in the tide pools and how he knew she was special, even then.

Clara turns squarely to him. "But is she ready? Can she be brought up to speed on the events since The Fall and learn about the Council?"

"I'll make certain that she's prepared," Aizen says. "But what about Ganymede? Don Credence is dead. His heir is, too. And the other dons do not hold such influence. There will be war."

"The boy," his mother says. "He's the key."

"He's troubled, Mom. He's barely whole. Barely sane," Aizen says. "He spoke about freeing his people. Ulysses did, too. But I don't understand what people they are referring to."

"I need time with him," she responds. "I must discover exactly what has been happening on this moon."

CHAPTER TWENTY - ONE

"Ulysses…" Samuel whispers as his friend's memories slip away and sounds of the real world return. But they are not the sounds of the missile site. The weight within his gut is wrong and the lighting is artificial. *This is not Earth.* He cracks open his eyes to find himself stripped of his armor and prostheses, and lying upon a white bed in a white room, with a white table and chair at its center. *Another prison,* he realizes, but he's neither chained nor cuffed. He presses hands into the mattress to sit up, but nothing happens. *Because I have no hands.* He raises his arms, feeling as if they still exist, but only one responds, and it stops at the elbow. He tries lifting his leg. Nothing happens. *Because I'm paralyzed.*

The bed automatically tips up, granting him a better view of his cell, but no one is there.

"Samuel Guilhadenpicardinesinkell," a voice perfectly pronounces.

He searches for where it might be coming from. But there is only silence now. "Yes?"

"How are you feeling?"

"Confused," he mutters.

"As one would expect," says the voice.

"What is this place?"

"You're being detained for medical study," says the voice. "In due time, you will be tried for your crimes against humanity."

Samuel thinks about that and scowls. "And what are my crimes?"

"You hijacked a refuse barge and attacked a seed bank, killing its personnel and stealing over two hundred million credits worth of endangered seed. Then, you attacked a federal security force, killing several high ranking Arkathy officers and freeing a war criminal. You illegally entered Earth, attacked native Terrans, and stole a priceless artifact. You were found in possession of black market armament and prostheses. And lastly, you unleashed an unknown weapon of mass destruction upon the Supreme Minister," the voice lists. "Do you deny this?"

"No," Samuel says into the white room. "But do you want to know why I did this? Do you even care?"

There is a long pause.

That's what I thought, Samuel thinks until a door appears in the wall across from him. A woman enters with a hardened expression. *She's been crying...*

"Do you know who I am?" she asks.

The same voice, Samuel realizes. "Another authority figure telling us we are wrong to defend ourselves?"

The woman tilts her head. "Us?" She approaches the white table and sits in its white chair. She waves a hand and his bed pulls to the table and tilts up. "You know, Samuel, I've met someone like you before," she says. "Though the circumstances were quite different."

"I guarantee you have not," Samuel says.

The woman folds her hands. "Is this *Samuel* I'm talking with right now. Or is this *Ulysses?* Maybe it's *Calvin?"* She leans back in her chair. "Or perhaps it's *Khasi?"*

How much does she know? Samuel thinks.

The woman gently sets an auto-syringe on the table. "Most people don't know what this is. But I do. Because Dione Sharpe told me herself."

Samuel feels rage bursting from within. "You don't know Dione! She died centuries ago!"

"So, Ulysses, you are in there..." the woman responds. "My name is Clara Ocol, and I'm an Investigative Biographer. And Samuel, I am not here to prosecute you." She breathes deeply. "I wish to hear your story, and those who's memories you have incorporated, to understand why you did these things. And then, I will publish your stories for the galaxy to read so that our society might learn from your plight."

"You wrote Zion's biography," comes the don's voice through Samuel.

"You know... I met him once as a child, when he came to establish new trade deals on Ganymede after The Arkathy Blockade."

"Just get to the point!" Ulysses grumbles, cutting off the don. "You want The Terran Files."

Clara seems unfazed. "We already have The Terran Files and know what they contain. But this is not about the files. This is about you."

"Bullshit!" Ulysses snaps. "You're going to use them to destroy us!"

Clara shakes her head. "We're returning them to the Terrans."

"So that they can destroy us!?"

"Ulysses," Clara calmly says. "My son says you're trying to save your people and that you might use information in The Terran Files to do so. However, System Sol has no idea who you are and why you're important. But I do. I know that the clones of Director Williams were tasked with rebuilding System Sol after The Fall. And that, during this time, laws and due process were cast aside. Horrific things happened, but humanity only sees the results. You, however, know exactly what happened and, more importantly, know how it happened. Your testimony can help bring about justice."

Samuel feels a third presence come to him and starts chuckling.

"You talk, and talk, and talk," Khasi says. "But you'll just parade us around like dogs. Dangle carrots in our faces. You did it with my people, you did it with Ulysses's people, and you're still doing it with Samuel's people."

Clara nods. "Khasi Sinam, I presume. I was hoping to talk with you."

"And why is that?" Khasi responds.

"Because I've heard of you before. But I could not figure from where until I was able to study the remains of Don Credence's yacht up close. That's when I remembered an interview I performed long ago with an old architect living on Ganymede who discovered a valuable material, one called Jupiter Marble. I must have listened to her ramble nonstop for several months about the beauty of material, form, and function, before she finally hinted at her family history. She said that she comes from a long line of heroes stretching all the way back to old Earth."

Samuel squirms trying to regain control.

"Who is this architect?" Khasi asks.

"Kandara Sagran," Clara responds. "She would like to talk with you. If you would be open to it."

Samuel feels Khasi's tug of war between joy and agony, and uses the moment to regain control.

"That was unfair," Samuel says.

"How so, Samuel?" Clara asks, immediately picking up on the change.

She's good... Samuel clenches his jaw. "You say, you want our truth, but what if nobody listens? They've never listened before."

"I will make certain that they do," Clara says.

Samuel tilts his head and studies Clara's strained eyes again. "What do you have to gain from this?"

Clara places her holotile on the table, opening a DNA strand. "Your genetic code appears to latch onto introduced DNA, morphing it into exact replicas. This is how you've been so easily walking the memories of others. But I'm not sure you understand what else this means."

"I can only walk the memories of those I share DNA with," Samuel says.

"But you can copy anyone's DNA, meaning that you can walk the memories of anyone living or in the past. And then, you become them."

Samuel knows it is true, knows he is no longer himself, but a hybrid creature.

"But your DNA can also be used to regrow organs and limbs," she says.

Samuel studies her red eyes again. "What does this mean to you personally?"

Clara clenches her jaw. "My husband was severely wounded by Ulysses during your fight with Aizen. Several of his organs must be replaced. And even then, we are not sure he will pull through." She breathes deeply. "We need your cells to regrow these organs."

"Aizen killed Ulysses," Samuel seethes. "Isn't this only fair?"

The dread in Clara's eyes is replaced by fury. But she calms, somehow a master of her own body. "If I could save your friend, I would. But memory immersion of this magnitude destroys the brain of whom it extracts from..."

Samuel looks to the floor.

It's okay, Sam, Ulysses says. *I'm with you now.*

"...Which is why I'm willing to help your story be heard in the most effective way I can. Through your biography," Clara says. "But we must work quickly. An emergency session of The Council of Colonies has been called and will take place in Ganymedan orbit to show them what the Supreme Minister did to your city."

Samuel becomes aware of the gravity again. "Where are we?"

Clara waves at the wall and it parts to reveal the burnt destruction of Hardsill and the fires still spreading into its vast fields. "Captain Witteksam of the Arkathy will be announcing Supreme Minister Hjordiana's removal from office and her arrest for the unsanctioned attack on your home," Clara says. "But we hope for several more arrests. Starting with Ganymedan Representatives Acton, Binhington, and Skaeters, for the long standing human rights violations against your people."

Samuel stares at the fires stretching into the fields, utterly stunned.

"Samuel..." Clara says. "For this to happen, I need to know what you know... what Don Credence knows... and what Ulysses knows. Will you help me?"

♦

Captain Witteksam enters Parliament floor to a stirring audience of more than seventeen-thousand representatives hailing from every corner of the galaxy. He takes Supreme Minister Hjordiana's usual position at a central podium. Representatives Acton, Binhington, and Skaeters of Ganymede enter and take places just behind him, their heads hung low in mourning.

Clara waits in Parliament Floor's entry tunnel, remembering the last time she was here competing for Zion's biography. Thalee stands beside her in white council dress, embroidered with Terran symbols, deep in thought.

"My dearest representatives," the captain rasps, letting his voice wash over them. "I come to you today with both great sorrow and great revelation. Sorrow for the people of Hardsill who have suffered a horrible attack under the guise of necessity." He motions to the charred remains of the city on holographic display behind him. "On behalf of Supreme Minister Hjordiana, I apologize deeply. And I apologize for myself, for not immediately intervening. For this mistake, I am forever haunted by the three and a half million lives lost..."

Representatives breathe heavily in their many biological ways, hanging upon the captain's words.

"...Within our Arkathy rights, we have stripped Supreme Minister Hjordiana of all power, effective immediately." The captain motions to himself. "And thus, her responsibilities have fallen upon me, until an election can be held one standard year from now, as mandated by the Council of Colonies..." The Arkathy captain takes a moment to collect himself. "But I will not be seeking reelection... No Arkathy will hold office in the Council of Colonies again... For our shame demands we step away..."

All breathing ceases.

"...But this is not justice. This is not resolution," the captain continues. "A question has plagued me these past four months. How could this have happened in today's universe? Are we not civilized? Are we not moral? And this begs another question. Is there something more than meets the eye on

Ganymede?"

The Ganymedan representatives shift uncomfortably in their seats.

"...And so, we investigated..."

Arkathy soldiers appear at the entrances, several behind Clara and Thalee in the tunnel. Confused whispers echo upon the chamber's marble.

"...To best illuminate our findings, I present to you, Special Investigative Biographer, Clara Ocol," the Arkathy Captain rasps.

Move! Clara thinks, as her name is mumbled thousands of times by representatives. She forces forth, her legs shaking, her adrenaline pumping. *It should feel the same as last time,* Clara thinks, but she knows the stakes are monumentally higher. She crosses parliament floor, taking in the immense audience.

The Captain patiently waits.

Clara approaches the podium and shakes the interim minister's hand in human custom, then taps two fingers against her chin in the Arkathy way.

The Captain grins and taps two fingers in return. Then, steps aside, motioning for Clara to take his place.

She takes the podium. "Thank you, Interim Minister Witteksam. And thank you, representatives, for granting me your audience today. What I am about to present to you challenges the very foundation of the Council of Colonies. For I have found this governance directly responsible for not only the destruction of the city you see below, but for centuries of human atrocity." Clara pauses. "Ganymede is not what we thought it was. It is not simply providing food for System Sol. There is a darker side, that until now, has remained out of sight and out of mind. But several of you here today know what I speak of, are actively working to perpetuate it, to conceal it, and reap the rewards..."

The Ganymedan representatives lurch to their feet behind Clara and scurry from their seats. More in the audience are heading for the exits, only to find them guarded. She recognizes Representatives Fordham and Vesta among them, and a stab of pain comes when she sees Representative Marcey of Venus.

"...The truth is," Clara continues. "Many of the luxuries we enjoy today are produced by a population of approximately five hundred and thirty-seven million undocumented laborers living in bondage in the fields you see burning. As we speak, they are fighting to put out the fires, to save their crops, their homes, and their livelihoods. To survive. All so you can enjoy a cup of coffee... Yet, they have no voice, no rights, and no identity. Until now..."

"...My findings are detailed in my latest biography entitled, *Samuel Kell,* chronicling the lives of unexpected leaders, including the late Don Credence of Hardsill, whose detailed records prove the atrocities enacted by our own council representatives to be true..."

Arkathy soldiers surround the escaping representatives.

"...Representatives Acton, Binhington, and Skaeters of Ganymede. Fordham of Puck. Vesta of Miranda. Marcey of Venus. You are a few among many who dealt with the Ganymedan cartels to ensure the continued oppression of these people. We have detailed records of these transactions and have matched them to your financial accounts. In some cases, we have direct recordings of these dealings. I suggest you contact your lawyers."

The looks on their faces tell stories, some grinning like children being caught. Others, like Representative Marcey, holding shame. Clara's heart aches for the man. *But he did what he did and must pay the price.*

"Thank you, Clara," Captain Witteksam says, and retakes the podium. He looks into the sea of representatives, focusing his attention upon those surrounded by his soldiers. "You have the right to remain silent..."

Clara steps back, feeling monumental weight lift from her shoulders, and takes a seat behind the captain. *I've kept my promise. Samuel will keep his. But this is only the beginning,* Clara knows, having found evidence suggesting a more widespread issue.

"Clara," comes a whisper. Thalee takes the seat next to her. She looks pale. "I..."

Clara clasps Thalee's hand. "Pretend like they do not exist, that you are talking to yourself in a mirror or practicing with Aizen. Nothing more."

Thalee breathes deeply. "Okay... With Aizen..."

With Aizen... Clara studies the Terran, knowing that she loves him as much as Aizen loves her. Her anxiety for them rises, knowing there will be pain and suffering. But then, she thinks about Jonathan, here on Ganymede, barely stabilized and still undergoing surgeries, and when they had first met. *Still worth it...*

Captain Witteksam's voice rises. "...But there is another great matter to discuss. It is a celebration, it is hope. May I present to you, Thalee Sicondra, representative elect of *Earth.*"

Gasps scatter across the council and Clara cannot tell if there will be mutiny or a standing ovation.

Thalee gives Clara a final terrified look, then takes slow, strong, yet graceful steps to the podium. Captain Witteksam steps aside. Thalee places a hand on the wood and looks upon the thousands of representatives. "Thank you… Minister Witteksam," she says in Interspeak, her Terran accent thick.

The representatives settle, captured by the exoticness of her voice.

"I am Thalee Sicondra. I am a Terran. As you would say," she pauses.

Clara sees the representatives lean forward, on the edges of their seats. *She has them already…*

"I come from a world that does not know what a council is. I have never seen this many people in one place before," she says and waves towards the audience. "And I am told there are hundreds of billions of us among the stars. So, what can my people offer to you? What difference can we make in your universe? I do not know this myself, for we are ignorant of what lies beyond Earth." She pauses. "But we know what humanity has endured for thousands of years before The Fall. We know what innovations were created and lost. We know everything that was forgotten."

A stirring comes.

Thalee raises her hand to hush them. "I understand your skepti-cism. You did not think this knowledge still existed. Like I did not know you existed." She raises a metal ring. "But here is our proof."

A hologram emits from the ring, captured by Parliament Floor's relay system and sent before every representative's seat. Images flash, of war and famine, of great celebrations and magnificent cities. Years scroll back from the moments preceding The Fall, depicting blazing battles between the Hermians and Terrans, then to The Great Expansion. Soon, humanity is confined to one world, but its cultures are immense, vast, and varying. More great world wars come and go. More moments of innovation pass by. Empires rise and fall – Usonian, British, Japanese, Ottoman, Spanish, Aztec, Mayan, Roman, Greek, Han, Tang, Mao, Czar, Mongol, Egyptian, Macedonian, Babylonian, Ethiopian, Indian…

The council erupts, until the images suddenly change to people sitting around tables hosting flatbread, dipping food into lentils and greens. Another of chefs gently carving raw fish follows. Cuisines so red with spice proceed those of incredible color. Legs of lamb, dumplings, stews, salads… Each radiates a culture so foreign, yet so familiar it hurts.

The Council of Colonies is now silent.

The food… Clara grins, imagining what Zion might say if he were here.

CHAPTER TWENTY - TWO

"She actually did it," Samuel whispers, watching on hologram as Clara identifies those responsible for his people's torture and the Ganymedan representatives being taken into custody on hologram.

Clara kept her word... Khasi says from within, just as surprised.

But will it make a difference? Ulysses asks.

No, Calvin answers. *It is but a grain of sand in the desert.*

"What the hell does that mean?" Samuel says.

Calvin sighs. *Ganymede is one of many work colonies strewn about the systems.*

Fuck... Ulysses responds.

Samuel studies his amputated body, feeling frustration overcome him. "I thought this was the endgame!" he shouts. "I thought this was what I sacrificed everything for! And now, you're telling me that it won't make a difference!?"

That's not what I'm saying, Calvin responds.

"What are you saying, then!?"

"That this is the beginning of something much greater..." comes a voice not within Samuel's head.

He snaps about, trying to determine where it came from. He fixates in the direction the coms had emitted during his conversation with Clara.

The wall parts and an ancient woman with impeccable posture, sitting in a hover-chair, enters.

"You have one hour, full privacy, as requested," says a guard at the door.

The woman nods gently and the wall seals tightly behind her.

Her chair slowly approaches Samuel's bed, and he cannot help but think about Ulysses's life.

"Beverly?" he whispers.

The old woman tilts her head. "An incredible guess, but no," she says. "I did meet Beverly once, long ago, as a child, when she was at the end of her life."

"Somehow, I know you," Samuel says.

"I assure you that you do not. But, I certainly know you."

"Why are you here?"

The old woman's eyes lock onto Samuel. "I came to speak with the man who started all this."

Samuel stares deeply into her eyes, eyes so familiar, yet so far away.

"Kandara?" Khasi gasps through Samuel.

"So, Khasi... You live again," the old woman says. "In a way."

"And, so do you…" Khasi responds, choking up. "In a way."

She sighs deeply. "I'm sorry Khasi, but I am not your daughter, and I am not a clone of her, but I do possess her genes. In fact, We owe everything to her, and by proxy, owe everything to you."

"We?" Samuel says.

Several suits of auto-armor suddenly appear around Samuel.

"Wh-who are you?" he barely mutters, noting that their armor holds a deep blackness.

"Everyone and no one," the old architect says.

Their helmets split down their middles, unveiling faces of several women, but they are the same woman, young and old, spanning all stages of life.

Tamarind!? Calvin shouts.

Joan!? Ulysses cries, then, *Genie!? Astrid!?*

Khasi grunts. *General Kase!*

It cannot be them! Calvin says as they spin about within Samuel's mind.

Samuel grasps his temples as intense pressure builds. *Shut up!* He screams within. *They're all of them and none of them!* The voices quiet. He takes a deep breath and removes his hands from his temples. Then, he looks at these women, and recognizes one from his own lifetime. Samuel gulps. "Mom?"

"Yes and no," Kandara Sagran says. "We've lived in the shadows time and time again, raised by our previous incarnations to pass on the torch through a process called, Parthenogenesis. We are several, but we are one. You may have met our previous selves, but you have not met us."

"How is that possible?" Samuel asks.

She sighs deeply. "I am sorry we have deceived you all. But we could not risk telling a soul until the timing was right. I promise to answer all your questions on the way."

"On the way to where?" Samuel asks.

"There are many more like you, Samuel, and more like me. And it's time we all got acquainted." She points at another set of auto-armor on the floor. "The revolution begins now."

◆

Jonathan rests upright in his cryotube with his eyes closed, peacefully sleeping.

I hope that's true, Aizen thinks, but cannot help sensing his father is fighting wildly within, trying to hold on to what glimmer of life remains. His body is stitched and bruised all across his torso and up his neck. *Now, we wait.*

Dr. Lee watches his holotile as cryogel fills Jonathan's chamber starting at his legs and crawling upwards.

Aizen can feel a bitter chill on his own legs. He clenches his jaw and looks to his mother. Her lips are tight and her eyes are hard. *Pretending to be strong,* he knows.

The cryogel is at his father's neck now, and his face tenses.

Aizen's heart leaps.

That's just a subconscious reaction, Dione says from within.

It becomes too much. Aizen's hands tremble and his eyes weep. He looks away.

Footsteps come racing down the hall and an alarm suddenly sounds, jolting Aizen from his anguish.

"Dr. Lee! We have an emergency!" someone cries.

The good doctor remains focused upon his holotile, but Aizen turns as a tech bursts into the room.

"Dr. Lee!" he shouts.

Clara whirls towards the tech. "Not now!"

"But it's Samuel!" the tech desperately says.

Aizen's stomach sinks. "Is he okay?"

The tech gives a blank look. "We don't know!"

Dr. Lee finally faces the tech with fury in his eyes. "Explain!"

"When we came to get Kandara Sangran after her visit, they were…" the tech looks around confused. "…Both gone."

Dr. Lee cocks his head. "His room is fully guarded! He's a cripple! Kandara was in a hover-chair! How can they be gone!?"

"I don't know, they just are."

"Dr. Lee, finish up here!" Clara says and faces Aizen. "We'll go investigate!"

His mother and the tech hustle down the hall. Aizen gives his father one last look before strutting after them.

"Were the guards subdued in any way?" his mother asks.

"No, nothing," says the tech.

"They had help from the inside," Aizen says. "Check the security feeds and hologram emitter to see if they were tampered with."

The tech peels off. Two guards stand at the doorway ahead.

Clara points at them. "Have you left this position?"

"No, mam," one says. "We even have food delivered to us."

"Was it opened any time other than to deliver food?" she follows up.

"Only when we came to retrieve Kandara Sagran."

Aizen grimaces. "That's when they escaped."

"Impossible," says the guard. "We were right here and we have disruption current to negate cloaking."

"Are they calibrated to detect Arkathy auto-armor?" his mother says.

"Yes," the guard responds.

"Kandara Sagran," she then mutters. "What if Jupiter Marble was somehow integrated into their cloaks?"

The guard's eyes widen. "Then, I don't know…"

Aizen's heart pounds. "Open the door!"

The guard clenches his jaw. "No."

"Open the damn door!" Dr. Lee snaps as he approaches out of breath.

The guard nods and flashes his badge. The unlocking of heavy deadbolts and a decompression hiss come. A vault-like door slides open to a sterile white room, with a bed that is made, as if never used. Upon the tabletop is a holotile with a name hanging in its projection, *"Aizen Ocol."*

Aizen cautiously approaches the tile. It emits a recognition laser to confirm his identity. Then, his name melts to, *"Mercy is your weakness! Your father is the price!"*

Horror runs through Aizen as he recalls the med-pack he gave Samuel, and how none of this would have happened if he just let the boy die. "This is all my fault…"

"No, Aizen," his mother says. "None of this is your doing."

"Dr. Lee," Aizen says. "Can you save my father without Samuel?"

Dr. Lee shakes his head. "We extracted many samples, but we need the boy present to perform trials."

"So, Dad dies," Aizen says. "Or is frozen forever…"

His mother's lip quivers.

"Nothing is certain either way," Dr. Lee desperately says. "We can start the research while Samuel is tracked down."

Aizen's heart pounds. "Then, there will be no mercy this time!" He brushes past Dr. Lee, races down the hall, and out the front door of the hospital.

Grassland stretches as far as the eye can see and Jupiter hangs low in the horizon. Aizen dashes into the tall grass, bounding like a gazelle of old Earth, quickly adjusting to Ganymede's gravity. Tears rain down his cheeks and a terrible groaning emits from his mouth. *Faster!* he orders himself, galloping through the field. Fires still rage in the distance and smoke fills his nose. He slips into meditation. *You can run faster!*

Grassland becomes lines of crops lush with beans that gently clack in the artificial wind.

Keep running! Hours pass. His legs burn and his breath is ragged. *Don't stop! Don't let up!* He opens his eyes again to see the Ganymedan sun setting at one horizon and Jupiter's glow increasing at the other. He focuses on its swirl, remembering the once magnificent storm during Justin's time. *Barely recognizable now.* Fields give way to tall grassland again. The soles of his feet burn. His mouth is parched. But then, chill air brushes against his skin that is not wind. He abruptly stops.

The sound of water churning, the murmurs of a crew working, and the winding and groaning of poorly maintained equipment, becomes apparent. When Aizen steps forth, the grass ends at a gargantuan pool of water.

"The wells," Aizen whispers.

Flood lights reflecting upon the water's rippling surface highlight a crew working across the way. Orders are shouted by a man atop a skiff as others align at the shore. An old crane reels something from the depths of Ganymede's ocean.

Aizen slips into meditation to find a glowing ball rising through a water column much like the one on Enceladus. *Thousands of something,* Aizen realizes. *Shrimp.* He opens his eyes to witness the surface bulge like a balloon and when the water tension breaks a netball emerges.

The crane groans as the netball swings to a metal platform at the well's edge. The bottom of the net releases, spilling thousands of creatures onto the platform. Workers dunk their hands into the shrimp, every few seconds tossing one back into the well.

Too small, pregnant, or not a shrimp at all, Aizen knows. The scent if smoke is overtaken by decay. *Similar to the tide pools.* He looks at the well's edge, then slowly kneels and peers into the water's blackness, knowing it is a sheer cliff to the moon's underground ocean. *But still...* Aizen slowly dips his hand into the frigid water and closes his eyes. Incredible points of life appear and he feels an oceanic current, though slow compared to Enceladus. *Here goes nothing...*

"Hello?" Aizen says, imagining himself emitting electricity.

Nothing.

"Hello…" he tries again. "Is anyone there?"

A group of lights, deep down, stop their movement.

"My name is Aizen… I'm alone," Aizen says, feeling its truth, knowing that the souls within him do not truly understand him. *Not like Dad did...*

...Aizen, returns. ...Aizen...Aizen...Aizen...Aizen.

"Aizen!" A shove comes to his shoulder.

He nearly tumbles into the well and pulls his hand from the water. He opens his eyes. *It's Thalee.*

"Everyone is looking for you," she shortly says.

"They always are," Aizen snips.

Thalee kneels next to him. "Are you going to run away every time things get difficult?"

Aizen feels his frustration rise. "My father is about to die! And the only person who can save him disappeared into thin air! I have a right to be upset!"

"But why did you run?" she asks.

He studies her. "How did you find me!?"

"Don't evade," she says with calm determination.

Aizen breaths deeply. "I don't know… I just needed to be alone."

"But you are never alone, right?"

"Because of them?" Aizen mutters.

"No…" Thalee says. "Because of your father."

"I guess he's technically in there, too," Aizen says.

"Not what I mean," Thalee responds. She gently places her palm on Aizen's chest. "No matter what happens, your father is here…" She places her other palm to her chest. "Just like Liontus is here. So, running is pointless."

Aizen frowns. "Do you know how many times we've lost our loved ones? Lost fathers, mothers, soul mates, and children? Not because of old age, but because of ill fate." Aizen pulls her hand from his chest. "I'm cursed to kill anyone I love…"

Thalee's eyes narrow. "Please, tell me you don't believe that."

"It must be true," Aizen says.

Her eyes harden. "Those were other people's lives. This is your life—"

"And my father is about to die because of me!" Aizen snaps.

"So what!" Thalee shouts back. "You cannot stop these things from happening! Death is part of existence! It's the most important part! For without death, you cannot truly appreciate life!"

Aizen looks into the water. "I will stop it from happening again."

"No, you can't," she says.

"I can if I never pass on my gifts," he says, feeling horrible dread. "If I never become a father."

Thalee is silent. She gently takes Aizen's hand and places it on her stomach. Then, she whispers, "Too late."

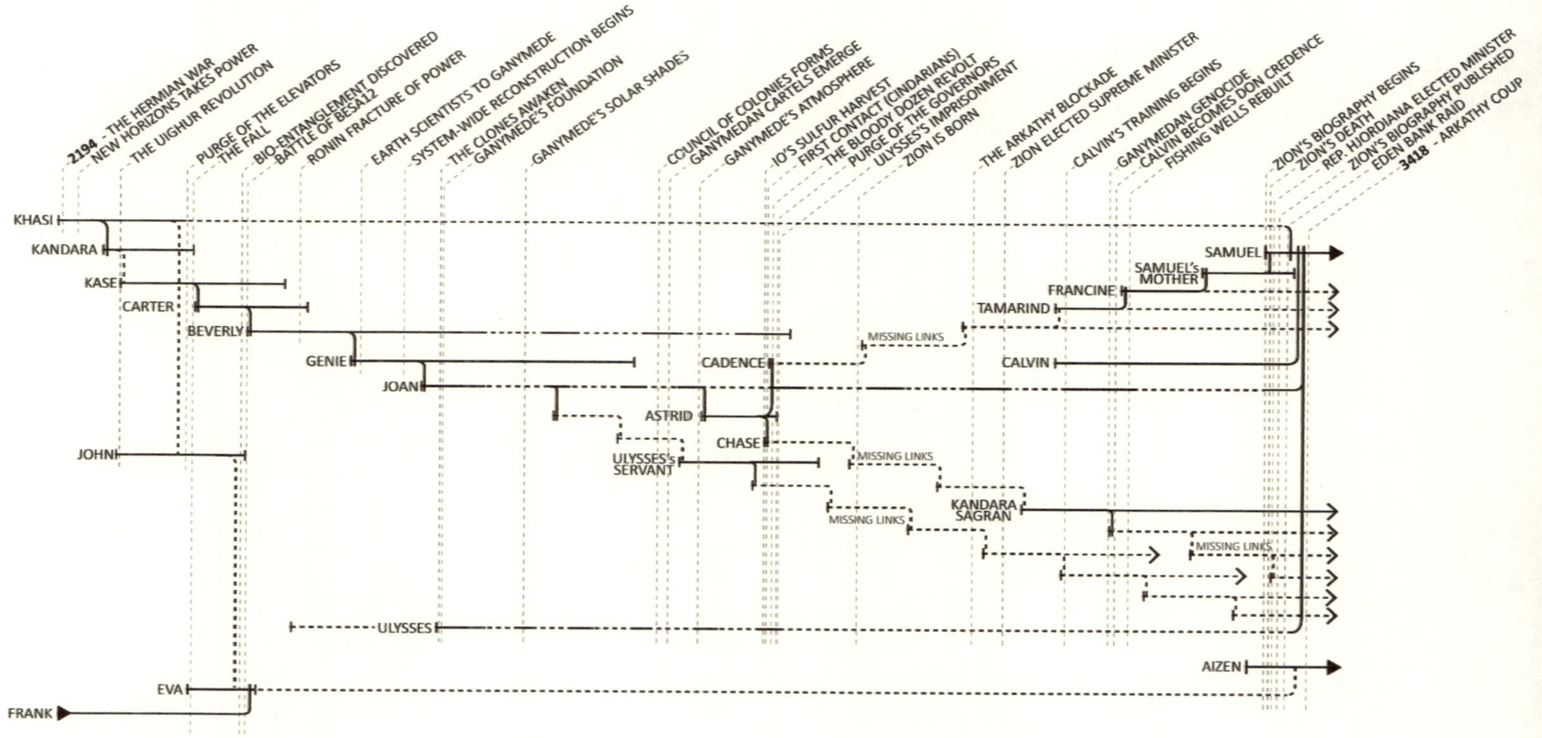

2194 - THE HERMIAN WAR
NEW HORIZONS TAKES POWER
THE UIGHUR REVOLUTION
PURGE OF THE ELEVATORS
THE FALL
BIO-ENTANGLEMENT DISCOVERED
BATTLE OF BESA12
RONIN FRACTURE OF POWER
EARTH SCIENTISTS TO GANYMEDE
SYSTEM-WIDE RECONSTRUCTION BEGINS
THE CLONES AWAKEN
GANYMEDE'S FOUNDATION
GANYMEDE'S SOLAR SHADES
COUNCIL OF COLONIES FORMS
GANYMEDAN CARTELS EMERGE
GANYMEDE'S ATMOSPHERE
IO'S SULFUR HARVEST
FIRST CONTACT (CINDARIANS)
THE BLOODY DOZEN REVOLT
PURGE OF THE GOVERNORS
ULYSSES'S IMPRISONMENT
ZION IS BORN
THE ARKATHY BLOCKADE
ZION ELECTED SUPREME MINISTER
CALVIN'S TRAINING BEGINS
GANYMEDAN GENOCIDE
CALVIN BECOMES DON CREDENCE
FISHING WELLS REBUILT
ZION'S BIOGRAPHY BEGINS
ZION'S DEATH
REP. HJORDIANA ELECTED MINISTER
ZION'S BIOGRAPHY PUBLISHED
EDEN BANK RAID
3418 - ARKATHY COUP
KHASI
KANDARA
KASE
CARTER
BEVERLY
GENIE
JOAN
JOHN
ULYSSES
EVA
FRANK
SAMUEL
SAMUEL's MOTHER
FRANCINE
TAMARIND
CALVIN
CADENCE
ASTRID
CHASE
ULYSSES's SERVANT
KANDARA SAGRAN
AIZEN
MISSING LINKS
MISSING LINKS
MISSING LINKS
MISSING LINKS

www.ingramcontent.com/pod-product-compliance
Lightning Source LLC
Chambersburg PA
CBHW030332010826
48973CB00004B/974